BE~
wo~
tio~
lite~
public ~ ~~~~~~~~~~~~ ~~~ ~~~ diverse intel-
lectual culture. The works included here, by more than forty women
writers, represent the ambitious range of their contributions to an
age galvanized by political change and controversy, revaluations
of aesthetic traditions, developments in scientific thought, new
religious movements, and emerging methodologies in social, ethno-
logical, and economic analysis. Women writers can be seen developing established literary forms—including the novel, the sonnet, the
philosophical poem, comic and tragic writing for the stage—in
innovative ways. They also write political polemic, educational
guides, prophecy, household and conduct guides, accounts of travel,
national history, science books, literary and art criticism, poetry
and prose for children, autobiography, reports from the colonies,
humour, and economics. More revealing still, everything included
in this volume was written for publication and forms part of a
publicly available debate.

As well as including selections from widely read writers such as
Frances Burney, Mary Wollstonecraft, Ann Radcliffe, Maria Edgeworth, Jane Austen, and Mary Shelley, this anthology brings readers
into contact with women of the intellectual stature and ambition of
the historian Catharine Macaulay, the charisma and drive of the
prophet Joanna Southcott, the notoriety of the courtesan Harriette
Wilson, and the spark and sensibility of the essayist Maria Jane
Jewsbury. Contributions by Jane Marcet on chemistry, Priscilla
Wakefield on botany, Sarah Siddons on acting, Anna Jameson on the
history of art, and Harriet Martineau on political economy demonstrate women's involvement in all aspects of the intellectual life of
the time.

FIONA ROBERTSON is a Reader in English Literature at the University of Durham. She is the author of *Legitimate Histories: Scott,
Gothic, and the Authorities of Fiction* (Clarendon Press, 1994), the
editor of Walter Scott's *The Bride of Lammermoor* (1991) and, with
Anthony Mellors, co-editor of Stephen Crane's *The Red Badge of
Courage and Other Stories* (1998), both published in Oxford World's
Classics. She has published articles on a range of authors and issues
in the Romantic period, and is writing the volume on *Literature of
the Romantic Period* for the new *Oxford English Literary History*.

OXFORD WORLD'S CLASSICS

*For over 100 years Oxford World's Classics have brought
readers closer to the world's great literature. Now with over 700
titles—from the 4,000-year-old myths of Mesopotamia to the
twentieth century's greatest novels—the series makes available
lesser-known as well as celebrated writing.*

*The pocket-sized hardbacks of the early years contained
introductions by Virginia Woolf, T. S. Eliot, Graham Greene,
and other literary figures which enriched the experience of reading.
Today the series is recognized for its fine scholarship and
reliability in texts that span world literature, drama and poetry,
religion, philosophy and politics. Each edition includes perceptive
commentary and essential background information to meet the
changing needs of readers.*

OXFORD WORLD'S CLASSICS

═══

Women's Writing
1778–1838
An Anthology

═══

Edited with an Introduction and Notes by
FIONA ROBERTSON

OXFORD
UNIVERSITY PRESS

OXFORD
UNIVERSITY PRESS

Great Clarendon Street, Oxford OX2 6DP

Oxford University Press is a department of the University of Oxford.
It furthers the University's objective of excellence in research, scholarship,
and education by publishing worldwide in

Oxford New York

Athens Auckland Bangkok Bogotá Buenos Aires Cape Town
Chennai Dar es Salaam Delhi Florence Hong Kong Istanbul Karachi
Kolkata Kuala Lumpur Madrid Melbourne Mexico City Mumbai Nairobi
Paris São Paulo Shanghai Singapore Taipei Tokyo Toronto Warsaw

with associated companies in Berlin Ibadan

Oxford is a registered trade mark of Oxford University Press
in the UK and in certain other countries

Published in the United States
by Oxford University Press Inc., New York

Selection, arrangement, editorial matter © Fiona Robertson 2001

The moral rights of the author have been asserted
Database right Oxford University Press (maker)

First published as an Oxford World's Classics paperback 2001

British Library Cataloguing in Publication Data

Data available

Library of Congress Cataloging in Publication Data

Data available

ISBN 0–19–283313–8

1 3 5 7 9 10 8 6 4 2

Typeset in Ehrhardt
by RefineCatch Limited, Bungay, Suffolk
Printed in Great Britain by
Cox & Wyman Ltd.
Reading, Berkshire

To my mother and her sisters

ACKNOWLEDGEMENTS

FOR enabling me to concentrate my research time on this project I gratefully acknowledge the award of a Sir James Knott Foundation Fellowship from the University of Durham. My reading and research relied on the collections of the Library of the University of Durham, Palace Green; the Bodleian Library, Oxford; and the British Library. For discussions, suggestions, and support of various kinds I would like to thank Tom Craik, Judith Luna, Pamela Knights, Pat Lawrence, Lionel Martin, Francis O'Gorman, Michael O'Neill, Struan Robertson, Andrew Sanders, and most of all Anthony Mellors.

CONTENTS

INTRODUCTION

'Knowledge and her Daughter': Restriction, Liberation, and Diversity in Women's Writing

In the collection of Anna Laetitia Barbauld's works edited in 1825 by her niece, Lucy Aikin, appears, tucked away, an enigmatic little fable entitled 'Knowledge and her Daughter'. Its ostensible heroine, the female divinity Knowledge, protects and educates primitive mankind, but finds her attempted extension of this role into marriage and motherhood sabotaged by a provokingly rebellious daughter. No critical tradition surrounds 'Knowledge and her Daughter': the tale was last included in print in 1884, in the final edition of Grace Ellis's collection of Barbauld's works. Yet it is an intrinsically valuable work, as well as one which suggests crucial questions and issues which affected women's writing during Barbauld's lifetime, such as the place of female intellect in a society dominated by male institutions, the proper boundaries of women's education, and the psychological uncertainty and self-division from which women may, in an idealized future, free themselves. This is Barbauld's tale:

Knowledge, the daughter of Jupiter, descended from the skies to visit man. She found him naked and helpless, living on the spontaneous fruits of the earth, and little superior to the ox that grazed beside him. She clothed and fed him; she built him palaces; she showed him the hidden riches of the earth, and pointed with her finger the course of the stars as they rose and set in the horizon. Man became rich with her gifts, and accomplished from her conversation. In process of time Knowledge became acquainted with the schools of the philosophers; and being much taken with their theories and their conversation, she married one of them. They had many beautiful and healthy children; but among the rest was a daughter of a different complexion from all the rest, whose name was Doubt. She grew up under many disadvantages; she had a great hesitation in her speech; a cast in her eye, which, however, was keen and piercing; and was subject to nervous tremblings. Her mother saw her with dislike: but her father, who was of the sect of the Pyrrhonists, cherished and taught her logic, in which she made a great progress. The Muse of History was much troubled with her intrusions: she would tear out whole leaves, and blot over many pages of her favourite works. With the divines her depredations were still worse: she was forbidden to enter a church; not-withstanding which, she would slip in under the surplice, and spend her time in making mouths at the priest. If she got at a library, she destroyed or blotted over the most valuable manuscripts. A most undutiful child; she was never better pleased than when she could unexpectedly trip up her mother's heels, or expose a rent or an unseemly patch in her flowing and ample garment. With mathematicians she never meddled; but in all other systems of knowledge she intruded herself, and her breath diffused a mist over the page which often left it scarcely legible. Her mother at length said to her, 'Thou art my child, and I know it is decreed that while I tread this earth thou must accompany my footsteps; but thou art mortal, I am immortal; and there will come a time when I shall be freed from thy intrusion, and shall pursue my glorious track from star to star, and from system to system, without impediment and without check.'[1]

As this anthology makes clear, there is no such thing as an exemplary woman's text, but 'Knowledge and her Daughter' is at the very least highly resonant, especially when the contexts of its pro-duction and reception are taken into account. Neither Grace Ellis nor Lucy Aikin comments on the tale, Aikin referring simply to the 'several little fancy pieces scattered among her familiar letters' and commenting in a general way that the 'allegorical or enigmatical style . . . seemed peculiarly adapted to her genius'.[2] It seems odd that Aikin, a feminist writer, should offer no response to the fable, but her silence, and her implicit domestication of these 'fancy pieces', are symptomatic of the tensions in Barbauld's troubled public career. Reviled and effectively silenced in the aftermath of her prophetic poem, *Eighteen Hundred and Eleven*, Barbauld had first come to public attention in 1773 with a volume of *Poems* and *Miscellaneous Pieces in Prose*, published jointly with her brother, John Aikin. The respectable brother-and-sister collaboration anticipates the fraternal frames built up around the work of Elizabeth Hamilton, Mary Lamb, Dorothy Wordsworth, and the astronomer Caroline Herschel.[3]

---

[1] Anna Laetitia Barbauld, 'Knowledge and her Daughter: A Fable', in *The Works of Anna Laetitia Barbauld*, ed. with Memoir by Lucy Aikin, 2 vols. (London: Longman, Hurst, Rees, Orme, Brown, and Green, 1825), ii. 236–7. Grace Ellis's collection first appeared in 1874: the 1884 edition of *Tales, Poems and Essays by Anna Laetitia Barbauld* was published in Boston by Roberts Brothers.

[2] *The Works of Anna Laetitia Barbauld*, ed. Aikin, vol. i, pp. lxx, lxix.

[3] Caroline Herschel's *Catalogue of Stars, Taken from Mr Flamsteed's Observations Contained in the Second Volume of the Historia Coelestis* (1797) presents her work as an addendum; and comes with a validating preface by her brother, William Herschel, in

As a revisionist text, 'Knowledge and her Daughter' is rewardingly difficult to judge. It handles its intervention in mythological tradition lightly, transferring the male Titan Prometheus' interest in helping mankind to a woman, Knowledge, while remaining within acceptable bounds (since the Greek and Roman gods of wisdom, Pallas Athene and Minerva, were women). Its feminist colours remain decorously furled. And, as is the case with many works by women, no clues survive about how it was read at the time, making it difficult to place even in the intellectual and artistic contexts to which it clearly belongs: in the liberationist aesthetics of William Blake, for example; in the questioning fantasies of Mary Shelley (for whom Barbauld's tale might seem to have been written); or in the aesthetic choices presented in John Keats's poem *Lamia* (in which philosophy claims its revenge on the feminine, with ambiguous results).

Partly because of these silences and elisions, Barbauld's fable is a particularly apposite starting-point for a consideration of women's writing. A tale of two intellectuals, it offers readers two competing types of womanhood, and, in exploring the relationship between them, sets up a dialectic of restriction and liberation which turns out to be highly creative. Although the final word is given to Knowledge, who looks forward to the eventual death of Doubt and to the continuation of her own glorious flight, the fable's moral—and its sympathies—remain ambivalent. Like Minerva, Knowledge seems to have sprung entirely from the brain of her father, Jupiter, king of all the gods: no mother is mentioned. Her intellectual drive is combined with appealing and traditional feminine qualities: she is nurturing, child-bearing, positive in her gifts of skill and enterprise. She is undermined, however, by Doubt, at least in the present imperfect state of society, her progress literally tripped up by the consequence of her domesticated desires. When the fable is read in this way, its closing vision can be seen as a fantasy of unimpeded intellectual and artistic expression, a liberation which has echoes in the endings of some of Barbauld's other works (such as 'A Summer Evening's Meditation'), and which is full of hope for women's intellectual and creative advancement.

But although Knowledge's vision transcends the restrictions of her present role, the scene-stealing figure of the fable is her stammering,

which he says he has kept an eye on the work in progress and has endeavoured to prevent errors from creeping in. Caroline Herschel discovered eight comets and in Feb. 1828 was awarded the gold medal of the Royal Astonomical Society.

squinting, transgressive daughter. This nervous intellectual has been educated by her father, himself a philosophical doubter, an adherent of Pyrrho, the Greek sceptical philosopher of the fourth century BC who taught that nothing was capable of proof and nothing real except physical sensations. Doubt makes all systems and institutions of knowledge 'scarcely legible'. She tears and blots the narratives of history, destroys precious manuscripts, and impishly disrupts the dignified performances of priesthood and matriarchy alike. Only mathematics is spared. An instinctive yet systematic revolutionary, Doubt focuses her efforts on the written narratives which support traditional society, narratives which she finds enshrined in historical works, libraries, and the Church. She offers an entirely different image of woman, excluded from established systems and institutions, unassimilable to polite society, an unlikely marriage prospect, and a rival for her father's attention and companionship. Which is the more fitting model of the woman writer, Knowledge or Doubt? Perhaps Barbauld's fable endorses neither, exploring more provocatively the creative spark between them. It is Doubt, after all, who jolts her mother back from domesticity into a reaffirmation of her universal quest; while Knowledge, in her time, has been a transgressive child, turning away from her all-powerful father to espouse a mortal husband who holds unconventional epistemological views. The fable's energy springs from a central, resentful, irony, that the one human being the otherwise sympathetic Knowledge cannot tolerate is her clever, unconventional daughter. And it ends with an assertion of 'immortal' authority, disturbing or reassuring, depending on one's perspective, but reinforcing the association between daughters, 'impediment' (like Doubt's disabilities), and restriction.

All of these competing interpretations of Barbauld's fable—privileging Knowledge, Doubt, or the symbiosis which is disguised by Doubt's 'different complexion'—open up legitimate approaches to the writing of the hundreds of women publishing during the period 1778–1838. During these years, and for many years afterwards, women's social, political, legal, and intellectual impediments were indeed serious obstacles. Electorally mute, women were debarred from membership of any political association or society. Their political influence was domestic and private—a situation which was far from new, but which was strikingly restrictive at a time when politics was increasingly a public concern. Once married, they had no legally protected control over their money and property, and no rights over their children.[4] Denied what Barbauld represents as the ability to see clearly, and straight, few received Doubt's—or Barbauld's—education, especially in the classical languages which opened up the traditional resources of learning in philosophy, political history, and the physical sciences.[5] How could their speech be anything other than hesitant and impaired? This anthology includes many pieces of writing which take up issues raised by 'Knowledge and her Daughter', and one of the purposes of this introduction is to draw attention to the connections between them. The most important feature which they all share with Barbauld's fable, however, is that they all respond to the creative and persuasive power of 'impediment'. While most women's social and educational opportunities were limited in this period, their writing seems energized rather than constrained by the declared experience, and rhetorical possibilities, of exclusion. Frances Burney builds a long novelistic career on being 'nobody'; the milkwoman-poet Ann Yearsley defines her identity by class exclusion; the prophet Joanna Southcott draws authenticity from being female, middle-aged, uneducated, and poor.[6] These 'exclusions' might have

[4] See Gillian Skinner, 'Women's Status as Legal and Civic Subjects: "A Worse Condition than Slavery Itself"?', in Vivien Jones (ed.), *Women and Literature in Britain 1700–1800* (Cambridge: Cambridge University Press, 2000), 91–110.

[5] Barbauld was educated by her father, a tutor of classics at the major Dissenting Academy in Warrington: further details are provided in the biographical introduction to her work, below. More generally, see Elizabeth Kowaleski-Wallace, 'Milton's Daughters: The Education of Eighteenth-Century English Women Writers', *Feminist Studies*, 12 (1986), 275–93.

[6] On Burney, see Catherine Gallagher, *Nobody's Story: The Vanishing Acts of Women Writers in the Market Place, 1670–1820* (Oxford: Clarendon Press, 1994), and in particular the argument that 'the apparent negativity in the rhetoric of these women writers—their emphasis on disembodiment, dispossession, and debt—points not to disabling self-doubts but to an important source of their creativity' (327); and Joanne Cutting-Gray, *Woman as 'Nobody' in the Novels of Fanny Burney* (Gainesville, Fla.: University of Florida Press, 1992). Yearsley's self-construction is considered by Mary Waldron in *Lactilla, Milkwoman of Clifton: The Life and Writings of Ann Yearsley, 1753–1806* (Athens, Ga.: University of Georgia Press, 1996), and Donna Landry, *The Muses of Resistance: Laboring-Class Women's Poetry in Britain, 1739–1796* (Cambridge: Cambridge University Press, 1990). For Southcott, see the discussion later in this introduction. In 'A History of the Precedent: Rhetorics of Legitimation in Women's Writing' (*Critical Inquiry*, 26 (2000), 309–27), Catherine Gallagher examines different stratagies used by women writers to establish, or obscure, their links with an intellectual tradition, paying particular attention to 'the oddness of the author's "orphan" rhetoric' (311) in the preface to Mary Wollstonecraft's *Vindication of the Rights of Woman*.

a basis in biographical and social fact, but they are also artistic and rhetorical choices.

The last part of the eighteenth century and the first part of the nineteenth form a distinctive period in women's cultural history. Jacqueline Pearson has recently analysed the prominence of the reading woman as a 'key icon' of a period during which literacy among women increased dramatically and the female reader began to constitute a significant portion, if not the majority, of the reading public.[7] The historian Linda Colley argues that the 'boundaries supposedly separating men and women were, in fact, unstable *and becoming more so*' during this time,[8] while Gary Kelly identifies a 'feminization of culture and civil society' accompanied by a marked increase in the number of women involved in print culture.[9] Women were highly visible in key social and political debates and innovative in all aspects of literary production, although they did not always relish this view of themselves. In her *Letters on the Female Mind*, Laetitia Matilda Hawkins contends that women have 'a pertinacity of opinion in dispute, and a provoking shrewdness that makes them most unpleasant arguers'. Highly pertinacious and shrewd herself, she compares women to lapdogs, suggesting that 'women ignorant were less a nuisance than . . . women informed', and that they may well find themselves ejected from the drawing-room if they become too excitable (p. 135 below). In this excitable time, the risks of social exclusion were genuine. In order to understand a broader range of women's writing than is usually available to readers, it is important to confront and question critical preconceptions about the boundaries of women's self-expression in this period: for example, the assumption that women's voices were necessarily marginalized and compromised both by publishing conditions and by social expectations; that they could not openly express dissent; that a patriarchal system suppressed female self-expression; or that women wrote best about issues within their immediate grasp, held back by a limited education from intervening in the most advanced and challenging ideas of their time. As literary canons evolve and are changed, the texts most commonly chosen for detailed analysis tend to confirm critical

---

[7] Jacqueline Pearson, *Women's Reading in Britain, 1750–1835: A Dangerous Recreation* (Cambridge: Cambridge University Press, 1999), 219.

[8] Linda Colley, *Britons: Forging the Nation 1707–1837* (New Haven: Yale University Press, 1992), 250.

[9] *Women, Writing, and Revolution 1790–1827* (Oxford: Clarendon Press, 1993), p. vi.

assumptions. This collection of texts works on the assumption that, when a fuller range of women's writing becomes available, their close involvement in the intellectual life of their times will become more apparent. As readers will find, women's attention to intellectual fashion becomes evident in all sorts of unexpected places, such as Jane Taylor's brilliant mix of Egyptology, antiquarianism, and modish natural history in 'The Toad's Journal'—a piece written for children—or in the adaptation of progressive views of history to the analysis of cookery in Christian Isobel Johnstone's *Cook and Housewife's Manual*, a work which purports to come from the pen of a character in a recent novel by Walter Scott. In fashioning its own view of what matters in women's writing at this time, this introduction confines itself to discussion of texts included in the anthology; but it will, I hope, become obvious that they are only part of an exceptionally rich intellectual and aesthetic milieu.

The women writers in this anthology were part of a period in which, as Percy Shelley expressed it, an 'electric life' burned in literature and thought.[10] The years between 1778 and 1838 were a time of intense intellectual vitality. In religion, the spread of Methodism and the growth of Evangelicalism within the Church of England brought increasing pressure on the Anglican establishment, while political pressure groups eventually secured the extension of civic liberties to Dissenters and Roman Catholics. The most prominent and iconographic figure of religious fervour in this period, however, was a woman, Joanna Southcott. In science, discoveries such as those of electricity and oxygen were accompanied by revisions in the systems by which knowledge was classified. The 'chemical revolution' led by Antoine Lavoisier in France in the 1770s, and the popularization of the sexual system of taxonomy developed by the Swedish botanist Carl Linnaeus, both led to new systems of description and analysis designed to make the terms of scientific discussion internationally understandable.[11] Women such as Jane

[10] From *A Defence of Poetry* (1821), *Shelley's Poetry and Prose*, ed. D. H. Reiman and S. Powers (New York: Norton, 1977).

[11] Jan Golinski has presented the first two decades of the nineteenth century as the heyday of chemistry, a period in which 'a series of startling discoveries was made, the rhetorical unity of the discipline was reconstructed in many textbooks and educational programs, and public audiences were recruited in unprecedented numbers for its support' (*Science as Public Culture: Chemistry and Enlightenment in Britain, 1760–1820* (Cambridge: Cambridge University Press, 1992), 286).

Marcet, author of *Conversations on Chemistry*, and Priscilla Wakefield, author of *An Introduction to Botany*, are traditionally seen as
'mere' educationalists in an age in which women were major contributors to the expanding market for children's books. They are
assumed to have reduced scientific advance to accessible, digestible,
instruction. But the systems they were describing were far from
fixed or universally accepted. Debates about scientific terminology
and experimental methodology forced them to intervene in, not just
replicate, scientific change.[12] At the same time, the suitability of such
study for women was open to doubt. Richard Polwhele attacks the
acceptability of 'bliss botanic' for women in *The Unsex'd Females: A
Poem* largely because of the influence of Erasmus Darwin's *Botanic
Garden*.[13] After Darwin's popularization of the sexuality of plants,
even the vegetable branch of natural history was not an entirely
innocent intellectual pursuit for women. Yet Marcet and Wakefield,
decorous as their language now sounds, vigorously claim women's
access to scientific enquiry.

The unleashing of creative and polemical energy represented by
the French Revolution made the 1790s an especially vocal decade,
and again women's voices were to the fore, as the work of Mary
Wollstonecraft and Helen Maria Williams demonstrates. Women
were especially vociferous in the movement to end the slave trade in
the British Empire.[14] Meanwhile, there was a gradual expansion
of British interests abroad, and experience of European colonies
and former colonies to be reported and analysed, as it is here by
Elizabeth Inchbald, Elizabeth Hamilton, Hannah Kilham, Harriet
Martineau, and Emma Roberts. Empire offered images of female
behaviour such as *sati* (the self-immolation of widows in India)

---

[12] See Londa Schiebinger, *The Mind Has No Sex? Women in the Origins of Modern
Science* (Cambridge, Mass.: Harvard University Press, 1989), and Judith Pascoe,
'Female Botanists and the Poetry of Charlotte Smith', in Carol Shiner Wilson and Joel
Haefner (eds.), *Re-Visioning Romanticism: British Women Writers, 1776–1837* (Philadel-
phia: University of Pennsylvania Press, 1994), 193–209.

[13] *The Unsex'd Females* (London: Cadell and Davies, 1798), 8–9.

[14] See Clare Midgley, *Women Against Slavery: The British Campaigns 1780–1870*
(London: Routledge, 1992), and Moira Ferguson, *Subject to Others: British Women
Writers and Colonial Slavery, 1670–1834* (New York: Routledge, 1992). For a discussion
of women's use of metaphors of empire and slavery, as well as their reflections on
practices such as *sati*, see Felicity Nussbaum, *Torrid Zones: Maternity, Sexuality, and
Empire in Eighteenth-Century English Narratives* (Baltimore: Johns Hopkins University
Press, 1995).

which focused attention on parallels and differences from British social custom. Within the British Isles, changing emphases on propriety and decorum, and a growing middle class anxious to acquire the manners of its social superiors, opened up to scrutiny the roles of women in the family, the workforce, and the moral economy. In the most public of domestic spheres, the sexual and marital misdemeanours of George, Prince of Wales, Prince Regent from 1811 and king from 1820 until 1830, brought sharply into focus the rights and wrongs of woman. The Prince illegally married the twice-widowed Roman Catholic Maria Fitzherbert in 1787; in 1795 he married Caroline of Brunswick, and they had a child, Charlotte, whose early death in childbirth in 1817 prompted a national outpouring of grief and provided a model of womanhood against which her mother could be tested. The Prince and Princess of Wales lived separately for many years, with the Prince's continuing affairs and domestic involvement with Mrs Fitzherbert securing public opinion on the side of his wife. Caroline travelled to Rome, Naples, and other Italian cities with a motley entourage of supporters and spies, and took a married Italian lover, Bartolomeo Pergami. She returned to England on her husband's accession to the throne in 1820, rallied enormous public support, resisted the bill to divorce her, and died suddenly in London in August 1821, a few weeks after being publicly excluded from her husband's coronation. As if Caroline's domestic wrongs were not enough, she allied herself with another wronged queen, dressing up as Mary, Queen of Scots, for one appearance in the House of Lords during her divorce trial. The story of Caroline of Brunswick brings into focus the extent to which political life in this time made use of an iconography of martyred female monarchy (most easily recognized in Edmund Burke's depiction of Marie Antoinette in his account of the French Revolution).[15] Caroline did not defend herself in print; but the writings of two of the Prince Regent's mistresses, Mary Robinson and Harriette Wilson, are

---

[15] See Anna Clark, 'Queen Caroline and the Sexual Politics of Popular Culture in London, 1820', *Representations*, 31 (1990), 47–68 and Flora Fraser, *The Unruly Queen: The Life of Queen Caroline* (London: Macmillan, 1996). Gary Kelly argues that 'the "Queen Caroline Affair" revived political language and imagery from the Revolution debate, revealed the importance of "domestic woman" in focusing social, political, ideological, and cultural conflicts in the Revolutionary aftermath, and marked a turning point toward the reform debate of the 1820s and 1830s' (*Women, Writing, and Revolution*, 172).

represented here, as well as extracts from the 'Life' of his discarded
wife, written by Mary Hays.

The broad range of women's concerns, and the different modes
which they employed to explore them, can be gauged by a preliminary look at works by the first three women included here—Frances
Burney, Catharine Macaulay, and Clara Reeve. In the opening letters
of her first novel, *Evelina*, Frances Burney uses the perspective of
an innocent young woman's entry into London society to make
startlingly waspish comments about male appearances and manners,
and to reveal the worrying lack of control which Evelina has over
her actions and choices. Even in her choice of dancing partner,
Evelina turns out to be entitled only to the power of refusal, and to
be reduced to blushing incoherence in public, in contrast to her
power of ordering and commenting on her experiences when she
writes them down. Later in the anthology, these issues are taken up
by Elizabeth Hamilton in the comically skewed account of an English ball in *Letters of a Hindoo Rajah* (in which men display 'heroic
apathy and indifference' and the women look like 'superannuated
dancing girls', p. 191), and by Maria Edgeworth in the cynical tale of
Lady Delacour from *Belinda*. Priscilla Wakefield, meanwhile, commenting on the scarcity of employment choices for women, echoes
Evelina's distaste for the effeminacy of male assistants in the
fashion-house (p. 200; Lady Delacour takes up the same idea,
pp. 234–5). If a dangerous and displacing world for women is beginning to emerge even in these early moments of *Evelina*, a still more
disturbing one is found in a strange piece of fatherly instruction
from Burney's later novel, *Camilla*. Here a young woman, Eugenia,
who has been left scarred by a childhood accident, is 'vanquished'
and/or 'soothed' by being taken to watch, as in a freak show, a
beautiful young madwoman, who gesticulates and slavers while
Eugenia's father is 'intently engaged in his observations'.[16] Female
mental and physical deformity is a recurrent concern in writings
included here. Barbauld gives Doubt a squint (an impediment others
seized on, in the 1790s, to attack Mary Hays), and Mary Shelley's
tale 'The Mortal Immortal' presents the ageing female body as a
type of monstrosity. Elizabeth Barrett, in sentimental tradition an

[16] Highly apposite to this episode is Elaine Showalter's discussion of depictions of
female insanity in the male rational discourse of the French Revolution, in *The Female
Malady: Women, Madness and English Culture, 1830–1980* (London: Virago, 1987), 1–4.

icon of impediment and of the liberation by love which can overcome it, experiments in the early writings included here with an
aesthetics based on fragmentation, limitation, and interrupted or
impaired vision; while Harriet Martineau's literary success was
achieved despite debilitating deafness. The performance of female
impairment used to educate Eugenia raises far more complex issues
than her father can see.

The second woman whose works are included here was as celebrated as Burney in an entirely different intellectual mode, and in
her later years as excoriated as Mary Wollstonecraft for the supposed
irregularities of her personal life. The republican historian Catharine
Macaulay is outstanding among women of her time in taking on an
ambitious narrative of national, political, and constitutional history.[17]
Contemporary reviews of her work show how odd this seemed. One
review of the first volume of her *History* thought its style 'so correct,
bold, and nervous, that we can discover no traces of a female pen . . .
and were we at liberty to suppose Mrs. Macaulay married, we might
suspect that her husband and she were joint Historians'.[18] Another
declared her work 'untinctured with the weakness of a female pen'.[19]
Hannah More wrote of her privately as 'not feminine either in her
writings or her manners; she was only a tolerably clever man'.[20] In
the extracts presented here, Macaulay builds on historical detail,
meticulously amassed through independent scholarly research, until
she can deliver brief sharp attacks on the corruption of individuals
and institutions, on the unwritten laws governing society (just as
they turned out to govern Evelina's first ball), on the moral torpidity
of 'the people' and the dangerous gullibility of 'the crowd'. In her
Letters on Education, Macaulay develops ideas about the enslavement
of women, the sexual double standard, and the education of daughters, which will seem familiar to readers of Wollstonecraft. She also

---

[17] As her biographer, Bridget Hill, observes: 'As a historian, a political polemicist, a
"learned lady" with scholarly pretensions, an independent and fearless critic of all she
thought wrong, Catharine Macaulay broke every rule in the eighteenth-century book on
how a woman should conduct herself and the role she should occupy.' *The Republican
Virago: The Life and Times of Catharine Macaulay, Historian* (Oxford: Clarendon Press,
1992), 130.

[18] *Monthly Review*, 29 (1763), 375.

[19] *European Magazine and London Review*, 4 (1783), 330.

[20] *The Letters of Hannah More*, ed. and introd. R. Brimley Johnson (London: John
Lane, The Bodley Head, 1925), 80.

makes connections between women and slavery which anticipate comments by Wollstonecraft, More, and several others throughout the period. Her lifelong passion, however, was to attack much wider social injustice and to pinpoint the origins of the state corruption which she saw poisoning all social behaviour. She is a revisionist historian first; a commentator on women's issues second.

In the first extracts included here, the focus of Macaulay's attack is the infamous South Sea Bubble of 1820, and in the course of her remarks on this great popular delusion an unexpected historical irony presents itself. In her account of the Bubble, she riskily reveals that her own grandfather had been one of the directors of the South Sea Company. Jacob Sawbridge was found guilty of fraudulent dealing and was expelled from the House of Commons. The revelation of a grandfather's imputed criminality is dangerous for any writer, but particularly so for a female historian negotiating the problematic expectations of scholarly impartiality. Macaulay risks the accusation that she is incapable of delivering 'public' history without confusing it with private family reputations. Macaulay was not, however, the only great eighteenth-century historian whose grandfather had been found guilty of fraudulent dealings in the South Sea affair. Edward Gibbon, grandfather of the celebrated author of *Decline and Fall of the Roman Empire*, was also a director of the Company, and like Jacob Sawbridge he was criminally charged and heavily fined. Like Macaulay, Gibbon wrote about his grandfather (in his *Memoirs of My Life and Writings*). Yet although both grandfathers are present in modern narratives of the Bubble, only one of their historian grandchildren is even mentioned. It is not Catharine Macaulay. Yet, as the Explanatory Notes of this anthology demonstrate, nineteenth-century accounts of the South Sea Bubble draw on Macaulay's details and examples, though silently: the section of her history included here was demonstrably influential. Partly because of this nineteenth-century elision, in modern accounts of the Bubble her testimony has become totally invisible. A piece of writing originally chosen for its outspoken engagement with the most traditionally 'male' of all subjects—historical, financial, constitutional, international, highly abstract (in that the South Sea Company never actually traded in anything)—turns out to satisfy the most simple of emotional requirements of an illustrative piece of women's writing—that it should have been most unaccountably neglected.

In contrast to the prominent public careers of Burney and Macaulay, Clara Reeve's writing life seems genteelly, if productively, spinsterish. Yet she too is a pioneer, this time of women's literary history. In *The Progress of Romance* Reeve evaluates the novels of Sarah Fielding, Charlotte Lennox, Frances Sheridan, Frances Brooke, Madame de Lafayette, Aphra Behn, and Mary Manley, among others.[21] She carefully explores the authority of the female critical voice, and her revaluation of romance opens up new literary possibilities for writers such as Ann Radcliffe, the publishing phenomenon of her generation. By setting Euphrasia's history of literary romance in the context of evening 'conversations', Reeve develops the mode of the conversation or explanatory dialogue used by Plato, Galileo, Berkeley, and Hume, and seized on by many women writers represented here (including Charlotte Smith, Priscilla Wakefield, and Jane Marcet). She gives the convention a novelistic twist, however, in making clear the sexual competition and raillery which accompany Euphrasia's intellectual efforts; and she includes several barbed asides on male intellectual tradition. According to Euphrasia, men copy each other and value intellectual imitation (p. 47), an idea which is taken up by Joanna Baillie in her discussion of male traditions of drama in the 'Introductory Discourse' of *Plays on the Passions*. The pressures on female originality—socially, intellectually, and creatively—are intense.

Goddesses and Grandmothers: The Range of Women's Writing Lives

One of the issues which arises most clearly from 'Knowledge and her Daughter' is the difficulty of setting up a woman's tradition: the female line in Barbauld's story is troubled, contentious, and blocked. It is not always possible to trace clear links between generations of women's writing, and is more difficult still when one is looking at too narrow a selection of what they wrote. Some women actively sought female guides and advisers, and wrote about their indebtedness to other women. Harriet Martineau, for example, explicitly traces her interest in political economy to the influence and encouragement of

---

[21] Laura L. Runge discusses what 'may be the first serious treatment of women novelists by a female critic' in *Gender and Language in British Literary Criticism 1660–1790* (Cambridge: Cambridge University Press, 1997), 158.

Jane Marcet, while Mary Robinson, claiming a creative identity for herself in her *Memoirs,* and describing a time in her life when (aged 15, and recently married) she was beset by predatory men, makes a point of anchoring her ambitions on the poems of Barbauld, exclaiming: 'I read them with rapture. I thought them the most beautiful poems I had ever seen, and considered the woman who could invent such poetry as the most to be envied of human creatures.'[22] When Clara Reeve has her critic-heroine Euphrasia ask 'What Goddess, or what Muse must I invoke to guide me through these vast, unexplored regions of fancy?' (p. 45), she expresses the difficulty of women's access to traditionally female figures of inspiration, and to literary precedents. Some women's experience of this tradition, however, suggests blind spots and deliberate occlusions. 'I look everywhere for grandmothers and see none' declared Elizabeth Barrett in a letter of 1845 (bafflingly, when one considers that the collection of sonnets for which she continues to be best known (*Sonnets from the Portuguese,* 1850) builds on the new fashion for sonnets created by Charlotte Smith in the 1770s and on the sonnet-sequence of Mary Robinson).[23] Virginia Woolf famously urged women to 'think back through [their] mothers',[24] but this can generate division and misrecognition, as it did for Knowledge and Doubt.

Appropriately, the women included in this anthology came from a range of backgrounds, had very different experiences of marriage and motherhood, different religious beliefs, and often starkly different degrees of success in the literary world. They are a mixture of lives cut short (Maria Jane Jewsbury died at 33, Laetitia Elizabeth Landon at 36, Mary Tighe and Mary Wollstonecraft at 38, Jane Austen and Felicia Hemans at 41, Mary Robinson at 42) and lives comfortably extended, sometimes well beyond the period in which they were most active as writers (Joanna Baillie died at 88, Frances Burney at 87, Dorothy Wordsworth at 84, Mary Hays and Mary Lamb at 83). Several of them were scandalous in their time: Catharine Macaulay, guilty of a happy marriage to a man twenty-six years her junior; Mary Wollstonecraft, mother of an illegitimate

---

[22] *Memoirs of Mary Robinson, 'Perdita',* ed. and introd. J. Fitzgerald Molloy (London: Gibbings, 1895), 69–70.

[23] *The Letters of Elizabeth Barrett Browning,* ed. Frederick G. Kenyon, 2 vols., 4th edn. (London: Smith Elder, 1898), i. 232.

[24] Virginia Woolf, *A Room of One's Own* (1929; rpt. Harmondsworth: Penguin, 1972), 72.

child; Mary Robinson, discarded mistress of the Prince of Wales and others; Harriette Wilson, who played her aristocratic lovers at their own game, but lost, in the end, all the same; Joanna Southcott, prophet to thousands and continually whispered against, especially when apparently pregnant at 64; Laetitia Elizabeth Landon, adored by her public but undermined by gossip and consigned to probably the most miserable end of any woman represented here. Many had deeply unhappy marriages, some—including Charlotte Smith, Felicia Hemans, and Anna Jameson—to men who decamped. 'Genius places a woman in an unnatural position; notoriety frightens away affection; and superiority has for its attendant fear, not love', Laetitia Elizabeth Landon reflected after the death of Hemans.[25] Both Sarah Siddons and Mary Robinson had serially unfaithful husbands. Mary Hays and Harriet Martineau were in love with men who died before they could marry, while for years Hannah More claimed an income in lieu of marriage from a man who had engaged himself to marry her but could never quite face up to it. (Which is worse—her powerlessness to act in this situation or the pragmatic acknowledgement of her financial entitlement?) Elizabeth Inchbald and Mary Tighe were married to men with whom they never managed to fall in love: Hannah Kilham's happy match lasted only for a few months, leaving her with an only daughter who died within a year. Anna Laetitia Barbauld's husband became insane and attacked her, committing suicide after they had separated. In her notorious *Memoirs*, Harriette Wilson traces the start of her professional promiscuity to the close observation of marital oppression: 'my dear mother's marriage had proved to me so forcibly, the miseries of two people of contrary opinions and character, torturing each other to the end of their natural lives, that, before I was ten years old, I decided, in my own mind, to live free as air from any restraint but that of my conscience' (p. 445). Many other writers, perhaps mindful of similar mismatches and their legal inescapability for women, chose not to marry at all.

Women's access to formal education, likewise, varied enormously. Depending on the situation and inclination of fathers or brothers, women might be educated at home either by a parent (Mary Tighe by her brilliant mother, Clara Reeve by her scholarly father, Jane

---

[25] 'On the Character of Mrs. Hemans's Writings', *New Monthly Magazine* (1835).

Taylor by both parents, who were professional writers and book-engravers) or by a tutor employed primarily for the sons of the family. Some of the links between writers in this anthology originate in their being educated in schools run by other women: Mary Robinson, Ann Radcliffe, and Laetitia Elizabeth Landon shared this experience. A home education sometimes meant a more varied one than was available in girls' schools: Felicia Hemans had a particularly impressive background in classical and modern languages, while Elizabeth Hamilton added to a boarding-school education the conversation and guidance of her orientalist brother, which continued to prompt her studies after his premature death. The educational goals of teaching establishments varied greatly, not only because of differences in the wealth of the parents (Charlotte Smith had an intellectually stimulating education, until her father gambled away his money), but also because of differences in educational belief. The writers in this anthology who came from Dissenting family backgrounds, for example, including Barbauld, Mary Hays, Mary Wollstonecraft, Helen Maria Williams, Dorothy Wordsworth, and Jane Taylor, along with the Quakers Priscilla Wakefield and Hannah Kilham, were brought up in an intellectual tradition which valued education in women and actively promoted it. Even so, Barbauld later turned down a proposal that she set up a college for women, arguing that women 'ought only to have such a general tincture of knowledge as to make them agreeable companions to a man of sense' and that 'to have too great a fondness for books is little favourable to the happiness of a woman'.[26] There were other educational modes available to adult women, however, which could change or intensify the interests of childhood. Jane Marcet traces her curiosity about chemistry to a series of public lectures at the Royal Institution: 'the establishment of those public institutions, open to both sexes, for the dissemination of philosophical knowledge . . . clearly prove that the general opinion no longer excludes women from an acquaintance with the elements of science'.[27] Mary Shelley also attended public lectures in science, the foundations of ideas explored in *Frankenstein*. Marcet's *Conversations on Chemistry* is full of the excitement and sense of new possibilities in experimental science, and it provides, in Mrs B., a female teacher who domesticates the

[26] *The Works of Anna Laetitia Barbauld*, ed. Aikin, vol. i, pp. xvii–xviii, xix.
[27] Jane Marcet, *Conversations on Chemistry* (1806), vol. i, p. ix.

performative enlightenment offered by brilliant public speakers like Humphry Davy. In effect, Marcet's all-female image of education conjures up an alternative to the difficulties women frequently experienced when they attempted to combine their intellectual endeavours with their domestic and social responsiblilites. As Harriet Martineau recalls in her *Autobiography*:

When I was young, it was not thought proper for young ladies to study very conspicuously; and especially with pen in hand. Young ladies (at least in provincial towns) were expected to sit down in the parlour to sew,—during which reading aloud was permitted,—or to practice their music; but so as to be fit to receive callers, without any signs of blue-stockingism which could be reported abroad.[28]

The 'signs of blue-stockingism' were any resemblance to the dominant British model of the woman intellectual in the 1750s and 1760s, the coterie of wealthy and well-connected London ladies known as the Bluestockings, which included Elizabeth Montagu, the highly learned classical scholar Elizabeth Carter, Hester Thrale, Elizabeth Boscawen, Hester Chapone, and Hannah More. This circle discussed freely with men, and the model was much imitated in provincial towns and cities.[29] It was also, as Martineau's testimony shows, much feared, especially by women themselves.

The diversity in women's publishing careers is just as marked as the diversity in their emotional and educational experiences. Wherever possible, this anthology strives to represent internal variety in the work of individual authors, giving extra space to writers such as Barbauld, Elizabeth Inchbald, and Jane Taylor, who excelled in different literary genres. Individual works had widely differing audiences and fortunes, however, ranging from the overwhelming attacks on Barbauld's prophetic poem *Eighteen Hundred and Eleven*, the intense sentimental appreciation of *Psyche* (the sensuous work of the acceptably dead Mary Tighe), and the widely read novels of Ann Radcliffe, Maria Edgeworth, and Jane Austen, to Hannah Kilham's reports on Sierra Leone and Harriet Martineau's observations on the United States. Some writers, such as Frances Burney, published work by subscription, so that the saleability of their works was

[28] *Harriet Martineau's Autobiography with Memorials by Maria Weston Chapman*, 3 vols., 2nd edn. (London: Smith, Elder, 1897), 100.

[29] Sylvia Haverstock Myers, *The Bluestocking Circle: Women, Friendship, and the Life of the Mind in Eighteenth-Century England* (Oxford: Clarendon Press, 1990).

directly connected to their social contacts. The subscription-list of
Camilla, which ran to over 1,100 names, included two royal dukes;
eminent politicians such as William Canning, Edmund Burke (who
subscribed for twenty sets), and Warren Hastings; all the surviving
Bluestockings of London and of the Anna Seward set in Lichfield;
the literary families of Norwich and of Bath, and the Edgeworths of
Edgeworthstown; the 21-year-old Jane Austen at the Rectory of
Steventon, Hampshire; and the established actor Sarah Siddons.[30]
Others relied on literary patrons, or had publishers who actively
promoted their work, as the prominent radical Dissenter Joseph
Johnson promoted the work of Mary Wollstonecraft, and the newspaper editor William Jerdan promoted the poems of Laetitia Elizabeth Landon. When they came to be reviewed, however, these works
often faced the blank wall of essentializing criticism. Reviewing
Frances Burney's last novel *The Wanderer; or, Female Difficulties* for
the *Edinburgh Review* in February 1815, one of the greatest critics of
this and any time, William Hazlitt, seizes the opportunity to com-
partmentalize the whole attempted range of female endeavour:

The surface of their minds, like that of their bodies, seems of a finer
texture than ours; more soft, and susceptible of immediate impression.
They have less muscular power,—less power of continued voluntary
attention,—or reason—passion and imagination: But they are more easily
impressed with whatever appeals to their senses or habitual prejudices.
The intuitive perception of their minds is less disturbed by any general
reasonings on causes or consequences. They learn the idiom of character
and manner, as they acquire that of language, by rote merely, without
troubling themselves about the principles.[31]

Laetitia Matilda Hawkins had offered much the same diagnosis of
the natural powers of the female mind, but Hazlitt's emphasis on a
necessarily degraded female reason was a step too far.

Yet, in spite of Hazlitt's scathing dismissal, writing was an increasingly acceptable occupation for women, although the tensions
between desirable or even respectable social conduct and women's
artistic expression were well recognized. (Indeed, in this same
review, Hazlitt makes it clear that Burney's body, like her writing,

---

[30] This approach is indebted to the pioneering chapter on Burney's subscription-list
in Amy Cruse, *The Englishman and his Books in the Early Nineteenth Century* (London:
Harrap, 1930).

[31] *Edinburgh Review*, 24 (Feb. 1815), 337.

has seen better days: women writers are engaging enough when young and pretty.) A particularly difficult medium was writing and performing for the stage. Theatres were run by men and dominated by men, and it was a vibrant time in theatre history, audiences drawn by lavish dramatic spectaculars, German-style sentimental melodrama, pacey comedies of modern manners, new tales of incest, parricide, and brooding guilt to rival the old. In this world some women, such as Elizabeth Inchbald and Sarah Siddons, flourished. From about 1800, however, women playwrights became a rarity.[32] The dramatist Joanna Baillie certainly believed that the criticism which descended upon her first volume of *Plays on the Passions* in 1798 was the result of her identity as author becoming known. 'John *any-body* would have stood higher with the critics than Joanna Baillie', she later reflected.[33] Even so, the dominance of women in certain areas of publication—particularly the novel, occasional poetry, and writing for children—shifted the grounds of women's literary production in this period. In terms of access to the public arena of publishing and performance, women's opportunities were significantly compromised in some respects and privileged in others. When it came to making a living by publication in the annuals and magazines, especially in the last twenty years of the period, women were prominent and successful. Elizabeth Barrett comments in a letter to Mary Russell Mitford that she considered the best-selling British poet of the nineteenth century, Felicia Hemans, 'too conventionally a lady, to be a great poetess—she was bound fast in satin riband'.[34] What had actually happened, as Barrett certainly recognized and resented, was that some areas of literary production had been claimed for women, and that Hemans's ladylike restrictions were the

[32] For information about this decline, see Ellen Donkin, *Getting into the Act: Women Playwrights in London, 1776–1829* (London: Routledge, 1995), 186. For an alternative view of women's stagecraft, see Catherine B. Burroughs, *Closet Stages: Joanna Baillie and the Theater Theory of British Romantic Women Writers* (Philadelphia: University of Pennsylvania Press, 1997), which considers the theory and practice of women's drama and the intersections of private and public stages in the theatrical nature of private behaviour as well as in closet dramas, private theatricals, tableaux vivants, and the mainstream London stage.

[33] *Collected Lettters of Joanna Baillie*, ed. Judith Bailey Slagle, i (Madison: Fairleigh Dickinson University Press, 1999), 12.

[34] *The Letters of Elizabeth Barrett Browning to Mary Russell Mitford: 1836–1854*, ed. Meredith B. Raymond and Mary Rose Sullivan, 3 vols. (Winfield, Kan.: Wedgestone Press, 1983), ii. 425.

key to her international popularity. 'Impediment', once again, could be a powerful language.

Aberration and the Dangerous Female Voice: The Case of Joanna Southcott

Although women's works of this period are frequently more direct and more hard-hitting than many readers might expect, they also carry the marks of the constraints under which most women wrote. After years of success as a playwright and actor, Elizabeth Inchbald—best known today for her novel *A Simple Story* and such a favourite of William Godwin that Mary Wollstonecraft took to calling her 'Mrs Perfection'—was able to support her two destitute sisters, one of whom was a prostitute, and to offer financial aid to other women. This aberrant behaviour exposed her to rumours of mental imbalance, against which she defended herself in a letter to her friend John Taylor in 1805:

That the world should say I have lost my senses, I can readily forgive, when I recollect that a few years ago it said the same of Mrs. Siddons. I am now fifty-two years old, and yet if I were to dress, paint, and visit, no one would call my understanding into question; or if I were to beg from all my acquaintance a guinea or two, as subscription for a foolish book, no one would accuse me of avarice. But because I choose that retirement suitable to my years, and think it my duty to support two sisters instead of one servant, I am accused of madness. I might plunge in debt, be confined in prison, a pensioner on 'The Literary Fund,' or be gay as a girl of eighteen, and yet be considered as perfectly in my senses; but because I choose to live in independence, affluence to me, with a mind serene and prospects unclouded, I am supposed to be mad.[35]

Since the death of her husband Inchbald—beautiful, engaging, and a stammerer, like Doubt—had resisted a number of suitors and carved out an independent role for herself in the complicated and compromising world of the London stage. A striking number of the women included in this anthology achieved comparable social, intellectual, and financial independence, often to the detriment of their so-called 'sanity'. As Inchbald recalls, Sarah Siddons was rumoured to have lapsed into insanity; while, during the silent years after the

---

[35] John Taylor, *Records of My Life* (New York: J. & J. Harper, 1833), 227–8.

publication of *The Italian* in 1797, Ann Radcliffe was thought to have suffered the same fate. Mary Lamb suffered periodic fits of insanity after killing her mother in 1796, and breakdowns in 'fragile' female sensibility feature in several extracts included here. More generally, Inchbald's comments draw attention to the policing of women's behaviour and the rigid expectations which governed it. Virginia Woolf memorably evokes the situation in her 1925 essay 'Harriette Wilson':

Across the broad continent of a woman's life falls the shadow of a sword. On one side all is correct, definite, orderly; the paths are strait, the trees regular, the sun shaded; escorted by gentlemen, protected by policemen, wedded and buried by clergymen, she has only to walk demurely from cradle to grave and no one will touch a hair of her head. But on the other side all is confusion. Nothing follows a regular course. . . . For in that strange land gentlemen are immune; any being of the male sex can cross from sun to shade with perfect safety.[36]

Woolf points out that in Wilson's shaded land she 'must protest till she is black in the face, and run up a whole fabric of lies into the bargain, before she can make good her claim to a share in the emotions of human kind'.[37] Being beyond the pale of acceptable female behaviour has stylistic consequences: it leads to displays of excess feeling, conspicuous fabrication, and hyperbole.

The rhetorical and personal consequences of exclusion are nowhere clearer than in the strange story of Joanna Southcott, the greatest religious phenomenon of her age. Southcott is at the very least an unusual test-case of the difficulties women's writing could face. In many ways she is too atypical and too extreme to be expressive of wider issues. Her work, however, and the considerable literature it generated, bring sharply and unsettlingly into focus general problems about women's sanity, motives, social worth, and public credibility. One of the first things she tells us in the extracts included here is that her own sister considers her out of her mind. She insists that readers remember her age, gender, and class. She develops a feminist theology in which she, 'the woman' (closely associated with the 'woman clothed in darkness' in the Book of Revelation), is to redeem Eve's mistake in placing her trust in Satan in the Garden of

---

[36] 'Harriette Wilson', from *The Moment: Collected Essays*, 4 vols. (London: Hogarth Press, 1966–7) iii. 227–31, 227.

[37] Ibid. 228.

Eden. In her most complex work, *A Dispute between the Woman and the Powers of Darkness*, she takes on Satan himself. In the preamble to this work, conspicuously aware of the boundaries of acceptable feminine speech, she reports that God has reprimanded her failure to record the blasphemous language of Satan in earlier works 'because I thought his words were too shocking to pen': 'I was *ordered* to pen every word *perfect* which he uttered' (p. 259). Far from being a passive amanuensis, however, Southcott revels in her own power of speech. As she tells Satan while he prepares to make his case: 'I am not ordered to sit and wait till thou art pleased to speak. I can pen all thou hast to say by four o'clock.' Exasperated by this homely ultimatum, Satan bursts out: 'Thou aggravating Devil! I will appeal to any man of sense, if thou art not enough to provoke the Devil, and enrage all Hell against thee: and now thou sittest and laughest at all thou art writing from me. I have not done;—don't be so ready with thy answers' (p. 263). In conversations which sound like marital disputes, Southcott pertinaciously remains uneducated, impulsive, garrulous, and stubborn. In an even more blatant reminder of her femininity, at the age of 64 she announced that she was pregnant with an immaculately conceived Messiah, to be called Shiloh. Rumours about her sexual indulgences had long been part of the attempt to discredit her, but this was an extreme development. She died a few months later. At her request and the insistence of her followers her body was kept warm for four days and four nights before a dissection to ascertain the truth of the pregnancy and the cause of death was performed. She was then buried at night, to avoid drawing crowds. The medical details (no established cause of death: appearance of pregnancy the result of flatulence and 'extensive omental fat') were publicly available, and were reported, for example, in Leigh Hunt's radical paper *The Examiner* early in 1815.[38] Not only did Southcott's body become the final test-case of her veracity, but problems of female 'inspiration', acceptable speech, and the right to speak openly about all the baffled or hostile clerics in the Church of England who had opposed and tricked her, were at the heart of her female testimony.

[38] Tim Marshall uses the 'medicalisation of death' evident in Southcott's dissection and the use or abuse of her body in cultural disseminations such as Thomas Rowlandson's 1814 cartoon 'A Medical Inspection. Or Miracles will never cease' to align the popular phenomenon of Southcottianism with the situation of the Creature in *Frankenstein* (*Murdering to Dissect: Grave-robbing*, Frankenstein *and the Anatomy Literature* (Manchester and New York: Manchester University Press, 1995), 188–98).

To a certain extent religious discourse is one in which women have always been able to play a part and to claim a voice, as mystics and prophets. In England alone, female prophets such as Eleanor Davies, Mary Cary, and Anna Trapuel were prominent in the revolutionary period of the civil wars and commonwealth in the seventeenth century: several women of the same period had announced that they were pregnant with a new Messiah. One of them, Mary Adams, was immediately imprisoned, and was publicly proclaimed to have given birth to a monster and to have killed herself. Elements in Southcott's story were far from new, therefore. Southcott, however, was a dangerously public figure, successfully promoted by a select group of male clerics and scholars, and making thousands of converts among educated and uneducated alike. The backlash against her reads like an extreme version of the rhetoric used to discredit women's writing, especially when that writing could be seen as 'enthusiastic' or improper. Consider the timely publication in 1814 of one D. Hughson's *The Life of Joanna Southcott: Illustrative of her Supposed Mission; her Erroneous Opinions and Delusive Prophecies; her Profaneness, Respecting her Pregnancy and the Birth of Shiloh: to which are added, the Observations of the Faculty on her Bodily Complaints; with Strictures on her Conduct, as far as it affects Religion, Morality, and the Public Mind.* This was the last major work to appear before Southcott's death later in the same year, and, in consequence, one of the last works in which she is still a problematic, living, threat. No sentimental retrospection blunts Hughson's language. He laments the intrusion into 'a period for useful knowledge' of 'the witless efflorescences of a distracted old woman', writing contemptuously of 'this antiquated Sibyl', 'this antiquated virgin', 'this disordered devotee to superstition'.[39] Hughson is suspicious of the financial side of Southcottian salvation and thinks she and her 'crafty adherents' impose on 'the unwary and weak-minded'.[40] He is especially scathing, however, about her ambition ('The terrific Buonaparte, who has for so long a period kept the prostrate world in slavery, appears but a very humble figure when compared with the colossal Joanna') and about her presumption in superseding centuries of male biblical exegesis. Like many intemperate attacks,

---

[39] Hughson's work was published in London by S. A. Oddy in 1814: quotations are taken from 3, 4, 5, 67.

[40] Ibid. 3.

Hughson's is a gift to the defence. He isolates exactly the qualities in Southcott's social position and manner of address which made her compelling. God might justifiably reply that her being 'a poor, uninstructed, and illiterate old woman'[41] was precisely his point. The indignation of Hughson's account, however, makes certain threats very clear. First, it is telling that he associates her, however scathingly, with Napoleon, the tyrant inheritor of popular revolution. Second, her gender, class, age, and lack of formal education are an affront to the public values of this progressive age. Third, she is a danger to lady readers, who might be led astray by certain references to the Lord as her husband. 'But there is reason to fear', he warns, 'that the delirium of sensuality is sometimes found combined with the frenzy of fanaticism, and that carnality may be gratified under the imagination of spirituality'.[42] As Cora Kaplan argues in 'Pandora's Box', sensuality in men is creatively legitimate, but '[n]o woman of the same time could offer such an artistic manifesto. In women the irrational, the sensible, even the imaginative are all drenched in an overpowering and subordinating sexuality.'[43]

What Women Said

In 'Writing a Love Tale', Maria Jane Jewsbury creates a 'room of her own' in a broken-down summer-house, busies herself with fitting it up with pictures and writing equipment, and then confronts the awful question: 'what had I got to say?' (p. 449). Carrying forward the strangely creative impediments suggested by 'Knowledge and her Daughter' and made manifest in the career of Joanna Southcott, how exactly did women writers make use of their situation, and what did they have to say? They have, first of all, as Jewsbury finds in her own tale, a great deal to say about the situation of women. From the beginning to the end of this anthology, images of women abound, often caught in tableaux of suffering, from Helen Maria Williams's depiction of Madame Roland on the scaffold and Ann Radcliffe's account of Mary, Queen of Scots, to Felicia Hemans's *Records of Woman* and the panoply of literary and legendary figures to whom Jewsbury appeals in her essay 'Woman's Love'. Versions of domestic

[41] Hughson, 102.
[42] Ibid. 89.
[43] Cora Kaplan, *Sea Changes: Culture and Feminism* (London: Verso, 1986), 158.

imprisonment range from the pathos of Ann Yearsley's poem 'The Captive Linnet' to the grim comedy of Maria Edgeworth's Lady Rackrent, a Jewish heiress married for money and locked in her room for years while her husband takes up pork suppers. Mary Russell Mitford, in many ways an affirmative writer about women, chooses a subject—life in a bustling rural village—which presents women in rewarding and influential domestic and community roles. But even her work is full of trapped women: in the first of her stories included here, the vibrant little girl Lizzy is shut up at home, crying 'let me out!' until Mitford and her dog Mayflower rescue her (p. 392). Later in the same story, Mitford contrasts the energetic walkers with the 'shivering lady with the invisible face' closed up in the coach: 'Hooded, veiled, and bonneted as she is, one sees from her attitude how miserable she would look uncovered' (p. 394). For all Mitford's studied innocence of tone, 'uncovered' unavoidably suggests the lady's unease with her own body.

In the different modes of art history and literary criticism, as well as in poems and stories which reflect self-consciously on female creativity, women writers interweave revisionism with decorum. Several works intervene in traditional male depictions of female figures, creating an alternative feminized perspective which sometimes—as in the case of Sarah Siddons's interpretation of the character of Lady Macbeth—turns out to have become thoroughly assimilated in later commentary. Siddons expresses conventional horror at the character of Lady Macbeth, but she is clearly aware of links between this character and the more general lot of women: she points out, for example, that Macbeth's heart is constantly 'eased', since he 'has been continually pouring out his miseries to his wife', who 'gives proofs of a naturally higher toned mind' (p. 222). No male critic has overlooked Macbeth's dependence on his wife, but Siddons's quietly acerbic turn of phrase opens up a whole domestic world of women's emotional labour. The poet Sappho is reimagined in works by Mary Robinson, Felicia Hemans, and Elizabeth Barrett, while Mary Tighe takes up the story of Psyche, showing in her emphasis on Psyche's envious sisters and the pulls of parental authority ways in which the ancient legend can be aligned with the language and common motifs of the modern domestic novel. In her 'Proem' she explicitly allies Psyche's plight with the modern female experience of love's 'thraldom', telling her readers to expect a tale 'In which your own distress is pictured | And all that weary way which you yourselves must tread' (p. 285). Felicia Hemans chooses the Bolognese sculptor Properzia Rossi to voice the ironies of the successful woman artist denied the human love she seeks, and, in this highly self-conscious poem, depicts the creation of her 'parting work', a marble statue of forsaken Ariadne. For all her desire for 'love's kind words to woman', however, Properzia Rossi recognizes that the reduction of her art to the image of a deserted woman is a betrayal of her gifts:

> Oh! I might have given
> Birth to creations of far nobler thought;
> I might have kindled, with the fire of heaven,
> Things not of such as die! But I have been
> Too much alone!

> (p. 417)

Like Mary Shelley in *Frankenstein*, Hemans bases an aesthetic of disappointment on the unattainability of happy family life. In another appreciation of the works of Renaissance Italy, Anna Jameson experiments with art criticism interwoven with the perspective of a lovelorn lady traveller in her popular travel-narrative *Diary of an Ennuyée*. Resonantly declaring 'I can only see with woman's eyes', Jameson considers representations of Judith, and sickens at the memory of Artemisia Gentileschi's painting *Judith and Holofernes*. Laetitia Elizabeth Landon, meanwhile, writes a whole neglected sequence of essays on the heroines of Walter Scott. Reflecting on the situation of Diana Vernon, heroine of *Rob Roy*, Landon suddenly bursts out: 'Take the life of girls in general; how they are cared for from their youth upwards. The nurse, the school, the home circle, environ their early years; they know nothing of real difficulties, or of real cares; and there is an old saying, that a woman's education begins after she is married' (p. 475). Like Siddons, Landon finds her attention to a fictional character difficult to separate from her consciousness of female restriction.

Women displayed a wide range of other social, economic, intellectual, and political interests, making use of their political marginality to offer criticism and commentary which is often creatively skewed. Many texts included here focus on cultural contrasts and misunderstandings, offering comparative social analysis by means of a description of an alien environment, whether this be the earth as seen by a space-traveller in Jane Taylor's short story 'How it Strikes a Stranger', England visited by a Hindu Rajah, or Sumatra, India, Ceylon, Sierra Leone, and the United States viewed through British eyes. Barbauld's poem *Eighteen Hundred and Eleven* offers the alienating perspective of an American tourist viewing the ruins of London; while Helen Maria Williams, returning to Britain from revolutionary France, feels like a foreigner. Hannah More's essay 'The White Slave Trade' hijacks the language of the anti-slavery movement to criticize the tyranny of fashion and the marriage market. Mary Lamb views the world of fashion from the perspective of an overworked seamstress, joining in Priscilla Wakefield's plea that women should employ women. Writing from an even more marginalized perspective, Harriette Wilson exposes the sexual weakness of the ruling class. Her account of a courtesan's life redirects the plot of both 'genuine' whore-biographies (confessionals ending on the scaffold or in religious conversion) and erotica mimicking them (like John Cleland's *Fanny Hill*), in that it avoids moralistic resolution and descriptions of sexual encounters alike. Wilson makes her writing an extension of her sexual compliance, since both are ways of making money: the courtesan seizes the pen. In another male-dominated tradition, closely associated with the oriental satires of Voltaire and Johnson, Elizabeth Hamilton adopts the perspective of a Hindu Rajah to attack the hypocrisies and complacency of the established order. Hamilton's Rajah is rapt with wonder at the supposed wisdom of the House of Lords and the upbringing of the king's sons, imagining 'how wise, learned, grave, and pious, these princely youths must be: their actions are doubtless the mirrors of decorum, and their lips the gates of wisdom!' (p. 189). When one remembers that one of the princes in question here is George, Prince of Wales, the full irony of this admiration becomes apparent. In Emma Roberts's account of the pronunciation of Anglo-Indian women, in which 'the mother, or rather father-tongue, has lost all its strength and beauty' (p. 536), language itself is recognized as a masculine and imperialist tool.

After the defamation and death of Catharine Macaulay, women avoided the ambitious genre of national and constitutional history, but they found ways of writing historically, all the same.[44] In her

---

[44] The best account is Bonnie G. Smith, *The Gender of History: Men, Women and Historical Practice* (Cambridge, Mass.: Harvard University Press, 2000), but there has also been interest by Janet Todd, Joan Scott, Elaine Showalter, and Jane Marcus in the ways in which women question 'male historiography'.

female biographies, Mary Hays emphasizes the feelings and motivations of her eminent women rather than their cultural contexts: the feminization of history was thereby part of a wider move to linger on the private rather than on the public events of the past. It is seen in Joanna Baillie's call for a drama of private feeling, and in Maria Edgeworth's repositioning of the historian as gossip in *Castle Rackrent*. Hays also, however, mixes the forms of history and the novel. In her account of Mary, Queen of Scots, she devotes several pages to an analysis of the probable causes and results of the breakdown of the Queen's love for her husband, Darnley, and to a partial justification of her involvement with Bothwell. The technique is empathetic, the language highly charged: 'In proportion to the sensibility of Mary was her disappointment, her humiliation, her abhorrence, and her despair.'[45] The links, and discontinuities, between history and fiction are taken up by Ann Radcliffe, Jane Porter, Sydney Owenson, and other women novelists. As part of the evasion of joined-up historical narrative, women in different genres produced self-declared 'sketches', as did Helen Maria Williams and Mary Russell Mitford in prose, or 'fragments', a favourite form for Elizabeth Barrett. Any commentary upon politics and contemporary society could be kept within the bounds of the feminine, while writers retained the right to be whimsical, or casual, partial, or avowedly subjective. Eventually, as in Hays's life of 'Caroline, Wife of George IV', the domesticated and feminized history proves capable again of addressing issues of urgent national importance.

A whole new area of social commentary is opened up by the selection of materials included here from women's writings on home economy, available for the first time alongside the various forms of traditionally 'high' literary and non-literary discourse. The introduction to the section 'Household Words' traces the rise of cookery books, household manuals, and marriage guidance written by women, and considers the significance of these publications for women readers in a changing society. It is important to notice in the present more general account, however, that these neglected books are full of social criticism and reflections on the role of women, in and outside the family. Their women authors write about preparations for a ball and the correct kind of 'light' supper required; about

[45] Hays, *Memoirs of Queens*, 104.

indigestion and biliousness; about the high price of butter relative to meat; about the depravity of servants; about women dieting; and about how best to extract husbands from public houses. They are lively and experimental works, some of them testing out different types of writing within their covers. In *The Home Book; or, Young Housekeeper's Assistant*, 'by a Lady', 40 out of 175 pages are devoted to a fictive-instructive hybrid, 'Henry and Clara; a Tale for Young Married Persons'. Novels instruct, and instruction manuals novelize. Far from keeping women firmly within the domestic sphere, these works aim to elevate their role and their responsibilities. While Felicia Hemans shocked William Wordsworth with her lack of domestic skill and Harriet Martineau worried about being that ludicrous creature, 'a literary lady who could not sew',[46] Emma Roberts, first encountered in this anthology as the author of *Scenes and Characteristics of Hindostan*, writes on domestic economy in order 'to show that a life devoted to literature is not incompatible with the study and practice of domestic economy' (p. 552). Indeed, many of the concerns raised in the 'Household Words' section bring into focus women's writings about the domestic elsewhere in the anthology, including Mary Lamb's declaration that 'Needlework and intellectual improvement are naturally in a state of warfare' (p. 338), and the deadening restriction of the all-female household in 'Margaret Green: The Young Mahometan', in which time is computed by needlework, the older women having 'no other chronology to reckon by, than in the recollection of what carpet, what sofa-cover, what set of chairs, were in the frame at that time' (p. 332).

In the increasingly popular genre of writing for children, meanwhile, women were prominent and revisionist. Beginning with Sarah Fielding's *The Governess, or, Little Female Academy* in 1749, fiction written specifically for children became an established part of women's literary enterprise. Mary Wollstonecraft, Anna Laetitia Barbauld, Sarah Trimmer, Maria Edgeworth, Ann and Jane Taylor, Mary Lamb, and Mary Sherwood built up significant œuvres in the genre. Educational works for children had their vehement opponents, including Samuel Taylor Coleridge and his friend Charles Lamb, who bursts out in a letter to Coleridge of 23 October 1802 against the banishment of old nursery classics by the 'nonsense'

---

[46] *Harriet Martineau's Autobiography*, 27.

of Anna Laetitia Barbauld and Sarah Trimmer, whose 'knowledge insignificant and vapid' has displaced the awakening of a child's powers by appeals to imagination and wonder. Lamb contends:

Science has succeeded to Poetry no less in the little walks of Children than with Men. —: Is there no possibility of averting this sore evil? Think what you would have been now, if instead of being fed with Tales and old wives fables in childhood, you had been crammed with Geography & Natural History? Damn them. I mean the cursed Barbauld Crew, those Blights & Blasts of all that is Human in man & child.[47]

Charles Lamb's emphasis on fact-crammed morality underestimates the complexity of women's writing for children, and especially its troubling comedy. In poems such as Jane Taylor's apparently sunny and complacent 'The Cow and the Ass', for example, the animals ape human manners and discuss their oppression by the human race. The cow's complaints are refuted by the ass, and she seems to concede to them; but she still considers him 'not very bright'.[48] The poem is also a comic observation of behaviour between men and women, and in this it is characteristic of the links between children's literature and other modes of women's writing. Several of the tales for children featured here focus on girls who are forced to make their own decisions, exposing the vulnerability of their confidence and judgement. Ann Radcliffe's depiction of the rising panic and irrationality of Emily St Aubert, heroine of *The Mysteries of Udolpho*, as she is shut up alone in a torture-chamber, or Mary Tighe's interest in the pressures on Psyche's faith, gain in resonance when they are read alongside the troubled tales of Mary Lamb's Elinor Forester and Margaret Green, and the unsettlingly luscious pre-sexual crimes of Mary Sherwood's greedy Emily. Girls' choices are made in the absence of parents, who may be dead or inadequate: in the same way, Jane Austen's Fanny Price and Anne Elliot need to learn to trust their own judgements, and Mary Shelley's infant-like Creature reaches out for its sleeping creator, only to be repelled and (like Barbauld's Doubt) instinctively loathed. Even when women are being 'educational' rather than imaginative, the darker side of their social situation comes to the fore; while in works such as Jane

---

[47] *Lamb as Critic*, ed. Roy Park (London: Routledge and Kegan Paul, 1980), 165.
[48] Revisions to the later texts of 'The Cow and the Ass', possibly by Jane Taylor's sister Ann, simplify the double-edged ending.

Marcet's series of *Conversations*—on natural philosophy, chemistry, and political economy—young girls prove themselves to possess not only active imaginations but also lively social consciences and considerable intellectual acumen.

There are, then, many different answers to Maria Jane Jewsbury's question, 'what had I got to say?'. Women's writing in this sixty-year period is strikingly varied and rich, and it resists simple statements about continuity and development. When individual genres of women's writing are considered, it is sometimes possible to identify broad changes in topic, tone, and emphasis across the period. Recent literary critics have been particularly attentive to women's poetry, suggesting that in the 1820s and 1830s women's writing became more conservative, with leading figures such as Hemans and Landon purveying a consciously sentimental new version of the self-styled 'poetess'.[49] Some argue that the poetry of Wordsworth, Byron, Keats, and others had effectively claimed introspection for men, taking from women the prerogative of emotional speech which had allowed Charlotte Smith to revitalize the sonnet. In prose fiction, comparably, critics have argued that the novel was triumphantly reclaimed for masculinity and seriousness by Walter Scott.[50] Analysts of women's polemical prose point to the devastating effect of William Godwin's biographical memoir of Mary Wollstonecraft, which made it possible for generations afterwards to associate feminist thinking irrevocably with sexual impropriety. In scientific discourse, women are said to have been increasingly marginalized in the drive towards professionalization and specialization. In economics and the social sciences, in contrast, their role is augmented, Harriet Martineau being claimed by several commentators as a significant founder of the discourse of the social sciences.[51] All these claims can be questioned, or at the very least complicated, by the range of work

---

[49] Glennis Stephenson, 'Poet Construction: Mrs Hemans, L. E. L., and the Image of the Nineteenth-Century Woman Poet', in Shirley Neuman and Glennis Stephenson (eds.), *ReImagining Women: Representations of Women in Culture* (Toronto: University of Toronto Press, 1993), 61–73.

[50] For example, Ina Ferris, *The Achievement of Literary Authority: Gender, History, and the Waverley Novels* (New York: Cornell University Press, 1991).

[51] See Lynn McDonald, *Women Founders of the Social Sciences* (Ottawa: Carleton University Press, 1994), and S. Hoecker-Drysdale, *Harriet Martineau: First Woman Sociologist* (Oxford and New York: Berg, 1992).

presented here. In social and political commentary, the heated debate of the 1790s is rekindled in the later 1820s and 1830s, its new outspokenness underpinned by women's reclamation of a language of feeling which is distinct from the language of eighteenth-century sensibility and more securely grounded in the domestic affections. Women had reclaimed the language of the heart, and they put it to political purpose. There is also less of a sense of division between women writers in these later decades. Whereas women's writing in the 'revolutionary decade' of the 1790s makes one aware of disputes and divisions (Hawkins rushing into print to admonish Williams, Hamilton satirizing women Jacobins in *Memoirs of Modern Philosophers*), in the 1820s and 1830s women increasingly endorse each other's work in public. Women were also making more of increased opportunities to travel, and it may be that the resurgence of political commentary evident in works by Martineau and Roberts reflects a shift in the genre of social observation, and, in turn, a shift in readers' desire to hear about ways of life in other lands. This shift is supported by a new confidence and sense of individual authority, however. Elizabeth Hamilton's *Letters of a Hindoo Rajah* is in part a tribute to her dead brother, an orientalist scholar and a soldier who had spent fourteen years in the east. In *Scenes and Characteristics of Hindostan*, however, Emma Roberts writes from her own experience, and on her own authority: her work does not purport to be a 'translation', or to be indebted to the scholarship of a man.

When Anna Laetitia Barbauld imagined the depredations of Doubt in the realms of history, divinity, and scholarly commentary and polemic, she anticipated key areas of women's revisionist work in the decades to follow. In their satirical and comic works, likewise, women tripped up those who claimed authority over them: parents, husbands, and social superiors. Doubt spares mathematics, but women writers tested and promulgated the new discourses of the sciences. Knowledge is an ambiguous figure, conservative in her views but revolutionary in her plans of escape and transcendence. Perhaps 'Knowledge and her Daughter' is an exemplary text after all.

NOTE ON THE ANTHOLOGY

THE sixty-year period represented in this volume was one in which the cultural power of the anthology—etymologically, a gathering of flowers—was coming into its own, with collections of ancient ballads, 'specimens' of poetry, and collected editions of plays and novels, all creating, and substantiating, literary traditions. Some women writers were prominent in these ventures: Elizabeth Inchbald wrote prefaces for the twenty-one volumes of Bell's *British Theatre*, while Anna Laetitia Barbauld edited the fifty-volume collection *British Novelists* and created an anthology of literary, moral, and didactic extracts for young women in *The Female Speaker* (1811). The final two decades of the period saw the rise of a different kind of specimen-collecting, this time in keepsakes, giftbooks, and annuals, some of which, like the *Forget-me-not*, implied analogies with the gathering of flowers. Aimed at the female consumer, these luxury goods arranged literary works into gifts and memorials, decorative and commemorative in their appeal. Meanwhile, throughout the period, young women were encouraged to botanize: to observe, classify, and draw flowers. Collections of elegant, instructive, or harmonious verse and prose were an increasingly powerful cultural force, and were also, in the private sphere of the journal and commonplace book, used to define the proper boundaries of the feminine. Putting together a selection of women's writing from this period means recognizing that the cultural position of literary 'specimens' and collections of specimens is of special importance at this time; and forces one to confront issues about literary history and the status of the literary which were central to the context in which these writings were produced. The purpose of this Note is to make explicit some of the principles and decisions which have shaped the volume.

The collection is defined first of all by the years which it spans. The years 1778 and 1838 are unencumbered dates, dates not immediately associated with revolutions in literary, political, or intellectual history, and they allow a freer play of texts than would be possible were the boundaries to be more prescriptive: for example, 1789/90 and 1830/32 (the dates commonly used to designate the

Romantic Period in Britain), or 1760 and 1821 (the dates of the accession and death of George III). The aim has been to give a sense of a period short enough to generate internal debate and to make that debate intelligible; but long enough to show changes of style, topic, and cultural assumptions and to suggest ways in which those changes affected women's writing. The starting date, 1778, has been chosen because during that year two monumental, but entirely different, publishing events took place. The first was the publication of the most celebrated novel of its age, Frances Burney's *Evelina*—the subtitle of which, 'The History of a Young Lady's Entrance into the World', has the additional advantage of being suitably inaugural. The second was a new direction in historical writing by the only woman historian of her time, Catharine Macaulay. The closing date of the anthology, 1838, is the year in which Laetitia Elizabeth Landon died, and in which she wrote her greatest lyric, 'Night at Sea', as well as the series of essays on the heroines of Walter Scott's novels which, unlike 'Night at Sea', have lain entirely unrecovered by feminist literary historiography. In mentioning these conjunctions I hope to begin to bring into focus the stark differences in the fortunes of women's writing which have driven the preparation of this anthology: the high visibility of certain aspects of women's achievement—a great society novel and an intense and poignant lyrical poem—and the continued invisibility of others (in this case political and constitutional history and literary criticism).

In between Burney and Macaulay and Landon, between the unassuming years 1778 and 1838, lie six decades of constant and often fierce debate about the capabilities of women, and a steady productivity in an impressive variety of literary and non-literary genres. Historical boundaries frequently make little lasting sense when used to characterize literature: they make even less sense when the boundaries of the 'literary' are questioned. I have tried to use the span of the anthology creatively, selecting texts which generate or respond to one another and which highlight development and change across the period as a whole, but I have avoided setting up a new self-contained 'period' with all the concentric forces that generates. In particular, my choice of texts destabilizes what might otherwise be assumed to be the chronological centre of the period 1778–1838, the enigmatic first decade of the nineteenth century, by bringing together for this decade some of the oddest and most startling works in the entire collection. And although key ideas and interests connect many of the items included, the anthology emphasizes diversity, choosing not to give special attention to any one area of women's thought.

Probably more arresting than the dates of the anthology, however, is its focus on gender. The critical ethics of separation by gender continue to be hotly debated, and collections of women's work remain vulnerable to attack from two apparently distinct positions: the argument that separation perpetuates ghettoization and the argument that women's writing possesses a distinctively female language and literary vocabulary. In practice, these arguments are difficult to separate, because the second is largely a positive version of the first. Both, however, presume that the broad outlines of women's published works are known: that we know the entity we describe. For many of the works included here, however, this is simply not the case. This selection shows, first of all, that women were involved in far more areas of public debate than we generally suppose; and, second, that they conspicuously lacked, and probably avoided, a common language or purpose, unless it suited them. It accepts a separatist format in order to focus attention on a range of writing which in fact breaks down traditional groupings, especially those which privilege the conventionally 'literary', even more so the 'poetical'. In this respect the anthology tests my working assumption that many of the genuine theoretical problems which beset collections of women's writing are a product of too closed an attention to particular literary forms. Jane Marcet has not so far made it into an anthology of early writings on chemistry, or Hannah Kilham into an anthology of African linguistics; so, for the time being, women they must be.

In terms of content, the aim has been to present a genuinely inclusive collection of literary and non-literary texts across genres, class differences, political hues, and varying degrees of contemporary or posthumous fame. At a much earlier stage in the recovery of women's texts, Elaine Showalter argued in 'Feminist Criticism in the Wilderness':

No theory, however suggestive, can be a substitute for the close and extensive knowledge of women's texts which constitutes our essential subject. Cultural anthropology and social history can perhaps offer us a terminology and a diagram of women's cultural situation. But feminist critics must use this concept in relation to what women actually wrote, not in relation to a theoretical, political, metaphoric, or visionary ideal of what women ought to write.[1]

This anthology is as open as possible to Showalter's demand, including in its selection women writing about money and political economy, natural history, travel, the cultures of the Americas, Africa, and the East. It includes writers in the evangelical tradition, prominent Dissenters, writers of educational tracts, books of advice and guidance, poets and dramatists. There is no attempt to privilege particular political views, especially views which might appear to modern readers to be attractively radical or combative of pre-feminist cultural assumptions. Radical writing can be formulaic, just as conformist writing can be creatively brittle. In keeping with Harriet Martineau's recognition that women were at the forefront of what she termed 'practical divinity', many of the texts turn on religious issues. Women novelists are fully represented, as befits the genre in which women made the most thoroughgoing contribution to the literary culture of the period. Individual women writers often wrote in several different literary and non-literary genres, and wherever possible an attempt has been made to acknowledge this. A versatile and accomplished writer such as Barbauld, for example, benefits greatly from being freed from the constraints of genre: visible for the first time in this anthology, her prose piece for children, 'True Magicians' (a visionary geography) contains an account of Britain in the dark ages which interacts with descriptions in her most famous poem, *Eighteen Hundred and Eleven*.

The selection of material has involved difficult decisions. It would be both impoverishing and misleading to exclude the best-known writers of the period, although my selections from Austen, Edgeworth, and Shelley are influenced by the ready availability of their works elsewhere, and I have set out to select from their work specimens which generate links and questions with other writers. The range of women writers now available to readers has expanded greatly in recent years, so that in addition to the problem of the securely canonical there are many difficulties surrounding the

---

[1] *New Feminist Criticism: Essays on Women, Literature, and Theory* (London: Virago, 1986), 266.

representation of work by writers such as Barbauld, Smith, Lamb, Hemans, and Landon. My aim has been to show a wider range of their work than is commonly anthologized: Lamb's stories for children as well as the much-anthologized 'On Needlework', Barbauld's and Landon's prose as well as their poetry, and a selection of what I consider to be Hemans's best lyrics. Entirely missing from the final selection are some important writers—Hester Lynch Piozzi, Hannah Cowley, Jane West, Amelia Opie, Jane Porter, Sara Coleridge, Caroline Norton—as well as a host of others who are distinctive and challenging. All one can reasonably say in exculpation is that they have made way for some unmissable pieces of writing. It would be easier to do justice to some writers in a themed collection: setting Mary Ann Radcliffe's *The Female Advocate; or, An Attempt to Recover the Rights of Women from Male Usurpation* (1799) next to Wollstonecraft and Wakefield, Caroline Norton's *A Voice from the Factories* (1836) next to Martineau, Eliza Fay's *Original Letters from India* (1817) next to Roberts, Anna Maria Falconbridge's *Two Voyages to Sierra Leone* (1794) next to Kilham, Lucy Aikin's historical works next to Macaulay and Hays, or the autobiographies of Ann Candler and Catharine Cappe next to Robinson. But this anthology does not select by theme. Sometimes omissions are dictated by pressures on particular parts of the anthology. In all justice, Frances Trollope's *Domestic Manners of the Americans* (1832) and Anna Jameson's *Winter Studies and Summer Rambles in Canada* (1838) should find a place here, and to move in the final sections of the anthology to a sudden concentration on travel and the analysis of colonial and post-colonial societies (Kilham, Martineau, Roberts) would be to represent a genuine trend in literary history. But it would also risk a sudden preponderance of North American travels.

In addition, some longer modes of women's published writing are especially resistant to adequate representation in extract form. Novels, in quality as well as quantity often the leading contribution of women writers at this time, typically require most, if not always all, of the space they occupied on the shelves of the circulating libraries. Plays, a less common mode for women but central to the careers of several women writers, can be difficult to wrench from specific contexts of performance and audience. Another major literary genre poses a somewhat different problem. Although women's poetry is fully represented here, in a selection which aims to demonstrate its variousness of form and style, it is not given the special prominence which has often been the case (and which carries forward traditional assumptions about the special status of poetry in the (male) Romantic period). There are now a number of high-quality anthologies of women's poetry in the eighteenth and nineteenth centuries, and while this privileging of a 'high', and often succinct, literary art is understandable in the context of hard-copy publishing and essential in the recovery and elucidation of a particular genre, it does not always make available the best of what women were writing. This anthology by no means includes all that I think valuable in women's poetry of the time—far from it—but it does enjoy the luxury of looking beyond poetry, safe in the knowledge that Charlotte Smith's *Beachy Head* and Laetitia Elizabeth Landon's *The Improvisatrice* now have assured readerships. The variety and excitement of women's prose (fictional, polemical, satirical, critical, devotional, historical), women's writing for and about the stage, women's contributions to science, economics, art criticism, and sociology—these seem to me to be more in need of a wider readership, and often appear to have allowed women more individuality than did poetry.

As will be apparent from the decisions described so far, the anthology faces up to some contentious omissions in order to champion other causes. The four special causes I am most aware of are Joanna Southcott, Jane Marcet, Maria Jane Jewsbury, and Emma Roberts (all predominantly prose writers, a further reflection perhaps of the valuable editorial work which has been done to recover women poets in recent years). Sometimes the entire œuvre of a writer calls out for new attention; at other times individual works demand inclusion. If Wollstonecraft is underrepresented here, it is because of Priscilla Wakefield's observations on female employment and the need for women to support the labour of women. If space has not been found for Joanna Baillie's Scottish lyrics, it is because readers will not be able to find Sarah Siddons's notes on Lady Macbeth anywhere else. Caroline Bowles and Sara Coleridge are much less famous than Elizabeth Barrett; but Barrett's macabre, troubling early poetry seems to me more interesting than theirs, and just as heavily overshadowed by her later productions.

A special feature of the selection is that all the works were prepared for publication at their authors' request. It is an anthology of public rather than private writing, setting out to demonstrate the extent and range of women's published contributions to the debates of their time, and electing not to supplement these with subsequently recovered letters, diaries, travel-accounts, or memoirs. This decision is less difficult to make in the context of widespread scholarly interest in making available such private works as the letters and journals of Eleanor Butler and Sarah Ponsonby, Catherine Talbot, Jane Johnston, Louisa Arrowsmith, and Anna Margaretta Larpent. But there is a more important principle at stake here. The decision to select works intended by their authors for publication means that no retrospective visibility is accorded to brilliant and sensitive writings such as Dorothy Wordsworth's Alfoxden and Grasmere journals, invaluable insights into daily literary life such as Maria Edgeworth's letters home from London, or miniature masterpieces of practicality such as Susanna Whatman's manuscript instructions to her house-staff. These are genuine losses, but they are made in order to establish an impression of a publishing culture for women which is not available when works are accorded an apparent equality of status entirely dependent on the recuperative efforts of a different age. Some of the most interesting works by women in this period were simply not available for public perusal. A case in point is the wealth of manuscript material left by Lady Louisa Stuart, daughter of George III's mentor and prime minister Lord Bute, and one of the most intellectually gifted women of her time. Stuart's social rank made publication seem undignified, and this compounded the difficulties of gender which are apparent from her family's lack of interest in her writing. If aristocratic women were discouraged from entering the public sphere as the intellectuals they often were in private, women of the labouring, artisan, and servant classes rarely had access to this sphere at all.

With these difficulties in mind, it becomes increasingly unsatisfactory to perpetuate the sometimes blurred distinction between published works and works to which we have long had privileged access, notably the journals and letters of the wives, sisters, and daughters of the central canonical male Romantic poets. The unpublished journals of Dorothy Wordsworth, in particular, have achieved a special exemplary and/or honorary status in women's writing of this period, and, more recently, strong claims have been made for the value of the letters and journals of Claire Clairmont. Clairmont is missing here and Wordsworth represented only by published poems and by her *Recollections of a Tour made in Scotland*, which she revised for publication in 1822. All anthologies build upon ideas which are current at the time of compilation: this one builds on the widespread current interest in interdisciplinary studies, in the creative relationship between literature and science, and in questioning the status of so-called high art. It is not, and cannot be, a re-creation of a period's literary culture. But by omitting works which were not in any sense part of that *public* culture it is easier to appreciate the variety of what women were publishing, and possible to take that range as a model for the kinds of writing an anthology ideally ought to include. Given that the exclusion of private writings might be expected to restrict what women felt able or willing to say, it is remarkable that their public voices speak so resonantly, contentiously, and variously, and that the modes of their writing should be so conspicuously inventive and diverse. In itself, this is a discovery worth making: we do not need to rescue women writers from the constraints imposed by publication, even though the world of publishing was a male world. Furthermore, the often-invoked division between a 'free' private expression and constrained public modes looks much less secure, and is clearly not specific to gender. (No woman of this period writes letters, even to her closest confidants, which are as racy, contemptuous, and coarse as some of Byron's; but then few men do, either.) Indeed, print seems to have granted women certain freedoms which were not readily available in private discourse.

In contrast to the difficult decisions which have shaped its content, the volume's internal organization is very simple. The works are grouped by author; and, within this grouping, by the date of the earliest selected work. So, the works of the first author, Burney, appear together, even though the extracts from *Camilla* belong to a much later period than the extracts from the second writer selected, Macaulay. The opportunity to group works by the same author, to encourage recognition of the range which is often so striking within, as well as across, the œuvres represented, seems more important than arrangement by date of publication alone, valuable as this can be—in Jerome McGann's *Romantic Period Verse*, for example—in raising awareness of Romantic chronology. Although no selection of any one author's work sets out to give a representative history of her writing, this arrangement nevertheless makes it possible to discern changes of direction and emphasis within some publishing careers. It also permits the essays introducing each author's work to take up more immediately questions of context (especially plot context, vital in the extracts from novels) and to set up dialogue between the extracts (including dialogue with works by other writers). Exceptions to this principle of organization have been kept to a minimum. Reeve is placed earlier than she should be because she is represented by extracts from a single work which precedes the majority of the works from Barbauld and Smith which follow it. Wollstonecraft (first extract 1791) is placed before Williams (first extract 1790) in order to allow her review of *A Simple Story* to follow the extracts from Inchbald's novel; and so that Williams immediately precedes Hawkins's *Letters on the Female Mind*, which is addressed to her. Radcliffe's *Journal of a Tour Made in the Summer of 1794* is allowed to precede the much better-known *Mysteries of Udolpho*: both originate in the same year, but the particular section selected from the *Journal* offers a new way of understanding the most iconic of Romantic Period novels. Siddons's acting notes on Lady Macbeth, published in 1834, are not dated, but by placing them after Baillie's comments on tragedy and the play *De Monfort*, in which Siddons acted, they are accorded an intellectual and personal context which is resonant for them and for her.

Finally, the secondary materials associated with a collection of this kind are potentially overpowering. The Chronology is designedly minimalist, seeking merely to signpost key events and the volume-length publications featured in the anthology: fuller information on each author's writing career is concentrated in the introductory biographical and critical accounts introducing the extracts. The Bibliography brings together items of special interest from a burgeoning critical field: it seeks to make early studies of authors who have not attracted a great deal of recent attention as visible to readers as a selection of more recent studies, and to direct readers to specialist bibliographies, reference guides, and relevant anthologies. The introductions to each author are selective, and take more for granted in the discussion of particularly well-known and established writers such as Austen than they do in the cases of, say, Macaulay and Southcott. They aim to provide essential biographical, social, and intellectual contexts for the writers, and immediate literary contexts for those extracts taken from longer works; as well as providing some added interest, since these are not writers easily contained by the samples of their work included here. Some of the selections made rely heavily on the Explanatory Notes. This is especially true of those which focus on women's intellectually weighty contributions to history, science, and criticism of art and literature. Sometimes—as in the lists of fashionable names given in the memoirs of Mary Robinson and Harriette Wilson—the tone and direction of apparently gossipy or 'high society' writing cannot be gauged without detailed guidance, and this I have attempted to provide. As so often happens, it is not always clear how interesting a piece of writing is until one comes to annotate it.

Wherever possible, I have taken first edition and first collected edition texts as the basis for my selection. I have intervened as little as possible, but have silently changed a handful of potentially puzzling spellings and punctuation marks (but not those spellings which are obvious variants of current forms).

SELECT BIBLIOGRAPHY

Bibliographies and Reference Works

Alston, Robin, *A Checklist of Women Writers 1801–1900: Fiction, Verse, Drama* (London: British Library, 1990).

Armstrong, Isobel, and Bristow, Joseph, with Cath Sharrock (eds.), *Nineteenth-Century Women Poets* (Oxford: Clarendon Press, 1997).

Ashfield, Andrew (ed.), *Romantic Women Poets 1770–1838: An Anthology* (Manchester: Manchester University Press, 1995).

Bell, Peter, *Regency Women: An Index to Biographies and Memoirs* (Edinburgh: Peter Bell, 1991).

Blain, Virginia, Clements, Patricia, and Grundy, Isobel (eds.), *The Feminist Companion to Literature in English: Women Writers from the Middle Ages to the Present* (London: Batsford, 1990).

Boos, Florence, *Bibliography of Women and Literature*, 2 vols. (New York and London: Holmes and Meier, 1989).

Faxon, Frederick W., *Literary Annuals and Gift Books: A Bibliography, 1823–1903* (Middlesex: PLA, 1973).

Feldman, Paula R. (ed.), *British Women Poets of the Romantic Era: An Anthology* (Baltimore: Johns Hopkins University Press, 1997).

Franklin, Caroline (ed.), *The Romantics: Women Poets 1770–1830*, 12 vols. (London: Routledge/Thoemmes Press, 1996).

Horwitz, Barbara J., *British Women Writers, 1700–1850: An Annotated Bibliography of Their Works and Works about Them*, Magill Bibliographies (Lanham, Md.: Scarecrow Press, 1997).

Hutchinson, Anne M. (ed.), *Editing Women* (Cardiff: University of Wales Press, 1998).

Jackson, J. R. de J., *Romantic Poetry by Women: A Bibliography 1770–1835* (Oxford: Clarendon Press, 1993).

Jump, Harriet Devine (ed.), *Women's Writing of the Romantic Period, 1789–1836: An Anthology* (Edinburgh: Edinburgh University Press, 1997).

Leighton, Angela, and Reynolds, Margaret (eds.), *Victorian Women Poets: An Anthology* (Oxford: Blackwell, 1995).

Lonsdale, Roger (ed.), *Eighteenth Century Women Poets: An Oxford Anthology* (Oxford: Oxford University Press, 1990).

Sage, Lorna (ed.), *The Cambridge Guide to Women's Writing in English* (Cambridge: Cambridge University Press, 1999).

Shattock, Joanne, *The Oxford Guide to British Women Writers* (Oxford: Oxford University Press, 1993).

Todd, Janet (ed.), *A Dictionary of British and American Women Writers 1660–1800* (London: Methuen, 1984).

Wu, Duncan (ed.), *Romantic Women Poets: An Anthology* (Oxford: Blackwell, 1997).

General Studies

Women's Writing, 1778–1838

Adburgham, Alison, *Women in Print: Writing Women and Women's Magazines from the Restoration to the Accession of Victoria* (London: Allen and Unwin, 1972).

Alexander, Meena, *Women in Romanticism: Mary Wollstonecraft, Dorothy Wordsworth and Mary Shelley* (London: Macmillan, 1989).

Benstock, Shari (ed.), *Feminist Issues in Literary Scholarship* (Bloomington, Ind.: Indiana University Press, 1987).

Bohls, Elizabeth A., *Women Travel Writers and the Language of Aesthetics, 1716–1818* (Cambridge: Cambridge University Press, 1995).

Burroughs, Catherine B., *Closet Stages: Joanna Baillie and the Theater Theory of British Romantic Women Writers* (Philadelphia: University of Pennsylvania Press, 1997).

Butler, Judith, *Gender Trouble: Feminism and the Subversion of Identity* (London: Routledge, 1990).

Cixous, Hélène, 'The Laugh of the Medusa', in Patricia Bizzel and Bruce Herzberg (eds.), *The Rhetorical Tradition: Readings from Classical Times to the Present* (Boston: Bedford-St Martin's, 1990), 1232–45.

Copeland, Edward, *Women Writing About Money* (Cambridge: Cambridge University Press, 1993).

Curran, Stuart, 'Women Readers, Women Writers', in Stuart Curran (ed.), *The Cambridge Companion to British Romanticism* (Cambridge: Cambridge University Press, 1993), 177–95.

David, D., *Intellectual Women and Victorian Patriarchy: Harriet Martineau, Elizabeth Barrett Browning, George Eliot* (Basingstoke: Macmillan, 1987).

DeJean, Joan, 'Fictions of Sappho', *Critical Inquiry*, 13 (1987), 589–612.

Dimand, Mary Ann, Dimand, Robert W., and Forget, Evelyn L. (eds.), *Women of Value: Feminist Essays on the History of Women in Economics* (Aldershot: Edward Elgar, 1995).

Donkin, Ellen, *Getting into the Act: Women Playwrights in London, 1776–1829* (London: Routledge, 1995).

Ellison, Julie, *Delicate Subjects: Romanticism, Gender, and the Ethics of Understanding* (Ithaca, NY: Cornell University Press, 1990).

Elwood, Anne Katharine, *Memoirs of the Literary Ladies of England*, 2 vols. (1843; New York: AMS, 1971).

Ezell, Margaret, *Writing Women's Literary History* (Baltimore: Johns Hopkins University Press, 1993).

Favret, Mary A., and Watson, Nicola J. (eds.), *At the Limits of Romanticism: Essays in Cultural, Feminist, and Materialist Criticism* (Bloomington, Ind.: Indiana University Press, 1994).

Feldman, Paula R., and Kelley, Theresa M. (eds.), *Romantic Women Writers: Voices and Countervoices* (Hanover, NH: University Press of New England, 1995).

Ferguson, Moira (ed.), *The First Feminists: British Women Writers 1578–1799* (Bloomington, Ind.: Indiana University Press, 1985).

Figes, Eva, *Sex and Subterfuge: Women Writers to 1850* (New York: Persea Books, 1982).

Finke, Laurie, *Feminist Theory, Women's Writing* (Ithaca, NY: Cornell University Press, 1985).

Folger Collective on Early Women Writers (eds.), *Women Critics, 1660–1820: An Anthology* (Bloomington, Ind.: Indiana University Press, 1995).

Fraiman, Susan, *Unbecoming Women: British Women Writers and the Novel of Development* (New York: Columbia University Press, 1993).

Gallagher, Catherine, *Nobody's Story: The Vanishing Acts of Women Writers in the Market Place, 1670–1820* (Oxford: Clarendon Press, 1994).

—— 'A History of the Precedent: Rhetorics of Legitimation in Women's Writing', *Critical Inquiry*, 26 (2000), 309–27.

Gilbert, Sandra, and Gubar, Susan, *The Madwoman in the Attic: The Woman Writer and the Nineteenth-Century Literary Imagination* (New Haven: Yale University Press, 1979).

—— —— (eds.), *Shakespeare's Sisters: Feminist Essays on Women Poets* (Bloomington, Ind.: Indiana University Press, 1979).

Greer, Germaine, *Slip-Shod Sibyls: Recognition, Rejection and the Woman Poet* (London: Penguin, 1995).

Hofkosh, Sonia, 'A Woman's Profession: Sexual Difference and the Romance of Authorship', *Studies in Romanticism*, 32 (1993), 245–72.

Homans, Margaret, *Bearing the Word: Language and Female Experience in Nineteenth-Century Women's Writing* (Chicago: University of Chicago Press, 1986).

Johnson, Claudia L., *Equivocal Beings: Politics, Gender, and Sentimentality in the 1790s* (Chicago: University of Chicago Press, 1995).

Jones, Vivien, *Women in the Eighteenth Century: Constructions of Femininity* (London: Routledge, 1990).

Kaplan, Cora, *Sea Changes: Culture and Feminism* (London: Verso, 1986).

Kelly, Gary, *Women, Writing, and Revolution 1790–1827* (Oxford: Clarendon Press, 1993).

Kowaleski-Wallace, Elizabeth, *Their Fathers' Daughters: Hannah More, Maria Edgeworth, and Patriarchal Complicity* (New York: Oxford University Press, 1991).

Landry, Donna, *The Muses of Resistance: Laboring-Class Women's Poetry in Britain, 1739–1796* (Cambridge: Cambridge University Press, 1990).

Lane, Maggie, *Literary Daughters* (New York: St Martin's Press, 1989).

Linkin, Harriet Kramer, and Behrendt, Stephen C. (eds.), *Romanticism and Women Poets: Opening the Doors of Perception* (Lexington, Ky.: University of Kentucky Press, 1999).

McDonald, Lynn, *Women Founders of the Social Sciences* (Ottawa: Carleton University Press, 1994).

McMillan, Dorothy (ed.), *The Scotswoman at Home and Abroad: Non-Fictional Writing 1700–1900* (Glasgow: Association for Scottish Literary Studies, 1999).

Mellor, Anne K. (ed.), *Romanticism and Feminism* (Bloomington, Ind.: Indiana University Press, 1988).

—— *Romanticism and Gender* (London: Routledge, 1993).

—— 'A Criticism of Their Own: Romantic Women Literary Critics', in John Beer (ed.), *Questioning Romanticism* (Baltimore: Johns Hopkins University Press, 1996), 29–48.

—— *Mothers of the Nation: Women's Political Writing in England, 1780–1830* (Bloomington, Ind.: Indiana University Press, 2000).

Moers, Ellen, *Literary Women* (Garden City, NY: Anchor, 1977).

Montefiore, Jen, *Feminism and Poetry: Language, Experience, Identity in Women's Writing* (New York: Pindar, 1987).

Myers, Mitzi, 'Little Girls Lost: Rewriting Romantic Childhood, Righting Gender and Genre', in Glenn Edward Sadler (ed.), *Teaching Children's Literature: Issues, Pedagogy, Resources* (New York: MLA, 1992), 131–42.

Myers, Sylvia Haverstock, *The Bluestocking Circle: Women, Friendship, and the Life of the Mind in Eighteenth-Century England* (Oxford: Clarendon Press, 1990).

Newton, Judith, *Women, Power and Subversion: Social Strategies in British Fiction, 1778–1860* (Athens, Ga.: University of Georgia Press, 1981).

—— and Rosenfelt, Deborah (eds.), *Feminist Criticism and Social Change: Sex, Class, and Race in Literature and Culture* (London: Methuen, 1985).

Pascoe, Judith, *Romantic Theatricality: Gender, Poetry, and Spectatorship* (Ithaca, NY: Cornell University Press, 1997).

Pearson, Jacqueline, *Women's Reading in Britain, 1750–1835: A Dangerous Recreation* (Cambridge: Cambridge University Press, 1999).

Poovey, Mary, *The Proper Lady and the Woman Writer: Ideology as Style in the Works of Mary Wollstonecraft, Mary Shelley and Jane Austen* (Chicago: University of Chicago Press, 1984).

Robinson, Daniel, 'Reviving the Sonnet: Women Romantic Poets and the Sonnet Claim', *European Romantic Review*, 6 (1995), 98–127.

Ross, Marlon B., *The Contours of Masculine Desire: Romanticism and the Rise of Women's Poetry* (New York: Oxford University Press, 1989).

Schiebinger, Londa, *The Mind Has No Sex? Women in the Origins of Modern Science* (Cambridge, Mass.: Harvard University Press, 1989).

Schofield, Mary Anne, and Macheski, Cecilia (eds.), *Fetter'd or Free? British Women Novelists, 1670–1815* (Athens, Oh.: University of Ohio Press, 1986).

—— —— (eds.), *Curtain Calls: British and American Women and the Theater 1660–1820* (Athens, Ga.: Ohio University Press, 1991).

Shevelov, Kathryn, *Women and Print Culture* (London: Routledge, 1989).

Smith, Bonnie G., *The Gender of History: Men, Women and Historical Practice* (Cambridge, Mass.: Harvard University Press, 2000).

Spencer, Jane, *The Rise of the Woman Novelist: From Aphra Behn to Jane Austen* (Oxford: Blackwell, 1986).

Spender, Dale, *Mothers of the Novel* (London: Pandora, 1986).

Spivak, Gayatri Chakravorty, 'Displacement and the Discourse of Woman', in Mark Krupnick (ed.), *Displacement: Derrida and After* (Bloomington, Ind.: Indiana University Press, 1983).

Still, J., and Worton, M. (eds.), *Textuality and Sexuality: Reading Theories and Practices* (Manchester: Manchester University Press, 1993).

Taylor, Irene, and Luria, Gina, 'Gender and Genre: Women in British Romantic Literature', in Marlene Springer (ed.), *What Manner of Woman: Essays on English and American Life and Literature* (Oxford: Blackwell, 1977), 98–123.

Thomson, Dorothy Lampen, *Adam Smith's Daughters* (Jericho, NY: Exposition-University Press, 1973).

Todd, Janet, *The Sign of Angellica: Women, Writing and Fiction 1660–1800* (London: Virago, 1989).

Turner, Cheryl, *Living by the Pen: Women Writers in the Eighteenth Century* (London: Routledge, 1992).

Ty, Eleanor, *Unsex'd Revolutionaries: Five Women Novelists of the 1790s* (Toronto: University of Toronto Press, 1993).

Walkowitz, Judith, Jehlen, Myra, and Chevigny, Bell, 'Patrolling the Borders: Feminist Historiography and the New Historicism', *Radical History Review*, 43 (1989), 23–43.

Williams, Jane, *The Literary Women of England* (London: Saunders and Otley, 1861).

Williamson, Marilyn L., 'Towards a Feminist Literary History', *Signs*, 10 (1984), 136–47

Wilson, Carol Shiner, and Haefner, Joel (eds.), *Re-Visioning Romanticism: British Women Writers, 1776–1837* (Philadelphia: University of Pennsylvania Press, 1994).

Cultural Contexts, 1778–1838

Adams, M. Ray, *Studies in the Literary Backgrounds of English Radicalism* (New York: Greenwood Press, 1968).

Anderson, Patricia, *The Printed Image and the Transformation of Popular Culture, 1790–1860* (Oxford: Clarendon Press, 1991).

Barker-Benfield, G. J., *The Culture of Sensibility: Sex and Society in Eighteenth-Century Britain* (Chicago: University of Chicago Press, 1992).

Bowers, Bege K., and Brothers, Barbara (eds.), *Reading and Writing Women's Lives: A Study of the Novel of Manners* (Ann Arbor: University of Michigan Press, 1990).

Brophy, Elizabeth Bergen, *Women's Lives and the Eighteenth Century English Novel* (Tampa, Fla.: University of South Florida Press, 1991).

Butler, Marilyn, *Jane Austen and the War of Ideas* (Oxford: Clarendon Press, 1975; revised edn., 1987).

—— *Romantics, Rebels and Reactionaries: English Literature and its Background 1760–1830* (Oxford: Oxford University Press, 1981).

Clark, Anna, 'Queen Caroline and the Sexual Politics of Popular Culture in London, 1820', *Representations*, 31 (1990), 47–68.

Copley, Stephen, and Whale, John (eds.), *Beyond Romanticism: New Approaches to Texts and Contexts 1780–1832* (London: Routledge, 1992).

Cox, Philip, *Gender, Genre, and the Romantic Poets* (Manchester: Manchester University Press, 1996).

Cruse, Amy, *The Englishman and his Books in the Early Nineteenth Century* (London: Harrap, 1930).

Davidoff, Leonore, and Hall, Catherine, *Family Fortunes: Men and Women of the English Middle Class, 1780–1850* (Chicago: University of Chicago Press, 1987).

Fergus, Jan, and Thaddeus, Janice Farrar, 'Women, Publishers, and Money, 1790–1820', *Studies in Eighteenth-Century Culture*, 17 (1987), 191–207.

Ferguson, Moira, *Subject to Others: British Women Writers and Colonial Slavery, 1670–1834* (New York: Routledge, 1992).

Fletcher, Anthony, *Gender, Sex and Subordination in England, 1500–1800* (New Haven: Yale University Press, 1995).

Fraser, Flora, *The Unruly Queen: The Life of Queen Caroline* (London: Macmillan, 1996).

Gallagher, Catherine, and Laquer, Thomas (eds.), *The Making of the Modern Body: Sexuality and Society in the Nineteenth Century* (Berkeley: University of California Press, 1987).

Gaull, Marilyn, *English Romanticism: The Human Context* (New York: Norton, 1988).

Golinski, Jan, *Science as Public Culture: Chemistry and Enlightenment in Britain, 1760–1820* (Cambridge: Cambridge University Press, 1992).

Hill, Bridget, *Women, Work, and Sexual Politics in Eighteenth-Century England* (Oxford: Blackwell, 1989).

Hofkosh, Sonia, *Sexual Politics and the Romantic Author* (Cambridge: Cambridge University Press, 1998).

Jones, Chris, *Radical Sensibility: Literature and Ideas in the 1790s* (London: Routledge, 1993).

Keener, Frederick M., and Lorsch, Susan E. (eds.), *Eighteenth Century Women and the Arts* (New York: Greenwood Press, 1988).

Klancher, Jon P., *The Making of English Reading Audiences, 1790–1832* (Madison: University of Wisconsin Press, 1987).

Knight, David M., *Ideas in Chemistry: A History of the Science* (London: Athlone Press, 1992).

—— *Science in the Romantic Era*, Variorum Collected Studies Series (Aldershot: Ashgate Variorum, 1998).

Kowaleski-Wallace, Elizabeth, 'Milton's Daughters: The Education of Eighteenth-Century English Women Writers', *Feminist Studies*, 12 (1986), 275–93.

Kucich, Greg, 'Romanticism and Feminist Historiography', *Wordsworth Circle*, 24 (1993), 133–40.

Landes, Joan B., *Women and the Public Sphere in the Age of the French Revolution* (Ithaca, NY: Cornell University Press, 1988).

Laqueur, Thomas, *Making Sex: Body and Gender from the Greeks to Freud* (Cambridge, Mass.: Harvard University Press, 1990).

Leranbaum, Miriam, '"Mistresses of Orthodoxy": Education in the Lives and Writings of Late Eighteenth-Century English Women Writers', *Proceedings of the American Philosophical Society*, 121 (1977), 281–301.

McBride, Theresa M., *The Domestic Revolution* (New York: Holmes and Meier, 1976).

McGann, Jerome J., *The Poetics of Sensibility: A Revolution in Literary Style* (Oxford: Oxford University Press, 1996).

Midgley, Clare, *Women Against Slavery: The British Campaigns 1780–1870* (London: Routledge, 1992).

Miller, Peter John, 'Eighteenth-Century Periodicals for Women', *History and Education Quarterly*, 11 (1971), 279–86.

Mitchell, Juliet, and Oakley, Ann (eds.), *The Rights and Wrongs of Women* (New York: Penguin, 1976).

Nussbaum, Felicity A., *The Autobiographical Subject: Gender and Ideology in Eighteenth-Century England* (Baltimore: Johns Hopkins University Press, 1989).

—— *Torrid Zones: Maternity, Sexuality, and Empire in Eighteenth-Century English Narratives* (Baltimore: Johns Hopkins University Press, 1995).

Outram, Dorinda, *The Body and the French Revolution: Sex, Class and Political Culture* (New Haven: Yale University Press, 1989).

Paulson, Ronald, *Representations of Revolution (1789–1820)* (New Haven: Yale University Press, 1983).

Prochaska, Frank K., *Women and Philanthropy in Nineteenth-Century England* (Oxford: Clarendon Press, 1980).

Rendall, Jane, *The Origins of Modern Feminism: Women in Britain, France and the United States 1780–1860* (London: Macmillan, 1985).

Richardson, Alan, and Hofkosh, Sonia (eds.), *Romanticism, Race, and Imperial Culture, 1780–1834* (Bloomington, Ind.: Indiana University Press, 1996).

Rogers, Katharine M., *Feminism in Eighteenth-Century England* (Brighton: Harvester, 1982).

Runge, Laura L., *Gender and Language in British Literary Criticism 1660–1790* (Cambridge: Cambridge University Press, 1997).

Scheuermann, Mona, *Her Bread to Earn: Women, Money and Society from Defoe to Austen* (Lexington, Ky.: University Press of Kentucky, 1993).

Shteir, Ann B., *Cultivating Women, Cultivating Science: Flora's Daughters and Botany in England, 1760–1860* (Baltimore: Johns Hopkins University Press, 1996).

Smith, Hilda L. (ed.), *Women Writers and the Early Modern British Political Tradition* (Cambridge: Cambridge University Press, 1998).

Thompson, E. P., *The Making of the English Working Class* (Harmondsworth: Penguin, 1963, 1980).

Thomson, D. L., *Adam Smith's Daughters* (New York: Exposition Press, 1973).

Todd, Janet, *Sensibility: An Introduction* (New York: Methuen, 1986).

Tompkins, Joyce M. S., *The Popular Novel in England, 1770–1800* (Lincoln, Nebr.: University of Nebraska Press, 1961).

Vickery, Amanda, *The Gentleman's Daughter: Women's Lives in Georgian England* (New Haven: Yale University Press, 1998).

Studies of Individual Writers

Texts and Primary Resources

Austen, Jane, *Letters*, ed. Deirdre Le Faye (Oxford: Oxford University Press, 1995).

Baillie, Joanna, *Collected Lettters*, ed. Judith Bailey Slagle, i (Madison: Fairleigh Dickinson University Press, 1999).

—— *A Selection of Poems and Plays*, ed. Keith Hanley and Amanda Gilroy (Brookfield, Vt.: Pickering and Chatto, 2001).

Barbauld, Anna Laetitia, *The Works of Anna Laetitia Barbauld*, ed. with Memoir by Lucy Aikin, 2 vols. (London: Longman, Hurst, Rees, Orme, Brown, and Green, 1825).

—— *The Poems of Anna Letitia Barbauld*, ed. William McCarthy and Elizabeth Kraft (Athens, Ga.: University of Georgia Press, 1994).

Barrett, Elizabeth, *The Letters of Elizabeth Barrett Browning*, ed. Frederick G. Kenyon, 2 vols., 4th edn. (London: Smith Elder, 1898).

—— *The Letters of Elizabeth Barrett Browning to Mary Russell Mitford: 1836–1854*, ed. Meredith B. Raymond and Mary Rose Sullivan, 3 vols. (Winfield, Kan.: Wedgestone Press, 1983).

Bass, Robert D., *The Green Dragoon: The Lives of Banastre Tarleton and Mary Robinson* (London: Alvin Redman, 1957).

Benger, Elizabeth (ed.), *Memoirs of Mrs Elizabeth Hamilton with Selections from her Correspondence and Unpublished Writings* (London: Longman, Hurst, Rees, Orme & Brown, 1818).

Biller, Sarah, *Hannah Kilham, Memoir of the Late Hannah Kilham; Chiefly Compiled from Her Journal, and Edited by Her Daughter-in-Law, Sarah Biller* (London: Darton and Harvey, 1837).

Blanchard, [Samuel] Laman, *The Life and Literary Remains of L.E.L.*, 2 vols. (London: Henry Colburn, 1841).

Boaden, James, *Memoirs of Mrs. Inchbald, Including her Familiar Correspondence with the Most Distinguished Persons of Her Time*, 2 vols. (London: Bentley, 1833).

Chorley, Henry F., *Memorials of Mrs. Hemans, with Illustrations of her Literary Character from her Private Correspondence*, 2 vols. (London: Saunders and Otley, 1836).

Hemans, Felicia, *Selected Poems*, ed. Gary Kelly and Susan Wolfson (Peterborough, Ont.: Broadview, 1997).

Jewsbury, Maria Jane, *Maria Jane Jewsbury: Occasional Papers*, selected with a Memoir by Eric Gillett (London: Oxford University Press, Humphrey Milford, 1932).

Lamb, Charles, and Lamb, Mary, *The Letters of Charles and Mary Anne Lamb*, ed. Edwin W. Marrs, 3 vols. (Ithaca, NY: Cornell University Press, 1975–8).

—— and —— *The Works of Charles and Mary Lamb*, ed. Thomas Hutchinson (London: Oxford University Press, Humphrey Milford, 1924).

McGann, Jerome, and Riess, Daniel (eds.), *Letitia Elizabeth Landon: Selected Writings* (Peterborough, Ont.: Broadview, 1997).

Macpherson, Gerardine, *Memoirs of the Life of Anna Jameson* (London: Longmans, Green, and Co., 1878).

Martineau, Harriet, *Selected Letters*, ed. Valerie Sanders (Oxford: Clarendon Press, 1990).

Mitford, Mary Russell, *Recollections of a Literary Life; or, Books, Places and People* (London: R. Bentley, 1852).

—— *The Letters of Mary Russell Mitford*, ed. R. Brimley Johnson (1925; Port Washington, Wash.: Kennikat Press, 1972).

'Memoir of Mrs. Hannah More', *The Works of Hannah More*, 6 vols. (London: H. Fisher, R. Fisher, and P. Jackson, 1834), i. 9–72.

More, Hannah, *The Letters of Hannah More*, ed. and introd. R. Brimley Johnson (London: John Lane, The Bodley Head, 1925).

—— *Selected Writings of Hannah More*, ed. Robert Hole (London: Pickering and Chatto, 1996).

Robinson, Mary, *Memoirs of Mary Robinson*, '*Perdita*', ed. and introd. J. Fitzgerald Molloy (London: Gibbings, 1895).

—— *The Poetical Works of Mary Robinson* (Providence, RI: Brown/NEH Women Writers Project, 1990).

—— *Selected Poems*, ed. Judith Pascoe (Peterborough, Ont.: Broadview Press, 2000).

Shelley, Mary Wollstonecraft, *The Journals of Mary Wollstonecraft Shelley*, ed. Paula R. Feldman and D. Scott Kilvert, 2 vols. (Oxford: Clarendon Press, 1987).

—— *The Letters of Mary Wollstonecraft Shelley*, ed. Betty T. Bennett, 3 vols. (Baltimore: Johns Hopkins University Press, 1980–8).

Smith, Charlotte, *The Poems of Charlotte Smith*, ed. Stuart Curran (Oxford: Oxford University Press, 1993).

Taylor, Isaac, *Memoirs and Poetical Remains of the Late Jane Taylor; with Extracts from her Correspondence* (London: B. J. Holdsworth, 1825; rpt. 1925, 1970).

Taylor, Jane, *Prose and Poetry*, introd. F. V. Barry (London: Humphrey Milford, 1925).

Wollstonecraft, Mary, *The Works of Mary Wollstonecraft*, ed. Janet Todd and Marilyn Butler, 7 vols. (London: Pickering and Chatto, 1989).

Wordsworth, Dorothy, *Journals of Dorothy Wordsworth*, ed. Mary Moorman (Oxford: Oxford University Press, 1971).

—— *Recollections of a Tour Made in Scotland*, ed. with notes and photographs by Carol Kyros Walker (New Haven: Yale University Press, 1997).

Wordsworth, William, and Wordsworth, Dorothy, *The Letters of William and Dorothy Wordsworth*, ed. Alan G. Hill (Oxford: Clarendon Press, 1993).

Critical Studies

Aaron, Jane, *A Double Singleness: Gender and the Writings of Charles and Mary Lamb* (Oxford: Clarendon Press, 1991).

Astin, Marjorie, *Mary Russell Mitford: Her Circle and Her Books* (London: N. Douglas, 1930).

Balleine, G. R., *Past Finding Out: The Tragic Story of Joanna Southcott and Her Successors* (London: SPCK, 1956).

Blanch, Lesley, *The Game of Hearts: Harriette Wilson and her Memoirs* (London: Century, 1955).

Brooks, Stella, 'The Sonnets of Charlotte Smith', *Critical Survey*, 4 (1992), 9–21.

Butler, Marilyn, *Maria Edgeworth: A Literary Biography* (Oxford: Clarendon Press, 1972).

Carhart, Margaret S., *The Life and Work of Joanna Baillie* (1923; London: Oxford University Press, 1970).

Clarke, Norma, *Ambitious Heights: Writing, Friendship, Love: The Jewsbury Sisters, Felicia Hemans and Jane Carlyle* (London: Routledge, 1990).

Cottom, Daniel, *The Civilised Imagination: A Study of Ann Radcliffe, Jane Austen, and Sir Walter Scott* (Cambridge: Cambridge University Press, 1985).

Cullins, Chris, 'Mrs Robinson and the Masquerade of Womanliness', in Veronica Kelly and Dorothea Von Mücke (eds.), *Body and Text in the Eighteenth Century* (Stanford, Calif.: Stanford University Press, 1994), 266–89.

Curran, Stuart, 'Charlotte Smith and British Romanticism', *South Central Review*, 11 (1994), 64–78.

Cutt, M. Nancy, *Mrs Sherwood and her Books for Children: A Study* (London: Oxford University Press, 1974).

Cutting-Gray, Joanne, *Woman as 'Nobody' in the Novels of Fanny Burney* (Gainesville, Fla.: University of Florida Press, 1992).

Demers, Patricia, *The World of Hannah More* (Lexington, Ky.: University Press of Kentucky, 1996).

—— '"For mine's a stubborn and a savage will": "Lactilla" (Ann Yearsley) and "Stella" (Hannah More) Reconsidered', *Huntington Library Quarterly*, 56 (1993), 135–50.

Devlin, Diana D., *The Novels and Journals of Fanny Burney* (New York: St Martin's Press, 1987).

Dickson, Mona, *The Powerful Bond: Hannah Kilham, 1774–1832* (London: Dennis Dobson, 1980).

Doody, Margaret Anne, *Frances Burney: The Life in the Works* (New Brunswick, NJ: Rutgers University Press, 1988).

Epstein, Julia, *The Iron Pen: Frances Burney and the Politics of Women's Writing* (Madison: University of Wisconsin Press, 1989).

Erskine, Mrs S., *Anna Jameson: Letters and Friendships 1812–60* (London: Unwin, 1915).

Favret, Mary A., 'Spectatrice as Spectacle: Helen Maria Williams at Home in the Revolution', *Studies in Romanticism*, 32 (1993), 273–95.

Ferguson, Moira, 'Resistance and Power in the Life and Writings of Ann Yearsley', *Eighteenth-Century: Theory and Interpretation*, 27 (1986), 247–68.

Fletcher, Loraine, *Charlotte Smith: A Critical Biography* (Basingstoke: Macmillan, 1998).

Ford, Charles Howard, *Hannah More: A Critical Biography* (New York: Peter Lang, 1996).

Fryckstedt, Monica, 'The Hidden Rill: The Life and Career of Maria Jane Jewsbury', *Bulletin of the John Rylands University Library of Manchester*, 66: 2 (Spring 1984), 177–203 and 67: 1 (Autumn 1984), 450–73.

Gillian, Thomas, *Harriet Martineau* (Boston: Twayne, 1985).

Henchy, P., *The Works of Mary Tighe* (Dublin: Bibliographic Society of Ireland, 1957).

Hilbish, Florence Anna May, *Charlotte Smith, Poet and Novelist (1749–1806)* (Philadelphia: University of Pennsylvania Press, 1941).

Hill, Bridget, *The Republican Virago: The Life and Times of Catharine Macaulay, Historian* (Oxford: Clarendon Press, 1992).

Hoecker-Drysdale, S., *Harriet Martineau: First Woman Sociologist* (Oxford and New York: Berg, 1992).

Hopkins, James K., *A Woman to Deliver Her People* (Austin, Tex.: University of Texas Press, 1982).

Hunter, Shelagh, *Harriet Martineau: The Poetics of Moralism* (Aldershot: Scolar Press, 1995).

Johnson, Claudia, *Jane Austen: Women, Politics, and the Novel* (Chicago: University of Chicago Press, 1988).

Johnston, Judith, *Anna Jameson: Victorian, Feminist, Woman of Letters* (Aldershot: Ashgate, 1997).

Jones, Chris, 'Helen Maria Williams and Radical Sensibility', *Prose Studies*, 12 (1989), 3–24.

Jump, Harriet Devine, *Mary Wollstonecraft: Writer* (Hemel Hempstead: Harvester, 1994).

Kelly, Gary, *Revolutionary Feminism: The Mind and Career of Mary Wollstonecraft* (Basingstoke: Macmillan, 1992).

Knight, H. C., *Jane Taylor: Her Life and Letters* (London: Nelson, 1880).

Kuczynski, Ingrid, 'Reading a Landscape: Ann Radcliffe's *A Journey Made in the Summer of 1794, Through Holland and the Western Frontier of Germany, With a Return Down the Rhine* (1795)', in Michael Gassenmeier *et al.* (eds.), *British Romantics as Readers: Intertextualities, Maps of Misreading, Reinterpretations* (Heidelberg: Carl Winter Universitätsverlag, 1998), 241–57.

Labbe, Jacqueline, 'Selling One's Sorrows: Charlotte Smith, Mary Robinson, and the Marketing of Poetry', *Wordsworth Circle*, 25 (1994), 68–71.

Leighton, Angela, *Elizabeth Barrett Browning* (Brighton: Harvester, 1986).

Levin, Susan, *Dorothy Wordsworth and Romanticism* (New Brunswick, NJ: Rutgers University Press, 1987).

Linkin, Harriet Kramer, 'Romanticism and Mary Tighe's *Psyche*: Peering at the Hem of Her Blue Stockings', *Studies in Romanticism*, 35 (1996), 55–72.

Littlewood, S. R., *Mrs Inchbald and her Circle* (London: Daniel O'Connor, 1921).

Lootens, Tricia, 'Hemans and Home: Victorianism, Feminine "Internal Enemies", and the Domestication of National Identity', *PMLA* 109 (1994), 238–53.

Mack, Anne, Rome, J. J., and Manneje, George [J. J. McGann], 'Literary History, Romanticism, and Felicia Hemans', *Modern Language Quarterly*, 54 (1993), 215–45.

Manvell, Roger, *Elizabeth Inchbald: England's Principal Woman Dramatist and Independent Woman of Letters in Eighteenth Century London: A Biographical Study* (Lanham, Md.: University Press of America, 1987).

Mellor, Anne K., *Mary Shelley: Her Life, Her Fictions, Her Monsters* (London: Methuen, 1988).

Miles, Robert, *Ann Radcliffe: The Great Enchantress* (Manchester: Manchester University Press, 1995).

Moskal, Jeanne, 'Ann Radcliffe's Lake District', *Wordsworth Circle*, 31 (2000), 56–62.

Norton, Ricter, *The Mistress of Udolpho: The Life of Ann Radcliffe* (Leicester: Leicester University Press, 1998).

Pichanick, Valerie, *Harriet Martineau: The Woman and her Work 1802–1876* (Ann Arbor: University of Michigan Press, 1980).

Riess, Daniel, 'Laetitia Landon and the Dawn of English Post-Romanticism', *Studies in English Literature*, 36 (1996), 807–27.

Roberts, Emma, 'Memoir of L.E.L.', *The Zenana and Minor Poems of L.E.L.* (London: Fisher, 1839).

Rodgers, Betsy, *Georgian Chronicle: Mrs Barbauld and her Family* (London: Methuen, 1958).

Rogers, Katharine M., 'Inhibitions on Eighteenth-Century Women Novelists: Elizabeth Inchbald and Charlotte Smith', *Eighteenth-Century Studies*, 11 (1977–8), 63–78.

Schnorrenberg, Barbara B., 'The Brood-Hen of Faction: Mrs Macaulay and Radical Politics, 1765–75', *Albion*, 11 (1979), 33–45.

Setzer, Sharon M., 'Mary Robinson's Sylphid Self: The End of Feminine Self-Fashioning', *Philological Quarterly*, 75 (1996), 501–20.

Stanton, Judith, 'Charlotte Smith's "Literary Business": Income, Patronage, and Indigence', *Age of Johnson*, 1 (1988), 375–401.

Stephenson, Glennis, 'Poet Construction: Mrs Hemans, L. E. L., and the Image of the Nineteenth-Century Woman Poet', in Shirley Neuman and Glennis Stephenson (eds.), *Reimagining Women: Representations of Women in Culture* (Toronto: University of Toronto Press, 1993), 61–73.

—— *Letitia Landon: The Woman Behind L. E. L.* (Manchester: Manchester University Press, 1995).

Sutherland, Kathryn, 'Hannah More's Counter-Revolutionary Feminism', in Kelvin Everest (ed.), *Revolution and Writing: British Literary Responses to the French Revolution* (Milton Keynes: Open University Press, 1991), 27–63.

Todd, Janet, *Mary Wollstonecraft: A Revolutionary Life* (London: Weidenfeld and Nicolson, 2000).

Tompkins, J. M. S., 'The Bristol Milkwoman', in *The Polite Marriage* (1938; Freeport, NY: Books for Libraries Press, 1969), 58–102.

Trinder, Peter, *Mrs Hemans* (Cardiff: University of Wales Press, 1984).

Ty, Eleanor, 'Engendering a Female Subject: Mary Robinson's (Re)Presentations of the Self', *English Studies in Canada*, 21 (1995), 407–31.

Waldron, Mary, *Lactilla, Milkwoman of Clifton: The Life and Writings of Ann Yearsley, 1753–1806* (Athens, Ga.: University of Georgia Press, 1996).

Withey, Lynne E., 'Catharine Macaulay and the Uses of History: Ancient

Rights, Perfectionism, and Propaganda', *Journal of British Studies*, 16 (1976), 59–83.

Yates, Gayle Graham, *Harriet Martineau on Women* (New Brunswick, NJ: Rutgers University Press, 1985).

Further Reading in Oxford World's Classics

Beeton, Isabella, *Mrs Beeton's Book of Household Management*, ed. Nicola Humble.

Burney, Fanny, *Camilla*, ed. Edward A. Bloom and Lilian D. Bloom.

—— *Cecilia*, ed. Peter Sabor and Margaret Anne Doody.

—— *Evelina*, ed. Edward A. Bloom.

Edgeworth, Maria, *Belinda*, ed. Kathryn Kirkpatrick.

—— *Castle Rackrent*, ed. George Watson.

Five Romantic Plays 1768–1821, ed. Paul Baines and Edward Burns.

Inchbald, Elizabeth, *A Simple Story*, ed. J. M. S. Tompkins.

Radcliffe, Ann, *The Mysteries of Udolpho*, ed. Bonamy Dobrée and Terry Castle.

Shelley, Mary, *Frankenstein* (the 1818 text), ed. Marilyn Butler.

Wollstonecraft, Mary, *A Vindication of the Rights of Woman/A Vindication of the Rights of Men*, ed. Janet Todd.

CHRONOLOGY

1778   Frances Burney's first novel, *Evelina*; Catharine Macaulay, *The History of England from the Revolution to the Present Time*; beginning of Mary Robinson's affair with the Prince of Wales.

1780   Anti-Catholic Gordon Riots in London.

1781   Defeat of British by Americans at Yorktown; Anna Laetitia Barbauld, *Hymns in Prose for Children*.

1783   Peace of Paris brings end to war with American colonies and recognizes their independence.

1784   James Watt invents steam engine; first volume of Charlotte Smith's *Elegiac Sonnets*.

1785   Failure of Bill for Parliamentary Reform; Edmund Cartwright patents power loom; Clara Reeve, *The Progress of Romance*.

1786   Birth of Mary Russell Mitford; birth of Harriette Wilson.

1787   American Constitution signed; foundation of the Association for the Abolition of the Slave Trade; Elizabeth Inchbald, *Such Things Are*.

1788   British settlement of Australia; beginning of trial of Warren Hastings; William Wiberforce first moves for parliamentary abolition of the slave trade.

1789   Fall of the Bastille in Paris (July); Declaration of Rights of Man and the Citizen (August); George Washington becomes US President.

1790   Lavoisier, table of chemical elements; hopes of reform in civic status of Dissenters defeated; Macaulay, *Letters on Education*: Helen Maria Williams, *Letters Written in France*.

1791   Flight of Louis XVI from Paris; recaptured at Varennes; riots in Birmingham; Inchbald, *A Simple Story*; Robinson, *Poems*; death of Macaulay.

1792   September Massacres in Paris followed by proclamation of Republic; Louis XVI put on trial; increased political activity across Britain instanced by formation of the London Corresponding Society and the Association for the Preservation of Liberty and Property Against Republicans and Levellers; Mary Wollstonecraft, *A Vindication of the Rights of Woman*.

1793   Execution of Louis XVI (January) and of Marie Antoinette

(October); France declares war on Britain (February); during Robespierre's Reign of Terror, Madame Roland executed and Helen Maria Williams imprisoned in Paris; trial and conviction of radicals in Scotland; Laetitia Matilda Hawkins, *Letters on the Female Mind*; birth of Felicia Hemans.

1794 Suspension of Habeas Corpus to increase state powers over those suspected of political sedition; overthrow and execution of Robespierre; Treason Trials in London end in acquittal; Ann Radcliffe, *The Mysteries of Udolpho*; birth of Anna Jameson; birth of Emma Roberts.

1795 Anti-radical legislation strengthened by Seditious Meetings Act and Treasonable Practices Act; Warren Hastings acquitted; establishment of Directory in France; introduction of Speenhamland system of poor relief; Radcliffe, *Journal of a Tour Made in the Summer of 1794*; Hannah More, first of series *Cheap Repository Tracts*.

1796 Britain at war with Spain; Napoleon leads French campaign of conquest in Italian states; Ann Yearsley, *The Rural Lyre*; Mary Wollstonecraft, *Letters Written during a Short Residence in Sweden, Norway, and Denmark*; Burney, *Camilla*; Mary Robinson, *Sappho and Phaon*; Elizabeth Hamilton, *Translation of the Letters of a Hindoo Rajah*; Priscilla Wakefield, *Introduction to Botany*.

1797 Naval mutinies; second volume of Smith's *Elegiac Sonnets*; death of Wollstonecraft; birth of Mary Wollstonecraft Godwin (later Shelley).

1798 Uprising in Ireland; further suspension of Habeas Corpus; Horatio Nelson leads British victory at battle of the Nile, defeating Napoleon's invasion of Egypt; first volume of Joanna Baillie's *Plays on the Passions*; Wakefield, *Reflections on the Present Condition of the Female Sex*.

1799 Napoleon overthrows Directory and becomes First Consul of France; anti-radical measures in Britain include suppression of London Corresponding Society and passing of the repressive 'Six Acts' and Combination Acts (to prevent formation of trade unions).

1800 Act of Union with Ireland; Jefferson becomes US President; foundation of Royal Institution of Science; Maria Edgeworth, *Castle Rackrent*, death of Robinson; birth of Maria Jane Jewsbury.

1801 Resignation of the Prime Minister, William Pitt the Younger, succeeded by Lord Addington; first Census in Britain (the population is 9,168,000); further suspension of Habeas Corpus; Maria Edgeworth, *Belinda*; Robinson, *Memoirs*; Joanna Southcott's first publication, *The Strange Effects of Faith*.

1802   Peace of Amiens brings temporary end to war with France; Southcott, *A Dispute between the Woman and the Powers of Darkness*; birth of Laetitia Elizabeth Landon; birth of Harriet Martineau.

1803   War resumes; Dorothy Wordsworth's tour of Scotland.

1804   Napoleon is declared Emperor of France (May); Pitt forms new ministry; Jane and Ann Taylor, *Original Poems for Infant Minds*.

1805   Victory and death of Nelson at battle of Trafalgar; French victory over Austria and Russia at Austerlitz; Mary Tighe, *Psyche*.

1806   Defeat of Prussia by French troops at Jena; Napoleon closes continental ports to British trade; complex political year following death of Pitt and Charles James Fox, leading to the 'ministry of all the talents', led by Lord Grenville; Jane Marcet, *Conversations on Chemistry*; Inchbald, first volumes of John Bell's *British Theatre*; death of Smith; death of Yearsley; birth of Elizabeth Barrett.

1807   Act abolishing the slave trade in the British Empire; France invades Spain and Portugal; death of Reeve.

1808   Beginning of Peninsular War against France; Hemans's first volume, *Poems*; Maria Eliza Rundell, *A New System of Domestic Cookery*.

1809   French victory over British troops at Corunna; beginning of Perceval's ministry; Charles and Mary Lamb, *Mrs Leicester's School*.

1810   Holland annexed by France; increasing fears over mental incapacity of George III; death of Tighe.

1811   Prince of Wales is declared Regent; Luddite riots against introduction of factory machinery in the Midlands.

1812   Assassination of the Prime Minister, Perceval; beginning of Lord Liverpool's ministry; French retreat from Moscow after failed invasion of Russia; declaration of war against the United States of America; removal of 'Elgin Marbles' to London; Anna Laetitia Barbauld, *Eighteen Hundred and Eleven*.

1813   Further setbacks for French as Spain is liberated by British troops under Wellington, followed by defeat in Holland, Italy, and Switzerland.

1814   Allies invade France, Napoleon abdicates and is exiled to Elba; First Treaty of Paris between France and Allies; peace with United States; Corn Law is passed by Parliament; Stephenson invents the steam engine; Jane Austen, *Mansfield Park*; death and dissection of Southcott.

1815   Napoleon escapes from exile and leads French army to defeat by Allies at Waterloo; Louis XVIII declared King of France.

1816   Economic and social distress in Britain follows the end of the war with France; riot at Spa Fields (December); Jane Taylor, *Essays in Rhyme on Morals and Manners*; Marcet, *Conversations on Political Economy*, death of Hamilton.

1817   Suspension of Habeas Corpus; Seditious Meetings Bill; Pentridge uprising in Derbyshire; death of Austen.

1818   Habeas Corpus restored; Austen, *Persuasion*; Mary Shelley, *Frankenstein*; Mary Sherwood, first parts of *The History of the Fairchild Family*.

1819   Violent suppression of meeting at St Peter's Fields, Manchester (Peterloo); legislation restricting freedom of press; Mary Russell Mitford, first parts of *Our Village*.

1820   Death of George III and accession of George IV (January); beginning of divorce trial of Caroline of Brunswick; discovery of Cato Street Conspiracy to assassinate ministers; revolutions in Spain, Portugal, and Naples; Landon, first published poem.

1821   Exclusion of Caroline from coronation of George IV (July), followed by her death (August); death of Napoleon; beginning of Greek War of Independence; foundation of London Co-operative Society; Mary Hays, *Memoirs of Queens*; death of Inchbald.

1822   Suicide of Lord Castlereagh; foundation of Royal Academy of Music; Hemans, *Welsh Melodies*.

1823   Beginning of penal reforms by the Home Secretary, Robert Peel; death of Radcliffe.

1824   Repeal of 1662 Poor Law Act; repeal of Combination Laws of 1799 and 1801; foundation of London Mechanics Institution; establishment of National Gallery; death of Taylor.

1825   Widespread financial crisis; opening of Darlington–Stockton passenger railway; Harriette Wilson, *Memoirs*; Jewsbury, *Phantasmagoria*; Mrs Parkes, *Domestic Duties*; death of Barbauld.

1826   Liverpool succeeded as Prime Minister by George Canning; riots in Lancashire protesting at the introduction of power looms; Barrett's first volume, *Essay on Mind, and Other Poems*; Anna Jameson, *The Diary of an Ennuyée*; Christian Isobel Johnstone, *The Cook and Housewife's Manual*.

1827   Greek Independence secured; foundation of University College London (first non-denominational university); death of Williams.

1828   Wellington becomes Prime Minister; repeal of Test and Corporation Acts; Hemans, *Records of Woman*; Hannah Kilham, *Report on a Recent Visit to the Colony of Sierra Leone*.

1829   Catholic Emancipation Act; establishment of Metropolitan Police Force.

1830   Death of George IV and accession of William IV; beginning of the reforming Whig ministry of Earl Grey; agricultural labourers' revolts in southern England, led by 'Captain Swing'; July Revolution in Paris; foundation of Royal Geographical Society; Felicia Hemans, *Songs of the Affections*.

1831   Parliamentary Reform Bill struggles through Commons but is defeated in Lords; riots in Bristol, Derby, Nottingham; beginnings of reform of working conditions for children in the Cotton Mills Act; death of Siddons.

1832   Successful passing of the Reform Act; Harriet Martineau, first parts of *Illustrations of Political Economy*; death of Wakefield; death of Kilham.

1833   Abolition of slavery; Barrett, *Prometheus Bound*; death of More.

1834   Poor Law Act; burning of Houses of Parliament in London; Thomas Campbell, *Life of Mrs Siddons*.

1835   Municipal Reform Act; Roberts, *Scenes and Characteristics of Hindostan*; death of Hawkins; death of Hemans.

1837   Death of William IV and accession of Victoria; Martineau, *Society in America*.

1838   Publication of the 'People's Charter'; Barrett, *The Seraphim*; death of Landon.

WOMEN'S WRITING

1778–1838

FRANCES BURNEY
(1752–1840)

The third of the six surviving children from the first marriage of the music teacher and historian of music Dr Charles Burney, Frances Burney was born in King's Lynn, Norfolk, and experimented in writing creatively at an early age, although she burned her childhood manuscripts on her fifteenth birthday in 1767. Her mother Esther Sleepe died when Burney was 10, and she disliked his second wife, Elizabeth Allen (m. 1767), against whom the Burney children developed a private emotional resistance or secret 'treason'. Largely self-educated, she acted as secretary and copyist of her father's work, and wrote out the manuscript of her first novel in a disguised hand because her own would have been identifiable by compositors who had prepared his books for the press. In 1778 she published her first novel, *Evelina; or, the History of a Young Lady's Entrance into the World*, anonymously, and on its success became a noted figure in the intellectual group which gathered around the Streatham home of Hester Lynch Piozzi (then Thrale); it included Samuel Johnson, who championed Burney's work, and Edmund Burke and Richard Brinsley Sheridan. Thrale thought Burney gave the impression of being an actress, part of a family on display, one in which each individual 'must write and read & be literary'.[1] On the recommendation of her father and a fatherly mentor, Samuel Crisp, she set aside a manuscript comedy, *The Witlings*, in 1779, possibly because it contained too recognizable a mockery of the leading Bluestocking Elizabeth Montagu. In the mid-1780s she had hopes of being proposed to by the Revd George Owen Cambridge, and aspects of her uncertainty and unhappiness are thought to be found in the experiences of the heroine of her third novel, *Camilla*.

Burney's literary reputation secured her the position, which she disliked, of Second Keeper of the Robes to Queen Charlotte, for which she was paid £200 per year and from which her father expected patronage and influence. During these unhappy five years, 1786–91 (unhappy for herself and for the court: Burney witnessed the supposed madness, now identified as porphyria, of the king, George III), she worked on three tragedies, one of which, *Edwy and Elgiva*, was performed, in 1795, with Kemble and Sarah Siddons among the players. Ill with unhappiness, she was eventually released from court, and granted a pension of £100 per annum for life by the queen, which secured her financial independence. In 1792 she met

[1] *Thraliana: The Diary of Mrs Hester Lynch Thrale*, ed. K. C. Balderston, 2 vols. (Oxford: Clarendon Press, 1942), 1. 399.

General Alexandre d'Arblay, a French émigré who had recently joined the little colony of French émigrés in Mickleham, Surrey, and in July 1793 married him in spite of her father's opposition; they had a son, Alexander, in 1794, and from 1802 to 1812 lived in France, unable to return because of the state of war between Britain and Napoleonic France. Her other novels are the extremely popular *Cecilia; or, Memoirs of an Heiress* (1782), *Camilla; or, a Picture of Youth* (1796), which was financially but not critically successful, and *The Wanderer; or, Female Difficulties* (1814), which was neither. She continued to write plays, including her comedy *Love and Fashion* which she withdrew just before its projected performance at Covent Garden in 1800, and the comedies *A Busy Day* (1800–1) and *The Woman-Hater* (1801), unperformed because of her removal to France in April 1802. Her *Memoirs* of her father appeared in 1832. Burney's much-admired *Diary*, published 1842–6, tells of court life, life in France, her mastectomy, undertaken without anaesthetic in September 1811, and life in Brussels during the days before and after the battle of Waterloo, in which her husband fought, and for which he was rewarded with the title of Comte d'Arblay. Her writings secured her an income, although not until *Camilla* did she negotiate anything like fair terms: she earned £20 for *Evelina*, £250 for *Cecilia*, and £2,000 for *Camilla*. From these earnings the d'Arblays financed the building of Camilla Cottage, West Humble, on land on the Norbury estate of their friends the Lockes, but they lost the cottage in 1814, William Locke having died in 1810 without formally securing to them the land they had leased for it. Burney's life was clouded by the deaths of her favourite sister Susanna in January 1800, her husband in May 1818, and her son in January 1837. She died in London on the anniversary of Susanna's death forty years earlier, and was buried next to her husband and son in Wolcot churchyard, Bath.

In the Preface to *Evelina* Burney reveals mixed feelings about the perceived literary status of novelists and the value of novels for young women. Her roll-call of inspirational novelistic precursors is exclusively male, and she makes no allusion to her own gender. Her statement that this three-volume novel (or series of letters, as it purports to be) is presented to the reading public 'with a very singular mixture of timidity and confidence, resulting from the peculiar situation of the editor', has, however, often been read as a tacit appeal to male protection made by a properly retiring young woman. Warning her readers that they are not to expect the fantasy-world of romance or the perfections of idealized characters from her novel, she describes its subject thus: 'a young female, educated in the most secluded retirement, makes, at the age of seventeen, her first appearance upon the great and busy stage of life; with a virtuous mind, a cultivated understanding, and a feeling heart, her ignorance of the forms, and inexperience in the manners, of the world, occasion all the little incidents which these volumes record.' The individuality and comic edge of the work were immediately admired, and although Burney was far from being the first to attempt to capture the immediacy of a young woman's response to her world and the men within it (the most important prototypes being Samuel Richardson's *Pamela* and *Clarissa*, both written, like *Evelina*, in the epistolary mode), Burney adroitly exploits the epistolary form to suggest experience in the process of being formed; of events which may be trivial, or not, because the future on which their significance depends is not yet known to the correspondent-narrators. In the following extract from the early part of the novel, the motherless heroine, Evelina Anville, abandoned by her father and brought up in ignorance of her true rank by a clergyman guardian, Mr Villars, writes to him of her first days in London in the company of a friend, Mrs Mirvan, and her daughter, Maria. Evelina's secluded but secure and affectionate upbringing in Dorset is acknowledged by Mr Villars to have made her manners rather rustic.

Burney's third novel, the five-volume *Camilla*, centres on the mistakes of its heroine, Camilla Tyrold, as her conduct is put to the test by the man she eventually marries, Edgar Mandlebert. Burney disliked thinking of it as a 'novel', writing to her father: 'It gives so simply the notion of a mere love story that I recoil a little from it. I mean this work to be sketches of character and morals put in action—not a romance.'[2] Burney worked on the novel in various drafts and different versions for several years. It is in parts more moralistic and more instructive than *Evelina*, and weaves into the traditional courtship plot episodes in which the hearts and minds of the Tyrold sisters are refined and corrected. In the following extract Camilla and her sister Eugenia, who has been facially disfigured by smallpox and crippled in a childhood accident (both the fault of her uncle, who in contrition makes her his sole heir), are treated to an educational circus-show in miniature, for the correction of the morally and emotional vitiating disappointments of female vanity. Eugenia is an interesting character for readers tracing the representation of women's education; she is a learned and well-read young woman who has been given a classical education after her disfigurement, and after an unhappy marriage turns to writing her memoirs. Anna Laetitia Barbauld, who was disappointed in *Camilla* as a whole, liked the story of Eugenia; while Jane Austen, who did like *Camilla*, makes a point in *Northanger Abbey* (ch. 7) of exposing the dullard John Thorpe's lack of appreciation of the oddities that lead to Eugenia's disfiguring accident: 'There is nothing in it but an old man's playing at see-saw and learning Latin. Upon my soul there is not.'

[2] Amy Cruse, *The Englishmen and his Books in the Early Nineteenth Century* (London: Harrap, 1930), 24.

⁓

From *Evelina* (1778)

LETTER X
Evelina to the Rev. Mr Villars

Queen-Ann-Street, London, Saturday, April 2

This moment arrived. Just going to Drury-Lane theatre.* The celebrated Mr Garrick performs Ranger.* I am quite in extacy. So is Miss
Mirvan. How fortunate, that he should happen to play! We would
not let Mrs Mirvan rest till she consented to go; her chief objection
was to our dress, for we have had no time to *Londonize* ourselves; but
we teized her into compliance, and so we are to sit in some obscure
place, that she may not be seen. As to me, I should be alike unknown
in the most conspicuous or most private part of the house.

I can write no more now. I have hardly time to breathe—only just
this, the houses and streets are not quite so superb as I expected.
However, I have seen nothing yet, so I ought not to judge.

Well, adieu, my dearest Sir, for the present; I could not forbear
writing a few words instantly on my arrival; though I suppose my
letter of thanks for your consent is still on the road.

Saturday Night

O my dear Sir, in what raptures am I returned! Well may Mr Garrick
be so celebrated, so universally admired—I had not any idea of so
great a performer.

Such ease! such vivacity in his manner! such grace in his motions!
such fire and meaning in his eyes!—I could hardly believe he had
studied a written part, for every word seemed spoke from the
impulse of the moment.

His action—at once so graceful and so free!—his voice—so clear,
so melodious, yet so wonderfully various in its tones—such
animation!—every look *speaks!*

I would have given the world to have had the whole play acted over
again. And when he danced—O how I envied Clarinda.* I almost
wished to have jumped on the stage and joined them.

I am afraid you will think me mad, so I won't say any more; yet I really believe Mr Garrick would make you mad too, if you could see him. I intend to ask Mrs Mirvan to go to the play every night while we stay in town. She is extremely kind to me, and Maria, her charming daughter, is the sweetest girl in the world.

I shall write to you every evening all that passes in the day, and that in the same manner as, if I could see, I should tell you.

Sunday

This morning we went to Portland chapel, and afterwards we walked in the Mall in St James's Park, which by no means answered my expectations: it is a long straight walk, of dirty gravel, very uneasy to the feet; and at each end, instead of an open prospect, nothing is to be seen but houses built of brick.* When Mrs Mirvan pointed out the *Palace* to me—I think I was never much more surprised.

However, the walk was very agreeable to us; every body looked gay, and seemed pleased, and the ladies were so much dressed, that Miss Mirvan and I could do nothing but look at them. Mrs Mirvan met several of her friends. No wonder, for I never saw so many people assembled together before. I looked about for some of *my* acquaintance, but in vain, for I saw not one person that I knew, which is very odd, for all the world seemed there.

Mrs Mirvan says we are not to walk in the Park again next Sunday, even if we should be in town, because there is better company in Kensington Gardens. But really if you had seen how much every body was dressed, you would not think that possible.

Monday

We are to go this evening to a private ball, given by Mrs Stanley, a very fashionable lady of Mrs Mirvan's acquaintance.

We have been *a shopping*, as Mrs Mirvan calls it, all this morning, to buy silks, caps, gauzes, and so forth.

The shops are really very entertaining, especially the mercers;* there seem to be six or seven men belonging to each shop, and every one took care, by bowing and smirking, to be noticed; we were conducted from one to another, and carried from room to room, with so much ceremony, that at first I was almost afraid to follow.

I thought I should never have chosen a silk, for they produced so many, I knew not which to fix upon, and they recommended them all so strongly, that I fancy they thought I only wanted persuasion to buy every thing they shewed me. And, indeed, they took so much trouble, that I was almost ashamed I could not.

At the milliners, the ladies we met were so much dressed, that I should rather have imagined they were making visits than purchases. But what most diverted me was, that we were more frequently served by men than by women; and such men! so finical, so affected! they seemed to understand every part of a woman's dress better than we do ourselves; and they recommended caps and ribbands with an air of so much importance, that I wished to ask them how long they had left off wearing them!

The dispatch with which they work in these great shops is amazing, for they have promised me a compleat suit of linen against the evening.*

I have just had my hair dressed.* You can't think how oddly my head feels; full of powder and black pins, and a great *cushion* on the top of it. I believe you would hardly know me, for my face looks quite different to what it did before my hair was dressed. When I shall be able to make use of a comb for myself I cannot tell, for my hair is so much entangled, *frizzled* they call it, that I fear it will be very difficult.

I am half afraid of this ball to-night, for, you know, I have never danced but at school; however, Miss Mirvan says there is nothing in it. Yet I wish it was over.

Adieu, my dear Sir; pray excuse the wretched stuff I write, perhaps I may improve by being in this town, and then my letters will be less unworthy your reading. Mean time I am,

Your dutiful and affectionate,

though unpolished,

EVELINA

Poor Miss Mirvan cannot wear one of the caps she made, because they dress her hair too large for them.

LETTER XI

Evelina in continuation

Queen-Ann-Street, April 5, Tuesday morning

I have a vast deal to say, and shall give all this morning to my pen. As to my plan of writing every evening the adventures of the day, I find it impracticable; for the diversions here are so very late, that if I begin my letters after them, I could not go to bed at all.

We past a most extraordinary evening. A *private* ball this was called, so I expected to have seen about four or five couple; but, Lord! my dear Sir, I believe I saw half the world! Two very large rooms were full of company; in one, were cards for the elderly ladies, and in the other, were the dancers. My mamma Mirvan, for she always calls me her child, said she would sit with Maria and me till we were provided with partners, and then join the card-players.

The gentlemen, as they passed and repassed, looked as if they thought we were quite at their disposal, and only waiting for the honour of their commands; and they sauntered about, in a careless indolent manner, as if with a view to keep us in suspense. I don't speak of this in regard to Miss Mirvan and myself only, but to the ladies in general; and I thought it so provoking, that I determined, in my own mind, that, far from humouring such airs, I would rather not dance at all, than with any one who should seem to think me ready to accept the first partner who would condescend to take me.

Not long after, a young man, who had for some time looked at us with a kind of negligent impertinence, advanced, on tiptoe, towards me; he had a set smile on his face, and his dress was so foppish, that I really believe he even wished to be stared at; and yet he was very ugly.

Bowing almost to the ground, with a sort of swing, and waving his hand with the greatest conceit, after a short and silly pause, he said, 'Madam—may I presume?'—and stopt, offering to take my hand. I drew it back, but could scarce forbear laughing. 'Allow me, Madam,' (continued he, affectedly breaking off every half moment) 'the honour and happiness—if I am not so unhappy as to address you too late—to have the happiness and honour—'

Again he would have taken my hand, but, bowing my head, I begged to be excused, and turned to Miss Mirvan to conceal my laughter. He then desired to know if I had already engaged myself to some more fortunate man? I said No, and that I believed I should not dance at all. He would keep himself, he told me, disengaged, in hopes I should relent; and then, uttering some ridiculous speeches of sorrow and disappointment, though his face still wore the same invariable smile, he retreated.

It so happened, as we have since recollected, that during this little dialogue, Mrs Mirvan was conversing with the lady of the house. And very soon after another gentleman, who seemed about six-and-twenty years old, gayly, but not foppishly, dressed, and indeed extremely handsome, with an air of mixed politeness and gallantry, desired to know if I was engaged, or would honour him with my hand. So he was pleased to say; though I am sure I know not what honour he could receive from me; but these sort of expressions, I find, are used as words of course, without any distinction of persons, or study of propriety.

Well, I bowed, and I am sure I coloured; for indeed I was frightened at the thoughts of dancing before so many people, all strangers, and, which was worse, *with* a stranger; however, that was unavoidable, for though I looked round the room several times, I could not see one person that I knew. And so, he took my hand, and led me to join in the dance.

The minuets were over before we arrived, for we were kept late by the milliner's making us wait for our things.*

He seemed very desirous of entering into conversation with me; but I was seized with such a panic, that I could hardly speak a word, and nothing but the shame of so soon changing my mind, prevented my returning to my seat, and declining to dance at all.

He appeared to be surprised at my terror, which I believe was but too apparent: however, he asked no questions, though I fear he must think it very odd; for I did not choose to tell him it was owing to my never before dancing but with a school-girl.

His conversation was sensible and spirited; his air and address were open and noble; his manners gentle, attentive, and infinitely engaging; his person is all elegance, and his countenance the most animated and expressive I have ever seen.

In a short time we were joined by Miss Mirvan, who stood next couple to us. But how was I startled, when she whispered me that my partner was a nobleman! This gave me a new alarm; how will he be provoked, thought I, when he finds what a simple rustic he has honoured with his choice! one whose ignorance of the world makes her perpetually fear doing something wrong!

That he should be so much my superior every way, quite disconcerted me; and you will suppose my spirits were not much raised, when I heard a lady, in passing us, say, 'This is the most difficult dance I ever saw.'

'O dear, then,' cried Maria to her partner, 'with your leave, I'll sit down till the next.'

'So will I too, then,' cried I, 'for I am sure I can hardly stand.'

'But you must speak to your partner first,' answered she; for he had turned aside to talk with some gentlemen. However, I had not sufficient courage to address him, and so away we all three tript, and seated ourselves at another end of the room.

But, unfortunately for me, Miss Mirvan soon after suffered herself to be prevailed upon to attempt the dance; and just as she rose to go, she cried, 'My dear, yonder is your partner, Lord Orville, walking about the room in search of you.'

'Don't leave me, then, dear girl!' cried I; but she was obliged to go. And then I was more uneasy than ever; I would have given the world to have seen Mrs Mirvan, and begged of her to make my apologies; for what, thought I, can I possibly say for myself in excuse for running away? he must either conclude me a fool, or half mad, for any one brought up in the great world, and accustomed to its ways, can have no idea of such sort of fears as mine.

I was in the utmost confusion, when I observed that he was every where seeking me, with apparent perplexity and surprise; but when, at last, I saw him move towards the place where I sat, I was ready to sink with shame and distress. I found it absolutely impossible to keep my seat, because I could not think of a word to say for myself, and so I rose, and walked hastily towards the card-room, resolving to stay with Mrs Mirvan the rest of the evening, and not to dance at all. But before I could find her, Lord Orville saw and approached me.

He begged to know if I was not well? You may easily imagine how much I was confused. I made no answer, but hung my head, like a fool, and looked on my fan!

He then, with an air the most respectfully serious, asked if he had been so unhappy as to offend me?

'No, indeed!' cried I: and then, in hopes of changing the discourse, and preventing his further inquiries, I desired to know if he had seen the young lady who had been conversing with me?

No;—but would I honour him with my commands to see for her?

'O by no means!'

Was there any other person with whom I wished to speak?

I said *no*, before I knew I had answered at all.

Should he have the pleasure of bringing me any refreshment?

I bowed, almost involuntarily. And away he flew.

I was quite ashamed of being so troublesome, and so much *above* myself as these seeming airs made me appear; but indeed I was too much confused to think or act with any consistency.

If he had not been swift as lightning, I don't know whether I should not have stolen away again; but he returned in a moment. When I had drunk a glass of lemonade, he hoped, he said, that I would again honour him with my hand, as a new dance was just begun. I had not the presence of mind to say a single word, and so I let him once more lead me to the place I had left.

Shocked to find how silly, how childish a part I had acted, my former fears of dancing before such a company, and with such a partner, returned more forcibly than ever. I suppose he perceived my uneasiness, for he intreated me to sit down again, if dancing was disagreeable to me. But I was quite satisfied with the folly I had already shewn, and therefore declined his offer, tho' I was really scarce able to stand.

Under such conscious disadvantages, you may easily imagine, my dear Sir, how ill I acquitted myself. But, though I both expected and deserved to find him very much mortified and dis-pleased at his ill fortune in the choice he had made, yet, to my very great relief, he appeared to be even contented, and very much assisted and encouraged me. These people in high life have too much presence of mind, I believe, to *seem* disconcerted, or out of humour, however they may feel: for had I been the person of the most con-sequence in the room, I could not have met with more attention and respect.

When the dance was over, seeing me still very much flurried, he led me to a seat, saying that he would not suffer me to fatigue myself from politeness.

And then, if my capacity, or even if my spirits had been better, in how animated a conversation might I have been engaged! It was then that I saw the rank of Lord Orville was his least recommendation, his understanding and his manners being far more distinguished. His remarks upon the company in general were so apt, so just, so lively, I am almost surprised myself that they did not re-animate me; but indeed I was too well convinced of the ridiculous part I had myself played before so nice an observer, to be able to enjoy his pleasantry: so self-compassion gave me feeling for others. Yet I had not the courage to attempt either to defend them, or to rally in my turn, but listened to him in silent embarrassment.

When he found this, he changed the subject, and talked of public places, and public performers; but he soon discovered that I was totally ignorant of them.

He then, very ingeniously, turned the discourse to the amusements and occupations of the country.

It now struck me, that he was resolved to try whether or not I was capable of talking upon *any* subject. This put so great a constraint upon my thoughts, that I was unable to go further than a monosyllable, and not even so far, when I could possibly avoid it.

We were sitting in this manner, he conversing with all gaiety, I looking down with all foolishness, when that fop who had first asked me to dance, with a most ridiculous solemnity, approached, and after a profound bow or two, said, 'I humbly beg pardon, Madam,—and of you too, my Lord,—for breaking in upon such agreeable conversation—which must, doubtless, be much more delectable—than what I have the honour to offer—but—'

I interrupted him—I blush for my folly,—with laughing; yet I could not help it; for, added to the man's stately foppishness, (and he actually took snuff between every three words) when I looked round at Lord Orville, I saw such extreme surprise in his face,—the cause of which appeared so absurd, that I could not for my life preserve my gravity.

I had not laughed before from the time I had left Miss Mirvan, and I had much better have cried then; Lord Orville actually stared at me; the beau, I know not his name, looked quite enraged. 'Refrain—Madam,' (said he, with an important air,) 'a few moments refrain!—I have but a sentence to trouble you with.—May I know to what accident I must attribute not having the honour of your hand?'

'Accident, Sir!' repeated I, much astonished.

'Yes, accident, Madam—for surely,—I must take the liberty to observe—pardon me, Madam,—it ought to be no common one—that should tempt a lady—so young a one too,—to be guilty of ill manners.'

A confused idea now for the first time entered my head, of something I had heard of the rules of assemblies; but I was never at one before,—I have only danced at school,—and so giddy and heedless I was, that I had not once considered the impropriety of refusing one partner, and afterwards accepting another. I was thunderstruck at the recollection: but, while these thoughts were rushing into my head, Lord Orville, with some warmth, said, 'This lady, Sir, is incapable of meriting such an accusation!'

The creature—for I am very angry with him,—made a low bow, and with a grin the most malicious I ever saw, 'My Lord, said he, far be it from me to *accuse* the lady, for having the discernment to distinguish and prefer—the superior attractions of your Lordship.'

Again he bowed, and walked off.

Was ever any thing so provoking? I was ready to die with shame. 'What a coxcomb!' exclaimed Lord Orville; while I, without knowing what I did, rose hastily, and moving off, 'I can't imagine, cried I, where Mrs Mirvan has hid herself!'

'Give me leave to see,' answered he. I bowed and sat down again, not daring to meet his eyes; for what must he think of me, between my blunder and the supposed preference?

He returned in a moment, and told me that Mrs Mirvan was at cards, but would be glad to see me; and I went immediately. There was but one chair vacant, so, to my great relief, Lord Orville presently left us. I then told Mrs Mirvan my disasters, and she good-naturedly blamed herself for not having better instructed me, but said she had taken it for granted that I must know such common customs. However, the man may, I think, be satisfied with his pretty speech, and carry his resentment no farther.

In a short time, Lord Orville returned. I consented, with the best grace I could, to go down another dance, for I had had time to recollect myself, and therefore resolved to use some exertion, and, if possible, appear less a fool than I hitherto had; for it occurred to me that, insignificant as I was, compared to a man of his rank and figure, yet, since he had been so unfortunate as to make choice of me for a partner, why I should endeavour to make the best of it.

The dance, however, was short, and he spoke very little; so I had no opportunity of putting my resolution in practice. He was satisfied, I suppose, with his former successless efforts to draw me out: or, rather, I fancied, he has been inquiring *who I was*. This again disconcerted me, and the spirits I had determined to exert, again failed me. Tired, ashamed, and mortified, I begged to sit down till we returned home, which we did soon after. Lord Orville did me the honour to hand me to the coach, talking all the way of the honour *I* had done *him!* O these fashionable people!

Well, my dear Sir, was it not a strange evening? I could not help being thus particular, because, to me, every thing is so new. But it is now time to conclude. I am, with all love and duty,

Your

EVELINA

From *Camilla* (1796)

Strictures on Beauty

To lengthen the airing, Mr Tyrold ordered the carriage by a new road; and to induce Eugenia to break yet another spell, in walking as well as riding, he proposed their alighting, when they came to a lane, and leaving the coach in waiting while they took a short stroll.

He walked between his daughters a considerable way, passing, wherever it was possible, close to cottages, labourers, and children. Eugenia submitted with a sigh, but held down her head, affrighted at every fresh object they encountered, till, upon approaching a small miserable hut, at the door of which several children were playing, an unlucky boy called, out, 'O come! come! look!—here's the little hump-back gentlewoman!'

She then, clinging to her father, could not stir another step, and cast upon him a look of appeal and reproach that almost overset him; but, after speaking to her some words of kindness, he urged her to go on, and alone, saying, 'Throw only a shilling to the senseless little crew, and let Camilla follow and give nothing, and see which will become the most popular.'

They both obeyed, Eugenia fearfully and with quickness casting amongst them some silver, and Camilla quietly walking on.

'O, I have got a sixpence!' cried one; 'and I've got a shilling!' said another; while the mother of the little tribe came from her wash-tub, and called out, 'God bless your ladyship!' and the father quitted a little garden at the side of his cottage, to bow down to the ground, and cry, 'Heaven reward you, good madam! you'll have a blessing go with you, go where you will!'

The children then, dancing up to Camilla, begged her charity; but

when, seconding the palpable intention of her father, she said she
had nothing for them, they looked highly dissatisfied, while they
redoubled their blessings to Eugenia.

'See, my child,' said Mr Tyrold, now joining them, 'how cheaply
preference, and even flattery, may be purchased!'

'Ah, Sir!' she answered, recovered from her terrour, yet deep in
reflection, 'this is only by bribery, and gross bribery, too! And what
pleasure, or what confidence can accrue from preference so earned!'

'The means, my dear Eugenia, are not beneath the objects: if it is
only from those who unite native hardness with uncultured minds
and manners, that civility is to be obtained by such sordid materials,
remember, also, it is from such only it can ever fail you. In the lowest
life, equally with the highest, wherever nature has been kind, sympathy springs spontaneously for whatever is unfortunate, and respect
for whatever seems innocent. Steel yourself, then, firmly to with-
stand attacks from the cruel and unfeeling, and rest perfectly secure
you will have none other to apprehend.'

The clear and excellent capacity of Eugenia, comprehended in
this lesson, and its illustration, all the satisfaction Mr Tyrold hoped
to impart; and she was ruminating upon it with abated despondence,
when, as they came to a small house, surrounded with a high wall,
Mr Tyrold, looking through an iron gate at a female figure who
stood at one of the windows, exclaimed—'What a beautiful creature!
I have rarely, I think seen a more perfect face.'

Eugenia felt so much hurt by this untimely sight, that, after a
single glance, which confirmed the truth of what he said, she bent
her eyes another way; while Camilla herself was astonished that her
kind father should call their attention to beauty, at so sore and critical a juncture.

'The examination of a fine picture,' said he, fixing his eyes upon
the window, and standing still at the iron gate, 'is a constant as well
as exquisite pleasure; for we look at it with an internal security, that
such as it appears to us today, it will appear again tomorrow, and
tomorrow, and tomorrow;* but in the pleasure given by the examination of a fine face, there is always, to a contemplative mind, some
little mixture of pain; an idea of its fragility steals upon our admiration, and blends with it something like solicitude; the consciousness
how short a time we can view it perfect, how quickly its brilliancy of
bloom will be blown, and how ultimately it will be nothing.—'

'You would have me, Sir,' said Eugenia, now raising her eyes, 'learn to see beauty with unconcern, by depreciating its value? I feel your kind intention; but it does not come home to me; reasoning such as this may be equally applicable to any thing else, and degrade whatever is desirable into insignificance.'

'No, my dear child, there is nothing, either in its possession or its loss, that can be compared with beauty; nothing so evanescent, and nothing that leaves behind it a contrast which impresses such regret. It cannot be forgotten, since the same features still remain, though they are robbed of their effect upon the beholder; the same complexion is there, though faded into a tint bearing no resemblance with its original state; and the same eyes present themselves to the view, though bereft of all the lustre that had rendered them captivating.'

'Ah, Sir! this is an argument but formed for the moment. Is not the loss of youth the same to every body? and is not age equally unwelcome to the ugly and to the handsome?'

'For activity, for strength, and for purposes of use, certainly, my dear girl, there can be no difference; but for motives to mental regret, there can be no comparison. To those who are commonly moulded, the gradual growth of decay brings with it its gradual endurance, because little is missed from day to day; hope is not roughly chilled, nor expectation rudely blasted; they see their friends, their connections, their contemporaries, declining by the same laws, and they yield to the immutable and general lot rather imperceptibly than resignedly; but it is not so with the beauty; her loss is not only general, but peculiar; and it is the peculiar, not the general evil, that constitutes all hardship. Health, strength, agility, and animal spirits, she may sorrowing feel diminish, but she hears everyone complain of similar failures, and she misses them unmurmuring, though not unlamenting; but of beauty, every declension is marked with something painful to self-love. The change manifested by the mirror might patiently be borne; but the change manifested in the eyes of every beholder gives a shock that does violence to every pristine feeling.'

'This may certainly, sir, be cruel; trying at least; but then,—what a youth has she first passed! Mortification comes upon her, at least, in succession; she does not begin the world with it—a stranger at all periods to anything happier!'

'Ah, my child! the happiness caused by personal attraction pays a dear after-price! The soldier who enters the field of battle requires not more courage, though of a different nature, than the faded beauty who enters an assembly-room. To be wholly disregarded, after engaging every eye; to be unassisted, after being habituated to seeing crowds anxiously offer their services; to be unheard, after monopolising every ear—can you, indeed, persuade yourself a change such as this demands but ordinary firmness? Yet the altered female who calls for it, has the least chance to obtain it; for even where nature has endowed her with fortitude, the world and its flatteries have almost uniformly enervated it, before the season of its exertion.'

'All this may be true,' said Eugenia, with a sigh; 'and to me, however sad in itself, it may prove consolatory; and yet—forgive my sincerity, when I own—I would purchase a better appearance at any price, any expence, any payment, the world could impose!'

Mr Tyrold was preparing an answer, when the door of the house, which he had still continued facing, was opened, and the beautiful figure, which had for some time retired from the window, rushed suddenly upon a lawn before the gate against which they were leaning.

Not seeing them, she sat down upon the grass, which she plucked up by hands full, and strewed over her fine flowing hair.

Camilla, fearing they should seem impertinent, would have retreated; but Eugenia, much struck, sadly, yet with earnestness compelled herself to regard the object before her, who was young, fair, of a tall and striking figure, with features delicately regular.

A sigh, not to be checked, acknowledged how little either reasoning or eloquence could subdue a wish to resemble such an appearance, when the young person, flinging herself suddenly upon her face, threw her white arms over her head, and sobbed aloud with violence.

Astonished, and deeply concerned, Eugenia internally said, alas! what a world is this! even beauty so exquisite, without waiting for age or change, may be thus miserable!

She feared to speak, lest she should be heard; but she looked up to her father, with an eye that spoke concession, and with an interest for the fair afflicted, which seemed to request his assistance.

He motioned to her to be quiet; when the young person, abruptly half rising, burst into a fit of loud, shrill, and discordant laughter.

Eugenia now, utterly confounded, would have drawn her father away; but he was intently engaged in his observations, and steadily kept his place.

In two minutes, the laugh ceased all at once, and the young creature, hastily rising, began turning round with a velocity that no machine could have exceeded.

The sisters now fearfully interchanged looks that shewed they thought her mad, and both endeavoured to draw Mr Tyrold from the gate, but in vain; he made them hold by his arms, and stood still.

Without seeming giddy, she next began to jump; and he now could only detain his daughters, by shewing them the gate, at which they stood, was locked.

In another minute, she perceived them, and, coming eagerly forward, dropt several low courtesies, saying, at every fresh bend— 'Good day!—Good day!—Good day!'

Equally trembling, they now both turned pale with fear; but Mr Tyrold, who was still immovable, answered her by a bow, and asked if she were well.

'Give me a shilling!' was her reply, while the slaver drivelled unrestrained from her mouth, rendering utterly disgusting a chin that a statuary might have wished to model.

'Do you live at this house!' said Mr Tyrold.

'Yes, please—yes, please—yes, please,' she answered, twenty times following, and almost black in the face before she would allow herself to take another breath.

A cat now appearing at the door, she seized it, and tried to twine it round her neck with great fondling, wholly unresisting the scratches which tore her fine skin.

Next, capering forward with it towards the gate, 'Look! look!' she cried, 'here's puss!—here's puss!—here's puss!'

Then, letting it fall, she tore her handkerchief off her neck,* put it over her face, strained it as tight as she was able, and tied it under her chin; and then struck her head with both her hands, making a noise that resembled nothing human.

'Take, take me away, my father!' cried Eugenia, 'I see, I feel your awful lesson! but impress it no further, lest I die in receiving it!'

Mr Tyrold immediately moved off without speaking; Camilla, penetrated for her sister, observed the same silence; and Eugenia, hanging upon her father, and absorbed in profound rumination, only by the depth of her sighs made her existence known; and thus, without the interchange of a word, slowly and pensively they walked back to the carriage.

Eugenia broke the silence as soon as they were seated: 'O, my father!' she exclaimed, 'what a sight have you made me witness! how dread a reproof have you given to my repining spirit! Did you know this unhappy beauty was at that house? Did you lead me thither purposely to display to me her shocking imbecility?'

'Relying upon the excellence of your understanding, I ventured upon an experiment more powerful, I well knew, than all that reason could urge; an experiment not only striking at the moment, but which, by playing upon the imagination, as well as convincing the judgment, must make an impression that can never be effaced. I have been informed for some time, that this poor girl was in our neighbourhood; she was born an idiot, and therefore, having never known brighter days, is insensible to her terrible state. Her friends are opulent, and that house is taken, and a woman is paid, to keep her in existence and in obscurity. I had heard of her uncommon beauty, and when the news reached me of my dear Eugenia's distress, the idea of this meeting occurred to me; I rode to the house, and engaged the woman to detain her unfortunate charge at the window till we appeared, and then to let her loose into the garden. Poor, ill fated young creature! it has been, indeed, a melancholy sight.'

'A sight,' cried Eugenia, 'to come home to me with shame!—O, my dear Father! your prescription strikes to the root of my disease!—shall I ever again dare murmur!—will any egotism ever again make me believe no lot so hapless as my own! I will think of her when I am discontented; I will call to my mind this spectacle of human degradation—and submit, at least with calmness, to my lighter evils and milder fate.'

'My excellent child! this is just what I expected from the candour of your temper, and the rectitude of your sentiments. You have seen, here, the value of intellects in viewing the horrour of their loss; and you have witnessed, that beauty, without mind, is more dreadful than any deformity. You have seized my application, and left me nothing to enforce; my dear, my excellent child! you have left for your fond Father nothing but tender approbation! With the utmost thankfulness to Providence, I have marked from your earliest childhood, the native justness of your understanding; which, with your studious inclination to sedentary accomplishments, has proved a reviving source of consolation to your mother and to me, for the cruel accidents we have incessantly lamented. How will that admirable mother rejoice in the recital I have to make to her! What pride will she take in a daughter so worthily her own, so resembling her in nobleness of nature, and a superior way of thinking! Her tears, my child, like mine, will thank you for your exertions! she will strain you to her fond bosom, as your father strains you at this moment!'

'Yes, Sir,' cried Eugenia, 'your kind task is now completed with your vanquished Eugenia! her thoughts, her occupations, her happiness, shall henceforth all be centred in filial gratitude and contentment.'

The affectionate Camilla, throwing her arms about them both, bathed each with the tears of joy and admiration, which this soothing conclusion to an adventure so severe excited.

CATHARINE MACAULAY
(1731–1791)

The republican historian and polemicist Catharine Macaulay (born Sawbridge, later Graham) was the most widely admired and most controversial woman intellectual of her time: she was the first English woman historian, and the initiator of a fundamental revaluation of seventeenth-century history which was crucial to the development of radical politics in America, France, and Britain. Macaulay was born into an established Whig family at the family home, Olantigh, near Ashford in Kent (destroyed by fire early in the twentieth century with the loss of Macaulay's papers), the third child and second daughter of John Sawbridge, a former officer in the Guards, and his second wife Elizabeth Wanley, who died in childbirth in 1733 at the age of 22. Macaulay's background was wealthy but the family's wealth had been founded by her disgraced financier grandfather, and was augmented by shrewd marriages and land purchases by her father and elder brother. She was 2 years old when her mother died, and her father took little subsequent interest in his four children. Instead Macaulay was educated by a governess and read extensively in her father's library. A vivid account of the young Catharine Sawbridge, and a detailed estimate of her intellectual significance, is given by Mary Hays (see below) in her essay on Macaulay in *Female Biography*, which presents

Macaulay as a 'lady, who, by her writings, and the powers of her mind, has reflected so much credit on her sex and country'. 'A female historian, by its singularity, could not fail to excite attention: she seemed to have stepped out of the province of her sex; curiosity was sharpened, and malevolence provoked.'[1] Mary Wollstonecraft thought of her as 'the woman of the greatest abilities, undoubtedly, that this country has ever produced'.[2] Macaulay's gender was a major preoccupation of her reviewers, and she anticipated this, referring in the introduction to the first volume of her *History of England from the Accession of James I to that of the Brunswick Line* (1763) to the supposed 'defects of a female historian', and appearing to endorse traditional ideas by saying that if her history fails to live up to her ambitions her plans at least have merit, 'and if the goodness of my head may justly be questioned, my heart will stand the test of the most critical examination' (pp. xviii, ix).

Macaulay was closely involved in political debate, and was a significant figure in the groups known as the Real Whigs and the supporters of John Wilkes. Among an impressive range of philosophical, historical, and political works, her major achievement is the eight-volume *History of England from the Accession of James I to that of the Brunswick Line* (1763–83), which evaluates the consequences—constitutional, political, and social—of the accession of William and Mary and in particular the flawed legacy of the Glorious Revolution: 'The plan of settlement was neither properly digested or maturely formed', she later explained in the first letter of *The History of England . . . in Letters* (5). Britain, she argued, was now at risk of despotic government because of an overthrow of Whig principles and because the post-Revolutionary settlement had granted the monarch too much power. Startling in its attack on the Revolution settlement, the *History* is also innovative in its methodology. The major previous accounts of the turbulent history of England in the seventeenth century were Clarendon's Tory *History of the Rebellion* (1702–4) and David Hume's *History of England* (1754–62). Macaulay had an unusually detailed grasp of source materials, especially tracts of the 1640s and 1650s, and was familiar with a wide range of seventeenth-century literature: she was innovative in ways unrelated to her gender. (Her greatest rival, Hume, had not used manuscripts or archival research.) Her personal library contained nearly five thousand tracts and sermons, mainly of the seventeenth and eighteenth centuries. Before the opening of the British Museum in 1759 it was difficult for any historian to gain access to primary source material.

---

[1] *Female Biography; or, Memoirs of Illustrious and Celebrated Women, of all Ages and Countries*, 6 vols. (London: for Richard Phillips by Thomas Davison, 1803), v. 287, 292.

[2] *A Vindication of the Rights of Woman*, ed. Miriam Brody Kramnick (Harmondsworth: Penguin, 1982), 206.

Macaulay's personal life came under intense scrutiny. In 1760, at the age of 29, she became the second wife of Dr George Macaulay, an eminent Scottish physician practising in London, fifteen years her senior and a friend of John and William Hunter, the uncles of Joanna Baillie; he died in 1766, leaving her with her only child, Catherine Sophia. Macaulay remained for several years in London before moving to Bath in 1774 in the hope of improving her always troublesome health. In about 1776 she and her young daughter accepted an invitation to share the house and use the library of the Revd Dr Thomas Wilson, rector of St Stephen's, Walbrook, a friend of her MP brother John, and, like John, a founder member of the Society of Supporters of the Bill of Rights, formed in 1769 to gather financial support for John Wilkes. Macaulay was 45, Wilson 73 and a widower since 1772. In April 1775 he formally adopted Catherine Sophia. Macaulay's years in Bath produced the first and only volume of *The History of England from the Revolution to the Present Time, in a Series of Letters to a Friend* (1778), addressed to Wilson, and included in the extracts here. It has a new, less scholarly, tone. The epistolary form of this innovative and sometimes disconcertingly informal history adopts the convention of a domestic, casual, intimate style often associated with women's 'histories' of the heart. Wilson, unfortunately, turned out to be an embarrassingly fervent admirer. He arranged an extravagant entertainment for her birthday in 1777 and had a statue of her erected in his church (which he promptly removed on her remarriage): his attentions brought ridicule upon them both. While in Bath, she took as her doctor Dr James Graham and met his younger brother William, a Scottish ship's steward whom she married in 1778 when he was 21. Amid the furore caused by the difference in age and class, fuelled by Wilson's angry threats to publish her letters to him and by rumours that she had been sexually involved with both Graham brothers and a purloiner of Wilson's money, her reputation was destroyed.

The opprobrium occasioned by Macaulay's marriage to Graham ironically makes it easier to see her intellectual importance and the extent to which her historical scholarship made her threatening. A satirical pamphlet, *The Female Patriot: An Epistle from C——t——e M——c——y to The Reverend Dr W——l——n On her late Marriage* (1779), presents her enthusiasm and boldness in writing history as a variant of indecorous libidinous warmth, while impugning her ambition ('To be imparadised in the arms of an immortal Historian, what a sentimental ne plus ultra!').[3] Another pamphlet, *A Bridal Ode on the Marriage of Catherine and Petruchio* (1779) affects amazement that Macaulay should give up her freedom

---

[3] (London: J. Bew, 1779), 28.

in order to be subjected to a husband's tyranny, politicizing the personal as it trivializes her histories' championing of the liberty of the subject:

> *Married!*—Can *Catherine's* Soul submit
> To *Non-Resistance?*—tamely quit
>   Her former *free* Domains?
> Can her *republican*, stiff Neck,
> Bend to the rude imperious Check
>   Of Tyrant Bits and Chains?[4]

She and her husband spent over a year in the United States, the 'empire of freedom' as she described it (*Address . . . on the Important Crisis of Affairs*, 26). Her American friend Mercy Otis Warren in 1805 published a *History of the American Revolution*, a task Macaulay had envisaged for herself. She spent ten days at Mount Vernon: Washington admired her work and her principles. In 1787 she wrote to Mercy Otis Warren that 'the History of your late glorious revolution is what I should certainly undertake were I again young'.[5] In 1777–8 she visited France. The last few years of her life were spent in Binfield near Reading in Berkshire: here she wrote her *Letters on Education*, and died after a long and painful illness.

Macaulay is now most often read for her *Letters on Education with Observations on Religious and Metaphysical Subjects* (1790), reviewed by Wollstonecraft in the *Analytical Review* for November 1790 and acknowledged in her *Vindication of the Rights of Woman* in 1792. *Letters on Education* shares key arguments with Wollstonecraft's *Vindication*, including that vice and virtue are the same for men and for women and that girls should be encouraged to take physical exercise. It is not devoted to the situation of women, however, instead giving Macaulay's views on the care of infants, slavery, capital punishment, animal welfare, and a range of other issues. At its centre is a formidable plan of reading for boys and girls alike. A chapter from this work is included in the selection here; but to focus on *Letters on Education* rather than on her important contributions to historical and political thought is, limitingly, to draw her in to a kind of 'acceptable' feminine discourse, even though what she says within this discourse is far from conventional. Her historical writings show her at her most challenging and most impressive, and it is on these that this selection concentrates.

The first two passages are from *The History of England from the Revolution to the Present Time, in a Series of Letters to a Friend* (1778). The tenor of this work, which was left incomplete, is, like that of her more ambitious

---

    [4] (London: J. Bew, 1779), 7–8.

    [5] Bridget Hill, *The Republican Virago: The Life and Times of Catharine Macaulay, Historian* (Oxford: Clarendon Press, 1992), 128.

and more formal histories, republican and revisionist. Macaulay traces the growth of state and private corruption in the years following the accession of William and Mary after the Glorious Revolution of 1688, and is especially rigorous in itemizing instances of popular blindness in the face of institutionalized trickery, such as the topic of the first two passages, the South Sea Company and its ruinous collapse in 1720. The episode has a personal relevance for Macaulay, as she reveals in her attempt to redeem the reputation of her grandfather, Jacob Sawbridge (one of the 'three capital sharpers of Europe', according to Daniel Defoe);[6] but it more potently draws forth her impatience of popular gullibility and greed, and supports her suspicion of new forms of tyranny. The next extract included here is from the conclusion to the final volume of the *History of England from the Accession of James I to that of the Brunswick Line* (1783), and the final extract is from her *Letters on Education* (1790).

~

From *The History of England from the Revolution to the Present Time, in a Series of Letters to a Friend* (1778)

LETTER V

The next important event which offers itself in this reign, my friend, is the sudden rise, and the as sudden fall, of the South Sea Company.* The pernicious policy introduced by William of borrowing money of the public, and settling certain taxes to pay the interest of the borrowed sum, had introduced a new kind of traffic into the kingdom, which was totally unknown to happier times.* When a nation is deeply in debt, public credit is ever precarious; and the rise and fall of stocks furnish an opportunity for needy adventures to prey on the hopes and the fears of individuals, whilst the growing necessities of the state give rise to a variety of inventions for raising the sums adequate to the exigencies of the occasion. This worst kind of gaming made a rapid progress in the kingdom; and at length the spirit of adventure, and the eager desire of becoming suddenly rich by the successful attempts of a few of the favoured sons of fortune, infected all ranks and all conditions of men through the whole society.

In the eleventh year of Queen Anne,* when the debt on the navy had amounted to above five millions, the two houses passed an act for

[6] Ibid. 4.

the throwing this and several other debts into one stock, amounting in the whole to nine millions four hundred and seventy-one thousand three hundred and twenty-five pounds, and a fund was formed for the paying an interest or an annuity of six per cent, till the principal should be paid: the yearly interest of the principal amounted to the sum of five hundred and sixty-eight thousand two hundred and seventy-nine pounds: all the duties upon wines, vinegar, tobacco, India goods, wrought silk, whale fins, &c. were perpetuated for the payment; and with this fund was granted the monopoly of a trade to the South Sea, or coast of Peru in Mexico, in South America;* and the several proprietors of the navy bills, debentures, and other public securities,* were incorporated into a company, called The South Sea Company.

It is said, my friend, that Sir John Blount, who had been bred a scrivener,* was the man who formed this South Sea scheme, which for a while threatened the destruction of public credit, and which fell so heavy on the heads of several individuals; it seems he had projected his plan on the famous Mississippi scheme, formed by Law, which in the preceding year had failed in France, and which had entailed ruin on many thousand families in that kingdom;* and yet Law's scheme was much more plausible, as it contained an exclusive trade to Louisiana; whereas the South Sea scheme, by the conditions of the peace of Utrecht, was deprived of any commercial advantage.*

In the natural state of humanity, my friend, I believe two thirds of any given society may be numbered in the classes of fools and madmen; but there sometimes reigns an epidemic madness, as well as an epidemic fever of a different kind, which, from being first partial, becomes general, and then universal; and I do not know any country where these instances are so often to be met with as in England. This was the state of the case in the year seventeen hundred and twenty; and favoured with this opportunity, Blount, and a few associates with very moderate talents, first imposed on the majority of the directors of the South Sea company, and then on the whole nation.

The tricks of the alley, although continually repeated, impose even at this time on a large number of credulous individuals;* but at the period I am now writing on, my friend, there were very few, even of the most wary, who had reason to laugh at his neighbour for becoming the dupe of shallow artifice, and the most contemptible impositions: the mere circulating a report that Gibraltar and Port Mahon would be exchanged for some places in Peru,* by which means the English trade to the South Sea would be protected and enlarged, operated with such power, that in five days the directors opened their books for a subscription of one million, at the rate of three hundred pounds for one hundred pounds capital; and an eager multitude crowded in such a manner to the subscription, that it exceeded two millions of capital stock: in a few days the stock advanced to three hundred and forty pounds, and the subscriptions were sold for double the price of the first payment. At length, by a repetition of the same arts, and the promise of high dividends, the stock was raised to one thousand: Exchange-alley was every day filled with a multitude of people of all conditions; and the general infatuation prevailed till the eighth day of December, when the stock fell. It was now that the tide of hope began to ebb; and in a few days the spirits of the adventurers were sunk so low, that on the twenty-ninth day of the same month, the stock fell from a thousand to one hundred and fifty pounds: several eminent goldsmiths and bankers, who had lent great sums on the occasion, were obliged to stop payment and abscond;* public credit sustained a shock; the nation was consequently thrown into a ferment, and the ravings of grief, disappointment, and despair, filled every place with noise, tumult, and confusion.

As several principal members of the ministry were deeply engaged in the support of the South Sea company, they employed their influence with the bank to support its credit; and at length that corporation, with much reluctance, agreed to subscribe into the stock of the South Sea company, valued at four hundred per cent, three millions five hundred thousand pounds, which the company were to repay to the bank on Lady-day and Michaelmas of the ensuing year.* Books were opened at the bank to take in a subscription for the support of public credit, and considerable sums of money were brought in; the stock rose, and the expedient effectually answered the design of the contrivers, by enabling them to realize, without any great loss: however, the ensuing bankruptcy of goldsmiths, and the sword-blade company, occasioned such a run upon the bank, that the money was paid away faster than it was received on subscription; and the directors of the bank, seeing themselves in danger of being involved in the ruin of the South Sea company, renounced an agreement which they were under no legal obligation to perform.

Disappointment and despair again seized the minds of the numerous adventurers; and the clamour of the people increasing to an alarming height, expresses were sent to the King, who was at this time in Hanover, to hasten his return.* His Majesty arrived in England on the eleventh day of December, and the parliament was assembled on the eighth of the preceding month. The South Sea business came immediately under consideration; the directors were ordered to produce an account of all their proceedings; a bill passed both houses, and was enacted into a law, for restraining the sub-governor, deputy-governor, directors, treasurer, under-treasurer, cashier, secretary, and accomptants of the South Sea company, from quitting the kingdom till the end of the next sessions of parliament; also for discovering their estates and effects, in order to prevent them from being transported or alienated; and a committee of secrecy was chosen by ballot to examine all the books, papers, and proceedings, relating to the execution of the South Sea act. The sub and deputy-governors, the directors and officers of the South Sea company, were examined at the bar of the house, and after the examination a bill was brought in, disabling them to enjoy any office in that company, or in the East-India company, or in the bank of England:* nor did the vengeance of parliament stop here; an order was made to secure the books and papers of Knight, Surman, and Turner;* the persons of Sir George Caswell, Sir John Blount, and Sir John Lambert, were taken into custody;* Sir Theodore Janssen, Mr Sawbridge, Sir Robert Chaplain, and Mr Eyles, were expelled the house, and apprehended;* orders were given to remove all directors of the South Sea company from the places they possessed under the government, and their estates were confiscated by act of parliament.

As my very worthy grandfather, Mr Jacob Sawbridge, was among those sufferers who were deemed public delinquents, whose estates were confiscated, whose persons were imprisoned, and who suffered the disgrace of disablement from bearing office, and expulsion from the house, I cannot leave this subject without informing you, my friend, if the concurrent testimony of all his contemporaries has not yet reached your ears, that my grandfather, though carried along with the tide of other men's iniquity, was so perfectly free from any intention or inclination to defraud the public, that he was never once accused of being let into the secret practices of Knight, and other of the guilty directors, that he always publicly and privately exclaimed against every unfair means taken by the direction to give an unnatural rise to the stock; and that it was generally acknowledged that the government, in order to appease the clamours of an enraged people, confounded the innocent with the guilty: and besides this, they were so shamefully partial in the distribution of justice, that several of the members of both houses of parliament, though deeply engaged with the directors in the notorious offences charged against them, escaped punishment. Mr Aislabie alone, who had been the most forward in the promoting the South Sea scheme, was expelled the house, and committed to the tower.*

After the vengeance of the public had been in some measure appeased by the ruin which had fallen on the estates and property of the projectors and directors of the South Sea scheme, the parliament entered into means for the repairing in some measure the loss which had been sustained by individuals. The capital stock of the company in their corporate capacity exceeded by thirteen millions the stock allotted to all the proprietors; seven millions of this stock was enacted by law to be paid to the public, and the remainder was to be divided among all the proprietors.

It was not only to the South Sea scheme that such a large number of families owed their ruin. The spirit of gaming once set afloat was excited by the chimerical scheme of every knavish projector: one of these vultures, without explaining the advantageous scheme he pretended to have formed, published proposals for a subscription, declaring, that every person paying two guineas should be entitled to a subscription of one hundred pounds: and can you believe it, my friend? in one forenoon he received a thousand of these subscriptions: in the evening he set out for another kingdom. New companies were every day formed, and the first nobility of the kingdom appeared at their head: the Prince of Wales was constituted governor of the Welch copper company; the Duke of Chandos of the York-building; and the Duke of Bridgwater* formed a third for building houses in London.

During the influence of these delusive hopes, the increase of luxury and vice kept more than equal pace with the imaginary increase of riches: individuals of the lowest class, lifted up in idea to the possession of large property, pampered themselves with rich dainties, with expensive wines, purchased sumptuous furniture, appeared in sumptuous equipages and apparel; and I have heard that it was in this period of vanity and extravagance that monopolizers first set an advanced price on the luxuries and even on the necessaries of life, and that the markets, by the arts and chicanery of trade, never recovered their usual moderation.

The presbyterians, the dissenters of all denominations, and the greater number of moralists, have dated the decline of virtue in England to the licentious days of Charles the Second: certain it is, that decency of manners, regard to public liberty and national good, received an irrecoverable check from the loose example of a profligate court, and from the scoffs and revilings of all those who, in a vulgar sense, were called great in the kingdom: and it is too true, my friend, that the aera of the Revolution,* instead of introducing a more correct and regular system of manners, only added to the profligacy then prevailing, the meaner vices of sordid rapacity and venal corruption.

It was now generally asserted, that every man had his price: the few instances which the times exhibited of self-denial, on the principles of honour and patriotism, were regarded as the effects of an enthusiastic lunacy; the electors paid no regard to their privileges, but as it enabled them to make a lucrative gain of their votes; the elected made the best market of their purchased seats; and opposition was now carried on without other motive than the bringing obscure men into notice, and enhancing the price of corruption: and yet, my friend, if ever the people of this country had reason to be in a more particular manner watchful of their political security and their national welfare, it was undoubtedly at this period, when they had a foreign prince on the throne; a prince, who was a stranger to the laws and constitution of Great-Britain; a prince, who, on all the principles which govern human affection, they had reason to expect was strongly attached to the arbitrary system of government which prevails in every German principality, and whose predilection for his native country must naturally be increased by the implicit obedience paid by all his hereditary subjects.

If any virtue had remained in England, these circumstances of well-grounded distrust would have awakened the attention and the caution of the people; but indeed it was so unfortunately the reverse, that for every law of the constitution, if there are any which yet remain unviolated, we are entirely indebted to the moderation or the timidity of our governors . . .

LETTER VI

Every law, my friend, relating to public or private property, and in particular penal statutes, ought to be rendered so clear and plain, and promulgated in such a manner to the public, as to give a full information of its nature and contents to every citizen. Ignorance of laws, if not wilful, is a just excuse for their transgression; and if the care of the government does not extend to the proper education of the subject, and to their proper information on the nature of moral turpitude and legal crimes, and to the encouragement of virtue, with what face of justice can they punish delinquency? But if, on the contrary, the citizens, by the oppression of heavy taxes, are rendered incapable, by the utmost exertion of honest industry, of bringing up or providing for a numerous family,—if every encouragement is given to licentiousness, for the purpose of amusing and debasing the minds of the people, or for raising a revenue on the vices of the subject;—is punishment in this case better than legal murder? Or, to use a strong, yet adequate expression, is it better than infernal tyranny?

Whilst the Commons were thus careless of all the just ends for which they were entrusted with their extensive privileges;—whilst seats in parliament were purchased at high prices, with a view of making the best penny of the public;—whilst the members of both houses were singly engaged in the business of raising money on the people, in order to exact a large share of the dividend;—it is no wonder that the only laws which could possibly restrain the abuses of representation, which could render the spirit of the constitution consistent with its forms, and fix dominion's limits to its end,— namely, laws to prevent pensioners from sitting in parliament,* and to restore the people to their ancient salutary privileges, by shortening the duration of parliaments, should be rejected with disdain by a venal majority.*

Before I leave this subject, my friend, I must observe to you, that Dr Sherlock, bishop of Bangor, afterwards translated to Sarum, and then to London,* made no scruple to argue avowedly in favour of that canker-worm in a state, that destroyer of every political constitution, that ruin to the morals of the people, Corruption, as a necessary part of administration; and declared, that an independent house of Commons, and an independent house of Lords, were as inconsistent with the English constitution as an independent or absolute King. This senseless assertion lies so open to conviction, since it is plain, if an independent house of Commons is inconsistent with our constitution that a dependent one is useless, expensive, dangerous, and burthensome, that it is not worth the making any observation upon it; only, that it proves to what a low state of depravity we were fallen, and how lost to every sense of what is just, fit, decent, and expedient, when one of the heads of the English church should venture to broach doctrines which would have scandalized every Pagan priest in the corruptest state of idolatry.

Suffer me to indulge my fancy for once, my friend, tho' I am writing on a serious subject. Methinks I hear you say, What was become of the voice of the people? Is it possible, that before their necks were quite bowed to the yoke, by repeated ineffectual exertions, by painful executions, and frightful examples of suffering patriotism;—is it possible, that the voice of the people, under such insulting injuries, should not have risen into a thunder which would have shaken the two houses of parliament, and by operation of fear have produced that reformation in the conduct of their government, which neither reason nor duty could have effected?—Why truly, my friend, in answer to these interrogations, I must inform you, that the people at this time were, as the people of Great-Britain always are, half stupid, half drunk, and half asleep: they tamely suffered all these insults with a patience which, in a good cause, would have done honour to the primitive saints of the Christian church: nay more, under the whig banners,* the churchmen and the dissenters of all denominations united their efforts to establish and secure the best of all possible governments, and to hand down the invaluable blessing of being bought and sold to the latest posterity. However, as all sublunary happiness must ever be in a fluctuating state, the people were at length, by great art and management, roused to a ferment; and this, as is always the case, on a subject in which their interest was no ways concerned; and the minister was defeated in the only salutary measure he had ever proposed to the consideration of parliament.*

It is the opinion of Davenant,* that master of all subjects which concern the welfare of commercial states, that excises are the most proper ways and means to support the government in a long war, because they would lie equally on the whole body of the people, and produce great sums, proportionable to the great wants of the public. Agreeable to this idea, my friend, the prime minister, Sir Robert Walpole, on the pretence of preventing frauds, perjuries, and false entries, in the levying the customs, in the year 1733 proposed that a partial excise on tobacco should be levied: in this proposition he joined the laws of the customs with those of the excise,* namely, that the farther subsidy of three farthings per pound charged upon imported tobacco should be still levied at the custom-house, and payable to his Majesty's civil list;* that then the tobacco should be lodged in warehouses to be appointed for that purpose by the commissioners of the excise; that the keeper of each warehouse, appointed likewise by the commissioners, should have one lock and key, and the merchant importer another; and that the tobacco should be thus secured until the merchant should find vent for it, either by exportation or home consumption; that the part designed for exportation should be weighed at the custom-house, discharged of the three farthings per pound which had been paid at its first importation, and then exported without farther trouble; that the portion destined for home consumption should, in presence of the warehouse-keeper, be delivered to the purchaser upon his paying the inland duty of four-pence per pound weight to the proper officer appointed to receive it, by which means the merchant would be eased of the inconvenience of paying the duty upon importation, or of granting bonds, and finding sureties for the payment before he had found a market for the commodity; that all penalties and forfeitures, so far as they formerly belonged to the crown, should for the future be applied to the use of the public; that appeals in this, as well as in all other cases relating to the excise, should be heard and determined by two or three of the judges to be named by his Majesty, and in the country by the judge of assize upon the next circuit, who should hear and determine such appeals in the most summary way, without the formality of proceedings in courts of law or equity.

Though Sir Robert Walpole's scheme, my friend, was defective in the grand point, which renders even an excise desirable in this country, namely, the discharging that train of dependents and leeches which help to suck the vitals of the commonwealth,* the custom-house officers, yet the opposition did not think fit to attack him on this defect, or to propose any amendment which might tend to relieve the constitution from a set of dependents which are more than sufficient to render ineffectual all the bars against prerogative. That it would introduce a general excise was the cry of the country party;* and the nation, though they had sat easy under innovations which gave up their power and their fortunes to the disposal of the crown and its dependents, took the alarm,—an alarm which was attended with such a ferment, that though the minister carried his point with the Commons by a majority of sixty-one voices, he was obliged to waive the advantage, and give up his triumph to the almost united voice of the people, who threatened him with the executing justice on his person in the rough way of popular coercion.

Thus the people, exerting with success their natural rights on a subject of little importance to the welfare of the community, left the lovers of mankind the melancholy sensation of bitterly regretting their unpardonable supineness on points in which the welfare of the constitution, and the freedom and the opulence of their posterity, were deeply interested. . . .

From *History of England from the Accession of James I to that of the Brunswick Line* (1783)

Closing Address

As a close to this long narration of national evils and national follies, so conspicuous in the mournful annals of the two last centuries, I appeal to the ingenuous and uncorrupted part of my countrymen, which class of historians have been the real friends of the constitution; those who, by humouring the prejudices of all factions, have left the judgment of the reader in such an embarrassed state as to be incapable of forming any just opinion of men, of measures, or of the true interest of their country; or those writers who, like myself, in an honest contempt of the ill-founded rage and resentment of all denominations of men and interests, have, through the whole course of my narrative, closely adhered to the purest principles of civil and religious freedom; have marked every deviation from constitutional rectitude; and have not only pointed out the destructive enormities of marked tyrants, but have endeavoured to direct the judgment of the public to the detection of those marked hypocrites, who, under the specious pretence of public good, have advanced their private interest and ambition on the ruin of all that is valuable to man.

From *Letters on Education* (1790)

No Characteristic Difference in Sex

The great difference that is observable in the characters of the sexes, Hortensia, as they display themselves in the scenes of social life, has given rise to much false speculation on the natural qualities of the female mind.—For though the doctrine of innate ideas, and innate affections, are in a great measure exploded by the learned, yet few persons reason so closely and so accurately on abstract subjects as through a long chain of deductions, to bring forth a conclusion which in no respect militates with their premises.

It is a long time before the crowd give up opinions they have been taught to look upon with respect; and I know many persons who will follow you willingly through the course of your argument, till they perceive it tends to the overthrow of some fond prejudice; and then they will either sound a retreat, or begin a contest in which the contender for truth, though he cannot be overcome, is effectually silenced, from the mere weariness of answering positive assertions, reiterated without end. It is from such causes that the notion of a sexual difference in the human character has, with a very few exceptions, universally prevailed from the earliest times, and the pride of one sex, and the ignorance and vanity of the other, have helped to support an opinion which a close observation of Nature, and a more accurate way of reasoning, would disprove.

It must be confessed, that the virtues of the males among the human species, though mixed and blended with a variety of vices and errors, have displayed a bolder and a more consistent picture of excellence than female species has hitherto done. It is on these reasons that, when we compliment the appearance of a more than ordinary energy in the female mind, we call it masculine, and hence it is, that Pope has elegantly said a *perfect woman's but a softer man.**
And if we take in the consideration, that there can be but one rule of moral excellence for beings made of the same materials, organized

after the same manner, and subjected to similar laws of Nature, we must either agree with Mr Pope, or we must reverse the proposition, and say, that *a perfect man is a woman formed after a coarser mold*. The difference that actually does subsist between the sexes, is too flattering for men to be willingly imputed to accident; for what accident occasions, wisdom might correct; and it is better, says Pride, to give up the advantages we might derive from the perfection of our fellow associates, than to own that Nature has been just in the equal distribution of her favours. These are the sentiments of the men; but mark how readily they are yielded to by the women; not from humility I assure you, but merely to preserve with character those fond vanities on which they set their hearts. No; suffer them to idolize their persons, to throw away their life in the pursuit of trifles, and to indulge in the gratification of the meaner passions, and they will heartily join in the sentence of their degradation.

Among the most strenuous asserters of a sexual difference in character, Rousseau is the most conspicuous, both on account of that warmth of sentiment which distinguishes all his writings, and the eloquence of his compositions:* but never did enthusiasm and the love of paradox, those enemies to philosophical disquisition, appear in more strong opposition to plain sense than in Rousseau's definition of this difference. He sets out with a supposition, that Nature intended the subjection of the one sex to the other: that consequently there must be an inferiority of intellect in the subjected party: but as man is a very imperfect being, and apt to play the capricious tyrant, Nature, to bring things nearer to an equality, bestowed on the woman such attractive graces, and such an insinuating address, as to turn the balance on the other scale. Thus Nature, in a giddy mood, recedes from her purposes, and subjects prerogative to an influence which must produce confusion and disorder in the system of human affairs. Rousseau saw this objection; and in order to obviate it, he has made up a moral person of the union of the two sexes, which, for contradiction and absurdity, outdoes every metaphysical riddle that was ever formed in the schools.* In short, it is not reason, it is not wit; it is pride and sensuality that speak in Rousseau, and, in this instance, has lowered the man of genius to the licentious pedant.

But whatever might be the wise purpose intended by Providence in such a disposition of things, certain it is, that some degree of inferiority, in point of corporal strength, seems always to have existed between the two sexes; and this advantage, in the barbarous ages of mankind, was abused to such a degree, as to destroy all the natural rights of the female species, and reduce them to a state of abject slavery. What accidents have contributed in Europe to better their condition, would not be to my purpose to relate; for I do not intend to give you a history of women; I mean only to trace the sources of their peculiar foibles and vices; and these I firmly believe to originate in situation and education only: for so little did a wise and just Providence intend to make the condition of slavery an unalterable law of female nature, that in the same proportion as the male sex have consulted the interest of their own happiness, they have relaxed in their tyranny over women; and such is their use in the system of mundane creation, and such their natural influence over the male mind, that were these advantages properly exerted, they might carry every point of any importance to their honour and happiness. However, till that period arrives in which women will act wisely, we will amuse ourselves in talking of their follies.

The situation and education of women, Hortensia, is precisely that which must necessarily tend to corrupt and debilitate both the powers of mind and body. From a false notion of beauty and delicacy, their system of nerves is depraved before they come out of their nursery; and this kind of depravity has more influence over the mind, and consequently over morals, than is commonly apprehended. But it would be well if such causes only acted towards the debasement of the sex; their moral education is, if possible, more absurd than their physical. The principles and nature of virtue, which is never properly explained to boys, is kept quite a mystery to girls. They are told indeed, that they must abstain from those vices which are contrary to their personal happiness, or they will be regarded as criminals, both by God and man; but all the higher parts of rectitude, every thing that ennobles our being, and that renders us both innoxious and useful, is either not taught, or is taught in such a manner as to leave no proper impression on the mind. This is so obvious a truth, that the defects of female education have ever been a fruitful topic of declamation for the moralist; but not one of this class of writers have laid down any judicious rules for amendment. Whilst we still retain the absurd notion of a sexual excellence, it will militate against the perfecting a plan of education for either sex. The judicious Addison animadverts on the absurdity of bringing a young lady up with no higher idea of the end of education than to make her agreeable to a husband, and confining the necessary excellence for this happy acquisition to the mere graces of person.*

Every parent and tutor may not express himself in the same manner as is marked out by Addison: yet certain it is, that the admiration of the other sex is held out to women as the highest honour they can attain; and whilst this is considered as their *summum bonum*,* and the beauty of their persons the chief *desideratum* of men, Vanity, and its companion Envy, must taint, in their characters, every native and every acquired excellence. Nor can you, Hortensia, deny, that these qualities, when united to ignorance, are fully equal to the engendering and rivetting all those vices and foibles which are peculiar to the female sex; vices and foibles which have caused them to be considered, in ancient times, as beneath cultivation, and in modern days have subjected them to the censure and ridicule of writers of all descriptions, from the deep thinking philosopher to the man of ton and gallantry, who, by the bye, sometimes distinguishes himself by qualities which are not greatly superior to those he despises in women.* Nor can I better illustrate the truth of this observation than by the following picture, to be found in the polite and gallant Chesterfield.* 'Women,' says his Lordship, 'are only children of a larger growth. They have an entertaining tattle, sometimes wit; but for solid reasoning, and good sense, I never in my life knew one that had it, or who acted or reasoned in consequence of it for four and twenty hours together. A man of sense only trifles with them, plays with them, humours and flatters them, as he does an engaging child; but he neither consults them, nor trusts them in serious matters.'*

CLARA REEVE
(1729–1807)

Born and brought up in Ipswich, Suffolk, Reeve was the eldest daughter among the eight children of the Revd William Reeve and his wife Hannah Smythies, daughter of George I's jeweller and goldsmith. By Reeve's own account, her father encouraged her to read parliamentary debates and studies of British, Greek, and Roman history when she was a child, and she went on to lead a retired but highly active and quietly influential literary life. After the death of her father in 1755 she lived with her mother and sisters in Colchester, and later back in Ipswich, where she died. In contrast to some women writers in this collection she was a latecomer to public attention, her first publication being a volume of poems, *Original Poems on Several Occasions* (1769; with a barbed preface suggesting that she had already suffered literary disappointment and ill treatment). After this she published a translation of Barclay's Latin romance *Argenis* (1621) as *The Phoenix* (1772), the popular novel *The Old English Baron* (the first edition of which, published in 1777, bore the title *The Champion of Virtue: A Gothic Story*), four other novels (two, like *The Old English Baron*, historical), and *Plans of Education, with Remarks on the Systems of Other Writers* (1792). Acknowledged in her own time as a woman of learning and information, Reeve is represented here by a work which deserves wider recognition, her innovative history of prose fiction *The Progress of Romance* (1785). Reeve's views on recent fiction, and especially her views on the relative merits of the novels of Samuel Richardson, aroused the wrath of the poet Anna Seward, and led to a heated exchange. Locally controversial, she is also ambitious in her range of reference and bold in her critical intervention in the as-yet-unwritten history of the modern novel.

Reeve is a much more revealing exemplum of the lot of the woman writer than has often been recognized by literary historians. Fatally devoid (as far as we know) of striking oddities of manner and opinion, she has suffered from critical assumptions which privilege creative excess—all of which she might have escaped, had she not written a novel declaring itself to be 'Gothic'. As a novelist (or 'ingenious authoress') Reeve is declared limited by Walter Scott in his 'Life' of her, from *Ballantyne's Novelist's Library* (1821–4), and she is still often regarded as a clumsily decorous and commonsensical imitator of Horace Walpole's proto-Gothic novel *The Castle of Otranto* (1764). Although several recent critics have revised this view of her fiction, her significance lies more surely in the literary analysis of fiction than in its creation. She is one of the most important voices in the eighteenth-century revaluation of romance and the construction of a tradition, and canon, of prose fiction. Her most important precursor is Richard Hurd; but Hurd's *Letters on Chivalry and Romance* (1752) are an educated individual's reflections on personal taste, while, as the extracts from *The Progress of Romance* included here demonstrate, Reeve intersperses her definitions of literary form with implicit and explicit engagements with the nature of critical authority itself. Her work is presented as a series of conversations between three friends, conducted over several evenings by the fireside. In this it resembles Madame de Genlis's *Theatre of Education* (also 1785). Eschewing the male influences of James Beattie and Thomas Warton, Reeve quietly ensures that the literary historians selected for special praise in *The Progress of Romance* are female (Elizabeth Rowe, 1674–1737, and Susannah Dobson, d. 1795). Running throughout *The Progress of Romance*, therefore, are a number of devices for the legitimation of the female critic. One of Reeve's most attentive recent readers, Laura Runge, contends that because of the increasing 'cultural investment in native female purity' in the last decades of the century, Reeve 'is subject to more restrictive codes regarding the proper language in which to deliver' her literary judgements.[1] Perhaps aware of such restrictive codes, Reeve prints as an appendix to *The Progress of Romance* an oriental tale, 'The History of Charoba, Queen of Ægypt', which reprises in acceptable fictional form some of the issues about female authority and the line of female tradition which are contested in the main body of the work.

In the extracts from the first sections of *The Progress of Romance* which follow, the leisured and domestically independent female critic, Euphrasia, is mocked and challenged throughout by her male friend Hortensius, many of whose remarks and interventions read as amused flirtation rather than as sustained intellectual debate, drawing attention to the polite social context in which amateur female criticism necessarily operates, and at the same time defusing any readerly anxiety about Euphrasia's intellectual self-assertiveness. Euphrasia is Reeve's spokeswoman, and, like her, has translated Barclay's *Argenis*. Euphrasia's female friend Sophronia, in contrast to the mocking Hortensius, champions her authority and is happy to adopt the role of attentive tutee. It is instructive to compare this triangulation of discursive voices with works such as Jane Marcet's *Conversations*. Reeve's decision to inject into the literary debate elements of novelistic attention to character and situation is carried forward by Marcet; the invasive male voice against which Reeve sets her woman of letters is a distinctive contribution, however, and may usefully be compared with male–female debate in Austen's novels (see *Persuasion*, below). A further interesting complication in the passages which follow is the common eighteenth-century assocation of romance with femininity and with a debased or outdated type of literature. Euphrasia claims authority for the female critic, but she also constructs a history and a continuing narrative for the feminized literary form of romance, asserting its importance in the history of the novel which, she argues, has seemed to displace it. Reeve's work thus helps create the aesthetic conditions for Ann Radcliffe's

---

[1] *Gender and Language in British Literary Criticism, 1660–1790* (Cambridge: Cambridge University Press, 1997), 155.

reappropriation and innovative redirection of romance in works such as *The Mysteries of Udolpho* (see Radcliffe, below).

~

From *The Progress of Romance* (1785)

EVENING I

Hortensius, Sophronia, Euphrasia

Euph. Hortensius, I am proud of a visit from you, tho' I am ignorant of the motive to which I am indebted for it.

Hort. What Madam, do you think you can give a challenge, and go off with impunity?—I am come hither to demand an explanation of your behaviour last Thursday evening at *Sophronia's* house; and I have brought her with me to be a witness to our dispute—of the defeat of one of us,—or perhaps of our compromise, and reconciliation.

Soph. Or that *Euphrasia* shall make a convert to her own opinion.

Euph. I am obliged to the occasion that brings you both to spend an hour with me.—Pray be seated my friends, and let me understand your meaning.—Surely I was not so presumptuous as to challenge *Hortensius*?

Hort. I will not suffer you either by raillery or compliment to evade my purpose.—In the course of our late conversation, you threw out several hints that struck me as either *new*, or *uncommon*, in respect to the works of the ancient and modern writers;—but what surprised me most of all, you seemed to degrade Epic poetry, and to place it on an equality with the old Romance.* I wish you to explain your sentiments on this head, for I cannot account for your defence of a kind of writings that are generally exploded. I little expected to hear *Euphrasia* ridicule the works of the great Ancients.—(You smile)—Yes Madam, raillery was the only weapon you deigned to use, in opposition to my arguments.—Yet you told me you had better reasons in reserve, but you did not choose then to enter upon the subject, as it would engross too much of our time and attention.

Euph. Your memory Sir, is very retentive, and there is no warding off your attack; perhaps I only seemed to degrade your favourites, and exalt the others, because I opposed opinions long received, and but little examined; while in reality I only meant to place each in their proper rank, both as to merit and utility.

Hort. To convince me of that, you must give me a full explanation of your opinions in respect to both, and also of the foundation of them.

Soph. I have promised in your behalf that you shall give *Hortensius* full satisfaction, and my honour is engaged for it—I know this is a subject you are not unprepared to speak upon.

Euph. Methinks you demand no trifling satisfaction for my Challenge, as it pleases you to call it. However I shall not refuse to comply with your request, if you can have patience to listen, while I investigate a subject of greater extent than perhaps you may suppose, and which though I am not quite unprepared for, I am afraid to begin.

Soph. My dear friend, it is your patience and not ours that will be tried. I am very desirous to hear this subject discussed, and to be informed by the conversation of two such opponents. I expect from *Euphrasia's* reading and observation much advantage to myself.

Hort. My expectations Madam, do not fall short of yours.

Euph. No compliments my good friends! my reading and observations are very much at your service, I wish they may afford you information or entertainment. I will confess to you that I have considered this subject deeply, and that I have written some remarks upon it.—I have made many extracts from different Authors, and collected materials of various kinds; always intending to methodize them one time or other.—I will bring my papers before you, communicate my remarks, propose my opinions; and either be confirmed in them by your approbation, or be silenced by your better arguments on the contrary side;—perhaps I may be enabled to strike out new lights upon the subject, when my imagination is corrected by the judgment of *Hortensius.*

Hort. No compliments I repeat. I wish I may be able to stand my ground. I find you are making great preparations against me, you are coming upon me armed with your papers and extracts.—Artillery and fire-arms against the small sword, the tongue.

Euph. A most warlike allusion! and the comparison holds good;

for if I should come to a close engagement, the small sword will destroy what may escape the artillery.

Hort. Fairly replied.—The attack is begun, I have questioned you closely, it is your part to maintain your own opinions. You have said that Romances are neither so contemptible, nor so dangerous a kind of reading, as they are generally represented—you have compared them to Epic poems.

Euph. Let me first entreat you my good friends to divest yourselves of common prejudices:—Excuse the expression.—Mankind in general are more biassed by names than things; and what is yet stranger, they are biassed by names to which they have not affixed an absolute and determinate meaning.—For instance—pray what do you understand by the word Romance?

Hort. By Romance I understand a wild, extravagant, fabulous Story.

Euph. Sophronia, favour me with an explanation of this word? It is not merely a question of idle curiosity.

Soph. I understand it to mean all those kind of stories that are built upon fiction, and have no foundation in truth.

Euph. You will please to reflect, that under this general denomination of Romance, a vast genus of composition is included, works of various kinds, merits, and tendencies. It is running some hazard, to praise or to decry in general terms, without being perfectly acquainted with the whole extent of the subject under consideration.

Hort. What is it necessary to read all the trash contained in this Genus, as it pleases you to call it, in order to speak of any part of it?

Euph. By no means, I will explain this point presently.—No writings are more different than the ancient *Romance* and modern *Novel*, yet they are frequently confounded together, and mistaken for each other. There are likewise great distinctions to be made between the *old Greek* Romances, those of the middle ages, and those of the fifteenth and sixteenth Centuries. Books of all these kinds have been enthusiastically read and admired; of late years they have been as absurdly censured and condemned. If read indiscriminately they are at best unprofitable, frequently productive of absurdities in manners and sentiments, sometimes hurtful to good morals; and yet from this Genus there may be selected books that are truly respectable, works of genius, taste, and utility, capable of improving the morals and manners of mankind.

Soph. I am entirely of your opinion, and give my testimony to this truth.

Euph. It seems to me that this Genus of composition has never been properly distinguished or ascertained; that it wants to be methodized, to be separated, classed, and regulated; and that a work of this kind would be both entertaining and useful.

Soph. Doubtless it would, and you give us hopes of seeing this accomplished.

Hort. I perceive that you are laying a deep foundation, but what kind of building you will raise upon it, I am impatient to hear.

Euph. If you will honour me with your attention, and sometimes give me your assistance, we will at leisure hours pursue this subject together. Let me bespeak your favour, by assuring you that I mean to do something more than merely to investigate *names*:—we will afterwards proceed to consider the beauties and defects of these writings, of the uses and abuses, and of their effects upon the manners of the times in which they were written. I propose to trace Romance to its Origin, to follow its progress through the different periods to its declension, to shew how the modern Novel sprung up out of its ruins, to examine and compare the merits of both, and to remark upon the effects of them.

Hort. Upon my word you do well to lay a deep foundation, the superstructure will require it: if it be well executed it will do you honour, and without a compliment, I think you equal to this undertaking.

Euph. You may be mistaken, and yet I may be entitled to your allowance,—the design may be good though the execution should fall short. I always mean more than I can express;—my materials increase upon me, insomuch that I fear I may be encumbered by the number and variety of them. I shall depend upon your assistance, and since you have opened my mouth upon the subject, you are bound in honour to correct my redundancies, and to supply my deficiencies.

Hort. What to furnish you with weapons for my defeat?

Euph. Not so, but to assist me in the course of my progress through the land of Romance. I purpose to remark upon the most eminent works of the kind, and to pay the tribute of praise to works of Genius and morality.

Hort. I respect both the motive and the end too much to discourage you, and you may depend upon every assistance in my power.

Euph. Let then the present conversation serve as an introduction to our progress, the next time we meet we will pursue the subject more closely.

Hort. Let it be at my house next Thursday ladies!

Soph. Agreed, and let the Thursday in every week be set apart for this purpose, till the progress is finished.

Euph. With all my heart.—I will readily attend you in turn.

Hort. I am much obliged to you, for your readiness to gratify my curiosity, and shall expect next Thursday with some impatience.—adieu Madam.

Euph. I shall depend upon you for encouragement when deserved,—correction where I am mistaken, and allowance where wanted.—adieu my friends.

EVENING VII

Hortensius, Sophronia, Euphrasia

Hort. We have now, I presume, done with the Romances, and are expecting your investigation of Novels.

Euph. It is now that I begin to be sensible in how arduous an undertaking I have engaged, and to fear I shall leave it unfinished.

Hort. Have no fears, Madam; we shall not suffer you to leave off presently. We expect the completion of the plan you have given us.

Soph. If I judge rightly, the conclusion is yet a great way off.

Euph. This is one of the circumstances that frighten me. If I skim over the subject lightly it will be doing nothing; and if I am too minute I may grow dull and tedious, and tire my hearers.

Hort. You must aim at the medium you recommended to us.

Euph. What Goddess, or what Muse must I invoke to guide me through these vast, unexplored regions of fancy?—regions inhabited by wisdom and folly,—by wit and stupidity,—by religion and profaneness,—by morality and licentiousness.—How shall I separate and distinguish the various and opposite qualities of these strange concomitants?—point out some as the objects of admiration and respect, and others of abhorrence and contempt?

Hort. The subject warms you already, and when that is the case, you will never be heard coldly.—Go on and prosper.

Euph. In this fairy land are many Castles of various Architecture.—Some are built in the air, and have no foundation at all,—others are composed of such heavy materials, that their own weight sinks them into the earth, where they lie buried under their own ruins, and leave not a trace behind,—a third sort are built upon a real and solid foundation, and remain impregnable against all the attacks of Criticism, and perhaps even of time itself.

Soph. So so!—we are indeed got into Fairy-land; it is here that I expect to meet with many of my acquaintance, and I shall challenge them whenever I do.

Euph. I hope that you will assist my labours.—I will drop the metaphor, and tell you that I mean to take notice only of the most eminent works of this kind:—to pass over others slightly and leave the worst in the depths of Oblivion.

The word *Novel* in all languages signifies something new. It was first used to distinguish these works from Romance, though they have lately been confounded together and are frequently mistaken for each other.

Soph. But how will you draw the line of distinction, so as to separate them effectually, and prevent future mistakes?

Euph. I will attempt this distinction, and I presume if it is properly done it will be followed,—If not, you are but where you were before. The Romance is an heroic fable, which treats of fabulous persons and things.—The Novel is a picture of real life and manners, and of the times in which it is written.* The Romance in lofty and elevated language, describes what never happened nor is likely to happen.—The Novel gives a familiar relation of such things, as pass every day before our eyes, such as may happen to our friend, or to ourselves; and the perfection of it, is to represent every scene, in so easy and natural a manner, and to make them appear so probable, as to deceive us into a persuasion (at least while we are reading) that all is real, until we are affected by the joys or distresses, of the persons in the story, as if they were our own.

Hort. You have well distinguished, and it is necessary to make this distinction.—I clearly perceive the difference between the Romance and Novel, and am surprized they should be confounded together.

Euph. I have sometimes thought it has been done insidiously, by those who endeavour to render all writings of both kinds contemptible.

Soph. I have generally observed that men of learning have spoken of them with the greatest disdain, especially collegians.*

Euph. Take care what you say my friend, they are a set of men who are not to be offended with impunity. Yet they deal in Romances, though of a different kind.—Some have taken up an opinion upon trust in others whose judgment they prefer to their own.—Others having seen a few of the worst or dullest among them, have judged of all the rest by them;—just as some men affect to despise our sex, because they have only conversed with the worst part of it.

Hort. Your sex knows how to retort upon ours, and to punish us for our offences against you.—Proceed however.

ANNA LAETITIA BARBAULD
(1743–1825)

One of the most interesting and versatile writers of her time, the Unitarian Dissenter and pacifist Anna Laetitia Barbauld excelled in writing in several major genres, of which the selection here is designed to be representative. Born Anna Laetitia Aikin at Kibworth Harcourt, Leicestershire, she was the eldest child and only daughter of the Presbyterian minister and Kibworth schoolmaster Dr John Aikin and his wife (also of a Presbyterian family) Jane Jennings, and grew up in an intellectual and stimulating family in which she became an early and fluent reader, linguist, and, like Clara Reeve, a scholar of Latin and Greek. This education was cemented when her father became a tutor at the newly established Dissenting Academy at Warrington, Lancashire, in 1758: she was encouraged by the radical scientist and polymath Joseph Priestley, who taught there from 1761 to 1767, and who later read her works in manuscript and circulated copies to friends. The personal and intellectual context of Warrington is important in her early works: many of her poems are addressed to female friends in this circle, in the tradition of the seventeenth-century poet Katherine Phillips.

The young Anna Laetitia Aikin was part of a network of Dissenters, intellectuals, and social thinkers, but she was also acutely aware of the differences between her educational opportunities and the medical training of her brother (and later literary collaborator) John (1747–1822), reflecting in a poem addressed to him in 1768 on her 'more humble works, and lower cares' until she has to admonish herself with 'But hush my heart! nor strive to soar too high'. In May 1774, aged 30, she married a former Warrington pupil and Dissenting cleric, Rochemont Barbauld, five years her junior, having just turned down Elizabeth Montagu's suggestion that they set up a Ladies' College. Instead, she and her husband kept a boys' school in his congregation in Palgrave, Suffolk (closed 1785). Samuel Johnson, revealing something of a gap between his idea of women's education and Barbauld's half-stifled wishes, retorted: 'If I had bestowed such an education on a daughter, and had discovered that she thought of marrying such a fellow, I would have sent her to the *Congress* [the American Continental Congress of 1775]';[1] but the early happiness of the marriage is suggested in many poems, especially 'To Mr Barbauld, with a Map of the Land of Matrimony'. After travelling in Europe they settled in Hampstead in 1787, where Anna Laetitia Barbauld took in pupils; and in Stoke Newington, London, home of many radical Dissenters and of her brother John, in 1802. For several years her husband's mental health deteriorated: an assault on his wife in February 1808 led to their separation, and he drowned himself in November the same year. In her widowhood Barbauld devoted herself to literary work and to a wide circle of literary friends based in London, including Joanna Baillie. Failing eyesight troubled her in the last years before her death in 1825. Her writings for children are based on many years' practical experience; in addition to their schoolteaching she and her husband adopted Charles, the 2-year-old son of her brother, in 1777, three years after their marriage. Some of her children's works, including *Lessons for Children of Two to Three Years Old* (1778), are addressed to Charles.

In December 1772 Joseph Johnson published Barbauld's first volume of thirty-three poems (dated 1773), which went into five editions by 1777

---

[1] Quoted in *The Poems of Anna Letitia Barbauld*, ed. William McCarthy and Elizabeth Kraft (Athens, Ga.: University of Georgia Press, 1994), p. xxii.

(new edn. 1792, American edn. 1820); in 1773, with her brother John, *Miscellaneous Pieces in Prose*, a collection to which she contributed admired essays on 'Inconsistency in our Expectations' and 'On Romances', with other pieces. While in Suffolk she published what has often been considered her best work, the highly popular *Hymns in Prose for Children* (1781), which long retained its popularity, and from which the first extract below is taken. The pieces were 'intended to be committed to memory, and recited' (Preface, p. iv). In the 1790s she published an important poem on the slave trade, *Epistle to William Wilberforce* (1791) and several political pamphlets, including *Sins of Government, Sins of the Nation* (1793). She contributed poems and essays to the *Monthly Magazine*, edited by her brother, from 1796. She edited the poetry of Mark Akenside (1794) and William Collins (1797), and the letters of Samuel Richardson (6 volumes, 1804). Her introductions to the novels she included in her fifty-volume *Edition, with Essay and Lives, of the British Novelists* (1810), one of the most important early collections of prose fiction, and the long prefatory essay 'On the Origin and Progress of Novel Writing' consolidate her standing as a critic of distinction and a significant figure in the development of a novelistic canon. A selection of poetry and prose for *The Female Speaker* (1811) was designed for the use of young women; and a year later she published the work which was to cut short her literary output, the much-criticized poem *Eighteen Hundred and Eleven*. After her death, her writings were edited by her niece Lucy Aikin (1781–1864), along with *A Legacy for Young Ladies*.

Barbauld's work was frequently slighted by male contemporaries. Samuel Tayor Coleridge later wrote of her dismissively in his *Notebooks* as 'Mistress Bare and Bald',[2] and with Elizabeth Inchbald she was one of Charles Lamb's 'two *bald* ladies'.[3] She also had staunch personal defenders. When Henry Crabb Robinson first met the Barbaulds in 1805 he described Mr Barbauld as weazen-faced, a great talker, 'fond of dwelling on controversial points in religion'. Mrs Barbauld, in contrast, 'bore the remains of great personal beauty. She had a brilliant complexion, light hair, blue eyes, a small elegant figure . . . Her excellence lay in the soundness and acuteness of her understanding, and in the perfection of her taste'.[4] She was a key figure for other women writers, particularly those steeped, as she was, in the intellectual traditions of Dissent. In the second essay of her 'Female Writers on Practical Divinity' (1822), Harriet

---

[2] *The Notebooks of Samuel Taylor Coleridge*, vol. 3, *1808–1819: Text*, ed. K. Coburn (London: Routledge and Kegan Paul, 1973), 3965.

[3] *Poems*, ed. McCarthy and Kraft, p. xxxiv.

[4] *Diary, Reminiscences, and Correspondence of Henry Crabb Robinson, Barrister-at-Law, F.S.A.*, selected and ed. Thomas Sadler, 3rd edn., 2 vols. (1872; New York: AMS Press, 1967), i. 118.

Martineau describes Barbauld as 'our first living female poet' (748), praising 'her powerful eloquence, her chaste enthusiasm, and her devotional feelings'. Contrasting her with Hannah More, who inspires awe in the reader, Martineau argues that Barbauld 'meets our ideas, and seems to express what had passed through our own minds, much more forcibly than we ourselves could have done'. Martineau pointedly regrets 'that her powers of writing should not have been more frequently employed'. She is also remembered with affection in Martineau's *Autobiography* as a woman marked by 'superiority'.

The first of the pieces selected below comes from *Hymns in Prose for Children*. After this, four poems demonstrate Barbauld's versatility and concentration of style. 'To a Little Invisible Being' is a magical threshold of a poem in style as well as in subject: Barbauld's consciousness of the physical jostles with a sentimental-moral treatment and with the mock-heroic. 'The Rights of Woman', a more public and declamatory piece, ends with the tenderness for married life which is evident in the several poems which she wrote for and to her husband. It is thought to have been provoked by Wollstonecraft's dismissal of one of her poems in *Vindication of the Rights of Woman*, and, as her recent editors McCarthy and Kraft point out, it was not among the poems Barbauld herself chose to publish, appearing only in Lucy Aikin's collection of 1825. The same, however, is true of several poems now regarded as central to Barbauld's œuvre. Barbauld's command of sensuous language, sometimes associated with feminine excess, is richly apparent in 'Inscription for an Ice-House' (composed *c.*1793) and 'To Mr [S. T.] C[oleridge]' (1797, first published in the *Monthly Magazine* in 1799): these works are rightly increasingly recognized as major contributions to Romantic poetry.

Continuing the fascination with magic found in 'Inscription for an Ice-House' is the little-known essay 'True Magicians', an imaginative survey of the arts of intellectual enquiry enclosed in a dream-vision. In the posthumous collection *A Legacy for Young Ladies* (1826), this is the opening piece, one of several, Lucy Aikin explains, 'found among her papers by the members of her own family'.[5] It is addressed to the young Sarah Carr (see note to page 57), and therefore can be dated to the first decade of the century. Barbauld uses the dream-vision, and the tradition of the prospect poem, again in *Eighteen Hundred and Eleven: A Poem*, completed by the beginning of December 1811 and published early in 1812 by Joseph Johnson. It blends Barbauld's visionary and political styles, and it was vehemently attacked in contemporary reviews because Barbauld's anti-

---

[5] *A Legacy for Young Ladies, Consisting of Miscellaneous Pieces, in Prose and Verse, by the Late Mrs Barbauld* (London: Longman, Hurst, Rees, Orme, Brown, and Green, 1826), p. iv.

war views were denounced as unpatriotic. Barbauld attacks the economic and social as well as military consequences of war: this was a war of blockaded ports and beleaguered colonies, and civilians were badly hit by food shortages and price inflation. 1810 was a year of bankruptcies; 1811 saw an upsurge in popular revolt and a crisis in the monarchy itself, this being the year in which George III was declared unable to rule and his son, the widely distrusted Prince of Wales, took over as Prince Regent. Barbauld looks into a future in which Britian's economy and culture have irretrievably declined, adopting a prophetic mode which led one reviewer to call her 'the Cassandra of the state'.[6] In the context of this anthology, such a view of her invites comparisons with Joanna Southcott, whose writings are also deeply intertwined with the fortunes of the war and with popular fears about it. Henry Crabb Robinson, who disliked the tone of *Eighteen Hundred and Eleven*, records: 'It provoked a very coarse review in the *Quarterly*, which many years afterwards Murray told me he was more ashamed of than any other article'.[7] John Wilson Croker's review for the *Quarterly Review* in June 1812 deplored the poem as party propaganda and considered it a satire only on the 'lady-author' herself. Defending the poem in a letter of November 1812 to Walter Scott, however, Joanna Baillie writes:

I think the meaning of Mrs Barbauld's poem is in some degree mistaken by you as it has been by many people. Tho' she condemns the system that has prevailed for many years of being constantly at war, she looks forward to the unhappy change which she supposes will take place in this country as a thing that must happen in the natural course of events in the course of ages, as we learn from experience learning & arts have travelled over the globe from one country to another remaining permanently nowhere, and not as a misfortune soon or suddenly to befall us. . . . Her hopes of the Americans I believe arises from her having had no connection with them and knowing little about them.[8]

The backlash produced by *Eighteen Hundred and Eleven* cut short Barbauld's career as a poet, and it is an important episode in the reception of women's interventions in political debate at this time. Her silencing recalls aspects of the diminution of Catharine Macaulay's reputation (just as her emphasis on economics and political structures, and her dislike of the public finance of warfare recalls Macaulay's concerns) and helps to bring into focus the limits imposed on women's direct, historically

---

[6] *Monthly Review*, NS 67 (1812), 428.

[7] *Diary, Reminiscences, and Correspondence of Henry Crabb Robinson*, i. 210.

[8] *Collected Letters*, ed. Judith Bailey Slagle, i (Madison: Farleigh Dickinson University Press, 1999), 314.

informed, and unsentimental intervention in the most crucial aspects of national culture. The copy-texts of all the works included here come from Lucy Aikin's collections.

~

From *Hymns in Prose for Children* (1781)

Hymn XI

The golden orb of the sun is sunk behind the hills, the colours fade away from the western sky, and the shades of evening fall fast around me.

Deeper and deeper they stretch over the plain; I look at the grass, it is no longer green; the flowers are no more tinted with various hues; the houses, the trees, the cattle, are all lost in the distance. The dark curtain of night is let down over the works of God; they are blotted out from the view as if they were no longer there.

Child of little observation! canst thou see nothing because thou canst not see grass and flowers, trees and cattle? Lift up thine eyes from the ground shaded with darkness to the heavens that are stretched over thy head; see how the stars one by one appear and light up the vast conclave.

There is the moon bending her bright horns like a silver bow, and shedding her mild light, like liquid silver, over the blue firmament.

There is Venus, the evening and the morning star; and the Pleiades, and the Bear that never sets, and the Pole star* that guides the mariner over the deep.

Now the mantle of darkness is over the earth; the last little gleam of twilight is faded away; the lights are extinguished in the cottage windows, but the firmament burns with innumerable fires; every little star twinkles in its place. If you begin to count them they are more than you can number; they are like the sands of the sea shore.

The telescope shows you far more, and there are thousands and ten thousands of stars which no telescope has ever reached.

Now Orion heaves his bright shoulder above the horizon, and Sirius, the dog-star,* follows him the brightest of the train.

Look at the milky way, it is a field of brightness; its pale light is composed of myriads of burning suns.

All these are God's families; he gives the sun to shine with a ray of his own glory; he marks the path of the planets, he guides their wanderings through the sky, and traces out their orbit with the finger of his power.

If you were to travel as swift as an arrow from a bow, and to travel on further and further still, for millions of years, you would not be out of the creation of God.

New suns in the depth of space would still be burning round you, and other planets fulfilling their appointed course.

Lift up thine eyes, child of earth, for God has given thee a glimpse of heaven.

The light of one sun is withdrawn, that thou mayest see ten thousand. Darkness is spread over the earth that thou mayest behold, at a distance, the regions of eternal day.

This earth has a variety of inhabitants; the sea, the air, the surface of the ground, swarm with creatures of different natures, sizes, and powers; to know a very little of them is to be wise among the sons of men.

What then, thinkest thou, are the various forms and natures and senses and occupations of the peopled universe?

Who can tell the birth and generation of so many worlds? who can relate their histories? who can describe their inhabitants?

Canst thou measure infinity with a line? canst thou grasp the circle of infinite space?

Yet all these depend upon God, they hang upon him as a child upon the breast of its mother; he tempereth the heat to the inhabitant of Mercury; he provideth resources against the cold in the frozen orb of Saturn. Doubt not that he provideth for all beings that he has made.

Look at the moon when it walketh in brightness; gaze at the stars when they are marshalled in the firmament, and adore the Maker of so many worlds.

The Rights of Woman (*c*.1792)

Yes, injured Woman! rise, assert thy right!
Woman! too long degraded, scorned, oppressed;
O born to rule in partial Law's despite,
Resume thy native empire o'er the breast!

Go forth arrayed in panoply divine;
That angel pureness which admits no stain;
Go, bid proud Man his boasted rule resign,
And kiss the golden sceptre of thy reign.

Go, gird thyself with grace; collect thy store
Of bright artillery glancing from afar;
Soft melting tones thy thundering cannon's roar,
Blushes and fears thy magazine of war.

Thy rights are empire: urge no meaner claim,—
Felt, not defined, and if debated, lost;
Like sacred mysteries, which withheld from fame,
Shunning discussion, are revered the most.

Try all that wit and art suggest to bend
Of thy imperial foe the stubborn knee;
Make treacherous Man thy subject, not thy friend;
Thou mayst command, but never canst be free.

Awe the licentious, and restrain the rude;
Soften the sullen, clear the cloudy brow:
Be, more than princes' gifts, thy favours sued;—
She hazards all, who will the least allow.

But hope not, courted idol of mankind,
On this proud eminence secure to stay;
Subduing and subdued, thou soon shalt find
Thy coldness soften, and thy pride give way.

Then, then, abandon each ambitious thought,
Conquest or rule thy heart shall feebly move,
In Nature's school, by her soft maxims taught,
That separate rights are lost in mutual love.

Inscription for an Ice-House* (c.1793)

Stranger, approach! within this iron door
Thrice locked and bolted, this rude arch beneath
That vaults with ponderous stone the cell; confined
By man, the great magician, who controuls
Fire, earth and air, and genii of the storm,
And bends the most remote and opposite things

To do him service and perform his will,—
A giant sits; stern Winter; here he piles,
While summer glows around, and southern gales
Dissolve the fainting world, his treasured snows
Within the rugged cave.—Stranger, approach!
He will not cramp thy limbs with sudden age,
Not wither with his touch the coyest flower
That decks thy scented hair. Indignant here,
Like fettered Sampson when his might was spent
In puny feats to glad the festive halls
Of Gaza's wealthy sons* or he who sat
Midst laughing girls submiss, and patient twirled
The slender spindle in his sinewy grasp;*
The rugged power, fair Pleasure's minister,
Exerts his art to deck the genial board;
Congeals the melting peach, the nectarine smooth,
Burnished and glowing from the sunny wall:
Darts sudden frost into the crimson veins
Of the moist berry; moulds the sugared hail:
Cools with his icy breath our flowing cups;
Or gives to the fresh dairy's nectared bowls
A quicker zest. Sullen he plies his task,
And on his shaking fingers counts the weeks
Of lingering Summer, mindful of his hour
To rush in whirlwinds forth, and rule the year.

*To Mr C[oleridge]** (1797)

Midway the hill of science, after steep
And rugged paths that tire the unpractised feet,
A grove extends; in tangled mazes wrought,
And filled with strange enchantment: dubious shapes
Flit through dim glades, and lure the eager foot
Of youthful ardour to eternal chase.
Dreams hang on every leaf: unearthly forms
Glide through the gloom; and mystic visions swim
Before the cheated sense. Athwart the mists,
Far into vacant space, huge shadows stretch
And seem realities; while things of life,

Obvious to sight and touch, all glowing round,
Fade to the hue of shadows. Scruples here,
With filmy net, most like the autumnal webs
Of floating gossamer, arrest the foot
Of generous enterprise; and palsy hope
And fair ambition with the chilling touch
Of sickly hesitation and blank fear.
Nor seldom Indolence these lawns among
Fixes her turf-built seat; and wears the garb
Of deep philosophy, and museful sits
In dreamy twilight of the vacant mind,
Soothed by the whispering shade; for soothing soft
The shades; and vistas lengthening into air,
With moonbeam rainbows tinted. Here each mind
Of finer mould, acute and delicate,
In its high progress to eternal truth
Rests for a space, in fairy bowers entranced;
And loves the softened light and tender gloom;
And, pampered with most unsubstantial food,
Looks down indignant on the grosser world,
And matter's cumbrous shapings. Youth beloved
Of Science—of the Muse beloved,—not here,
Not in the maze of metaphysic lore,
Build thou thy place of resting! Lightly tread
The dangerous ground, on noble aims intent;
And be this Circe of the studious cell
Enjoyed, but still subservient.* Active scenes
Shall soon with healthful spirit brace thy mind;
And fair exertion, for bright fame sustained,
For friends, for country, chase each spleen-fed fog
That blots the wide creation—
Now heaven conduct thee with a parent's love!

True Magicians (pub. 1826)

*To Miss C.**

My dear Sarah,—I have often reflected, since I left you, on the wonderful powers of magic exhibited by you and your sister. The dim obscurity of that grotto hollowed out by your hands under the laurel hedge, where you used to mix the ingredients of your incantations, struck us with awe and terror; and the broom which you so often brandished in your hands made you look very like witches indeed. I must confess, however, that some doubts have now and then arisen in my mind, whether or no you were truly initiated in the secrets of your art; and these suspicions gathered strength after you had suffered us and yourself to be so drenched as we all were on that rainy Tuesday; which, to say the least, was a very odd circumstance, considering you had the command of the weather. As I was pondering these matters alone in the chaise between Epsom and London, I fell asleep and had the following dream.

I thought I had been travelling through an unknown country, and came at last to a thick wood cut out into several groves and avenues, the gloom of which inspired thoughtfulness, and a certain mysterious dread of unknown powers came upon me. I entered however one of the avenues, and found it terminated in a magnificent portal, through which I could discern confusedly among thick foliage, cloistered arches and Grecian porticos, and people walking and conversing amongst the trees. Over the portal was the following inscription: '*Here dwell the true magicians. Nature is our servant. Man is our pupil. We change, we conquer, we create.*'

As I was hesitating whether or no I should presume to enter, a pilgrim, who was sitting under the shade, offered to be my guide, assuring me that these magicians would do me no harm, and that so far from having any objection to be observed in their operations, they were pleased with any opportunity of exhibiting them to the curious. In therefore I went, and addressed the first of the magicians I met with, who asked me whether I liked panoramas. On replying that I thought them very entertaining, she took me to a little eminence and bade me look round. I did so, and beheld the representation of the beautiful value of Dorking, with Norbury-park and Box-hill to the

north, Reigate to the east, and Leith tower with the Surrey hills to
the south.* After I had admired for some time the beauty and accur-
acy of the painting, a vast curtain seemed to be drawn gradually up,
and my view extended on all sides. On one hand I traced the wind-
ings of the Thames up to Oxford, and stretched my eye westward
over Salisbury Plain, and across the Bristol Channel into the romantic country of South Wales; northward the view extended to Lincoln
cathedral, and York minster towering over the rest of the churches.
Across the Sussex downs I had a clear view of the British Channel,
and the opposite coast of France, with its ports blockaded by our
fleets.* As the horizon of the panorama still extended, I spied the
towers of Notre Dame, and the Tuileries, and my eye wandered at
large over 'The vine-covered hills and gay regions of France,' quite
down to the source of the Loire.* At the same time the great Atlantic
ocean opened to my view; and on the other hand I saw the lake of
Geneva, and the dark ridge of Mount Jura, and discovered the summits of the Alps covered with snow; and beyond, the orange groves
of Italy, the majestic dome of St Peter's, and the smoking crater of
Vesuvius. As the curtain still rose, I stretched my view over the
Mediterranean, the scene of ancient glory, the Archipelago studded
with islands, the shores of the Bosphorus, and the gilded minarets
and cypress groves of Constantinople. Throwing back a look to the
less attractive north, I saw pictured the rugged, broken coast of
Norway, the cheerless moors of Lapland, and the interminable desolation of the plains of Siberia. Turning my eye again southward, the
landscape extended to the plains of Barbary, covered with date-trees;
and I discerned the points of pyramids appearing above the horizon,
and saw the Delta and the seven-mouthed Nile.* In short, the curtain
still rose, and the view extended further and further till the panorama took in the whole globe. I cannot express to you the pleasure I
felt as I saw mountains, seas, and islands, spread out before me.
Sometimes my eye wandered over the vast plains of Tartary, sometimes it expatiated in the savannahs of America. I saw men with dark
skins, white cotton turbans wreathed about their heads, and long
flowing robes of silk; others almost naked under a vertical sun. I saw
whales sporting in the northern seas, and elephants trampling
amidst fields of maize and forests of palm-trees. I seemed to have put
a girdle about the earth, and was gratified with an infinite variety of
objects which I thought I never could be weary of contemplating. At

length, turning towards the magician who had entertained me with such an agreeable exhibition, and asking her name, she informed me it was *Geography*.

My attention was next arrested by a sorceress, who, I was told, possessed the power of calling up from the dead whomsoever she pleased, man or woman, in their proper habits and figures, and obliging them to converse and answer questions. She held a roll of parchment in her hand, and had an air of great dignity. I confess that I felt a little afraid; but having been somewhat encouraged by the former exhibition, I ventured to ask her to give me a specimen of her power, in case there was nothing unlawful in it. 'Whom,' said she, 'do you wish to behold?' After considering some time, I desired to see Cicero, the Roman orator.* She made some talismanic figures on the sand, and presently he rose to my view, his neck and head bare, the rest of his body in a flowing toga, which he gathered round him with one hand, and stretching out the other very gracefully, he recited to me one of his orations against Catiline.* He also read to me—which was more than I could in reason have expected—several of his familiar letters to his most intimate friends. I next desired that Julius Cæsar might be called up: on which he appeared, his hair nicely arranged, and the fore part of his head, which was bald, covered with wreaths of laurel; and he very obligingly gave me a particular account of his expedition into Gaul.* I wished to see the youth of Macedon, but was a little disappointed in his figure, for he was low in stature and held his head awry; but I saw him manage Bucephalus with admirable courage and address, and was afterwards introduced with him into the tent of Darius, where I was greatly pleased with the generosity and politeness of his behaviour.* I afterwards expressed some curiosity to see a battle, if I might do it with safety, and was gratified with the sea-fight of Actium.* I saw, after the first onset, the galleys of Cleopatra turning their prows and flying from the battle, and Antony, to his eternal shame, quitting the engagement and making sail after her. I then wished to call up all the kings of England, and they appeared in order, one after the other, with their crowns and the insignia of their dignity, and walked over the stage for my amusement much like the descendants of Banquo in Macbeth.* Their queens accompanied them, trailing their robes upon the ground, and the bishops with their mitres, and judges, and generals, and eminent persons of every class. I asked many questions as they passed, and received a great deal of information relative to the laws, manners, and transactions of past times. I did not, however, always meet with direct answers to my questions. For instance, when I called up Homer, and after some other conversation asked him where he was born, he only said, 'Guess!'* And when I asked Louis the Fourteenth who was the man in the iron mask,* he frowned and would not tell me. I took a great deal of pleasure in calling up the shades of distinguished people in different ages and countries, making them stand close by one another, and comparing their manners and costume. Thus I measured Catharine of Russia against Semiramis, and Aristotle against Lord Bacon.* I could have spent whole years in conversation with so many celebrated persons, and promised myself that I would often frequent this obliging magician. Her name, I found, was in heaven *Clio*, on earth *History*.

I saw another, who was making a charm for two friends, one of whom was going to the East Indies: they were bitterly lamenting that when they were parted at so great a distance from each other they could no longer communicate their thoughts, but must be cut off from each other's society. Presenting them with a talisman inscribed with four-and-twenty black marks, 'Take this,' she said; 'I have breathed a voice upon it: by means of this talisman you shall still converse, and hear one another as distinctly, when half the globe is between you, as if you were talking together in the same room.' The two friends thanked her for such an invaluable present, and retired. Her name was *Abracadabra*.

I was next invited to see a whispering-gallery,* of a most curious and uncommon structure. To make the experiment of its powers, a young poet of a very modest appearance, who was stealing along in a retired walk, was desired to repeat a verse in it. He applied his lips to the wall, and whispered in a low voice, '*Rura mihi et rigui placeant in vallibus amnes*.'* The sound ran along the walls for some time in a kind of low whisper; but every minute it grew louder and louder, till at length it was echoed and re-echoed from every part of the gallery, and seemed to be pronounced by a multitude of voices at once, in different languages, till the whole dome was filled with the sound. There was a strong smell of incense. The gallery was constructed by *Fame*.

The good pilgrim next conducted me to a cave where several sorceresses, very black and grim, were amusing themselves with making lightning, thunder, and earthquakes. I saw two vials of cold liquor mixed together, and flames burst forth from them. I saw some insignificant-looking black grains, which would throw palaces and castles into the air. I saw—and it made my hair stand on end—a headless man, who lifted up his arm and grasped a sword. I saw men flying through the air, without wings, over the tops of towns and castles, and come down unhurt. The cavern was very black, and the smoke and fires and mephitic blasts and sulphureous vapours that issued from it, gave the whole a very tremendous appearance. I did not stay long, but as I retired I saw *Chemistry* written on the walls in letters of flame, with several other names which I do not now remember.

My companion whispered me that some of these were suspected of communication with the evil genii, and that the demon of War had been seen to resort to the cave. 'But now,' said the pilgrim, 'I will lead you to enchanters who deserve all your veneration, and are even more beneficent than those you have already seen.' He then led me to a cavern that opened upon the sea shore: it blew a terrible storm, the waves ran mountains high, the wind roared, and vessels were driven against each other with a terrible shock. A female figure advanced and threw a little oil upon the waves; they immediately subsided, the winds were still, the storm was laid, and the vessels pursued their course in safety. 'By what magic is this performed?' exclaimed I. 'The magician is *Meekness*,' replied my conductor; 'she can smooth the roughest sea, and allay the wildest storm.'

My view was next directed to a poor wretch, who lay groaning in a most piteous manner, and crushed to the earth with a mountain on his breast; he uttered piercing shrieks, and seemed totally unable to rise or help himself. One of these good magicians, whose name I found was *Patience*, advanced and struck the mountain with a wand; on which, to my great surprise, it diminished to a size not more than the load of an ordinary porter, which the man threw over his shoulders, with something very like a smile, and marched off with a firm step and very composed air.

I must not pass over a charmer of a very pleasing appearance and lively aspect. She possessed the power (a very useful one in a country so subject to fogs and rains as this is) of gilding a landscape with sunshine whenever she breathed upon it. Her name was *Cheerfulness*. Indeed you may remember that your papa brought her down with him on that very rainy day when we could not go out at all, and he played on his flute to you and you all danced.

I was next struck, on ascending an eminence, with a most dreary landscape. All the flat country was one stagnant marsh. Amidst the rushy grass lay the fiend Ague, listless and shivering: on the bare and bleak hills sat Famine, with a few shells of acorns before her, of which she had eaten the fruit. The woods were tangled and pathless; the howl of wolves was heard. A few smoky huts, or caves, not much better than the dens of wild beasts, were all the habitations of men that presented themselves. 'Miserable country!' I exclaimed; 'step-child of nature!' 'This,' said my conductor, 'is Britain as our ancestors possessed it.' 'And by what magic,' I replied, 'has it been converted into the pleasant land we now inhabit?' 'You shall see,' said he. 'It has been the work of one of our most powerful magicians. Her name is *Industry*.' At the word, she advanced and waved her wand over the scene. Gradually the waters ran off into separate channels, and left rich meadows covered with innumerable flocks and herds. The woods disappeared, except what waved gracefully on the tops of the hills, or filled up the unsightly hollows. Wherever she moved her wand, roads, bridges, and canals laid open and improved the face of the country. A numerous population, spread abroad in the fields, were gathering in the harvest. Smoke from warm cottages ascended through the trees, pleasant towns and villages marked the several points of distance. Last, the Thames was filled with forests of masts, and proud London appeared with all its display of wealth and grandeur.

I do not know whether it was the pleasure I received from this exhilarating scene, or the carriage having just got upon the pavement, which awakened me; but I determined to write out my dream, and advise you to cultivate your acquaintance with all the true *Arts of Magic*.

Eighteen Hundred and Eleven: A Poem (1812)

Still the loud death drum, thundering from afar,
O'er the vext nations pours the storm of war:*
To the stern call still Britain bends her ear,
Feeds the fierce strife, the alternate hope and fear;
Bravely, though vainly, dares to strive with Fate,
And seeks by turns to prop each sinking state.

Colossal power with overwhelming force
Bears down each fort of Freedom in its course;
Prostrate she lies beneath the Despot's sway,
While the hushed nations curse him—and obey.*

Bounteous in vain, with frantic man at strife,
Glad Nature pours the means—the joys of life;
In vain with orange blossoms scents the gale,
The hills with olives clothes, with corn the vale;
Man calls to Famine, nor invokes in vain,
Disease and Rapine follow in her train;
The tramp of marching hosts disturbs the plough,
The sword, not sickle, reaps the harvest now,
And where the Soldier gleans the scant supply,
The helpless Peasant but retires to die;
No laws his hut from licensed outrage shield,
And war's least horror is the ensanguined field.

Fruitful in vain, the matron counts with pride
The blooming youths that grace her honoured side;
No son returns to press her widow'd hand,
Her fallen blossoms strew a foreign strand.
—Fruitful in vain, she boasts her virgin race,
Whom cultured arts adorn and gentlest grace;
Defrauded of its homage, Beauty mourns,
And the rose withers on its virgin thorns.
Frequent, some stream obscure, some uncouth name
By deeds of blood is lifted into fame;
Oft o'er the daily page some soft one bends
To learn the fate of husband, brothers, friends,
Or the spread map with anxious eye explores,
Its dotted boundaries and penciled shores,
Asks *where* the spot that wrecked her bliss is found,
And learns its name but to detest the sound.

And think'st thou, Britain, still to sit at ease,
An island Queen amidst thy subject seas,
While the vext billows, in their distant roar,
But soothe thy slumbers, and but kiss thy shore?
To sport in wars, while danger keeps aloof,
Thy grassy turf unbruised by hostile hoof?

So sing thy flatterers;* but, Britain, know,
Thou who hast shared the guilt must share the woe.
Nor distant is the hour; low murmurs spread,
And whispered fears, creating what they dread;
Ruin, as with an earthquake shock, is here,
There, the heart-witherings of unuttered fear,
And that sad death, whence most affection bleeds,
Which sickness, only of the soul, precedes.
Thy baseless wealth dissolves in air away,
Like mists that melt before the morning ray:
No more on crowded mart or busy street
Friends, meeting friends, with cheerful hurry greet;
Sad, on the ground thy princely merchants bend
Their altered looks, and evil days portend,
And fold their arms, and watch with anxious breast
The tempest blackening in the distant West.*

Yes, thou must droop; thy Midas dream is o'er;
The golden tide of Commerce leaves thy shore,
Leaves thee to prove the alternate ills that haunt
Enfeebling Luxury and ghastly Want;
Leaves thee, perhaps, to visit distant lands,
And deal the gifts of Heaven with equal hands.

Yet, O my Country, name beloved, revered,
By every tie that binds the soul endeared,
Whose image to my infant senses came
Mixt with Religion's light and Freedom's holy flame!
If prayers may not avert, if 'tis thy fate
To rank amongst the names that once were great,
Not like the dim cold Crescent shalt thou fade,
Thy debt to Science and the Muse unpaid;*
Thine are the laws surrounding states revere,
Thine the full harvest of the mental year,
Thine the bright stars in Glory's sky that shine,
And arts that make it life to live are thine.
If westward streams the light that leaves the shores,
Still from thy lamp the streaming radiance pours.*
Wide spreads thy race from Ganges to the pole,
O'er half the western world thy accents roll:

Nations beyond the Apalachian hills
Thy hand has planted and thy spirit fills:
Soon as their gradual progress shall impart
The finer sense of morals and of art,
Thy stores of knowledge the new states shall know,
And think thy thoughts, and with thy fancy glow;
Thy Lockes, thy Paleys* shall instruct their youth,
Thy leading star direct their search for truth;
Beneath the spreading Platan's tent-like shade,
Or by Missouri's rushing waters laid,
'Old father Thames' shall be the Poet's theme,
Of Hagley's woods the enamoured virgin dream,*
And Milton's tones the raptured ear enthrall,
Mixt with the roaring of Niagara's fall;
In Thomson's glass the ingenuous youth shall learn
A fairer face of Nature to discern;*
Nor of the Bards that swept the British lyre
Shall fade one laurel, or one note expire.
Then, loved Joanna, to admiring eyes
Thy storied groups in scenic pomp shall rise;*
Their high soul'd strains and Shakespear's noble rage
Shall with alternate passion shake the stage.
Some youthful Basil from thy moral lay
With stricter hand his fond desires shall sway;
Some Ethwald, as the fleeting shadows pass,
Start at his likeness in the mystic glass;*
The tragic Muse resume her just controul,
With pity and with terror purge the soul,
While wide o'er transatlantic realms thy name
Shall live in light, and gather *all* its fame.

Where wanders Fancy down the lapse of years
Shedding o'er imaged woes untimely tears?
Fond moody Power! as hopes—as fears prevail,
She longs, or dreads, to lift the awful veil,
On visions of delight now loves to dwell,
Now hears the shriek of woe or Freedom's knell:
Perhaps, she says, long ages past away,
And set in western waves our closing day,

Night, Gothic night, again may shade the plains
Where Power is seated, and where Science reigns;*
England, the seat of arts, be only known
By the grey ruin and the mouldering stone;
That Time may tear the garland from her brow,
And Europe sit in dust, as Asia now.*

Yet then the ingenuous youth whom Fancy fires
With pictured glories of illustrious sires,
With duteous zeal their pilgrimage shall take
From the blue mountains,* or Ontario's lake,
With fond adoring steps to press the sod
By statesmen, sages, poets, heroes trod;
On Isis' banks to draw inspiring air,
From Runnymede to send the patriot's prayer;
In pensive thought, where Cam's slow waters wind,
To meet those shades that ruled the realms of mind;*
In silent halls to sculptured marbles bow,
And hang fresh wreaths round Newton's awful brow.*
Oft shall they seek some peasant's homely shed,
Who toils, unconscious of the mighty dead,
To ask where Avon's winding waters stray,
And thence a knot of wild flowers bear away;
Anxious inquire where Clarkson, friend of man,
Or all-accomplished Jones* his race began;
If of the modest mansion aught remains
Where Heaven and Nature prompted Cowper's strains;*
Where Roscoe, to whose patriot breast belong
The Roman virtue and the Tuscan song,
Led Ceres to the black and barren moor
Where Ceres never gained a wreath before:*
With curious search their pilgrim steps shall rove
By many a ruined tower and proud alcove,
Shall listen for those strains that soothed of yore
Thy rock, stern Skiddaw, and thy fall, Lodore;*
Feast with Dun Edin's classic brow their sight,
And 'visit Melross by the pale moonlight.'*

But who their mingled feelings shall pursue
When London's faded glories rise to view?

The mighty city, which by every road,
In floods of people poured itself abroad;
Ungirt by walls, irregularly great,
No jealous drawbridge, and no closing gate;
Whose merchants (such the state which commerce brings)
Sent forth their mandates to dependent kings;
Streets, where the turban'd Moslem, bearded Jew,
And wooly Afric, met the brown Hindu;
Where through each vein spontaneous plenty flowed,
Where Wealth enjoyed, and Charity bestowed.
Pensive and thoughtful shall the wanderers greet
Each splendid square, and still, untrodden street;
Or of some crumbling turret, mined by time,
The broken stair with perilous step shall climb,
Thence stretch their view the wide horizon round,
By scattered hamlets trace its ancient bound,
And, choked no more with fleets, fair Thames survey
Through reeds and sedge pursue his idle way.

With throbbing bosoms shall the wanderers tread
The hallowed mansions of the silent dead,
Shall enter the long isle and vaulted dome
Where Genius and where Valour find a home;
Awe-struck, midst chill sepulchral marbles breathe,
Where all above is still, as all beneath;
Bend at each antique shrine, and frequent turn
To clasp with fond delight some sculptured urn,
The ponderous mass of Johnson's form to greet,
Or breathe the prayer at Howard's sainted feet.*

Perhaps some Briton, in whose musing mind
Those ages live which Time has cast behind,
To every spot shall lead his wondering guests
On whose known site the beam of glory rests:
Here Chatham's eloquence in thunder broke,
Here Fox persuaded, or here Garrick spoke;*
Shall boast how Nelson, fame and death in view,
To wonted victory led his ardent crew,
In England's name enforced, with loftiest tone,
Their duty,—and too well fulfilled his own:*

How gallant Moore, as ebbing life dissolved,
But hoped his country had his fame absolved.*
Or call up sages whose capacious mind
Left in its course a track of light behind;
Point where mute crowds on Davy's lips reposed,
And Nature's coyest secrets were disclosed;*
Join with their Franklin, Priestley's injured name,
Whom, then, each continent shall proudly claim.*

Oft shall the strangers turn their eager feet
The rich remains of ancient art to greet,
The pictured walls with critic eye explore,
And Reynolds be what Raphael* was before.
On spoils from every clime their eyes shall gaze,
Egyptian granites and the Etruscan vase;*
And when midst fallen London, they survey
The stone where Alexander's ashes lay,*
Shall own with humbled pride the lesson just
By Time's slow finger written in the dust.
There walks a Spirit o'er the peopled earth,*
Secret his progress is, unknown his birth;
Moody and viewless as the changing wind,
No force arrests his foot, no chains can bind;
Where'er he turns, the human brute awakes,
And, roused to better life, his sordid hut forsakes:
He thinks, he reasons, glows with purer fires,
Feels finer wants, and burns with new desires:
Obedient Nature follows where he leads;
The steaming marsh is changed to fruitful meads;
The beasts retire from man's asserted reign,
And prove his kingdom was not given in vain.
Then from its bed is drawn the ponderous ore,
Then Commerce pours her gifts on every shore,
Then Babel's towers and terraced gardens rise,
And pointed obelisks invade the skies;*
The prince commands, in Tyrian purple drest,
And Egypt's virgins weave the linen vest.*
Then spans the graceful arch the roaring tide,
And stricter bounds the cultured fields divide.

Then kindles Fancy, then expands the heart,
Then blow the flowers of Genius and of Art;
Saints, heroes, sages, who the land adorn,
Seem rather to descend than to be born;
Whilst History, midst the rolls consigned to fame,
With pen of adamant inscribes their name.

The Genius now forsakes the favoured shore,
And hates, capricious, what he loved before;
Then empires fall to dust, then arts decay,
And wasted realms enfeebled despots sway;
Even Nature's changed; without his fostering smile
Ophir no gold, no plenty yields the Nile;*
The thirsty sand absorbs the useless rill,
And spotted plagues from putrid fens distill.
In desert solitudes then Tadmor sleeps,
Stern Marius then o'er fallen Carthage weeps;*
Then with enthusiast love the pilgrim roves
To seek his footsteps in forsaken groves,
Explores the fractured arch, the ruined tower,
Those limbs disjointed of gigantic power;
Still at each step he dreads the adder's sting,
The Arab's javelin, or the tiger's spring;
With doubtful caution treads the echoing ground,
And asks where Troy or Babylon is found.

And now the vagrant Power no more detains
The vale of Tempe, or Ausonian plains;*
Northward he throws the animating ray,
O'er Celtic nations bursts the mental day:
And, as some playful child the mirror turns,
Now here now there the moving lustre burns;
Now o'er his changeful fancy more prevail
Batavia's dykes than Arno's purple vale,*
And stinted suns, and rivers bound with frost,
Than Enna's plains or Baia's viny coast;*
Venice the Adriatic weds in vain,
And Death sits brooding o'er Campania's plain;*
O'er Baltic shores and through Hercynian groves,
Stirring the soul, the mighty impulse moves;*

Art plies his tools, and Commerce spreads her sail,
And wealth is wasted in each shifting gale.
The sons of Odin tread on Persian looms,
And Odin's daughters breathe distilled perfumes;*
Loud minstrel Bards, in Gothic halls, rehearse
The Runic rhyme, and 'build the lofty verse':*
The Muse, whose liquid notes were wont to swell
To the soft breathings of the Æolian shell,
Submits, reluctant, to the harsher tone,
And scarce believes the altered voice her own.*
And now, where Caesar saw with proud disdain
The wattled hut and skin of azure stain,
Corinthian columns rear their graceful forms,
And light varandas brave the wintry storms,
While British tongues the fading fame prolong
Of Tully's eloquence and Maro's song.*
Where once Bonduca whirled the scythed car,
And the fierce matrons raised the shriek of war,*
Light forms beneath transparent muslins float,
And tutored voices swell the artful note.
Light-leaved acacias and the shady plane
And spreading cedar grace the woodland reign;
While crystal walls the tenderer plants confine,
The fragrant orange and the nectared pine;
The Syrian grape there hangs her rich festoons,
Nor asks for purer air, or brighter noons:
Science and Art urge on the useful toil,
New mould a climate and create the soil,
Subdue the rigour of the northern Bear,*
O'er polar climes shed aromatic air,
On yielding Nature urge their new demands,
And ask not gifts but tribute at her hands.

London exults:—on London Art bestows
Her summer ices and her winter rose;
Gems of the East her mural crown adorn,
And Plenty at her feet pours forth her horn;
While even the exiles her just laws disclaim,
People a continent, and build a name:

August she sits, and with extended hands
Holds forth the book of life to distant lands.

But fairest flowers expand but to decay;
The worm is in thy core, thy glories pass away;
Arts, arms and wealth destroy the fruits they bring;
Commerce, like beauty, knows no second spring.
Crime walks thy streets, Fraud earns her unblest bread,
O'er want and woe thy gorgeous robe is spread,
And angel charities in vain oppose:
With grandeur's growth the mass of misery grows.
For see,—to other climes the Genius soars,
He turns from Europe's desolated shores;
And lo, even now, midst mountains wrapt in storm,
On Andes' heights he shrouds his awful form;
On Chimborazo's summits treads sublime.*
Measuring in lofty thought the march of Time;
Sudden he calls:—''Tis now the hour!' he cries,
Spreads his broad hand, and bids the nations rise.
La Plata hears amidst her torrents' roar;
Potosi hears it, as she digs the ore:*
Ardent, the Genius fans the noble strife,
And pours through feeble souls a higher life,
Shouts to the mingled tribes from sea to sea,
And swears—Thy world, Columbus, shall be free.*

CHARLOTTE SMITH
(1749–1806)

Born into an affluent family in King Street, just off St James's Square, London, Charlotte Turner was the eldest of the three children of Nicholas Turner, who had inherited two estates in Sussex and Surrey, and his wife Anna Towers, who died in childbirth when Charlotte was 3. She was brought up by her aunt, Lucy Towers, at her father's estate at Bignor Park, Sussex. During a happy childhood she went to school in Chichester and Kensington, London, and became a voracious reader as well as accomplished in drawing, dancing, and acting. Her lifelong interest in

botany accompanied a skill and precision in close observation which
was encouraged by her drawing lessons. These fortunate circumstances
and prospects rapidly changed, however. In 1761 her father sold the
Surrey estate, a consequence of his increasing involvement in gambling,
and removed Charlotte and her sister Catherine (later the writer Catherine Anne Dorset) from school. In 1764 he remarried, for money, a
woman who took a jealous dislike to his clever and attractive daughter,
and a superficially suitable marriage was arranged for Charlotte at the
age of 15, to Benjamin Smith, improvident son of a successful West
Indies merchant. They married in February 1765 and had twelve children (ten of whom survived infancy), but it was to be an incompatible
and financially ruinous match for the bride. She had additional sources
of grief. Her first son died on the day, or the day following, the birth of
her second, a gifted and sensitive boy who in turn died at the age of
10. Smith's earliest surviving sonnets date from this time, the late
1770s and early 1780s. In 1795 she lost her favourite daughter, Augusta,
aged 20; three other sons also predeceased her, but it was Augusta's
loss which haunted the last eleven years of her life, and to which she
continually returned. One of her poems about Augusta is included
here.

When Benjamin Smith's wealthy father died in 1776, he left a will so
complicated in its various provisions (intended to protect his grandchildren from his son's spendthrift ways) that no settlement was
forthcoming from it until 1813, years after Charlotte Smith's death. The
ensuing legal battles, thought to be a major inspiration for the Jarndyce
litigation in Charles Dickens's novel *Bleak House* (1852–3), sapped her
energy for the rest of her life, and the family's finances were precarious. In
1783–4 she shared her husband's seven-month imprisonment for debt,
and in 1784 published at her own expense a volume of *Elegiac Sonnets*
which were well received, and to which she added in the several subsequent editions until they numbered ninety-two sonnets in all. In the
Preface to the first edition, Smith, like Mary Robinson later, comments on
the difficulty of the 'legitimate' (Petrarchan) sonnet in English, and
emphasizes her poems as spontaneous products of personal sensibility:
'Some very melancholy moments have been beguiled by expressing in
verse the sensations those moments brought.' The publication of the
third edition in 1786 prompted Anna Seward's 'Advice to Mrs Smith: A
Sonnet', in which Seward cautions Smith against dwelling on the passions
depicted by Petrarch and Goethe and against letting 'foreign taste or tales
enchain | The genuine freedom of [her] flowing line'. Her reputation was
firmly established, however. In 1787, settled in Sussex after a period of
enforced economy in a dilapidated chateau in Normandy, she separated

from her husband and set out to support herself and her children by writing. The success of her first novel, *Emmeline, or the Orphan of the Castle* (1788), led to the publication of nine others, all intellectually and socially alert, and often interpreted in closely autobiographical terms; she also translated Prevost's *Manon Lescaut* and a selection of prison-tales translated from Gayot de Pitaval's *Causes Célèbres* as *The Romance of Real Life* (1787). Her sonnets are only the most widely known of her poems: the longer works *The Emigrants* (1793) and the posthumously published, unfinished *Beachy Head* (1807) are increasingly admired. She also wrote six volumes for children: two poems from these are included here. In the later 1790s Smith befriended Elizabeth Inchbald, Mary Hays, and the novelist Eliza Fenwick, but suffered increasingly from rheumatism, and was frequently confined to bed in the last few years of her life. The symptoms accompanying her final illness suggest ovarian cancer. Her estranged husband, who had continually sought to obtain money from her literary ventures, died a few months before her in a debtors' prison in Scotland.

More than any of the writers introduced so far, Charlotte Smith earned her living by writing, and although some of her ideas challenged convention, she was careful to observe essential proprieties in order to secure sales. Her writing in different genres developed acceptable vehicles for advanced ideas. In the 1792 preface to her novel *Desmond*, she questions the wisdom that women should have nothing to say about politics 'in a world where they are subject of such mental degradation; where they are censured as affecting masculine knowledge if they happen to have any understanding; or despised as insignificant triflers if they have none' (6). Speaking of her own writing, she points out: '*I* however, may safely say, that it was in the *observance*, not in the *breach* of duty, *I* became an author' (7). As a poet, Smith was innovative and influential. In a footnote to 'Stanzas Suggested in a Steamboat off St Bees' Head' (1833), Wordsworth called her 'a lady to whom English verse is under greater obligations than are likely to be either acknowledged or remembered. She wrote little, and that little unambitiously, but with true feeling for rural nature, at a time when nature was not much regarded by English Poets'.[1] In fact, Smith's poetic output was far from 'little' or unambitious, and it has recently received far more critical recognition than Wordsworth anticipated. Her prose, meanwhile, is one of the difficult omissions of this anthology. Smith was one of Jane Austen's favourite writers, and her novels helped shape the taste for Gothic fiction represented here by Ann Radcliffe. Although most of her novels are out of print, and fully deserving of a

---

[1] *The Poetical Works of William Wordsworth*, ed. Ernest de Selincourt and Helen Darbishire, 5 vols. (Oxford: Clarendon Press, 1940–9), iv. 403.

wider readership, they are rewarding as narrative wholes rather than in excerpts. They lack the episodic immediacy which marks out, for all their differences in style, the passages from Burney, Inchbald, Radcliffe, Edgeworth, and Austen included here. I have chosen to represent Smith's voluminous literary output with six of the influential *Elegiac Sonnets*, her 'Ode to the Missel Thrush' from *Conversations Introducing Poetry* (1804), and the fable 'The Jay in Masquerade' from *The History of Birds* (1807), all with Smith's own notes. In the sonnets, Smith's poetic persona describes herself as imprisoned and oppressed (by social constraints and by her own capacity for feeling): she writes of treasures, like the glow-worm, destroyed by man's desire to possess them; and of a natural world which seems to offer discrete images of connection with the human, but which is also mysterious and transient. 'Ode to the Missel Thrush' is a more joyous piece, and in its original setting, as part of *Conversations Introducing Poetry*, the thrush is presented as an alternative to that overburdened poetic bird, the nightingale. The final stanza shows how precarious the joys of 'Hope and Fortitude' might be, however. 'The Jay in Masquerade' combines Smith's delight in natural description with a warning tale of 'pilfering' in literature, unexpectedly bringing back into focus the vexed issues of literary originality and authenticity, crucial to the debate on female claims to masculinized 'genius' but here used to chide male ambition. Not for Smith is the archetype of vanity to be a young woman of fashion. The lively, glancing style is full of amusing detail but Smith continues to emphasize the importance of individuality and liberty, describing a zone of freedom and sociability presided over by a protective woman (whose ultimate responsibility for the apparently unmanned estate, or for the 'collecting' of foreign species of bird, however, is left unclear).

≈

From *Elegiac Sonnets* (1784–1797)

The partial Muse has from my earliest hours

The partial Muse has from my earliest hours
    Smiled on the rugged path I'm doom'd to tread,
And still with sportive hand has snatch'd wild flowers,
    To weave fantastic garlands for my head:
But far, far happier is the lot of those
    Who never learn'd her dear delusive art;

Which, while it decks the head with many a rose,
    Reserves the thorn, to fester in the heart.
For still she bids soft Pity's melting eye
    Stream o'er the ills she knows not to remove,
Points every pang, and deepens every sigh
    Of mourning Friendship, or unhappy Love.
Ah! then, how dear the Muse's favours cost,
If those paint sorrow best—who feel it most![1]

To a Nightingale[2]

Poor melancholy bird—that all night long
    Tell'st to the Moon thy tale of tender woe;
    From what sad cause can such sweet sorrow flow,
And whence this mournful melody of song?

Thy poet's musing fancy would translate
    What mean the sounds that swell thy little breast,
    When still at dewy eve thou leavest thy nest,
Thus to the listening night to sing thy fate.

Pale Sorrow's victims wert thou once among,
    Tho' now released in woodlands wild to rove?
    Say—hast thou felt from friends some cruel wrong,
Or died'st thou—martyr of disastrous love?
Ah! songstress sad! that such my lot might be,
To sigh, and sing at liberty—like thee!

Written in the Church-Yard at Middleton in Sussex

Press'd by the Moon, mute arbitress of tides,
    While the loud equinox its power combines,
    The sea no more its swelling surge confines,
But o'er the shrinking land sublimely rides.
The wild blast, rising from the Western cave,
    Drives the huge billows from their heaving bed;

---

[1] 'The well-sung woes shall soothe my pensive ghost; | He best can paint them who shall feel them most.' Pope's 'Eloisa to Abelard', l. 366.
[2] The idea from the 43rd Sonnet of Petrarch. *Secondo parte.* 'Quel rosigniuol, che si soave piagne.'

Tears from their grassy tombs the village dead,[1]
And breaks the silent sabbath of the grave!
With shells and sea-weed mingled, on the shore
    Lo! their bones whiten in the frequent wave;
    But vain to them the winds and waters rave;
They hear the warring elements no more:
While I am doom'd—by life's long storm opprest,
To gaze with envy on their gloomy rest.

The Glow-Worm

When on some balmy-breathing night of Spring
    The happy child, to whom the world is new,
Pursues the evening moth, of mealy wing,*
    Or from the heath-bell beats the sparkling dew;
He sees before his inexperienced eyes
    The brilliant Glow-worm, like a meteor, shine
On the turf-bank;—amazed, and pleased, he cries,
    'Star of the dewy grass![2]—I make thee mine!'—
Then, ere he sleep, collects 'the moisten'd' flower,[3]
    And bids soft leaves his glittering prize enfold
And dreams that Fairy-lamps illume his bower:
    Yet with the morning shudders to behold
His lucid treasure, rayless as the dust!
—So turn the world's bright joys to cold and blank disgust.

Written in a Tempestuous Night, on the Coast of Sussex*

The night-flood rakes upon the stony shore;
    Along the rugged cliffs and chalky caves
Mourns the hoarse Ocean, seeming to deplore
    All that are buried in his restless waves—
Mined by corrosive tides, the hollow rock
    Falls prone, and rushing from its turfy height,

[1] Middleton is a village on the margin of the sea, in Sussex, containing only two or three houses. There were formerly several acres of ground between its small church and the sea, which now, by its continual encroachments, approaches within a few feet of this half-ruined and humble edifice. The wall, which once surrounded the churchyard, is entirely swept away, many of the graves broken up, and the remains of bodies interred washed into the sea; whence human bones are found among the sand and shingles on the shore.

[2] 'Star of the earth,' Dr Darwin.*

[3] 'The moisten'd blade—' Walcot's beautiful 'Ode to the Glow-worm'.*

Shakes the broad beach with long-resounding shock,
    Loud thundering on the ear of sullen Night;
Above the desolate and stormy deep,
    Gleams the wan Moon, by sloating mist opprest;
Yet here while youth, and health, and labour sleep,
    Alone I wander—Calm untroubled rest,
    'Nature's soft nurse,'* deserts the sigh-swoln breast,
And shuns the eyes, that only wake to weep!

Reflections on Some Drawings of Plants

I can in groups these mimic flowers compose,
    These bells and golden eyes, embathed in dew;
Catch the soft blush that warms the early Rose,
    Or the pale Iris cloud with veins of blue;
Copy the scallop'd leaves, and downy stems,
    And bid the pencil's varied shades arrest
Spring's humid buds, and Summer's musky gems:
    But, save the portrait on my bleeding breast,
I have no semblance of that form adored,
    That form, expressive of a soul divine,
    So early blighted; and while life is mine,
With fond regret, and ceaseless grief deplored—
    That grief, my angel! with too faithful art
Enshrines thy image in thy Mother's heart.*

Ode to the Missel Thrush[1] (1804)

The winter solstice scarce is past,
Loud is the wind, and hoarsely sound

[1] Missel Thrush. *Turdus visivorous*. Mr White, in his account of singing birds, puts this among those whose song ceases before Midsummer.* It is certainly an error. This remarkable bird, which cannot be mistaken for any other, began to sing so early as the second week of January; and now I hear him uttering a more clamorous song, the 8th of July, between the flying showers. Whenever the weather is windy or changeable, he announces it by a variety of loud notes. There is only one bird of this kind within hearing, who sang last year to the beginning of August. His food consists of berries and insects, but principally, the former. The fruit of the Hawthorn, *Mesphilus*, Elder, *Sambucas*, Spindletree, *Euonymus*, Sloe, *Prunus*, and Holly, *Ilex*, occasionally supply him; but the Misseltoe, *Viscum*, from whence he takes his name of *viscivorous*, is his favourite food. As birdlime is often made of its glutinous berries, and this thrush is supposed to encrease the Misseltoe by depositing the seeds he has swallowed on other trees, he is said in a Latin proverb to propagate the means of his own destruction.

The mill-streams in the swelling blast,
And cold and humid is the ground;
When, to the ivy, that embowers
Some pollard tree, or sheltering rock,
The troop of timid warblers flock,
And, shuddering, wait for milder hours.

While thou! the leader of their band,
Fearless salut'st the opening year;
Not stay'st, till blow the breezes bland
That bid the tender leaves appear.
But, on some rowering elm or pine,
Waving elate thy dauntless wing,
Thou joy'st thy love notes wild to sing,
Impatient of St Valentine!

Oh, herald of the Spring! while yet
No harebell scents the woodland lane,
Nor starwort fair,* nor violet,
Braves the bleak gust and driving rain,
'Tis thine, as thro' the copses rude
Some pensive wanderer sighs along,
To soothe him with thy cheerful song,
And tell of Hope and Fortitude!

For thee then, may the hawthorn bush,
The elder, and the spindle tree,
With all their various berries blush,
And the blue sloe abound for thee!
For thee, the coral holly glow
Its arm'd and glossy leaves among,
And many a branched oak be hung
With thy pellucid misseltoe.

Still may thy nest, with lichen lin'd,
Be hidden from the invading jay,
Nor truant boy its covert find,
To bear thy callow young away;
So thou, precursor still of good,
O, herald of approaching Spring,
Shalt to the pensive wanderer sing
Thy song of Hope and Fortitude.

The Jay in Masquerade (1807)

Within a park's area vast,
    Where grassy slopes and planted glades,
Where the thron'd chesnuts, cones, and mast,*
    Strew'd the wide woodland's mingled shades;
From antler'd oaks the acorns shower'd,
    As blew the sharp October breeze;
And from the lighter ashes pour'd
    With the first frost their jetty keys.*
Attracted there a countless throng
    Of birds resorted to the woods,
With various cries, and various song,
    Cheering the cultur'd solitudes.
In the high elms gregarious rooks
    Were heard, loud clam'ring with the daw;
And alders, crowding on the brooks,
    The willow wren and halcyon saw;*
And where, through reeds and sedges steal
    With slower course th' obstructed tide,
The shieldrake, and the timid teal,
    And water rail, and widgeon hide.*
The lake's blue wave in plumy pride
    The swan repell'd with ebon foot,
And ducks Muscovian, scarlet-eyed,
    Sail'd social with the dusky coot.
The partridge on the sunny knowl
    Securely call'd her running brood,
And here at large the turkeys prowl
    As free as in their native wood;
With quick short note the pheasant crow'd,
    While, scudding through the paddocks spacious,
In voice monotonous and loud,
    Was seen the guinea fowl pugnacious.
The mistress who presided here
    Each bird indigenous protected;
While many a feather'd foreigner
    Was from remoter climes collected.
A Jay among these scenes was hatch'd,

Who fancied that indulgent nature
His grace and beauty ne'er had match'd,
    Not ever form'd so fair a creature.
His wings, where blues of tend'rest shade
    Declin'd so gradually to jet;
Plumes like gray clouds, that o'er the red
    Float when the summer sun is set;
Like Sachem's diadem,* a crest
    Rising to mark him for dominion;
In short, that never bird possess'd
    Such charms, was his confirm'd opinion.
Till wand'ring forth one luckless day,
    'Twas his ill fortune to behold
A peacock to the sun display,
    Above his lovely shells of gold,
Those shafts, so webb'd, and painted so,
    That they seem'd stol'n from Cupid's wing,
And dipp'd in the ethereal bow
    That shines above the show'rs of spring;
And, as the light intensely beam'd,
    Or as they felt the rustling zephyr,
The em'rald crescents brightly gleam'd
    Round lustrous orbs of deep'ning sapphire.
Still, on the peacock as he gaz'd,
    The Jay beheld some beauty new,
While high his green panache he rais'd,
    And waved his sinuous neck of blue;
And still with keen and jealous eyes,
    The restless, vain, impatient Jay
Or perches near, or round him flies,
    And marks his manners and his way.
For where his shiv'ring train is spread,
    Or near the ant-hills in the copse,
Or in the grass along the mead,
    Some radiant feather often drops;
And these, where'er they chanc'd to fall,
    The Jay, with eagerness the prize
Hasten'd to seize, collecting all
    These snowy shafts with azure eyes,

Fancying that all this plumage gay
    He could so manage, as to place
Around his form, and thus display
    The peacock's hues, the peacock's grace.
He tried, and so adorn'd appear'd,
    Amazing all the folk of feather;
Who, while they gazed at him, were heard
    To join in ridicule together,
Gibing and taunting, as they press
    Around, and mock his senseless trouble,
While some pluck off his borrow'd dress,
    Geese hiss, ducks quack, and turkies gobble.
Shrill screams the stare, and long and loud
    The yaffil laughs from aspin gray;*
Til scarce escaping from the crowd
    With his own plumes, he skulks away.

Be what you are, nor try in vain,
    To reach what nature will deny,
Factitious Art can ne'er attain
    The grace of young Simplicity.
And ye, whose transient fame arises
    From that which others write or say,
Learn hence, how common sense despises
    The pilf'ring literary Jay.

ELIZABETH INCHBALD
(1753–1821)

Born Elizabeth Simpson, the second-youngest of the nine children of a farmer, John Simpson, and his wife Mary Rushbrook, at Standingfield, near Bury St Edmunds in Suffolk, Inchbald was an actor, dramatist, and novelist. Her family were Catholics, a faith she retained by education and conviction. Despite a pronounced stutter which impeded her chances of succeeding in an acting career, she ran away from home at 19 to seek work on the London stage, and a few months later, in June 1772, married Joseph Inchbald, a portrait-painter and actor seventeen years her senior, and a fellow Catholic. The match seems to have been partly a defensive move on Elizabeth Inchbald's part, and it was not happy. In September 1772 she made her theatrical debut in Bristol, playing Cordelia to her husband's Lear. With him she toured the country, undertaking many dramatic roles, and forming friendships with leading threatrical figures including Sarah Siddons and her brother John Philip Kemble. She first began writing plays during a brief residence in Paris in 1776. Her husband died suddenly of a heart attack in 1779, and Inchbald continued her threatrical career for a further ten years, appearing at Covent Garden for the first time in 1780 and consolidating her acting by writing comedies and farces in the 1780s and 1790s. She retired from the stage in 1789. Her personal situation had continued to have its perils—the theatre manager Thomas Harris moved from attempted seduction to attempted rape during her time at Covent Garden—but Inchbald was an astute manager of her two careers of writing and acting, and used them together to achieve the best deals for herself. A measure of her success is that she left the considerable fortune of £6,000 when she died.

Inchbald was the friend of several leading radical writers and a member of the lively London intellectual set which included Mary Wollstonecraft, Mary Hays, and the publisher Joseph Johnson. The writers William Godwin and Thomas Holcroft are both thought to have proposed marriage to her. Later, Wollstonecraft was rather waspish about Godwin's friendship with Inchbald, writing to him on 24 August 1796: 'As you are to dine with Mrs Perfection today, it would be dangerous not to remind you of my existence.'[1] Wollstonecraft's and Godwin's daughter Mary Shelley recalls his describing her as 'a piquante mixture between a lady and a milkmaid'.[2] A confirmed Londoner, she moved frequently from lodgings to lodgings in her later years, and in 1819 retired to the mainly Catholic establishment of Kensington House, Kensington, where she lived for the last two years of her life. She had written her memoirs, and in 1786 had been offered £1,000 for their publication. An expanded version, in four volumes, was offered to the publisher Constable through William Godwin's mediation in 1818, but Constable declined them. She later burned them on the advice of her confessor.

Including her first play, *Polygamy* (1781), and her first success, a topical farce called *The Mogul Tale; or, The Descent of the Balloon* (1784), which earned her £100, Inchbald wrote twenty-one plays, eighteen of which were published, but achieved a more lasting success with the publication of the first of her two novels, *A Simple Story*, in 1791. A more avowedly

[1] Roger Manvell, *Elizabeth Inchbald: England's Principal Women Dramatist and Independent Woman of Letters in Eighteenth Century London: A Biographical Study* (Lanham, Md.: University Press of America, 1987), 99.
[2] Ibid. 107.

political novel, *Nature and Art*, followed in 1796. The rather weary Preface to *A Simple Story* invites readers to see novel-writing as a welcome release from her theatrical toils—it was also a more safely feminine mode. Inchbald laments that it has been her destiny 'to be occupied throughout her life, in what has the least suited either her inclination or capacity— with an invincible impediment in her speech, it was her lot for thirteen years to gain a subsistence by public speaking—and, with the utmost detestation to the fatigue of inventing, a constitution suffering under a sedentary life, and an education confined to the narrow boundaries prescribed her sex, it has been her fate to devote a tedious seven years to the unremitting labour of literary productions'. Despite these avowed feelings, it would be wrong to allow the brilliance of *A Simple Story* to overshadow Inchbald's writings for the stage and her dramatic criticism, which she developed at length in the introductions to the twenty-five volumes of John Bell's *The British Theatre*, edited between 1806 and 1809. These pieces are especially interesting for their awareness of the practicalities of acting, an edge which is evident in her preface to the work of the most respected woman dramatist of the age, Joanna Baillie.

The selection from Inchbald's work given here allows space for one of the rapidly paced chapters of *A Simple Story* (in its first-edition state) while emphasizing first of all her writing for and about the stage. Although her most often-remembered play is *Lovers' Vows* (1798), the adaptation from Kotzebue which is rehearsed to such effect in Austen's *Mansfield Park* (see below), Inchbald turned most naturally to incidental comedy. *Such Things Are* (performed 1787, published 1788) was popular, new productions frequently being staged: there are records of a London production in 1824. The play earned her £900. The extract from the first scene of *Such Things Are* is introduced by her own 'Remarks' on it from *The British Theatre* collection. The play was based on the work of the prison reformer John Howard, and examines the impact of tyrannical rule on Indian society, but it also sparkles with marital dispute. The exchanges between Sir Luke and Lady Tremor combine critique of the tyranny of the Sultan's sovereignty and of the domestic tyranny created by the misunderstandings between men and women:

Lady Tremor. Pray, Mr Haswell, is it true that the Sultan cut off the head of one of his wives the other day because she said to him—'I won't?'
Sir Luke. Do, my dear, be silent.
Lady Tremor. I won't.
Sir Luke. O, that the Sultan had you instead of me!
Lady Tremor. And with my head off, I suppose?

Sir Luke. No, my dear; in that state, I shou'd have no objection to you myself.

(I. i.)

The extract from *Such Things Are* is followed by Inchbald's unconventionally astringent 'Remarks' on Joanna Baillie's play *De Monfort* (see the extract from Baillie, below). Inchbald loved the stage and was suspicious of Baillie's theoretical pronouncements upon it. She could also claim direct experience of the way in which Baillie's tragedy came across to an audience: she had taken a box at Drury Lane for the first night of *De Monfort*, and wrote afterwards to a friend: 'That fine play, supported by the most appropriate acting of Kemble and Siddons, is both dull and highly improbable in the representation'.[3] Throughout her prefaces she is keen to allow the theatre its own rules: something can work theatrically which no theoretical approach would find viable, and audience reaction is a primary constituent of theatrical success, not a secondary consideration.

Inchbald's dramatic writing is marked by an assured handling of dialogue, a characteristic which is instrumental in the immediacy of *A Simple Story*. She started work on this novel in February 1777 and finished a first version of it, probably only the first two volumes of the eventual four-volume work, in 1779. She offered it for publication, but it was rejected. Ten years later she added the second half of the story, which tells of Miss Milner's daughter, Matilda, and her reputation as a dramatist ensured it publication this time. It was published by George Robinson in 1791, and earned Inchbald £200. According to her biographer James Boaden, Dorriforth/Lord Elmwood is based on the actor John Philip Kemble, to whom the married Inchbald was strongly attracted and who remained a lifelong friend. Inchbald herself, however, maintained that the novel was 'all invention' with the exception of the character of Dorriforth's former tutor Sandford, whom she modelled on her first confessor.

In the extract given here, Miss Milner, who has fallen in love with her guardian, Mr Dorriforth, while he is still a Roman Catholic priest, is adapting to the change of fortune which has seen him give up his vocation and turn to thoughts of marriage. The woman he considers to be a suitable wife, however, is not Miss Milner, but the coldly perfect Miss Fenton. Exacerbating Miss Milner's feelings is the knowledge that his choice is wholeheartedly endorsed by his former tutor, Mr Sandford, her most scathing and powerful detractor. Observing these tangled and unexpressed passions is Mrs Horton, an elderly widow who keeps house for Dorriforth and disapproves of his sprightly ward; and her kindly

---

[3] Ellen Donkin, *Getting Into the Act: Women Playwrights in London, 1776–1829* (London: Routledge, 1995), 163.

spinster niece Miss Woodley, affectionately attached to both Miss Milner and Dorriforth and the only person to know that Miss Milner loves him.

In January 1810 Maria Edgeworth wrote to Inchbald: 'I never read any novel—I except none—I never read any novel that affected me so strongly, or that so completely possessed me with the belief in the real existence of all the people it represents . . . I believed all to be real, and was affected as I should be by the real scenes if they had passed before my eyes.'[4] This is all the more extraordinary because Inchbald uses so few conventional methods of making characters 'real' to us: we know the colour of nobody's hair, read nobody's private journal, hear the narrator's considered views of no character for longer than two sentences. In some ways it is a difficult novel from which to select extracts, because it moves with such apparent effortlessness from one subtly observed exchange to the next. Selecting extracts, however, turns out to be a telling test of Inchbald's skill, because it reveals the clarity of design and psychological grasp which makes every incident quite capable of standing alone. 'When Dale Spender published her pioneering and polemical *Mothers of the Novel: 100 good women writers before Jane Austen* she made claims for several writers whose reputations she helped to re-establish, but her strongest words are reserved for Inchbald as novelist: 'The absence of Elizabeth Inchbald from the literary tradition is not only a loss—it is a disgrace'.[5]

~

Remarks on *Such Things Are* (1806)

The writer of this play was, at the time of its production, but just admitted to the honours of an anthoress, and wanted experience to behold her own danger, when she attempted the subject on which the work is founded.* Her ignorance was her protection. Had her fears been greater, or proportioned to her task, her success had been still more hazardous. A bold enterprize requires bold execution; and as skill does not always unite with courage, it is often advantageous, where cases are desperate, not to see with the eye of criticism: chance will sometimes do more for rash self-importance, than that judgment, which is the parent of timidity.

Such was the consequence on the first appearance of this

---

[4] Quoted by James Boaden, *Memoirs of Mrs Inchbald, Including her Familiar Correspondence with the Most Distinguished Persons of Her Time*, 2 vols. (London: Bentley, 1833), ii. 152.

[5] (London: Pandora, 1986), 215.

comedy—its reception was favourable beyond the usual bounds of favour bestowed upon an admired play, and the pecuniary remuneration equally extraordinary.

There was novelty, locality, and invention in 'Such Things are;' and the audience forgave, or, in their warmth of approbation, overlooked, improbability in certain events, incorrectness of language, and meanness, bordering on vulgarity, in some of the characters.

As the scene is placed in the East Indies, where the unpolished of the British nation so frequently resort to make their fortune, perhaps the last mentioned defect may be more descriptive of the manners of the English inhabitants of that part of the globe, than had elegance of dialogue, and delicacy of sentiment, been given them. Nevertheless, a more elevated style of conversation and manners in Sir Luke and Lady Tremor would not have been wholly improper, and would assuredly have been much more pleasing; especially to those who may now sit in judgment upon the work, as readers, and cold admirers of that benevolence, no longer the constant theme of enthusiastic praise, as when this drama was first produced.

When this play was written, in 1786, Howard, the hero of the piece, under the names of Haswell, was on his philanthropic travels through Europe and parts of Asia, to mitigate the sufferings of the prisoner.* His fame, the anxiety of his countrymen for the success of his labours, and their pride in his beneficent character, suggested to the author a subject for the following pages. The scene chosen for its exhibition is the island of Sumatra;* where the English settlement, the system of government, modes and habits of the natives, the residents, and the visitors of the isle, may well reconcile the fable and incidents of the drama to an interesting degree of possibility.

From *Such Things Are* (1787)

ACT THE FIRST SCENE I

A Parlour at Sir Luke Tremor's

Enter Sir Luke, *followed by* Lady Tremor.

Sir Luke. I tell you, madam, you are two and thirty.

Lady. I tell you, sir, you are mistaken.

Sir Luke. Why, did not you come over from England exactly sixteen years ago?

Lady. Not so long.

Sir Luke. Have not we been married, the tenth of next April, sixteen years?

Lady. Not so long.

Sir Luke. Did you not come over the year of the great eclipse?*— answer me that.

Lady. I don't remember it.

Sir Luke. But I do—and shall remember it as long as I live.—The first time I saw you was in the garden of the Dutch envoy: you were looking through a glass at the sun—I immediately began to make love to you, and the whole affair was settled while the eclipse lasted—just one hour, eleven minutes, and three seconds.

Lady. But what is all this to my age?

Sir Luke. Because I know you were at that time near seventeen, and without one qualification except your youth, and your fine clothes.

Lady. Sir Luke, Sir Luke, this is not to be borne!

Sir Luke. Oh! yes—I forgot—you had two letters of recommendation from two great families in England.

Lady. Letters of recommendation!

Sir Luke. Yes; your character—that, you know, is all the fortune we poor Englishmen, situated in India, expect with a wife, who crosses the sea at the hazard of her life, to make us happy.

Lady. And what but our characters would you have us bring?— Do you suppose any lady ever came to India, who brought along with her friends or fortune?

Sir Luke. No, my dear: and what is worse, she seldom leaves them behind.

Lady. No matter, Sir Luke: but if I delivered to you a good character—

Sir Luke. Yes, my dear, you did: and if you were to ask me for it again, I can't say I could give it you.

Lady. How uncivil! how unlike are your manners to the manners of my Lord Flint!

Sir Luke. Ay, you are never so happy as when you have an opportunity of expressing your admiration of him—A disagreeable, nay, a very dangerous man—one is never sure of one's self in his presence—he carries every thing he hears to the ministers of our suspicious Sultan—and I feel my head shake whenever I am in his company.

Lady. How different does his lordship appear to me?—To me he is all *politesse*.

Sir Luke. Politesse! how should you understand what is real *politesse?* You know your education was very much confined.

Lady. And if it *was* confined?—I beg, Sir Luke, you will cease these reflections: you know they are what I can't bear!—[*Walks about in a passion*]—Pray, does not his lordship continually assure me, I might be taken for a countess, were it not for a certain little grovelling toss I have caught with my head? which I learnt of you—learnt by looking so much at you.

Sir Luke. And now, if you don't take care, by looking so much at his lordship, you may catch some of his defects.

Lady. I know of very few he has.

Sir Luke. I know of many—besides those he assumes.

Lady. Assumes!

Sir Luke. Yes: Do you suppose he is as forgetful as he pretends to be?—no, no; but because he is a favourite with the Sultan, and all our great men, he thinks it genteel or convenient to have no memory; and yet, I'll answer for it, he has one of the best in the universe.

Lady. I cannot credit your charge.

Sir Luke. Why, though he forgets his appointments with his tradesmen, did you ever hear of his forgetting to go to court when a place was to be disposed of? Did he ever mistake, and send a bribe to a man out of power? Did he ever forget to kneel before the prince of this island, or to look in his highness's presence like the statue of Patient-resignation, in humble expectation?

Lady. Dear Sir Luke—

Sir Luke. Sent from his own country in his very infancy, and brought up in the different courts of petty arbitrary princes here in Asia, he is the slave of every rich man, and the tyrant of every poor one.

Lady. 'Petty princes!'—'tis well his highness, our Sultan, does not hear you.

Sir Luke. 'Tis well he does not—Don't you repeat what I say: but you know how all this fine country is harassed and laid waste by a set of princes—Sultans, as they style themselves, and I know not what—who are for ever calling out to each other, 'That's mine,' and 'That's mine;'—and 'You have no business here,' and 'You have no business there;'—and '*I* have business every where. [*Strutting.*]—Then, 'Give *me* this,' and 'Give *me* that;'—and 'Take this,' and 'Take that.'

[*Makes Signs of fighting.*

Lady. A very elegant description, truly.

Sir Luke. Why, you know 'tis all matter of fact: and Lord Flint, brought up from his youth among these people, has not one *trait* of an Englishman about him: he has imbibed all this country's cruelty; and I dare say wou'd mind no more seeing me hung up by my thumbs, or made to dance upon a red hot gridiron.—

Lady. That is one of the tortures I never heard of!—O! I should like to see that of all things!

Sir Luke. Yes, by keeping this man's company, you'll soon be as cruel as he is: he will teach you every vice. A consequential, grave, dull—and yet with that degree of levity which dares to pay addresses to a woman, even before her husband.

Lady. Did not you declare, this minute, his lordship had not a *trait* of his own country about him?

Sir Luke. As you observe, that last *is* a *trait* of his own country.

Enter Servant *and* Lord Flint.

Serv. Lord Flint—

[*Exit* SERVANT.

Lady. My lord, I am extremely glad to see you: we were just mentioning your name.

Lord. Were you, indeed, madam? You do me great honour.

Sir Luke. No, my lord—no great honour.

Lord. Pardon me, Sir Luke.

Sir Luke. But, I assure you, my lord, in what I said I did *myself* a great deal.

Lady. Yes, my lord; and I'll acquaint your lordship what it was.

[*Going up to him.*

Sir Luke. [*Pulling her aside.*] Why, you wou'd not inform against me, sure! Do you know what would be the consequence? My head must answer it.

[*Frightened.*

Lord. Nay, Sir Luke, I insist upon knowing.

Sir Luke. [*To her.*] Hush! hush!—No, my lord, pray excuse me: your lordship, perhaps, may think what I said did not come from my heart; and I assure you, upon my honour, it did.

Lady. O, yes—that I am sure of.

Lord. I am extremely obliged to you.

[*Bowing.*

Sir Luke. O, no, my lord, not at all—not at all. [*Aside to her.*] I'll be extremely obliged to *you*, if you will be silent.—Pray, my lord, are you engaged out to dinner to-day? for her ladyship and I are.

Lady. Yes, my lord, and we should be happy to find your lordship of the party.

Lord. 'Engaged out to dinner?'—Egad, very likely—very likely: but if I am, I have positively forgotten where.

Lady. We are going to—

Lord. No—I think, now you put me in mind of it—I think I have company to dine with me. I am either going out to dinner, or have company to dine with me; but I really can't tell which: however, my people know—but I can't recollect.

Sir Luke. Perhaps your lordship *has* dined: can you recollect whether you have?

Lord. No, no—I have not dined—What's o'clock?

Lady. Perhaps, my lord, you have not breakfasted?

Lord. O, yes; I've breakfasted—I think so—but, upon my word, these things are of such slight consequence, they are very difficult to remember.

Sir Luke. They are, indeed, my lord—and I wish all my family wou'd entirely forget them.

Lord. What did your ladyship say was o'clock?

Lady. Exactly twelve, my lord.

Lord. Bless me! I ought to have been somewhere else then—an absolute engagement.—I have broke my word—a positive appointment.

Lady. Shall I send a servant?

Lord. No, no, no, no—by no means—it can't be helped now; and they know my unfortunate failing: besides, I'll beg their pardon, and that will be ample satisfaction.

Lady. You are very good, my lord, not to leave us.

Lord. I cou'd not think of leaving you so soon—the happiness I enjoy in your society is so extreme—

Sir Luke. That were your lordship to go away now, you might never remember to come again.

Remarks on *De Monfort* (1807)

Amongst the many female writers of this and other nations, how few have arrived at the elevated character of a woman of genius!

The authoress of 'De Monfort' received that rare distinction, upon this her first publication.

There was genius in the novelty of her conception, in the strength of her execution; and though her play falls short of dramatic excellence, it will ever be rated as a work of genius.

Joanna Baillie, in her preface to her first publication, displays knowledge, taste, and judgment, upon the subject of the drama, to a very high degree: still, as she observes, 'theory and practice are very different things;' and, perhaps, so distinct is the art of criticism, from the art of producing plays, that no one critic so good as herself, has ever written a play half so good as the following tragedy.

Authors may think too profoundly, as well as too superficially—and if a dramatic author, with the most accurate knowledge of the heart of man, probe it too far, the smaller, more curious, and new-created passions, which he may find there, will be too delicate for the observation of those who hear and see in a mixed, and, sometimes, riotous, company.

The spirit, the soul, the every thought and sensation of the first character in this piece, De Monfort, is clearly discerned by the reader, and he can account for all the events to which they progressively lead: but the most attentive auditor, whilst he plainly beholds effects, asks after causes; and not perceiving those diminutive seeds of hatred, here described, till swollen, they extend to murder, he conceives the hero of the tragedy to be more a pitiable maniac, than a man acting under the dominion of natural propensity.

Even to the admiring reader of this work, who sees the delineation of nature in every page, it may perchance occur, that disease must have certain influence with hate so rancorous; for rooted antipathy, without some more considerable provocation than is here adduced, is very like the first unhappy token of insanity.

Strike not upon one particular chord in all De Monfort's feelings, and he is a noble creature; but from this individual string vibrates all that is mean and despicable in man. Thus is the mind of the lunatic generally tyrannized by one obstinate idea.

Though hatred be the passion described in this tragedy, pride was its origin, and envy its promoter—The school-boy, who, by his ridicule, wounded the self-importance of his playfellow, might, we find, have been forgiven, had not good fortune bestowed, on this Rezenvelt, unexpected riches, social qualities, and friends, to rival those possessed by Monfort, his former superior.

From hence is derived this most admirable moral—The proud man, yielding to every vice which pride engenders, descends, in the sequel of his arrogance, to be the sport of his enemy, the pity of his friends, to receive his life a gift from the man he abhors, and to do a midnight murder!

Still the author's talents invest with dignity this cowardly assassin, and he inspires a sublime horror to the last moment of his existence—and even when extended as a corse.

The character of Rezenvelt is well drawn; and, in one scene, gives an excellent sample of the writer's powers in comedy; in that comic dialogue, at least, which has most pleasant effect, when dispersed through a tragedy.

On Jane De Monfort she has bestowed some of her very best poetic descriptions; and, from the young Page's first account of the 'queenly' stranger, has given such a striking resemblance of both the person and mièn of Mrs Siddons, that it would almost raise a suspicion she was, at the time of the writing, designed for the representation of this noble female.

This drama, of original and very peculiar formation, plainly denotes that the authoress has studied theatrical productions as a reader more than as a spectator; and it may be necessary to remind her—that Shakspeare gained his knowledge of the effect produced from plays upon an audience, and profited, through such attainment, by his constant attendance on dramatic representations, even with the assiduity of a performer.

From *A Simple Story* (1791)

As soon as the first transports of despair were over, Miss Milner suffered herself to be once more in hope—she found there were no other means to support her life; and to her no small joy, her friend, Miss Woodley, was much less severe on the present occasion than she expected.—No engagement between mortals, was, in Miss Woodley's opinion, binding like that entered into with heaven; and whatever vows Lord Elmwood had made to another, she justly supposed, no woman's love for him, equalled Miss Milner's—it was prior to all others too, and that established a claim, at least to contend for success; and in a contention, what rival would not fall before her?

It was not difficult to guess who this rival was; or if they were a little time in suspense, Miss Woodley soon arrived at the certainty, by inquiring of Mr Sandford; who, unsuspicious why she asked, readily informed her the intended Lady Elmwood, was no other than Miss Fenton; and that her marriage with his lordship would be solemnized as soon as the mourning for the late Lord Elmwood was expired.—This last intelligence made Miss Woodley shudder— however, she repeated it to Miss Milner, word for word.

'Happy! happy, woman!' exclaimed Miss Milner of Miss Fenton;

'she has received the first fond impulses of his heart, and has had the transcendent happiness of teaching him to love!'

'By no means,' returned Miss Woodley, finding there was no other method to comfort her; 'do not suppose Lord Elmwood's marriage is the result of love—it is no more than a duty, a necessary piece of business, and this you may plainly see by the wife on whom he has fixed.—Miss Fenton was thought a proper match for his cousin, and this same propriety, you must perceive still exists.'

It was easy to convince Miss Milner all her friend said was truth, for she wished it to be so. 'And oh!' she exclaimed, 'could I but stimulate passion, in the place of propriety—do you think my dear Miss Woodley,' (and she looked with such begging eyes, it was impossible not to answer as she wished,) 'do you think it would be unjust to Miss Fenton, were I to inspire her destined husband with a passion which she may not have inspired, and which I believe she herself cannot feel?'

Miss Woodley paused a minute, and then answered, 'No;'—but there was a hesitation in her manner of delivery—she did say, 'No,' but she looked as if she was afraid she ought to have said 'Yes.'— Miss Milner, however, did not wait to give her time to recall the word, or to alter its meaning by adding others to it, but run on eagerly, and declared, 'As that was her opinion, she would abide by it, and do all she could to supplant her rival.'—In order, nevertheless, to justify this determination, and satisfy the conscience of Miss Woodley, they both concluded, Miss Fenton's heart was not engaged in the intended marriage, and consequently she was indifferent whether it took place or not.

Since the death of the late earl,* that young lady had not been in town; nor had the present lord been near the spot where she resided since the week her lover died; of course, nothing like love could be declared at so early a period; and if it had been made known since, it must only have been by letter, or by the deputation of Mr Sandford, who they knew had been once in the country to visit her; but how little he was qualified to enforce a tender passion, was a comfortable reflection.

Revived with these conjectures, of which some were true, and others false; the very next day a dark gloom overspread their bright prospects, on Mr Sandford's saying, as he entered the breakfast-room,

'Miss Fenton, ladies, desired me to present her compliments to you.'

'Is she in town?' asked Mrs Horton.

'She came to town yesterday morning,' returned Sandford, 'and is at her brother's, in Ormond street; my lord and I supped there last night, and that made us so late home.'

His lordship entered soon after, and confirmed what had been said, by bowing to his ward, and telling her, 'Miss Fenton had charged him with her kindest respects.'

'How does poor Miss Fenton look?' Mrs Horton asked Lord Elmwood.

To which question Sandford replied, 'Beautiful—she looks beautifully.'

'She has got over her uneasiness, I suppose then?' said Mrs Horton—not knowing she was asking the question before her new lover.

'Uneasy!' replied Sandford, 'uneasy at any trial this world can send? that had been highly unworthy of her.'

'But sometimes women do fret at such things,' replied Mrs Horton innocently.

Lord Elmwood asked Miss Milner—'If she meant to ride, this charming day?'

While she was hesitating—

'There are very different kinds of women,' (answered Sandford, directing his discourse to Mrs Horton,) 'there is as much difference between some women, as between good and evil spirits.'

Lord Elmwood asked Miss Milner again—if she took an airing?

She replied, 'No.'

'And beauty,' continued Sandford, 'when endowed upon spirits that are evil, is a mark of their greater, their more extreme wickedness.—Lucifer was the most beautiful of all the angels in paradise—'

'How do you know?' said Miss Milner.

'But the beauty of Lucifer' (continued Sandford, in perfect neglect and contempt of her question,) 'was an aggravation of his guilt; because it shewed a double share of ingratitude to the Divine Creator of that beauty.'

'Now you talk of angels,' said Miss Milner, 'I wish I had wings; and I should like to fly through the park this morning.'

'You would be taken for an angel in good earnest,' said Lord Elmwood.

Sandford was angry at this little compliment, and cried, 'Then instead of the wings, I would advise the serpent's skin.'*

'My lord,' cried she, 'does not Mr Sandford use me ill?'—Vext with other things, she felt herself extremely hurt at this, and made the appeal almost in tears.

'Indeed, I think he does,' answered his lordship, and he looked at Sandford as if he was displeased.

This was a triumph so agreeable to her, she immediately pardoned the offence; but the offender did not so easily pardon her.

'Good morning, ladies,' said his lordship, rising to go away.

'My lord,' said Miss Woodley, 'you promised Miss Milner to accompany her one evening to the opera; this is opera night.'

'Will you go, my lord?' asked Miss Milner, in a voice so soft, he seemed as if he wished, but could not resist it.

'I am to dine at Mr Fenton's to-day,' he replied, 'and if he and his sister will go; and you will allow them part of your box, I will promise to come.'

This was a condition that did not please her, but as she felt a strong desire to see him in the company of his intended bride, (for she fancied she could perceive his most secret sentiments, could she once see them together) she answered not ungraciously, 'Yes, my compliments to Mr and Miss Fenton, and I hope they will favour me with their company.'

'Then, madam, if they come, you may expect me—else not.' And he bowed and left the room.

All the day was passed in anxious expectation by Miss Milner, what would be the event of the evening; for upon the skill of her penetration that evening, all her future prospects she thought depended.—If she saw by his looks, his words, or assiduity, he loved Miss Fenton, she flattered herself she would never think of him again with hope; but if she observed him treat her with inattention or indifference, she meant to cherish from that moment the fondest expectations.—Against that short evening her toilet was consulted the whole day; and the alternate hope and fear which fluttered at her heart, gave a more than usual brilliancy to her eyes, and more than usual bloom to her complexion.—But in vain was her beauty; vain all the pains she had taken to decorate that beauty; vain the many looks she cast towards her box-door to see it open; Lord Elmwood did not come.

The music was discord—every thing she saw, was disgusting—in a word, she was miserable.

She longed impatiently for the curtain to drop, because she was uneasy where she was—yet she asked herself, 'Shall I be less unhappy at home? yes, at home I shall see Lord Elmwood, and that will be happiness—but he will behold me with neglect, and that will be misery.—Ungrateful man! I will no longer think of him,' she said to herself.—Or could she have thought of him without joining in the same idea Miss Fenton, her anguish had been supportable; but while she pictured them as lovers, the tortures of the rack give but a few degrees more pain than she endured.

There are but few persons who ever felt the real passion of jealousy, because few have felt the real passion of love; but to those who have experienced them both, jealousy not only affects the mind, but every fibre of the frame is a victim to it; and Miss Milner's every limb ached, with agonizing torment, while Miss Fenton, courted and beloved by Lord Elmwood, was present to her imagination.

The moment the opera was finished, she flew hastily down stairs, as if to fly from the sufferings she experienced.—She did not go into the coffee-room, though repeatedly persuaded by Miss Woodley, but waited at the door till her carriage drew up.

Piqued—heart-broken—full of resentment to the object of her uneasiness; as she stood inattentive to all that passed, a hand gently laid hold of her's, and the most humble and insinuating voice said, 'Will you permit me to hand you to your carriage?' She was awaked from her reverie, and found Lord Frederick Lawnly by her side.*— Her heart, just then melting with tenderness to another, was perhaps more accessible than heretofore, or bursting with resentment, thought this the moment to retaliate. Whatever passion reigned that instant, it was favourable to the desires of Lord Frederick, and she looked as if she was glad to see him; he beheld this with the rapture and the humility of a lover; and though she did not feel the slightest love in return, she felt a gratitude proportionate to the insensibility with which she had been treated by her guardian, and Lord Frederick was not very erroneous if he mistook this gratitude for a latent spark of affection. The mistake, however, did not force from him his respect: he handed her to her carriage, bowed lowly, and disappeared. Miss Woodley wished to divert her thoughts from the object which could only make her wretched, and as they rode home, by many encomiums upon Lord Frederick, endeavoured to incite her to a regard for him; Miss Milner was displeased at the attempt, and exclaimed,

'What, love a rake, a man of professed gallantry? impossible.—To me, a common rake is as odious, as a common prostitute is to a man of the nicest feelings.—Where can be the pride of inspiring a passion, fifty others can equally inspire? or the transport of bestowing favours, where the appetite is already cloyed by fruition of the self-same enjoyments?'

'Strange,' cried Miss Woodley, 'that you, who possess so many follies incident to your sex, should, in the disposal of your heart, have sentiments so contrary to women in general.'

'My dear Miss Woodley,' returned she, 'put in competition the languid love of a debauchee, with the vivid affection of a sober man, and judge which has the dominion? Oh! in my calendar of love, a solemn lord chief justice, or a devout archbishop ranks before a licentious king.'

Miss Woodley smiled at an opinion which she knew half her sex would laugh at; but by the air of sincerity with which it was delivered, she was convinced, her late behaviour to Lord Frederick was but the mere effect of chance.

Lord Elmwood's carriage drove to his door just at the time her's did; Mr Sandford was with him, and they were both come from passing the evening at Mr Fenton's.

'So, my lord,' said Miss Woodley, as soon as they met in the apartment, 'you did not come to us.'

'No,' answered his lordship, 'I was sorry; but I hope you did not expect me.'

'Not expect you, my lord?' cried Miss Milner, 'did not you say you would come?'

'If I had, I certainly should have come,' returned he, 'but I only said so conditionally.'

'That I am witness to,' cried Sandford, 'for I was present at the time, and his lordship said it should depend upon Miss Fenton.'

'And she, with her gloomy disposition,' said Miss Milner, 'chose to sit at home.'

'Gloomy disposition?' repeated Sandford, 'She is a young lady with a great share of sprightliness—and I think I never saw her in better spirits than she was this evening, my lord?'

Lord Elmwood did not speak.

'Bless me, Mr Sandford,' cried Miss Milner, 'I meant no reflection upon Miss Fenton's disposition; I only meant to censure her taste for staying at home.'

'I think,' replied Sandford, 'a much greater censure should be passed upon those, who prefer rambling abroad.'

'But I hope, ladies, my not coming,' said his lordship, 'was no cause of inconvenience to you; you had still a gentleman with you, or I should certainly have come.'

'Oh! yes, two gentlemen,' answered the young son of Lady Evans, a lad from school, whom Miss Milner had taken along with her, and to whom his lordship had alluded.

'What two?' asked Lord Elmwood.

Neither Miss Milner or Miss Woodley answered.

'You know, madam,' said young Evans, 'that handsome gentleman who handed you into your carriage, and you called my lord.'

'Oh! he means Lord Frederick Lawnly,' said Miss Milner carelessly, but a blush of shame spread over her face.

'And did he hand you into your coach?' asked his lordship, earnestly.

'By mere accident, my lord,' Miss Woodley replied, 'for the crowd was so great—'

'I think, my lord,' said Sandford, 'it was very lucky you were *not* there.'*

'Had Lord Elmwood been with us, we should not have had occasion for the assistance of any other,' said Miss Milner.

'Lord Elmwood has been with you, madam,' returned Sandford, 'very frequently, and yet—'

'Mr Sandford,' said his lordship, interrupting him, 'it is near bed-time, your conversation keeps the ladies from retiring.'

'Your lordship's does not,' said Miss Milner, 'for you say nothing.'

'Because, madam, I am afraid to offend.'

'But does not your lordship also hope to please? and without risking the one, it is impossible to arrive at the other.'

'I think, at present, the risk of one would be too hazardous, and so I wish you a good night.' And he went out of the room somewhat abruptly.

'Lord Elmwood,' said Miss Milner, 'is very grave—he does not look like a man who has been passing his evening with the woman he loves.'

'Perhaps he is melancholy at parting from her,' said Miss Woodley.

'More likely offended,' said Sandford, 'at the manner in which that lady has spoken of her.'

'Who, I?' cried Miss Milner, 'I protest I said nothing but—'

'Nothing, madam? did not you say she was gloomy?'

'But, what I thought—I was going to add, Mr Sandford.'

'When you think unjustly, you should not express your thoughts.'

'Then, perhaps, I should never speak.'

'And it were better you did not, if what you say, is to give pain.— Do you know, madam, that my lord is going to be married to Miss Fenton?'

'Yes,' answered Miss Milner.

'Do you know that he loves her?'

'No,' answered Miss Milner.

'How, madam! do you suppose he does not?'

'I suppose he does, yet I don't know it.'

'Then supposing he does, how can you have the imprudence to find fault with her before him?'

'I did not—to call her gloomy, was, I knew, to praise her both to him and to you, who admire such tempers.'

'Whatever her temper is, *every one* admires it; and so far from its being what you have described, she has a great deal of vivacity; vivacity which proceeds from the heart.'

'No, if it proceeded, I should admire it too; but it rests there, and no one is the better for it.'

'Come, Miss Milner,' said Miss Woodley, 'it is time to retire; you and Mr Sandford must finish your dispute in the morning.'

'Dispute, madam!' said Sandford, 'I never disputed with any one beneath a doctor of divinity in my life.—I was only cautioning your friend not to make light of virtues, which it would do her honour to possess.—Miss Fenton is a most amiable young woman, and worthy just such a husband as my Lord Elmwood will make her.'

'I am sure,' said Miss Woodley, 'Miss Milner thinks so—she has a high opinion of Miss Fenton—she was at present only jesting.'

'But, madam, jests are very pernicious things, when delivered with a malignant sneer.—I have known a jest destroy a lady's reputation—I have known a jest give one person a distaste for another—I have known a jest break off a marriage.'

'But I suppose there is no apprehension of that, in the present case?' said Miss Woodley—wishing he might answer in the affirmative.

'Not that I can foresee,' replied he.—'No, Heaven forbid; for I look upon them to be formed for each other—their dispositions, their pursuits, their inclinations the same.—Their passions for each other just the same—pure—white as snow.'

'And I dare say, not warmer,' replied Miss Milner.

He looked provoked beyond measure.

'Dear Miss Milner,' cried Miss Woodley, 'how can you talk thus? I believe in my heart you are only envious my lord did not offer himself to you.'

'To her!' said Sandford, affecting an air of the utmost surprise, 'to her? Do you think his lordship received a dispensation from his vows to become the husband of a coquette—a—' he was going on.

'Nay, Mr Sandford,' cried Miss Milner, 'I believe my greatest crime in your eyes, is being a heretic.'*

'By no means, madam—it is the only circumstance that can apologize for your faults; and had you not that excuse, there would be none for you.'

'Then, at present, there is an excuse—I thank you, Mr Sandford; this is the kindest thing you ever said to me. But I am vext to see you are sorry, you have said it.'

'Angry at your being a heretic?' he resumed, 'Indeed I should be much more concerned to see you a disgrace to our religion.'

Miss Milner had not been in a good humour during the whole evening—she had been provoked to the full extent of her patience several times; but this harsh sentence hurried her beyond all bounds, and she arose from her seat in the most violent agitation, and exclaimed, 'What have I done to be treated thus?'

Though Mr Sandford was not a man easily intimidated, he was on this occasion evidently alarmed; and stared about him with so strong an expression of surprise, that it partook in some degree of fear.—Miss Woodley clasped her friend in her arms, and cried with the tenderest affection and pity, 'My dear Miss Milner, be composed.'

Miss Milner sat down, and was so for a minute; but her dead silence was nearly as alarming to Sandford as her rage had been; and he did not perfectly recover himself till he saw a flood of tears pouring down her face; he then heaved a sigh of content that it had so ended, but in his heart resolved never to forget the ridiculous affright into which he had been put.—He stole out of the room without uttering a syllable—But as he never retired to rest before he had repeated a long form of evening prayers, so when he came to that part which supplicates 'Grace for the wicked,' he named Miss Milner's name, with the most fervent devotion.

MARY WOLLSTONECRAFT
(1759–1797)

Brought up in London, the eldest daughter among the seven children of Edward Wollstonecraft, an English weaver, and his Irish wife Elizabeth Dixon, Mary Wollstonecraft had an unhappy and unsettled childhood. The family moved from Spitalfields to unsuccessful attempts at gentleman farming in Essex and Yorkshire, returning to London in 1775, when they settled in Hoxton, famous for the Dissenting Academy where her future husband, the philosopher William Godwin, studied. Wollstonecraft always worked for a living, first of all as a companion to an elderly widow in Bath. After the death of her mother (whom she returned to London to nurse) in 1781, she set up a school for girls with her sisters and close friend Fanny Blood in Islington: it quickly relocated to Newington Green, where Wollstonecraft became part of an active and stimulating Dissenting community. The school closed in 1786, debts and disarray exacerbated by the recently married Fanny Blood's death in childbirth. During this period Wollstonecraft put her practical experience to public use in *Thoughts on the Education of Daughters*, which was accepted by the radical publisher Joseph Johnson and appeared in 1787. Johnson took a great interest in her work, and she wrote many articles and reviews (including the review of Inchbald selected here) for his periodical *The Analytical Review*. From late in 1787 Wollstonecraft spent a year as a governess to Lord and Lady Kingsborough's family in Ireland: she was dismissed, probably because the Kingsborough daughters became over-ardently attached to her. Back in London, and living rent-free in a house provided by Johnson, she quickly published other educational works, including *Original Stories from Real Life* (1788) and *The Female Reader* (1789), as well as her only completed novel, *Mary: A Fiction* (1788). Her prominence in Johnson's social and intellectual circle increased with the publication of her prompt response to Edmund Burke's *Reflections on the Revolution in France* (*A Vindication of the Rights of Men*, 1790), followed in 1792 by *A Vindication of the Rights of Woman*. In 1791 she met William Godwin and Thomas Paine, was strongly drawn to the painter Henry Fuseli, who rejected her, and in 1792–3 lived in Paris with the American land-speculator Gilbert Imlay. Their child Fanny was born in Le Havre in 1794, after which Wollstonecraft returned to London, making a plea-for-help suicide bid in her efforts to win Imlay back. Her successful travel-book *Letters Written During a Short Residence in Sweden, Norway and Denmark* (1796) originated in the business visit she undertook on his behalf, but by this time he was living with another woman, and on her return to London she made another, more serious, attempt at suicide, thwarted by wherrymen who recovered her from the Thames.

At this juncture Wollstonecraft's friend and admirer Mary Hays (see Hays, below) reintroduced her to the radical philosopher, political theorist, and novelist William Godwin, and they became lovers, marrying in March 1797 when Wollstonecraft was pregnant. On 10 September she died of an infection incurred in childbirth ten days after the birth of their daughter Mary (later Mary Shelley; see Shelley, below). Wollstonecraft and Godwin had included among their close friends Mary Robinson, the novelists Eliza Fenwick and Amelia Alderson, and they had a wide circle of intellectual and political acquaintance. Mary Hays, whose obituary of Wollstonecraft appeared in the *Monthly Magazine*, described her death as a 'public loss', lamenting the adversities and sorrows she had to face but praising her 'philosophic mind' as well as her 'exquisite sensibility' and 'ardent, ingenuous, unconquerable spirit'. For Hays, she mattered not only for her 'exertions to awaken in the minds of her oppressed sex a sense of their degradation', but more fundamentally for her ability to trace social and domestic evil to its root in 'the defects of civil institutions'.[1] Wollstonecraft left an incomplete novel, *The Wrongs of Woman; or, Maria*, which Godwin edited and published in 1798 as part of his *Memoirs and Posthumous Works*, a principled and dangerously plaindealing work which caused outrage among contemporary readers and reviewers, and lastingly damaged Wollstonecraft's reputation, exposing her to the effects of the truth about her relationship with Imlay, her first daughter's illegitimacy, and her unconventional relationship with Godwin. Opponents of Wollstonecraft's ideas used her approach to relationships as a way of associating female free-thinking with sexual immorality: the slur was to inhibit many expressions of feminist thought.

[1] 'Deaths in and near London', *The Monthly Magazine, and British Register, for 1797* (1798), 232–3.

Wollstonecraft's writings are widely available and frequently discussed. Although their necessarily brief representation here does insufficient justice to their seriousness and force, her works benefit from the context of other women's writing, even though she herself seems rather to ally herself with a male tradition of polemic. Her reflections on female sensibility, and in particular on the influence of Rousseau, link her to several other writers included here, who share her suspicion of the dubious honour conferred by the feeling heart. Wollstonecraft is more explicit, however, as Hays's obituary recognizes, in seeing the poisoned chalice of sensibility as part of wider and more fundamental social injustices. This can be seen in the first piece selected here, her review of *A Simple Story*, with its pithily impatient reflections on women's fondness for the trappings of sensibility. Perhaps evasively, the review concentrates on the second half of Inchbald's novel, which deals with Miss Milner's daughter Matilda and her estrangement from her father: Wollstonecraft wishes it to be a more pointedly improving work than it is, and she laments the collusion of women's writing with male ideology, but she feels herself to be on firmer ground in attacking the second half. Wollstonecraft clearly recognizes the appeal of Miss Milner to a literary audience, and chooses not to dwell upon the complications of sympathy and instruction set up by Inchbald's shrewd and questioning characterization. The second extract, from *A Vindication of the Rights of Woman*, reveals a more confident, self-controlled, polemic, continually referring back to the practical organization of education which profoundly interested Wollstonecraft. Male fictions of femininity prove to be a slower-moving target than Inchbald's contradictory heroine, and allow Wollstonecraft to link the situation of women with that of slaves and a feminized standing army (soldiers permanently waiting for military action, rather than enlisted to deal with it). Finally, an extract from *Letters from Sweden* shows Wollstonecraft's revealingly charged reaction to women who seem to be creatures merely of flesh. Insisting on the importance of mind, she reverts in a logic of half-expressed sexual jealousy to Gilbert Imlay's descriptions of the 'country girls' of America: it is a short extract, but one full of stylistic and intellectual conflict and unease.

~

Review of *A Simple Story* (1791)

The plan of this novel is truly dramatic, for the rising interest is not broken, or even interrupted, by any episode, nor is the attention so divided, by a constellation of splendid characters, as to make the reader at a loss to say which is the hero of the tale.

Mrs I. had evidently a very useful moral in view, namely to show the advantage of a good education;* but it is to be lamented that she did not, for the benefit of her young readers, inforce it by contrasting the characters of the mother and daughter, whose history must warmly interest them. It were to be wished, in fact, in order to insinuate a useful moral into thoughtless unprincipled minds, that the faults of the vain, giddy miss Milner had not been softened, or rather gracefully withdrawn from notice by the glare of such splendid, yet salacious virtues, as flow from sensibility. And to have rendered the contrast more useful still, her daughter should have learned (to prove that a cultivated mind is a real advantage) how to bear, nay, rise above her misfortunes, instead of suffering her health to be undermined by the trials of her patience, which ought to have strengthened her understanding. Why do all female writers, even when they display their abilities, always give a sanction to the libertine reveries of men? Why do they poison the minds of their own sex, by strengthening a male prejudice that makes women systematically weak? We alluded to the absurd fashion that prevails of making the heroine of a novel boast of a delicate constitution; and the still more ridiculous and deleterious custom of spinning the most picturesque scenes out of fevers, swoons, and tears.

The characters in the Simple Story are marked with a discriminating outline, and little individual traits are skilfully brought forward, that produce some natural and amusing scenes. Lively conversations abound, and they are, in general, written with the spirited vivacity and the feminine ease that characterizes the conversation of an agreeable well-bred woman. The author has even the art to render dialogues interesting that appear to have only the evanescent spirit, which mostly evaporates in description, to recommend them.

From *A Vindication of the Rights of Woman* (1792)

The Prevailing Opinion of a Sexual Character Discussed

To account for, and excuse the tyranny of man, many ingenious arguments have been brought forward to prove, that the two sexes, in the acquirement of virtue, ought to aim at attaining a very different character: or, to speak explicitly, women are not allowed to have sufficient strength of mind to acquire what really deserves the name of virtue. Yet it should seem, allowing them to have souls, that there is but one way appointed by Providence to lead *mankind* to either virtue or happiness.

If then women are not a swarm of ephemeron triflers, why should they be kept in ignorance under the specious name of innocence? Men complain, and with reason, of the follies and caprices of our sex, when they do not keenly satirize our headstrong passions and groveling vices.—Behold, I should answer, the natural effect of ignorance! The mind will ever be unstable that has only prejudices to rest on, and the current will run with destructive fury when there are no barriers to break its force. Women are told from their infancy, and taught by the example of their mothers, that a little knowledge of human weakness, justly termed cunning, softness of temper, *outward* obedience, and a scrupulous attention to a puerile kind of propriety, will obtain for them the protection of man; and should they be beautiful, every thing else is needless, for, at least, twenty years of their lives.

Thus Milton describes our first frail mother; though when he tells us that women are formed for softness and sweet attractive grace, I cannot comprehend his meaning, unless, in the true Mahometan strain, he meant to deprive us of souls, and insinuate that we were beings only designed by sweet attractive grace, and docile blind obedience, to gratify the senses of man when he can no longer soar on the wing of contemplation.*

How grossly do they insult us who thus advise us only to render ourselves gentle, domestic brutes! For instance, the winning softness so warmly, and frequently, recommended, that governs by obeying. What childish expressions, and how insignificant is the being—can it be an immortal one? who will condescend to govern by such sinister methods! 'Certainly,' says Lord Bacon, 'man is of kin to the beasts by his body; and if he be not of kin to God by his spirit, he is a base and ignoble creature!'* Men, indeed, appear to me to act in a very unphilosophical manner when they try to secure the good conduct of women by attempting to keep them always in a state of childhood. Rousseau was more consistent when he wished to stop the progress of reason in both sexes, for if men eat of the tree of knowledge, women will come in for a taste; but, from the imperfect cultivation which their understandings now receive, they only attain a knowledge of evil.

Children, I grant, should be innocent; but when the epithet is applied to men, or women, it is but a civil term for weakness. For if it be allowed that women were destined by Providence to acquire human virtues, and by the exercise of their understandings, that stability of character which is the firmest ground to rest our future hopes upon, they must be permitted to turn to the fountain of light, and not forced to shape their course by the twinkling of a mere satellite. Milton, I grant, was of a very different opinion; for he only bends to the indefeasible right of beauty, though it would be difficult to render two passages which I now mean to contrast, consistent. But into similar inconsistencies are great men often led by their senses.

> 'To whom thus Eve with *perfect beauty* adorn'd.
> My Author and Disposer, what thou bidst
> *Unargued* I obey; so God ordains;
> God is *thy law, thou mine:* to know no more
> Is Woman's *happiest* knowledge and her *praise*.'*

These are exactly the arguments that I have used to children; but I have added, your reason is now gaining strength, and, till it arrives at some degree of maturity, you must look up to me for advice—then you ought to *think*, and only rely on God.

Yet in the following lines Milton seems to coincide with me; when he makes Adam thus expostulate with his Maker.

> 'Hast thou not made me here thy substitute,
> And these inferior far beneath me set?
> Among *unequals* what society
> Can sort, what harmony or true delight?
> Which must be mutual, in proportion due
> Giv'n and receiv'd; but in *disparity*
> The one intense, the other still remiss
> Cannot well suit with either, but soon prove
> Tedious alike: of *fellowship* I speak
> Such as I seek, fit to participate
> All rational delight—'*

In treating, therefore, of the manners of women, let us, disregarding sensual arguments, trace what we should endeavour to make them in order to co-operate, if the expression be not too bold, with the supreme Being.

By individual education, I mean, for the sense of the word is not precisely defined, such an attention to a child as will slowly sharpen the senses, form the temper, regulate the passions as they begin to ferment, and set the understanding to work before the body arrives at maturity; so that the man may only have to proceed, not to begin, the important task of learning to think and reason.

To prevent any misconstruction, I must add, that I do not believe that a private education can work the wonders which some sanguine writers have attributed to it. Men and women must be educated, in a great degree, by the opinions and manners of the society they live in. In every age there has been a stream of popular opinion that has carried all before it, and given a family character, as it were, to the century. It may then fairly be inferred, that, till society be differently constituted; much cannot be expected from education. It is, however, sufficient for my present purpose to assert, that, whatever effect circumstances have on the abilities, every being may become virtuous by the exercise of its own reason; for if but one being was created with vicious inclinations, that is positively bad, what can save us from atheism? or if we worship a God, is not that God a devil?

Consequently, the most perfect education, in my opinion, is such an exercise of the understanding as is best calculated to strengthen the body and form the heart. Or, in other words, to enable the individual to attain such habits of virtue as will render it independent. In fact, it is a farce to call any being virtuous whose virtues do not result from the exercise of its own reason. This was Rousseau's opinion respecting men:* I extend it to women, and confidently assert that they have been drawn out of their sphere by false refinement, and not by an endeavour to acquire masculine qualities. Still the regal homage which they receive is so intoxicating, that till the manners of the times are changed, and formed on more reasonable principles, it may be impossible to convince them that the illegitimate power, which they obtain, by degrading themselves, is a curse, and that they must return to nature and equality, if they wish to secure the placid satisfaction that unsophisticated affections impart. But for this epoch we must wait—wait, perhaps, till kings and nobles, enlightened by reason, and, preferring the real dignity of man to childish state, throw off their gaudy hereditary trappings: and if then women do not resign the arbitrary power of beauty—they will prove that they have *less* mind than man.

I may be accused of arrogance; still I must declare what I firmly believe, that all the writers who have written on the subject of female education and manners from Rousseau to Dr Gregory,* have contributed to render women more artificial, weak characters, than they would otherwise have been; and, consequently, more useless members of society. I might have expressed this conviction in a lower key; but I am afraid it would have been the whine of affectation, and not the faithful expression of my feelings, of the clear result, which experience and reflection have led me to draw. . . .

Many are the causes that, in the present corrupt state of society, contribute to enslave women by cramping their understandings and sharpening their senses. One, perhaps, that silently does more mischief than all the rest, is their disregard of order.

To do every thing in an orderly manner, is a most important precept, which women, who, generally speaking, receive only a disorderly kind of education, seldom attend to with that degree of exactness that men, who from their infancy are broken into method, observe. This negligent kind of guesswork, for what other epithet can be used to point out the random exertions of a sort of instinctive common sense, never brought to the test of reason? prevents their generalizing matters of fact—so they do to-day, what they did yesterday, merely because they did it yesterday.

This contempt of the understanding in early life has more baneful consequences than is commonly supposed; for the little knowledge which women of strong minds attain, is, from various circumstances, of a more desultory kind than the knowledge of men, and it is acquired more by sheer observations on real life, than from comparing what has been individually observed with the results of experience generalized by speculation. Led by their dependent situation and domestic employments more into society, what they learn is rather by snatches; and as learning is with them, in general, only a secondary thing, they do not pursue any one branch with that persevering ardour necessary to give vigour to the faculties, and clearness to the judgment. In the present state of society, a little learning is required to support the character of a gentleman; and boys are obliged to submit to a few years of discipline. But in the education of women, the cultivation of the understanding is always subordinate to the acquirement of some corporeal accomplishment; even while enervated by confinement and false notions of modesty, the body is prevented from attaining that grace and beauty which relaxed half-formed limbs never exhibit. Besides, in youth their faculties are not brought forward by emulation; and having no serious scientific study, if they have natural sagacity it is turned too soon on life and manners. They dwell on effects, and modifications, without tracing them back to causes; and complicated rules to adjust behaviour are a weak substitute for simple principles.

As a proof that education gives this appearance of weakness to females, we may instance the example of military men, who are, like them, sent into the world before their minds have been stored with knowledge or fortified by principles. The consequences are similar; soldiers acquire a little superficial knowledge, snatched from the muddy current of conversation, and, from continually mixing with society, they gain, what is termed a knowledge of the world; and this acquaintance with manners and customs has frequently been confounded with a knowledge of the human heart. But can the crude fruit of casual observation, never brought to the test of judgment, formed by comparing speculation and experience, deserve such a distinction? Soldiers, as well as women, practise the minor virtues with punctilious politeness. Where is then the sexual difference; when the education has been the same? All the difference that I can discern, arises from the superior advantage of liberty, which enables the former to see more of life.

It is wandering from my present subject, perhaps, to make a political remark; but, as it was produced naturally by the train of my reflections, I shall not pass it silently over.

Standing armies can never consist of resolute, robust men;* they may be well disciplined machines, but they will seldom contain men under the influence of strong passions, or with very vigorous faculties. And as for any depth of understanding, I will venture to affirm, that it is as rarely to be found in the army as amongst women; and the cause, I maintain, is the same. It may be further observed, that officers are also particularly attentive to their persons, fond of dancing, crowded rooms, adventures, and ridicule.[1] Like the *fair* sex, the business of their lives is gallantry.—They were taught to please, and they only live to please. Yet they do not lose their rank in the distinction of sexes, for they are still reckoned superior to women, though

---

[1] Why should women be censured with petulant acrimony, because they seem to have a passion for a scarlet coat? Has not education placed them more on a level with soldiers than any other class of men?

in what their superiority consists, beyond what I have just mentioned, it is difficult to discover.

The great misfortune is this, that they both acquire manners before morals, and a knowledge of life before they have, from reflection, any acquaintance with the grand ideal outline of human nature. The consequence is natural; satisfied with common nature, they become a prey to prejudices, and taking all their opinions on credit, they blindly submit to authority. So that if they have any sense, it is a kind of instinctive glance, that catches proportions, and decides with respect to manners; but fails when arguments are to be pursued below the surface, or opinions analyzed.

May not the same remark be applied to women? Nay, the argument may be carried still further, for they are both thrown out of a useful station by the unnatural distinctions established in civilized life. Riches and hereditary honours have made cyphers of women to give consequence to the numerical figure; and idleness has produced a mixture of gallantry and despotism into society, which leads the very men who are the slaves of their mistresses to tyrannize over their sisters, wives, and daughters. This is only keeping them in rank and file, it is true. Strengthen the female mind by enlarging it, and there will be an end to blind obedience; but, as blind obedience is ever sought for by power, tyrants and sensualists are in the right when they endeavour to keep women in the dark, because the former only want slaves, and the latter a play-thing. The sensualist, indeed, has been the most dangerous of tyrants, and women have been duped by their lovers, as princes by their ministers, whilst dreaming that they reigned over them. . . .

It is difficult for us purblind mortals to say to what height human discoveries and improvements may arrive when the gloom of despotism subsides, which makes us stumble at every step; but, when morality shall be settled on a more solid basis, then, without being gifted with a prophetic spirit, I will venture to predict that woman will be either the friend or slave of man. We shall not, as at present, doubt whether she is a moral agent, or the link which unites man with brutes. But, should it then appear, that like the brutes they were principally created for the use of man, he will let them patiently bite the bridle, and not mock them with empty praise; or, should their rationality be proved, he will not impede their improvement merely to gratify his sensual appetites. He will not, with all the graces of rhetoric, advise them to submit implicitly their understanding to the guidance of man. He will not, when he treats of the education of women, assert that they ought never to have the free use of reason, nor would he recommend cunning and dissimulation to beings who are acquiring, in like manner as himself, the virtues of humanity.

Surely there can be but one rule of right, if morality has an eternal foundation, and whoever sacrifices virtue, strictly so called, to present convenience, or whose *duty* it is to act in such a manner, lives only for the passing day, and cannot be an accountable creature.

The poet then should have dropped his sneer when he says,

> 'If weak women go astray,
> The stars are more in fault than they.'*

For that they are bound by the adamantine chain of destiny is most certain, if it be proved that they are never to exercise their own reason, never to be independent, never to rise above opinion, or to feel the dignity of a rational will that only bows to God, and often forgets that the universe contains any being but itself and the model of perfection to which its ardent gaze is turned, to adore attributes that, softened into virtues, may be imitated in kind, though the degree overwhelms the enraptured mind.

If, I say, for I would not impress by declamation when Reason offers her sober light, if they be really capable of acting like rational creatures, let them not be treated like slaves; or, like the brutes who are dependent on the reason of man, when they associate with him; but cultivate their minds, give them the salutary, sublime curb of principle, and let them attain conscious dignity by feeling themselves only dependent on God. Teach them, in common with man, to submit to necessity, instead of giving, to render them more pleasing, a sex to morals.

Further, should experience prove that they cannot attain the same degree of strength of mind, perseverance, and fortitude, let their virtues be the same in kind, though they may vainly struggle for the same degree; and the superiority of man will be equally clear, if not clearer; and truth, as it is a simple principle, which admits of no modification, would be common to both. Nay, the order of society as it is at present regulated would not be inverted, for woman would then only have the rank that reason assigned her, and arts could not be practised to bring the balance even, much less to turn it.

These may be termed Utopian dreams.—Thanks to that Being who impressed them on my soul, and gave me sufficient strength of mind to dare to exert my own reason, till, becoming dependent only on him for the support of my virtue, I view, with indignation, the mistaken notions that enslave my sex.

I love man as my fellow; but his scepter, real, or usurped, extends not to me, unless the reason of an individual demands my homage; and even then the submission is to reason, and not to man. In fact, the conduct of an accountable being must be regulated by the operations of its own reason, or on what foundation rests the throne of God?

It appears to me necessary to dwell on these obvious truths, because females have been insulated, as it were; and, while they have been stripped of the virtues that should clothe humanity, they have been decked with artificial graces that enable them to exercise a short-lived tyranny. Love, in their bosoms, taking place of every nobler passion, their sole ambition is to be fair, to raise emotion instead of inspiring respect; and this ignoble desire, like the servility in absolute monarchies, destroys all strength of character. Liberty is the mother of virtue, and if women be, by their very constitution, slaves, and not allowed to breathe the sharp invigorating air of freedom, they must ever languish like exotics, and be reckoned beautiful flaws in nature.

As to the argument respecting the subjection in which the sex has ever been held, it retorts on man. The many have always been enthralled by the few; and monsters, who scarcely have shewn any discernment of human excellence, have tyrannized over thousands of their fellow-creatures. Why have men of superior endowments submitted to such degradation? For, is it not universally acknowledged that kings, viewed collectively, have ever been inferior, in abilities and virtue, to the same number of men taken from the common mass of mankind—yet, have they not, and are they not still treated with a degree of reverence that is an insult to reason? China is not the only country where a living man has been made a God.* *Men* have submitted to superior strength to enjoy with impunity the pleasure of the moment—*women* have only done the same, and therefore till it is proved that the courtier, who servilely resigns the birthright of a man, is not a moral agent, it cannot be demonstrated that woman is essentially inferior to man because she has always been subjugated.

Brutal force has hitherto governed the world, and that the science of politics is in its infancy, is evident from philosophers scrupling to give the knowledge most useful to man that determinate distinction.

I shall not pursue this argument any further than to establish an obvious inference, that as sound politics diffuse liberty, mankind, including woman, will become more wise and virtuous.

From *Letters Written During a Short Residence in Sweden, Norway and Denmark* (1796)

LETTER IV

The severity of the long Swedish winter tends to render the people sluggish; for, though this season has its peculiar pleasures, too much time is employed to guard against its inclemency. Still, as warm clothing is absolutely necessary, the women spin, and the men weave, and by these exertions get a fence to keep out the cold. I have rarely passed a knot of cottages without seeing cloth laid out to bleach; and when I entered, always found the women spinning or knitting.

A mistaken tenderness, however, for their children, makes them, even in summer, load them with flannels; and, having a sort of natural antipathy to cold water, the squalid appearance of the poor babes, not to speak of the noxious smell which flannel and rugs retain, seems a reply to a question I had often asked—Why I did not see more children in the villages I passed through? Indeed the children appear to be nipt in the bud, having neither the graces nor charms of their age. And this, I am persuaded, is much more owing to the ignorance of the mothers than to the rudeness of the climate. Rendered feeble by the continual perspiration they are kept in, whilst every pore is absorbing unwholesome moisture, they give them, even at the breast, brandy, salt fish, and every other crude substance, which air and exercise enables the parent to digest.

The women of fortune here, as well as every where else, have nurses to suckle their children; and the total want of chastity in the lower class of women frequently renders them very unfit for the trust.

You have sometimes remarked to me the difference of the manners of the country girls in England and in America;* attributing the reserve of the former to the climate—to the absence of genial suns. But it must be their stars, not the zephyrs gently stealing on their senses, which here lead frail women astray*—Who can look at these rocks, and allow the voluptuousness of nature to be an excuse for gratifying the desires it inspires? We must, therefore, find some other cause beside voluptuousness, I believe, to account for the conduct of the Swedish and American country girls; for I am led to conclude, from all the observations I have made, that there is always a mixture of sentiment and imagination in voluptuousness, to which neither of them have much pretension.

The country girls of Ireland and Wales equally feel the first impulse of nature, which, restrained in England by fear of delicacy, proves that society is there in a more advanced state. Besides, as the mind is cultivated, and taste gains ground, the passions become stronger, and rest on something more stable than the casual sympathies of the moment. Health and idleness will always account for promiscuous amours; and in some degree I term every person idle, the exercise of whose mind does not bear some proportion to that of the body.

The Swedish ladies exercise neither sufficiently; of course, grow very fat at an early age; and when they have not this downy appearance, a comfortable idea, you will say, in a cold climate, they are not remarkable for fine forms. They have, however, mostly fine complexions; but indolence makes the lily soon displace the rose. The quantity of coffee, spices, and other things of that kind, with want of care, almost universally spoil their teeth, which contrast but ill with their ruby lips.

The manners of Stockholm are refined, I hear, by the introduction of gallantry; but in the country, romping and coarse freedoms, with coarser allusions, keep the spirits awake. In the article of cleanliness, the women, of all descriptions, seem very deficient; and their dress shews that vanity is more inherent in women than taste.

The men appear to have paid still less court to the graces. They are a robust, healthy race, distinguished for their common sense and turn for humour, rather than for wit or sentiment. I include not, as you may suppose, in this general character, some of the nobility and officers, who having travelled, are polite and well informed.

I must own to you, that the lower class of people here amuse and interest me much more than the middling, with their apish good breeding and prejudices. The sympathy and frankness of heart conspicuous in the peasantry produces even a simple gracefulness of deportment, which has frequently struck me as very picturesque;* I have often also been touched by their extreme desire to oblige me, when I could not explain my wants, and by their earnest manner of expressing that desire. There is such a charm in tenderness!—It is so delightful to love our fellow-creatures, and meet the honest affections as they break forth. Still, my good friend, I begin to think that I should not like to live continually in the country, with people whose minds have such a narrow range. My heart would frequently be interested; but my mind would languish for more companionable society.

The beauties of nature appear to me now even more alluring than in my youth, because my intercourse with the world has formed, without vitiating my taste. But, with respect to the inhabitants of the country, my fancy has probably, when disgusted with artificial manners, solaced itself by joining the advantages of cultivation with the interesting sincerity of innocence, forgetting the lassitude that ignorance will naturally produce. I like to see animals sporting, and sympathize in their pains and pleasures. Still I love sometimes to view the human face divine, and trace the soul, as well as the heart, in its varying lineaments.*

A journey to the country, which I must shortly make, will enable me to extend my remarks.—Adieu!

HELEN MARIA WILLIAMS
(1762–1827)

The daughter of Charles Williams, an army officer, and his wife Helen Hay, Helen Maria Williams was born in London. In 1769 her father died and she moved with her mother to Berwick-on-Tweed, Northumberland, and later to Scotland. She returned to London in 1781, and in 1788 went to France to visit her sister, Cecilia, who had married a Protestant minister: she was to spend much of the rest of her life in France. She became a friend of leading Girondins, especially Madame Roland, and when this group was purged in 1793 was imprisoned for six months (at first in the Luxembourg Prison, later in her own home) under the regime of

Robespierre and was in danger of joining her friends at the guillotine. On her release in 1794 she spent six months in Switzerland with John Hurford Stone (1763–1818), an English radical and Unitarian who was at that time married. He divorced his wife, and there may have been a secret marriage with Williams. She returned to France after the fall of Robespierre, at first supported the rise to power of Napoleon Bonaparte, but became increasingly disillusioned by the decline of revolution into empire and autocracy. She and Stone became French citizens in 1817: after Stone's death the following year she lived partly with her French nephew, a Protestant pastor, in Amsterdam, but died in Paris and was buried next to Stone in Père-Lachaise. At first in tune with much British intellectual opinion in supporting the French Revolution, Williams was increasingly reviled for her political views and her unconventional personal life. Britain and France were at war from 1793, and her revolutionary sympathies were enough to brand her a traitor to her country.

Williams became famous for her sensibility, praised in William Wordsworth's first published work, the sonnet 'On Seeing Miss Helen Maria Williams Weep at a Tale of Distress' (1787), but her work always had a political edge. Her early published poems criticized war (*Edwin and Eltruda: A Legendary Tale*, 1782) and imperialism (*Peru*, 1784), celebrated the end of the war with the American colonies (*An Ode on the Peace*, 1783), and opposed slavery (*On the Bill for Regulating the Slave Trade*, 1788). She established herself as a poet, especially with the important collection *Poems* (1786: new edition 1791) before turning to prose fiction with *Julia: a Novel* (1790) and *Perourou, the Bellows-Mender* (1801); she also translated the travels and researches of Alexander von Humboldt. The core of her work is the several series of letters and accounts describing revolutionary and post-revolutionary France. The first and most influential of these, *Letters Written from France, in the Summer of 1790, to a Friend in England: Containing Various Anecdotes Relative to the French Revolution; and Memoirs of Mons. and Madame du F——* (1790), was an important early firsthand account of the Revolution and helped to shape British responses to events in Paris. It was followed by five other collections of reports and responses, tracing the changing political situation, and Williams's changing attitude towards it, up to 1819.

Looking back on her early enthusiasm for the Revolution in *A Narrative of Events which have taken place in France, from the Landing of Napoleon Bonaparte, on the 1st of March, 1815, till the Restoration of Louis XVIII* (1815), Williams explains: 'To my then youthful imagination, the day-star of liberty seemed to rise on the vine-covered hills of France, only to shed benedictions on humanity. I dreamt of prison-doors thrown open,—of dungeons visited by the light of day—of the peasant oppressed no longer—of equal rights, equal laws, a golden age, in which all that lived were to be happy. But how soon did these beautiful illusions vanish, and this star of liberty set in blood!' (7–8). Williams persuades her readers through her willingness to discuss politics in such emotional terms, and through her lack of awkwardness about sentimentality. Although it is too long to be represented here, the story with which she accompanied the first of her *Letters Written from France* is typical of her technique. She devotes much of the book to the love-story of her friends Augustin du Fossé and Monique Coquerel, claiming them as a parable of the oppressive old regime, and allying the sentimental reader with the struggle against tyranny and injustice, politicizing feeling. Williams's decision to tell a story which, she says, has 'the air of a romance' (193) is characteristic: 'I can assure you, that when a proposition is addressed to my heart, I have some quickness of perception. I can then decide, in one moment, points upon which philosophers and legislators have differed in all ages: nor could I be more convinced of the truth of any demonstration in Euclid, than I am, that, that system of politics must be the best, by which those I love are made happy' (196). Williams also emphasizes the importance of women in the Revolution, claiming that 'we often act in human affairs like those secret springs in mechanism, by which, though invisible, great movements are regulated' (*Letters Written in France*, 38). She presents female sensibility as the only safeguard against the cruelties and cold detachment produced by the Revolution; by emphasizing women's powers of sympathy, fidelity, and compassion, she challenges the politically suspect excesses of sensibility. She also shows women as the greatest victims of the aftermath of revolution, especially during the Terror, and the extracts given here highlight that aspect of her argument. As Stuart Curran puts it, she was 'the foremost mythologizer of the heroic martyrdom of Madame Roland'.[1]

In turn, Williams has often been described in precisely the terms she invites. Reviewing *Letters Written in France* for the *Analytical Review* in December 1790, Wollstonecraft termed Williams's reflections on the Revolution 'truly feminine'. Recognizing the significance of the epistolary form for women, she praised Williams's 'sincerity' and 'tender' heart, 'true to every soft emotion'.[2] That tender heart was, however, a highly effective mediator between Williams's radical views and the political resistance of her readers. It allowed her to write the most compelling of contemporary eyewitness accounts of France, creating a rhetoric in which she could exaggerate, be proved wrong, change her mind, and retain her authority as a witness. Williams is genuinely her readers' 'correspondent'

---

[1] 'Women Readers, Women Writers', in Stuart Curran (ed.), *The Cambridge Companion to British Romanticism* (Cambridge: Cambridge University Press, 1993), 186.

[2] *Analytical Review*, 8 (1790), 431, 432.

in Paris, and her work, often confined to the debate on the French Revolution, is in fact more clearly appreciated if it is seen as an innovative contribution to the emerging role of the female journalist. The extracts included here are from Williams's immediate response to the Revolution, in the 1790 *Letters Written in France*, and from her account of the death of Madame Roland in *Letters from France* (1792–6). The text retains her under-accented French and incorporates her translations of it.

~

From *Letters Written in France* (1790)

LETTER IX

Yesterday I received your letter, in which you accuse me of describing with too much enthusiasm the public rejoicings in France, and prophesy that I shall return to my own country a fierce republican. In answer to these accusations, I shall only observe, that it is very difficult, with common sensibility, to avoid sympathizing in general happiness. My love of the French revolution, is the natural result of this sympathy, and therefore my political creed is entirely an affair of the heart; for I have not been so absurd as to consult my head upon matters of which it is so incapable of judging. If I were at Rome, you would not be surprized to hear that I had visited, with the warmest reverence, every spot where any relics of her ancient grandeur could be traced; that I had flown to the capitol, that I had kissed the earth on which the Roman senate sat in council: And can you then expect me to have seen the Federation at the Champ de Mars, and the National Assembly of France, with indifference?* Before you insist that I ought to have done so, point out to me, in the page of Roman history, a spectacle more solemn, more affecting, than the Champ de Mars exhibited, or more magnanimous, more noble efforts in the cause of liberty than have been made by the National Assembly. Whether the new form of government, establishing in France, be more or less perfect than our own,

> 'Who shall decide, when doctors disagree,
> And soundest casuists doubt, like you and me?'*

I fancy we had better leave the determination of this question in the hands of posterity. In the mean time, I wish that some of our political critics would speak with less contempt, than they are apt to do, of the new constitution of France, and no longer repeat after one another the trite remark, that the French have gone too far, because they have gone farther than ourselves; as if it were not possible that that degree of influence which is perfectly safe in the hand of the executive part of our government, might be dangerous, at this crisis, to the liberty of France. But be this as it may, it appears evident that the temple of Freedom which they are erecting, even if imperfect in some of its proportions, must be preferable to the old gloomy Gothic fabric which they have laid in ruins.* And therefore, when I hear my good countrymen, who guard their own rights with such unremitting vigilance, and who would rather part with life than liberty, speak with contempt of the French for having imbibed the noble lesson which England has taught, I cannot but suspect that some mean jealousy lurks beneath the ungenerous censure. I cannot but suspect, that, while the fair and honourable traders of our commercial country act with the most liberal spirit in their ordinary dealings with other nations, they wish to make a monopoly of liberty, and are angry that France should claim a share of that precious property; by which, however, she may surely be enriched, without our being impoverished. The French, on the contrary, seem to have imbibed, with the principles of liberty, the strongest sentiments of respect and friendship towards that people, whom they gratefully acknowledge to have been their masters in this science. They are, to use their own phrase, 'devenus sous des Anglois,' [Williams translates: 'Become madly fond of the English'] and fondly imagine that the applause they have received from a society of philosophers in our country, is the general voice of the nation.*

Whether the new constitution be composed of durable materials or not, I leave to politicians to determine; but it requires no extraordinary sagacity to pronounce, that the French will henceforth be free. The love of liberty has pervaded all ranks of the people, who, if its blessings must be purchased with blood, will not shrink from paying the price:

> 'While ev'n the peasant boasts his rights to scan,
> And learns to venerate himself as man.'*

The enthusiastic spirit of liberty displays itself, not merely on the days of solemn ceremonies—occupies not only every serious deliberation—but is mingled with the gaiety of social enjoyment. When they converse, liberty is the theme of discourse; when they dance, the figure of the cotillon is adapted to a national tune;* and when they sing, it is but to repeat a vow of fidelity to the constitution, at which all who are present instantly join in chorus, and sportively lift up their hands in confirmation of this favourite sentiment.

In every street, you see children performing the military exercise, and carrying banners made of paper of the national colours, wearing grenadiers caps of the same composition, and armed, though not like Jack the Giant-killer, with swords of sharpness.*

Upon the whole, liberty appears in France adorned with the freshness of youth, and is loved with the ardour of passion. In England she is seen in her matron state, and, like other ladies at that period, is beheld with sober veneration.

With respect to myself, I must acknowledge, that, in my admiration of the revolution in France, I blend the feelings of private friendship with my sympathy in public blessings; since the old constitution is connected in my mind with the image of a friend confined in the gloomy recesses of a dungeon, and pining in hopeless captivity; while, with the new constitution, I unite the soothing idea of his return to prosperity, honours, and happiness.*

LETTER XXVI

London

We left France early in September, that we might avoid the equinoctial gales;* but were so unfortunate as to meet, in our passage from Dieppe to Brighton, with a very violent storm. We were two days and two nights at sea, and beat four and twenty hours off the coast of Brighton; and it would be difficult for you, who have formed your calculations of time on dry land, to guess what is the length of four and twenty hours in a storm at sea. At last, with great difficulty, we landed on the beach, where we found several of our friends and acquaintance, who, supposing that we might be among the passengers, sympathised with our danger, and were anxious for our preservation.

Before the storm became so serious as to exclude every idea but that of preparing to die with composure, I could not help being diverted with the comments on French customs, and French politics, which passed in the cabin. 'Ah,' says one man to his companion, 'one had need to go to France, to know how to like old England when one gets back again.'—'For my part,' rejoined another, 'I've never been able to get drunk once the whole time I was in France—not a drop of porter to be had—and as for their victuals, they call a bit of meat of a pound and a half, a fine piece of roast beef.'—'And pray,' added he, turning to one of the sailors, 'What do you think of their National Assembly?'—'Why,' says the sailor, 'if I ben't mistaken, the National Assembly has got some points from the wind.'*

I own it has surprized me not a little, since I came to London, to find that most of my acquaintance are of the same opinion with the sailor. Every visitor brings me intelligence from France full of dismay and horror. I hear of nothing but crimes, assassinations, torture, and death. I am told that every day witnesses a conspiracy; that every town is the scene of a massacre; that every street is blackened with a gallows, and every highway deluged with blood. I hear these things, and repeat to myself, Is this the picture of France? Are these the images of that universal joy, which called tears into my eyes, and made my heart throb with sympathy?—To me, the land which these mighty magicians have suddenly covered with darkness, where, waving their evil wand, they have reared the dismal scaffold, have clotted the knife of the assassin with gore, have called forth the shriek of despair, and the agony of torture; to me, this land of desolation appeared drest in additional beauty beneath the genial smile of liberty. The woods seemed to cast a more refreshing shade, and the lawns to wear a brighter verdure, while the carols of freedom burst from the cottage of the peasant, and the voice of joy resounded on the hill, and in the valley.

Must I be told that my mind is perverted, that I am become dead to all sensations of sympathy, because I do not weep with those who have lost a part of their superfluities, rather than rejoice that the oppressed are protected, that the wronged are redressed, that the captive is set at liberty, and that the poor have bread? Did the universal parent of the human race, implant the feelings of pity in the heart, that they should be confined to the artificial wants of vanity, the ideal deprivations of greatness; that they should be fixed beneath the dome of the palace, or locked within the gate of the chateau; without extending one commiserating sigh to the wretched hamlet, as if its famished inhabitants, though not ennobled by *man*, did not bear, at least, the ensigns of nobility stamped on our nature by God?

Must I hear the charming societies, in which I found all the elegant graces of the most polished manners, all the amiable urbanity of liberal and cultivated minds, compared with the most rude, ferocious, and barbarous levellers that ever existed? Really, some of my English acquaintance, whatever objections they may have to republican principles, do, in their discussions of French politics, adopt a most free and republican style of censure. Nothing can be more democratical than their mode of expression, or display a more levelling spirit, than their unqualified contempt of *all* the leaders of the revolution.

It is not my intention to shiver lances, in every society I enter, in the cause of the National Assembly. Yet I cannot help remarking, that, since that Assembly does not presume to set itself up as an example to this country, we seem to have very little right to be furiously angry, because they think proper to try another system of government themselves. Why should they not be suffered to make an experiment in politics? I have always been told, that the improvement of every science depends upon experiment. But I now hear that, instead of their new attempt to form the great-machine of society upon a simple principle of general amity upon the FEDERATION of its members, they ought to have repaired the feudal wheels and springs, by which their ancestors directed its movements. Yet if mankind had always observed this retrograde motion, it would surely have led them to few acquisitions in virtue, or in knowledge; and we might even have been worshipping the idols of paganisin at this moment. To forbid, under the pains and penalties of reproach, all attempts of the human mind to advance to greater perfection, seems to be proscribing every art and science. And we cannot much wonder that the French, having received so small a legacy of public happiness from their forefathers, and being sensible of the poverty of their own patrimony, should try new methods of transmitting a richer inheritance to their posterity.

Perhaps the improvements which mankind may be capable of making in the art of politics, may have some resemblance to those they have made in the art of navigation. Perhaps our political plans may hitherto have been somewhat like those ill-constructed misshapen vessels, which, unfit to combat with the winds and waves, were only used by the antients to convey the warriors of one country to despoil and ravage another neighbouring state; which only served to produce an intercourse of hostility, a communication of injury, an exchange of rapine and devastation.—But it may possibly be within the compass of human ability to form a system of politics, which, like a modern ship of discovery, built upon principles that defy the opposition of the tempestuous elements ('and passions are the elements of life'—)* instead of yielding to their fury makes them subservient to its purpose, and sailing sublimely over the untracked ocean, unites those together whom nature seemed for ever to have separated, and throws a line of connection across the divided world.

One cause of the general dislike in which the French revolution is held in this country, is the exaggerated stories which are carefully circulated by such of the aristocrats as have taken refuge in England. They are not all, however, persons of this description. There is now a young gentleman in London, nephew to the Bishop de Sens, who has lost his fortune, his rank, all his high expectations, and yet who has the generosity to applaud the revolution, and the magnanimity to reconcile himself to personal calamities, from the consideration of general good; and who is 'faithful found' to his country, 'among the faithless.'* I hope this amiable young Frenchman will live to witness, and to share the honours, the prosperity of that regenerated country; and I also hope that the National Assembly of France will answer the objections of its adversaries in the manner most becoming its own dignity, by forming such a constitution as will render the French nation virtuous, flourishing, and happy.

From *Letters from France* (1792–1796)

At this period one of the most accomplished women that France has produced perished on the scaffold. This lady was Madame Roland, the wife of the late minister.* On the 31st of May he had fled from his persecutors, and his wife who remained was carried to prison. The wits observed on this occasion, that the body of Roland was missing, but that he had left his soul behind. Madame Roland was indeed possessed of the most distinguished talents, and a mind highly cultivated by the study of literature. I had been acquainted with her since

I first came to France, and had always observed in her conversation the most ardent attachment to liberty, and the most enlarged sentiments of philanthropy; sentiments which she developed with an eloquence peculiar to herself, with a flow and power of expression which gave new graces and new energy to the French language. With these extraordinary endowments of mind she united all the warmth of a feeling heart, and all the charms of the most elegant manners. She was tall and well shaped, her air was dignified, and although more than thirty-five years of age she was still handsome. Her countenance had an expression of uncommon sweetness, and her full dark eyes beamed with the brightest rays of intelligence. I visited her in the prison of St Pelagie,* where her soul, superior to circumstances, retained its accustomed serenity, and she conversed with the same animated cheerfulness in her little cell as she used to do in the hotel of the minister. She had provided herself with a few books, and I found her reading Plutarch.* She told me she expected to die; and the look of placid resignation with which she spoke of it, convinced me that she was prepared to meet death with a firmness worthy of her exalted character. When I enquired after her daughter, an only child of thirteen years of age, she burst into tears; and at the overwhelming recollection of her husband and her child, the courage of the victim of liberty was lost in the feelings of the wife and the mother.

Immediately after the murder of the Gironde she was sent to the Conciergerie, like them to undergo the mockery of a trial, and like them to perish.* When brought before the revolutionary tribunal she preserved the most heroical firmness, though she was treated with such barbarity, and insulted by questions so injurious to her honour, that sometimes the tears of indignation started from her eyes. This celebrated woman, who at the bar of the national convention had by the commanding graces of her eloquence forced even from her enemies the tribute of applause and admiration, was now in the hands of vulgar wretches, by whom her fine talents, far from being appreciated, were not even understood. I shall transcribe a copy of her defence taken from her own manuscript. With keen regret I must add, that some papers in her justification, which she sent me from her prison, perhaps with a view that at some happier period, when the voice of innocence might be heard, I should make them public, I was compelled to destroy, the night on which I was myself arrested;* since, had they been found in my possession, they would inevitably have involved me in her fate. Before I took this resolution, which cost me a cruel effort, I employed every means in my power to preserve those precious memorials, in vain; for I could find no person who would venture to keep them amidst the terrors of domiciliary visits, and the certainty, if they were found, of being put to death as an accomplice of the writer. But her fair fame stands in no need of such testimonials; her memory is embalmed in the minds of the wise and good, as one of those glorious martyrs who have sealed with their blood the liberties of their country. After hearing her sentence, she said, 'Vous me jugez digne de partager le fort des grands hommes que vous avez assassines. Je tacherai de porter a l'echafaud le courage qu'ils y ont montre.' [Williams translates: 'You think me worthy, then, of sharing the fate of those great men whom you have assassinated. I will endeavour to go to the scaffold with the courage which they displayed.']

On the day of her trial she dressed herself in white: her long dark hair flowed loosely to her waist, and her figure would have softened any hearts less ferocious than those of her judges.* On her way to the scaffold she was not only composed, but sometimes assumed an air of gaiety, in order to encourage a person who was condemned to die at the same time, but who was not armed with the same fortitude.

When more than one person is led at the same time to execution, since they can suffer only in succession, those who are reserved to the last are condemned to feel multiplied deaths at the sound of the falling instrument, and the sight of the bloody scaffold. To be the first victim was therefore considered as a privilege, and had been allowed to Madame Roland as a woman. But when she observed the dismay of her companion, she said to him, 'Allez le premier: que je vous epargne au moins la douleur de voir couler mon sang.' [Williams translates: 'Go first: let me at least spare you the pain of seeing my blood shed.'] She then turned to the executioner, and begged that this sad indulgence might be granted to her fellow sufferer. The executioner told her that he had received orders that she should perish first. 'But you cannot, I am sure,' said she with a smile, 'refuse the last request of a lady.' The executioner complied with her demand. When she mounted the scaffold, and was tied to the fatal plank, she lifted up her eyes to the statue of Liberty, near which the guillotine was placed, and exclaimed, 'Ah Liberte, comme on t'a jouee!' [Williams translates: 'Ah Liberty! how hast thou been sported with!'] The next moment she perished. But her name will be recorded in the annals of history, as one of those illustrious women whose superior attainments seem fitted to exalt her sex in the scale of being.

She had predicted that her husband would not survive her loss, and her prediction was fulfilled. Roland, who had concealed himself till this period, no sooner heard the fate of his wife, whose influence over his mind had often been a subject of reproach amongst his enemies, than, feeling that life was no longer worth possessing, he put an end to his existence.* His body was found in a wood near the high-road between Paris and Rouen: the papers which were in his pocket-book were sent to the committee of general safety, and have never seen the light. His unhappy daughter found an asylum with an old friend of her proscribed parents, who had the courage to receive her at a period when it was imminently dangerous to afford her protection. But the time probably now draws near when this child will be adopted by her country, and an honourable provision will be made for her, as a testimony of national gratitude towards those who gave her birth.*

LAETITIA MATILDA HAWKINS
(1759–1835)

The daughter of an upwardly mobile writer and lawyer, John Hawkins (the son of a carpenter), and his wealthy wife Sidney Storer, Laetitia Matilda Hawkins was born in London and was educated by her father, for whom she acted as an occasional amanuensis. There are Burneyesque elements in her background, her involvement in her father's work, and her subsequent life, but Hawkins's father never achieved the recognition she thought he deserved, and Hawkins herself never made the transition from ladylike anonymity to literary fame. Sir John Hawkins published his *General History of the Science and Practice of Music* (1776) in the same year as Charles Burney and suffered, not entirely fairly, by the comparison; he went on to publish memoirs of Dr Johnson which were eclipsed by James Boswell's (in fairness, unbeatable) *Life*. His daughter observed these literary and intellectual circles and later published accounts of them in her *Anecdotes* (1822). She kept her novel-writing secret from her family, published her first novel anonymously when still in her teens, and tells us that she wrote several others. Her literary life intensified on the death of her father in 1789 and mother in 1793; after this Hawkins lived with her brother Henry in Twickenham. She published, anonymously, *Letters on the Female Mind* in 1793; later, the novels *The Countess and Gertrude, or Modes of Discipline* (1811), *Roseanne, or a Father's Labour Lost* (1814), *Heraldine, or Opposite Proceedings* (1821), and *Annaline, or Motive-Hunting* (1824). They are organized thematically and feature idealized heroines; like all her works, however, they are dedicated to women and reveal limited support for women's education. Hawkins is also thought to have published devotional works in the manner of Hannah More. Her *Anecdotes* of her father and members of the Johnson circle were reviewed by Thomas De Quincey; her *Memoirs* (1824) include more miscellaneous observations and information.

The previously unassigned periodical *The Female Preceptor. Containing Essays, Chiefly on the Duties of the Female Sex; with a Variety of Useful and Polite Literature, Poems, &c.* 'conducted by a Lady' (5 volumes, 1814–15) may now be identified as the work of Hawkins, and it greatly extends her significance as a commentator on women's affairs. The first address, 'On the Female Mind', signed H.M.W., comes from *Letters on the Female Mind*. In a striking passage, Hawkins suggests that the limits on female intellectual endeavour are clearly indicated by the distorting effect thought has on the female countenance. This argument, which leaps off the page today, probably caused little consternation at the time. Indeed, it was a little old-fashioned. A review of the first volume of Catharine Macaulay's *History* in the *Monthly Review* in 1763 had included in its recommendation that each sex stick with its 'characteristical excellence' the observation that 'intense thought spoils a lady's features; it banishes *les ris et les grâces*, which form all the enchantment of a female face'.[1]

There are not many recollections of Hawkins. In the final instalment of his *Graybeard's Gossip on his Literary Acquaintance* (1848), the novelist and humorist Horace Smith recalls the 'profoundly pious' Hawkins as one of the 'Curiosities of Literature', opining: 'Such of my readers as are well-stricken in years and possess good memories may recall a certain Miss Hawkins, the authoress of [various novels] which found special favour with serious people many years ago.' He relates an anecdote of being approached by Hawkins for advice on 'a religious novel in which she had made considerable progress, the principal personage whereof was Jesus Christ!'[2] If Horace Smith was right (and he is likely to have been: he himself wrote novels set in pre-Christian and early Christian times, and would have been an obvious person for Hawkins to consult about such an endeavour), Hawkins might by now have secured a place in literary history

---

[1] *Monthly Review*, 29 (1763), 373.   [2] *New Monthly Magazine*, 82 (1848), 335–6.

as the originator of a new kind of historical fiction. However, this anecdote is all that has survived of her novel, unless it awaits discovery in the Hawkins family papers. She abandoned the project and died soon afterwards.

The following extracts from her *Letters on the Female Mind* (1793), addressed to Helen Maria Williams, are indicative of her mixed and sometimes contradictory views on the proper social and intellectual roles of women. In the passages preceding the extracts Hawkins declares that 'I know no useful, and I am sure there is no ornamental science or study, that is not within the reach of a feminine capacity' (11); she goes on to list arithmetic, geography, natural philosophy, natural history, civil history, biography, as well as 'the attainment of all the languages a female inclination *points* to' (that is, not Latin or Greek), as being 'proper' additions to musical taste and ability, skill in 'the imitative arts', and the physical grace honed by dancing (13). Throughout her account she is anxious to avoid excess ambition in female intellect and especially concerned about women's improper involvement in politics; at the same time, she speaks most eloquently about the checks and balances of female ability in the context of male approval and 'permission'. Her adoption of the insider's voice, in which women are 'we', is another complication in the effect of her argument, for it assumes an intimacy which, if it undermines Helen Maria Williams's sentimental immediacy, nevertheless links the feminine with personal expression.

Hawkins has mixed views on the abilities and role of women, arguing for the inferiority of female intellect but seeing female eloquence, because addressed to the heart rather than to the head, as dangerous in its power over 'the passions of man' (24). She warns against the violent exertion of the female mind, likening the spectacle to seeing 'a beautiful, delicately formed horse, whose powers were misapplied to the drawing an enormous burden' (27). At the same time, some of her underlying assumptions about the importance of women's companionship with men and their role as members of society, are not out of keeping with Wollstonecraft's. Women must fulfil duties taught by religion, but this is a higher role than the decorative and palliative roles commonly expected of them: 'we are not what we should be if we desire solely to please those of the other sex; we must please *ourselves*—a more difficult task to a well-informed mind, than it can possibly be made appear to one that is not so' (28). There are signs, also, that Hawkins assumed that in the ongoing progress of mankind women's roles would change: she criticizes her contemporaries not by absolute standards but because, she argues, 'we have overstepped the limits assigned us; we have anticipated the progress of time, and before we have well attained the apex of perfection, are precipitating ourselves down the steep descent of degeneracy' (29). To argue for social progress is to adopt a familiar pattern of Enlightenment history, but to add notions of perfection is to introduce a version of Godwinian perfectibility which jars with some of Hawkins's more conservative attitudes; while the 'steep descent of degeneracy' draws on scientific and economic models as well as on historical and sociological models of decline and fall.

~

From *Letters on the Female Mind* (1793)

LETTER I

In this first address to you, I would confine myself to the consideration of this simple proposition—*What are the objects on which the female genius may be most properly exercised?* But this question involves in it one previous to it, and that is, *What are the peculiar properties of the female mind?* which, with your leave, we will first regard.

It cannot, I think, be truly asserted, that the intellectual powers know no difference of sex. Nature certainly intended a distinction; but it is a distinction that is far from degrading us. Instances, without doubt, may be adduced, where talents truly masculine, and of superior masculine excellence, have been bestowed on the softer sex; but they are so rare, that the union is not to be looked for. In general, and almost universally, the feminine intellect has less strength but more acuteness; consequently, in our exercise of it, we shew less perseverance and more vivacity. We are not formed for those deep investigations that tend to the bringing into light reluctant truth; but when once she has appeared, when *vēra incessu patuit Dea*,* then it is within the female province to give her spirit and decoration, which the less flexible and less volatile male mind would fail in attempting.

That we were not designed for the exertion of intense thought, may be fairly inferred from the effect it produces on the countenance and features. The contracted brow, the prolated visage, the motionless eye-ball, and the fixed attitude, though they may give force and dignity to the strong lines of the male countenance, can give nothing to soft features that is not unpleasant: no other idea can be conveyed but that of Armida accoutred in Clarinda's armour:* the new character is unsuitable and unmanageable, not only useless but oppressive.

In contemplating this subject, I have always imagined this difference to subsist between the minds of the different sexes. Male genius fetches its treasures from the depths of science, and the accumulated wisdom of ages: the female finds her's in the lighter regions of fancy and the passing knowledge of the day. There are, unquestionably, approximations between them that render it sometimes difficult to ascertain the precise point at which they diverge, as in all other works of the creation links are found which form, by regular gradations, the various dissimilarities of being into one regular progression; but still the generic and specific distinction exists, though to our obtuse faculties scarcely perceptible but when magnified by some degrees of distance.

In this age of liberality and refinement in female education, (for which no one is more thankful than myself) whatever is ingenious, shrewd, elegant, and sportive; whatever requires pathos and the energy of plaintive eloquence, may be looked for from our young women; and their invention renders the field assigned them a source of inexhaustible production, in which, while by confining their attention, they do not weaken their powers, they need fear no rival; but if they prefer the mine to the flowery face of nature, if they will dig for casual diamonds instead of weaving fragrant garlands, let them not be disappointed if they fail, or angry if the trespass is retorted more to their harm.

When I confine the powers of women to lighter subjects of exertion, I would not be understood as insinuating, that they are incapable of any thing *serious:* I mean only that they misapply them, when, descending below the level of necessity, they fancy they find pleasure in what they are not fitted to comprehend. Dividing subjects of thought into *abstruse, serious,* and *light,* I consider only the former and the latter as peculiarly appropriated by either sex; the center is common to both: it is the key-note uniting two chords, equally useful and necessary to both.

The peculiar properties of the female mind I should therefore reckon acuteness of perception, vivacity of imagination, and a concatenation of invention that disdains all limit. The corporeal part of our composition here lends its aid, and while it produces, perhaps, only pains to the body, adds every possible intellectual charm to the mind: our irritable nerves are our torments and our grace; what we conceive quickly and clearly, we feel exquisitely; natural eloquence gives to these feelings the power of conveying themselves to others, and gratified with the incontrovertible testimony of our power, we are apt to suppose it of a species very different from what it really is: we take it for strength, when it is only the property of penetration; we fancy we wield a pike, when it is but a needle; and we suppose the world subdued by our arguments, when it has yielded only to our persuasions.

If this desultory sketch is believed to comprehend nearly the whole brief catalogue of female powers, where shall we look for subjects fitted to their exertions? Let not the advocate for female excellence be alarmed; the field is ample, and little is excluded from its boundary; every shrub, every flower of literature is contained within it; forest trees only are excluded: and surely no woman, who has ever contemplated the oak, will complain that she is not permitted to bear it away from its native soil.

LETTER II

Admitting, then, that there are some few things locked up from female research, it remains to discover what those are. Whatever our *personal* strength is unequal to, will, I suppose, be granted me, as improper for our sex to engage in. To navigate a ship, or to build a church, have not yet been the objects of our emulation. The practice of physic in its extent, the toil of pleading at the bar, and the vigils of other occupations, have not yet held forth allurements, sufficient to attract us. Divinity has an aspect less attractive than almost any other study, when operating on a lively imagination, and I trust no ladies will think me injurious to their rights, if I dismiss it from the catalogue of their studies.

Perhaps I shall be thought to make an inconsistent concession, if I give it as my opinion that polemics are not the *most* unfit study a woman can give in to;* the inclination to it being but rare, it would more readily be exiled than admitted; but I see no invincible obstacle to a woman's making some figure in such a controversy, provided she is thoroughly versed in the dead languages, which are as attainable by us as by our masters. An extensive acquaintance with the writings of the fathers, a complete deduction of church-history, and a sedulous research into the scriptures, are the requisites in polemics; and a strong inclination might acquire all these; but where is the woman that has that inclination? Or would it be possible for a mind to be thus enlightened without perceiving that it was assuming a character utterly devoid of all those graces that constitute the perfection of the weaker sex?

The study, my dear madam, which I place in the climax of unfitness, is that of *politics*; and so strongly does it appear to me barred against the admission of females, that I am astonished that they ever ventured to approach it. To constitute a sound judgement in the interests of states and kingdoms, I should think it necessary that a boy (for I have no idea of a girl now) after having been carefully instructed at home, should be sent to run the gauntlope of a public school,* where he would learn mankind in miniature. He would see the jarring interests, the circumventing fraud, the open violence of the great world, brought there under his eye; his feelings would be blunted by the collision he must meet with, and his reasoning faculties would come out unbiassed by them, which, however unamiable, I need not say is requisite to a passage through the bustling world. Leaving school, he is sent to a university, where he acquires the theory of politics from the historians and legislators of antiquity: he is taught to prepare his weapons for the 'wordy war,'* and dismissed to compare what he has only on the *ipse dixit* of his instructors,* with what is to be found in practice:—he travels, lives in those places where he has the best prospect of society, gets as near the springs and wheels of government as he can—contemplates all its forms, its changes, and its interests, and returns to his country to apply his experience to her necessities. Through how much of all this discipline can a woman go? You will grant it a path impenetrable to her; that nine women out of ten would sacrifice their health, if not their lives, in the attempt to explore the various governments of various climates; but you will contend, that all I have set down is not necessary. How will you supply the want of any part of it? There is but one way, my dear madam, in which it can be even *speciously* supplied. We must either learn by our own experience, or that of others—the first is not possible in this instance, the last is a method proverbially condemned; but, I believe I may assert, it is the only method open to a woman, and that every *female* politician is a *hearsay* politician. . . .

We well know, that in the subordinate classes of life, the hand that is accustomed to the exertion of its muscular strength, is unapt afterwards to those things that require only pliancy, and so it is with our minds:—if we are to be politicians, if we are to place our amusements in the *arena* of contention, let it be of what kind it may, adieu to all the charms of female tenderness and female *weakness*, for even that has charms. Instead of founding the motives of our conduct on the laws of instructed nature, and looking to our hearts for the impulses of duty, we shall, if we are good wives, be so, because the well-being of a state is connected with our virtue; not because the affection we feel towards the man we are devoted to, makes the discharge of our duty to him a gratification to us, and the breach of it impossible;—we shall be careful mothers, if such cares are not beneath our notice, because we hope to rear a progeny of patriots, or, perhaps, I should rather say, of pertinacious disputants. The examples of Portia and Cornelia will be our models and our justification;* and we shall, in our newly-acquired feminine virility, defy the modern world to blame what our ancestors so applauded, not considering that there is a wide difference between a fluctuating republic, and a settled form of government; that where a state is in its infancy, or in its renovation, the powers of every one are called on to make its nurture or improvement their first care; but that where, thanks to the goodness of Providence! every thing out of our own dwelling is settled comfortably for us; where we are not called on to fight *pro aris et focis** our interference can do no good, but may do much harm; just as in the building a house, every one employed in it may be meritoriously diligent, and must be diligent to be meritorious; but when it is completed, when the surveyor has pronounced it ready for habitation, if the bricklayer insists that the chimnies are too low, and load them with more bricks, if the mason will lay weights of stone where they are not wanted, and some will strengthen and others decorate, according to their own whim or *interest*, their interference can deserve no praise, their labours are only detrimental; and well is it for such busy folks if, in the mean time, their own dwellings are not miserably out of repair.

There is another consideration I could adduce, as a strong argument against our giving into those studies and pursuits that tend to annihilate the distinctions between male and female genius. However men may admire our talents, and wonder at our attainments, they are seldom pleased with us for entering the lists with them.* There is a natural jealousy of right on their part that leads them to resent the infringement; and on the side of woman there is, I am sorry to say, a pertinacity of opinion in dispute, and a provoking shrewdness that makes them most unpleasant arguers. We have not the strength or deep voice of the mastiff, but we have the loco-motive quickness, and the snappishness of the fondled creature a modern naturalist has stiled *The Comforter*.* We cannot make ourselves feared, but we may be despised or hated: we may be intolerably troublesome while we mean no harm; and as the dear Chloe, or the charming Bijou,* are occasionally excluded from the drawing-room for their exertions, those whom nature, notwithstanding all modern levelling, has made our lords and masters, may recollect, that women ignorant were less a nuisance than they find women informed; and that, therefore, it is for their ease and interest to exile them from the field of literature.—That this is not impossible, a comparison of the ladies of Elizabeth's days, with the generation preceding our's, will prove.—It is not to be presumed that our *rights*, if we have any, are unalienable: it is as yet far from decided, that we are morally and collectively the *better* for being *wiser*. Let us then, if we do not love darkness, be very careful to do nothing to provoke our superiors to take away the lamp they had allowed us.

ANN RADCLIFFE
(1764–1823)

Born Ann Ward, the only child of a London haberdasher, William Ward, and his wife Ann Oates, Radcliffe became the most celebrated and best-selling novelist of the 1790s. The family moved from Holborn to Bath in 1773, where her father took over the management of a shop selling goods by Josiah Wedgwood and his partner Thomas Bentley. Bentley, a scientist and friend of Samuel Taylor Coleridge, was Ann Oates's uncle by marriage. After attending a school kept by the writers Sophia and Harriet Lee in Bath, she married the journalist and later newspaper proprietor William Radcliffe in January 1787 and settled near London. They had no children. Encouraged by her husband, Radcliffe started to write fiction and poetry, publishing her first novel two years after her marriage. In spite of her fame, Radcliffe took no part in literary society and after the publication of *The Italian* in 1797 it was widely rumoured that she had died or gone insane. She was actually listed in the deaths columns in 1809. As Julie Kavanagh pointed out in 1863: 'She who could allow herself to be proclaimed dead or insane and not remonstrate, was no ordinary woman':[1] when Christina Rossetti wanted to write a biography of her, however, she found the dearth of information about her life an insuperable obstacle. The fact seems to be that Radcliffe found herself comfortably off after the deaths of her parents in 1798 and 1800, and had earned enough from her hugely successful novels to write as and when she pleased. She was paid £500 for *The Mysteries of Udolpho* and £800 for *The Italian*. Imitations of her work were so widespread that she might have believed it more than usually difficult to produce another original success: in addition, she is reported to have thought successful authorship incompatible with true ladyhood.

Radcliffe's withdrawal from writing is all the more unusual because she had her husband's active encouragement, and because her critical as well as creative engagement with literature is so apparent in everything she wrote. In addition to the innovative chapter-epigraphs which aligned all her novels with other literature, her posthumously published essay 'On the Supernatural in Poetry' (1826) is an adroit piece of literary criticism, as well as being an innovative account of the different operations of 'terror' and 'horror' in literature. Because information about her life is so restricted, and so dependent upon a single source—the account written almost certainly by her husband for the *Annual Biography and Obituary*—it is very difficult to offer explanations, especially if one considers (as Robert Miles does in his critical study of Radcliffe),[2] that the views ascribed to Radcliffe in that account may well have been those of her husband; that they might be the narrative against which her writing struggled, rather than the narrative of that writing. One rumour was that she was confined by insanity to Haddon Hall in Derbyshire, near Hardwick, described in the extract below from her *Journey*, and where she, like Sophia Lee before her, thought that Mary, Queen of Scots, had been imprisoned. The insanity story resurfaced when she died, and was the occasion of her husband's corrective obituary. These rumours are interesting in their assumption of the extreme imaginative pressure involved in the creation of her tales of terror, and in their evident desire to make Radcliffe's life fit her fiction.

Radcliffe was an accomplished poet, although much of her best work is incorporated in her novels; *St Alban's Abbey, a Metrical Tale* (1826), and

---

[1] *English Women of Letters: Biographical Sketches*, 2 vols. (London: Hurst and Blackett, 1863), i. 250.

[2] *Ann Radcliffe: The Great Enchantress* (Manchester: Manchester University Press, 1995), 26–8.

the poems collected after her death are exceptions. Her fame rests on her novels. *The Castles of Athlin and Dunbayne: A Highland Story* (1789), a routine romance, was followed by the sketchy but more suggestive *A Sicilian Romance* (1790) and the most intellectually engaged of her novels, *The Romance of the Forest* (1791); but it was *The Mysteries of Udolpho* (1794) which established her fame as a terror-romancer, and *The Italian* (1797) which is now most often cited as her masterpiece. Responding to criticism of the historical inaccuracy of her work, she wrote a more carefully researched piece, *Gaston de Blondeville*, not published until 1826, three years after her death: it is also the only one of her works to feature a genuine ghost. Her essay 'On the Supernatural in Poetry' was also published posthumously, in the *New Monthly Magazine* in 1826. As Robert Miles reminds us, 'Radcliffe's is the œ uvreof a young woman; her major novels were published between the ages of 25 and 33'.[3]

Radcliffe took only one journey outside England, travelling with her husband to the Alps via Holland and the German Rhineland. She was 30, and had just secured an astonishing £500 advance for *The Mysteries of Udolpho*; he had just been fired from the editorship of *The Morning Post*. What seemed like a lull in the war with France in 1794 turned increasingly dangerous for British travellers during the Radcliffes' expedition, and they were refused entry to Switzerland when an error in their passport led the Austrian lieutenant in charge to accuse them of espionage. From this excursion developed Radcliffe's neglected but fascinating travel-narrative, *A Journey Made in the Summer of 1794, Through Holland and the Western Frontier of Germany . . . To which are added Observations During a Tour to the Lakes* (1795). It was avidly received, going into three editions in the year of its publication, and the first set of extracts selected here is taken from it, showing Radcliffe confronting a dark episode in England's past and a worrying social contrast in its incipiently industrial present.

In the *Journey*, when the Radcliffes return from France they are immediately 'cheered by the faintly seen coast of England' (368) and view 'the bolder features of the English coast', where 'Shakespeare's cliff' strikes them with particular grandeur, and they consider that 'There are, perhaps, few prospects of sea and shore more animated and magnificent than this' (369). As they move north, and further back into English history, however, contrasts emerge which are less simple, emotionally and historically, than the contrast between Britain and France which so exhilarates them on their return. In Derbyshire Radcliffe visits Hardwick Hall, which at this time presented itself to visitors, misleadingly, as one of the prisons of Mary, Queen of Scots. Her account of the Elizabethan building and its relics of Mary Stuart is part of the tradition of

---

[3] Ibid. 27.

sentimental tourism, but also part of a reinterpretation of the image of the Scottish queen undertaken by many women in the eighteenth and nineteenth centuries. It was, moreover, a reinterpretation made more pressing and politically and emotionally more complex by the execution of Marie Antoinette in 1793, the year before the Radcliffes' travels. Radcliffe's reaction to Hardwick, as she renders it for publication, fetishizes relics, an emotional response predicated on a perhaps comfortable sense of loss (it certainly makes her representations of Catholicism in her novels more interesting). Alive, Mary, like Marie Antoinette, would presumably provoke more mixed feelings. The evocation of Mary's situation here, however, suggests that her appearance in Sophia Lee's historical-Gothic novel *The Recess* (1783–5) is actually far more significant in the development of Radcliffe's—and through her Gothic's—depiction of the imprisoned and victimized heroine than critics have recognized. To see Mary in the context of Radcliffe's *Journey*, moreover, as the passage included here moves from historical guilt to Manchester and what Radcliffe presents as its unnameable dark double, the slave port of Liverpool, is to allow the wider implications of Radcliffe's presentation of Mary Stuart to come into play.

Radcliffe's nervous and expressive sweep from Hardwick Hall to the slave trade offers an unusual but revealing introduction to the better-known narrative tensions and secret guilts of her most celebrated novel, *The Mysteries of Udolpho*. In the extract from the third volume of this novel, the heroine, Emily St Aubert, has long been held in the remote Italian castle of Udolpho by its owner, Montoni, a sinister aristocrat who has married Emily's aunt and only living protector, and who has designs on Emily's extensive fortune. Emily's aunt has come to recognize the folly of her marriage, but is powerless to escape from it or from the castle; while Emily, realizing that Montoni means to force her into marriage with one of his impoverished aristocratic cronies, desperately seeks to escape and to be reunited with her absent beloved, Valancourt. The extract here takes up the story as Emily is forbidden access to her aunt, who has, she fears, been incarcerated or worse in some hidden part of the castle. One of the castle attendants, Barnardine, offers to help Emily escape, but in order to do this she must trust entirely to him and meet him alone and in darkness. 'She blamed herself for suffering her romantic imagination to carry her so far beyond the bounds of probability,' Radcliffe's narratorial voice comments, 'and determined to endeavour to check its rapid flights, lest they should sometimes extend into madness. Still, however, she shrunk from the thought of meeting Barnardine, on the terrace, at midnight.' Emily's situation is an extreme version of the dilemmas facing women of her time in real life, and her heightened sensibility makes her both cypher and victim, linking her to Helen Maria Williams's revolutionary narratives.

Like many heroines in this anthology and throughout women's writing of the period, she is a solitary but intellectually resourceful female striving to escape a male threat which is always just about to reveal itself as sexual, but which is so entangled with the bastions of male social power— architectural, legal, political, religious—that the oppressive atmosphere of impending rape and murder comes to seem her own imaginative creation, her own fault. By putting together *A Journey Made in the Summer of 1794* and *The Mysteries of Udolpho*, however, it can be seen that Emily's transgressive midnight ramble and horrified spectatorship, and her haunted imagination afterwards, are a characteristic of that type of historical nightmare described by Thomas De Quincey as 'an eternity not coming, but past and irrevocable',[4] and which impels the deconstructed historical fiction of Nathaniel Hawthorne's *The Scarlet Letter* (1850). The relics of Mary, Queen of Scots, evoke both immediacy and distance, feelings which are essential to the narrative techniques, the setting, the plot, and the haunted, rather than historical, fictional past of *The Mysteries of Udolpho*.

❧

From *A Journey Made in the Summer of 1794* (1795)

Derbyshire and Lancashire

Our vessel was bound to Deal, and, leaving Dover and its cliffs on the south, we entered that noble bay, which the rich shores of Kent open for the sea.* Gentle hills, swelling all round from the water, green with woods, or cultivation, and speckled with towns and villages, with now and then the towers of an old fortress, offered a landscape particularly cheering to eyes accustomed to the monotonous flatness of Dutch views. And we landed in England under impressions of delight more varied and strong than can be conceived, without referring to the joy of an escape from districts where there was scarcely an home for the natives, and to the love of our own country, greatly enhanced by all that had been seen of others.

Between Deal and London, after being first struck by the superior appearance and manners of the people to those of the countries we had been lately accustomed to, a contrast too obvious as well as too often remarked to be again insisted upon, but which made all the

---

[4] Letter to Mary Russell Mitford, 1844, quoted in Grevel Lindop, *The Opium Eater: A Life of Thomas De Quincey* (London: Dent, 1981), 354.

ordinary circumstances of the journey seem new and delightful, the difference between the landscapes of England and Germany occurred forcibly to notice. The large scale, in which every division of land appeared in Germany, the long corn grounds, the huge stretches of hills, the vast plains and the wide vallies could not but be beautifully opposed by the varieties and undulations of English surface, with gently swelling slopes, rich in verdure, thick inclosures, woods, bowery hop grounds, sheltered mansions, announcing the wealth, and substantial farms, with neat villages, the comfort of the country. English landscape may be compared to cabinet pictures, delicately beautiful and highly finished; German scenery to paintings for a vestibule, of bold outline and often sublime, but coarse and to be viewed with advantage only from a distance.*

Northward, beyond London, we may make one stop, after a country, not otherwise necessary to be noticed, to mention Hardwick, in Derbyshire, a seat of the Duke of Devonshire, once the residence of the Earl of Shrewsbury, to whom Elizabeth deputed the custody of the unfortunate Mary.* It stands on an easy height, a few miles to the left of the road from Mansfield to Chesterfield, and is approached through shady lanes, which conceal the view of it, till you are on the confines of the park. Three towers of hoary grey then rise with great majesty among old woods, and their summits appear to be covered with the lightly shivered fragments of battlements, which, however, are soon discovered to be perfectly carved open work, in which the letters E. S. frequently occur under a coronet, the initials, and the memorials of the vanity, of Elizabeth, Countess of Shrewsbury, who built the present edifice.* Its tall features, of a most picturesque tint, were finely disclosed between the luxuriant woods and over the lawns of the park, which, every now and then, let in a glimpse of the Derbyshire hills. The scenery reminded us of the exquisite descriptions of Harewood,

The deep embowering shades, that veil Elfrida;*

and those of Hardwick once veiled a form as lovely as the ideal graces of the Poet, and conspired to a fate more tragical than that, which Harewood witnessed.

In front of the great gates of the castle court, the ground, adorned by old oaks, suddenly sinks to a darkly shadowed glade, and the view opens over the vale of Scarsdale, bounded by the wild mountains of the Peak. Immediately to the left of the present residence, some ruined features of the antient one, enwreathed with the rich drapery of ivy, give an interest to the scene, which the later, but more historical structure heightens and prolongs. We followed, not without emotion, the walk, which Mary had so often trodden, to the folding doors of the great hall, whose lofty grandeur, aided by silence and seen under the influence of a lowering sky, suited the temper of the whole scene. The tall windows, which half subdue the light they admit, just allowed us to distinguish the large figures in the tapestry, above the oak wainscoting, and shewed a colonnade of oak supporting a gallery along the bottom of the hall, with a pair of gigantic elk's horns flourishing between the windows opposite to the entrance. The scene of Mary's arrival and her feelings upon entering this solemn shade came involuntarily to the mind; the noise of horses' feet and many voices from the court; her proud yet gentle and melancholy look, as, led by my Lord Keeper, she passed slowly up the hall; his somewhat obsequious, yet jealous and vigilant air, while, awed by her dignity and beauty, he remembers the terrors of his own Queen; the silence and anxiety of her maids, and the bustle of the surrounding attendants.*

From the hall a stair-case ascends to the gallery of a small chapel, in which the chairs and cushions, used by Mary, still remain, and proceeds to the first story, where only one apartment bears memorials of her imprisonment, the bed, tapestry and chairs having been worked by herself.* This tapestry is richly embossed with emblematic figures, each with its title worked above it, and, having been scrupulously preserved, is still entire and fresh. . . .

A short passage leads from the state apartment to her own chamber, a small room, overlooked from the passage by a window, which enabled her attendants to know, that she was contriving no means of escape through the others into the court. The bed and chairs of this room are of black velvet, embroidered by herself; the toilet of gold tissue; all more decayed than worn, and probably used only towards the conclusion of her imprisonment here, when she was removed from some better apartment, in which the antient bed, now in the state-room, had been placed. The date 1599 is once or twice inscribed in this chamber; for no reason, that could relate to Mary, who was removed hence in 1584, and fell, by the often-blooded hands of Elizabeth, in 1587.*

These are the apartments, distinguished by having been the residence of so unhappy a personage. On the other side of the mansion, a grand gallery occupies the length of the whole front, which is 165 feet, and contains many portraits, now placed carelessly on chairs, or the floor; amongst them an head of Sir Thomas More, apparently very fine; heads of Henries the Fourth, Seventh and Eighth; a portrait of Lady Jane Gray, meek and fair, before a harpsichord, on which psalm-book is opened; at the bottom of the gallery, Elizabeth, slyly proud and meanly violent; and, at the top, Mary, in black, taken a short time before her death, her countenance much faded, deeply marked by indignation and grief, and reduced as if to the spectre of herself, frowning with suspicion upon all who approached it; the black eyes looking out from their corners, thin lips, somewhat aquiline nose and beautiful chin.*

What remains of the more antient building is a ruin, which, standing nearly on the brink of the glade, is a fine object from this. A few apartments, though approached with difficulty through the fragments of others, are still almost entire, and the dimensions of that called the Giant's Chamber are remarkable for the beauty of their proportion.

From Hardwick to within a few miles of Middleton,* the beauty of the country declines, while the sublimity is not perfected; but, from the north-west brow of Brampton Moor, the vast hills of Derbyshire appear in wild and ghastly succession. Middleton, hewn out of the grey rocks, that impend over it, and scarcely distinguishable from them, is worth notice for its very small and neat octagon church, built partly by brief and partly by a donation from the Duke of Devonshire.* The valley, or rather chasm, at the entrance of which it stands, is called Middleton Dale, and runs, for two miles, between perpendicular walls of rock, which have more the appearance of having been torn asunder by some convulsive rent of the earth, than any we have elsewhere seen. The strata are horizontal, and the edges of each are often distinct and rounded; one of the characteristics of granite. Three grey rocks, resembling castles, project from these solid walls, and, now and then, a lime-kiln, round like a bastion, half involves in smoke a figure, who, standing on the summit, looks the Witch of the Dale, on an edge of her cauldron, watching the workings of incantation.

The chasm opened, at length, to a hill, whence wild moorish

mountains were seen on all sides, some entirely covered with the dull purple of heath, others green, but without enclosures, except sometimes a stone wall, and the dark sides of others marked only by the blue smoke of weeds, driven in circles near the ground.

Towards sun-set, from a hill in Cheshire, we had a vast view over part of that county and nearly all Lancashire, a scene of fertile plains and gentle heights, till some broad and towering mountains, at an immense distance, were but uncertainly distinguished from the clouds. Soon after, the cheerful populousness of the rich towns and villages in Lancashire supplied objects for attention of a different character; Stockport first, crowded with buildings and people, as much so as some of the busiest quarters in London, with large blazing fires in every house, by the light of which women were frequently spinning, and manufacturers issuing from their workshops and filling the steep streets, which the chaise rolled down with dangerous rapidity; then an almost continued street of villages to Manchester, some miles before which the road was busy with passengers and carriages, as well as bordered by handsome country houses; and, finally for this day, Manchester itself; a second London; enormous to those, who have not seen the first, almost tumultuous with business, and yet well proved to afford the necessary peacefulness to science, letters and taste.* And not only for itself may Manchester be an object of admiration, but for the contrast of its useful profits to the wealth of a neighbouring place, immersed in the dreadful guilt of the Slave Trade,* with the continuance of which to believe national prosperity compatible, is to hope, that the actions of nations pass unseen before the Almighty, or to suppose extenuation of crimes by increase of criminality, and that the eternal laws of right and truth, which smite the wickedness of individuals, are too weak to struggle with the accumulated and comprehensive guilt of a national participation in robbery, cruelty and murder.

From *The Mysteries of Udolpho* (1794)

During the remainder of the day, Emily's mind was agitated with doubts and fears and contrary determinations, on the subject of meeting this Barnardine on the rampart, and submitting herself to his guidance, she scarcely knew whither. Pity for her aunt and anxiety for herself alternately swayed her determination, and night came, before she had decided upon her conduct. She heard the castle clock strike eleven—twelve—and yet her mind wavered. The time, however, was now come, when she could hesitate no longer: and then the interest she felt for her aunt overcame other considerations, and, bidding Annette follow her to the outer door of the vaulted gallery, and there await her return, she descended from her chamber. The castle was perfectly still, and the great hall, where so lately she had witnessed a scene of dreadful contention,* now returned only the whispering footsteps of the two solitary figures gliding fearfully between the pillars, and gleamed only to the feeble lamp they carried. Emily, deceived by the long shadows of the pillars and by the catching lights between, often stopped, imagining she saw some person, moving in the distant obscurity of the perspective; and, as she passed these pillars, she feared to turn her eyes toward them, almost expecting to see a figure start out from behind their broad shaft. She reached, however, the vaulted gallery, without interruption, but unclosed its outer door with a trembling hand, and, charging Annette not to quit it and to keep it a little open, that she might be heard if she called, she delivered to her the lamp, which she did not dare to take herself because of the men on watch, and, alone, stepped out upon the dark terrace. Every thing was so still, that she feared, lest her own light steps should be heard by the distant sentinels, and she walked cautiously towards the spot, where she had before met Barnardine, listening for a sound, and looking onward through the gloom in search of him. At length, she was startled by a deep voice, that spoke near her, and she paused, uncertain whether it was his, till it spoke again, and she then recognized the hollow tones of Barnardine, who had been punctual to the moment, and was at the appointed place, resting on the rampart wall. After chiding her for not coming sooner, and saying, that he had been waiting nearly half an hour, he desired Emily, who made no reply, to follow him to the door, through which he had entered the terrace.

While he unlocked it, she looked back to that she had left, and, observing the rays of the lamp stream through a small opening, was certain, that Annette was still there. But her remote situation could little befriend Emily, after she had quitted the terrace; and, when Barnardine unclosed the gate, the dismal aspect of the passage beyond, shewn by a torch burning on the pavement, made her shrink from following him alone, and she refused to go, unless Annette might accompany her. This, however, Barnardine absolutely refused to permit, mingling at the same time with his refusal such artful circumstances to heighten the pity and curiosity of Emily towards her aunt, that she, at length, consented to follow him alone to the portal.

He then took up the torch, and led her along the passage, at the extremity of which he unlocked another door, whence they descended, a few steps, into a chapel, which, as Barnardine held up the torch to light her, Emily observed to be in ruins, and she immediately recollected a former conversation of Annette, concerning it, with very unpleasant emotions.* She looked fearfully on the almost roofless walls, green with damps, and on the gothic points of the windows, where the ivy and the briony had long supplied the place of glass, and ran mantling among the broken capitals of some columns, that had once supported the roof. Barnardine stumbled over the broken pavement, and his voice, as he uttered a sudden oath, was returned in hollow echoes, that made it more terrific. Emily's heart sunk; but she still followed him, and he turned out of what had been the principal aisle of the chapel. 'Down these steps, lady,' said Barnardine, as he descended a flight, which appeared to lead into the vaults; but Emily paused on the top, and demanded, in a tremulous tone, whither he was conducting her.

'To the portal,' said Barnardine.

'Cannot we go through the chapel to the portal?' said Emily.

'No, Signora, that leads to the inner court, which I don't choose to unlock. This way, and we shall reach the outer court presently.'

Emily still hesitated; fearing not only to go on, but, since she had gone thus far, to irritate Barnardine by refusing to go further.

'Come, lady,' said the man, who had nearly reached the bottom of the flight, 'make a little haste; I cannot wait here all night.'

'Whither do these steps lead?' said Emily, yet pausing.

'To the portal,' repeated Barnardine, in an angry tone, 'I will wait no longer.' As he said this, he moved on with the light, and Emily, fearing to provoke him by further delay, reluctantly followed. From the steps, they proceeded through a passage, adjoining the vaults, the walls of which were dropping with unwholesome dews, and the vapours, that crept along the ground, made the torch burn so dimly, that Emily expected every moment to see it extinguished, and Barnardine could scarcely find his way. As they advanced, these vapours thickened, and Barnardine, believing the torch was expiring, stopped for a moment to trim it. As he then rested against a pair of iron gates, that opened from the passage, Emily saw, by uncertain flashes of light, the vaults beyond, and, near her, heaps of earth, that seemed to surround an open grave. Such an object, in such a scene, would, at any time, have disturbed her; but now she was shocked by an instantaneous presentiment, that this was the grave of her unfortunate aunt, and that the treacherous Barnardine was leading herself to destruction. The obscure and terrible place, to which he had conducted her, seemed to justify the thought; it was a place suited for murder, a receptacle for the dead, where a deed of horror might be committed, and no vestiage appear to proclaim it. Emily was so overwhelmed with terror, that, for a moment, she was unable to determine what conduct to pursue. She then considered, that it would be vain to attempt an escape from Barnardine, by flight, since the length and the intricacy of the way she had passed would soon enable him to overtake her, who was unacquainted with the turnings, and whose feebleness would not suffer her to run long with swiftness. She feared equally to irritate him by a disclosure of her suspicions, which a refusal to accompany him further certainly would do; and, since she was already as much in his power as it was possible she could be, if she proceeded, she, at length, determined to suppress, as far as she could, the appearance of apprehension, and to follow silently whither he designed to lead her. Pale with horror and anxiety, she now waited till Barnardine had trimmed the torch, and, as her sight glanced again upon the grave, she could not forbear enquiring, for whom it was prepared. He took his eyes from the torch, and fixed them upon her face without speaking. She faintly repeated the question, but the man, shaking the torch, passed on; and she followed, trembling, to a second flight of steps, having ascended which, a door delivered them into the first court of the castle. As they crossed it, the light shewed the high black walls around them, fringed with long grass and dank weeds, that found a scanty soil among the mouldering stones; the heavy buttresses, with, here and there, between them, a narrow grate, that admitted a freer circulation of air to the court, the massy iron gates, that led to the castle, whose clustering turrets appeared above, and, opposite, the huge towers and arch of the portal itself. In this scene the large, uncouth person of Barnardine, bearing the torch, formed a characteristic figure. This Barnardine was wrapt in a long dark cloak, which scarcely allowed the kind of half-boots, or sandals, that were laced upon his legs, to appear, and shewed only the point of a broad sword, which he usually wore, slung in a belt across his shoulders. On his head was a heavy flat velvet cap, somewhat resembling a turban, in which was a short feather; the visage beneath it shewed strong features, and a countenance furrowed with the lines of cunning and darkened by habitual discontent.

The view of the court, however, reanimated Emily, who, as she crossed silently towards the portal, began to hope, that her own fears, and not the treachery of Barnardine, had deceived her. She looked anxiously up at the first casement, that appeared above the lofty arch of the portcullis; but it was dark, and she enquired, whether it belonged to the chamber, where Madame Montoni was confined. Emily spoke low, and Barnardine, perhaps, did not hear her question, for he returned no answer; and they, soon after, entered the postern door of the gate-way, which brought them to the foot of a narrow stair-case, that wound up one of the towers.

'Up this stair-case the Signora lies,' said Barnardine.

'Lies!' repeated Emily faintly, as she began to ascend.

'She lies in the upper chamber,' said Barnardine.

As they passed up, the wind, which poured through the narrow cavities in the wall, made the torch flare, and it threw a stronger gleam upon the grim and sallow countenance of Barnardine, and discovered more fully the desolation of the place—the rough stone walls, the spiral stairs, black with age, and a suit of antient armour, with an iron visor, that hung upon the walls, and appeared a trophy of some former victory.

Having reached a landing-place, 'You may wait here, lady,' said he, applying a key to the door of a chamber, 'while I go up, and tell the Signora you are coming.'

'That ceremony is unnecessary,' replied Emily, 'my aunt will rejoice to see me.'

'I am not so sure of that,' said Barnardine, pointing to the room he had opened: 'Come in here, lady, while I step up.'

Emily, surprised and somewhat shocked, did not dare to oppose him further, but, as he was turning away with the torch, desired he would not leave her in darkness. He looked around, and, observing a tripod lamp, that stood on the stairs, lighted and gave it to Emily, who stepped forward into a large old chamber, and he closed the door. As she listened anxiously to his departing steps, she thought he descended, instead of ascending, the stairs; but the gusts of wind, that whistled round the portal, would not allow her to hear distinctly any other sound. Still, however, she listened, and, perceiving no step in the room above, where he had affirmed Madame Montoni to be, her anxiety increased, though she considered, that the thickness of the floor in this strong building might prevent any sound reaching her from the upper chamber. The next moment, in a pause of the wind, she distinguished Barnardine's step descending to the court, and then thought she heard his voice; but, the rising gust again overcoming other sounds, Emily, to be certain on this point, moved softly to the door, which, on attempting to open it, she discovered was fastened. All the horrid apprehensions, that had lately assailed her, returned at this instant with redoubled force, and no longer appeared like the exaggerations of a timid spirit, but seemed to have been sent to warn her of her fate. She now did not doubt, that Madame Montoni had been murdered, perhaps in this very chamber; or that she herself was brought hither for the same purpose. The countenance, the manners and the recollected words of Barnardine, when he had spoken of her aunt, confirmed her worst fears. For some moments, she was incapable of considering of any means, by which she might attempt an escape. Still she listened, but heard footsteps neither on the stairs, or in the room above; she thought, however, that she again distinguished Barnardine's voice below, and went to a grated window, that opened upon the court, to enquire further. Here, she plainly heard his hoarse accents, mingling with the blast, that swept by, but they were lost again so quickly, that their meaning could not be interpreted; and then the light of a torch, which seemed to issue from the portal below, flashed across the court, and the long shadow of a man, who was under the arch-way, appeared upon the pavement. Emily, from the hugeness of this sudden portrait, concluded it to be that of Barnardine; but other deep tones, which passed in the wind, soon convinced her he was not alone, and that his companion was not a person very liable to pity.

When her spirits had overcome the first shock of her situation, she held up the lamp to examine, if the chamber afforded a possibility of an escape. It was a spacious room, whose walls, wainscoted with rough oak, shewed no casement but the grated one, which Emily had left, and no other door than that, by which she had entered. The feeble rays of the lamp, however, did not allow her to see at once its full extent; she perceived no furniture, except, indeed, an iron chair, fastened in the centre of the chamber, immediately over which, depending on a chain from the ceiling, hung an iron ring. Having gazed upon these, for some time, with wonder and horror, she next observed iron bars below, made for the purpose of confining the feet, and on the arms of the chair were rings of the same metal. As she continued to survey them, she concluded, that they were instruments of torture, and it struck her, that some poor wretch had once been fastened in this chair, and had there been starved to death. She was chilled by the thought; but, what was her agony, when, in the next moment, it occurred to her, that her aunt might have been one of these victims, and that she herself might be the next! An acute pain seized her head, she was scarcely able to hold the lamp, and, looking round for support, was seating herself, unconsciously, in the iron chair itself; but suddenly perceiving where she was, she started from it in horror, and sprung towards a remote end of the room. Here again she looked round for a seat to sustain her, and perceived only a dark curtain, which, descending from the ceiling to the floor, was drawn along the whole side of the chamber. Ill as she was, the appearance of this curtain struck her, and she paused to gaze upon it, in wonder and apprehension.

It seemed to conceal a recess of the chamber; she wished, yet dreaded, to lift it, and to discover what it veiled: twice she was withheld by a recollection of the terrible spectacle her daring hand had formerly unveiled in an apartment of the castle,* till, suddenly conjecturing, that it concealed the body of her murdered aunt, she seized it, in a fit of desperation, and drew it aside. Beyond, appeared a corpse, stretched on a kind of low couch, which was crimsoned with human blood, as was the floor beneath. The features, deformed by death, were ghastly and horrible, and more than one livid wound appeared in the face. Emily, bending over the body, gazed, for a moment, with an eager, frenzied eye; but, in the next, the lamp dropped from her hand, and she fell senseless at the foot of the couch.

When her senses returned, she found herself surrounded by men, among whom was Barnardine, who were lifting her from the floor, and then bore her along the chamber. She was sensible of what passed, but the extreme languor of her spirits did not permit her to speak, or move, or even to feel any distinct fear. They carried her down the stair-case, by which she had ascended; when, having reached the arch-way, they stopped, and one of the men, taking the torch from Barnardine, opened a small door, that was cut in the great gate, and, as he stepped out upon the road, the light he bore shewed several men on horseback, in waiting. Whether it was the freshness of the air, that revived Emily, or that the objects she now saw roused the spirit of alarm, she suddenly spoke, and made an ineffectual effort to disengage herself from the grasp of the ruffians, who held her.

Barnardine, meanwhile, called loudly for the torch, while distant voices answered, and several persons approached, and, in the same instant, a light flashed upon the court of the castle. Again he vociferated for the torch, and the men hurried Emily through the gate. At a short distance, under the shelter of the castle walls, she perceived the fellow, who had taken the light from the porter, holding it to a man, busily employed in altering the saddle of a horse, round which were several horsemen, looking on, whose harsh features received the full glare of the torch; while the broken ground beneath them, the opposite walls, with the tufted shrubs, that overhung their summits, and an embattled watch-tower above, were reddened with the gleam, which, fading gradually away, left the remoter ramparts and the woods below to the obscurity of night.

'What do you waste time for, there?' said Barnardine with an oath, as he approached the horsemen. 'Dispatch—dispatch!'

'The saddle will be ready in a minute,' replied the man who was buckling it, at whom Barnardine now swore again, for his negligence, and Emily, calling feebly for help, was hurried towards the horses, while the ruffians disputed on which to place her, the one designed for her not being ready. At this moment a cluster of lights issued from the great gates, and she immediately heard the shrill voice of Annette above those of several other persons, who advanced. In the same moment, she distinguished Montoni and Cavigni,* followed by a number of ruffian-faced fellows, to whom she no longer looked with terror, but with hope, for, at this instant, she did not tremble at the thought of any dangers, that might await her within the castle, whence so lately, and so anxiously she had wished to escape. Those, which threatened her from without, had engrossed all her apprehensions.

A short contest ensued between the parties, in which that of Montoni, however, were presently victors, and the horsemen, perceiving that numbers were against them, and being, perhaps, not very warmly interested in the affair they had undertaken, galloped off, while Barnardine had run far enough to be lost in the darkness, and Emily was led back into the castle. As she re-passed the courts, the remembrance of what she had seen in the portal-chamber came, with all its horror, to her mind; and when, soon after, she heard the gate close, that shut her once more within the castle walls, she shuddered for herself, and, almost forgetting the danger she had escaped, could scarcely think, that any thing less precious than liberty and peace was to be found beyond them.

Montoni ordered Emily to await him in the cedar parlour, whither he soon followed, and then sternly questioned her on this mysterious affair. Though she now viewed him with horror, as the murderer of her aunt, and scarcely knew what she said in reply to his impatient enquiries, her answers and her manner convinced him, that she had not taken a voluntary part in the late scheme, and he dismissed her upon the appearance of his servants, whom he had ordered to attend, that he might enquire further into the affair, and discover those, who had been accomplices in it.

Emily had been some time in her apartment, before the tumults of her mind allowed her to remember several of the past circumstances. Then, again, the dead form, which the curtain in the portal-chamber had disclosed, came to her fancy, and she uttered a groan, which terrified Annette the more, as Emily forbore to satisfy her curiosity, on the subject of it, for she feared to trust her with so fatal a secret, lest her indiscretion should call down the immediate vengeance of Montoni on herself.

Thus compelled to bear within her own mind the whole horror of the secret, that oppressed it, her reason seemed to totter under the intolerable weight. She often fixed a wild and vacant look on Annette, and, when she spoke, either did not hear her, or answered from the purpose. Long fits of abstraction succeeded; Annette spoke repeatedly, but her voice seemed not to make any impression on the sense of the long agitated Emily, who sat fixed and silent, except that, now and then, she heaved a heavy sigh, but without tears.

Terrified at her condition, Annette, at length, left the room, to inform Montoni of it, who had just dismissed his servants, without having made any discoveries on the subject of his enquiry. The wild description, which this girl now gave of Emily, induced him to follow her immediately to the chamber.

At the sound of his voice, Emily turned her eyes, and a gleam of recollection seemed to shoot athwart her mind, for she immediately rose from her seat, and moved slowly to a remote part of the room. He spoke to her in accents somewhat softened from their usual harshness, but she regarded him with a kind of half curious, half terrified look, and answered only 'yes,' to whatever he said. Her mind still seemed to retain no other impression, than that of fear.

Of this disorder Annette could give no explanation, and Montoni, having attempted, for some time, to persuade Emily to talk, retired, after ordering Annette to remain with her during the night, and to inform him, in the morning, of her condition.

When he was gone, Emily again came forward, and asked who it was, that had been there to disturb her. Annette said it was the Signor—Signor Montoni. Emily repeated the name after her, several times, as if she did not recollect it, and then suddenly groaned, and relapsed into abstraction.

With some difficulty, Annette led her to the bed, which Emily examined with an eager, frenzied eye, before she lay down, and then, pointing, turned with shuddering emotion, to Annette, who, now more terrified, went towards the door, that she might bring one of the female servants to pass the night with them; but Emily, observing her going, called her by name, and then in the naturally soft and plaintive tone of her voice, begged, that she, too, would not forsake her.—'For since my father died,' added she, sighing, 'every body forsakes me.'

'Your father, ma'amselle!' said Annette, 'he was dead before you knew me.'

'He was, indeed!' rejoined Emily, and her tears began to flow. She now wept silently and long, after which, becoming quite calm, she at length sunk to sleep, Annette having had discretion enough not to interrupt her tears. This girl, as affectionate as she was simple, lost in these moments all her former fears of remaining in the chamber, and watched alone by Emily, during the whole night.

HANNAH MORE
(1745–1833)

Hannah More was the fourth of the five daughters of Jacob More, master of the free school at Stapleton, Gloucestershire, and Mary Grace, a farmer's daughter. Being brought up among the elder daughters of an educated family, she leapt ahead of the expected acquirements and developed a habit of learning from others and a precosity which turned out to be the foundation of a long and varied intellectual, creative, and religious life. Her father taught her mathematics and Latin; and when her sisters established a school she learnt Italian and Spanish. She was one of the best-known and possibly the most frequently read of women writers of her time, and during her long life she published a greater variety of works, in more varied contexts, than can adequately be represented here. More's prominence may be gauged by the fact that in the *Dictionary of National Biography* the longest entry for a writer included in this anthology is devoted to her; it was, moreover, written by the project's originator, Sir Leslie Stephen, himself.

For six years Hannah More was engaged to be married, but instead received an annuity from her irresolute suitor. With this degree of financial independence she visited London and became part of a circle which included the great actor David Garrick, Dr Johnson, Horace Walpole, and members of the Bluestocking circle, of which she wrote in the celebrated poem 'Bas Bleu' (1784); she wrote poems and tragedies, one of which, *Percy* (1777), had a successful theatre run. She wrote critically on the theatre and on her own plays in her 'General Preface' and 'Preface to Tragedies' in *The Works of Hannah More* (1830). She later renounced theatre-going and turned to writing religious and instructive works. Increasingly involved with Evangelical thinkers and activists, she was a friend of the anti-slavery campaigner William Wilberforce and published a long poem, *Slavery*, in 1788. With her sisters, she established a Sunday School in Cheddar (the village which appeared as 'Weston' in her later writings); other schools followed, established in ten parishes by 1791. Her tract warning of the dangers of Tom Paine and the principles of the French Revolution, *Village Politics, by Will Chip* (1793), is a well-known contribution to the revolutionary debates of the 1790s, and was followed by a series of cheap tracts written for the edification of the poor. The 114 monthly *Cheap Respository Tracts* (1795–7), written by More, her sisters, and her friends, and including ballads, biblical tales, and educational tales, achieved a huge circulation in Britain and the United States: Marilyn Gaull has called it 'her most successful venture and perhaps the most successful publishing venture of all time'.[1] By 1796 sales were running at 2 million a month. After the cessation of More's series, the Religious Tracts Society was established in 1799 to carry forward her example. A novel, *Coelebs in Search of a Wife* (1809), earned her £2,000; she left about £30,000 on her death. Other important works include *Strictures on the Modern System of Female Education* (1799), *Practical Piety* (1811), *Christian Morals* (1813), and *Moral Sketches* (1819). In Harriet Martineau's first publication, a series of three articles signed 'Disciplus', the first two of which consider More and Barbauld as leading 'Female Writers on Practical Divinity' (1822), Martineau praises *Practical Piety* and analyses More's *Essay on St Paul*. She also suggests that Protestanism may be the key to the superiority of British women moralists: 'Compare the elevated and noble works of Mrs Hannah More with the qualified morality, the affected feeling, the long-drawn-out sentiments of Madame Genlis; though I believe both to be women of great talents and sincere piety.'[2]

As Mitzi Myers first pointed out in her ground-breaking essay on More, 'Hannah More's Tracts for the Times: Social Fiction and Female Ideology',[3] More's reactionary agenda in the Tracts achieved more than she envisaged, establishing a new style and a readership which created as it castigated an emergent working-class audience. She also wrote a great deal about the situation of women in circumstances too poor or too unremarkable to have attracted much attention in the past. Some of her women have gone to the bad in various ways, but more of them are seen struggling with expanding families or idle husbands or a lack of useful information about household management.

More's prodigious output is represented here by the didactic poem from the *Cheap Repository Tracts* series, 'The Riot; or, Half a Loaf is Better than No Bread' (1795), which is said to have succeeded in stopping a food riot in Bristol; and by her essay 'The White Slave Trade' (1805) in which she influentially represents the subjection of women to fashionable codes of appearance and deportment as an economic oppression analogous to slavery. Both are based on the 1830 collected text. Later on in the anthology, in the section 'Household Words', substantial extracts are given from a little-known but significant tract, *The Cottage Cook*, from January 1797 (more modishly but limitingly retitled 'A Cure for Melancholy' in some collected editions of her works). It was the first in a series of 'Mrs Jones' tracts, *The Sunday School* and the two-part *History of Hester Wilmot*. More's characteristic blend of morality and practicality is often

---

[1] *English Romanticism: The Human Context* (New York: Norton, 1988), 48.
[2] *The Monthly Repository of Theology and General Literature*, 17 (1822), 594.
[3] In Mary Anne Schofield and Cecilia Macheski (eds.), *Fetter'd or Free? British Women Novelists, 1670–1815* (Athens, Oh.: University of Ohio Press, 1986), 264–84.

sampled in works which address the great public issues of the day; here it is deployed in a tale of female domestic economy which presents in miniature many of More's precepts for the role of women in society. As Kathryn Sutherland has argued, 'Mrs Jones literally revolutionises the obscure village of Weston to which she has retired': 'In place of the general public redirection demanded by the radical pamphleteers, [More] sets a limited and particularised social reform based on caring, enduring, and the redemptive power of women's actions.'[4]

~

The Riot; or, Half a Loaf is Better than No Bread.
In a Dialogue between Jack Anvil and Tom Hod
To the Tune of 'A Cobbler there was'
Written in 1795, a Year of Scarcity and Alarm

'Come, neighbours, no longer be patient and quiet,
Come let us go kick up a bit of a riot;
I am hungry, my lads, but I've little to eat,
So we'll pull down the mills and seize all the meat:*
I'll give you good sport, boys, as ever you saw,
So a fig for the justice, a fig for the law.'   *Derry down*

Then his pitchfork Tom seized—'Hold a moment,' says Jack,
'I'll show thee thy blunder, brave boy, in a crack.
And if I don't prove we had better be still,
I'll assist thee straightway to pull down every mill;
I'll show thee how passion thy reason does cheat,
Or I'll join thee in plunder for bread and for meat.   *Derry down*

'What a whimsy to think thus our bellies to fill,
For we stop all the grinding by breaking the mill!
What a whimsy to think we shall get more to eat
By abusing the butchers who get us the meat!
What a whimsy to think we shall mend our spare diet
By breeding disturbance, by murder and riot!   *Derry down*

'Because I am dry, 'twould be foolish, I think,
To pull out my tap and to spill all my drink;

⁴ 'Hannah More's Counter-Revolutionary Feminism', in Kelvin Everest (ed.), *Revolution and Writing: British Literary Responses to the French Revolution* (Milton Keynes: Open University Press, 1991), 39, 38.

Because I am hungry and want to be fed,
That is sure no wise reason for wasting my bread;
And just such wise reasons for mending their diet
Are used by those blockheads who rush into riot.   *Derry down*

'I would not take comfort from others' distresses,
But still I would mark how God our land blesses;
For though in Old England the times are but sad,
Abroad I am told they are ten times as bad;
In the land of the Pope there is scarce any grain,
And 'tis still worse, they say, both in Holland and Spain. *Derry down*

'Let us look to the harvest our wants to beguile,
See the lands with rich crops how they everywhere smile!
Meantime to assist us, by each western breeze,
Some corn is brought daily across the salt seas.
We'll drink little tea, no whisky at all,
But patiently wait and the prices will fall.   *Derry down*

'But if we're not quiet, then let us not wonder
If things grow much worse by our riot and plunder;
And let us remember, whenever we meet,
The more ale we drink, boys, the less we shall eat.
On those days spent in riot, *no* bread you brought home:
Had you spent them in labour, you must have had *some*. *Derry down*

'A dinner of herbs, says the wise man,* with quiet
Is better than beef amid discord and riot.
If the thing can't be helped, I'm a foe to all strife,
And pray for a peace every night of my life;
But in matters of state not an inch will I budge,
Because I conceive I'm no very good judge.   *Derry down*

'But though poor, I can work, my brave boy, with the best,
Let the King and the Parliament manage the rest;
I lament both the war and the taxes together,
Though I verily think they don't alter the weather.
The King, as I take it with very good reason,
May prevent a bad law but can't help a bad season. *Derry down*

'The Parliament-men, although great is their power,
Yet they cannot contrive us a bit of a shower;

And I never yet heard, though our rulers are wise,
That they know very well how to manage the skies;
For the best of them all, as they found to their cost,
Were not able to hinder last winter's hard frost.   *Derry down*

'Besides, I must share in the wants of the times,
Because I have had my full share in its crimes;
And I'm apt to believe the distress which is sent
Is to punish and cure us of all discontent.
But harvest is coming—potatoes will come!
Our prospect clears up. Ye complainers be dumb!   *Derry down*

'And though I've no money and though I've no lands,
I've a head on my shoulders and a pair of good hands;
So I'll work the whole day and on Sundays I'll seek
At church how to bear all the wants of the week.
The gentlefolks too will afford us supplies;
They'll subscribe—and they'll give up their puddings and pies.
                                                        Derry down

'Then before I'm induced to take part in a riot,
I'll ask this short question—What shall I get by it?
So I'll e'en wait a little till cheaper the bread,
For a mittimus hangs o'er each rioter's head;*
And when of two evils I'm asked which is best,
I'd rather be hungry than hanged, I protest.'   *Derry down*

Quoth Tom, 'Thou art right; if I rise, I'm a Turk',*
So he threw down his pitchfork and went to his work.

The White Slave Trade (1805)

Hints towards forming a Bill for the Abolition of the White Female Slave Trade, in the Cities of London and Westminster

Whereas many members of both Houses of Parliament have long been indefatigably labouring to bring in a bill for the amelioration of the condition of slaves in our foreign plantations, as well as for the entire abolition of the trade itself;* and whereas it is presumed that the profound attention of these sage legislators to this great foreign evil prevents their attending to domestic grievances of the same nature; it is, therefore, humbly requested, that whilst these benevolent senators are thus meritoriously exerting themselves for the deliverance of our black brethren, the present writer may be permitted to suggest the following loose hints of a bill for the abolition of slavery at *home*; a slavery the more interesting, as it is to be feared that it may in some few instances be found to involve the wives, daughters, aunts, nieces, cousins, mothers, and grandmothers even of these very zealous abolitionists themselves. . . .

In our West India plantations, the lot of slaves is of all descriptions: here it is uniform. In our islands there are diversities of masters; if some are cruel, others are kind; and the worst are mortal. Here there is one, arbitrary, universal tyrant, and like the Lama of Thibet he never dies. His name is FASHION. Here, indeed, the original subjection is voluntary, but, once engaged, the subsequent servility of the slaves keeps pace with the tyranny of the despot. They hug their chains, and because they are gilt and shining, this prevents them, not from feeling, but from acknowledging that they are heavy. With astonishing fortitude they carry them about, not only without repining, but as their glory and distinction. A few females, indeed, are every where to be found who have manfully resisted the tyrant, but they are people *whom nobody knows*. As the free people are the minority, and as, in this one instance, the minority are peaceable persons, no one envies them an exemption from chains, and their freedom is considered only as a proof of their insignificance.

I propose to take up the question, as was done in the black slave trade, on the two notorious grounds of *inhumanity* and *impolicy*,* and first of the first, as our good old divines say.* Here are great multitudes of beautiful white creatures, forced away annually, like their prototypes in Africa, from all the endearing connections of domestic life, separated from their husbands, dragged from their children, till these last are old enough to be also engaged as slaves in the same labour: nay, in some respects, their condition is worse than that of their African brethren; for, if they are less restricted in the article of food, they are more abridged in that of rest.

It is well known that in some of our foreign plantations, under mild masters, the slaves have, in one instance, more indulgence than the English despot here allows to the white. Some of *them* have at least the Sunday to themselves, in which they may either serve God or attend to their own families. Here, the tyrant allows of no such alleviation. So far from it, his rigour peculiarly assigns the Sabbath for acts of superior fatigue and exertion, such as long journeys, crowded markets, &c. And whereas, in our foreign plantations, slaves too frequently do the work of horses, in the system of domestic slavery horses partake of the labour of the slave without diminishing his sufferings; many hundreds being regularly condemned, after the labours of the day are closed, to transport the slaves to the scene of their nightly labours,* which scene shifts so often, that there is scarcely an interval of rest; so that the poor animals are exposed the greater part of the night to all the rigours of a northern winter.

Again, if the African slaves go nearly naked, their burning clime prevents the want of covering from being one of their greatest hardships: whereas, though the female slaves of London and Westminster were aforetime comfortably clothed, and were allowed by the despot to accommodate their dress to the season, wearing the lightest raiment in the hottest weather, and thick silks trimmed with skins of beasts in cold and frost; now nakedness is of all seasons, and many of the most delicate females are allowed so little clothing as to give pain to the humane beholder.* In the most rigorous seasons, they are so exposed as to endanger their own health, and shock the feelings of others, both on the score of compassion and delicacy.

The younger slaves are condemned to violent bodily labour, from midnight to sunrise. For this public service they are many years preparing by a severe drill under a great variety and succession of posture-masters. . . . Greater compassion, indeed, seems to be shown to the more aged slaves, who are nightly allowed to sit, and do their work at a multitude of tables provided for that purpose. Some of these employments are quiet enough, well suited to weakness and imbecility, and just serve to keep the slaves out of harm's way; but at other tables, the labour of the slave is most severe; and though you cannot perceive their fetters, yet they must undoubtedly be firmly chained to the spot, as appears by their inability to quit it; for by their long continuance in the same attitude one can hardly suppose them to be at liberty.*

But if their bodies labour less than those of the more active slaves, they seem to suffer the severest agitations of mind; their colour often changes, their lips tremble, and their voice falters; and no wonder, for sometimes all they have in the world is at stake, and depends on the next slight motion of the hand. In one respect the comparison between the African and this part of the London slave trade fails: the former, though incompatible with the *spirit* of our laws, yet is not, alas! carried on in direct opposition to the *letter* of them; whereas these tables, at which some of the English slaves are so cruelly exercised, have the cannon of an act of parliament planted directly in their face; and the oddity of the thing is, that the act is not, as in most other cases, made by one set of people and broken by another, but in many instances the law-maker is the law-breaker.*

Many of these elderly female slaves excuse their constant attendance in the public markets, (for it is thought that, at a certain age, they might be emancipated if they wished it,) by asserting the necessity of their attendance, 'till their daughters are disposed of. They are often heard to lament the hardship of this slavery, and to anticipate the final period of their labours; but it is observable, that not only when their daughters, but even their grand-daughters, are taken off their hands, they still continue, from the mere force of habit, and when they are past their labour, to hover about the markets.

A multitude of fine fresh young slaves are annually imported at the age of seventeen or eighteen; or, according to the phrase of the despot, *they come out.** This despot so completely takes them in as to make these lovely young creatures believe that the assigned period at which they lose the gaiety and independence of their former free life is, in fact, the day of their emancipation.

I come now to the question of *impolicy*. This white slavery, like the black, is evidently an injury to fair and lawful commerce, for the time spent in training and overworking these fair slaves might be better employed in promoting the more profitable articles of health, beauty, simplicity, modesty, and industry; articles which many think would fetch a higher price, and by which traffic, both the slave and the slave-owner would be mutually benefitted.

Those who take up this question on this ground maintain also that it does not answer to the slave holders; for that the markets are so glutted that there is less chance of a good bargain, in the best sense of the word, where there are so many competitors, and where there is so little opportunity of discriminating, than if the young slaves were disposed of by private contract; in which the respective value of each individual could be more exactly ascertained.

In the article of policy also, the slaves themselves are not only great losers; youth and beauty, by this promiscuous huddling of slaves together, failing to attract attention; but moreover youth and beauty are so soon impaired by hard labour, foul air, and late hours, that those who are not early disposed of, on the novelty of a first appearance, soon become withered, and are apt to lie a good while upon hands.

One strong argument brought to prove the impolicy of the African slave trade is, that it is a most improvident waste of the human species. What devastation is made in the human frame among our *white* slaves, by working over hours, by loss of sleep, want of clothing, fetid atmospheres, being crammed in the holds of smaller ships without their proper proportion of inches—what havoc, I say, is made by all those, and many other causes, let all the various baths and watering places, to which these poor exhausted slaves are sent every summer to recruit, after the working season is over, declare.

Some candid members, in imitation of Mr Dundas, have hoped for a *gradual abolition*, concluding that if no interference took place, the evil was become so great, it must needs be cured by its very excess; the event, however, has proved so far otherwise, that the grievance is actually grown worse and worse.

And whereas aforetime the slaves were comfortably covered, and were not obliged to labour through the *whole* night, nor to labour *every* night, nor to labour at several places in the *same* night; and whereas, aforetime, the hold in which they were confined was not obliged to receive more slaves than it could contain; it is now a notorious fact, that their clothing is stripped off in the severest weather; that their labours are protracted 'till the morning; and that since the late great increase of trade, three hundred panting slaves are often crammed into an area which cannot conveniently accommodate more than fourscore, to the great damage of the healths and lives of His Majesty's fair and faithful subjects.

From all the above causes it is evident, that the white slave trade has increased, is increasing, and ought to be diminished.*

Till, therefore, there be some hope that a complete abolition may be effected, the following regulations are humbly proposed:—

Regulation 1. That no slave be allowed to spend more than three hours in preparing her chains, beads, and other implements for the nightly labour.

2. That no slave be allowed to paint her person of more than two colours for any market.

3. That each slave be at least allowed sufficient covering for the purposes of decency, if not for those of health and comfort.

4. That no *little* slave be compelled to destroy her shape, and ruin her health, by being fastened to different instruments of torture, for the state of extracting sweet sounds, till some time after she can walk alone: and that in her subsequent progress she be not obliged to sit or stand at it more than half her waking hours.

5. That no slave be put under more than four posture masters, in order to teach her such attitudes and exercises as shall enable her to fetch more money in the markets.

6. That no slave be carried to more than three markets on the same night.

7. That no trader be allowed to press more slaves into one *hold* than three times as many as it will contain.

8. That the same regard to comfort, which has led the black factor to allow the African slaves a ton to a man,* be extended to the white slaves, not allowing them less than one chair to five slaves.

9. That no white slave *driver*, or horses, be allowed to stand in the street more than five hours in a dry night, or four in a rainy one.

10. That every elderly female slave, as soon as her youngest grandchild is fairly disposed of, be permitted to retire from her more public labours, without any fine or loss of character, or any other punishment from the despot.

To conclude:—the BLACK SLAVE TRADE has been taken up by its opposers, not only on the ground of inhumanity and impolicy, but on that of RELIGION also. On the first two points alone have we ventured to examine the question of the WHITE SLAVE TRADE. It would be a folly to enquire into it on this last principle; it *can* admit of no such discussion, as in this view it could not stand its ground for a single moment; for if that principle were allowed to operate, mitigations nearly approaching to abolition must inevitably and immediately take place.

MARY ROBINSON
(1758–1800)

Born Mary Darby, the strikingly beautiful younger daughter of Nicholas Darby, a merchant and the captain of a Bristol whaler, and Hetty Vanacott, Robinson began her education at the school in Bristol kept by Hannah More's sisters. On her father's return from Labrador, where he had set up a whale fishery, the family, their finances depleted, moved to London, where Mary Robinson attended the Chelsea school of Meribah Lorrington, an able woman who encouraged her in her writing. Lorrington's alcoholism prompted Mary's removal first to a school in Battersea and then to Oxford-house, Marylebone, where she made contacts which led to her introduction to the great actor and theatre manager David Garrick, who promoted her career on the stage. In April 1773, aged 14, she was married to an articled clerk, Thomas Robinson, whom her family, wrongly, believed to be wealthy. After her marriage she moved on the margins of fashionable society, frequenting the pleasure gardens of Vauxhall and Ranelagh and finding herself the object of pursuit by various men of fashion, including the infamous rake, Lord Lyttleton. Her only surviving child, Maria Elizabeth, was born in 1774; a second daughter, Sophia, died, aged six weeks, in 1777. In 1775–6 her husband was imprisoned in Fleet Prison for debt for fifteen months, and Robinson shared his imprisonment; the poems which she wrote in these months were published as *Poems* (1775).

After these interruptions she returned to her acting career, helped by Garrick, the actor William Brereton, and the playwright Sheridan, and between 1776 and 1780 she took lead parts in many plays, gaining particular admiration in the so-called 'breeches parts' (such as Viola and Rosalind). It was while playing Perdita in *The Winter's Tale* in 1778 that she attracted the attention of the Prince of Wales, becoming the first of his many mistresses. He was 17, she three years older: the story of his pursuit, though not its end, is told in one of the extracts from her work included here. As she points out, she had long known of her husband's infidelity and promiscuity. The bond for £20,000 which was to be the reward for her compliance was never honoured, and the Prince deserted her within a year for another mistress, Elizabeth Armistead. Robinson spent several months in Paris after their separation, meeting the queen, Marie Antoinette. In 1783 the influence of another reported lover, the Whig leader Charles James Fox, brought her a pension of £500 a year, but it was constantly in arrears. In 1781 she became involved in a longer but intermittently insecure relationship with Colonel Banastre Tarleton, a dashing and celebrated former officer in the Dragoon Guards and a veteran of the American war, with whom she lived in Paris for several years before settling in Brighton. During their long relationship he became an MP for Liverpool, but he was also a gambler and they led a life of extravagance and debt. Tarleton gave her up on securing a marriage to an heiress, the illegitimate daughter of the Duke of Ancaster, in 1798. A long illness, the result of a miscarriage or careless midwifery in her early twenties (probably when she abruptly left her husband to follow Tarleton to France in 1783), resulted in a paralysis of the legs which increasingly crippled her. Laetitia Matilda Hawkins's *Memoirs* include memorable though extremely unsympathetic descriptions of Robinson in the aftermath of her relationship with the Prince, affecting diverting styles of dress for the admiration of the London *ton*, and in the later days of her paralysis. She died impoverished, having been arrested and imprisoned for a debt of £63 a few months before. During the winter before her death in December 1800 she met and befriended Samuel Taylor Coleridge, who gave her a manuscript copy of 'Kubla Khan': she was also an intimate friend of William Godwin (through whom she knew Mary Wollstonecraft and Mary Hays), and of the novelists Jane Porter, Eliza Fenwick, Elizabeth Gunning, and Elizabeth Parsons (all of whom stayed with her in the months before her death at her cottage in Englefield Green, near Windsor). Porter, perhaps the greatest and in many ways the most unlikely of her friends, wrote an unpublished 'Character of the Late Mrs Robinson' (among the manuscripts of the Carl H. Pforzheimer Collection of Shelley and his Circle).

Robinson became a prolific writer, associated with the style of mannered and ornamental sentiment of the Della Cruscan poets. She wrote frequently for the London newspaper the *Morning Post*, which became under the editorship of Daniel Stuart a leading publisher of poetry including works by Wordsworth, Coleridge, and Southey. Judith Pascoe has analysed the importance of 'the peculiar aggregate of newsmaking and personality worship' of the *Morning Post* during the years of Robinson's association with it, and the way it both facilitated and was shaped by Robinson's performative self-presentation.[1] In 1799 she took over from Robert Southey as its poetry editor, and something of a poetry celebrity, the paper keeping readers informed of her state of health and her latest works. She had considerable influence in this capacity. Her poems for the *Morning Post* appeared under a range of pseudonyms—'Laura Maria', 'Oberon', 'Sappho', 'Julia', 'Lesbia', 'Portia', 'Bridget', 'Tabitha

---

[1] Judith Pascoe, 'Mary Robinson and the Literary Marketplace', in Paula R. Feldman and Theresa M. Kelley (eds.), *Romantic Women Writers: Voices and Countervoices* (Hanover, NH: University Press of New England, 1995), 252–68.

Bramble'—and these were used to some extent as distinctive poetic personae. She published several long poems and collections of shorter works, most notably *Poems* (1791), *Lyrical Tales* (1800), and the sequence of forty-four sonnets *Sappho and Phaon* (1796). Her satire on female gamblers, *Nobody*, was performed in 1794 but not published; *The Sicilian Lover: A Tragedy* (1796) was never acted. Her seven novels began with *Vancenza* (1792), which sold out in a day, and included several historical works and tales featuring the wrongs of woman. As 'Anne Frances Randall' she published in 1799 *A Letter to the Women of England, on the Injustice of Mental Subordination. With Anecdotes*. In this tract, Robinson's method is to juxtapose conventional claims about women with stark observations on social custom. Arguing with a freedom which could never be hers when writing as the notorious 'Perdita', she rests her case on stinging rebuke and unexpected connections: 'The most celebrated painters have uniformly represented angels as of no sex. Whether this idea originates in theology, or imagination, I will not pretend to determine; but I will boldly assert that there is something peculiarly unjust in condemning woman to suffer every earthly insult, while she is allowed a sex; and only permitting her to be happy, when she is divested of it.'[2] After Robinson's death her daughter Maria Elizabeth (herself a novelist) collected poems by Robinson and others as *The Wild Wreath* (1804), and published an edition of her mother's poems, arranged by Robinson before her death, in 1806.

In 1791 a review of Robinson's *Poems* in the *Gentleman's Magazine* was 'inclined to apprehend that, had she been less distinguished by her personal graces and accomplishments, by the impression which her beauty and captivating manners have generally made, her poetical taste might have been confined in its influence, and might have excited the complacent approbation of her friends, with little attention, and with less reward, from the public'.[3] Yet Robinson is now increasingly regarded as a central figure in the poetry of the Romantic period. The selection of her poems given here aims to show something of the range of her work, from the social criticism of 'January, 1795' (the text taken from its original appearance in the *Morning Post* on 29 January 1795, signed 'Portia'), via the representation of passion in classical guise in selected sonnets from *Sappho and Phaon*, to the reflective and imaginative 'Ode' to the infant Derwent Coleridge. Of these, the series of 'legitimate' (that is, Petrarchan) sonnets, *Sappho and Phaon*, most clearly engages with issues of women's writing. Robinson presents Sappho's scant extant works as 'the standard for the pathetic, the glowing, and the

[2] Mary Robinson (as 'Anne Frances Randall'), *A Letter to the Women of England, on the Injustice of Mental Subordination* (London: Longman and Rees, 1799), 15.

[3] *Gentleman's Magazine*, 61 (1791), 560.

amatory', her mind as 'so exquisitely tender, so sublimely gifted'.[4] Seen in its own time, Jerome McGann argues, as a work with 'serious and radical philosophical pretensions', *Sappho and Phaon* redefines the woman poet and also replaces Homer with Sappho as 'the paradigm naïve writer of ancient Greece'.[5] Above all, Robinson aligns herself with Sappho, implicitly claiming poetic greatness and a tragic end brought about by a lover's betrayal.

Finally, extracts from the unfinished and posthumously published *Memoirs of the Late Mrs Robinson Written by Herself* emphasize female reflection, self-possession, and victimization, and make a case for the inspiration and imagination of her literary work. They set out to redeem a reputation hopelessly tarnished from the 1780s on, and to redirect attention away from Robinson the fallen beauty and towards Robinson the creative and courageous artist. In dealing with her relationship with the Prince of Wales they have to find an acceptable language of sensibility which exerts a highly revealing pressure on the self-image of the woman writer, and it is interesting that they stop short at this point. In the process Robinson also has a great deal to say, and more to suggest, about the treatment of women as marital possessions, about the sexual double standard, and about the lack of protection afforded to women by a society which supposedly honours them.

~

January, 1795 (1795)

I

Pavement slip'ry; People sneezing;
Lords in ermine, beggars freezing;
Nobles, scarce the Wretched heeding;
Gallant Soldiers—fighting—bleeding!

II

Lofty Mansions, warm and spacious;
Courtiers, cringing and voracious:
Titled Gluttons, dainties carving;
Genius, in a garret, starving!*

---

[4] *Selected Poems*, ed. Judith Pascoe (Peterborough, Ont.: Broadview Press, 2000), 152.
[5] *The Poetics of Sensibility: A Revolution in Literary Style* (Oxford: Oxford University Press, 1996), 95, 100.

III

Wives, who laugh at passive Spouses;
Theatres, and Meeting-houses;
Balls, where simpring Misses languish;
Hospitals, and groans of anguish.

IV

Arts and Sciences bewailing;
Commerce drooping, Credit failing!*
Placemen, mocking subjects loyal;*
Separations; Weddings Royal!*

V

Authors, who can't earn a dinner;
Many a subtle rogue, a winner!
Fugitives, for shelter seeking;
Misers hoarding, Tradesmen breaking!

VI

Ladies gambling, night and morning;
Fools, the works of Genius scorning!
Ancient Dames for Girls mistaken,
Youthful Damsels—quite forsaken!

VII

Some in luxury delighting;
More in talking than in fighting;
Lovers old, and Beaux decrepid;
Lordlings, empty and insipid.

VIII

Poets, Painters, and Musicians;
Lawyers, Doctors, Politicians;
Pamphlets, Newspapers, and Odes,
Seeking Fame, by diff'rent roads.

IX

Taste and Talents quite deserted;
All the laws of Truth perverted;
Arrogance o'er Merit soaring!
Merit, silently deploring!

X

Gallant Souls with empty purses;
Gen'rals, only fit for Nurses!
Schoolboys, smit with Martial spirit,
Taking place of vet'ran merit!

XI

Honest men, who can't get places;
Knaves, who shew unblushing faces;
Ruin hasten'd. Peace retarded!
Candour spurn'd, and Art rewarded!

From *Sappho and Phaon* (1796)

*Sappho Discovers her Passion**

Why, when I gaze on Phaon's beauteous eyes,
    Why does each thought in wild disorder stray?
    Why does each fainting faculty decay,
And my chilled breast in throbbing tumults rise?*
Mute on the ground my lyre neglected lies,
    The muse forgot, and lost the melting lay;
    My downcast looks, my faltering lips betray
That, stung by hopeless passion, Sappho dies!
    Now on a bank of cypress let me rest;
Come, tuneful maids, ye pupils of my care,
    Come, with your dulcet numbers soothe my breast;
And as the soft vibrations float on air,
    Let pity waft my spirit to the blest
To mock the barb'rous triumphs of despair!

Contemns its Power

Oh how can Love exulting Reason quell!
    How fades each nobler passion from his gaze!
    E'en fame, that cherishes the poet's lays,
That fame ill-fated Sappho loved so well.
Lost is the wretch who in his fatal spell
    Wastes the short summer of delicious days,

And from the tranquil path of wisdom strays
In passion's thorny wild, forlorn to dwell.
  Oh ye who in that sacred temple smile
Where holy Innocence resides enshrined,
  Who fear not sorrow and who know not guile,
Each thought composed, and ev'ry wish resigned—
  Tempt not the path where Pleasure's flow'ry wile,
In sweet but pois'nous fetters, holds the mind.

Describes the Characteristics of Love

Is it to love, to fix the tender gaze,
  To hide the timid blush, and steal away?
  To shun the busy world, and waste the day
In some rude mountain's solitary maze?
Is it to chant *one* name in ceaseless lays,
  To hear no words that other tongues can say,
  To watch the pale moon's melancholy ray,
To chide in fondness, and in folly praise?
  Is it to pour th' involuntary sigh,
To dream of bliss, and wake new pangs to prove;
  To talk, in fancy, with the speaking eye,
Then start with jealousy, and wildly rove?
  Is it to loathe the light, and wish to die?
For these I feel, and feel that they are love.

Invokes Reason

Come, Reason, come, each nerve rebellious bind!
  Lull the fierce tempest of my fev'rish soul;
  Come with the magic of thy meek control
And check the wayward wand'rings of my mind!
Estranged from thee, no solace can I find;
  O'er my rapt brain, where pensive visions stole,
  Now passion reigns and stormy tumults roll—
So the smooth sea obeys the furious wind!
  In vain philosophy unfolds his store,
O'erwhelmed is ev'ry source of pure delight;
  Dim is the golden page of wisdom's lore;
All nature fades before my sick'ning sight:

For what bright scene can fancy's eye explore
Midst dreary labyrinths of mental night?

To the Aeolian Harp*

Come, soft Aeolian harp, while zephyr plays
 Along the meek vibration of thy strings,
 As twilight's hand her modest mantle brings,
Blending with sober grey the western blaze!
Oh prompt my Phaon's dreams with tend'rest lays
 Ere night o'ershade thee with its humid wings,
 While the lorn Philomel his sorrow sings
In leafy cradle, red with parting rays!*
 Slow let thy dulcet tones on ether glide,
So steals the murmur of the am'rous dove;
 The mazy legions swarm on ev'ry side,
To lulling sounds the sunny people move!*
 Let not the wise their little world deride—
The smallest sting can wound the breast of love.*

To Phaon

Oh I could toil for thee o'er burning plains,
 Could smile at poverty's disastrous blow,
 With thee could wander midst a world of snow
Where one long night o'er frozen Scythia reigns.*
Severed from thee, my sick'ning soul disdains
 The thrilling thought, the blissful dream to know,
 And canst thou give my days to endless woe,
Requiring sweetest bliss with cureless pains?
 Away, false fear, nor think capricious fate
Would lodge a daemon in a form divine!*
 Sooner the dove shall seek a tiger mate
Or the soft snowdrop round the thistle twine;
 Yet, yet, I dread to hope, nor dare to hate,
Too proud to sue, too tender to resign!

Laments Her Early Misfortunes

Why do I live to loathe the cheerful day,
   To shun the smiles of fame, and mark the hours
   On tardy pinions move, while ceaseless show'rs
Down my wan cheek in lucid currents stray?
My tresses all unbound, nor gems display,
   Nor scents Arabian; on my path no flow'rs
   Imbibe the morn's resuscitating pow'rs,
For one blank sorrow saddens all my way!
   As slow the radiant sun of reason rose,
Through tears my dying parents saw it shine;*
   A brother's frailties swelled the tide of woes,
And, keener far, maternal griefs were mine!*
   Phaon, if soon these weary eyes shall close,
Oh must that task, that mournful task, be thine?

Phaon Forsakes Her

Wild is the foaming sea, the surges roar,
   And nimbly dart the livid lightnings round!
   On the rent rock the angry waves rebound—
Ah me, the less'ning bark is seen no more!
Along the margin of the trembling shore,
   Loud as the blast my frantic cries shall sound,
   My storm-drenched limbs the flinty fragments wound,
And o'er my bleeding breast the billows pour!
   Phaon return! Ye winds, oh waft the strain
To his swift bark! Ye barb'rous waves forbear,
   Taunt not the anguish of a lover's brain,
Nor feebly emulate the soul's despair!
   For howling winds and foaming seas in vain
Assail the breast when passion rages there!

Her Address to the Moon

Oh thou, meek orb that, stealing o'er the dale,
   Cheer'st with thy modest beams the noon of night,
   On the smooth lake diffusing silv'ry light,
Sublimely still and beautifully pale!

What can thy cool and placid eye avail
    Where fierce despair absorbs the mental sight,
    While inbred glooms the vagrant thoughts invite
To tempt the gulf where howling fiends assail?
    Oh night, all nature owns thy tempered pow'r;
Thy solemn pause, thy dews, thy pensive beam;
    Thy sweet breath whisp'ring in the moonlight bow'r,
While fainting flowrets kiss the wand'ring stream!
    Yet vain is ev'ry charm, and vain the hour,
That brings to madd'ning love no soothing dream!

Her Reflections on the Leucadian Rock Before She Perishes*

While from the dizzy precipice I gaze,
    The world receding from my pensive eyes,
    High o'er my head the tyrant eagle flies,
Clothed in the sinking sun's transcendent blaze!
The meek-eyed moon midst clouds of amber plays
    As o'er the purpling plains of light she hies,
    Till the last stream of living lustre dies
And the cool concave owns her tempered rays!*
    So shall this glowing, palpitating soul
Welcome returning Reason's placid beam,
    While o'er my breast the waves Lethean roll*
To calm rebellious Fancy's fev'rish dream;
    Then shall my lyre disdain love's dread control,
And loftier passions prompt the loftier theme!

From *Memoirs of the Late Mrs Robinson Written by Herself* (1801)

I had then been married more than four years, my daughter Maria
Elizabeth nearly three years old. I had been then seen and known
at all public places from the age of fifteen; yet I knew as little of the
world's deceptions as though I had been educated in the deserts of
Siberia. I believed every woman friendly, every man sincere, till I
discovered proofs that their characters were deceptive.

I had now performed two seasons, in tragedy and comedy, with Miss Farren and the late Mr Henderson.* My first appearance in Palmira (in Mahomet) was with the Zaphna of Mr J. Bannister,* the preceding year; and, though the extraordinary comic powers of this excellent actor and amiable man have established his reputation as a comedian, his first essay in tragedy was considered as a night of the most distinguished promise. The Duchess of Devonshire still honoured me with her patronage and friendship,* and I also possessed the esteem of several respectable and distinguished females.

The play of *The Winter's Tale* was this season commanded by their Majesties.* I never had performed before the royal family; and the first character in which I was destined to appear was that of Perdita. I had frequently played the part, both with the Hermione of Mrs Hartley* and of Miss Farren: but I felt a strange degree of alarm when I found my name announced to perform it before the royal family.

In the green-room I was rallied on the occasion; and Mr Smith,* whose gentlemanly manners and enlightened conversation rendered him an ornament to the profession, who performed the part of Leontes, laughingly exclaimed, 'By Jove, Mrs Robinson, you will make a conquest of the Prince; for to-night you look handsomer than ever.' I smiled at the unmerited compliment, and little foresaw the vast variety of events that would arise from that night's exhibition!

As I stood in the wing opposite the Prince's box, waiting to go on the stage, Mr Ford, the manager's son, and now a respectable defender of the laws, presented a friend who accompanied him; this friend was Lord Viscount Malden, now Earl of Essex.*

We entered into conversation during a few minutes, the Prince of Wales all the time observing us, and frequently speaking to Colonel (now *General*) Lake, and to the Honourable Mr Legge, brother to Lord Lewisham,* who was in waiting on his Royal Highness. I hurried through the first scene, not without much embarrassment, owing to the fixed attention with which the Prince of Wales honoured me. Indeed, some flattering remarks which were made by his Royal Highness met my ear as I stood near his box, and I was overwhelmed with confusion.

The Prince's particular attention was observed by every one, and I was again rallied at the end of the play. On the last curtsy, the royal family condescendingly returned a bow to the performers; but just as the curtain was falling, my eyes met those of the Prince of Wales;

and with a look that I *never shall forget*, he gently inclined his head a second time; I felt the compliment, and blushed my gratitude.

During the entertainment Lord Malden never ceased conversing with me! He was young, pleasing, and perfectly accomplished. He remarked the particular applause which the Prince had bestowed on my performance; said a thousand civil things; and detained me in conversation till the evening's performance was concluded.

I was now going to my chair,* which waited, when I met the royal family crossing the stage. I was again honoured with a very marked and low bow from the Prince of Wales. On my return home, I had a party to supper; and the whole conversation centred in encomiums on the person, graces, and amiable manners of the illustrious Heir-apparent.

Within two or three days of this time, Lord Malden made me a morning visit. Mr Robinson was not at home, and I received him rather awkwardly. But his lordship's embarrassment far exceeded mine. He attempted to speak—paused, hesitated, apologised; I knew not why. He hoped I would pardon him; that I would not mention something he had to communicate: that I would consider the peculiar delicacy of his situation, and then act as I thought proper. I could not comprehend his meaning, and therefore requested that he would be explicit.

After some moments of evident rumination, he tremblingly drew a small letter from his pocket. I took it, and knew not what to say. It was addressed to PERDITA. I smiled, I believe rather sarcastically, and opened the *billet*. It contained only a few words, but those expressive of more than common civility; they were signed FLORIZEL.*

'Well, my lord, and what does this mean?' said I, half angry.

'Can you not guess the writer?' said Lord Malden.

'Perhaps yourself, my lord,' cried I, gravely.

'Upon my honour, no,' said the Viscount. 'I should not have dared so to address you on so short an acquaintance.'

I pressed him to tell me from whom the letter came. He again hesitated; he seemed confused, and sorry that he had undertaken to deliver it.

'I hope that I shall not forfeit your good opinion,' said he; 'but——'

'But what, my lord?'

'I could not refuse—for the letter is from the Prince of Wales.'

I was astonished; I confess that I was agitated; but I was also somewhat sceptical as to the truth of Lord Malden's assertion. I returned a formal and a doubtful answer, and his lordship shortly after took his leave.

A thousand times did I read this short but expressive letter. Still I did not implicitly believe that it was written by the Prince; I rather considered it as an experiment made by Lord Malden, either on my vanity or propriety of conduct. On the next evening the Viscount repeated his visit. We had a card-party of six or seven, and the Prince of Wales was again the subject of unbounded panegyric. Lord Malden spoke of his Royal Highness's manners as the most polished and fascinating; of his temper as the most engaging; and of his mind, the most replete with every amiable sentiment. I heard these praises, and my heart beat with conscious pride, while memory turned to the partial but delicately respectful letter which I had received on the preceding morning. . . .

However flattering it might have been to female vanity to know that the most admired and most accomplished Prince in Europe was devotedly attached to me; however dangerous to the heart such idolatry as his Royal Highness, during many months, professed in almost daily letters, which were conveyed to me by Lord Malden, still I declined any interview with his Royal Highness. I was not insensible to all his powers of attraction; I thought him one of the most amiable of men. There was a beautiful ingenuousness in his language, a warm and enthusiastic adoration, expressed in every letter, which interested and charmed me. During the whole spring, till the theatre closed, this correspondence continued, every day giving me some new assurance of inviolable affection.

After we had corresponded some months without ever speaking to each other (for I still declined meeting his Royal Highness, from a dread of the *éclat* which such a connection would produce, and the fear of injuring him in the opinion of his royal relatives), I received, through the hands of Lord Malden, the Prince's portrait in miniature, painted by the late Mr Meyer.* This picture is now in my possession. Within the case was a small heart cut in paper, which I also have; on one side was written, *Je ne change qu'en mourant.** On the other, *Unalterable to my Perdita through life*.

During many months of confidential correspondence, I always offered his Royal Highness the best advice in my power; I disclaimed every sordid and interested thought; I recommended him to be patient till he should become his own master; to wait till he knew more of my mind and manners, before he engaged in a public attachment to me; and, above all, to do nothing that might incur the displeasure of his Royal Highness's family. I entreated him to recollect that he was young, and led on by the impetuosity of passion; that should I consent to quit my profession and my husband, I should be thrown entirely on his mercy. I strongly pictured the temptations to which beauty would expose him; the many arts that would be practised to undermine me in his affections; the public abuse which calumny and envy would heap upon me; and the misery I should suffer, if, after I had given him every proof of confidence, he should change in his sentiments towards me. To all this I received repeated assurances of inviolable affection; and I most firmly believe that his Royal Highness meant what he professed—indeed, his soul was too ingenuous, his mind too liberal, and his heart too susceptible, to deceive premeditatedly, or to harbour even for a moment the idea of deliberate deception.

At every interview with Lord Malden I perceived that he regretted the task he had undertaken; but he assured me that the Prince was almost frantic whenever he suggested a wish to decline interfering. Once I remember his lordship's telling me that the late Duke of Cumberland had made him a visit early in the morning, at his house in Clarges Street, informing him that the Prince was most wretched on my account, and imploring him to continue his services only a short time longer. The Prince's establishment was then in agitation: at this period his Royal Highness still resided in Buckingham House.*

A proposal was now made that I should meet his Royal Highness at his apartments, in the disguise of male attire. I was accustomed to perform in that dress, and the Prince had seen me, I believe, in the character of the Irish Widow.* To this plan I decidedly objected. The indelicacy of such a step, as well as the danger of detection, made me shrink from the proposal. My refusal threw his Royal Highness into the most distressing agitation, as was expressed by the letter which I received on the following morning. Lord Malden again lamented that he had engaged himself in the intercourse, and declared that he had himself conceived so violent a passion for me that he was the most miserable and unfortunate of mortals.

During this period, though Mr Robinson was a stranger to my

epistolary intercourse with the Prince, his conduct was entirely neg-lectful. He was perfectly careless respecting my fame and my repose; passed his leisure hours with the most abandoned women, and even my own servants complained of his illicit advances. I remember one, who was plain even to ugliness; she was short, ill-made, squalid, and dirty; once, on my return from a rehearsal, I found that this woman was locked with my husband in my chamber. I also knew that Mr. Robinson continued his connection with a female who lodged in Maiden Lane,* and who was only one of the few that proved his domestic apostacy.

His indifference naturally produced an alienation of esteem on my side, and the increasing adoration of the most enchanting of mortals hourly reconciled my mind to the idea of a separation. The unbounded assurances of lasting affection which I received from his Royal Highness in many scores of the most eloquent letters, the contempt which I experienced from my husband, and the perpetual labour which I underwent for his support, at length began to weary my fortitude. Still I was reluctant to become the theme of public animadversion, and still I remonstrated with my husband on the unkindness of his conduct.

[End of Robinson's narrative]

ANN YEARSLEY
(1753–1806)

Born into a farm-labouring family in Clifton, Bristol, the daughter of John Cromarty and his wife Ann, a milkwoman, Ann Yearsley had no formal education, but was taught to read by her mother and to write by her brother, and developed a taste for reading and in particular for the poetry of Milton, Young, and Pope. She married John Yearsley, a local man who seems to have been slightly her social superior, at 21 and had six children in the next ten years. The reasons for the family's economic decline are not clear, but the Yearsleys were in want by 1783. The poverty of the family and the literary interests of Yearsley were brought to the attention of Hannah More by her cook, and More encouraged and helped Yearsley, and successfully sought subscribers to a volume of her poems, published as *Poems on Several Occasions* in 1785. Addressing the leading

Bluestocking Elizabeth Montagu in the Prefatory Letter to this collection of Yearsley's 'wild wood notes', More describes them, like the work of 'all unlettered Poets, abounding in imagery, metaphor, and personification; her faults, in this respect, being rather those of superfluity than of want'. The two fell out over More's handling of the profits (more than £600), which she placed in the funds with herself and Elizabeth Montagu as trustees. Yearsley used the prefaces to later editions of this work, and to subsequent publications, including *Poems on Various Subjects and Other Pieces* (1787), to complain of More's behaviour. Addressing her subscribers directly and appending a copy of the Deed of Trust by which More had appropriated her money, Yearsley testified that More had called her 'a savage' and had burned the manuscripts of her poems. By this time she had won the patronage of Frederick Augustus Hervey, Bishop of Derry and Earl of Bristol, to whom she dedicated *A Poem on the Inhumanity of the Slave Trade* in 1788. Her attempts to continue a literary career were only intermittently successful, however. In January 1793 she set up as proprietor of a circulating library at the Clifton Hotwells, but gave it up, possibly because of ill health, in 1797; had a historical tragedy, *Earl Goodwin*, performed in Bath and Bristol in 1789 and printed in 1791; published a historical novel, *The Royal Captives: A Fragment of Secret History* (1795); wrote substantial poems on Louis XVI (1793) and Marie Antoinette (1795), and a collection of verse, *The Rural Lyre* (1796). In 1789–90 a public feud with a rich lawyer and former mayor of Bristol, Levi Eames, whose servant had whipped two of her sons for trespass, spilled out into verse, further embroiling her in controversy. After the death of her husband in 1803 she moved to Melksham in Wiltshire to be near her only surviving son, John, and lived probably with one or more of her daughters for the remaining few years of her life. She was buried in Clifton churchyard.

Yearsley was patronized as an uneducated poet, a supposedly natural prodigy, but her creation of a poetic role for herself as 'Lactilla' makes plain her interest in classical and pastoral models and left her vulnerable to charges of risible pretension. A writer with impeccable classicist credentials might have made 'Lactilla' a faux-naïve questioning of the fanciful clumsiness of pastoral soubriquets, and the milkwoman of Clifton a mirror held to the shepherdess of the Petit Trianon; but Yearsley is interesting partly because she muddies boundaries, and because she seems at once to shun and to court individualism. Recent critics have warned against preoccupation with natural genius, pointing out, as Mary Waldron does, Yearsley's use of poetic models and her lack of interest in traditionally popular forms such as folk poetry and ballad.[1] Her writings champion the rights of those

---

[1] *Lactilla, Milkwoman of Clifton: The Life and Writings of Ann Yearsley, 1753–1806* (Athens, Ga.: University of Georgia Press, 1996), 116.

deemed insignificant in the social system: she frequently foregrounds her own limitations as a speaker in order to emphasize that opinions and feelings are to be found in the traditionally illiterate and inarticulate.

She is represented in this collection by two poems from the *Rural Lyre* collection. 'The Captive Linnet' encapsulates Yearsley's combination of libertarian themes and classical dressing, and suggests how difficult it could be to categorize her: is she the linnet, captive and victimized, or the friend of Mycias, an ambivalent figure who could be a fellow liberator but who is just as likely to have been the cause of the linnet's plight? More experimental and surprising, 'Soliloquy' moves from the incidental domesticity of its immediate setting through a nervous improvisation to the more settled sonorities of the poised close for which Yearsley characteristically strives: of mainstream Romantic poems, Coleridge's (later) 'Frost at Midnight' seems closest, but the reflective moment in both is indebted to Cowper; and Yearsley's meditation arises from a brief, but still recognizable, family exchange.

~

The Captive Linnet (1796)

Mycias, behold this bird! see how she tires—
Breaks her soft plumes, and springs against the wires!
A clown more rude than gracious brought her here
To pine in silence, and to die in snare.
Her haunt she well remembers: ev'ry morn
Her sweet note warbled from the blowing thorn
That hangs o'er yon cool wave; responses clear
Her sisters gave, and sprang through upper air.
E'en now (by habit gentler made), at eve,
A time when men their green dominions leave,
They sit, and call her near her fav'rite spray,
Meet no reply, and pensive wing their way.
This wound in friendship dear affections heal,
Their young require them: to their nests they steal;
Nurse them with warmth, with hope, with true delight,
And teach the danger of an early flight,—
Delicious toil! raptures that never cloy!
A mother only can define her joy.

Perhaps, dear Mycias, this poor mourner's breast
Was yesternight on her weak offspring prest!—

The down scarce breaking on their tender skin,
Their eyes yet clos'd, their bodies cold and thin;
Waiting when she would kindly warmth impart,
And take them trembling to her gen'rous heart.
Where are they now, sweet captive? Who'll befriend
Thy mourning children, as the storms descend?
The winds are bleak, thy mossy cradle's torn—
Hark! they lament thee, hungry and forlorn!
Each shiv'ring brother round his sister creeps,
Deep in the nest thy little daughter sleeps.
Again the blast, that tears the oak, comes on:
Thy rocking house, thy family are gone!
One to an hungry weasel falls a prey;
Another chirps, but not to hail the day:
Too weak to live, he seeks no casual aid,
And dies, rememb'ring thee, beneath the shade.
Where could thy daughter go? More weak and shrill
Her voice was heard. The ants forsake their hill.—
Through that republic Addison display'd,*
When he unsated hunger virtue made,
And gave, unwisely, ant-like souls to man—
The barb'rous rumour of misfortune ran.
Alike pourtray'd in hist'ry and in verse,
For prey industrious, obdurate and fierce:
Voracious columns move! The victim's voice
Invites her foes, who sting her, and rejoice.
Keenly their riots on her frame begin:
She tries to shake them from her downy skin;
Their organs touch her springs of being—Strife
She holds not with her fate—she trembles out of life.

O Mycias! What hath yon barbarian gain'd,
Who with malicious joy this linnet chain'd?
Could she at morn salute his untun'd ear?
When dull with vice could she the gaoler cheer;
Hail him with strains of liberty; proclaim,
With harmony he hates, her maker's name:
Or peck from him the crumb withheld so long,
That her heart sicken'd e'en at freedom's song?

No: see, she droops, rejects his aid—confin'd—
Her dreary cage she scorns, and dies resign'd.

Mycias! thus spreads unseen more ling'ring woe,
Than e'en thy sympathising soul must know:
Wisely ordain'd! He mocks the proffer'd cure,
Who bids his friend one fruitless pang endure:
Since pity turns to anguish, when denied,
And troubles swell, which must in death subside.
Ah! fly the scene; secure that guilt can find
In brutal force no fetter for the mind!
True! Violated thus, it feels the chain,
Rises with languor, and lies down with pain;
Yet bless'd in trembling to one mighty WHOLE,
DEATH is the field of VICTORY for the SOUL.

Soliloquy (1796)

*Begun from the circumstance of the moment, and prolonged as the images of
memory arose in the mind of the author, February 27, 1795*

Author to her son. Go you to bed, my boy.

Son. Do you write to-night?

Author. I do.

Son (laying his watch on the table). See, how late!

Author. No matter—You can sleep.

How patiently toils on this little watch!
My veins beat to its motion. Ye who sing
Of atoms, rest, and motion,[1] say, why Time
Sets in this toy a larum to my heart.*
O sacred Time! thy moment goes not down
But I go with it! Sixty coming hours
Are with us poor expectants of more price
Than sixty years sunk to oblivion. Rise,
Dear Memory, silent fascinating pow'r,
Hated by many: I will be thy slave,

---

[1] Mechanical philosophy is that which undertakes to account for the phenomena of
nature from the principles of mechanics, taking in the consideration of motion, rest,
figure, size, &c. This is also called the corpuscular philosophy.*

Thy willing slave. Then lead thy shadows round,
Forever sacred to my pensive mind.

Instructive Spirit, hail! For thee I call
Mild Contemplation, from the barren rock
Where mourns the ship-wreck'd mariner, to trim
My midnight lamp. Hail, much rever'd in death!
Thou knew'st to chart the moral world, and bend
The springs of thought to wisdom: thou wert wont
In life to smile, when wilder than the bard
On Cambria's height I struck the lyre:* my sigh,
Made harsh and inharmonious by despair,
Thou taught'st to break with melody. This hour,
Led on by Contemplation, I behold
Thine eyes that beam'd benevolence, thy heart
Once rich with fine regard. Ah me! that heart
'Mid this inhospitable scene was mine!

Couldst thou declare how long the storms of fate
Shall beat around me, when I may repose,
Or be as thou art! I have read the code
Of statutes form'd by man for future worlds;
And found his plan, so pompously display'd,
One lot of heterogeneous fragment. Man
Adores in fancy, violates in fact,
Laws serving his frail being. Yon pale moon
Forsakes the mountain top, to bring us round
Her renovated splendour; nature works
Obedient and unseen forever: we
May meet in spheres remote—If not, farewel!
I feel and know, those wishes can arise
But from affections growing with my life,
Mingling with hope, oppress'd by fear. The change
Fulfill'd in thee may chill me; ev'ry thought
Oblit'rate; vision, fancy forms, be doom'd
To sink, like beaming glory in the west;
Whilst space contracts on my weak eye, and heav'ns,
By human artists coloured, fade away,
As life goes gently from my beating heart.

Grant this could be—the import were no more
Than as an atom 'mid the vast profound
Impell'd, not swerving from the whole. Suppose,
This frame dissolving, to the busy winds
My ashes fled dividing: shall I know
To mourn?—How like my brethren I display
Conjecture without end!—Impatient pow'r
Of thought! where wouldst thou fly? Return, return!
Nor lose thy strength in phrensy, nor resign
The form I love.—This watch is down! Ye points,
Attun'd to motion by the art of man,
As tell-tales of his doings, can ye mark
Eternity by measur'd remnants? No.—
Fallacious in your working, ye would say,
With us, the life of man is but a day.

ELIZABETH HAMILTON
(1758–1816)

Born in Belfast, the youngest of the three children of the Scottish merchant Charles Hamilton and his Irish wife Katherine Mackay, Elizabeth
Hamilton was brought up by her paternal aunt and uncle on their farm in
Stirlingshire after her father's death in 1759: her elder sister and brother
remained with their mother in Belfast, and Hamilton saw her mother only
a few times before she died in 1767. She gives details of her early life with
her Presbyterian aunt and Episcopalian uncle, and her education, in a
'Biographical Fragment' included in Elizabeth Benger's 1818 *Memoirs of
the Late Mrs Elizabeth Hamilton*. Between 1766 and 1769 she was well but
not classically educated at a mixed boarding-school in Stirling, where she
seems to have been both studious and spirited. She also took lessons in
Edinburgh in 1769 from Dr Moyse, a lecturer on experimental philosophy. In the 'Preliminary Dissertation' to the work sampled here, *Letters
of a Hindoo Rajah*, she comments on 'that narrow and contracted path'
commonly 'allotted to the female mind', recalling: 'From her earliest
instructors, she imbibed the idea that toward a strict performance of the
several duties of life, Ignorance was neither a necessary, nor an useful
auxiliary, but on the contrary, that she ought to view every new idea as an
acquisition, and to seize, with avidity, every proper opportunity for
making the acquirement' (pp. lvii, lviii).

On the departure of her idolized soldier brother Charles (1753–92) for a fourteen-year tour of duty in India in 1772 she established a correspondence with him which educated her in his growing orientalist interests and scholarship. When he returned in 1786 he translated and edited *An Historical Relation of the Origin, Progress, and Final Dissolution of the Rohilla Afghans in the Northern Provinces of Hindostan: Compiled from a Persian Manuscript and Other Original Papers* (1787) and Hamilton helped him with research for his four-volume translation of one of the two chief commentaries on Muslim law, *The Hedaya, or Guide: A Commentary on the Mussulman Laws* (1791). When her uncle died in 1788 she spent about two years living with Charles and with her elder sister in London, where she found 'opportunities for instruction, of a nature still more pleasing' than the books which had been the main resource of her life in the country (p. lviii). Through Charles she met other members of the London Asiatic Society, and her intellectual circle included leading Orientalists of the day. Both she and Charles were supporters of the impeached (and eventually acquitted) former Governor-General of Bengal, Warren Hastings, and she used her works, especially *Letters of a Hindoo Rajah* (which was dedicated to him), to make this support public.

The death of Charles Hamilton from typhus in March 1792 was a defining event for her, one which 'transformed the cheerful haunt of domestic happiness into the gloomy abode of sorrow, and changed the energy of Hope into the listlessness of despondency' ('Preliminary Dissertation', p. lix). Continuing his orientalist scholarship, she published the anti-Jacobin *Translation of the Letters of a Hindoo Rajah; Written Previous to, and During the Period of his Residence in England. To which is prefixed a Preliminary Dissertation on the History, Religion, and Manners, of the Hindoos* (2 vols., London: G. G. and J. Robinson) in 1796, which went into five editions by 1811 and was well received critically. Another satirical novel, *Memoirs of Modern Philosophers*, (which includes, in the central character of Bridgetina Botherim, a portrait of Mary Hays) followed in 1800; then a range of historical, educational, and theoretical works. In 1796 Hamilton and her widowed sister had settled in Bath, but from 1804 they lived in Edinburgh, supported by a government pension in recognition of her literary work and of her 'promulgation of religious sentiment', awarded in 1804; and her best-known work, the novel *The Cottagers of Glenburnie* (1808), is the product of her desire to improve the welfare of the Scottish working classes. Hamilton was involved in the establishment of the Female House of Industry in Edinburgh, for which she wrote in 1809 *Exercises in Religious Knowledge; for the Instruction of Young Persons*. In poor health, and suffering from eye disease and gout, she travelled south, dying in Harrogate, where, in token of the high esteem in which she was held in her own time, there is a monument to her memory. Joanna Baillie and Maria Edgeworth were friends and admirers (Hamilton, despite illness, visited Edgeworth in Edgeworthstown during a three-month visit to Ireland in 1813, and Edgeworth wrote an essay on the 'Character and Writings of Mrs Elizabeth Hamilton' for the *Gentleman's Magazine* in 1816: Edgeworth's letters to her have not survived).

Letters of a Hindoo Rajah—Hamilton's 'black baby', as she called it—is in the tradition of the satirical 'oriental' letter associated with Montesquieu (*Lettres persanes*) and Goldsmith, and an innovative extension of the oriental tale. Like works criticizing British society of the 1790s, such as Robert Bage's *Hermsprong*, it assumes the perspective of a non-European looking for the first time at a society to which he expects to aspire: Jane Taylor (see below), was also interested in this device. Hamilton's work is distinguished from many other oriental tales first of all by its unabashed and detailed orientalist scholarship. In her contextualizing 'Preliminary Dissertation' on Hindu history, religion, and manners, Hamilton takes up her brother's anthropological interests, and explicitly addresses the problem that these are presumptious acquisitions for a feminine mind. In defending herself against this charge Hamilton grounds her work in hearth and home; but she makes it clear that in this hearth and home lurk, too commonly unseen, female intellectual and social interests which make scholarship a suitable resolution for the pain of loss. The striking and important feature of the 'Preliminary Dissertation' is its emphasis on the stability of Indian institutions, the caste system and the structures of Hindu belief, arguing for a complex coherence in a society frequently dismissed as chaotic. This offering of India is of great significance historically, and can also be seen as offering an alternative feminized order to the masculine traditions of India's colonizers.

In the *Letters* themselves, Zāārmilla, Rajah of Almora, confides in his friend Kisheen Neêay Māāndāāra his delight in the conversation of his English friend Captain Percy (a character based on Charles Hamilton), and his desire to visit the wonderful land of justice and order Percy describes. The account of British parliamentary and social organization is highly ironic, and doubts begin to enter the mind of the Rajah himself as he enters into some of the social gatherings of the British in India. He is especially taken aback by the behaviour of the British women. Hamilton refers in the 'Preliminary Dissertation' to the 'narrow and contracted path' which tradition has 'allotted to the female mind' (p. lvii). The Rajah sees little to suggest that they have any minds at all.

∽

From *Translation of the Letters of a Hindoo Rajah* (1796)

Thou knowest, O Māāndāāra, how my mind has ever thirsted after knowledge.* Thou knowest with what ardour I have ever performed my *Poojab Seraswatee*,[1] and that, at an age when few young men have read the Beids of the Shaster,[2] I had not only studied the sacred pages, but had perused every famous writing in the Shanscrit language.

The acquisition of the Persic tongue opened to me a door of knowledge which I was not slow to enter. History, for some time, became my favourite study. But what did the history of states and empires present to my view? Alas! what, but the weakness and the guilt of mankind? I beheld the few, whom fortune had unhappily placed in view of the giddy eminences of life, putting the reins of ambition into the bloody hand of cruelty, lash through torrents of perfidy and slaughter, till, perhaps, overthrown in their career, they were trampled on by others who were running the same guilty race: or if they survived to reach the goal they aimed at, living but to breathe the air of disappointment, and then drop into the sea of oblivion. Such is the history of the few whose guilty passions, and atrocious deeds have raised them to *renown*, and to whom the stupid multitude, the willing instruments of their ambition, the prey of their avarice, and the sport of their pride, have given the appellation of *heroes*.

To the great body of the people I never could perceive that it made any difference who it was that held the scorpion whip of oppression, as into whatever hand it was by them conveyed, they were equally certain of feeling the severity of its sting. Meditating on these things, the deep sigh of despondency has burst from my heart. Can it be, said I to myself, that the omnipotent and eternal Ruler of the universe should create such multitudes for no other purpose but to swell the triumphs of a fellow mortal, whose glory rises in proportion to the misery he inflicts upon the human race? Surely, by what I learn from the actions of the princes of the earth, virtue is a shadow, and the love of it, which I have heretofore cherished in my breast, is nothing but the illusive phantom of a dream!

By conversing with my English guest I got a different view of human nature. Through the medium of the Persic literature it

---

[1] Worship to Seraswatee, the Goddess of Letters.   [2] Scripture of the Hindoos.

appeared universally darkened by depravity. In the history of Europe
it assumed a milder form. In Europe man has not always, as in Asia,
been degraded by slavery, or corrupted by the possession of despotic
power. Whole nations have *there* acknowledged the rights of human
nature, and while they did so have attained to the summit of true
glory. The Romans, whom the Persian writers represent as the
lawless invaders, and fearless conquerors of the world;* and the
Greeks, whom they load with every opprobrium, were in fact
nations of heroes. Spurning the chain of slavery, they wisely
thought that human nature was too imperfect to be entrusted with
unlimited authority; while they performed Poojah to the Goddess
of Liberty,* their hearts were enlarged by the possession of every
virtue. She taught them the art of victory; strengthened their
nerves in the day of battle; and, when they returned from the field
of conquest, she gave sweetness to the banquets of simplicity, and
rendered poverty honourable by her smiles. At length, Wealth
and Luxury, the enemies of the Goddess, entered their dominions,
and enticed the people from the worship of Liberty; who, offended
by their infidelity, entirely forsook their country, making Happiness
and Virtue the companions of her flight. On a re-examination of
the conduct of these illustrious heroes, who, while their nation
performed Poojah to Liberty, had gained the summit of fame;
Percy pointed out to my view many imperfections, which while my
breast was enflamed by the first ardour of admiration, had escaped
my notice. The love of Liberty itself, that glorious plant as he
called it, which is properly cultivated never fails to produce the
fruits of virtue, sprung not (he said) in the Grecian, or the Roman
breast, from the pure soil of universal benevolence, but from the
rank roots of pride and selfishness. It never therefore extended to
embrace the human race. This perfection of virtue was unknown
in the world, till taught by the religion of Christ. This last assertion
of Percy's, appeared to me as a prejudice unfounded in truth. But
such are ever the hasty conclusions of ignorance. I had been taught to
believe that the pure doctrine of benevolence, and mercy, was
unknown to all but the favoured race of Brahma, that the Christian
faith like that of the Mussulmans,* was a narrow system of superstitious adherence to the wildest prejudices, engendering hatred, and
encouraging merciless persecution against all who differed from
them. Nothing can be more erroneous than this idea of Christianity.

By the indulgence of my English friend I was favoured with the perusal of the Christian Shaster.[3] The precepts it contains, are simple, pure, and powerful, all addressed to the heart; and calculated for restoring the universal peace and happiness which has been banished from the earth, since the days of the Sottee Jogue.[4]

The love of liberty in a people who are taught by the fundamental precepts of their Shaster, 'to do to others as they would have others do to them,' rises above the narrow spirit of selfishness, and extendeth to embrace the human race! Benevolent people of England! it is their desire, that all should be partakers of the same blessings of liberty, which they themselves enjoy. It was doubtless with this glorious view, that they sent forth colonies to enlighten, and instruct, the vast regions of America. To disseminate the love of virtue and freedom, they cultivated the trans-Atlantic isles: and to rescue *our* nation from the hands of the oppressor, did this brave, and generous people visit the shores of Hindostan!*

You may imagine how desirous I was to become acquainted with some particulars concerning the form of government, laws, and manners, of this highly favoured nation. Provided the above particulars are *true*, it is of course to expect, that they must all be formed after the model of perfection; and such, according to my conception of the accounts of Percy, they undoubtedly are.

It having pleased Brahma to create them all of one cast, among them are no distinctions, but such as are the reward of virtue. It is not there as in the profligate court of Delhi,* where great riches, a supple adherence to the minister, and a base and venal approbation of the measures of the court can lead to titles and distinction. No. In England, the honours of nobility are invariably bestowed according to intrinsic merit. The titles and privileges of these heroes of the first class, descend to their children. We may well suppose what care is bestowed on the education of these young nobles, whose minds are moulded into wisdom, at Universities instituted for the purpose.

---

[3] Scriptures.

[4] The age of purity. The Hindoos reckon the duration of the world by four Jogues, or distinct ages. The Sottee Jogue, or age of purity, is said to have lasted 3,200,000 years, when the life of man is said to have extended to 100,000 years. The Tirtah Jogue, or age in which one third of mankind were reprobate, which consisted of 2,400,000 years. The Dwaper Jogue, in which one half of the human race became depraved, endured 1,600,000 years. And the Collee Jogue, in which all mankind are corrupted, is the present era. See Halhed's Gentoo Laws.*

Where vice and folly are *alike* unknown: and where the faculties of a young man, might have as *great* a chance, of getting leave to rust in ignorance, as to be lost in dissipation! From these seminaries of virtue, they are called to the Senate of the nation; where they debate with all the gravity, and the interest, that might be expected from their early habits of serious thought, and deep investigation. The sons of the King, at an early age, take their seats in that tribunal, from whose decision there lies no appeal.* As their example is supposed to animate the young Nobility, it may well be imagined how wise, learned, grave, and pious, these princely youths must be: their actions are doubtless the mirrors of decorum, and their lips the gates of wisdom!

The equality of human beings in the sight of God, being taught by their religion, it is a fundamental maxim of their policy, that no laws are binding, which do not obtain the consent of the people. All laws are therefore issued by the sanction of their representatives; every separate district, town, and community, choosing from among themselves, the persons most distinguished for *piety*, *wisdom*, *learning*, and *integrity*, impart to them the power of acting in the name of the whole.*

About four hundred of these eminent men, each of whom to all the requisites of a Hindoo magistrate,[5] unites the knowledge of a Christian philosopher, form what is termed the third estate.*

Uninfluenced by the favour of party, uncontaminated by the base motives of avarice or ambition, they pursue with steady steps the path of equity, and have nothing so much at heart as the public welfare. No war can be engaged in, and no taxes imposed, but by the consent of these patriot chiefs. Judge then, my friend, how light the burden must be, that is laid on by these representatives, these brothers of the people. Never can such men as these be instrumental in sending war, with all its attendant miseries, into the nations of the earth: all of whom they are taught by their Shaster to consider as brethren. In

[5] It is ordained that 'the magistrate shall keep in subjection to himself his *Lust*, *Anger*, *Avarices*, *Folly*, *Drunkenness*, and *Pride*: he who cannot keep these passions under his own subjection, how shall he be able to nourish and instruct the people? Neither shall he be seduced by the pleasures of the chace, nor be addicted to play, nor always employed in dancing, singing, and playing on musical instruments. Nor shall he go to any place without a cause, nor dispraise any person without knowing his faults, nor shall he envy another person's superior merit, nor shall say that such persons as are men of capacity are men of no capacity, &c.' See Code of Gentoo Laws, page 52.

Asia we behold the gory monster, ever ready to stalk forth with destructive stride at the voice of ruthless tyranny, but in Europe, Princes are the friends of peace, and the fathers of their people. . . .

At the house of the Governor General,* I was introduced, by Captain Grey, to several gentlemen, both in the civil and military departments. They were all extremely kind, and obliging to me, and appeared to be no strangers to those laws of hospitality, of which our nation has long considered itself as the exclusive possessor.

I was invited by the Governor General himself, to a notch,* or, as they express it, *a ball*; which was to be given in the evening, in a house appropriated to that purpose. On enquiry, I found that the dancers were to be all *English*; a circumstance that delighted me, as I have hitherto had no opportunity of seeing any of their females.

I waited with impatience for the hour which was to take us to the place appointed; but as neither Captain Grey, nor any of his friends, had the same degree of curiosity, the greater part of the company were assembled before we reached the room. When we entered it, amazement, and delight, took possession of my soul. It is impossible to convey to you, by words, any idea of the beautiful objects that surrounded me: but you may judge of the transcendent power of their charms, when I tell you, that they shone forth with invincible lustre, in spite of the deformity of a dress, which appears to have been invented by envy, with an intention of disfiguring the fairest works of nature. These lovely creatures, to the number of about one hundred, were seated on benches in the European fashion, and smiled, and talked, to the gentlemen who addressed them, with great spirit, and vivacity: but this I did not wonder at; as I had been told by Grey, that they all either *were*, or, *had been Dancers*:* and, you know, women of that profession are seldom at a loss for conversation.

The great man having entered, and received the compliments of the company after the manner of his nation, which consists of very little ceremony, the dancing commenced. But judge of my astonishment, when I beheld the dancing girls led out—not by their masters—but—debasing meanness! each by an English Chief! Sincere as my respect for the Governor General certainly is, I could not restrain my indignation at seeing Chiefs, and military Commanders of high rank and authority, thus publicly degrading themselves by dancing for his amusement. How inconsistent, thought I, is the conduct of mortals! These men, who plume themselves upon their notions of liberty, and independence, submit, without reluctance, to an indignity, to which the Omrahs of the empire, who, in the days of its greatness, surrounded the royal Musmud, and prostrated themselves to salute the dust, which was shaken from the feet of royalty, would sooner have died than have submitted!* Though, on the part of the English Chiefs, it appeared entirely voluntary, yet I thought I could perceive that many of them felt sufficient repugnance to this degrading business, which they went through with that sort of heroic apathy and indifference, which you have beheld in a criminal of our nation when about to be hanged. Indeed, I never saw a dance so very little amusing. The gestures of the women were as little graceful as their dress; and had it not been for the extreme beauty of their countenances, I confess, I should soon have been tired with looking at them.

A gentleman, whom I had seen in the morning, told me, that his wife wished to be introduced to me. The request surprised me, but as I knew the gentleman to be a personage of high rank and character, I prepared to follow him. He conducted me to the opposite side of the room, and led me up to a group of Bibbys,* whom I had mistaken for superannuated dancing girls, but whom I now, to my infinite astonishment, discovered to be the wives of men of rank and eminence, whose names, according to the custom of their country, they bore. I could not find myself in the presence of these ladies without experiencing a considerable degree of embarrassment; this was by no means the case with them; like other females, they all spoke at once, and seemed endowed with much loquacity. They looked at me with steady countenances, totally void of that modest timidity, which is the most inestimable gem in female beauty. That glare of colouring, which, at first fight, caught my soul in the net of astonishment, lost, by degrees, its power of enchantment. And as the nightingale,[6] after having viewed, with short-lived rapture, the splendour of the gaudy tulip, returns with fresh delight to the contemplation of his beloved rose; so did my soul, in the midst of this blaze of western beauty, turn to the remembrance of the gentle graces, and endearing charms of my beloved Prymaveda! The loveliness of eyes, sparkling in beauty, may attract our admiration, but the

[6] This simile, the Rajah seems to have borrowed from the Persian. Of all the poetical fables of the East, none is so frequently alluded to, in the compositions of the Persian writers, as that which supposes the nightingale to be violently enamoured with the rose.

bare recollection of those which beamed with the softness of tender affection, is yet more precious to the soul!

Lost in these reflections, I became insensible to the scene around me; and incommoded by the extreme heat of the room, I took the first opportunity of departing. The green horses of Surraya had seen me perform my morning ablutions in the sacred stream,* before my friend Grey returned from this nocturnal festival.

PRISCILLA WAKEFIELD
(1751–1832)

Born Priscilla Bell, the eldest daughter of Daniel Bell and his wife Catharine Barclay (a granddaughter of the important Quaker apologist Robert Barclay), she was brought up in Tottenham, London. In 1771 she married Edward Wakefield, a city merchant, and with him had two sons and a daughter, Isabel. She was an innovative philanthropist, especially interested in facilitating savings in working families. She founded several savings or what she called 'frugality' banks, working with the Friendly Society of Tottenham which she established in 1798. In 1791 she established a charity to help women in childbirth. She was well connected, quick-witted, and extremely active in furthering opportunities for others: it was Wakefield, for example, who facilitated the decisive move in the career of the young painter John Constable, by encouraging him to make contacts in London and giving him a letter of introduction to Joseph Farington in 1799. Correspondence between the two shows that she continued to promote his success.

Her writings were predominantly educational and written for children. The success of her first book, *Juvenile Anecdotes* (1795, 1798), encouraged her to go on to produce several popular works dealing with travel and science. *The Juvenile Travellers* (1801), *A Family Tour Through the British Empire* (1804), *Excursions in North America* (1806), *The Traveller in Africa* (1814), and *The Traveller in America* (1817) develop the techniques of introducing children to geographical and sociological information. Her work in natural history, and botany in particular, is more significant still. *An Introduction to Botany, in a Series of Familiar Letters, with Illustrative Engravings* (1796) had reached an eleventh edition by 1841 and was translated into French in 1801. It presented itself as especially advantageous to women. Other educational works in natural history include *An Introduction to the Natural History and Classification of Insects, in a Series of Letters*

(1816), *Domestic Recreation, or Dialogues Illustrative of Natural and Scientific Subjects* (1805), *Instinct Displayed, or Facts Exemplifying the Sagacity of Various Species of Animals* (1811), and *A Catechism of Botany* (1817).

For adults she wrote *Reflections on the Present Condition of the Female Sex* (1798), a practical and informed piece of writing which considers the opportunities and desirable education and training for women in the upper, middle, and working classes. For genteel women she suggests literature ('a respectable and pleasing employment, for those who possess talents, and an adequate degree of mental cultivation', 125), painting ('historic, portrait, and miniature'), engraving, statuary, modelling (clay, not catwalk), music, landscape illustration, and gardening, 'with strictures on a theatrical life', which she deems unsuitable, although the fact that women have excelled on the stage she sees as 'proving that the abilities of the female sex are equal to nobler labours than are usually undertaken by women' (136). Wakefield's four class divisions are pragmatic but not absolute: it is clear that she considered education and preparation for suitable employment to be advantageous in all spheres of life, and that women's training allowed them to be 'improvable' in terms of social position. Training women to teach 'would be a far more valuable gift than a moderate dowry, which, when once consumed, is irrecoverable, whilst a talent, that can be resumed at discretion, is like a bank, to which application may always be made' (156). She also claims for all women 'the true dignity of a rational being' (139). Extracts from this work follow a sample of her scientific education-by-letters in *An Introduction to Botany*, in which one sister, Felicia, writes to another, Constance, of the instruction given by her governess, Mrs Snelgrove. The children therefore teach each other, an incentive to learning and to active assimilation of adult instruction. In the Preface to the work Wakefield explains her motivation as a desire 'to cultivate a taste in young persons for the study of nature, which is the most familiar means of introducing suitable ideas of the attributes of the Divine Being, by exemplifying them in the order and harmony of the visible creation'; to this religious aim she adds a Wollstonecraftian flavour, however, by emphasizing activity in the fresh air as the primary advantage of botanical study for girls. She hopes above all to counteract the temptations to female 'levity and idleness' by encouraging women to '[employ] their faculties rationally'.

~

From *An Introduction to Botany, in a Series of Familiar Letters* (1796)

LETTER II

Shrubbery, February 10

The morning being fine tempted us abroad. Botany supplied us with subjects for conversation. Mrs Snelgrove took the opportunity of remarking, that a perfect plant consists of the root, the trunk or stem, the leaves, the supports, flower and fruit; (for botanically speaking) by fruit in herbs, as well as in trees, is understood the whole formation of the seed: and as each part needs a particular explanation to a novice, she began her lecture by pointing out the uses of the root. The first, and most obvious, is that of enabling the plant to stand firmly in the ground, by serving as a balance to the head. By what means could the enormous oaks in the park be kept upright and fixed, but by their extensive, turgid roots: they serve as a counterpoise against the weight of the trunk and branches. The chief nourishment of the plant is received by the radicle, or fibrous part of the roots, that, like so many mouths, absorb the nutricious juices from the earth. The root also performs the part of a parent, by preserving the embryo plants in its bosom, during the severity of winter, in form of bulbs or buds: bulbs are properly but large buds, eyes, or gems, including the future plants. Nature is an oeconomist,* and is sparing of this curious provision, against the cold, where it is unnecessary. In warm countries, few plants are furnished with winter buds. Roots are distinguished by different names, according to their forms; as fibrous, bulbous, and tuberous, with many other lesser distinctions, expressive of their manner of growth.

The next part of a plant, that claims our notice, is the trunk or stem, which rises out of the root, and supports the flower, leaves, &c. The trunk of trees and shrubs, (and it is supposed, that the stem of the more diminutive kinds of plants, in the same manner) consists of several distinct parts; as the bark, the wood, the sap-vessels, corresponding to the blood-vessels in animals; the pith, the tracheae or air vesicles, and the web or tissue; each of these parts has its peculiar use, and its construction is admirably adapted to its purpose. The bark of plants seems to perform the same offices to them, that the skin does to animals; it clothes and defends them from injury, inhales the moisture of the air, and extracts, or conveys from the plant the superfluity of moist particles. The cause of evergreens retaining their foliage during the winter, is supposed to arise from an abundant quantity of oil in their barks, which preserves them from the effects of cold. The bark (as well as the wood) is supplied with innumerable vessels, which convey the fluids to and from every part of the plant; the wood also is furnished with others, which contain air, and is distributed throughout its substance. The stability of trees and shrubs consists in the wood, which corresponds with the bones of animals. The seat of life seems to reside in the pith or medullary substance,* which is a fine tissue of vessels originating in the centre. The fluids of plants are the sap, analogous to the blood of animals; and the proper juice, which is of various colours and consistence in different individuals; as white or milky in the dandelion, resinous in the fir, and producing gum in cherry or plum trees, &c. Hoping that I have given you such a clear description of the root and stem, as will enable you to form a general idea of their parts and uses, I shall proceed to leaves, which contribute, at the same time, to the benefit and ornament of the plant. I need not tell you, that the variety of their forms and manner of growth is great; your own observation has long since informed you of this particular, and prepared you to understand the terms by which botanists arrange them, according to their forms and shapes; as simple, compound, rough, smooth, round, oval, heart shaped, &c. these minutiae must be learned by referring to plates. Leaves are supposed to answer the purpose of lungs, and, by their inclination to be moved by the wind, in some degree, serve also those of muscles and muscular motions. They are very porous on both their surfaces, and inhale and exhale freely. The annual sunflower is an extraordinary instance of this fact; it is said to perspire nineteen times as much as a man, in twenty-four hours.* Fine weather encourages the perspiration of vegetables; but in heavy, moist, and wet weather, the inhalation exceeds. The effluvia of plants is thought unwholesome to persons of delicate constitutions, but particularly so at night and in a dull state of the atmosphere; but it is worth observing, that the air emitted from the leaves is never prejudicial; that which is noxious proceeds from the corollas only.*

The next parts to be considered, are the supports or props; by these are meant certain external parts of plants, which are useful to support and defend them from enemies and injuries, or for the secretion of some fluid, that is baneful or disagreeable to those insects that would otherwise hurt them. They are divided into seven kinds: 1st, Tendrils; small spiral strings, by which some plants, that are not strong enough to stand alone, sustain themselves by embracing trees, shrubs, or other supports; the honeysuckle and birdweed afford examples of this. 2dly, Floral leaves; are small leaves placed near the flower, smaller, and mostly of a different form from those of the plant. 3dly, Scales; small leafy appendages, situated on either side, or a little below the leaf, to protect it, when first emerging from the bud. 4thly, Foot stalks; these support the leaf, and defend and convey nourishment to the infant bud. 5thly, Flower stalks, or foot stalks, to the flower and fruit. 6thly, Arms; a general term for the offensive parts of plants, such as thorns, prickles, stings, &c. 7thly, Pubes; a name applied to the defensive parts of plants, such as hairs, wool, a certain hoary whiteness, hooks, bristles, glands, clamminess, and viscidity. In order to enliven a dry detail of names, and a mere description of parts, Mrs Snelgrove favoured me with an account of some curious contrivances of nature, observed in some particular plants, for their defence against insects, or larger animals, that would, without this precaution, greatly annoy them; and as I know the pleasure you take in such recitals, I shall repeat them to you, before I close this long letter. The viscous matter, which surrounds the stalks, under the flowers of the catchfly, prevents various insects from plundering the honey, or devouring the pollen, which fertilizes the seed. In the dionaea muscipula, or Venus's fly-trap, there is a still more wonderful means of preventing the depredations of insects. The leaves are armed with long teeth, like the antenna of insects, and lie spread upon the ground round the stem; they are so irritable, that when an insect creeps upon them, they fold up, and crush or pierce it to death. The flower of the arum muscivorum has the smell of carrion, which invites the flies to lay their eggs in the chamber of the flower; but the worms, which are hatched from these eggs, are unable to make their escape from their prison, being prevented by the hairs pointing inwards, which has given the name of fly-eater to this flower. The same purpose is effected in the dypsacus, vulgarly called teazel, by a bason or receptacle of water, placed round each joint of the stem.

The nauseous and pungent juices of some vegetables, and the

fragrance of others, are bestowed upon them in common with thorns and prickles for their defence against the depredation of animals. Many trees and shrubs supply grateful food to a variety of creatures, and would be quickly devoured, were they not armed with thorns and stings, which protect them not only against some kinds of insects, but also against the naked mouths of quadrupeds. It is worth remarking, as a farther analogy between plants and animals, that the former frequently lose their thorns, &c. by cultivation, as wild animals are deprived of their ferocity, by living in a domestic state, under the government and protection of man. My letter is already spun out to a tedious length, I must, therefore, reserve the description of the fructification till a future opportunity.—Adieu: your

FELICIA.

From *Reflections on the Present Condition of the Female Sex* (1798)

It is asserted by Doctor Adam Smith, that every individual is a burthen upon the society to which he belongs, who does not contribute his share of productive labour for the good of the whole.* The Doctor, when he lays down this principle, speaks in general terms of man, as a being capable of forming a social compact for mutual defence, and the advantage of the community at large. He does not absolutely specify, that both sexes, in order to render themselves beneficial members of society, are equally required to comply with these terms; but since the female sex is included in the idea of the species, and as women possess the same qualities as men, though perhaps in a different degree, their sex cannot free them from the claim of the public for their proportion of usefulness. That the major part of the sex, especially of those among the higher orders, neglect to fulfil this important obligation, is a fact that must be admitted, and points out the propriety of an enquiry into the causes of their deficiency.

The indolent indulgence and trifling pursuits in which those who are distinguished by the appellation of gentlewomen, often pass their lives, may be attributed, with greater probability, to a contracted education, custom, false pride, and idolizing adulation, than to any defect in their intellectual capacities. The contest for equality in the mental capacity of the sexes, has been maintained, on each side of the question, with ingenuity; but as a judgment only can be formed from facts, as they arise in the present state of things, if the experiments have been fairly tried, the rare instances of extraordinary talents, which have been brought forward to support the system of equality, must yield to the irrestistible influence of corporeal powers. Which leads to a conclusion, that the intellectual capacities of each sex, are wisely adapted to their appropriate purposes, and that, laying aside the invidious terms of superiority and inferiority, the perfection of mind in man and in woman, consists in a power to maintain the distinguishing characteristics of excellence in each. But this concession by no means proves, that even in this enlightened age and country, the talents of women have ever been generally exerted to the utmost extent of their capacity, or that they have been turned towards the most useful objects; neither does it imply, that the cultivation they receive, is adequate to bring into action the full strength of those powers, which have been bestowed on them by nature. The intellectual faculties of the female mind have too long been confined by narrow and ill-directed modes of education, and thus have been concealed, not only from others, but from themselves, the energies of which they are capable. The exigence of circumstances in private life has called forth numberless examples of female prudence, magnanimity and fortitude, which demonstrated no less a clearness of conception, than a warmth of feeling, reflecting equal honour upon the heads, and upon the hearts of the sex. Neither has history been silent in recording memorable instances of female capacity, in all the various branches of human excellence.

These united testimonies are surely sufficient to justify an opinion, that the imperfect contributions to the mass of public activity have not arisen from a want of ability to be useful, but from some defect of another kind, which it is necessary to discover, that a remedy may be found, and applied to the evil.

In civilized nations it has ever been the misfortune of the sex to be too highly elevated, or too deeply depressed; now raised above the condition of mortals, upon the score of their personal attractions; and now debased below that of reasonable creatures, with respect to their intellectual endowments. The result of this improper treatment has been a neglect of the mental powers, which women really possess, but know not how to exercise; and they have been contented to barter the dignity of reason, for the imaginary privilege of an empire, of the existence of which they can entertain no reasonable hope beyond the duration of youth and beauty.

Of the few who have raised themselves to pre-eminence by daring to stray beyond the accustomed path, the envy of their own sex, and the jealousy or contempt of the other, have too often been the attendants; a fate which doubtless has deterred others from attempting to follow them, or emulate, even in an inferior degree, the distinction they have attained.

But notwithstanding these disadvantages, and others of less perceptible influence, the diffusion of Christianity, and the progress of civilization, have raised the importance of the female character; and it has become a branch of philosophy, not a little interesting, to ascertain the offices which the different ranks of women are required to fulfil. Their rights and their duties have lately occupied the pens of writers of eminence; the employments which may properly exercise their faculties, and fill up their time in a useful manner, without encroaching upon those professions, which are appropriate to men, remain to be defined. There are many branches of science, as well as useful occupations, in which women may employ their time and their talents, beneficially to themselves and to the community, without destroying the peculiar characteristic of their sex, or exceeding the most exact limits of modesty and decorum. Whatever obliges them to mix in the public haunts of men, or places the young in too familiar a situation with the other sex; whatever is obnoxious to the delicacy and reserve of the female character, or destructive, in the smallest degree, to the strictest moral purity, is inadmissible. The sphere of feminine action is contracted by numberless difficulties, that are no impediments to masculine exertions. Domestic privacy is the only sure asylum for the juvenile part of the sex; nor can the grave matron step far beyond that boundary with propriety. Unfitted, by their relative situation in society, for many honourable and lucrative employments, those only are suitable for them, which can be pursued without endangering their virtue, or corrupting their manners.

But, under these restrictions, there may be found a multitude of objects adapted to the useful exertions of female talents, which it will be the principal design of these Reflections to point out, after making some remarks upon the present state of female education, and suggesting some improvements towards its reformation.

And here the author may perhaps be allowed to express her hope, that among the numbers of the female world, who appear to be satisfied with inferiority, many require only to be awakened to a true sense of their own real consequence, to be induced to support it by a rational improvement of those hours, which they have hitherto wasted in the most frivolous occupations. The promotion of so useful a design, is the only apology for intruding her opinions upon the subject; and it will be esteemed her highest recompence, should her observations contribute to its accomplishment. . . .

Men monopolize not only the most advantageous employments, and such as exclude women from the exercise of them, by the publicity of their nature, or the extensive knowledge they require, but even many of those, which are consistent with the female character. Another heavy discouragement to the industry of women, is the inequality of the reward of their labour, compared with that of men, an injustice which pervades every species of employment performed by both sexes.[1]

In employments which depend upon bodily strength the distinction is just; for it cannot be pretended that the generality of women can earn as much as men, where the produce of their labour is the result of corporeal exertion; but it is a subject of great regret, that this inequality should prevail, even where an equal share of skill and application are exerted. Male-stay-makers, mantua-makers, and hair-dressers are better paid than female artists of the same professions; but surely it will never be urged as an apology for this disproportion, that women are not as capable of making stays, gowns, dressing hair, and similar arts, as men; if they are not superior to them, it can only be accounted for upon this principle, that the prices they receive for their labour are not sufficient to repay them for the expence of qualifying themselves for their business, and that they sink under the mortification of being regarded as artizans of

[1] This abuse is in no instance more conspicuous, than in the wages of domestic servants. A footman, especially of the higher kind, whose most laborious task is to wait at table, gains, including clothes, vails, and other perquisites, at least £50 per annum, whilst a cook-maid, who is mistress of her profession, does not obtain £20, though her office is laborious, unwholesome, and requires a much greater degree of skill than that of a valet. A similar disproportion is observable among the inferior servants of the establishment.

inferior estimation, whilst the men, who supplant them, receive all the encouragement of large profits and full employment, which is ensured to them by the folly of fashion. The occasion for this remark is a disgrace upon those who patronize such a brood of effeminate beings in the garb of men; when sympathy with their humbler sisters should direct them to act in a manner exactly opposite, by holding out every incitement to the industry of their own sex. This evil indeed calls loudly upon women of rank and fortune for redress: they should determine to employ women only, wherever they can be employed; they should procure female instructors for their children; they should frequent no shops that are not served by women; they should wear no clothes that are not made by them; they should reward them as liberally as they do the men who have hitherto supplanted them. Let it be considered a common cause to give them every possible advantage. For once let fashion be guided by reason, and let the mode sanction a preference to women in every profession, to which their pretensions are equal with those of the other sex. This is a patronage which the necessitous have a right to expect from the rich and powerful, whether they are poor by birth, or are unfortunately become so by that mutability of fortune to which every rank is liable.

JOANNA BAILLIE
(1762–1851)

The descendant of an old Scottish family, Joanna Baillie was born in Bothwell, Lanarkshire; her twin died a few hours after birth. Her father, James Baillie, was a minister and later professor of divinity at Glasgow, and her mother, Dorothea Hunter, was the sister of the eminent surgeons and anatomists William and John Hunter. The course of Joanna Baillie's domestic life was much influenced by the career of her elder brother Matthew, who followed in their uncles' path and became a physician in London, then one of the court physicians of George III, and inherited their uncle William's School of Anatomy in Great Windmill Street, London. At the age of 10 she was sent with her sister Agnes to a boarding-school in Glasgow. She had only very recently acquired an interest in reading after being confined to bed after an accident, and the move to school showed her starting to develop her abilities. She vividly describes her developing love of plays and acting, and her fascination with the as-yet-unseen Sarah Siddons, in manuscript 'Memoirs written to please my nephew, William Baillie'.[1] In 1784, five years after the death of her father, she moved with her mother and Agnes to London to live with her brother Matthew, and in 1791, on Matthew's marriage, settled in Hampstead, where she was to live for the rest of her life with her mother (who died in 1806) and sister.

In addition to a close and lively family life with Matthew, his wife, and their children, Baillie had many literary friends and acquaintances: Anna Laetitia Barbauld was a close neighbour and Barbauld's niece and biographer Lucy Aikin an intimate friend. She knew Sarah Siddons and Maria Edgeworth well. Walter Scott, whom she met in 1806, was one of her greatest literary admirers and a close friend; while the poet Samuel Rogers wrote of her in 1791 as 'a very pretty woman with a broad Scotch accent'.[2] Annabella Milbanke, who married Byron, was a friend and Baillie defended her unreservedly on the break-up of the marriage. A measure of her centrality in the literary life of the day is that when, in 1823, she published a collection of poems solicited to raise money for a friend in need, it included new poems contributed by Hemans, Barbauld, Anna Maria Porter, Anne Grant of Laggan, Wordsworth, Scott, Southey, Thomas Campbell, Rogers, and George Crabbe. 'She had enjoyed a fame almost without parallel, and had outlived it', was Martineau's sympathetic analysis of her elderly years in Hampstead, 'yet was her serenity never disturbed, nor her merry humour in the least dimmed'.[3]

Baillie was in her teens when she developed a taste for reading plays, but her literary work began in earnest when she moved to London and was inspired by her uncle John's wife, the poet Anne Home Hunter, who directed her to recent publications. She borrowed French and English plays from the British Library. She has claims as a poet: her first publication *Poems; Wherein it is Attempted to Describe Certain Views of Nature and of Rustic Manners* (1790) was followed by several other collections, notably *Metrical Legends of Exalted Characters* (1821). She also contributed many lyrics to George Thomson's collections of Scottish, Irish, and Welsh song (different publications appeared between 1804 and 1822). Unusually for a woman writer of this time, and to the horror of her friend Scott, in 1831 she branched out into religious controversy with *A View of the General*

---

[1] Wellcome Institute for the History of Medicine Library: printed in Dorothy McMillan (ed.), *The Scotswoman at Home and Abroad: Non-Fictional Writing 1700–1900* (Glasgow: Association for Scottish Literary Studies, 1999), 96–105.

[2] Margaret S. Carhart, *The Life and Work of Joanna Baillie* (1923; London: Oxford University Press, 1970), 13.

[3] *Harriet Martineau's Autobiography with Memorials by Maria Weston Chapman*, 3 vols., 2nd edn. (London: Smith, Elder, 1897), i. 358.

Tenour of the New Testament Regarding the Nature and Dignity of Jesus Christ.

Her greatest fame, however, was as a dramatist and theorist of drama. She wrote twenty-six plays, some of them the most celebrated of all Romantic-period dramas. In 1798 appeared (anonymously) the first series of *A Series of Plays: in which it is attempted to delineate the stronger passions of the mind. Each passion being the subject of a Tragedy and a Comedy*, in the Preface of which Baillie developed her theories and proposed practice of drama. Baillie proposed to treat each 'passion', such as hatred and fear, in a tragedy and a comedy: William Hazlitt described her, in consequence of this schematization of feeling, as 'a Unitarian in poetry'.[4] Baillie acknowledged authorship in the third edition of 1800; the revelation of her femininity caused a literary sensation. Two other series of plays on the passions appeared in 1802 and 1812. Among her other plays are a Scottish tragedy, *The Family Legend* (1812), which confirmed her status as the leading female dramatist of her day, a collection of *Miscellaneous Plays* in 1804, and *The Bride* and *The Martyr* in 1826.

Baillie's Preface to *Plays on the Passions* is one of the key documents of Romantic-period literary criticism. In a detailed and wide-ranging argument, it contends that the exercise of sympathy with human nature is needed to make all types of moral work (including poetry, history, and philosophy) interesting. In history, 'the transactions of men become interesting to us only as we are made acquainted with men themselves' (16); to do this, slight circumstances and habits may be more revealing than public events. Romance-writing, meanwhile, exists precisely to supply what history does not always reveal: 'what men are in the closet as well as the field, by the blazing hearth, and at the social board, as well as in the council and the throne' (18). Poetry deals in idealizations, but even here, 'let one simple trait of the human heart, one expression of passion genuine and true to nature, be introduced, and it will stand forth alone in the boldness of reality, whilst the false and unnatural around it, fades away upon every side' (21). For Baillie, in no art form is this as essential as it is in the drama. To represent 'real and natural characters' is imperative. She criticizes writers of tragedy for creating characters in the grip of strong passions without showing how those passions developed, and without combining them with 'all that timidity, irresolution, distrust, and a thousand delicate traits, which make the infancy of every great passion more interesting, perhaps, than its full-blown strength' (38–9). This is the agenda of her most celebrated play, the tragedy of hatred, *De Monfort*.

---

[4] Lecture 'On the Living Poets' from *Lectures on the English Poets* (1818), in *The Complete Works of William Hazlitt*, ed. P. P. Howe, 21 vols. (London: J. M. Dent, 1930–4), v. 147.

In the 'Memoirs written to please my nephew, William Baillie', she records: 'De Monfort was written more rapidly and with more interruption from visitors & the gaeities of a Country Town, while at the time of the annual fair that lasted several weeks, frequent opportunities of seeing a very good company of actors in a small Theatre, brought scenery and stage effect more under my consideration.'[5] The piece was shown to her brother Matthew, and she was encouraged by him and by the critic Archibald Alison, to whom he sent another play of hers, *Basil*. After the publication of the volume, it was John Kemble's idea to put on *De Monfort* at Drury Lane. First performed in 1800 with Sarah Siddons and Kemble in the leading roles, it proved resistant to stage success. Siddons relished her role as the tragic hero's sister, however: 'Make me some more Jane de Monforts'.[6] She liked the role so much that after its rapid and gender-related removal from the public stage, she continued for several years to give solo readings from it at private gatherings. Baillie was regarded by some astute female contemporaries as having introduced to the stage a new type of female character. Hester Thrale Piozzi based her hunch about the gender of the author upon this one character, writing to a friend: 'I felt it was a woman's writing; no man makes female characters respectable—no man of the present day I mean, they only make them lovely.'[7]

~

From *Plays on the Passions* (1798)

Introductory Discourse

In whatever age or country the Drama might have taken its rise, tragedy would have been the first-born of its children. For every nation has its great men, and its great events upon record; and to represent their own forefathers struggling with those difficulties, and braving those dangers, of which they have heard with admiration, and the effects of which they still, perhaps, experience, would certainly have been the most animating subject for the poet, and the most interesting for his audience, even independently of the natural inclination we all so universally shew for scenes of horror and

---

[5] McMillan (ed.), *The Scotswoman at Home and Abroad*, 102.

[6] 'Life of Joanna Baillie', *The Dramatic and Poetical Works of Joanna Baillie*, 2nd edn. (London: Longman, 1853), p. xi.

[7] Ellen Donkin, *Getting into the Act: Women Playwrights in London, 1776–1829* (London: Routledge, 1995), 166.

distress, of passion and heroick exertion. Tragedy would have been the first child of the Drama, for the same reasons that have made the heroick ballad, with all its battles, murders, and disasters, the earliest poetical compositions of every country.

We behold heroes and great men at a distance, unmarked by those small but distinguishing features of the mind, which give a certain individuality to such an infinite variety of similar beings, in the near and familiar intercourse of life. They appear to us from this view like distant mountains, whose dark outlines we trace in the clear horizon, but the varieties of whose roughened sides, shaded with heath and brushwood, and seamed with many a cleft, we perceive not. When accidental anecdote reveals to us any weakness or peculiarity belonging to them, we start upon it like a discovery. They are made known to us in history only, by the great events they are connected with, and the part they have taken in extraordinary or important transactions. Even in poetry and romance, with the exception of some love story interwoven with the main events of their lives, they are seldom more intimately made known to us. To Tragedy it belongs to lead them forward to our nearer regard, in all the distinguishing varieties which nearer inspection discovers; with the passions, the humours, the weaknesses, the prejudices of men. It is for her to present to us the great and magnanimous hero, who appears to our distant view as a superior being, as a God, softened down with those smaller frailties and imperfections which enable us to glory in, and claim kindred to his virtues. It is for her to exhibit to us the daring and ambitious man, planning his dark designs, and executing his bloody purposes, mark'd with those appropriate characteristicks, which distinguish him as an individual of that class; and agitated with those varied passions, which disturb the mind of man when he is engaged in the commission of such deeds. It is for her to point out to us the brave and impetuous warrior struck with those visitations of nature, which, in certain situations, will unnerve the strongest arm, and make the boldest heart tremble. It is for her to shew the tender, gentle, and unassuming mind animated with that fire which, by the provocation of circumstances, will give to the kindest heart the ferocity and keenness of a tiger. It is for her to present to us the great and striking characters that are to be found amongst men, in a way which the poet, the novelist, and the historian can but imperfectly attempt. But above all, to her, and to her only it belongs to unveil to us the human mind under the dominion of those strong and fixed passions, which, seemingly unprovoked by outward circumstances, will from small beginnings brood within the breast, till all the better dispositions, all the fair gifts of nature are borne down before them. Those passions which conceal themselves from the observation of men; which cannot unbosom themselves even to the dearest friend; and can, often times, only give their fulness vent in the lonely desert, or in the darkness of midnight. For who hath followed the great man into his secret closet, or stood by the side of his nightly couch, and heard those exclamations of the soul which heaven alone may hear, that the historian should be able to inform us? and what form of story, what mode of rehearsed speech will communicate to us those feelings, whose irregular bursts, abrupt transitions, sudden pauses, and half-uttered suggestions, scorn all harmony of measured verse, all method and order of relation?

On the first part of this task her Bards have eagerly exerted their abilities: and some amongst them, taught by strong original genius to deal immediately with human nature and their own hearts, have laboured in it successfully. But in presenting to us those views of great characters, and of the human mind in difficult and trying situations which peculiarly belong to Tragedy, the far greater proportion, even of those who may be considered as respectable dramatick poets, have very much failed. From the beauty of those original dramas to which they have ever looked back with admiration, they have been tempted to prefer the embellishments of poetry to faithfully delineated nature. They have been more occupied in considering the works of the great Dramatists who have gone before them, and the effects produced by their writings, than the varieties of human character which first furnished materials for those works, or those principles in the mind of man by means of which such effects were produced. Neglecting the boundless variety of nature, certain strong outlines of character, certain bold features of passion, certain grand vicissitudes, and striking dramatick situations have been repeated from one generation to another; whilst a pompous and solemn gravity, which they have supposed to be necessary for the dignity of tragedy, has excluded almost entirely from their works those smaller touches of nature, which so well develope the mind; and by showing men in their hours of state and exertion only, they have consequently shewn them imperfectly. Thus, great and magnanimous heroes, who bear with majestick equanimity every vicissitude of fortune; who in every temptation and trial stand forth in unshaken virtue, like a rock buffeted by the waves; who encompast with the most terrible evils, in calm possession of their souls, reason upon the difficulties of their state; and, even upon the brink of destruction, pronounce long eulogiums on virtue, in the most eloquent and beautiful language, have been held forth to our view as objects of imitation and interest; as though they had entirely forgotten that it is only from creatures like ourselves that we feel, and therefore, only from creatures like ourselves that we receive the instruction of example.[1]. . .

From this general view, which I have endeavoured to communicate to my reader, of tragedy, and those principles in the human mind upon which the success of her efforts depends, I have been led to believe, that an attempt to write a series of tragedies, of simpler construction, less embellished with poetical decorations, less constrained by that lofty seriousness which has so generally been considered as necessary for the support of tragick dignity, and in which the chief object should be to delineate the progress of the higher passions in the human breast, each play exhibiting a particular passion, might not be unacceptable to the publick. And I have been the more readily induced to act upon this idea, because I am confident, that tragedy, written upon this plan, is fitted to produce stronger moral effect than upon any other. I have said that tragedy in representing to us great characters struggling with difficulties, and placed in situations of eminence and danger, in which few of us have any chance of being called upon to act, conveys its moral efficacy to our minds by the enlarged views which it gives to us of human nature, by the admiration of virtue, and execration of vice which it excites, and

[1] To a being perfectly free from all human infirmity our sympathy refuses to extend. Our Saviour himself, whose character is so beautiful, and so harmoniously consistent; in whom, with outward proofs of his mission less strong than those that are offered to us, I should still be compelled to believe, from being utterly unable to conceive how the idea of such a character could enter into the imagination of man, never touches the heart more nearly than when he says, 'Father, let this cup pass from me.'* Had be been represented to us in all the unshaken strength of these tragick heroes, his disciples would have made fewer converts, and his precepts would have been listened to coldly. Plays in which heroes of this kind are held forth, and whose aim is, indeed, honourable and praise-worthy, have been admired by the cultivated and refined, but the tears of the simple, the applauses of the young and untaught have been wanting.

not by the examples it holds up for our immediate application. But in opening to us the heart of man under the influence of those passions to which all are liable, this is not the case. Those strong passions that, with small assistance from outward circumstances, work their way in the heart, till they become the tyrannical masters of it, carry on a similar operation in the breast of the Monarch, and the man of low degree. It exhibits to us the mind of man in that state when we are most curious to look into it, and is equally interesting to all. Discrimination of character is a turn of mind, tho' more common than we are aware of, which every body does not possess; but to the expressions of passion, particularly strong passion, the dullest mind is awake; and its true unsophisticated language the dullest understanding will not misinterpret. To hold up for our example those peculiarities in disposition, and modes of thinking which nature has fixed upon us, or which long and early habit has incorporated with our original selves, is almost desiring us to remove the everlasting mountains, to take away the native land-marks of the soul; but representing the passions brings before us the operation of a tempest that rages out its time and passes away. We cannot, it is true, amidst its wild uproar, listen to the voice of reason, and save ourselves from destruction; but we can foresee its coming, we can mark its rising signs, we can know the situations that will most expose us to its rage, and we can shelter our heads from the coming blast. To change a certain disposition of mind which makes us view objects in a particular light, and thereby, oftentimes, unknown to ourselves, influences our conduct and manners, is almost impossible; but in checking and subduing those visitations of the soul, whose causes and effects we are aware of, every one may make considerable progress, if he proves not entirely successful. Above all, looking back to the first rise, and tracing the progress of passion, points out to us those stages in the approach of the enemy, when he might have been combated most successfully; and where the suffering him to pass may be considered as occasioning all the misery that ensues.

From *De Monfort: A Tragedy* (1798)

ACT TWO, SCENE II

De Monfort's apartments. Enter De Monfort, with a disordered air, and
his hand pressed upon his forehead, followed by Jane.

De Mon. No more, my sister, urge me not again:
My secret troubles cannot be revealed.*
From all participation of its thoughts
My heart recoils: I pray thee be contented.

Jane. What, must I, like a distant humble friend,
Observe thy restless eye, and gait disturb'd,
In timid silence, whilst with yearning heart
I turn aside to weep? O no! De Monfort!
A nobler task thy noble mind will give;
Thy true intrusted friend I still shall be.

De Mon. Ah, Jane, forbear! I cannot e'en to thee.

Jane. Then fy upon it! fy upon it, Monfort!
There was a time when e'en with murder stain'd,
Had it been possible that such dire deed
Could e'er have been the crime of one so piteous,
Thou would'st have told it me.

De Mon. So would I now—but ask of this no more.
All other trouble but the one I feel
I had disclos'd to thee. I pray thee spare me.
It is the secret weakness of my nature.

Jane. Then secret let it be; I urge no farther.
The eldest of our valiant father's hopes,
So sadly orphan'd, side by side we stood,
Like two young trees, whose boughs, in early strength,
Screen the weak saplings of the rising grove,
And brave the storm together—
I have so long, as if by nature's right,
Thy bosom's inmate and adviser been,
I thought thro' life I should have so remain'd,
Nor ever known a change. Forgive me, Monfort,
A humbler station will I take by thee:
The close attendant of thy wand'ring steps;

The cheerer of this home, by strangers sought;
The soother of those griefs I must not know,
This is mine office now: I ask no more.

 De Mon. Oh Jane! thou dost constrain me with thy love!
Would I could tell it thee!

 Jane. Thou shalt not tell me. Nay, I'll stop mine ears,
Nor from the yearnings of affection wring
What shrinks from utt'rance. Let it pass, my brother.
I'll stay by thee; I'll cheer thee, comfort thee:
Pursue with thee the study of some art,
Or nobler science, that compels the mind
To steady thought progressive, driving forth
All floating, wild, unhappy fantasies;
Till thou, with brow unclouded, smil'st again,
Like one who from dark visions of the night,
When th'active soul within its lifeless cell
Holds its own world, with dreadful fancy press'd
Of some dire, terrible, or murd'rous deed,
Wakes to the dawning morn, and blesses heaven.

 De Mon. It will not pass away: 'twill haunt me still.

 Jane. Ah! say not so, for I will haunt thee too;
And be to it so close an adversary,
That, tho' I wrestle darkling with the fiend,
I shall o'ercome it.

 De Mon.   Thou most gen'rous woman!
Why do I treat thee thus? It should not be—
And yet I cannot—O that cursed villain!
He will not let me be the man I would.

 Jane. What say'st thou, Monfort? Oh! what words are these?
They have awak'd my soul to dreadful thoughts.
I do beseech thee speak!

   (*He shakes his head and turns from her; she following him.*)

By the affection thou didst ever bear me,
By the dear mem'ry of our infant days;
By kindred living ties, ay, and by those
Who sleep i'the tomb, and cannot call to thee,
I do conjure thee speak.

(*He waves her off with his hand, and covers his face with the other, still turning from her.*)

Ha! wilt thou not?

(*Assuming dignity.*) Then, if affection, most unwearied love,
Tried early, long, and never wanting found,
O'er gen'rous man hath more authority,
More rightful power than crown and sceptre give,
I do command thee.

(*He throws himself into a chair greatly agitated.*)

De Monfort, do not thus resist my love.
Here I entreat thee on my bended knees.

(*Kneeling.*)

Alas! my brother!

(De Monfort *starts up, and catching her in his arms, raises her up, then placing her in the chair, kneels at her feet.*)

De Mon. Thus let him kneel who should the abased be,
And at thine honour'd feet confession make.
I'll tell thee all—but oh! thou wilt despise me.
For in my breast a raging passion burns,
To which thy soul no sympathy will own.
A passion which hath made my nightly couch
A place of torment; and the light of day,
With the gay intercourse of social man,
Feel like th' oppressive airless pestilence.
O Jane! thou wilt despise me,

Jane.   Say not so:
I never can despise thee, gentle brother.
A lover's jealousy and hopeless pangs
No kindly heart contemns.

De Mon.   A lover, say'st thou?
No, it is hate! black, lasting, deadly hate;
Which thus hath driv'n me forth from kindred peace,
From social pleasure, from my native home,
To be a sullen wand'rer on the earth,
Avoiding all men, cursing and accurs'd.

Jane. De Monfort, this is fiend-like, frightful, terrible!
What being, by th' Almighty Father form'd,

Of flesh and blood, created even as thou,
Could in thy breast such horrid tempest wake,
Who art thyself his fellow?
Unknit thy brows, and spread those wrath-clench'd hands:
Some sprite accurst within thy bosom mates
To work thy ruin. Strive with it, my brother!
Strive bravely with it; drive it from thy breast:
'Tis the degrader of a noble heart;
Curse it, and bid it part.

    De Mon. It will not part.   (*His hand on his breast.*)
                           I've lodged it here too long;
With my first cares I felt its rankling touch,
I loath'd him when a boy.

    Jane. Who did'st thou say?

    De Mon.   Oh! that detested Rezenvelt!
E'en in our early sports, like two young whelps
Of hostile breed, instinctively reverse,
Each 'gainst the other pitch'd his ready pledge,
And frown'd defiance. As we onward pass'd
From youth to man's estate, his narrow art,
And envious gibing malice, poorly veil'd
In the affected carelessness of mirth,
Still more detestable and odious grew.
There is no living being on this earth
Who can conceive the malice of his soul,
With all his gay and damned merriment,
To those, by fortune or by merit plac'd
Above his paltry self. When, low in fortune,
He look'd upon the state of prosp'rous men,
As nightly birds, rous'd from their murky holes,
Do scowl and chatter at the light of day,
I could endure it; even as we bear
Th'impotent bite of some half-trodden worm,
I could endure it. But when honours came,
And wealth and new-got titles fed his pride;
Whilst flatt'ring knaves did trumpet forth his praise,
And grov'ling idiots grinn'd applauses on him;
Oh! then I could no longer suffer it!

It drove me frantick.—What! what would I give!
What would I give to crush the bloated toad,
So rankly do I loathe him!

Jane. And would thy hatred crush the very man
Who gave to thee that life he might have ta'en
That life which thou so rashly did'st expose
To aim at his! Oh! this is horrible!

De Mon. Ha! thou hast heard it, then? From all the world,
But most of all from thee, I thought it hid.

Jane. I heard a secret whisper, and resolv'd
Upon the instant to return to thee.
Did'st thou receive my letter?

De Mon. I did! I did! 'twas that which drove me hither.
I could not bear to meet thine eye again.

Jane. Alas! that, tempted by a sister's tears,
I ever left thy house! these few past months,
These absent months, have brought us all this woe.
Had I remain'd with thee it had not been.
And yet, methinks, it should not move you thus.
You dar'd him to the field: both bravely fought;
He more adroit disarm'd you; courteously
Return'd the forfeit sword, which, so return'd,
You did refuse to use against him more;
And then, as says report, you parted friends.

De Mon. When he disarm'd this curs'd, this worthless hand
Of its most worthless weapon, he but spar'd
From dev'lish pride, which now derives a bliss
In seeing me thus fetter'd, sham'd, subjected
With the vile favour of his poor forbearance;
Whilst he securely sits with gibing brow*
And basely bates me, like a muzzled cur
Who cannot turn again.——
Until that day, till that accursed day,
I knew not half the torment of this hell,
Which burns within my breast. Heaven's lightning blast him!

Jane. O this is horrible! Forbear, forbear!
Lest heaven's vengeance light upon thy head,

For this most impious wish.

De Mon.   Then let it light.
Torments more fell than I have felt already
It cannot send. To be annihilated;
What all men shrink from; to be dust, be nothing,
Were bliss to me, compar'd to what I am.

Jane. Oh! would'st thou kill me with these dreadful words?

De Mon. (*Raising his arms to heaven*). Let me but once upon his ruin look,
Then close mine eyes for ever!

(Jane, *in great distress, staggers back, and supports herself upon the side
    scene. De Monfort, alarm'd, runs up to her with a soften'd voice*.)

Ha! how is this? thou'rt ill; thou'rt very pale.
What have I done to thee? Alas, alas!
I meant not to distress thee.—O my sister!

Jane. (*Shaking her head*.) I cannot speak to thee.

De Mon.   I have kill'd thee.
Turn, turn thee not away! look on me still!
Oh! droop not thus, my life, my pride, my sister!
Look on me yet again.

Jane.   Thou too, De Monfort,
In better days, wert wont to be my pride.

De Mon. I am a wretch, most wretched in myself,
And still more wretched in the pain I give.
O curse that villain! that detested villain!
He hath spread mis'ry o'er my fated life:
He will undo us all.

Jane. I've held my warfare through a troubled world,
And borne with steady mind my share of ill;
For then the helpmate of my toil wert thou.
But now the wane of life comes darkly on,
And hideous passion tears thee from my heart,
Blasting thy worth.—I cannot strive with this.

De Mon. (*Affectionately*.) What shall I do?

Jane.   Call up thy noble spirit,
Rouse all the gen'rous energy of virtue;

And with the strength of heaven-endued man,
Repel the hideous foe. Be great; be valiant.
O, if thou could'st! E'en shrouded as thou art
In all the sad infirmities of nature,
What a most noble creature would'st thou be!

De Mon. Ay, if I could: alas! alas! I cannot.

Jane. Thou can'st, thou may'st, thou wilt.
We shall not part till I have turn'd thy soul.

Enter Manuel.

De Mon. Ha! some one enters. Wherefore com'st thou here?

Man. Count Freberg waits your leisure.

De Mon. (*Angrily.*) Be gone, be gone.—I cannot see him now.

[Exit Manuel.

Jane. Come to my closet; free from all intrusion,
I'll school thee there; and thou again shalt be
My willing pupil, and my gen'rous friend;
The noble Monfort I have lov'd so long,
And must not, will not lose.

De Mon. Do as thou wilt; I will not grieve thee more.

[Exeunt.

SARAH SIDDONS
(1755–1831)

Born Sarah Kemble, the eldest of the twelve children of the actor and manager Roger Kemble and his wife Sarah Ward, Siddons was the foremost tragic actress of her age. The Kemble children were all brought up in unsettled and sometimes makeshift circumstances as their parents' theatrical company toured the provinces, but in professional terms the experience was invaluable. Siddons's brothers Charles Kemble and John Philip Kemble also became celebrated actors. In 1773 she married William Siddons, an actor in her parents' company, obtaining reluctant consent from her parents. They had seven children, only five of whom survived infancy, and all of whom predeceased her. Her first biographer, James Boaden, repeats persistent contemporary rumours that the marriage was unhappy;

despite her fame, Siddons led an arduous domestic as well as professional life, and her husband was a known philanderer. She herself, however, was linked with the painter Thomas Lawrence, and in 1809 was accused in print of adulterous behaviour, this time by an outraged wife, her fellow actor Catherine Galindo. More importantly, her fame brought her into contact with a wide range of privileged and educated people, and she included among her close friends Hester Thrale Piozzi, Elizabeth Inchbald, Joanna Baillie, the sculptor Anne Damer, and the family of Sir Ralph Milbanke, whose daughter Annabella married Byron. She is perceptively as well as sympathetically described by Joanna Baillie:

Her manner is too solemn & her voice too deep for familiar society, and having her mind little stored except with what is connected with her profession, and thinking at the same time that every one who spoke to her expected to hear her mouth utter some striking thing, she uttered many things not very well suited to the occasion; but I think she has a mind which has been occupied in observing what past within itself, and has therefore drawn her acting from a deeper source than actors generally do, besides her native talent for expressing emotions; and I think she has a quick perception of humour & character in other's [*sic*], at least she tells a humorous anecdote, not withstanding her deep toned voice, very droly.[1]

Siddons first performed on stage at the age of 11, playing Ariel in *The Tempest*, and continued to act throughout her teens. One of her performances in 1774 caught the attention of the great actor and manager David Garrick, who hired her for the Drury Lane company at £5 a week. She made her debut on the London stage at Drury Lane in 1775, playing Portia in *The Merchant of Venice*, but was not much admired, and returned to the provincial theatres for seven years. Her fame began in 1782 and lasted well beyond her official retirement in 1812 (her farewell performance was as Lady Macbeth at Covent Garden), although a brief return to the stage in 1819 was not a success. Her most celebrated role was as Lady Macbeth. 'We speak of Lady Macbeth, while we are in reality thinking of Mrs. S.', writes Charles Lamb in an essay on Shakespeare's tragedies.[2] Her dignity on and off stage did a great deal to reclaim acting as a respectable occupation for a woman, and in the many paintings of her she became a noble but passionately intense embodiment of female theatricality.[3]

Siddons is not at all known as a writer, and her presence in this collection is the result of a decision which has come to seem natural in modern

[1] *Collected Letters*, ed. Judith Bailey Slagle, i (Madison: Fairleigh Dickinson University Press, 1999), 390.

[2] 1812; originally published in the fourth number of Leigh Hunt's short-lived periodical *The Reflector*: rpt. in *Lamb as Critic*, ed. Roy Park (London: Routledge and Kegan Paul, 1980), 87.

[3] For the paintings, see Robyn Asleson (ed.), *A Passion for Performance: Sarah Siddons and her Portraitists* (Los Angeles: J. Paul Getty Museum, 1999).

publishing, but which was highly unusual for a woman of her time. Late in her life, Siddons asked the poet and editor Thomas Campbell, a man of enlightened political views and a central figure in public literary culture, to be her official biographer, granting him access to memoranda and documents which he incorporated in his *Life of Mrs Siddons* (1834): the papers she gave him are now in the Henry E. Huntington Library, San Marino, California. Campbell's *Life* is easy to criticize. Cyrus Redding called it 'a biography on stilts'.[4] Campbell clearly followed Siddons's wishes, however, in making available her critical observations on the part with which she had become identified. Her notes on the character of Lady Macbeth are not working notes or *aides-mémoires*. They envisage an audience of their own. Unfortunately for Siddons, Campbell has slipped to the literary margins of his age, and the notes on the character of Lady Macbeth which he made public are not available in any collection other than this. One writer who very much wanted to publish a biography of Siddons was Anna Jameson (see Jameson, below), and Siddons's niece and fellow actor Frances Anne Kemble always regretted Campbell's discouragement of Jameson, believing that the biography that might have been 'would have been written in a spirit of far higher artistic discrimination, and with infinitely more sympathy with the woman and with the actress'.[5] A sketch of Siddons's character appeared in Jameson's four-volume *Visits and Sketches* (1830). Ironically, Frances Anne Kemble had no faith in her aunt's literary or critical powers, suggesting that 'If that great actress had possest the order of mind capable of conceiving and producing a philosophical analysis of any of the wonderful poetical creations which she so wonderfully embodied, she would surely never have been able to embody them as she did'.[6] However tempting it is to wish for her a female biographer of the intellectual stature and perception of Anna Jameson, Siddons's inner life of criticism and reflection was well served by Campbell.

More recently, *The Reminiscences of Sarah Kemble Siddons* were edited by William Van Lennep in 1942. They reveal strong feelings about individual performances and audience reaction as well as about 'the degrading humiliations incidental to the profession of the Drama'.[7] They also show an intellectual and theatrical energy which belies her sometimes monumental and melancholy image. She obviously made meticulous preparation and was highly analytical of her performances. 'Remarks on the

[4] Cyrus Redding, *Literary Reminiscences and Memoirs of Thomas Campbell*, 2 vols. (London: James J. Skeet, 1860), ii. 288.

[5] Gerardine Macpherson, *Memoirs of the Life of Anna Jameson* (London: Longmans, Green, and Co., 1878), 62.

[6] Ibid. 17.

[7] *The Reminiscences of Sarah Kemble Siddons 1773–1785*, ed. with foreword by William Van Lennep (Cambridge, Mass.: Widener Library, 1942), 32.

Character of Lady Macbeth', published in the second volume of Campbell's *Life* (as are her notes on performing Constance in *King John*), is an intriguing document, a rationale for her professional interpretation of a role which Campbell describes as her 'masterpiece'. 'It was an era in one's life to have seen her in it.' Siddons found what she called 'the grand fiendish part' difficult, emotional empathy being blocked, so that 'to adopt this character, must be an effort of the judgement alone'.[8] Recent analysts of women's theatre, including Catherine Burroughs, have noted the importance of Siddons's 'Remarks' as the record of an individual actor's thorough intellectual preparation for a role and as an example of what we would now call method acting. Siddons encourages actors to suppose an extra-textual psychological life for their characters, including, in the case of Lady Macbeth, a past history of high dignity and command, a childhood and early married life in which nobody seriously opposed her wishes. She focuses on Lady Macbeth's role as a wife. Traditionally seen as a horrific aberration from womanhood and performed as a kind of monster, Lady Macbeth becomes, in Siddons's interpretation, someone at least partially recognizable to audiences. She changed the dramatic and critical history of the character; so much so, perhaps, that some of her remarks on Lady Macbeth seem familiar to us before we read them.

~

Remarks on the Character of Lady Macbeth (pub. 1834)

In this astonishing creature one sees a woman in whose bosom the passion of ambition has almost obliterated all the characteristics of human nature; in whose composition are associated all the subjugating powers of intellect and all the charms and graces of personal beauty. You will probably not agree with me as to the character of that beauty; yet, perhaps, this difference of opinion will be entirely attributable to the difficulty of your imagination disengaging itself from that idea of the person of her representative which you have been so long accustomed to contemplate. According to my notion, it is of that character which I believe is generally allowed to be most captivating to the other sex,—fair, feminine, nay, perhaps, even fragile—

> 'Fair as the forms that, wove in Fancy's loom,
> Float in light visions round the poet's head.'*

[8] Campbell, *Life of Mrs Siddons*, ii. 37.

Such a combination only, respectable in energy and strength of mind, and captivating in feminine loveliness, could have composed a charm of such potency as to fascinate the mind of a hero so dauntless, a character so amiable, so honourable as *Macbeth*,—to seduce him to brave all the dangers of the present and all the terrors of a future world; and we are constrained, even whilst we abhor his crimes, to pity the infatuated victim of such a thraldom. His letters, which have informed her of the predictions of those preternatural beings who accosted him on the heath, have lighted up into daring and desperate determinations all those pernicious slumbering fires which the enemy of man is ever watchful to awaken in the bosoms of his unwary victims. To his direful suggestions she is so far from offering the least opposition, as not only to yield up her soul to them, but moreover to invoke the sightless ministers of remorseless cruelty to extinguish in her breast all those compunctious visitings of nature which otherwise might have been mercifully interposed to counteract, and perhaps eventually to overcome, their unholy instigations. But having impiously delivered herself up to the excitements of hell, the pitifulness of heaven itself is withdrawn from her, and she is abandoned to the guidance of the demons whom she has invoked. . . .

THE THIRD ACT

The golden round of royalty now crowns her brow, and royal robes enfold her form; but the peace that passeth all understanding is lost to her for ever, and the worm that never dies already gnaws her heart.

> 'Nought's had—all's spent,
> Where our desire is had without content.
> 'Tis safer to be that which we destroy,
> Than by destruction dwell in doubtful joy.'*

Under the impression of her present wretchedness, I, from this moment, have always assumed the dejection of countenance and manners which I thought accordant to such a state of mind; and, though the author of this sublime composition has not, it must be acknowledged, given any direction whatever to authorize this assumption, yet I venture to hope that he would not have disapproved of it. It is evident, indeed, by her conduct in the scene which succeeds the mournful soliloquy, that she is no longer the presumptuous, the determined creature, that she was before the assassination of the King: for instance, on the approach of her husband, we behold for the first time striking indications of sensibility, nay, tenderness and sympathy; and I think this conduct is nobly followed up by her during the whole of their subsequent eventful intercourse. It is evident, I think, that the sad and new experience of affliction has subdued the insolence of her pride, and the violence of her will; for she comes now to seek him out, that she may, at least, participate in his misery. She knows, by her own woeful experience, the torment which he undergoes, and endeavours to alleviate his sufferings by the following inefficient reasonings:

> 'How now, my lord—why do you keep alone?
> Of sorriest fancies your companions making?
> Using those thoughts which should indeed have died
> With them they think on. Things without all remedy
> Should be without regard. What's done, is done.'*

Far from her former habits of reproach and contemptuous taunting, you perceive that she now listens to his complaints with sympathizing feelings; and, so far from adding to the weight of his affliction the burthen of her own, she endeavours to conceal it from him with the most delicate and unremitting attention. But it is in vain; as we may observe in his beautiful and mournful dialogue with the physician on the subject of his cureless malady: 'Canst thou not minister to a mind diseased?' &c.* You now hear no more of her chidings and reproaches. No; all her thoughts are now directed to divert his from those sorriest fancies, by turning them to the approaching banquet, in exhorting him to conciliate the goodwill and good thoughts of his guests, by receiving them with a disengaged air, and cordial, bright, and jovial demeanour. Yes; smothering her sufferings in the deepest recesses of her own wretched bosom, we cannot but perceive that she devotes herself entirely to the effort of supporting him.

Let it be here recollected, as some palliation of her former very different deportment, she had, probably, from childhood commanded all around her with a high hand; had uninterruptedly, perhaps, in that splendid station, enjoyed all that wealth, all that nature had to bestow; that she had, possibly, no directors, no controllers, and that in womanhood her fascinated lord had never once opposed her inclinations. But now her new-born relentings, under the rod of chastisement, prompt her to make palpable efforts in order to support the spirits of her weaker, and, I must say, more selfish husband. Yes; in gratitude for his unbounded affection, and in commiseration of his sufferings, she suppresses the anguish of her heart, even while that anguish is precipitating her into the grave which at this moment is yawning to receive her. . . .

THE FIFTH ACT

Behold her now, with wasted form, with wan and haggard countenance, her starry eyes glazed with the ever-burning fever of remorse, and on their lids the shadows of death. Her ever-restless spirit wanders in troubled dreams about her dismal apartment; and, whether waking or asleep, the smell of innocent blood incessantly haunts her imagination:

> 'Here's the smell of the blood still.
> All the perfumes of Arabia will not sweeten
> This little hand.'*

How beautifully contrasted is this exclamation with the bolder image of *Macbeth*, in expressing the same feeling!

> 'Will all great Neptune's ocean wash the blood
> Clean from this hand?'*

And how appropriately either sex illustrates the same idea!

During this appalling scene, which, to my sense, is the most so of them all, the wretched creature, in imagination, acts over again the accumulated horrors of her whole conduct. These dreadful images, accompanied with the agitations they have induced, have obviously accelerated her untimely end; for in a few moments the tidings of her death are brought to her unhappy husband. It is conjectured that she died by her own hand. Too certain it is, that she dies, and makes no sign. I have now to account to you for the weakness which I have, a few lines back, ascribed to *Macbeth*; and I am not quite without hope that the following observations will bear me out in my opinion. Please to observe, that he (I must think pusillanimously, when I compare his conduct to her forbearance,) has been continually pouring out his miseries to his wife. His heart has therefore been eased, from time to time, by unloading its weight of woe; while she, on the contrary, has perseveringly endured in silence the uttermost anguish of a wounded spirit.

> 'The grief that does not speak
> Whispers the o'erfraught heart, and bids it break.'*

Her feminine nature, her delicate structure, it is too evident, are soon overwhelmed by the enormous pressure of her crimes. Yet it will be granted, that she gives proofs of a naturally higher toned mind than that of *Macbeth*. The different physical powers of the two sexes are finely delineated, in the different effects which their mutual crimes produce. Her frailer frame, and keener feelings, have now sunk under the struggle—his robust and less sensitive constitution has not only resisted it, but bears him on to deeper wickedness, and to experience the fatal fecundity of crime.

> 'For mine own good—All causes shall give way.
> I am in blood so far stepp'd in, that should I wade no more,
> Returning were as tedious as go o'er.'*

Henceforth, accordingly, he perpetrates horrors to the day of his doom.

In one point of view, at least, this guilty pair extort from us, in spite of ourselves, a certain respect and approbation. Their grandeur of character sustains them both above recrimination (the despicable accustomed resort of vulgar minds,) in adversity; for the wretched husband, though almost impelled into this gulph of destruction by the instigations of his wife, feels no abatement of his love for her, while she, on her part, appears to have known no tenderness for him, till, with a heart bleeding at every pore, she beholds in him the miserable victim of their mutual ambition. Unlike the first frail pair in Paradise, they spent not the fruitless hours in mutual accusation.*

MARIA EDGEWORTH
(1767–1849)

Maria Edgeworth was born in Black Bourton, Oxfordshire, at the house of her mother's parents, where she spent much of her infancy. She was the daughter of the writer Richard Lovell Edgeworth and Anna Maria Elers, the first of his four wives. Her mother died when Maria was 5, and her father quickly remarried: the emotional impact made Maria unruly, and when the family returned to Ireland she was sent to school in England. On the death of his second wife in 1780 Edgeworth married her sister, and in 1782 Maria accompanied them back to the family estate at Edgeworthstown, County Longford, where she kept her father's accounts, dealt with his tenants, and took charge of the education of her brother Henry. She remained throughout her life actively involved with the financial management of the estate, and was entrusted with negotiations and planning. A talented scholar in French and Italian, she began translating the works of Madame de Genlis and composing her own literary work, either in collaboration with, or with the approval of, her father. Much of her work, especially in the early years, was educational, in keeping with her father's keen interest in its theory and practice. They both had a practical interest in the upbringing of children: once Edgeworth was established in his fourth marriage, Maria was the eldest of twenty-two children, and had written stories and instructive tales for them which she was to publish in the series *The Parent's Assistant* (from 1796) and *Early Lessons* (from 1801). Her first renown came with the co-publication with her father of the two-volume *Practical Education* (1798).

At the same time, Maria Edgeworth was establishing herself as an author for adults and as a novelist—before Scott, the most admired novelist of her day and a key figure in the transformation of the novel from a light form of entertainment (especially when practised by women) to a serious, morally directed, sociologically and historically engaged, culturally central form of literature. Her work was reviewed in the weightiest periodicals, and she calculated that she earned £11,062. 8s.10d. from sales and copyrights. The three tales in *Letters to Literary Ladies* (1795) defended education for women but were suspicious of fiction-writing. Her career as an independent novelist began in 1800 with *Castle Rackrent*, an innovative regional tale recording the customs of Ireland a generation back and published in the year of Ireland's union with England, and continued with *Belinda* (1801), *Popular Tales* (1804), *The Modern Griselda* (1805), *Leonora* (1806), *Tales of Fashionable Life* (two series, 1809 and 1812), *Patronage*

(1814), *Harrington* and *Ormond* (1817), and *Helen* (1834). With her father, she defended Irish dialect in *Irish Bulls* (1802). From a constant base in Edgeworthstown she made extended visits to Paris, London, and Edinburgh: in Paris in 1802–3 Edgeworth rejected a proposal of marriage from a Swedish diplomat, Edelcrantz, with whom she had fallen in love, because she did not want to leave her father and the Irish estate. She also kept up correspondences with Anna Laetitia Barbauld, Elizabeth Inchbald, and several other writers and thinkers, the dearest of them probably being Walter Scott. When her father died in 1817 she completed the memoirs on which he had been working: they were published in 1820. She also took an active role in managing the family estate in the wake of the financial crash of 1825, and in helping Irish peasants during the famine of 1846. Edgeworth was a prolific letter-writer, kept up literary correspondences and friendships, and was sharp and intellectually curious in a way which bordered on eccentricity. The most respected woman writer of her day, a moralist and social critic of acknowledged distinction, her energy and emotionalism could be disconcerting. The novelist and critic John Gibson Lockhart describes Edgeworth during her visit to Walter Scott at Abbotsford in 1823 as 'a little, dark, bearded, sharp, withered, active, laughing, talking, impudent, fearless, outspoken, honest, Whiggish, unchristian, good-tempered, kindly, ultra-Irish body'.[1]

Castle Rackrent is a turning-point in the history of the novel. In the Preface Edgeworth reveals a close affinity with the ideas expressed by Joanna Baillie in the 'Introductory Discourse' to *Plays on the Passions* (see Baillie, above). The two admired each other's work. Edgeworth, posing as a male 'editor', moots a domesticization of 'public', implicitly masculine, history, and emphasizes private feelings and motivations. The heroes of history, she complains, do not speak or act like living individuals; more problematic still, public behaviour is less revealing of character than 'careless conversations' and 'half-finished sentences'. So much for formal effect in the subject; the teller, too, should set art aside: 'a plain unvarnished tale is preferable to the most highly ornamented narrative'. Instead of learned historians, the reader can more readily trust a narrator modelled upon the local gossip. Edgeworth makes no mention of her gender, and the tale is to be told by a man; but the Preface is part of an ongoing domesticizing and personalizing of historical narrative in which women writers were closely involved. The novel purports to be a transcription by the editor of the family reminiscences of an Irish butler, Thady McQuirk, who has served successive Lords of the Anglo-Irish Rackrent family and traces their fortunes and misfortunes. In the extract

[1] *The Letters of Sir Walter Scott*, ed. H. J. C. Grierson *et al.*, 12 vols. (London: Constable, 1932–7), viii. 56 n.

below he describes the ruthlessly mercenary marriage of Sir Kit Condy. The representation of the Jewish heiress is more sympathetic and more innovative than it looks in retrospect; although Edgeworth is celebrated for her championing of Irish life and manners, she is also to be credited with the introduction to nineteenth-century fiction of a less prejudiced attitude towards minority and socially disadvantaged groups. Her later novel *Harrington* advanced the sympathetic representation of Jewish characters in fiction.

The second extract from Edgeworth's work is taken from one of her liveliest social novels. In *Belinda* (1801), the heroine, Belinda Portman, is sent to live in London with the fashionable Lady Delacour, who, as is revealed in the extract here, is an enticingly witty and highly intelligent observer of—and partaker in—social foibles. She has failed relationships with her husband and daughter, believes she is dying of breast cancer (wrongly, as it turns out), and, in consequence of her illness, has an opium habit. Also introduced in this extract, in Lady Delacour's words, is the assertive cross-dressing feminist Harriet Freke. *Belinda* is such a rich source of discussion of the social, intellectual, and emotional world of women—Anne K. Mellor calls it 'a textbook example of the new feminine Romantic ideology'[2]—that it has been included here in preference to lesser-known works by Edgeworth, such as the individual stories in collections such as *Popular Tales*. Edgeworth takes on Rousseau (the heroine's beloved, Clarence Hervey, has secretly trained up a Rousseau-style child of nature to be his bride), Wollstonecraft, Hays, Burney, Pope (the heroine's name alludes to *The Rape of the Lock*), and more. Quite simply, too, as the confessions of Lady Delacour show, *Belinda* is very well written.

∼

From *Castle Rackrent* (1800)

It was a very spirited letter to be sure: Sir Kit sent his service, and the compliments of the season, in return to the agent, and he would fight him with pleasure to-morrow, or any day, for sending him such a letter, if he was born a gentleman, which he was sorry (for both their sakes) to find (too late) he was not. Then, in a private postscript, he condescended to tell us, that all would be speedily settled to his satisfaction, and we should turn over a new leaf, for he was going to be married in a fortnight to the grandest heiress in England

---

[2] *Romanticism and Gender* (London: Routledge, 1993), 44.

and had only immediate occasion at present for £200, as he would not choose to touch his lady's fortune for travelling expences home to Castle Rackrent, where he intended to be, wind and weather permitting, early in the next month; and desired fires, and the house to be painted, and the new building to go on as fast as possible, for the reception of him and his lady before that time; with several words besides in the letter, which we could not make out, because, God bless him! he wrote in such a flurry. My heart warmed to my new lady when I read this; I was almost afraid it was too good news to be true; but the girls fell to scouring, and it was well they did, for we soon saw his marriage in the paper to a lady with I don't know how many tens of thousand pounds to her fortune: then I watched the post-office for his landing; and the news came to my son of his and the bride being in Dublin, and on the way home to Castle Rackrent. We had bonfires all over the country, expecting him down the next day, and we had his coming of age still to celebrate, which he had not time to do properly before he left the country; therefore a great ball was expected, and great doings upon his coming, as it were, fresh to take possession of his ancestors' estate. I never shall forget the day he came home: we had waited and waited all day long till eleven o'clock at night, and I was thinking of sending the boy to lock the gates, and giving them up for that night, when there came the carriages thundering up to the great hall door. I got the first sight of the bride; for when the carriage door opened, just as she had her foot on the steps, I held the flam full in her face to light her,* at which she shut her eyes, but I had a full view of the rest of her, and greatly shocked I was, for by that light she was little better than a blackamoor,* and seemed crippled, but that was only sitting so long in the chariot. 'You're kindly welcome to Castle Rackrent, my lady,' says I (recollecting who she was); 'did your honour hear of the bonfires?' His honour spoke never a word, nor so much as handed her up the steps—he looked to me no more like himself than nothing at all; I know I took him for the skeleton of his honour: I was not sure what to say next to one or t'other, but seeing she was a stranger in a foreign country, I thought it was right to speak cheerful to her, so I went back again to the bonfires. 'My lady,' says I, as she crossed the hall, 'there would have been fifty times as many, but for fear of the horses and frightening your ladyship: Jason and I forbid them, please your honour.' With that she looked at me a little bewildered. 'Will I have a fire lighted in the state room to-night?' was the next question I put to her, but never a word she answered, so I concluded she could not speak a word of English, and was from foreign parts. The short and the long of it was I couldn't tell what to make of her; so I left her to herself, and went straight down to the servants' hall to learn something for certain about her. Sir Kit's own man was tired, but the groom set him a talking at last, and we had it all out before ever I closed my eyes that night. The bride might well be a great fortune—she was a *Jewish* by all accounts, who are famous for their great riches. I had never seen any of that tribe or nation before, and could only gather, that she spoke a strange kind of English of her own, that she could not abide pork or sausages, and went neither to church or mass. Mercy upon his honour's poor soul, thought I; what will become of him and his, and all of us, with his heretic blackamoor at the head of the Castle Rackrent estate! I never slept a wink all night for thinking of it; but before the servants I put my pipe in my mouth, and kept my mind to myself; for I had a great regard for the family; and after this, when strange gentlemen's servants came to the house, and would begin to talk about the bride, I took care to put the best foot foremost, and passed her for a nabob in the kitchen,* which accounted for her dark complexion and every thing.

The very morning after they came home, however, I saw how things were plain enough between Sir Kit and my lady, though they were walking together arm in arm after breakfast, looking at the new building and the improvements. 'Old Thady,' said my master, just as he used to do, 'how do you do?' 'Very well, I thank your honour's honour,' said I; but I saw he was not well pleased, and my heart was in my mouth as I walked along after him. 'Is the large room damp, Thady?' said his honour. 'Oh, damp, your honour! how should it but be as dry as a bone,' says I, 'after all the fires we have kept in it day and night? it's the barrack-room your honour's talking on.'* 'And what is a barrack-room, pray, my dear?' were the first words I ever heard out of my lady's lips. 'No matter, my dear!' said he, and went on talking to me, ashamed like I should witness her ignorance. To be sure, to hear her talk one might have taken her for an innocent,* for it was, 'what's this, Sir Kit? and what's that, Sir Kit?' all the way we went. To be sure, Sir Kit had enough to do to answer her. 'And what do you call that, Sir Kit?' said she, 'that, that looks like a pile of black bricks, pray, Sir Kit?' 'My turf stack, my dear,' said my master, and bit his lip. Where have you lived, my lady, all your life, not to know a turf stack when you see it, thought I, but I said nothing. Then, by-and-bye, she takes out her glass, and begins spying over the country. 'And what's all that black swamp out yonder, Sir Kit?' says she. 'My bog, my dear,' says he, and went on whistling. 'It's a very ugly prospect, my dear,' says she. 'You don't see it, my dear,' says he, 'for we've planted it out, when the trees grow up in summer time,' says he. 'Where are the trees,' said she, 'my dear?' still looking through her glass. 'You are blind, my dear,' says he; 'what are those under your eyes?' 'These shrubs,' said she. 'Trees,' said he. 'May be they are what you call trees in Ireland, my dear,' said she; 'but they are not a yard high, are they?' 'They were planted out but last year, my lady,' says I, to soften matters between them, for I saw she was going the way to make his honour mad with her—'they are very well grown for their age, and you'll not see the bog of Allyballycarricko'shaughlin at-all-at-all through the screen, when once the leaves come out. But, my lady, you must not quarrel with any part or parcel of Allybal-lycarricko'shaughlin, for you don't know how many hundred years that same bit of bog has been in the family; we would not part with the bog of Allyballycarricko'shaughlin upon no account at all; it cost the late Sir Murtagh two hundred good pounds to defend his title to it and boundaries against the O'Learys who cut a road through it.' Now one would have thought this would have been hint enough for my lady, but she fell to laughing like one out of their right mind, and made me say the name of the bog over for her to get it by heart, a dozen times—then she must ask me how to spell it, and what was the meaning of it in English—Sir Kit standing by whistling all the while; I verily believed she laid the corner stone of all her future misfortunes at that very instant; but I said no more, only looked at Sir Kit.

There was no balls, no dinners, no doings; the country was all disappointed—Sir Kit's gentleman said in a whisper to me, it was all my lady's own fault, because she was so obstinate about the cross. 'What cross?' says I; 'is it about her being a heretic?' 'Oh, no such matter,' says he; 'my master does not mind her heresies, but her diamond cross, it's worth I can't tell you how much; and she has thousands of English pounds concealed in diamonds about her, which she as good as promised to give up to my master before he married, but now she won't part with any of them, and she must take the consequences.'

Her honey-moon, at least her Irish honey-moon, was scarcely well over, when his honour one morning said to me, 'Thady, buy me a pig!' and then the sausages were ordered, and here was the first open breaking-out of my lady's troubles. My lady came down herself into the kitchen, to speak to the cook about the sausages, and desired never to see them more at her table. Now my master had ordered them, and my lady knew that. The cook took my lady's part, because she never came down into the kitchen, and was young and innocent in housekeeping, which raised her pity; besides, said she, at her own table, surely, my lady should order and disorder what she pleases; but the cook soon changed her note, for my master made it a principle to have the sausages, and swore at her for a Jew herself, till he drove her fairly out of the kitchen; then, for fear of her place, and because he threatened that my lady should give her no discharge without the sausages, she gave up, and from that day forward always sausages, or bacon, or pig meat in some shape or other, went up to table; upon which my lady shut herself up in her own room, and my master said she might stay there, with an oath: and to make sure of her, he turned the key in the door, and kept it ever after in his pocket. We none of us ever saw or heard her speak for seven years after that:[1] he

---

[1] This part of the history of the Rackrent family can scarcely be thought credible; but in justice to honest Thady, it is hoped the reader will recollect the history of the celebrated Lady Cathcart's conjugal imprisonment.*—The Editor was acquainted with Colonel M'Guire, Lady Cathcart's husband; he has lately seen and questioned the maidservant who lived with Colonel M'Guire during the time of Lady Cathcart's imprisonment. Her ladyship was locked up in her own house for many years; during which period her husband was visited by the neighbouring gentry, and it was his regular custom at dinner to send his compliments to Lady Cathcart, informing her that the company had the honour to drink her ladyship's health, and begging to know whether there was any thing at table that she would like to eat? the answer was always, 'Lady Cathcart's compliments, and she has every thing she wants.' An instance of honesty in a poor Irish woman deserves to be recorded:—Lady Cathcart had some remarkably fine diamonds, which she had concealed from her husband, and which she was anxious to get out of the house, lest he should discover them. She had neither servant nor friend to whom she could entrust them; but she had observed a poor beggar woman; who used to come to the house; she spoke to her from the window of the room in which she was confined; the woman promised to do what she desired, and Lady Cathcart threw a parcel, containing the jewels, to her. The poor woman carried them to the person to whom they were directed; and several years afterwards, when Lady Cathcart recovered her liberty, she received her diamonds safely.

At Colonel M'Guire's death her ladyship was released. The editor, within this year, saw the gentleman who accompanied her to England after her husband's death. When she first was told of his death, she imagined that the news was not true, and that it was told only with an intention of deceiving her. At his death she had scarcely clothes

carried her dinner himself. Then his honour had a great deal of company to dine with him, and balls in the house, and was as gay and gallant, and as much himself as before he was married; and at dinner he always drank my lady Rackrent's good health, and so did the company, and he sent out always a servant, with his compliments to my lady Rackrent, and the company was drinking her ladyship's, health, and begged to know if there was any thing at table he might send her; and the man came back, after the sham errand, with my lady Rackrent's compliments, and she was very much obliged to Sir Kit—she did not wish for any thing, but drank the company's health. The country, to be sure, talked and wondered at my lady's being shut up, but nobody chose to interfere or ask any impertinent questions, for they knew my master was a man very apt to give a short answer himself, and likely to call a man out for it afterwards;* he was a famous shot; had killed his man before he came of age, and nobody scarce dared look at him whilst at Bath. Sir Kit's character was so well known in the country, that he lived in peace and quietness ever after, and was a great favourite with the ladies, especially when in process of time, in the fifth year of her confinement, my lady Rackrent fell ill, and took entirely to her bed, and he gave out that she was now skin and bone, and could not last through the winter. In this he had two physicians' opinions to back him (for now he called in two physicians for her), and tried all his arts to get the diamond cross from her on her death-bed, and to get her to make a will in his favour of her separate possessions; but there she was too tough for him. He used to swear at her behind her back, after kneeling to her to her face, and call her in the presence of his gentleman his stiff-necked Israelite, though before he married her, that same gentleman told me he used to call her (how he could bring it out, I don't know) 'my pretty Jessica!'* To be sure it must have been hard for her to guess what sort of a husband he reckoned to make her. When she was lying, to all expectation, on her death-bed of a broken heart, I could not but pity her, though she was a Jewish; and considering too it was

sufficient to cover her; she wore a red wig, looked scared, and her understanding seemed stupefied; she said that she scarcely knew one human creature from another; her imprisonment lasted above twenty years. These circumstances may appear strange to an English reader; but there is no danger in the present times, that any individual should exercise such tyranny as Colonel M'Guire's with impunity, the power being now all in the hands of government, and there being no possibility of obtaining from parliament an act of indemnity for any cruelties.

no fault of hers to be taken with my master so young as she was at the Bath, and so fine a gentleman as Sir Kit was when he courted her; and considering too, after all they had heard and seen of him as a husband, there were now no less than three ladies in our county talked of for his second wife, all at daggers drawn with each other, as his gentleman swore, at the balls, for Sir Kit for their partner,—I could not but think them bewitched; but they all reasoned with themselves, that Sir Kit would make a good husband to any Christian but a Jewish, I suppose, and especially as he was now a reformed rake; and it was not known how my lady's fortune was settled in her will, nor how the Castle Rackrent estate was all mortgaged, and bonds out against him, for he was never cured of his gaming tricks; but that was the only fault he had, God bless him.

My lady had a sort of fit, and it was given out she was dead, by mistake: this brought things to a sad crisis for my poor master,—one of the three ladies showed his letters to her brother, and claimed his promises, whilst another did the same. I don't mention names. Sir Kit, in his defence, said he would meet any man who dared to question his conduct, and as to the ladies, they must settle it amongst them who was to be his second, and his third, and his fourth, whilst his first was still alive, to his mortification and theirs. Upon this, as upon all former occasions, he had the voice of the country with him, on account of the great spirit and propriety he acted with. He met and shot the first lady's brother; the next day he called out the second, who had a wooden leg; and their place of meeting by appointment being in a new ploughed field, the wooden-leg man stuck fast in it. Sir Kit, seeing his situation, with great candour fired his pistol over his head; upon which the seconds interposed, and convinced the parties there had been a slight misunderstanding between them; thereupon they shook hands cordially, and went home to dinner together. This gentleman, to show the world how they stood together, and by the advice of the friends of both parties, to re-establish his sister's injured reputation, went out with Sir Kit as his second, and carried his message next day to the last of his adversaries: I never saw him in such fine spirits as that day he went out—sure enough he was within ames-ace of getting quit handsomely of all his enemies;* but unluckily, after hitting the toothpick out of his adversary's finger and thumb, he received a ball in a vital part, and was brought home, in little better than an hour after the affair, speechless on a hand-barrow, to my lady. We got the key out of his pocket the first thing we did, and my son Jason ran to unlock the barrack-room, where my lady had been shut up for seven years, to acquaint her with the fatal accident. The surprise bereaved her of her senses at first, nor would she believe but we were putting some new trick upon her, to entrap her out of her jewels, for a great while, till Jason bethought himself of taking her to the window, and showed her the men bringing Sir Kit up the avenue upon the hand-barrow, which had immediately the desired effect; for directly she burst into tears, and pulling her cross from her bosom, she kissed it with as great devotion as ever I witnessed; and lifting up her eyes to heaven, uttered some ejaculation, which none present heard; but I take the sense of it to be, she returned thanks for this unexpected inter-position in her favour when she had least reason to expect it. My master was greatly lamented: there was no life in him when we lifted him off the barrow, so he was laid out immediately, and *waked* the same night.* The country was all in an uproar about him, and not a soul but cried shame upon his murderer; who would have been hanged surely, if he could have been brought to his trial, whilst the gentlemen in the country were up about it; but he very prudently withdrew himself to the continent before the affair was made public. As for the young lady, who was the immediate cause of the fatal accident, however innocently, she could never show her head after at the balls in the county or any place; and by the advice of her friends and physicians, she was ordered soon after to Bath, where it was expected, if any where on this side of the grave, she would meet with the recovery of her health and lost peace of mind. As a proof of his great popularity, I need only add, that there was a song made upon my master's untimely death in the newspapers, which was in every body's mouth, singing up and down through the country, even down to the mountains, only three days after his unhappy exit. He was also greatly bemoaned at the Curragh, where his cattle were well known;* and all who had taken up his bets formerly were particularly inconsolable for his loss to society. His stud sold at the cant at the greatest price ever known in the county;* his favourite horses were chiefly disposed of amongst his particular friends, who would give any price for them for his sake; but no ready money was required by the new heir, who wished not to displease any of the gentlemen of the neighbourhood just upon his coming to settle amongst them; so a long credit was given where requisite, and the cash has never been gathered in from that day to this.

But to return to my lady:—She got surprisingly well after my master's decease. No sooner was it known for certain that he was dead, than all the gentlemen within twenty miles of us came in a body, as it were, to set my lady at liberty, and to protest against her confinement, which they now for the first time understood was against her own consent. The ladies too were as attentive as possible, striving who should be foremost with their morning visits; and they that saw the diamonds spoke very handsomely of them, but thought it a pity they were not bestowed, if it had so pleased God, upon a lady who would have become them better. All these civilities wrought little with my lady, for she had taken an unaccountable prejudice against the country, and every thing belonging to it, and was so partial to her native land, that after parting with the cook, which she did immediately upon my master's decease, I never knew her easy one instant, night or day, but when she was packing up to leave us. Had she meant to make any stay in Ireland, I stood a great chance of being a great favourite with her; for when she found I understood the weathercock, she was always finding some pretence to be talking to me, and asking me which way the wind blew, and was it likely, did I think, to continue fair for England. But when I saw she had made up her mind to spend the rest of her days upon her own income and jewels in England, I considered her quite as a foreigner, and not at all any longer as part of the family. She gave no vails to the servants at Castle Rackrent at parting,* notwithstanding the old proverb of '*as rich as a Jew*', which, she being a Jewish, they built upon with reason. But from first to last she brought nothing but misfortunes amongst us; and if it had not been all along with her, his honour, Sir Kit, would have been now alive in all appearance. Her diamond cross was, they say, at the bottom of it all; and it was a shame for her, being his wife, not to show more duty, and to have given it up when he condescended to ask so often for such a bit of a trifle in his distresses, especially when he all along made it no secret he married for money. But we will not bestow another thought upon her. This much I thought it lay upon my conscience to say, in justice to my poor master's memory.

From *Belinda* (1801)

Lady Delacour's History

After dinner, Lady Delacour, having made Belinda protest and blush, and blush and protest, that her head was not running upon the twisted note, began the history of her life and opinions in the following manner.

'I do nothing by halves, my dear—I shall not tell you my adventures, as Gil Blas told his to the archbishop of Grenada—skipping over the *useful* passages—because you are not an archbishop, and I should not have the grace to put on a sanctified face, if you were.* I am no hypocrite, and have nothing worse than folly to conceal. That's bad enough—for a woman who is known to play the fool, is always suspected of playing the devil. But I begin where I ought to end, with my moral, which I dare say you are not impatient to anticipate—I never read or listened to a moral at the end of a story in my life—manners for me, and morals for those that like them. My dear, you will be woefully disappointed, if in my story you expect any thing like a novel. I once heard a general say, that nothing was less like a review than a battle; and I can tell you, that nothing is more unlike a novel than real life. Of all lives, mine has been the least romantic. No love in it, but a great deal of hate. I was a rich heiress— I had, I believe, a hundred thousand pounds, or more; and twice as many caprices. I was handsome and witty—or, to speak with that kind of circumlocution which is called humility, the world, the partial world, thought me a beauty, and a *bel esprit*. Having told you my fortune, need I add, that I, or it, had lovers in abundance—of all sorts and degrees—not to reckon those, it may be presumed, who died of concealed passions for me. I had sixteen declarations and proposals in form—then what in the name of wonder, or of common sense, which by the by is the greatest of wonders—what in the name of common sense made me marry lord Delacour? Why, my dear, you—no, not *you*, but any girl who is not used to have a parcel of admirers, would think it the easiest thing in the world to make her choice; but let her judge by what she feels when a dexterous mercer or linen-draper produces pretty thing after pretty thing—and this is so becoming, and this will wear for ever—as he swears; but then that's so fashionable—the novice stands in a charming perplexity, and after examining, and doubting and tossing over half the goods in the shop, it's ten to one, when it begins to get late, the young lady, in a hurry, pitches upon the very ugliest and worst thing that she has seen. Just so it was with me and my lovers, and just so—"Sad was the hour, and luckless was the day"* I pitched upon viscount Delacour, for my lord and judge. He had just at that time lost at Newmarket more than he was worth in every sense of the word;* and my fortune was the most convenient thing in the world to a man in his condition. Lozenges are of sovereign use in some complaints. The heiress lozenge is a specific in some consumptions. You are surprized that I can laugh and jest about such a melancholy thing as my marriage with lord Delacour; and so am I, especially when I recollect all the circumstances—for though I bragged of there being no love in my history, there was when I was a goose or a gosling of about eighteen—just your age, Belinda, I think—something very like love playing about my heart, or my head. There was a certain Henry Percival, a Clarence Hervey of a man—* no, he had ten times the sense, begging your pardon, of Clarence Hervey—his misfortune, or mine, was that he had too much sense—he was in love with me but not with my faults; now I, wisely considering, that my faults were the greatest part of me, insisted upon his being in love with my faults. He wouldn't or couldn't—I said wouldn't—he said couldn't. I had been used to see the men about me lick the dust—for it was gold dust. Percival made wry faces—Lord Delacour made none. I pointed him out to Percival as an example—it was an example he would not follow. I was provoked, and I married, in hopes of provoking the man I loved. The worst of it was, I did not provoke him as much as I expected. Six months afterward, I heard of his marriage with a very amiable woman. I hate those *very amiable women*. Poor Percival! I should have been a very happy woman, I fancy, if I had married you—for I believe you were the only man who ever really loved me—but all that is over now! Where were we? O, I married my lord Delacour, knowing him to be a fool, and believing that, for this reason, I should find no trouble in governing him. But what a fatal mistake!—a fool, of all animals in the creation, is the most difficult to govern. We set out in the fashionable world, with a mutual desire to be as extravagant as possible. Strange, that with this similarity of taste we could never agree! Strange, that this similarity of taste was the cause of our perpetual quarrels! During the first year of our marriage, I had always the upper hand in these disputes, and the last word; and I was content. Stubborn as the brute was, I thought I should in time break him in. From the specimens you have seen, you may guess that I was even then a tolerable proficient in the dear art of *self-justification*—I had almost gained my point, just broken my lord's heart, when one fair morning, I unluckily told his man Champfort, that he knew no more how to cut hair than a sheep-shearer. Champfort, who is conceit personified, took mortal offence at this; and the devil, who is always at hand to turn anger into malice, put it into Champfort's head, to put it into my lord's head, that the world thought "My lady governed him". My lord took fire. They say the torpedo, the coldest of cold creatures,* sometimes gives out a spark—I suppose, when electrified with anger. The next time that innocent I insisted upon my lord Delacour's doing or not doing—I forget which—the most reasonable thing in the world, my lord turns short round, and answers, "My lady Delacour, I am not a man to be governed by a wife." And from that time to this, the words "I am not a man to be governed by a wife" have been written in his obstinate face, as all the world who can read the human countenance may see. My dear, I laugh, but even in the midst of laughter, there is sadness. But you don't know what it is—I hope you never may—to have an obstinate fool for a bosom friend.

'I at first flattered myself, that my lord's was not an inveterate, incurable malady, but from his obvious weakness, I might have seen that there was no hope; for cases of obstinacy are always dangerous in proportion to the weakness of the patient. My lord's case was desperate. Kill or cure, was my humane or prudent maxim. I determined to try the poison of jealousy, by way of an alternative. I had long kept it in petto as my ultimate remedy.* I fixed upon a proper subject—a man with whom I thought that I could coquette to all eternity, without any danger to myself—a certain colonel Lawless—as empty a coxcomb as you would wish to see. The world, said I to myself, can never be so absurd as to suspect lady Delacour with such a man as this, though her lord may, and will, for nothing is too absurd for him to believe. Half my theory proved just—that is saying a great deal for any theory. My lord swallowed the remedy that I had prepared for him, with an avidity, and a *bonhommie*, which it did me good to behold—my remedy operated beyond my most sanguine expectations. The poor man was cured of his obstinacy, and became stark mad with jealousy. Then indeed I had some hopes of him; for a madman can be managed, a fool cannot. In a month's time, I made him quite docile. With a face longer than the weeping philosopher's, he came to me one morning, and assured me, he would do every thing. I pleased, provided I would consult my own honour and his, and give up colonel Lawless.

' "Give up!"—I could hardly forbear laughing at the expression. I replied, "that as long as my lord treated me with becoming respect. I had never in thought or deed, given him just cause of complaint; but that I was not a woman to be insulted, or to be kept, as I had hitherto been, in leading-strings, by a husband". My lord, flattered, as I meant he should be with the idea, that it was possible he should be suspected of keeping a wife in leading-strings, fell to making protestations—"he hoped his future conduct would prove, &c." Upon this hint, I gave the reins to my imagination, and full drive I went into a fresh career of extravagance; if I were checked, it was *an insult*, and I began directly to talk of *leading strings*. This ridiculous game I played successfully enough, for some time, till at length, though naturally rather slow at calculation, he actually discovered, that if we lived at the rate of twenty thousand a year, and had only ten thousand a year to spend, we should, in due time, have nothing left. This notable discovery he communicated to me one morning, after a long preamble. When he had finished prosing, I agreed, that it was demonstrably just, that he should retrench his expenses; but that it was equally unjust and impossible, that I could make any reformation in my civil list. That economy was a word which I had never heard of in my life, till I married his lordship; that, upon second recollection, it was true, I had heard of such a thing as national economy; and that it would be a very pretty, though rather hackneyed topic of declamation for a maiden speech in the house of lords. I therefore advised him to reserve all he had to say upon this subject for the noble lord upon the woolsack;* nay, I very graciously added, that upon this condition, I would go to the house myself, to give his arguments and eloquence a fair hearing, and that I would do my best to keep myself awake. This was all mighty playful and witty; but it happened that my lord Delacour, who never had any great taste for wit, could not this unlucky morning at all relish it. Of course I grew angry, and reminded him, with an indelicacy which his want of generosity justified, that an heiress, who had brought a hundred thousand pounds into his family, had some right to amuse herself, and that it was not my fault if elegant amusements were more expensive than others.

'Then came a long criminating and recriminating chapter. It was "My lord, your Newmarket blunders."—"My lady, your cursed *theatricals*."—"My lord, I have surely a right"—"and my lady, I have surely as good a right."

'But, my dear, Belinda, however we might pay one another, we could not pay all the world with words. In short, after running through thousands, and tens of thousands, we were actually in distress for money. Then came selling of lands, and I don't know what devices, for raising money, according to the mode of lawyers and attorneys. It was quite indifferent to me, how they got money, provided that they got it for us. By what art these gentlemen raised money, I never troubled myself to inquire; it might have been the black art, for any thing I know to the contrary. I know nothing of business. So I signed all the papers they brought to me; and I was mighty well pleased to find, that by so easy an expedient as writing, "T. C. H. Delacour", I could command money at will. I signed, and signed, till at last I was with all due civility informed that my signature was no longer worth a farthing; and when I came to inquire into the cause of this phenomenon, I could no wise understand what my lord Delacour's lawyer said to me. He was a prig, and I had not patience either to listen to him, or to look at him. I sent for an old uncle of mine, who used to manage all my money matters before I was married: I put the uncle and the lawyer into a room together with their parchments, to fight the matter out, or to come to a right understanding if they could. The last it seems was quite impossible. In the course of half an hour, out comes my uncle in such a rage! I never shall forget his face—all the bile in his body had gotten into it—he had literally no whites to his eyes. "My dear uncle," said I, "What is the matter? Why you are absolutely gold stick in waiting."*

' "No matter what I am, child," said the uncle, "I'll tell you what you are with all your wit—a dupe—'tis a shame for a woman of your sense to be such a fool, and to know nothing of business—and if you knew nothing yourself, could not you send for me?"

' "I was too ignorant to know that I knew nothing," said I; but I will not trouble you with all the said Is and said hes. I was made to understand, that if lord Delacour were to die the next day, I should live a beggar. Upon this I grew serious, as you may imagine. My uncle assured me that I had been grossly imposed upon by my lord and his lawyer, and that I had been swindled out of my senses, and out of my dower. I repeated all that my uncle said, very faithfully, to lord Delacour; and all that either he or his lawyer could furbish out by way of answer was, that "necessity had no law".* Necessity, it must be allowed, though it might be the mother of law, was never with my lord the mother of invention. Having now found out that I had a good right to complain, I indulged myself in it most gloriously. In short, my dear, we had a comfortable family quarrel—love quarrels are easily made up—but of money quarrels there is no end. From the moment these money quarrels commenced, I began to hate lord Delacour—before I had only despised him. You can have no notion to what meanness extravagance reduces men. I have known lord Delacour shirk, and look so shabby, and tell so many lies to people about a hundred guineas—a hundred guineas! What do I say? About twenty, ten, five! O, my dear, I cannot bear the thoughts of it! But I was going on to tell you that my good uncle, and all my relations, quarrelled with me for having ruined myself, as they said—but I said, they quarrelled with me for fear I should ask them for some of their "vile trash". Accordingly I abused and ridiculed them, one and all; and for my pains, all my acquaintance said that "lady Delacour was a woman of a vast deal of spirit".

'We were relieved from our money embarrassments by the timely death of a rich nobleman; to whose large estate my lord Delacour was heir at law.* I was intoxicated with the idle compliments of all my acquaintance, and I endeavoured to console myself for misery at home, by gayety abroad. Ambitious of pleasing universally, I became the worst of slaves—a slave to the world. Not a moment of my time was at my own disposal—not one of my actions; I may say, not one of my thoughts, was my own. I was obliged to find things "charming" every hour, which tired me to death; and every day it was the same dull round of hypocrisy and dissipation. You wonder to hear me speak in this manner, Belinda, but one must speak the truth sometimes; and this is what I have been saying to Harriet Freke* continually—continually, for these ten years past. Then why persist in the same kind of life, you say? Why, my dear, because I could not stop—I was fit for this kind of life, and for no other—I could not be happy at *home*, for what sort of a companion could I have made of lord Delacour? By this time he was tired of his horse Potatoes, and his horse Highflier, and his horse Eclipse, and Goliah, and Jenny Grey, &c. and he had taken to hard drinking, which soon turned him as you see, quite into a beast. I forgot to tell you, that I had three children during the first five years of my marriage. The first was a boy; he was born dead; and my lord, and all his odious relations, laid the blame upon me; because I would not be kept prisoner half a year by an old mother of his, a vile Cassandra, who was always prophesying that my child would not be born alive.* My second child was a girl, but a poor diminutive, sickly thing. It was the fashion at this time for fine mothers to suckle their own children—so much the worse for the poor brats. Fine nurses never made fine children. There was a prodigious rout made about the matter; a vast deal of sentiment and sympathy, and compliments and inquiries; but after the novelty was over, I became heartily sick of the business; and at the end of about three months my poor child was sick too—I don't much like to think of it—it died. If I had put it out to nurse, I should have been thought by my friends an unnatural mother—but I should have saved its life. I should have bewailed the loss of the infant more, if lord Delacour's relations and my own had not made such lamentations upon the occasion, that I was stunned. I couldn't or wouldn't shed a tear, and I left it to the old dowager to perform in public, as she wished, the part of chief mourner,* and to comfort herself in private, by lifting up her hands and eyes, and railing at me as the most insensible of mothers. All this time I suffered more than she did; but that is what she shall never have the satisfaction of knowing. I determined, that if ever I had another child I would not have the barbarity to nurse it myself. Accordingly, when my third child, a girl, was born, I sent it off immediately to the country, to a stout healthy, broad-faced nurse, under whose care it grew and flourished; so that at three years old, when it was brought back to me, I could scarcely believe the chubby little thing was my own child. The same reasons which convinced me I ought not to nurse my own child, determined me, *a plus forte raison*,* not to undertake its education. Lord Delacour could not bear the child because it was not a boy. The girl was put under the care of a governess, who plagued my heart out with her airs and *tracasseries* for three or four years;* at the end of which time, as she turned out to be lord Delacour's mistress in form, I was obliged—in form—to beg she would leave my house, and I put her pupil into better hands, I hope, at a celebrated academy for young ladies. There she will, at any rate, be better instructed than she could be at home. I beg your pardon, my dear, for this digression on nursing and schooling, but I wanted only to explain to you why it was, that when I was weary of the business, I still went on in a course of dissipation. You see I had nothing at home, either in the shape of husband or children, to engage my affections. I believe it was this "aching void" in my heart which made me, after looking abroad some time for a bosom friend, take such a prodigious fancy to Mrs Freke. She was just then coming into fashion—she struck me the first time I met her, as being downright ugly; but there was a wild oddity in her countenance which made one stare at her, and she was delighted to be stared at—especially by me—so we were mutually agreeable to each other—I as starer, and she as stare. Harriet Freke had, without comparison, more assurance than any man or woman I ever saw. She was downright brass—but of the finest kind— Corinthian brass—She was one of the first who brought what I call *harum scarum* manners into fashion.* I told you that she had assurance—*impudence* I should have called it, for no other word is strong enough. Such things as I have heard Harriet Freke say! You will not believe it; but her conversation at first absolutely made me, like an old fashioned fool, wish I had a fan to play with. But to my astonishment, all this *took* surprisingly with a set of fashionable young men. I found it necessary to reform my manners. If I had not taken heart of grace, and publicly abjured the heresies of *false delicacy*, I should have been excommunicated—Lady Delacour's sprightly elegance—allow me to speak of myself in the style in which the newspaper writers talk of me—Lady Delacour's sprightly elegance was but pale—not to say *faded* pink, compared with the scarlet of Mrs Freke's dashing audacity. As my rival, she would on certain ground have beaten me hollow; it was therefore good policy to make her my friend. We joined forces, and nothing could stand against us. But I have no right to give myself credit for good policy in forming this intimacy; I really followed the dictates of my heart or my imagination. There was a frankness in Harriet's manner, which I mistook for artlessness of character. She spoke with such unbounded freedom on certain subjects, that I gave her credit for unbounded sincerity on all subjects. She had the talent of making the world believe *that* virtue to be invulnerable by nature, which disdained the common outworks of art for its defence. I, amongst others, took it for granted, that the woman who could make it her sport to "touch the brink of all we hate",* must have a stronger head than other people. I have since been convinced, however, of my mistake. I am persuaded that few can touch the brink without tumbling headlong down the precipice. Don't apply this, my dear, *literally*, to the person of whom we were speaking. I am not base enough to betray her secrets, however I may have been provoked by her treachery. Of her character and history you shall hear nothing, but what is necessary for my own justification. The league of amity between us was scarcely ratified, before my lord Delacour came with his wise remonstrating face, to beg me "to consider what was due to my own honour and his". Like the cosmogony-man in the Vicar of Wakefield,* he came out over and over with this cant phrase, which had once stood him in stead. "Do you think my lord," said I, "that because I give up poor Lawless to oblige you, I shall give up all common sense, to suit myself to your taste? Harriet Freke is visited by every body, but old dowagers and old maids. I am neither an old dowager nor an old maid. The consequence is obvious, my lord." Pertness in dialogue, my dear, often succeeds better with my lord than wit. I therefore saved the sterling gold, and bestowed upon him nothing but counters*—I tell you this to save the credit of my taste and judgment. But to return to my friendship for Harriet Freke. I, of course, repeated to her every word which had passed between my husband and me. She out-Heroded Herod upon the occasion;* and laughed so much at what she called my folly in *pleading guilty* in the Lawless cause, that I was downright ashamed of myself, and purely to prove my innocence, I determined, upon the first convenient opportunity, to renew my intimacy with the colonel. The opportunity which I so ardently desired of redeeming my independence, was not long wanting—Lawless, as my stars (which you know are always more in fault than ourselves)* would have it, returned just at this time from the continent, where he had been with his regiment; he returned with a wound across his forehead, and a black fillet which made him look something more like a hero, and ten times more like a coxcomb, than ever.* He was in fashion at all events, and amongst other ladies, Mrs Luttridge—odious Mrs Luttridge! smiled upon him. The colonel, however, had taste enough to know the difference between smile and smile; he laid himself and his laurels at my feet, and I carried him and them about in triumph.

Wherever I went, especially to Mrs Luttridge's, envy and scandal joined hands to attack me, and I heard wondering and whispering wherever I went. I had no object in view but to provoke my husband, therefore conscious of the purity of my intentions, it was my delight to brave the opinion of the wondering world. I gave myself no concern about the effect my coquetry might have upon the object of this flirtation—poor Lawless!—heart—I took it for granted he had none. How should a coxcomb come by a heart—vanity I knew he had in abundance, but this gave me no alarm, as I thought that if it should ever make him forget himself—I mean, forget what was due to me— I could, by one flash of my wit, strike him to the earth, or blast him for ever. One night we had been together at Mrs Luttridge's—she, amongst other good things, kept a faro bank*—and I am convinced, cheated—be that as it may, I lost an immensity of money, and it was my pride to lose with as much gayety as any body else could win; so I was, or appeared to be, in uncommonly high spirits, and Lawless had his share of my good humour. We left Mrs Luttridge's together early; about half past one. As the colonel was going to hand me to my carriage, a smart-looking young man, as I thought, came up close to the coach door, and stared me full in the face: I was not a woman to be disconcerted at such a thing as this, but I really was startled when the young fellow jumped into the carriage after me: I thought he was mad: I had only courage enough to scream. Lawless seized hold of the intruder to drag him out, and out he dragged the youth, exclaiming in a high tone, "What is the meaning of all this, sir? Who the devil are you? My name's Lawless—who the devil are you?" The answer to this was a convulsion of laughter. By the laugh, I knew it to be Harriet Freke, "Who am I! only a Freke!" cried she, "Shake hands." I gave her my hand, into the carriage she sprang, and desired the colonel to follow her: Lawless laughed, we all laughed, and drove away. "Where do you think I've been?" said Harriet, "in the gallery of the House of Commons; almost squeezed to death these four hours; but I swore I'd hear Sheridan's speech* to night, and I did. Betted fifty guineas I would, with Mrs Luttridge, and have won. Fun and Freke for ever, huzza!" Harriet was mad with spirits, and so noisy and unmanageable that, as I told her, I was sure she was drunk. Lawless, in his silly way, laughed incessantly, and I was so taken up with her oddities, that, for some time, I did not perceive we were going the Lord knows where; till, at last, when the 'larum of Harriet's voice ceased for an instant, I was struck with the strange sound of the carriage! "Where are we? Not upon the stones, I'm sure," said I, and putting my head out of the window, I saw we were beyond the turnpike. "The coachman's drunk as well as you, Harriet," said I; and I was going to pull the string to stop him, but Harriet had hold of it. "The man is going very right," said she, "I've told him where to go. Now don't fancy that Lawless and I are going to run away with you. All that is unnecessary now-a-days, thank God!" To this I agreed, and laughed for fear of being ridiculous. "Guess where you are going," said Harriet. I guessed and guessed, but could not guess right; and my merry companions were infinitely diverted with my perplexity and impatience, more especially, as I believe, in spite of all my efforts, I grew rather graver than usual. We went on to the end of Sloane-street, and quite out of town;* at last we stopped. It was dark, the footman's flambeau was out, I could only just see by the lamps, that we were at the door of a lone, odd looking house. The house door opened, and an old woman appeared with a lantern in her hand.

'"Where is this farce or freak, or whatever you call it, to end?" said I, as Harriet pulled me into the dark passage along with her.

'Alas! my dear Belinda,' said lady Delacour, pausing; 'I little foresaw where or how it was to end: but I am not come yet to the tragical part of my story, and as long as I can laugh, I will. As the old woman and her miserable blue light went on before us. I could almost have thought of sir Bertrand, or of some German *horrifications*,* but I heard Lawless, who never could help laughing at the wrong time, bursting behind me, with a sense of his own superiority.

'"Now you will learn your destiny, lady Delacour?" said Harriet, in a solemn tone.

'"Yes! from the celebrated Mrs W——, the modern dealer in art magic," said I, laughing, "for now I guess whereabouts I am." Colonel Lawless's laugh broke the spell. "Harriet Freke, never whilst you live expect to succeed in *the sublime*." Harriet swore at the colonel, for the veriest *spoil-sport* she had ever seen, and she whispered to me. "The reason he laughs is, because he is afraid of our suspecting the truth of him, that he believes *tout de bon* in conjuration, and the devil, and all that."* The old woman, whose cue I found was to be dumb, opened a door at the top of a narrow staircase, and pointing to a tall figure, completely enveloped in fur, left us to our fate. I will not trouble you with a pompous description of all the mummery of the scene, my dear, as I despair of being able to frighten you out of your wits. I should have been downright angry with Harriet Freke for bringing me to such a place, but that I knew women of the first fashion had been with Mrs W——before us—some in sober sadness—some by way of frolic. So as there was no fear of being ridiculous, there was no shame, you know, and my conscience was quite at ease. Harriet had no conscience, so she was always at ease; and never more so than in male attire, which she had been told became her particularly. She supported the character of a young rake with such spirit and *truth*, that I am sure no common conjurer could have discovered any thing feminine about her. She rattled on with a set of nonsensical questions; and among other things, she asked, "How soon will lady Delacour marry again after her lord's death?"

'"She will never marry after her lord's death," answered the oracle. "Then she will marry during his life time," said Harriet. "True," answered the oracle. Colonel Lawless laughed; I was angry; and the colonel would have been quiet, for he was a gentleman, but there was no such thing as managing Mrs Freke, who, though she had laid aside the modesty of her own sex, had not acquired the decency of the other. "Who is to be lady Delacour's second husband?" cried she. "You'll not offend any of the present company by naming the man." "Her second husband I cannot name," replied the oracle, "but let her beware of a Lawless lover." Mrs Freke and colonel Lawless, encouraged by her, triumphed over me without mercy; I may say, without shame! Well, my dear, I am in a hurry to have done with all this: though I "doated upon folly",* yet I was terrified at the thoughts of any thing worse. The idea of a divorce, the public brand of shameful life, shocked me, in spite of all my real and all my assumed levity. O that I had, at this instant, dared to *be myself*! But my fear of ridicule was greater than my fear of vice. "Bless me, my dear lady Delacour," whispered Harriet, as we left this house, "what can make you in such a desperate hurry to get home? You gape and fidget—one would think you had never sat up a night before in your life. I verily believe you are afraid to trust yourself with us. Which of us are you afraid of; Lawless, or me, or *yourself*?" There was a tone of contempt in the last words, which piqued me to the quick; and, however strange it may seem, I was now anxious only to convince Harriet that I was not afraid of myself. False shame made me act, as if I had no shame. You would not suspect me of knowing any thing of false shame, but depend upon it, my dear, many, who appear to have as much assurance as I have, are secretly its slaves. I moralize, because I am come to a part of my story, which I should almost be glad to omit—but I promised you, that there should be no sins of omission. It was light, but not broad daylight, when we got to Knightsbridge.* Lawless encouraged, for I cannot deny it, by the levity of my manner, as well as of Harriet's, was in higher and more familiar spirits than I ever saw him. Mrs Freke desired me to set her down at her sister's who lived in Grosvenor Place. I did so, and I beg you to believe, that I was in an agony to get rid of my colonel at the same time; but you know, I could not, before Harriet Freke, absolutely say to him—"Get out!" Indeed, to tell things as they were, it was scarcely possible to guess by my manner, that I was under any anxiety—I acted my part so well, or so ill. As Harriet Freke jumped out of the coach, a cock crowed in the area of her sister's house.* "There!" cried Harriet, "do you hear the cock crow, lady Delacour? Now it's to be hoped your fear of goblins is over—else I would not be so cruel, as to leave the pretty dear all alone." "All alone," answered I, "your friend the colonel is much obliged to you for making nobody of him." "My friend the colonel," whispered Harriet, leaning with her bold masculine arms folded upon the coach door, "My friend the colonel is much obliged to me, I'm sure, for remembering what the cunning, or the knowing woman told us just now, that you and he are—or are to be—one and the same person. So when I said I left you alone, I was not guilty of a bull, was I?"* I had the grace to be heartily ashamed of this speech, and called out in utter confusion "to Berkeley square. But where shall I set you down, colonel? Harriet, good morning—don't forget you are in man's clothes." I did not dare to repeat the question of "where shall I set you down, colonel?" at this instant, because Harriet gave me such an arch sneering look, as much as to say—still afraid of yourself! We drove on—I'm persuaded that the confusion which, in spite of all my efforts, broke through my affected levity, encouraged Lawless, who was naturally a coxcomb and a fool, to believe that I was actually his—else he never could have been so insolent. In short, my dear, before we had got through the turnpike gate, I was downright obliged to say to him, "Get out!"—which I did with a degree of indignation, that quite astonished him. He muttered something about ladies knowing their minds—and I own, though I went off with flying colours, I secretly blamed myself as much as I did him, and I blamed Harriet more than I did either. I sent for her the next day as soon as I could, to consult her. She expressed such astonishment, and so much concern, at this catastrophe of our night's frolic, and blamed herself with so many oaths, and execrated Lawless for a coxcomb so much to the ease and satisfaction of my conscience, that I was confirmed in my good opinion of her, and indeed felt for her the most lively affection and esteem—for observe, with me esteem ever followed affection; instead of affection following esteem. Woe be to all, who in morals preposterously put the cart before the horse! But to proceed with my history—all fashionable historians stop to make reflections, supposing that no one else can have the sense to make any. My *esteemed* friend agreed with me, that it would be best for all the parties concerned to hush up this business; that as Lawless was going out of town in a few days, to be elected for a borough,* we should get rid of him in the best way possible, without "more last words"—that he had been punished sufficiently on the spot, and that to punish twice for the same offence, once in private and once in public, would be contrary to the laws of English men and English women, and in my case would be contrary to the evident dictates of prudence—because I could not complain, without calling up lord Delacour, to call Lawless out. This I could not do without acknowledging that his lordship had been in the right, in warning me about *his honour and my own*, which old phrase I dreaded to hear for the ninety-ninth time; besides, lord Delacour was the last man in the world I should have chosen for my knight—though unluckily he was my lord. Besides, all things considered, I thought the whole story might not tell so well in the world for me, tell it which way I would. We therefore agreed, that it would be most expedient to hold our tongues. We took it for granted, that Lawless would hold his, and as for my people, they knew nothing, I thought, or if they did, I was sure of them. How the thing got abroad, I could not at the time conceive, though now I am well acquainted with the baseness and treachery of the woman I called my friend. The affair was known, and talked of every where the next day, and the story was told especially at odious Mrs Luttridge's, with such exaggerations as drove me almost mad. I was enraged, inconceivably enraged with Lawless, from whom I imagined the reports originated.

'I was venting my indignation against him in a room full of

company, where I had just made my story good, when a gentleman, to whom I was a stranger, came in breathless, with the news that colonel Lawless was killed in a duel by lord Delacour—that they were carrying him home to his mother's, and that the body was just going by the door. The company all crowded to the windows immediately, and I was left standing alone, till I could stand no longer. What was said or done after this, I do not remember—I only know, that when I came to myself, the most dreadful sensation I even experienced was, the certainty that I had the blood of a fellow creature to answer for. I wonder,' said lady Delacour, breaking off at this part of her history, and rising suddenly, 'I wonder what is become of Marriott?—surely it is time for me to have my drops. Miss Portman, have the goodness to ring, for I *must* have something immediately.' Belinda was terrified at the wildness of her manner. Lady Delacour became more composed, or put more constraint upon herself, at the sight of Marriott—Marriott brought from the closet in her lady's room the drops, which lady Delacour swallowed with precipitation. Then she ordered coffee, and afterward *chasse-café*,* and at last, turning to Belinda with a forced smile, she said—

'Now shall the princess Scheherazade go on with her story?'*

JOANNA SOUTHCOTT
(1750–1814)

Described in the *Dictionary of National Biography* not as writer, religious thinker, or self-styled prophet but simply as 'fanatic', Joanna Southcott was the fourth daughter of a farmer, William Southcott, and his second wife Hannah, and was born and brought up in the village of Gittisham, near Ottery St Mary in Devon. Her major intervention in public religious life was made in spite of centuries of opposition: 'Let your women keep silence in the churches: for it is not permitted unto them to speak; but they are commanded to be under obedience, as also saith the law', pronounced Paul (1 Corinthians 14:34). As a child she worked in the farm dairy, and after the death of her mother she went to work in a shop in Honiton, then was a servant in the household of a country squire before taking a succession of jobs in domestic service in Exeter. She was eagerly sought in marriage, and out of it, and had a succession of offers from eligible farmers, one of whom, Noah Bishop, was a clear favourite. Her reputation seems to have been sullied by jealous gossip, however, and she remained single. An early enthusiasm for religion became increasingly strong; as well as regular church attendance she went to Wesleyan services and joined the Methodist Society in 1791.

In 1792 she made her first public prophecy, that the locusts of Abaddon would descend on the world, suffered an extreme nervous agitation, and, recovering at the house of her sister Susanna in Plymtree, outside Exeter, began to write down prophecies. Her sister discouraged her; whereupon Southcott began to seal up her prophecies so that they could only be opened after the events she described. When she was able to return to Exeter in 1793 she set out to convince local clergymen of the truth of her prophecies, and continued to write and to secure her work with a distinctive seal. One clergyman, the Revd Mr Pomeroy, was for a while a supporter of her claims, but Southcott remained on the fringe of acceptable religious thinking until the publication, by an Exeter printer in 1801, of *The Strange Effects of Faith*, a ninepenny pamphlet of 48 pages which included an account of her life and of her campaign to be taken seriously. She invested £100 of her savings in its publication. As well as her characteristic mixture of narrative and 'dictated' verses of advice and prophecy it contains the first of many reflections on her gender: 'What a wonder does this appear, that the secrets of the Lord should be revealed to a woman. A wonder so great to many, that they cannot believe it' (73–4). The reason for it is that Southcott is to compensate for Eve's mistake and take revenge on Satan who duped her.

Readers convinced by this work introduced Southcott's claims to three established clergymen who in 1802 satisfied her long-proclaimed ambition to be 'tried'. Further trials followed in 1803 and 1804. In 1802 she moved to Paddington, London, and began to issue to her believers sealed certificates of salvation, signed by her: ten thousand had been applied for by 1805. The practice stopped in 1808, but the notoriety it created did not. She was often associated with the prophet Richard Brothers, but later dissociated herself from his ideas. In 1803 she met an 18 year old, Henry ('Joseph') Prescott, whose dreams she interpreted; and later in the same year she toured the midland and northern counties, gathering believers. The Exeter Dissenter William Tozer opened a chapel for her followers in Southwark, London, in 1805. In all she published sixty-five books of prophecy and commentary, including three *Continuations* of *The Strange Effects of Faith* (1802–3), *The First Book of the Sealed Prophecies* and *The Second Book of the Sealed Prophecies* (1803), *Letters and Communications* (1804), and *The True Explanation of the Bible* (1804–10). It has been estimated that almost three-quarters of her followers were women.

In *The Third Book of Wonders* (1813) Southcott announced that she had been chosen to bring forth the second Christ, 'Shiloh'; preparations were enthusiastic and elaborate, but her supposed pregnancy at the age of sixty-four was protracted, and she became ill. She was examined by nine doctors in August 1814; six of them thought that her symptoms would have indicated pregnancy in a younger woman. She died in December 1814, and at her request her body was kept warm for four days before an autopsy and a secretive night-time burial.

Some of the malicious 'biographical' accounts of Southcott are discussed in the Introduction. Of all the women writers represented in this collection, however, she has one of the strongest claims to a lasting and international influence. The 1843 pamphlet *A Call to the Believers in the Divine Mission of the Lord to Joanna Southcott, stimulating them to do their duty to their God, their King, their Country, their Families, and Themselves* refers to her as 'the martyred bride of Jesus, our beloved Mother' (17) and praises the inspiring language of the verse prophecies. *The Vision of Judgment; or, the Return of Joanna from her Trance* (1829) is only one of a multitude of protestations of continuing faith; but there is a concomitant mocking tradition, typified by the mischievous *A Full Account of the Ghost of Joanna Southcott With her Nightly Preambles, and her Merry Song* (n.d.: ?1815) which testifies to early traditions of her haunting the countryside (and the taverns of the Elephant and Castle area of London). Southcottian believers, disputants, and revivalists have kept her name alive. The table of Southcottian sects in G. R. Balleine's *Past Finding Out: The Tragic Story of Joanna Southcott and her Successors,*[1] traces groups such as the Old Southcottians, the New and Latter House of Israel, The New Eve, and the Followers of Zion Ward (Shilohites). In her own time, the London engraver William Sharp became a Southcottian, and recommended her to William Blake; Blake was not convinced, however, being, as the painter Flaxman observed to Henry Crabb Robinson, 'not fond of playing second fiddle'.[2] Blake's epigram 'On the Virginity of the Virgin Mary and Joanna Southcott', thought to date from 1807–9, suggests her continuing currency. Among her contemporaries, some not especially interested in her religious importance recognized in her story elements of a wider social significance: in his 1817 essay 'What is the People?', for example, William Hazlitt places establishment scorn of Southcott in the context of the ideological use of biblical teaching to keep the poor in their place. For Byron, in *Don Juan*, Southcott is simply a way of attacking Wordsworth: 'And the new births of both their stale virginities | Have proved but

---

[1] (London: SPCK, 1956), 147.

[2] *Diary, Reminiscences, and Correspondence of Henry Crabb Robinson, Barrister-at-law, F.S.A.*, selected and ed. Thomas Sadler, 3rd edn., 2 vols. (1872; New York: AMS Press, 1967), i. 247.

dropsies, taken for divinities' (iii. 95). A 'Memoir of Joanna Southcott' published in volume 4 of *The Female Preceptor* (1814), probably by Laetitia Hawkins, calls Southcott 'a *disgrace to her sex*' (361) even though it not entirely ironically classes the prediction of the coming of Shiloh 'amongst the wonders of the present day'.

The question of female authority is central to Southcott's work. In *Sound an Alarm in my Holy Mountain* (1804), God reveals to Southcott that the completion of his plan for mankind depends upon woman—that revelation to a man will not do, at all: 'Therefore have I made all her Prophecies more true and plain . . . than any prophecies given to man, that you may now begin to see the woman is your Helpmate for your Good. But if all were given plain and true to man, they would not want, nor receive the woman for their good; but judge they knew all themselves' (62). The question of gender is therefore closely bound up in Southcott's work with the question of style and address: her crises of narratorial authority, and the 'plain' relationship she seeks to establish with her readers, are familiar issues in women's writing, and Southcott, still dismissed as a disastrously naïve stylist, deserves closer attention. Southcott's attempts to win credence from established church figures seems to detract from her own authority: she is constantly seeking approval from male establishments. But she also undermines them, often saying that God told her before a particular approach that it was doomed to failure.

Southcott's writings (later dictated) are voluminous and repetitive ('running on like a parrot', as Satan complains in *A Dispute between the Woman and the Powers of Darkness* (1802), 15), interspersing personal prose with verse prophecy. They are represented here by extracts from her first book, *The Strange Effects of Faith*, describing her struggle to be listened to in Exeter; from the Second Part of the same work, in which she deals with the accusations of her detractors and in particular with the claim that she is mad; and from *A Dispute between the Woman and the Powers of Darkness*, in which she expands on the argument, presented many times in her published work, that because mankind first fell through the errors of Eve its deliverance from Satan must likewise be accomplished through the agency of a woman, Southcott herself. In the first day's dispute, Satan, at this stage calling himself merely 'Satan's Friend', tempts Southcott by referring to her love of writing and by seeking to arouse her envy of writers whose works are highly regarded and sell well: 'dost thou not know *many* have had thousands of pounds for being clever in writing and singing, and get rich thereby, and caressed in the first companies, and their books sell faster than they could write them; while thine lay by; and thou hast but a few friends to keep thee alive?' (9). After Southcott's spirited defence of her faith in the truth of her works, Satan is provoked to exclaim 'Don't say no more of one thing's contradicting another: for that is like thy writings, and the Bible: full of contradictions throughout' (11).

∽

From *The Strange Effects of Faith* (1801)

As I have began [*sic*] to publish to the world, I shall give some short account of my Life, which hath been singular, from my youth up to this day. I shall omit former particulars, and begin with informing the Reader, that, in 1792, I was strangely visited, by day and night, concerning what was coming upon the whole earth. I was then ordered to set it down in writing. I obeyed, though not without strong external opposition; and so it has continued to the present time.

In 1792, my Sister told me, I was growing out of my senses. She said, 'You say there will be a war. Who shall we go to war with? the French are destroying themselves.* As to the dearth of provision you speak of, you are wrong; for corn will come down very low; I could not make 4*s*. 6*d*. a bushel of the best of the wheat this year. As to the distresses of the nation, you are wrong there; for England was never in a more flourishing state than it is at present.*—I answered, 'Well, if it be of God, it will come to pass, however likely or unlikely it may appear at present. If not, I shall hurt no one but myself by writing it. I am the fool, and must be the sufferer, if it be not of God. If it be of God, I would not refuse for the world, and am determined to err on the safest side.' My Sister thought she should err on the safest side, by preventing me from doing it; and said, I should not do it in her house. However, I took advantage of her absence; and, in 1792, I wrote of what has since followed in this nation and all others; but the end is not yet—I left my writings at Plymtree, and came back to Exeter.*

In 1793, the war broke out; and in this year, three remarkable things happened, which I had written of in 1792. These events strengthened my judgment that it was of God; for it was said, 'Whatever I put into thy mouth, I will do upon the earth.'

In 1793, I told the Rev. Mr L. how I had been warned of what was coming. After hearing me in silence, he said, 'It comes from the Devil; for not one thing you have mentioned will come to pass. You have the war in your favour, which is all that will come true of your prophecies; and the war will be over in a quarter of a year. It is from the Devil, to disturb your peace: Satan hath a design to sift you as wheat.* Yet I believe you to be a good woman; your friends speak of you in the highest terms; but what you have said will never come true. Besides, if it were, the Lord would never have revealed it to you. There are a thousand in Exeter, whom I could point out, to whom the Lord would have revealed it before he would to you.'—Of these observations I had been warned, before I saw him; yet it made a deep impression on my heart, tears and prayers were my private companions. But the next day, I was answered, 'Who made him a judge? He neither knows thee, nor thy forefathers, who walked before me with a perfect and upright heart.' Thus the feeling of my heart was deeply answered; with further sayings used by him, which at present I shall not mention. . . .

The May following,* two things happened, as [I] had predicted. I went to the above Minister's house, and put a letter into his hand, saying, 'Sir, as you doubt what spirit I am led by, be pleased to keep this letter till the end of the year; you will then judge of its truth.' This he consented to do—At the end of 1798, what I had written of came to pass. He then said to me, 'Formerly, if it were asked of a Prophet, how the wars would tend; he could tell. Now, if you can inform me of what will happen in Italy or England, I shall believe you.'*—The next day, I was earnest in prayer, that the Lord would answer his enquiries; and they were so. I sent him the answer, which was completely fulfilled, as to Italy and England, in 1797; but the three great sheets of writing, which I gave him, foretold affairs for years to come, and spoke much of the present period.

The following spring 1797, I sent a letter to a second Dignitary of the Exeter Cathedral. His servant returned it to me, saying his master would not be in Exeter to receive it till the next week. I then sent it again, and met the like disappointment; but the letter was left. I was now answered, that I should have the same dissatisfaction when he came to Exeter; and that both Dignitaries would treat my letters with contempt.

> 'Thus, both will thee deceive.
> But shall they laugh thee unto shame,
> For what thou dost believe?

If they agree to laugh at thee,
　　Their laughter I shall turn;
And in the end, thou'lt find these men,
　　Like thee, will sorely mourn.
Thou build'st so high, that none can fly,
　　To rob thee of thy brood;
The fowler's net cannot come nigh;
　　Nor can the shooter's load.
Tho' heavy charges men prepare,
　　And point them from their breast,
They are afraid to let them off,
　　Lest they their aim should miss.
Besides they fear, I may be there;
　　And terror stops the blow:
Thus I thee guard from ev'ry snare,
　　And that they all shall know.'

In this manner, from simple types and shadows, I was foretold how every man would act; and that I had nothing to fear, as no man should hurt me, if the truth of my writings should provoke them to anger.

These promises, and the proofs of the truth of my writings, strengthened my confidence in the Lord; but I have often marvelled, why I was ordered to send to Ministers who would not give themselves the trouble of searching out the truth; and, for this reason, have often doubted whether the calling were of God, or not. But the pondering of my heart was thus answered:

'How can the fruit be ever try'd?
How can the truth be e'er apply'd?
The godly men will so decay,
If I shall prove as weak as thee.
I say, the fruit shall surely fall:
Let . . . stand* and hear his call;
And now a Moses let him be,
Or else my judgments all shall see:
Then all together you may feast
　　And all together fast:
I'll bring a myst'ry in the end,
　　That shall for ever last.'

These words were delivered to me in 1796, in answer to a sermon, preached on the 29th of May, by the first mentioned Dignitary to whom I had sent a letter. I fancied, that he reproached me in his sermon; and his words pierced my heart. I marvelled, that a Gentleman, to whom I had appealed, should decline seeing me, to convince me of my error, if I were wrong; and in solitary tears, I repeated the words of David,

> 'Since godly men decay, O Lord,
>   Do thou my cause defend;
> For scarce these wretched times afford
>   One just and faithful friend.'*

I was answered,

> 'Since godly men do so decay,
>   And thou dost sore complain,
> Then the good Shepherd shall appear,
>   The sheep for to redeem:
> For faithful lab'rers now shall come
>   And in my vineyard go:
> My harvest it is hast'ning on,
>   Which ev'ry soul shall know.'

After this, it was said to me, 'As men increase thy sorrows, I will increase their's; and the general burden shall increase, till men take the load from thee.'—Yet I marvelled, how the 12th chapter of Revelations could be fulfilled, of the woman travailing in birth, and longing to be delivered:* But the wonders John saw in heaven must take place on earth.

> What wonders then must here appear
>   To an enlighten'd race,
> When ev'ry myst'ry is made clear,
>   And seen without a glass.*
> No veil between them being seen,
>   No wonders you'll behold;
> For all alike is clearly bright,
>   As pearly streets with gold.
> Should wonders there to you appear,
>   You'll wonder then of all.

> To see them clothed with the sun,
> Could wonder none at all.

Such is the mystery to man—(that a woman should be clothed with the Sun of Righteousness, who is now coming with healing in his wings)—because they know not the Scriptures, which indicate, that, to fulfil all righteousness, the woman must be a helpmate to man, to complete his happiness.* This men marvel at, because they never conceived what the Lord hath in store for them, in fulfilling his promise given to woman.

> So men, I see, do stand in wonder,
>   While angels also gaze:
> Satan broke man's bliss asunder;
>   Man wandereth in a maze.
> So, with amaze, you all may gaze:
>   The angels wonder here,
> You cannot see the mystery,
>   Nor find the Bible clear.
> There Eden's tree, you all shall see,
>   Preserved for your sake:
> The flaming sword is God's own word,
>   'Twill break the serpent's neck.

Thus, by types, shadows, dreams, and visions, I have been led on from 1792, to the present day; whereby the mysteries of the Bible, with the future destinies of nations have been revealed to me, which will all terminate in the Second Coming of Christ; and the Day of Judgment, when the seven thousand years are ended.*

From *The Strange Effects of Faith, Second Part* (1802)

I know the things that I have published are hard to be understood, and full as hard to be believed, which makes some marvel at them, and cast various constructions upon them. Some say, they see no prophecies in them; others, that it is from the devil; whilst some attribute it to fallen angels, and others conceive it as from myself alone, asserting that all my foreknowledge is drawn from the Bible, and that I am out of my senses. I shall answer every one according to their different words.

Those that see no prophecies in them, do not understand what they read, the book is full of prophecies throughout; the letters I sent to the ministers, and what was written in 1792, is deep of prophecy, and speaketh of all nations in distress and war: the shadow is begun, and the substance is hastening on; but I cannot make the blind to see, 'till it please the Lord to reveal to them the truth; and if they cannot see it no other way, the Lord will open their eyes by the truth.

Now I shall answer those who say it is from the devil. If satan is divided against himself, how then can his kingdom stand? And how came satan to know in 1792 what the Lord would do upon the earth, when it is concealed from the angels, in heaven, 'till the Lord is pleased to disclose it to them, and to send them down to warn mankind thereof. But if I, by the spirit of the devil, am become a true believer in Christ, by what spirit is the world become unbelievers in the gospel of Christ and their Bibles? believing that their Bibles will never be fulfilled in any other way than their judgments point out, and that is no way at all. For while one is inclined to this way, and another is inclined to that, no man's judgment can be true; so it is impossible to fulfil the Bible to the judgments of men, and therefore it must be fulfilled to the judgments of God. But where is the man that knows his decrees? For it is written by the Prophets, 'in the latter days the Lord will do marvellous things amongst them; the wisdom of the wise men shall perish, the understanding of the prudent men shall be hid':* then how can men tell how to fulfil their Bibles, seeing their understandings are hid? Who by searching can find out God? or who can find out the Almighty to perfection? Yet the world is led to believe they can, from their knowledge and learning, find out the mysteries of the Bible, which no man can maintain by arguments: their Bible is true, if they have wisdom to find it out. Now I ask mankind, by what spirit they are led to believe things contrary to the Bible, and say I am led to believe the Scriptures, consistent with the truth thereof, by the spirit of the devil? May not he that sitteth in the heavens laugh, to hear the folly of mankind, whom the Lord hath pronounced dead as to every knowledge and perfection of him, say he is alive to all the knowledge of God, contrary to the written word of God, which the different opinions of mankind verifyeth and proveth. So let God be true, and every man a liar, who saith he can fulfil his Bible by learning; and let those who say I am led by the devil, prove it by the word of God, if they can, and I will give it up.

Now I shall answer those who say, it is from fallen angels, who wish to gain themselves in favour with God. This to me is as great an error as the former, for then the division must have taken place in hell already.* But can fallen angels, after rebelling against God in heaven, and, joining with the devil, work in the hearts of men upon earth to break the commands of God, ever think to gain themselves in favour with God again? This to me is unlikely in the first place; in the second more unlikely; to think by mocking of God, by coming as an angel of light, pretending he is the maker and judge of all men, and that all power in heaven, earth, and hell is his, should ever gain him in favour with God: I say, this appears so improbable to me, that if the fallen angels think it, they must have lost their senses as well as their glory. I conceive, therefore, those thoughts to be the production of a weaker head than mine, to judge the spirit came from God, for I cannot build my faith upon no such sandy foundation.*

Now I shall answer those who say, I am, or shall be, out of my senses. This I grant is true; for out of my senses proceed all my writings; and so far from any sense or knowledge I have of myself, so high as the heavens are above the earth, and how much farther they will go, I cannot tell; but this I know, they are gone so far, they never will come back to the senses of men, while they are of so many different opinions. No judge will give up his cause to a divided jury, and I must be no judge of my own cause, if I gave it up to a divided people: For the first minister I ever spoke to on the subject said, it was from God; the second, that it was from the devil; the third minister said, the latter gentleman had not shewn his sense in what he had spoken; the fourth declared, that it was not from the devil, and if not of God, it was of myself; other ministers said, it was the disorder of a confused brain, and this disorder had so increased over the land, that every one felt the fatal effects thereof; and I feel it to my sorrow, for the truth of all my writings lies before me, and I know I must go through evil report and through good report, through honour and through dishonour, as counted a fool, yet making some wise; the bees gather honey from the bitterest herbs; and those whose minds go deep, will get wisdom from my foolishness, should it prove from the devil, as some insinuate; but if of God, as I judge it is, it will strengthen their faith to stand in the evil day, and give them courage and faith to stand against all the wiles of the devil; for it is by faith ye must be saved. I have already told you, and I now again tell you, the end of all things is at hand, by which is meant, that satan's kingdom is to be destroyed, that all nations will be called in, the fulfilment of the Gentiles, and the calling in of the Jews.*

A Dispute between the Woman and the Powers of Darkness (1802)

Introduction

This book may appear strange to some of my readers, to say, it is a Dispute between me and the Powers of Darkness. Though some may marvel, as they have already done, when I said the Lord would give liberty to Satan to come and offer whatever arguments he had to plead against the justice of his sentence, as being bound not to tempt any that were sealed;* and *I was ordered* to pen his words, whatever blasphemy he might speak against the Lord, and the justice of his sentence; for the Lord said I should not *do* as I did in 1792, refuse to write his blasphemy, out of a wrong zeal for religion; because I thought his words were too shocking to pen: but now I was *commanded* to banish these fears; because it would make religion become sinful. Therefore I was *ordered* to pen every word *perfect* which he uttered. The Powers of Darkness broke in upon me three or four days in the house where I was then sojourning; I was ordered to leave that house *the second day of August*, and go to a place prepared for me, *alone* by myself. Some, disputed with me, saying, they could not believe it was the command of the Lord, that I should pen the words of the Devil, after I had been writing by the Spirit of (God) the Lord. This appeared to them contrary to reason: but I was answered by the Spirit of the Lord, if I refused to obey, what I had already done was to no purpose. The Lord HIMSELF contended with Satan about Job;* and our Saviour suffered HIMSELF to be tempted forty days by the Devil,* and disputed with him. And shall the creature be more holy than his Creator? Shall man be more holy than his God? If the Lord has been contending with Satan for man near six thousand years, should I be too holy to contend with the Devil, for my Maker, seven days? If so we must all perish. For we must fight and overcome, that we may have part in the Tree of Life. For as the dispute *began* with the Devil and the woman,* it must *end* with the Devil and the woman: and the command was given to me that which ever stood out to the end should conquer. If my words stood last, and I held out with arguments, in stedfast faith, against the Devil for seven days, then the woman should *be freed* and Satan should *fall*. But if I gave up to the Devil, and Satan conquered in *the seven days*, then Satan's kingdom must stand, and the woman must fall. So seven days was to end the dispute between the woman and Satan; and men were then to judge what a powerful adversary the woman had to contend with. But I was promised, the Lord would be with me, by day and by night; that he would not leave me, nor forsake me;—his right hand should support me, and that the Powers of Darkness should not be permitted to appear visibly to me whilst I was alone. For he that hath said to the proud waves of the sea, hitherto shall ye go and no farther, had set bounds for Satan to go as far as he would in temptations, but no farther; and that he should not appear or hurt me, unless I gave up my faith in the Lord. *This*, with many strong promises made to me, I read to the three ministers and other gentlemen, who saw things in a different light from those who thought it *wrong* to contend with the Devil at all. They said, whatever the Lord *commanded was right*; and they had not a doubt but he would keep me according to his promise; and they should be in earnest prayer for me all the time. All my friends that knew of it said the same: So I went *the second day of August*, accompanied by my friends, to a place prepared for me, to be alone by myself; and I was forbidden to see any *for three days*. The third day the ministers were ordered to come, that if Satan had *aught* to say for himself in person, he might then appear: so they attended, according to the directions given; but Satan did not appear; and therefore he was afterwards forbidden. If he would not come boldly before men, he should not be permitted to come *in person* before a woman alone. So I had nothing to fear from his appearance; but was commanded only to write his words.

Now I shall inform my readers what made me stand out so stedfast and firm in faith against the Devil and all his threatenings. I well knew if my calling was of God, as I judged it to be, and I had prophecied in His Name, He would keep me from the Powers of Darkness according to His Word, and not forsake me in the trying hour. I well knew Satan's malice was greater than his power:—for the power that is *almighty to save*, is the Lord alone. And though I had been foiled in a few things, to keep me humble before the Lord, and to try the talents of the learned, that we might walk *by faith* and not *by sight*; for it is said to me in my sealed writings,

> Men's wisdom high I mean to try,
> And all their conduct too.

Now if every word was to come in a straight line, neither men's wisdom or faith could ever be tried at all. For the great A line a child could read,* and if my writings had all come in that manner, they could not have been consistent with the Bible. For it is written, in the latter days, I shall do marvellous things amongst them. 'The wisdom of the wise men shall perish, and the understanding of the prudent men shall be hid.' But was the Lord to put all His prophecies in a plain line, then He must deal ungenerously with the Jews: as Isaiah speaks both of the first and second coming of Christ in his Prophecies, without distinguishing one from the other, by saying, which was the first and which was the last.* So these reasons being assigned to me kept me always humble before the Lord, in a steady faith, mixed with fear, and always in prayer, that I might not be led by any wrong spirit. But now is come the fiery trial with the Devil. I well knew if I was deceived in my writings, as not coming from the Lord, He must have forsaken me, and Satan would have destroyed me as he threatened: and I would sooner have died than live to say, *the Lord saith*, if He had not spoken, or deceived worthy and good men that believed in them as coming from the Lord. So I ran the hazard of my life to know in whom I had believed. The world have judged me;— but they do not know me;—I am no impostor to deceive either God or man. By my own master I well knew I must stand or fall. If the Lord was my master, I knew I should *stand*: but if Satan had been my master, as he said, I knew I should fall. So now I will rejoice in the God of my salvation, who hath delivered me out of the mouth of the lion, and out of the Paw of the Bear, and I trust he will deliver me from the uncircumcised in heart, ear, and life.*

> So I myself am now the judge;
> Men's wisdom is too weak;
> If they believe that Hell below
> Such language e'er could speak

As is in my other books. For now I shall shew you in this what *the language* of Hell is, which I was *ordered by the Lord* to pen, and put in print:—To shew you that the woman mentioned in the Revelations *must* tread down Satan under her feet by strength of arguments,* and by faith in CHRIST JESUS, OUR BLESSED LORD AND SAVIOUR. So let men read the following book and judge for themselves, and I shall judge for myself. The Lord also is my judge, and is witness against my foes. My readers must observe, that the seven days dispute between me and Satan, while I was alone, begins as follows. What was said previous to my coming here, you will have either at the end of this book or in another; as *all* is ordered to be put in print. That the last may be first, and the first last. Satan conquered the woman at first: but the woman has conquered him *at last*.

The Fourth Day's Dispute

Satan. Thou eternal bitch! Thou runnest on so fast the Devil cannot overtake thee.

Joanna. Neither do I want to have him. But as I am *ordered* to pen his words, I shall pen them. But I will not sit waiting for them. If he cannot find arguments ready, let him keep silence; and hear, what I have to say for myself, my Maker, and dear Redeemer.

Satan. Damn thy Redeemer, and thee too; is my power to be overthrown by the desire of a cursed woman? Now I tell thee if God does not renounce that promise, I will bring in a bill against Him and shame Him to His Face.* Thou knowest not what is behind. Thou sayest I am a Devil, and so I tell thee now I will be one. Thou sayest my reign is short, and it shall be powerful. I have not done,—so don't be too ready with thy answers. I see thy laughter, and I will turn it into mourning. The seven days are not yet up; and *dare* Foley or Bruce to rob me of my time allowed me:* I shall speak for myself all this day and not wait for thy answers.

Joanna. Thou art silent; and I shall begin. I will not wait one minute for thy words. I hear when thou stoppest, and then my answer is ready. This day if thou hast aught to say for thyself, or against the Most High, bring it forth, and *I am ordered* by the Lord to pen it. But I am not ordered to sit and wait till thou art pleased to speak. I can pen all thou hast to say by four o'clock. But if thou hast more to say than I can pen by that time, I will pen it after: but not if thou keepest silence before for thy pleasure, thou shalt then for mine.

Satan. Thou aggravating Devil! I will appeal to any man of sense, if thou art not enough to provoke the Devil, and enrage all Hell against thee: and now thou sittest and laughest at all thou art writing from me. I have not done;—don't be so ready with thy answers. I will keep thee on till night, if I make thee write nonsense. I will mock thee now; for know: thou art commanded to pen all I say: and so I shall say on, God is a God.

Joanna. Thou sayest God is a God. I answer, a just God, a good God, an holy, and a true God. Heaven and Earth will set forth His praises: but thou sayest, Satan, I am enough to provoke the Devil. And didst thou not provoke the woman to wrath at first, when thou deceivedst her with lies and broughtest misery upon her? Didst thou not provoke the woman to anger and indignation against thee, when thou workedst in the hearts of men by thy hellish power to crucify her Son? Look at Calvary.—Look at the Cross.—See there, the dear, and dying Lord, crucified, pierced with spears, and hanging on the cursed tree, which thy hellish arts had worked on man to bring on Him. See all the sufferings that He went thro' and see if this was not enough to enrage the woman; and provoke her to wrath and indignation against thee *to laugh at thy calamities, and mock when thy fear cometh.* It is just and right, Satan, that thou shouldst feel the weight of the woman's wrath and indignation against thee, who seekedst her ruin from the first. And now thou hast tried, by every art hell can invent, to seek it at last. Now, Satan, look to Calvary, *and there behold her dying Lord*, and see if justice doth not demand thy guilty blood:—and the woman's wrath and indignation on thy head. Thou serpent to the woman, her woes of sorrow *must now* come on thee. Now answer for thyself, if thou canst.

Satan. Was not God an eternal fool to let Him suffer, if He could prevent it?

Joanna. God suffered His Son to take the blame man cast on his Maker, in Paradise. For as thy arts, O Satan, brought death on man, and he cast it on his Maker, for giving him the woman. He took it and shared the fate with man. But know, the Lord promised then, the Serpent should share the fate the woman cast on him: and now thou must share thy fate with Jezebel—For she forged lies to destroy

Naboth, and gained his vineyard;* and thou hast forged lies the same—and thou must be cast down as she was, and share thy fate with thy followers, as Christ did with his followers.

Satan. Stop thy damned eternal tongue, thou runnest on so fast, all the Devils in Hell cannot keep up with thee. Thou sayest Christ suffered with His followers, and I shall with mine. If Christ was such a fool to submit, I will not submit to no such laws. I did not make them: and now I will break them. For I will work in Earth and Hell to war, before I will stoop to suffer like Jezebel. Thy tongue is ready for an answer, but I have not done yet.

Joanna. Thy tongue is silent, and I will not wait one moment to hear what thou hast to say. Thou breakedst the law at first: and when thou knewest the law of God, that He had made;—if thou bruizest His heel, He shall bruize thy head.* Now thou wast ready enough to enter into Judas to fulfil the law of the first part, that the Lord had made to bruize his heel. Now God, in justice to His own honour and great name, must bruize thy head, to fulfil the last part. For, as Christ submitted to the first—so thou must submit to the last. So, if thou art a king, shew thy honour as a king, and die quietly with thy followers, as Christ did with His followers. So now, see the Gallows and the Fires which thy followers have been brought to by following thee, O Satan.* —And now it is but just and right for thee to share the fate with them. And if thou deniest the justice of God in this sentence, thou deniest all that is right and just. Then a just God must take justice into his own Hands.

Satan. A woman's tongue no man can tame. God hath done something to chuse a bitch of a woman, that will down-argue the Devil, and scarce give him room to speak—for the sands of a glass do not run faster than thy tongue. It is better to dispute with a thousand men than with one woman. Thy assurance and ignorance protect thee. Thou payest no more regard to the greatness of Satan, than thou wouldest to a chattering woman like thyself. So I must confess I was a fool there, ever to enter into dispute with thee, knowing what a chattering fool thou art; all men are tired of thy tongue; and now thou hast tired the Devil's also. Therefore, do shut up, and say no more for thy own shame; but I know there is no shame in thee, if the Devil do not shame thee now. Pomeroy said, thou toldst too fast; Manley said, thou toldst too fast; Mossop said, thou toldst too fast;

and Bruce* said the same: and men and women have tried to shame thee out of it. But I hope, if none else can't shame thee, the Devil will shame thee, as not to answer again. For, as thy paper is nearly ended, I will get a-head of thee now, if thou answerest again; unless thou art like a mad fool without any shame at all. So I will see what thou hast got to say, and answer in a few words: for I hate so many as thou answerest—one word of a sort is enough.

Joanna. One word of a sort I will answer. If man can't tame a woman's tongue, how shall the Devil? If God hath done *something* to chuse a woman to dispute with Satan at last, Satan did *something* to dispute with the woman at first, if Satan down-argued the woman at first, she ought to down-argue him at last. If Satan scarce gave the woman room to speak or think at first, the woman ought not to give him room to speak or think at the last. If Satan thought fit to dispute with the woman at first, he hath thought it fit to dispute with her at last. If Satan thought it better to dispute with twenty men than with one woman, why did he not appear when there was but three men, to plead for himself? If Satan paid no regard to the weakness and ignorance of the woman at first—the weakness and ignorance of the woman will pay no regard to him at last. If he took the advantage of her weakness, she will take the advantage of her strength. If Satan pleaded the promises of God against her, she will plead the promises of God for her. If Satan repents of his folly at last, he ought to have repented at first, that ever he entered into dispute with her. If he knew what a weak ignorant creature she was at first to believe in his words, he might know when the voice of the Lord came to her, to bid her claim the promise, to be as God's, knowing good from evil, she would be as ready to believe the latter as the former, and rely on that promise, and claim it. If the woman's fall has tired men, I hope it will tire the Devil also. If a Devil could not shame her at first, how shall he shame her at last? If he was not ashamed to enter into dispute with her, why should he be ashamed of her words? If they are *right*, they cannot shame the woman; and if they are *wrong* they cannot shame the Devil. For he glorieth in what the woman doth, that is wrong; so if the Woman is not ashamed of herself, the Devil cannot shame her. If she is not ashamed to say much before men she does regard, she cannot be ashamed to say much to the Devil, that she does not love, nor fear, *but* DESPISE. [*To this Satan made no answer for several hours*: But Joanna heard a whispering to this purpose,] *Christ is in her*, or she would have never made so ready an answer, and we may as well leave her. [This she penned—and, after some time, Satan thus broke in upon her.]

Satan. Who dost thou judge said Christ was in thee, or thou couldst not give so ready an answer?

Joanna. I said, I did not know.

Satan. Then now, I tell thee, it was the Angels of the Lord: and they said they would leave thee, and thou wantest no guard. So, now I tell thee, thou art in my power! and death, and hell, is thy portion, if thou answerest me again.

Joanna. The Lord never forsakes any who trust in Him; and He will not do it now. He hath promised to be with me—but, as thou wishest most to converse with men, why wast thou such a coward not to appear when they were present?

Satan. To make God the liar:—because He said, they should see wondrous things; and I was determined to give Him the lie. Dost thou think I would appear by God's appointment? No—I would not.

Joanna. The Lord did not command thee to appear; but if thou judgest thyself injured, or wronged, He gave thee liberty to appear and answer for thyself; and, as thou sayest it is best to dispute with men, thou oughtest to have appeared when they were present.

Satan. Then I will appear visible now.

Joanna. That is, if the Lord will let thee.

Satan. Is the Lord my keeper?

Joanna. It would be happy for thee, O Satan, if He had been thy keeper.

Satan. I would sooner be in Hell flames for ever, than stoop to any superior power to my own.

Joanna. Then into the flames thou oughtest to go. If the long-suffering mercies of God towards thee, and His not entering into strict judgment with thee, is of no avail, but thou art still hardened, thy destruction is just.

Satan. How can I say any thing, if thou sayest so much? Thou givest ten words for one.

Joanna. Thou wilt not speak to any purpose at all—only a few provoking words, without sense or reason. Bring forth thy arguments why thou art unjustly dealt with; that the world may judge thee.

End of the Fourth Day's Disputation.

JANE TAYLOR
(1783–1824)

Born in London, Jane Taylor was the second daughter of the engraver Isaac Taylor, of Ongar in Essex, and his wife Ann Martin. The Taylors were a Dissenting family, and a highly literary and enterprising one; Isaac Taylor wrote pamphlets and set up a Sunday School, while Ann Taylor wrote volumes of advice for mothers, including *Maternal Solicitude for a Daughter's Best Interests* (1814). There were eventually eleven children. Much of Jane Taylor's childhood was spent in Lavenham, Suffolk, with her elder sister Ann and brother Isaac, and later in Colchester, where their father became the minister of a Methodist congregation. The Taylor children were strictly educated but highly imaginative, producing stories, verse, and plays. From 1797 Jane and Ann joined in the family enterprise of engraving book illustrations.

The younger Taylors, especially Jane, became innovative and influential shapers of writing for children. Ann Taylor had had contributions published in an annual, *The Minor's Pocket Book*, which in 1804 published the first of her sister's works to appear in print. At the request of the Quaker publishers Darton and Harvey a joint publication followed, *Original Poems for Infant Minds by Several Young Persons* (1804). The majority were by Ann and Jane. In following Watts and Blake in writing in poetry, the Taylors distinguished themselves from the usual genre of women writing for children, which was prose. The poems proved popular in Britain and abroad—Walter Scott's four small children had them by heart—as did the next joint publication, *Rhymes for the Nursery* (1806). Even greater success followed *Hymns for Infant Minds* (1810), although Jane Taylor's contributions to this volume are less important than her sister's. In spring 1812 the Taylor family moved to Ongar in Essex. In 1813, after joint work on such collections as *Signor Topsy Turvey's Wonderful Magic Lantern* (1810) and *Original Hymns for Sunday Schools* (1812), Ann Taylor married, and Jane and Isaac left home for the West Country, spending two years in

Ilfracombe and three in Marazion, Cornwall. Jane Taylor went on to write independently, publishing *Display, a Tale for Young People* (1815), *Essays in Rhyme, on Morals and Manners* (1816), and many contributions in verse and prose from 1816 to 1822 to *The Youth's Magazine*, later published together as the two-volume *Contributions of QQ* (1824). In 1816 Jane Taylor had returned to Ongar and spent the rest of her life there, with occasional visits to London and Hastings and a pilgrimage to Olney in 1823. Increasingly ill, with breast cancer, she devoted herself to parish work, and died at the age of 40 without being able to take up the many offers from publishers triggered by the great popularity of her verses for children.

Jane Taylor described her way of working to her sister Ann: 'I try to conjure up some child into my presence, address her suitably, as well as I am able, and when I begin to flag, I say to her, "There, love, now you may go".'[1] This awareness of the changes in a child's attention and in her own creative energy helps to explain the mixture of lightness and intensity in her work. Taylor often seems to write primarily to instruct, but her interest is caught by the tiny detail, the oddity, and sometimes the ludicrousness of situations, and it is these things which captured the imagination of children and parents alike. Admired by leading literary figures of the day, including Maria Edgeworth, her works influenced generations of writers and illustrators for children. Illustrations by Kate Greenaway in 1883 testified to, and helped to extend, their popularity. They also found their way into other writings, to a greater extent than is usual for children's literature at this time. Critical and comic variations on 'The Star' are to be found in Lewis Carroll's *Alice's Adventures in Wonderland* (1865), while Robert Browning drew on 'How it Strikes a Stranger' for his late poem 'Rephan' (1889).

The extracts here begin with the Preface and selected poems (by Jane Taylor) from *Original Poems, for Infant Minds*; and the metrically and comically brilliant dialogue 'The Cow and the Ass'. It then includes her most famous poem, 'The Star', from *Rhymes for the Nursery*, the imaginative and influential prose tale 'How it Strikes a Stranger', and the delightful archaeological-antiquarian whimsy, 'The Toad's Journal', from *Contributions of QQ*. While the paired poems 'Morning' and 'Evening', and 'The Poppy' and 'The Violet', from *Original Poems, for Infant Minds* suggest absolute judgements about right and wrong behaviour (albeit of a kind which children often find appealing), Taylor allows into her poems the awareness that the operations and creatures of the natural world have an existence outside human moralizing, and this becomes one of the most interesting features of her later writing. 'The Cow and the Ass' debates animal rights, but the human beings who profit from the animals' labour

[1] F. V. Barry, *Poetry and Prose* (London: Humphrey Milford, 1925), p. xii.

end up seeming secondary to the sparring and rivalry of the debaters themselves. 'The Star' responds to the need to make the phenomena of nature proof of the greatness of God, but it also conveys the mystery and remoteness of a possible other world. In 'How it Strikes a Stranger' a visitor from one such world visits earth, and, in a tradition already encountered in this anthology in Elizabeth Hamilton's *Letters of a Hindoo Rajah*, comments on the strange practices he finds there. In 'The Toad's Journal' Taylor gives three quite distinct voices—the voice of the mock-antiquarian editor, the voice of the inveterately idle toad, and the voice of the work-ethic moralist who tries to confine the toad in the moral polarities familiar from 'The Poppy' and 'The Violet'. The moralist is keen to have the final say, but her promotion of useful labour has already been subtly undermined by the comically pointless notion of 'work' epitomized by the antiquarian; while, in the end, making the most of time and making absolutely nothing of it are both irrelevant in the context of the 'dream' of life's 'vale of tears'.

❦

From *Original Poems, for Infant Minds* (1804)

Preface

If a hearty affection for that interesting little race, the race of children, be any recommendation, the writers of the following pages are well recommended; and if to have studied, in some degree, their capacities, habits, and wants, with a wish to adapt these simple verses to their real comprehensions, and probable improvement:—if this have any further claim to the indulgence of the public, it is the last and greatest they attempt to make. The deficiency of the compositions as poetry, is by no means a secret to their authors; but it was thought desirable to abridge every poetic freedom and figure, and even every long-syllabled word, which might give, perhaps, a false idea to their little readers, or at least make a chasm in the chain of conception. Images, which to us are so familiar that we forget their imagery, are insurmountable stumbling-blocks to children, who have none but literal ideas; and though it may be allowable to introduce a simple kind, which a little maternal attention will easily explain, and which may tend to excite a taste for natural and poetic beauty, every thing superfluous it has been a primary endeavour to avoid. . . .

Morning

Awake, little girl, it is time to arise,
    Come shake drowsy sleep from your eye;
The lark is loud warbling his notes to the skies,
    And the sun is far mounted on high.

O come, for the fields with gay flow'rets o'erflow,
    The dew-drop is trembling still,
The lowing herds graze in the pastures below,
    And the sheep-bell is heard from the hill.

O come, for the bee has flown out of his bed,
    To begin his employment anew;
The spider is weaving her delicate thread,
    Which brilliantly glitters with dew.

O come, for the ant has crept out of her cell,
    Again to her labour she goes:
She knows the true value of moments too well
    To taste them in idle repose.

Awake, little sleeper, and do not despise
    Of insects instruction to ask,
From your pillow, with good resolutions arise,
    And cheerfully go to your task.

Evening

Little girl, it is time to retire to your rest,
    The sheep are put into the fold,
The linnet forsakes us and flies to her nest,
    To shelter her young from the cold.

The owl has flown out from his lonely retreat,
    And screams through the tall shady trees;
The nightingale takes on the hawthorn his seat,
    And sings to the evening breeze.

The sun, too, now seems to have finish'd his race,
    And sinks once again to his rest;
But though we no longer can see his bright face,
    He leaves a gold streak in the west.

Little girl, have you finished your daily employ,
    With industry, patience, and care?
If so, lay your head on your pillow with joy,
    No thorn to disturb shall be there.

The moon through your curtains shall cheerfully peep,
    Her silver beam dance on your eyes,
And mild evening breezes shall fan you to sleep,
    Till bright morning bids you arise.

The Poppy

High on a bright and sunny bed,
    A scarlet poppy grew;
And up it held its staring head,
    And thrust it full in view.

Yet no attention did it win
    By all these efforts made,
And less unwelcome had it been
    In some retired shade.

For though within its scarlet breast
    No sweet perfume was found,
It seem'd to think itself the best
    Of all the flow'rs around.

From this may I a hint obtain,
    And take great care indeed,
Lest I appear as pert and vain,
    As is this gaudy weed.

The Violet

Down in a green and shady bed,
    A modest violet grew,
Its stalk was bent, it hung its head,
    As if to hide from view.

And yet it was a lovely flow'r,
    Its colours bright and fair;
It might have grac'd a rosy bow'r,
    Instead of hiding there.

Yet there it was content to bloom,
 In modest tints array'd;
And there diffus'd its sweet perfume,
 Within the silent shade.

Then let me to the valley go,
 This pretty flow'r to see;
That I may also learn to grow
 In sweet humility.

The Cow and the Ass (1805)

Beside a green meadow a stream used to flow,
So clear, one might see the white pebbles below;
To this cooling brook the warm cattle would stray,
To stand in the shade on a hot summer's day.

A cow, quite oppressed by the heat of the sun,
Came here to refresh, as she often had done,
And standing quite still, stooping over the stream,
Was musing perhaps; or perhaps she might dream.

But soon a brown ass, of respectable look,
Came trotting up also, to taste of the brook,
And to nibble a few of the daisies and grass:
'How d'ye do?' said the cow; 'How d'ye do?' said the ass.

'Take a seat,' said the cow, gently waving her hand;
'By no means, dear madam,' said he, 'while you stand.'
Then stooping to drink, with a complaisant bow,
'Ma'am, your health,' said the ass:—'Thank you, sir,' said the cow.

When a few of these compliments more had been passed,
They laid themselves down on the herbage at last;
And waiting politely (as gentlemen must),
The ass held his tongue, that the cow might speak first.

Then, with a deep sigh, she directly began,
'Don't you think, Mr Ass, we are injured by man?
'Tis a subject which lies with a weight on my mind:
We really are greatly oppressed by mankind.

'Pray what is the reason (I see none at all)
That I always must go when Jane chooses to call?
Whatever I'm doing ('tis certainly hard)
I'm forced to leave off, to be milked in the yard.

'I've no will of my own, but must do as they please,
And give them my milk to make butter and cheese;
Sometimes I endeavour to kick down the pail,
Or give her a box on the ear with my tail.'

'But, Ma'am,' said the ass, 'not presuming to teach—
Oh dear, I beg pardon—pray finish your speech;
Excuse my mistake,' said the complaisant swain,
'Go on, and I'll not interrupt you again.'

'Why, sir, I was just then about to observe,
Those hard-hearted tyrants no longer I'll serve;
But leave them for ever to do as they please,
And look somewhere else for their butter and cheese.'

Ass waited a moment, his answer to scan,
And then, 'Not presuming to teach,' he began,
'Permit me to say, since my thoughts you invite,
I always saw things in a different light.

'That you afford man an important supply,
No ass in his senses would ever deny:
But then, in return, 'tis but fair to allow,
They are of *some* service to you, Mistress Cow.

''Tis their pleasant meadow in which you repose,
And they find you a shelter from wintery snows.
For comforts like these, we're indebted to man;
And for him, in return, should do all that we can.'

The cow, upon this, cast her eyes on the grass,
Not pleased to be schooled in this way by an ass:
'Yet,' said she to herself, 'though he's not very bright,
I really believe that the fellow is right.'

The Star (1806)

Twinkle, twinkle, little star,
How I wonder what you are!
Up above the world so high,
Like a diamond in the sky.

When the blazing sun is gone,
When he nothing shines upon,
Then you show your little light,
Twinkle, twinkle, all the night.

Then the trav'ller in the dark,
Thanks you for your tiny spark:
He could not see which way to go,
If you did not twinkle so.

In the dark blue sky you keep,
And often through my curtains peep,
For you never shut your eye,
'Till the sun is in the sky.

As your bright and tiny spark,
Lights the trav'ller in the dark, —
Though I know not what you are,
Twinkle, twinkle, little star.

How it Strikes a Stranger (1821)

In a remote period of antiquity, when the supernatural and the marvellous obtained a readier credence than now, it was fabled that a
stranger of extraordinary appearance was observed pacing the streets
of one of the magnificent cities of the east, remarking with an eye of
intelligent curiosity every surrounding object. Several individuals
gathering around him, questioned him concerning his country and
his business but they presently perceived that he was unacquainted
with their language, and he soon discovered himself to be equally
ignorant of the most common usages of society. At the same time the
dignity and intelligence of his air and demeanour forbade the idea
of his being either a barbarian or a lunatic. When at length he

understood by their signs that they wished to be informed hence he came, he pointed with great significance to the sky; upon which the crowd concluding him to be one of their deities, were proceeding to pay him divine honours: but he no sooner comprehended their design, than he rejected it with horror: and bending his knees and raising his hands towards heaven in the attitude of prayer, gave them to understand that he also was a worshipper of the powers above.

After a time, it is said, that the mysterious stranger accepted the hospitalities of one of the nobles of the city; under whose roof he applied himself with great diligence to the acquirement of the language, in which he made such surprising proficiency, that in a few days he was able to hold intelligent intercourse with those around him. The noble host now resolved to take an early opportunity of satisfying his curiosity respecting the country and quality of his guest; and upon his expressing this desire, the stranger assured him that he would answer his inquiries that evening after sunset. Accordingly, as night approached, he led him forth upon the balconies of the palace, which overlooked the wealthy and populous city. Innumerable lights from its busy streets and splendid palaces were now reflected in the dark bosom of its noble river; where stately vessels laden with rich merchandize from all parts of the known world, lay anchored in the port. This was a city in which the voice of the harp and of the viol, and the sound of the millstone were continually heard: and craftsmen of all kinds of craft were there; and the light of a candle was seen in every dwelling; and the voice of the bridegroom and the voice of the bride were heard there. The stranger mused awhile upon the glittering scene, and listened to the confused murmur of mingling sounds. Then suddenly raising his eyes to the starry firmament, he fixed them with an expressive gaze, on the beautiful evening star which was just sinking behind a dark grove that surrounded one of the principal temples of the city. 'Marvel not,' said he to his host, 'that I am wont to gaze with fond affection on yonder silvery star. That was my home; yes, I was lately an inhabitant of that tranquil planet; from whence a vain curiosity has tempted me to wander. Often had I beheld with wondering admiration, this brilliant world of yours, ever one of the brightest gems of our firmament: and the ardent desire I had long felt to know something of its condition, was at length unexpectly gratified. I received permission and power from above to traverse the mighty void, and to direct my course to this distant sphere. To that permission, however, one condition was annexed, to which my eagerness for the enterprise induced me hastily to consent; namely, that I must thenceforth remain an inhabitant of this strange earth, and undergo all the vicissitudes to which its natives are subject. Tell me therefore, I pray you, what is the lot of man; and explain to me more fully than I yet understand, all that I hear and see around me.'

'Truly, Sir,' replied the astonished noble, 'although I am altogether unacquainted with the manners and customs, products and privileges of your country, yet, methinks I cannot but congratulate you on your arrival in our world; especially since it has been your good fortune to alight on a part of it affording such various sources of enjoyment as this our opulent and luxurious city. And be assured it will be my pride and pleasure to introduce you to all that is most worthy the attention of such a distinguished foreigner.'

Our adventurer, accordingly, was presently initiated in those arts of luxury and pleasure which were there well understood. He was introduced, by his obliging host, to their public games and festivals; to their theatrical diversions, and convivial assemblies: and in a short time he began to feel some relish for amusements, the meaning of which, at first, he could scarcely comprehend. The next lesson which it became desirable to impart to him, was the necessity of acquiring wealth as the only means of obtaining pleasure. A fact which was no sooner understood by the stranger, than he gratefully accepted the offer of his friendly host to place him in a situation in which he might amass riches. To this object he began to apply himself with diligence; and was becoming in some measure reconciled to the manners and customs of our planet, strangely as they differed from those of his own, when an incident occurred which gave an entirely new direction to his energies.

It was but a few weeks after his arrival on our earth, when walking in the cool of the day with his friend in the outskirts of the city, his attention was arrested by the appearance of a spacious enclosure near which they passed; he inquired the use to which it was appropriated.

'It is,' replied the nobleman, 'a place of public interment.'

'I do not understand you,' said the stranger.

'It is the place,' repeated his friend, 'where we bury our dead.'

'Excuse me, Sir,' replied his companion, with some embarrassment. 'I must trouble you to explain yourself yet further.'

The nobleman repeated the information in still plainer terms.

'I am still at a loss to comprehend you perfectly,' said the stranger, turning deadly pale. 'This must relate to something of which I was not only totally ignorant in my own world, but of which I have, as yet, had no intimation in yours. I pray you, therefore, to satisfy my curiosity; for if I have any clue to your meaning, this, surely, is a matter of more mighty concernment than any to which you have hitherto directed me.'

'My good friend,' replied the nobleman, 'you must be indeed a novice amongst us, if you have yet to learn that we must all, sooner or later, submit to take our place in these dismal abodes; nor will I deny that it is one of the least desirable of the circumstances which appertain to our condition; for which reason it is a matter rarely referred to in polished society, and this accounts for your being hitherto uninformed on the subject. But truly, Sir, if the inhabitants of the place whence you came are not liable to any similar misfortune, I advise you to betake yourself back again with all speed; for be assured there is no escape here; nor could I guarantee your safety for a single hour.'

'Alas,' replied the adventurer, 'I must submit to the conditions of my enterprise; of which, till now, I little understood the import. But explain to me, I beseech you, something more of the nature and consequences of this wondrous metamorphosis, and tell me at what period it most commonly happens to man.'

While he thus spoke, his voice faultered, and his whole frame shook violently; his countenance was pale as death, and a cold dew stood in large drops, upon his forehead.

By this time his companion, finding the discourse becoming more serious than was agreeable, declared that he must refer him to the priests for further information; this subject being very much out of his province.

'How!' exclaimed the stranger, 'then I cannot have understood you;—do the priests only die?—are not you to die also?'

His friend evading these questions, hastily conducted his importunate companion to one of their magnificent temples, where he gladly consigned him to the instructions of the priesthood.

The emotion which the stranger had betrayed when he received the first idea of death, was yet slight in comparison with that which he experienced as soon as he gathered from the discourses of the priests, some notion of immortality; and of the alternative of happiness or misery in a future state. But this agony of mind was exchanged for transport when he learned, that by the performance of certain conditions before death, the state of happiness might be secured; his eagerness to learn the nature of these terms, excited the surprise and even the contempt of his sacred teachers. They advised him to remain satisfied for the present with the instructions he had received, and to defer the remainder of the discussion till the morrow.

'How!' exclaimed the novice, 'say you not that death may come at any hour!—may it not then come this hour;—and what if it should come before I have performed these conditions! Oh! withhold not this excellent knowledge from me a single moment!'

The priests suppressing a smile at his simplicity, then proceeded to explain their Theology to their attentive auditor: but who shall describe the ecstacy of his happiness when he was given to understand, that the required conditions were, generally, of easy and pleasant performance; and that the occasional difficulties or inconveniences which might attend them, would entirely cease with the short term of his earthly existence. 'If, then, I understand you rightly,' said he to his instructors, 'this event which you call death, and which seems in itself strangely terrible, is most desirable and blissful. What a favour is this which is granted to me, in being sent to inhabit a planet in which I can die!' The priests again exchanged smiles with each other; but their ridicule was wholly lost upon the enraptured stranger.

When the first transports of his emotion had subsided, he began to reflect with sore uneasiness on the time he had already lost since his arrival.

'Alas, what have I been doing!' exclaimed he. 'This gold which I have been collecting, tell me, reverend priests, will it avail me any thing when the thirty or forty years are expired which, you say, I may possibly sojourn in your planet!'

'Nay,' replied the priests, 'but verily you will find it of excellent use so long as you remain in it.'

'A very little of it shall suffice me,' replied he: 'for consider, how soon this period will be past: what avails it what my condition may be for so short a season? I will be take myself from this hour, to the grand concerns of which you have charitably informed me.'

Accordingly, from that period, continues the legend, the stranger devoted himself to the performance of those conditions on which, he was told, his future welfare depended; but in so doing, he had an opposition to encounter wholly unexpected, and for which he was even at a loss to account. By thus devoting this chief attention to his chief interests, he excited the surprise, the contempt, and even the enmity of most of the inhabitants of the city; and they rarely mentioned him but with a term of reproach, which has been variously rendered in all the modern languages.

Nothing could equal the stranger's surprise at this circumstance; as well as that of his fellow citizens appearing, generally, so extremely indifferent as they did to their own interests. That they should have so little prudence and forethought as to provide only for their necessities and pleasures for that short part of their existence in which they were to remain in this planet, he could consider only as the effect of disordered intellect; so that he even returned their incivilities to himself, with affectionate expostulation, accompanied by lively emotions of compassion and amazement.

If ever he was tempted for a moment to violate any of the conditions of his future happiness, he bewailed his own madness with agonizing emotions: and to all the invitations he received from others to do any thing inconsistent with his real interests, he had but one answer,—'Oh,' he would say, 'I am to die!—I am to die!'

The Toad's Journal (1822)

It is related by Mr Belzoni in the interesting narrative of his late discoveries in Egypt, that having succeeded in clearing a passage to the entrance of an ancient temple, which had been for ages buried in the sand, the first object that presented itself, upon entering, was a toad of enormous size;* and (if we may credit the assertions of some naturalists respecting the extraordinary longevity of these creatures, when in a state of solitary confinement)* we may believe that it was well stricken in years.

Whether the subjoined document was entrusted to our traveller by the venerable reptile as a present to the British Museum, or with the more mercantile view of getting it printed in London, in preference to Alexandria, on condition of receiving one per cent on the profits, after the sale of the 500th edition, (provided the publisher should by that time be at all remunerated for his risk and trouble,) we pretend not to say.* Quite as much as can be vouched for is, the MSS being faithfully rendered from the original hieroglyphic character.

(*The dates are omitted.*)

—'Crawled forth from some rubbish, and wink'd with one eye;
Half opened the other, but could not tell why:
Stretched out my left leg, as it felt rather queer,
Then drew all together and slept for a year.
Awakened, felt chilly—crept under a stone;
Was vastly contented with living alone.
One toe became wedged in the stone like a peg,
Could not get it away—had the cramp in my leg:
Began half to wish for a neighbour at hand
To loosen the stone, which was fast in the sand;
Pull'd harder—then dozed, as I found 'twas no use;—
Awoke the next summer, and lo! it was loose.
Crawled forth from the stone, when completely awake;
Crept into a corner, and grinned at a snake.
Retreated, and found that I needed repose;
Curled up my damp limbs and prepared for a doze:
Fell sounder to sleep than was usual before,
And did not awake for a century or more;
But had a sweet dream, as I rather believe:—
Methought it was light, and a fine summer's eve;
And I in some garden deliciously fed,
In the pleasant moist shade of a strawberry bed.
There fine speckled creatures claimed kindred with me,
And others that hopped, most enchanting to see.
Here long I regaled with emotion extreme;—
Awoke—disconcerted to find it a dream;
Grew pensive;—discovered that life is a load;
Began to be weary of being a toad:
Was fretful at first, and then shed a few tears.'—
Here ends the account of the first thousand years.

MORAL

To find a moral where there's none
Is hard indeed, yet must be done:
Since only morals sound and sage
May grace this consecrated page:
Then give us leave to search a minute,
Perhaps for one that is not in it.

How strange a waste of life appears
This wondrous reptile's length of years!
Age after age afforded him
To wink an eye, or move a limb,
To doze and dream;—and then to think
Of noting this with pen and ink;
Or hieroglyphic shapes to draw,
More likely, with his hideous claw;
Sure length of days might be bestowed
On something better than a toad!
Had his existence been eternal
What better could have filled his journal?

True, we reply; our ancient friend
Seems to have lived to little end;
This must be granted;—nay the elf
Seems to suspect as much himself.
Refuse not then to find a teacher
In this extraordinary creature:
And learn at least, whoe'er you be,
To moralize as well as he.
It seems that life is all a void,
On selfish thoughts alone employed;
That length of days is not a good,
Unless their use be understood;
While if good deeds one year engage,
That may be longer than an age;
But if a year in trifles go,
Perhaps you'd spend a thousand so.
Time cannot stay to make us wise,
We must improve it as it flies;
The work is ours, and they shall rue it
Who think that time will stop to do it.

And then, again, he lets us know
That length of days is length of woe.
His long experience taught him this,
That life affords no solid bliss:
Or if of bliss on earth you scheme,
Soon you shall find it but a dream;
The visions fade, the slumbers break,
And then you suffer wide awake.
What is it but a vale of tears,
Though we should live a thousand years?

MARY TIGHE
(1772–1810)

Born into a moderately wealthy, well-connected, and intellectual Dublin family, Mary Blachford was educated by her mother, Theodosia Tighe Blachford, who came from an aristocratic family and was prominent in the Irish Methodist movement. In the 'Sonnet Addressed to My Mother' which opens *Psyche; or, the Legend of Love*, she emphasizes her mother's intellectual influence upon her: 'to thee belong The graces which adorn my first wild song'. Her father William Blachford, a clergyman and librarian of Marsh's Library and St Patrick's Library, died when she was only a few months old. Tighe's work is marked throughout by her familiarity with a wide range of European literature.

In 1793 Mary Blachford married her cousin, Henry Tighe, of Woodstock, County Wicklow, who represented Inistoge in the Irish Parliament from 1790 until its dissolution by the Act of Union in 1800. According to her mother, she was in love with another man, and was never happy with her husband. The Tighes moved to London where he trained as a barrister and she, strikingly beautiful, was admired by his friends. She turned increasingly to literary pursuits, and during visits to the home of her mother's family in Rosanna, County Wicklow, between 1801 and 1803, she wrote the poem which was to make her name, *Psyche; or, the Legend of Love*. It circulated in manuscript from 1802 and was printed in 1805 for private circulation only: a year after her death, her brother-in-law William Tighe edited it for publication in *Psyche, with Other Poems* (1811), which quickly went into several editions. The work was widely admired, and its sensuousness was a significant influence on Keats. Tighe was ill with tuberculosis from 1804; she moved from London first to Dublin, where she met Sydney Owenson and other prominent Irish writers, then to Rosanna, and finally to Woodstock, where she died in the house of William Tighe. Years later her grave was visited by her admirer Felicia Hemans, one of whose poems about Tighe ('I stood where the life of song lay low') is included in the selection from Hemans later in this volume. Tighe's manuscript works include a novel, *Selena*, poems, and prose recollections privately published by William Tighe in 1811 as *Mary, a Series of Reflections during Twenty Years*. Her diary was destroyed.

Tighe's Preface to *Psyche* describes her subject as 'the beautiful ancient allegory of Love and the Soul', and insists that the poem has 'only pictured innocent love, such love as the purest bosom might confess'. It tells the story of the love-god Cupid and the fair mortal Psyche, told by Apuleius in *The Golden Ass* and often retold in whole or in part. It is a well-known story, often treated allegorically, but even when allegorical is inescapably sexual, and predicated on the strength of female as well as male sexual desire: a potentially dangerous story, in other words, for a woman writer. Tighe's Preface, accordingly, sets out to defuse some potential criticisms. Apologetic about allegory, it declares that she has steered away from any ambitious intellectual superstructure by making her meaning 'perfectly obvious'. It draws attention to the difficulties of the Spenserian stanza ('by no means well adapted to the English language'). It also sees off some competitors, listing, after Apuleius, tales of Cupid and Psyche by Molière, Jean de la Fontaine, Du Moustier, and Giambattista Marino, but then insisting that Tighe has 'taken nothing' from them. This opening account seems to have been highly effective in shaping readers' appreciation of the work. The *Quarterly Review* thought that *Psyche* had 'few rivals in delicacy of sentiment, style, or versification',[1] and, rather than aligning it with contemporary literature, reviewers set it in the context of the romances of Ariosto, Tasso, and Spenser.

When one turns from the Preface to the poem itself, however, different alignments emerge, and Tighe can be seen to develop concerns which link her with her contemporaries. For example, she significantly elaborates on the part of the story in which Psyche, banished by Cupid, strives to appease the wrath of Venus. Psyche becomes a sort of female knight-errant, traversing a landscape of obstacles and tests of faith which shows the influence of Bunyan's *Pilgrim's Progress* amid its more romance-led components. Although the genre in which she writes seems to separate her entirely from Clara Reeve, Tighe, like Reeve, is investigating the traditions of romance-narrative from the point of view of the female writer. Psyche's eventual success, and consequent marriage, meanwhile, link

---

[1] *Quarterly Review* 5 (May 1811), 471–85, quoted from 480.

Tighe's poem to a different tradition of women's writing, recalling the trials of Burney's Evelina and Camilla. The evil suggestions of Psyche's sisters, likewise, a traditional component of the ancient story, take on new life in the context of the novel of manners, in which young women test out the limits of their duty of obedience to the family, and must decide, sometimes with disastrous consequences, between the claims of a lover and of family advisers or female intimates. Amid Tighe's linguistic luxuries and mythological remoteness lies a recognizable, though sublimated, tale of female education and endeavour, and an arena of sexual politics familiar from novels. Despite her disavowal of high intellectual claims in the Preface, finally, Tighe chooses a story in which the heroine had traditionally been allegorized as 'mind' (hence the etymology of 'psychology'). Tighe's reinterpretation of the tale therefore has a contribution to make to contemporary debates on the role of women, albeit in a designedly oblique and defensibly decorative way. Critical reaction to it certainly suggests that Tighe had wooed her readers into a sensuous suspension of disbelief, but she had also shown later women poets such as Felicia Hemans, Laetitia Landon, and Elizabeth Barrett that the narrative conventions of romance, an elaborate though traditional stanza-form, and a new way of making women's emotional struggles central to narrative as well as to lyric poetry could be valid and popular forms for modern poetry.

∽

From *Psyche; or, the Legend of Love* (1805)

Proem

Let not the rugged brow the rhymes accuse,
Which speak of gentle knights and ladies fair,
Nor scorn the lighter labours of the muse—
Who yet for cruel battles would not dare
The low-strung chords of her weak lyre prepare,
But loves to court repose in slumbery lay,
To tell of goodly bowers and gardens rare,
Of gentle blandishments and amorous play,
And all the lore of love in courtly verse essay.

And ye whose gentle hearts in thraldom held
The power of mighty love already own,
When you the pains and dangers have beheld

Which erst your lord hath for his Psyche known,
For all your sorrows this may well atone—
That he you serve the same hath suffered;
And sure, your fond applause the tale will crown
In which your own distress is pictured,
And all that weary way which you yourselves must tread.

Most sweet would to my soul the hope appear,
That sorrow in my verse a charm might find,
To smooth the brow long bent with bitter cheer,
Some short distraction to the joyless mind
Which grief, with heavy chain, hath fast confined
To sad remembrance of its happier state;
For to myself I ask no boon more kind
Than power another's woes to mitigate,
And that soft soothing art which anguish can abate.

And thou, sweet sprite, whose sway doth far extend,
Smile on the mean historian of thy fame!
My heart in each distress and fear befriend,
Nor ever let it feel a fiercer flame
Than innocence may cherish free from blame,
And hope may nurse, and sympathy may own;
For as thy rights I never would disclaim,
But true allegiance offered to thy throne,
So may I love but one, by one beloved alone.

That anxious torture may I never feel
Which, doubtful, watches o'er a wandering heart—
Oh who that bitter torment can reveal
Or tell the pining anguish of that smart?
In those affections may I ne'er have part,
Which easily transferred can learn to rove;
No, dearest Cupid, when I feel thy dart,
For thy sweet Psyche's sake may no false love
The tenderness I prize lightly from me remove!

Canto II

ARGUMENT

Introduction—dangers of the world—Psyche conveyed by zephyrs awakes once more in the paternal mansion—envy of her sisters—they plot her ruin—inspire her with suspicion and terror—Psyche's return to the Palace of Love—her disobedience—Love asleep—Psyche's amazement— the flight of Love—sudden banishment of Psyche from the island of Pleasure—her lamentations—comforted by Love—temple of Venus— task imposed on Psyche conditional to her reconciliation with Venus— Psyche soothed and attended by Innocence—Psyche wandering as described in the opening of the first Canto

Oh happy you who, blessed with present bliss,
See not with fatal prescience future tears,
Nor the dear moment of enjoyment miss
Through gloomy discontent, or sullen fears
Foreboding many a storm for coming years;
Change is the lot of all. Ourselves with scorn
Perhaps shall view what now so fair appears;
And wonder whence the fancied charm was born
Which now with vain despair from our fond grasp is torn!

Vain schemer, think not to prolong thy joy!
But cherish while it lasts the heavenly boon;
Expand thy sails! Thy little bark shall fly
With the full tide of pleasure; though it soon
May feel the influence of the changeful moon,
It yet is thine! Then let not doubts obscure
With cloudy vapours veil thy brilliant noon,
Nor let suspicion's tainted breath impure
Poison the favouring gale which speeds thy course secure!

Oh Psyche, happy in thine ignorance,
Couldst thou but shun this heart-tormenting bane!
Be but content, nor daringly advance
To meet the bitter hour of threatened pain.
Pure spotless dove, seek thy safe nest again;
Let true affection shun the public eye
And quit the busy circle of the vain,
For there the treacherous snares concealéd lie;
Oh timely-warned escape—to safe retirement fly!

Bright shone the morn, and now its golden ray
Dispelled the slumbers from her radiant eyes,
Yet still in dreams her fancy seems to play,
For lo, she sees with rapture and surprise
Full in her view the well-known mansion rise,
And each loved scene or first endearment hails;
The air that first received her infant sighs
With wondering ecstasy she now inhales,
While every trembling nerve soft tenderness assails.

See from the dear pavilion where she lay,
Breathless she flies with scarce-assuréd feet,
Swift through the garden wings her eager way,
Her mourning parents' ravished eyes to greet
With loveliest apparition strange and sweet.
Their days of anguish all o'erpaid they deem
By one blessed hour of ecstasy so great;
Yet doubtingly they gaze, and anxious seem
To ask their raptured souls, 'Oh is this all a dream?'

The wondrous tale attentively they hear,
Repeated oft in broken words of joy;
She in their arms embraced, while every ear
Hangs on their Psyche's lips, and earnestly
On her is fixed each wonder-speaking eye;
Till the sad hour arrives which bids them part,
And twilight darkens o'er the ruddy sky;
Divinely urged they let their child depart,
Pressed with a fond embrace to each adoring heart.

Trusting that wedded to a spouse divine
Secure is now their daughter's happiness,
They half-contentedly their child resign,
Check the complaint, the rising sigh suppress,
And wipe the silent drops of bitterness.
Nor must she her departure more delay,
But bids them now their weeping Psyche bless;
Then back to the pavilion bends her way
Ere in the fading west quite sinks expiring day.

But while her parents listen with delight,
Her sisters' hearts the Furies agitate;*

They look with envy on a lot so bright,
And all the honours of her splendid fate,
Scorning the meanness of their humbler state;
And how they best her ruin may devise
With hidden rancour much they meditate,
Yet still they bear themselves in artful guise,
While mid the feigned caress, concealed the venom lies.

By malice urged, by ruthless envy stung,
With secret haste to seize their prey they flew,
Around her neck as in despair they clung;
Her soft complying nature well they knew,
And trusted by delaying to undo;
But when they found her resolute to go,
Their well-laid stratagem they then pursue,
And, while they bid their treacherous sorrows flow,
Thus fright her simple heart with images of woe.

'Oh hapless Psyche, thoughtless of thy doom!
Yet hear thy sisters who have wept for thee
Since first a victim to thy living tomb;
Obedient to the oracle's decree,
Constrained we left thee to thy destiny.
Since then no comfort could our woes abate;
While thou wert lulled in false security
We learned the secret honours of thy fate,
And heard prophetic lips thy future ills relate.

'Yet fearing never to behold thee more,
Our filial care would fain the truth conceal;
But from the sage's cell this ring we bore,
With power each latent magic to reveal.
Some hope from hence our anxious bosoms feel
That we from ruin may our Psyche save,
Since Heaven propitious to our pious zeal,
Thee to our frequent prayers in pity gave,
That warned, thou yet mayst shun thy sad untimely grave.

'Oh how shall we declare the fatal truth?
How wound thy tender bosom with alarms?
Tell how the graces of thy blooming youth,
Thy more than mortal, all-adoréd charms

Have lain enamoured in a sorcerer's arms?
Oh Psyche, seize on this decisive hour,
Escape the mischief of impending harms!
Return no more to that enchanted bower,
Fly the magician's arts, and dread his cruel power.

'If yet reluctant to forego thy love,
Thy furtive joys and solitary state,
Our fond officious care thy doubts reprove,
At least let some precaution guard thy fate,
Nor may our warning love be prized too late.
This night thyself thou mayst convince thine eyes:
Hide but a lamp, and cautiously await
Till in deep slumber thy magician lies,
This ring shall then disclose his foul deformities.

'That monster by the oracle foretold,
Whose cursèd spells both gods and men must fear,
In his own image thou shalt then behold,
And shuddering hate what now is prized so dear;
Yet fly not then, though loathsome he appear,
But let this dagger to his breast strike deep;
Thy coward terrors then thou must not hear,
For if with life he rouses from that sleep
Nought then for thee remains, and we must hopeless weep.'

Oh have you seen, when in the northern sky
The transient flame of lambent lightning plays,*
In quick succession lucid streamers fly,
Now flashing roseate, and now milky rays,
While struck with awe the astonished rustics gaze?
Thus o'er her cheek the meeting signals move,
Now pale with fear, now glowing with the blaze
Of much indignant, still confiding love,
Now horror's lurid hue with shame's deep blushes strove.

On her cold passive hand the ring they place,
And hide the dagger in her folding vest,
Pleased the effects of their dire arts to trace
In the mute agony that swells her breast,
Already in her future ruin blessed—
Conscious that now their poor deluded prey

Should never taste again delight or rest,
But, sickening in suspicion's gloom decay,
Or urged by terrors rash, their treacherous will obey.

While yet irresolute with sad surprise,
Mid doubt and love she stands in strange suspense;
Lo, gliding from her sisters' wondering eyes
Returning zephyrs gently bear her thence;
Lost all her hopes, her joys, her confidence,
Back to the earth her mournful eyes she threw
As if imploring pity and defence;
While bathed in tears her golden tresses flew,
As in the breeze dispersed they caught the precious dew.

Illumined bright now shines the splendid dome,
Melodious accents her arrival hail;
But not the torches' blaze can chase the gloom,
And all the soothing powers of music fail;
Trembling she seeks her couch with horror pale,
But first a lamp conceals in secret shade,
While unknown terrors all her soul assail.
Thus half their treacherous counsel is obeyed,
For still her gentle soul abhors the murderous blade.

And now, with softest whispers of delight,
Love welcomes Psyche still more fondly dear;
Not unobserved, though hid in deepest night,
The silent anguish of her secret fear.
He thinks that tenderness excites the tear
By the late image of her parents' grief,
And half-offended seeks in vain to cheer;
Yet while he speaks, her sorrows feel relief,
Too soon more keen to sting from this suspension brief!

Allowed to settle on celestial eyes,
Soft Sleep exulting now exerts his sway,
From Psyche's anxious pillow gladly flies
To veil those orbs, whose pure and lambent ray
The powers of heaven submissively obey.
Trembling and breathless then she softly rose
And seized the lamp where it obscurely lay,

With hand too rashly daring to disclose
The sacred veil which hung mysterious o'er her woes.

Twice, as with agitated step she went,
The lamp expiring shone with doubtful gleam,
As though it warned her from her rash intent;
And twice she paused, and on its trembling beam
Gazed with suspended breath, while voices seem
With murmuring sound along the roof to sigh;
As one just waking from a troublous dream,
With palpitating heart and straining eye,
Still fixed with fear remains, still thinks the danger nigh.

Oh, daring muse, wilt thou indeed essay
To paint the wonders which that lamp could show?
And canst thou hope in living words to say
The dazzling glories of that heavenly view?
Ah well I ween, that if with pencil true
That splendid vision could be well expressed,
The fearful awe imprudent Psyche knew
Would seize with rapture every wondering breast,
When Love's all-potent charms divinely stood confessed.

All imperceptible to human touch,
His wings display celestial essence light,
The clear effulgence of the blaze is such,
The brilliant plumage shines so heavenly bright
That mortal eyes turn dazzled from the sight;
A youth he seems in manhood's freshest years;
Round his fair neck, as clinging with delight,
Each golden curl resplendently appears,
Or shades his darker brow, which grace majestic wears.

Or o'er his guileless front the ringlets bright
Their rays of sunny lustre seem to throw—
That front than polished ivory more white!
His blooming cheeks with deeper blushes glow
Than roses scattered o'er a bed of snow,
While on his lips, distilled in balmy dews
(Those lips divine that even in silence know
The heart to touch), persuasion to infuse
Still hangs a rosy charm that never vainly sues.

The friendly curtain of indulgent sleep
Disclosed not yet his eyes' resistless sway,
But from their silky veil there seemed to peep
Some brilliant glances with a softened ray,
Which o'er his features exquisitely play,
And all his polished limbs suffuse with light.
Thus through some narrow space the azure day
Sudden its cheerful rays diffusing bright,
Wide darts its lucid beams, to gild the brow of night.

His fatal arrows and celestial bow
Beside the couch were negligently thrown,
Nor needs the god his dazzling arms to show
His glorious birth, such beauty round him shone
As sure could spring from Beauty's self alone;
The gloom which glowed o'er all of soft desire,
Could well proclaim him Beauty's cherished son;
And Beauty's self will oft these charms admire,
And steal his witching smile, his glance's living fire.

Speechless with awe, in transport strangely lost,
Long Psyche stood with fixed adoring eye;
Her limbs immoveable, her senses tossed
Between amazement, fear, and ecstasy,
She hangs enamoured o'er the deity,
Till from her trembling hand extinguished falls
The fatal lamp—he starts—and suddenly
Tremendous thunders echo through the halls,
While ruin's hideous crash bursts o'er the affrighted walls.

Dread horror seizes on her sinking heart,
A mortal chillness shudders at her breast,
Her soul shrinks fainting from death's icy dart,
The groan scarce uttered dies but half expressed,
And down she sinks in deadly swoon oppressed.
But when at length awaking from her trance,
The terrors of her fate stand all confessed,
In vain she casts around her timid glance,
The rudely frowning scenes her former joys enhance.

No traces of those joys, alas, remain;
A desert solitude alone appears.

No verdant shade relieves the sandy plain,
The widespread waste no gentle fountain cheers,
One barren face the dreary prospect wears;
Nought through the vast horizon meets her eye
To calm the dismal tumult of her fears,
No trace of human habitation nigh:
A sandy wild beneath; above, a threatening sky.

The mists of morn yet chill the gloomy air
And heavily obscure the clouded skies;
In the mute anguish of a fixed despair
Still on the ground immoveable she lies;
At length, with lifted hands and streaming eye,
Her mournful prayers invoke offended Love:
'Oh let me hear thy voice once more', she cries,
'In death at least thy pity let me move,
And death, if but forgiven, a kind relief will prove.

'For what can life to thy lost Psyche give,
What can it offer but a gloomy void?
Why thus abandoned should I wish to live?
To mourn the pleasure which I once enjoyed,
The bliss my own rash folly hath destroyed?
Of all my soul most prized, or held most dear,
Nought but the sad remembrance doth abide,
And late repentance of my impious fear—
Remorse and vain regret what living soul can bear?

'Oh art thou then indeed for ever gone?
And art thou heedless of thy Psyche's woe?
From these fond arms for ever art thou flown,
And unregarded must my sorrows flow!
Ah, why too happy did I ever know
The rapturous charms thy tenderness inspires?
Ah why did thy affections stoop so low?
Why kindle in a mortal breast such fires,
Or with celestial love inflame such rash desires?

'Abandoned thus for ever by thy love,
No greater punishment I now can bear,
From fate no farther malice can I prove;
Not all the horrors of this desert drear,

Nor death itself can now excite a fear;
The peopled earth a solitude as vast
To this despairing heart would now appear;
Here then, my transient joys for ever past,
Let thine expiring bride thy pardon gain at last!'

Now prostrate on the bare unfriendly ground,
She waits her doom in silent agony;
When lo, the well-known soft celestial sound
She hears once more with breathless ecstasy.
'Oh yet too dearly loved, lost Psyche! Why
With cruel fate wouldst thou unite thy power,
And force me thus thine arms adored to fly?
Yet cheer thy drooping soul, some happier hour
Thy banished steps may lead back to thy lover's bower.

'Though angry Venus we no more can shun,
Appease that anger and I yet am thine!
Lo, where her temple glitters to the sun;
With humble penitence approach her shrine,
Perhaps to pity she may yet incline;
But should her cruel wrath these hopes deceive,
And thou, alas, must never more be mine,
Yet shall thy lover ne'er his Psyche leave,
But, if the Fates allow, unseen thy woes relieve.

'Stronger than I, they now forbid my stay;
Psyche beloved, adieu!' Scarce can she hear
The last faint words, which gently melt away;
And now more faint the dying sounds appear,
Borne to a distance from her longing ear,
Yet still attentively she stands unmoved
To catch those accents which her soul could cheer,
That soothing voice which had so sweetly proved
That still his tender heart offending Psyche loved!

And now the joyous sun had cleared the sky,
The mist dispelled revealed the splendid fane;
A palmy grove majestically high
Screens the fair building from the desert plain;
Of alabaster white and free from stain
Mid the tall trees the tapering columns rose;

Thither, with fainting steps and weary pain,
Obedient to the voice at length she goes,
And at the threshold seeks protection and repose.

Round the soft scene immortal roses bloomed,
While lucid myrtles in the breezes play;*
No savage beast had ever yet presumed
With foot impure within the grove to stray,
And far from hence flies every bird of prey;
Thus, mid the sandy Garamantian wild,*
When Macedonia's lord pursued his way,
The sacred temple of great Ammon smiled,
And green encircling shades the long fatigue beguiled.*

With awe that fearfully her doom awaits
Still at the portal Psyche timid lies,
When lo, advancing from the hallowed gates
Trembling she views with reverential eyes
An aged priest. A myrtle bough supplies
A wand, and roses bind his snowy brows.
'Bear hence thy feet profane!' he sternly cries,
'Thy longer stay the goddess disallows;
Fly, nor her fiercer wrath too daringly arouse!'

His pure white robe imploringly she held,
And, bathed in tears, embraced his sacred knees;
Her mournful charms relenting he beheld,
And melting pity in his eye she sees.
'Hope not', he cries, 'the goddess to appease;
Retire at awful distance from her shrine,
But seek the refuge of those sheltering trees,
And now thy soul with humble awe incline
To hear her sacred will, and mark the words divine.

'Presumptuous Psyche, whose aspiring soul
The god of Love has dared to arrogate;
Rival of Venus, whose supreme control
Is now asserted by all-ruling fate,
No suppliant tears her vengeance shall abate
Till thou hast raised an altar to her power
Where perfect happiness, in lonely state,

Has fixed her temple in secluded bower,
By foot impure of man untrodden to this hour!

'And on the altar must thou place an urn
Filled from immortal beauty's sacred spring,
Which foul deformity to grace can turn,
And back to fond affection's eyes can bring
The charms which fleeting fled on transient wing;
Snatched from the rugged steep where first they rise,
Dark rocks their crystal source o'ershadowing,
Let their clear water sparkle to the skies
Where cloudless lustre beams which happiness supplies!

'To Venus thus for ever reconciled
(This one atonement all her wrath disarms),
From thy loved Cupid then no more exiled
There shalt thou, free from sorrow and alarms,
Enjoy for ever his celestial charms.
But never shalt thou taste a pure repose
Nor ever meet thy lover's circling arms
Till all subdued that shall thy steps oppose—
Thy perils there shall end, escaped from all thy foes.'

With meek submissive woe she heard her doom,
Nor to the holy minister replied;
But in the myrtle grove's mysterious gloom
She silently retired her grief to hide.
Hopeless to tread the waste without a guide,
All unrefreshed and faint from toil she lies;
When lo, her present wants are all supplied—
Sent by the hand of Love a turtle flies
And sets delicious food before her wondering eyes.*

Cheered by the favouring omen, softer tears
Relieve her bosom from its cruel weight.
She blames the sad despondence of her fears;
When still protected by a power so great,
His tenderness her toils will mitigate.
Then with renewéd strength at length she goes,
Hoping to find some skilled in secret fate,
Some learnéd sage who haply might disclose
Where lay that blissful bower, the end of all her woes.

And as she went—behold, with hovering flight
The dove preceded still her doubtful way;
Its spotless plumage of the purest white,
Which shone resplendent in the blaze of day,
Could even in darkest gloom a light display—
Of heavenly birth, when first to mortals given,
Named Innocence. But ah, too short its stay;
By ravenous birds it fearfully was driven
Back to reside with Love, a denizen of heaven.

Now through the trackless wild, o'er many a mile
The messenger of Cupid led the fair
And cheered with hope her solitary toil,
Till now a brighter face the prospects wear,
Past are the sandy wastes and deserts bare,
And many a verdant hill and grassy dale,
And trace that mortal culture might declare,
And many a wild wood dark and joyous vale
Appeared her soul to soothe, could soothing scenes avail.

But other fears her timid soul distress
Mid strangers unprotected and alone,
The desert wilderness alarmed her less
Than cities, thus unfriended and unknown;
But where the path was all by moss o'ergrown,
There still she chose her solitary way,
Where'er her faithful dove before had flown
Fearful of nought she might securely stray,
For still his care supplied the wants of every day.

And still she entered every sacred grove
And homage paid to each divinity,
But chief the altar of almighty Love
Weeping embraced with fond imploring eye;
To every oracle her hopes apply,
Instructions for her dangerous path to gain—
Exclaiming oft, with a desponding sigh,
'Ah, how through all such dangers, toil and pain,
Shall Psyche's helpless steps their object e'er attain?'

And now remote from every peopled town
One sultry day a cooling bower she found;

There, as I whilom sung,* she laid her down,
Where rich profusion of gay flowers around
Had decked with artless show the sloping ground;
There the wild rose and modest violet grow,
There all thy charms, Narcissus, still abound!*
There wrapped in verdure fragrant lilies blow,
Lilies that love the vale, and hide their bells of snow.

Thy flowers, Adonis, bright vermilion show;*
Still for his love the yellow crocus pines;
There, while indignant blushes seem to glow,
Beloved by Phoebus his Acanthus shines;*
Reseda still her drooping head reclines
With faithful homage to his golden rays,*
And, though mid clouds their lustre he resigns,
An image of the constant heart displays,
While silent still she turns her fond pursuing gaze.

And every sweet that Spring with fairy hands
Scatters in thy green path, enchanting May,
And every flowering shrub there clustering stands
As though they wooed her to a short delay,
Yielding a charm to soothe her weary way;
Soft was the tufted moss, and sweet the breeze,
With lulling sound the murmuring waters play,
With lulling sound from all the rustling trees
The fragrant gale invites to cool refreshing ease.

There as she sought repose, her sorrowing heart
Recalled her absent love with bitter sighs;
Regret had deeply fixed the poisoned dart
Which ever rankling in her bosom lies;
In vain she seeks to close her weary eyes—
Those eyes still swim incessantly in tears,
Hope in her cheerless bosom fading dies,
Distracted by a thousand cruel fears,
While banished from his love for ever she appears.

Oh thou best comforter of that sad heart
Whom fortune's spite assails—come, gentle sleep,
The weary mourner soothe! For well the art
Thou knowest in soft forgetfulness to steep

The eyes which sorrow taught to watch and weep;
Let blissful visions now her spirits cheer,
Or lull her cares to peace in slumbers deep,
Till from fatigue refreshed and anxious fear
Hope like the morning star once more shall reappear.

DOROTHY WORDSWORTH
(1771–1855)

Born in Cockermouth, Cumbria, Dorothy Wordsworth was the only daughter among the five children of John Wordsworth—an attorney and the law agent of the Cumberland landowner Lord Lowther, later the Earl of Lonsdale—and his wife Ann Cookson, the daughter of a Penrith linen-draper. She was separated from her father and brothers on the early death of their mother in 1778, and was sent to live in Halifax with the larger family of her mother's cousin, Elizabeth Threlkeld, whom she always referred to as 'aunt'. She had a stable and stimulating upbringing in Halifax among the Dissenting chapel congregation of which her aunt and friends were part: the haberdasher's shop which her aunt ran also housed the Halifax Old Subscription Library, and Dorothy Wordsworth became a keen reader. For three years she was educated at a boarding-school outside Halifax; then, on the sudden death of her father late in 1783, returned to live with her 'aunt' and to attend the day-school of Martha and Hannah Mellin. Her father died intestate, and he was owed £5,000 by his employer, Lord Lowther; his executors, Dorothy Wordsworth's uncles, spent twenty years trying to recover this money in a series of complex legal suits, and it was only paid, with interest, when the Earl of Lonsdale himself died. As a result, money was a problem for the Wordsworth family, and Dorothy's education and comfort the obvious economies. To her distress, in May 1787 she was removed, aged 15, to live in Penrith with her maternal grandparents. Here she came to know her brothers again, and made new friends, notably Mary Hutchinson; she also acquired a family tutor in the shape of her uncle, the Revd William Cookson, a fellow of St John's College, Cambridge. When William Cookson married in 1788, Dorothy went to live with him and his wife in his new parish of Forncett St Peter, Norfolk, where she set up a Sunday School, befriended William Wilberforce, and was active in parish work and the nursery.

In 1795 she and her brother William realized a long-standing plan to set up house together, living rent-free in Racedown Lodge in Dorset and looking after a little boy, Basil Montagu. In 1797 they befriended Samuel Taylor Coleridge, who described Dorothy in a letter: 'Her information various—her eye watchful in minutest observation of nature—and her taste a perfect electrometer—it bends, protrudes, and draws in at subtlest beauties and most recondite faults'.[1] To be near Coleridge they moved to Alfoxden House, Somerset, where Dorothy kept the 'Alfoxden Journal' (20 January to 22 May 1798). William and Dorothy spent the winter of 1798–9 travelling in Germany, and on their return settled at the cottage at Town End, Grasmere (later called Dove Cottage), where in May 1800 Dorothy began her 'Grasmere Journal'. Throughout these years she was intermittently unwell, but extremely active, visiting France with William in 1802. She continued to play a central part in her brother's household and thinking after his marriage to Mary Hutchinson in October 1802, and devoted herself to their children.

The Wordsworths moved to Allan Bank in 1808, to Grasmere Rectory (where two of the children, Catharine and Thomas, died) in 1811, and in 1813 to Rydal Mount, near Ambleside; in 1820 made a continental tour; and Dorothy visited Scotland again in 1822 and the Isle of Man in 1828. She became increasingly conservative and religious as she grew older. Dorothy had been subject to attacks of illness since 1801, had problems with her teeth (the remaining few were replaced with a false set in 1820), and became dangerously ill in 1829. After this, she was repeatedly ill, and in 1835 showed clear signs of mental disorientation. For twenty years she suffered 'pre-senile dementia of a type similar to Alzheimer's disease', according to modern diagnosis.[2] She survived so long—outliving her brother—because of the careful nursing of her sister-in-law Mary, and the stimulus of continued involvement in the daily affairs of William and Mary's family.

Apart from the connections and friendships formed through her brother, Dorothy Wordsworth was close to Mary Lamb, whose situation harmonized with her own in key respects, met Joanna Baillie in London, and knew Maria Jane Jewsbury well, staying with her family in Manchester in 1828. She did not feel tempted to join the ranks of literary women, however, resisting friends' appeals for publication with the declaration 'I should detest the idea of setting myself up as an Author'.[3] With the exception of a few poems published in her brother's collections, Dorothy Wordsworth's work was not known outside her own circle until long after her death. Both her brother and Coleridge drew on her journals for details and ideas in their own poetry, and sections of her prose were incorporated

---

[1] Robert Gittings and Jo Manton, *Dorothy Wordsworth* (Oxford: Clarendon, 1985), 65.
[2] Ibid. 271.
[3] Ibid. 188.

into William's *Guide to the Lakes* (1822). She is both well known to Romanticists and unusually difficult to place, partly because she seems to write for a private audience and to show little interest in the rewards or tribulations of the independently published author.

The first sample of her published writing selected here is taken from *Recollections of a Tour Made in Scotland*, completed in 1805, revised in 1806 and 1822, and published in 1874. Reading it during a visit to Rydal Mount in 1833, Henry Crabb Robinson was disappointed: 'She travelled with her brother and Coleridge. Had she but filled her volume with their conversation, rather than minute description!'⁴ The tour, for which they hired a horse and an 'Irish Jaunting Car' (an open cart) lasted six weeks, from 15 August to 25 September 1803, and the Wordsworths separated from Coleridge after two. It seems to have been an attempt to reproduce the closeness which had led to such an upsurge in poetic activity during the Quantock walks, but Coleridge was ill and resistant, and ended up touring Scotland alone on foot. Dorothy and William visited Inverary, Glencoe and Killiecrankie, the Trossachs, Edinburgh, and the Border regions. Dorothy kept some notes and maps made during the journey, and on her return began to write a series of recollections, though she abandoned the work for long periods, only finishing it at the end of May 1805. The final stages of writing were overshadowed by the death of her brother John, captain of the *Earl of Abergavenny*, which sank on 5 February 1805. The narrative was written for family and friends, who made copies of it. She was urged to consider publication, and in 1822 William Wordsworth wrote to the poet Samuel Rogers, following up Rogers's admiration for the work and asking Rogers to secure a publisher. Dorothy Wordsworth was fully involved in this move, and wrote to Rogers stipulating that she be paid at least £200 for the copyright, money which she hoped to use to finance a planned visit to Italy. The fair copy she prepared for the press was 'very much revised in the interests of supposed respectability. All references to William's general clumsiness, for instance, were carefully removed for this intended publication.'⁵ Obviously Rogers's efforts were unsuccessful, but Dorothy Wordsworth at this stage clearly intended this to be her first independent claim to a public readership. The *Recollections* were first published, edited by John Campbell Shairp, in 1874, and this is the text given here.

The first of the two poems included here, 'Address to a Child, During a Boisterous Winter Evening', was written in 1805–7 for William's eldest

---

⁴ *Diary, Reminiscences, and Correspondence of Henry Crabb Robinson, Barrister-at-Law, F.S.A.*, selected and ed. Thomas Sadler, 3rd edn., 2 vols. (1872; New York: AMS Press, 1967), ii. 140.

⁵ Gittings and Manton, *Dorothy Wordsworth*, 148.

child John and published in William's *Poems* of 1815. The poem was described as 'By a female Friend of the Author', and 'Johnny' became 'Edward'. The second, describing the 'Floating Island' at Hawkshead, is from the 1820s and was published in William's collection *Poems, Chiefly of Early and Late Years; Including The Borderers, a Tragedy* (London: Edward Moxon, 1842), in which it was signed 'D.W.'.

∾

From *Recollections of a Tour Made in Scotland* (1805)

[*Wednesday, August 24th*—] . . . As we advanced we perceived less of the coldness of poverty, the hills not having so large a space between them and the lake. The surface of the hills being in its natural state, is always beautiful; but where there is only a half cultivated and half peopled soil near the banks of a lake or river, the idea is forced upon one that they who do live there have not much of cheerful enjoyment.

But soon we came to just such a place as we had wanted to see. The road was close to the water, and a hill, bare, rocky, or with scattered copses rose above it. A deep shade hung over the road, where some little boys were at play; we expected a dwelling-house of some sort; and when we came nearer, saw three or four thatched huts under the trees, and at the same moment felt that it was a paradise. We had before seen the lake only as one wide plain of water;* but here the portion of it which we saw was bounded by a high and steep, heathy and woody island opposite, which did not appear like an island, but the main shore, and framed out a little oblong lake apparently not so broad as Rydale-water,* with one small island covered with trees, resembling some of the most beautiful of the holms of Windermere,* and only a narrow river's breadth from the shore. This was a place where we should have liked to have lived, and the only one we had seen near Loch Lomond. How delightful to have a little shed concealed under the branches of the fairy island! the cottages and the island might have been made for the pleasure of each other. It was but like a natural garden, the distance was so small; nay, one could not have forgiven any one living there, not compelled to daily labour, if he did not connect it with his dwelling by some feeling of domestic attachment, like what he has for the orchard where his children play. I thought, what a place for William!* he might row himself over with twenty strokes of the oars, escaping from the business of the house, and as safe from intruders, with his boat anchored beside him, as if he had locked himself upon the strong tower of a castle. We were unwilling to leave this sweet spot; but it was so simple, and therefore so rememberable, that it seemed almost as if we could have carried it away with us. It was nothing more than a small lake enclosed by trees at the ends and by the way-side, and opposite by the island, a steep bank on which the purple heath was seen under low oak coppice-wood, a group of houses over-shadowed by trees, and a bending road. There was one remarkable tree, an old larch with hairy branches, which sent out its main stem horizontally across the road, an object that seemed to have been singled out for injury where everything else was lovely and thriving, tortured into that shape by storms, which one might have thought could not have reached it in that sheltered place.

We were now entering into the Highlands. I believe Luss is the place where we were told that country begins;* but at these cottages I would have gladly believed that we were there, for it was like a new region. The huts were after the Highland fashion, and the boys who were playing wore the Highland dress and philabeg.* On going into a new country I seem to myself to waken up, and afterwards it surprises me to remember how much alive I have been to the distinctions of dress, household arrangements, etc. etc., and what a spirit these little things give to wild, barren, or ordinary places. The cottages are within about two miles of Luss. Came in view of several islands; but the lake being so very wide, we could see little of their peculiar beauties, and they, being large, hardly looked like islands.

Passed another gentleman's house, which stands prettily in a bay,* and soon after reached Luss, where we intended to lodge. On seeing the outside of the inn we were glad that we were to have such pleasant quarters. It is a nice-looking white house, by the road-side;* but there was not much promise of hospitality when we stopped at the door: no person came out till we had shouted a considerable time. A barefooted lass showed me up-stairs, and again my hopes revived; the house was clean for a Scotch inn,* and the view very pleasant to the lake, over the top of the village—a cluster of thatched houses among trees, with a large chapel in the midst of them. Like most of the Scotch kirks which we had seen, this building resembles a big house; but it is a much more pleasing building than they generally are, and has one of our rustic belfries, not unlike that at Ambleside, with two bells hanging in the open air. We chose one of the back rooms to sit in, being more snug, and they looked upon a very sweet prospect—a stream tumbling down a cleft or glen on the hill-side, rocky coppice ground, a rural lane, such as we have from house to house at Grasmere, and a few out-houses. We had a poor dinner, and sour ale; but as long as the people were civil we were contented.

Coleridge was not well, so he did not stir out, but William and I walked through the village to the shore of the lake. When I came close to the houses, I could not but regret a want of loveliness correspondent with the beauty of the situation and the appearance of the village at a little distance; not a single ornamented garden. We saw potatoes and cabbages, but never a honeysuckle. Yet there were wild gardens, as beautiful as any that ever man cultivated, overgrowing the roofs of some of the cottages, flowers and creeping plants. How elegant were the wreaths of the bramble that had 'built its own bower' upon the riggings in several parts of the village;* therefore we had chiefly to regret the want of gardens, as they are symptoms of leisure and comfort, or at least of no painful industry. Here we first saw houses without windows, the smoke coming out of the open window-places; the chimneys were like stools with four legs, a hole being left in the roof for the smoke, and over that a slate placed upon four sticks—sometimes the whole leaned as if it were going to fall. The fields close to Luss lie flat to the lake, and a river, as large as our stream near the church at Grasmere, flows by the end of the village, being the same which comes down the glen behind the inn; it is very much like our stream—beds of blue pebbles upon the shores.

We walked towards the head of the lake, and from a large pasture field near Luss, a gentle eminence, had a very interesting view back upon the village and the lake and islands beyond. We then perceived that Luss stood in the centre of a spacious bay, and that close to it lay another small one, within the larger, where the boats of the inhabitants were lying at anchor, a beautiful natural harbour. The islands, as we look down the water, are seen in great beauty. Inch-ta-vannach, the same that framed out the little peaceful lake which we had passed in the morning, towers above the rest.* The lake is very wide here, and the opposite shores not being lofty the chief part of the permanent beauty of this view is among the islands, and on the near shore, including the low promontories of the bay of Luss, and the village;

and we saw it under its dullest aspect—the air cold, the sky gloomy, without a glimpse of sunshine.

On a splendid evening, with the light of the sun diffused over the whole islands, distant hills, and the broad expanse of the lake, with its creeks, bays, and little slips of water among the islands, it must be a glorious sight.

Up the lake there are no islands; Ben Lomond terminates the view, without any other large mountains; no clouds were upon it, therefore we saw the whole size and form of the mountain, yet it did not appear to me so large as Skiddaw does from Derwent-water.* Continued our walk a considerable way towards the head of the lake, and went up a high hill, but saw no other reach of the water. The hills on the Luss side become much steeper, and the lake, having narrowed a little above Luss, was no longer a very wide lake where we lost sight of it.

Came to a bark hut by the shores, and sate for some time under the shelter of it. While we were here a poor woman with a little child by her side begged a penny of me, and asked where she could 'find quarters in the village.' She was a travelling beggar, a native of Scotland, had often 'heard of that water,' but was never there before. This woman's appearance, while the wind was rustling about us, and the waves breaking at our feet, was very melancholy: the waters looked wide, the hills many, and dark, and far off—no house but at Luss. I thought what a dreary waste must this lake be to such poor creatures, struggling with fatigue and poverty and unknown ways!

We ordered tea when we reached the inn, and desired the girl to light us a fire; she replied, 'I dinna ken whether she'll gie fire,' meaning her mistress. We told her we did not wish her mistress to give fire, we only desired her to let her make it and we would pay for it. The girl brought in the tea-things, but no fire, and when I asked if she was coming to light it, she said 'her mistress was not varra willing to gie fire.' At last, however, on our insisting upon it, the fire was lighted: we got tea by candlelight, and spent a comfortable evening. I had seen the landlady before we went out, for, as had been usual in all the country inns, there was a demur respecting beds, notwithstanding the house was empty, and there were at least half-a-dozen spare beds. Her countenance corresponded with the unkindness of denying us a fire on a cold night, for she was the most cruel and hateful-looking woman I ever saw. She was overgrown with fat, and was sitting with her feet and legs in a tub of water for the dropsy,—probably brought on by whisky-drinking.* The sympathy which I felt and expressed for her, on seeing her in this wretched condition—for her legs were swollen as thick as mill-posts—seemed to produce no effect: and I was obliged, after five minutes' conversation, to leave the affair of the beds undecided. Coleridge had some talk with her daughter, a smart lass in a cotton gown, with a bandeau round her head, without shoes and stockings. She told Coleridge with some pride that she had not spent all her time at Luss, but was then fresh from Glasgow.

It came on a very stormy night; the wind rattled every window in the house, and it rained heavily. William and Coleridge had bad beds, in a two-bedded room in the garrets, though there were empty rooms on the first floor, and they were disturbed by a drunken man, who had come to the inn when we were gone to sleep.

Thursday, August 25th.—We were glad when we awoke to see that it was a fine morning—the sky was bright blue, with quick-moving clouds, the hills cheerful, lights and shadows vivid and distinct. The village looked exceedingly beautiful this morning from the garret windows—the stream glittering near it, while it flowed under trees through the level fields to the lake. After breakfast, William and I went down to the water-side. The roads were as dry as if no drop of rain had fallen, which added to the pure cheerfulness of the appearance of the village, and even of the distant prospect, an effect which I always seem to perceive from clearly bright roads, for they are always brightened by rain, after a storm; but when we came among the houses I regretted even more than last night, because the contrast was greater, the slovenliness and dirt near the doors; and could not but remember, with pain from the contrast, the cottages of Somersetshire, covered with roses and myrtle, and their small gardens of herbs and flowers. While lingering by the shore we began to talk with a man who offered to row us to Inch-ta-vannach; but the sky began to darken; and the wind being high, we doubted whether we should venture, therefore made no engagement; he offered to sell me some thread, pointing to his cottage, and added that many English ladies carried thread away from Luss.

Presently after Coleridge joined us, and we determined to go to the island. I was sorry that the man who had been talking with us was not our boatman; William by some chance had engaged another. We had two rowers and a strong boat; so I felt myself bold, though there was a great chance of a high wind. The nearest point of Inch-ta-vannach is not perhaps more than a mile and a quarter from Luss; we did not land there, but rowed round the end, and landed on that side which looks towards our favourite cottages, and their own island, which, wherever seen, is still their own. It rained a little when we landed, and I took my cloak, which afterwards served us to sit down upon in our road up the hill, when the day grew much finer, with gleams of sunshine. This island belongs to Sir James Colquhoun,* who has made a convenient road, that winds gently to the top of it.

We had not climbed far before we were stopped by a sudden burst of prospect, so singular and beautiful that it was like a flash of images from another world. We stood with our backs to the hill of the island, which we were ascending, and which shut out Ben Lomond entirely, and all the upper part of the lake, and we looked towards the foot of the lake, scattered over with islands without beginning and without end. The sun shone, and the distant hills were visible, some through sunny mists, others in gloom with patches of sunshine; the lake was lost under the low and distant hills, and the island lost in the lake, which was all in motion with travelling fields of light, or dark shadows under rainy clouds. There are many hills, but no command-ing eminence at a distance to confine the prospect, so that the land seemed endless as the water.

What I had heard of Loch Lomond, or any other place in Great Britain, had given me no idea of anything like what we beheld: it was an outlandish scene—we might have believed ourselves in North America. The islands were of every possible variety of shape and surface—hilly and level large and small, bare, rocky, pastoral, or covered with wood. Immediately under my eyes lay one large flat island, bare and green, so flat and low that it scarcely appeared to rise above the water, with straggling peat-stacks and a single hut upon one of its out-shooting, promontories—for it was of a very irregular shape, though perfectly flat. Another, its next neighbour, and still nearer to us, was covered over with heath and coppice-wood, the surface undulating, with flat or sloping banks towards the water, and hollow places, cradle-like valleys, behind. These two islands, with Inch-ta-vannach, where we were standing, were intermingled with the water, I might say interbedded and interveined with it in a manner that was exquisitely pleasing. There were bays innumerable, straits or passages like calm rivers, landlocked lakes, and, to the main water, stormy promontories. The solitary hut on the flat green island seemed unsheltered and desolate, and yet not wholly so, for it was but a broad river's breadth from the covert of the wood of the other island. Near to these is a miniature, an islet covered with trees, on which stands a small ruin that looks like the remains of a religious house; it is overgrown with ivy, and were it not that the arch of a window or gateway may be distinctly seen, it would be difficult to believe that it was not a tuft of trees growing in the shape of a ruin, rather than a ruin overshadowed by trees. When we had walked a little further we saw below us, on the nearest large island, where some of the wood had been cut down, a hut, which we conjectured to be a bark hut. It appeared to be on the shore of a little forest lake, enclosed by Inch-ta-vannach, where we were, and the woody island on which the hut stands.

Beyond we had the same intricate view as before, and could discover Dumbarton rock with its double head.* There being a mist over it, it had a ghost-like appearance—as I observed to William and Coleridge, something like the Tor of Glastonbury from the Dorsetshire hills.* Right before us, on the flat island mentioned before, were several small single trees or shrubs, growing at different distances from each other, close to the shore, but some optical delusion had detached them from the land on which they stood, and they had the appearance of so many little vessels sailing along the coast of it. I mention the circumstance, because, with the ghostly image of Dumbarton Castle, and the ambiguous ruin on the small island, it was much in the character of the scene, which was throughout magical and enchanting—a new world in its great permanent outline and composition, and changing at every moment in every part of it by the effect of sun and wind, and mist and shower and cloud, and the blending lights and deep shades which took the place of each other, traversing the lake in every direction. The whole was indeed a strange mixture of soothing and restless images, of images inviting to rest, and others hurrying the fancy away into an activity still more pleasing than repose. Yet, intricate and homeless, that is, without lasting abiding-place for the mind, as the prospect was, there was no perplexity; we had still a guide to lead us forward.

Wherever we looked, it was a delightful feeling that there was something beyond. Meanwhile, the sense of quiet was never lost sight of; the little peaceful lakes among the islands might make you forget that the great water, Loch Lomond, was so near; and yet are more beautiful, because you know that it is so: they have their own bays and creeks sheltered within a shelter. When we had ascended to the top of the island we had a view up to Ben Lomond, over the long, broad water without spot or rock; and, looking backwards, saw the islands below us as on a map. This view, as may be supposed, was not nearly so interesting as those we had seen before. We hunted out all the houses on the shore, which were very few: there was the village of Luss, the two gentlemen's houses, our favourite cottages, and here and there a hut; but I do not recollect any comfortable-looking farm-houses, and on the opposite shore not a single dwelling. The whole scene was a combination of natural wildness, loveliness, beauty, and barrenness, or rather bareness, yet not comfortless or cold; but the whole was beautiful. We were too far off the more distant shore to distinguish any particular spots which we might have regretted were not better cultivated, and near Luss there was no want of houses.

After we had left the island, having been so much taken with the beauty of the bark hut and the little lake by which it appeared to stand, we desired the boatman to row us through it, and we landed at the hut. Walked upon the island for some time, and found out sheltered places for cottages. There were several woodmen's huts, which, with some scattered fir-trees, and others in irregular knots, that made a delicious murmuring in the wind, added greatly to the romantic effect of the scene. They were built in the form of a cone from the ground, like savages' huts, the door being just large enough for a man to enter with stooping. Straw beds were raised on logs of wood, tools lying about, and a forked bough of a tree was generally suspended from the roof in the middle to hang a kettle upon. It was a place that might have been just visited by new settlers. I thought of Ruth and her dreams of romantic love:

> And then he said how sweet it were,
> A fisher or a hunter there,
> A gardener in the shade,
> Still wandering with an easy mind,
> To build a household fire and find
> A home in every glade.*

We found the main lake very stormy when we had left the shelter of the islands, and there was again a threatening of rain, but it did not come on. I wanted much to go to the old ruin, but the boatmen were in a hurry to be at home. They told us it had been a stronghold built by a man who lived there alone, and was used to swim over and make depredations on the shore,—that nobody could ever lay hands on him, he was such a good swimmer, but at last they caught him in a net. The men pointed out to us an island belonging to Sir James Colquhoun, on which were a great quantity of deer.

Arrived at the inn at about twelve o'clock, and prepared to depart immediately: we should have gone with great regret if the weather had been warmer and the inn more comfortable. When we were leaving the door, a party with smart carriage and servants drove up, and I observed that the people of the house were just as slow in their attendance upon them as on us, with one single horse and outlandish Hibernian vehicle.*

Address to a Child,
During a Boisterous Winter Evening (1805–7)

What way does the Wind come? What way does he go?
He rides over the water, and over the snow,
Through wood, and through vale; and o'er rocky height
Which the goat cannot climb takes his sounding flight.
He tosses about in every bare tree,
As, if you look up, you plainly may see;
But how he will come, and whither he goes
There's never a Scholar in England knows.

He will suddenly stop in a cunning nook,
And rings a sharp larum;—but if you should look
There's nothing to see but a cushion of snow
Round as a pillow, and whiter than milk,
And softer than if it were covered with silk.

Sometimes he'll hide in the cave of a rock,
Then whistle as shrill as the buzzard cock;
—Yet seek him,—and what shall you find in the place?
Nothing but silence and empty space,

Save, in a corner, a heap of dry leaves,
That he's left for a bed for beggars or thieves!

As soon as 'tis daylight, to-morrow, with me
You shall go to the orchard, and then you will see
That he has been there, and made a great rout,
And cracked the branches, and strewn them about;
Heaven grant that he spare but that one upright twig
That looked up at the sky so proud and big
All last summer, as well you know,
Studded with apples, a beautiful show!

Hark! over the roof he makes a pause,
And growls as if he would fix his claws
Right in the slates, and with a huge rattle
Drive them down, like men in a battle:
—But let him range round; he does us no harm
We build up the fire, we're snug and warm;
Untouch'd by his breath see the candle shines bright,
And burns with a clear and steady light;
Books have we to read,—hush! that half-stifled knell,
Methinks 'tis the sound of the eight o'clock bell.

—Come, now we'll to bed! and when we are there
He may work his own will, and what shall we care?
He may knock at the door,—we'll not let him in,
May drive at the windows,—we'll laugh at his din;
Let him seek his own home wherever it be;
Here's a *cozie* warm House for Edward and me.

Floating Island (1820s)*

Harmonious Powers with Nature work
On sky, earth, river, lake and sea;
Sunshine and cloud, whirlwind and breeze,
All in one duteous task agree.

Once did I see a slip of earth
(By throbbing waves long undermined)
Loosed from its hold; how, no one knew,
But all might see it float, obedient to the wind;

Might see it, from the mossy shore
Dissevered, float upon the Lake,
Float with its crest of trees adorned
On which the warbling birds their pastime take.

Food, shelter, safety, there they find;
There berries ripen, flowerets bloom;
There insects live their lives, and die;
A peopled world it is; in size a tiny room.

And thus through many seasons' space
This little Island may survive;
But Nature, though we mark her not,
Will take away, may cease to give.

Perchance when you are wandering forth
Upon some vacant sunny day,
Without an object, hope, or fear,
Thither your eyes may turn—the Isle is passed away;

Buried beneath the glittering Lake,
Its place no longer to be found;
Yet the lost fragments shall remain
To fertilize some other ground.

JANE MARCET
(1769–1858)

Born Jane Haldimand, the only daughter of Francis Haldimand, a rich
Swiss merchant based in London, and his wife Jane Pickersgill, at the age
of 30 she married the physician and scientific writer Alexander Marcet,
from Geneva, who became a Fellow of the Royal Society in 1815 and died
in 1822. Marcet shared her husband's scientific interests, and set out to
encourage female education in science by writing instruction for children
in the form of 'conversations'. *Conversations on Natural Philosophy* was
designed as the preparatory volume, but was not published until 1819.
Long before this, her *Conversations on Chemistry* (1806) proved popular in
Britain and the United States (an estimated 160,000 copies were sold in
the United States before 1853), and went into several editions. Even more
influential was her *Conversations on Political Economy* (1816), which was

praised by the economists Jean-Baptiste Say, Thomas Malthus, David Ricardo, and J. R. McCulloch, and became a major influence on Harriet Martineau. The two became friends in 1833, and Marcet encouraged Martineau's work. An earlier reader of Marcet was Maria Edgeworth, who read *Conversations on Chemistry* when she was 9, much to Marcet's surprise when the two became friends in London in 1813. Edgeworth's first impressions are recorded in a letter to her sister: 'Mrs Marcet herself is plain, and has not an agreeable voice or fashionable appearance, but she is sensible in conversation and unaffected' (18 May 1813).[1] Admiration grew on further acquaintance: 'Mrs Marcet has quite won the hearts and heads of all this family', she reports on another visit in 1822. 'I never knew any woman except Mrs E[dgeworth: her stepmother] who had so much *accurate* information and who can give it out in narration so clearly, so much for the pleasure and benefit of others without the least ostentation or mock humility. What she knows she knows without fear or hesitation and stops and tells you she knows no more whenever she is not certain' (7 and 5 January 1822).[2] The same qualities shine in Marcet's published works.

Jane Marcet's educational output was large, and because of her unusual and wholly undeserved obscurity it is worth making its range clear. The format of her most famous works lent itself to adaptation in *Conversations on Vegetable Physiology* (1829), *Willy's Holidays, or Conversations on Different Kinds of Government* (1836), *Conversations for Children on Land and Water* (1838), *Conversations on the History of England for Children* (1842), *Conversations on Language for Children* (1844), and *Rich and Poor: Dialogues on a Few of the First Principles of Political Economy* (1851). Other works for children included *Stories for Young Children* (1831), *Stories for Very Young Children* (1832), *Mary's Grammar* (1835), the *Game of Grammar* (1842), *Lessons on Animals, Vegetables and Minerals* (1844), *Mother's First Book: Reading Made Easy* (1845), *Willy's Travels on the Railroad* (1847), and *Mrs M.'s Story-book* (1858). Later contributions to political economy were *John Hopkins's Notions of Political Economy* (1833), designed (unlike the earlier *Conversations*) specifically to further 'the improvement of the labouring classes' (Advertisement) and *Rich and Poor* (1851).

Conversations on Chemistry is in several different respects a work of great inventiveness and panache. Marcet's Preface is modest, deflecting anticipated criticism by praising the public institutions whose lecture series have opened up scientific knowledge to women, and hoping that she will be better able to inspire others by committing her new impressions of

---

[1] Maria Edgeworth, *Letters from England 1813–1844*, ed. Christina Colvin (Oxford: Clarendon Press, 1971), 64.

[2] Ibid. 312, 308.

nature to paper while they are fresh and strong. But her understanding of her subject allows her to structure the work with understated rigour; while the conversations themselves are anything but flat, for her two girls, Caroline and Emily, have distinctive personalities and respond with wit and intelligence to the information imparted by their instructor, Mrs B. Furthermore, Marcet is interested not just in the packaging of information but also in stimulating a wider intellectual curiosity. In the opening pages of the work, Caroline and Emily question the usefulness of chemistry for women while Mrs B. reflects on the development of the discipline itself. As can be seen later in the work, the principles which the girls learn here are applied to broader social issues, such as the resources of the natural world and the effect of industrial manufacture on the environment. The acquisition of scientific understanding is part of a much wider moral and social education, and often it is Caroline (and, more rarely, Emily) who initiates the most interesting discussions.

The next extracts are from the lengthy Conversation X of *Conversations on Political Economy*, entitled 'On the Condition of the Poor'. In the Preface to this work, Marcet muses that political economy is rarely taught to the young; she has 'attempted to bring within the reach of young persons a science which no English writer has yet presented in an easy and familiar form' (p. v). The conversation here between Caroline and Mrs B. begins with Caroline's musings on the topic of the last conversation, on the dangers of expanding population. She turns the conversation to the social implications of an imbalance between population and economic growth. In the second extract from *Conversations on Political Economy*, Mrs B. enumerates the practical difficulties faced by emigrants and discourages the practice in general, while allowing it to be necessary in cases of religious persecution (that is, in France and Spain). The conversation then turns to matters closer to home. Mrs B. goes on to laud, and Caroline to welcome, Friendly Societies and savings schemes for the working classes. Mrs B. explains that interest-paying bank savings accounts for the poor discourage wasteful expenditure and reduce the 'tax on the rich' imposed by the charitable desire to relieve penury and want. She also extols the virtues of education in promoting industry and independence among the poor. Caroline is impatient for more immediate results, while Mrs B. advises against the impulsive charity Caroline's tender-heartedness impels, instructing her that parish relief increases economic dependency and that the tax on the rich decreases the wages of the poor.

Marcet is an educational writer, but she also creates, in the characters of the two little girls, a discursive context in which knowledge really does have to show itself to be useful. Caroline learns quickly, but she questions pertinently, and as a result Marcet's different *Conversations* are far more intellectually engaged than many of the question-and-answer models from which they developed. They are also an antidote to any assumption that women's education *had* to be narrow. Marcet never openly declared her opinions about the social role of women, but readers of the extracts below might well feel that she did not have to.

∾

From *Conversations on Chemistry* (1806)

On the General Principles of Chemistry

MRS B.

Having now acquired some elementary notions of NATURAL PHIL-OSOPHY,* I am going to propose to you another branch of science, to which I am particularly anxious that you should devote a share of your attention. This is CHEMISTRY, which is so closely connected with Natural Philosophy, that the study of the one must be incomplete without some knowledge of the other; for it is obvious that we can derive but a very imperfect idea of bodies from the study of the general laws by which they are governed, if we remain totally ignorant of their intimate nature.

CAROLINE

To confess the truth, Mrs B., I am not disposed to form a very favourable idea of chemistry, nor do I expect to derive much enter-tainment from it. I prefer those sciences that exhibit nature on a grand scale, to those which are confined to the minutiæ of petty details. Can the studies which we have lately pursued, the general properties of matter, or the revolutions of the heavenly bodies, be compared to the mixing up of a few insignificant drugs?

MRS B.

I rather imagine that your want of taste for chemistry proceeds from the very limited idea you entertain of its object. You confine the chemist's laboratory to the narrow precincts of the apothecary's shop, whilst it is subservient to an immense variety of other useful purposes. Besides, my dear, chemistry is by no means confined to works of art. Nature also has her laboratory, which is the universe, and there she is incessantly employed in chemical operations. You are surprised, Caroline; but I assure you that the most wonderful and the most interesting phenomena of nature are almost all of them produced by chemical powers. Without entering therefore into the minute details of practical chemistry, a woman may obtain such a knowledge of the science, as will not only throw an interest on the common occurrences of life, but will enlarge the sphere of her ideas, and render the contemplation of nature a source of delightful instruction.

CAROLINE

If this is the case, I have certainly been much mistaken in the notion I had formed of chemistry. I own that I thought it was chiefly confined to the knowledge and preparation of medicines.

MRS B.

That is only a branch of chemistry, which is called Pharmacy; and though the study of it is certainly of great importance to the world at large, it properly belongs to professional men, and is therefore the last that I should advise you to study.

EMILY

But did not the chemists formerly employ themselves in search of the philosopher's stone, or the secret of making gold?*

MRS B.

These were a particular set of misguided philosophers, who dignified themselves with the name of Alchemists, to distinguish their pursuits from those of the common chemists, whose studies were confined to the knowledge of medicines.

But, since that period, chemistry has undergone so complete a revolution, that, from an obscure and mysterious art, it is now become a regular and beautiful science, to which art is entirely subservient.* It is true, however, that we are indebted to the alchemists for many very useful discoveries, which sprung from their fruitless attempts to make gold, and which undoubtedly have proved of infinitely greater advantage to mankind than all their chimerical pursuits.

The modern chemists, far from directing their ambition to the imitation of one of the least useful productions of inanimate nature, aim at copying almost all her operations, and sometimes even form combinations, the model of which is not to be found in her own productions. They have little reason to regret their inability to make gold (which is often but a false representation of riches), whilst by their innumerable inventions and discoveries, they have so greatly stimulated industry and facilitated labour, as prodigiously to increase the luxuries as well as the necessaries of life.

EMILY

But I do not understand by what means chemistry can facilitate labour; is not that rather the province of the mechanic?

MRS B.

There are many ways by which labour may be rendered more easy, independently of mechanics; but even the machine the most wonderful in its effects, the steam engine, cannot be understood without the assistance of chemistry.* In agriculture, a chemical knowledge of the nature of soils, and of vegetation, is highly useful; and in those arts which relate to the comforts and conveniences of life, it would be endless to enumerate the advantages which result from the study of this science.

CAROLINE

But, pray, tell us more precisely in what manner the discoveries of chemists have proved so beneficial to society?

MRS B.

That would be an unfair anticipation; for you would not comprehend the nature of such discoveries and useful applications, so well as you will do hereafter. Without a due regard to method, we cannot expect to make any progress in chemistry. I wish to direct your observation chiefly to the chemical operations of Nature; but those of Art are certainly of too high importance to pass unnoticed. We shall therefore allow them also some share of our attention.

EMILY

Well, then, let us now set to work regularly. I am very anxious to begin.

MRS B.

The object of chemistry is to obtain a knowledge of the intimate nature of bodies, and of their mutual action on each other. You find therefore, Caroline, that this is no narrow or confined science, which comprehends every thing material within our sphere.

CAROLINE

On the contrary, it must be inexhaustible; and I am at a loss to conceive how any proficiency can be made in a science whose objects are so numerous.

MRS B.

If every individual substance was formed of different materials, the study of chemistry would indeed be endless: but you must observe that the various bodies in nature are composed of certain elementary principles, which are not very numerous.

CAROLINE

Yes; I know that all bodies are composed of fire, air, earth, and water; I learnt that many years ago.

MRS B.

But you must now endeavour to forget it. I have already informed you what a great change chemistry has undergone since it has become a regular science. Within these thirty years especially, it has experienced an entire revolution, and it is now proved that neither fire, air, earth, nor water, can be called elementary bodies.* For an elementary body is one that cannot be decomposed; that is to say, separated into other substances; and fire, air, earth, and water, are all of them susceptible of decomposition.

EMILY

I thought that decomposing a body was dividing it into its minutest parts. And if so, I do not understand why an elementary substance is not capable of being decomposed, as well as any other.

MRS B.

You have misconceived the idea of *decomposition*; it is very different from mere *division*: the latter simply reduces a body into parts, but the former separates it into the various ingredients, or materials, of which it is composed. If we were to take a loaf of bread, and separate the several ingredients of which it is made, the flour, the yeast, the salt, and the water, it would be very different from cutting the loaf into pieces, or crumbling it to atoms.

EMILY

I understand you now very well. To decompose a body is to separate from each other the various elementary substances of which it consists.

CAROLINE

But flour, water, and the other materials of bread, according to your definition, are not elementary substances?

MRS B.

No, my dear; I mentioned bread rather as a familiar comparison, to illustrate the idea, than as an example.

The elementary substances of which a body is composed, are called the *constituent* parts of that body; in decomposing it, therefore, we separate its constituent parts. If, on the contrary, we divide a body by chopping it to pieces, or even by grinding or pounding it to the finest powder, each of these small particles will still consist of a portion of the several constituent parts of the whole body: these we call the *integrant* parts; do you understand the difference?

EMILY

Yes, I think, perfectly. We *decompose* a body into its *constituent* parts; and *divide* it into its *integrant* parts.

MRS B.

Exactly so. If therefore a body consist of only one kind of substance, though we may divide it into its integrant parts, it is not possible to decompose it. Such bodies are therefore called *simple* or *elementary*, as they are the elements of which all other bodies are composed. *Compound bodies* are such as consist of more than one of these elementary principles.

From *Conversations on Political Economy* (1816)

On the Condition of the Poor

CAROLINE

In our last conversation, Mrs B., you pointed out the evils arising from an excess of population; they have left a very melancholy impression on my mind.* I have been reflecting ever since whether there might be any means of averting them, and of raising subsistence to the level of population, rather than suffering population to sink to the level of subsistence. Though we have not the same resource in land as America; yet we have large tracts of waste land, which by being brought into cultivation would produce an additional stock of subsistence.

MRS B.

You forget that industry is limited by the extent of capital, and that no more labourers can be employed than we have the means of maintaining; they work for their daily bread, and without obtaining it, they neither could nor would work. All the labourers which the capital of the country can maintain being disposed of, the only question is, whether it be better to employ them on land already in a state of cultivation, or in breaking up and bringing into culture new lands; and this point may safely be trusted to the decision of the landed proprietors, as it is no less their interest than that of the labouring classes that the greatest possible quantity of produce should be raised. To a certain extent it has been found more advantageous to lay out capital in improving the culture of old land, rather than to employ it in bringing new land into tillage; because the soil of the waste land is extremely poor and ungrateful, and requires a great deal to be laid out on it before it brings in a return. But there is often capital sufficient for both these purposes, and of late years we have seen not only prodigious improvements in the processes of agriculture throughout the country, but a great number of commons inclosed and cultivated.*

CAROLINE

I fear you will think me inconsistent, but I cannot help regretting the inclosure of commons; they are the only resource of the cottagers for the maintenance of a few lean cattle. Let me once more quote my favourite Goldsmith:

> Where then, ah where shall poverty reside,
> To 'scape the pressure of contiguous pride?
> If to some common's fenceless limits stray'd,
> He drives his flock to pick the scanty blade,
> Those fenceless fields the sons of wealth deride,
> And e'en the bare worn common is deny'd.*

MRS B.

You should recollect that we do not admit poets to be very good authority in political economy. If, instead of feeding a few lean cattle, a common can, by being inclosed, fatten a much greater number of fine cattle, you must allow that the quantity of subsistence will be increased, and the poor though in a less direct manner, will fare the better for it. Labourers are required to inclose and cultivate those commons, the neighbouring cottagers are employed for that purpose, and this additional demand for labour turns to their immediate advantage. They not only receive an indemnity for their loss of right of common, but they find purchasers for the cattle they can no longer maintain, in the proprietors of the new inclosures.

When Finchley Common was inclosed, it was divided amongst the inhabitants of that parish;* and the cottagers and little shop-keepers sold the small slips of land which fell to their share to men of greater property, who thus became possessed of a sufficient quantity to make it answer to them to inclose and cultivate it; and the poorer classes were amply remunerated for their loss of commonage by the sale of their respective lots.

CAROLINE

But if we have it not in our power to provide for a redundant population by the cultivation of our waste lands, what objection is there to sending those who cannot find employment at home, to seek a maintenance in countries where it is more easily obtained, where there is a greater demand for labour? Or why should they not found new colonies in the yet unsettled parts of America?

MRS B.

Emigration is undoubtedly a resource for an overstocked population; but one that is adopted in general with great reluctance by individuals; and is commonly discouraged by governments, from an apprehension of its diminishing the strength of the country.

CAROLINE

It might be wrong to encourage emigration to a very great extent; I meant only to provide abroad for those whom we cannot maintain at home.

MRS B.

Under an equitable government there is little danger of emigration ever exceeding that point. The attachment to our native land is naturally so strong, and there are so many ties of kindred and association to break through before we can quit it, that no slight motive will induce a man to expatriate himself. . . .

But to return to the population of England; the more we find ourselves unable to provide for an overgrown population, the more desirous we should be to avail ourselves of those means which tend to prevent the evil;—such, for instance, as a general diffusion of knowledge, which would excite greater attention in the lower classes to their future interests.

CAROLINE

Surely you would not teach political economy to the labouring classes, Mrs B.?

MRS B.

No; but I would endeavour to give the rising generation such an education as would render them not only moral and religious, but industrious, frugal, and provident. In proportion as the mind is informed, we are able to calculate the consequences of our actions: it is the infant and the savage who live only for the present moment; those whom instruction has taught to think, reflect upon the past and look forward to the future. Education gives rise to prudence, not only by enlarging our understandings, but by softening our feelings, by humanizing the heart, and promoting amiable affections. The rude and inconsiderate peasant marries without either foreseeing or caring for the miseries he may entail on his wife and children; but he who has been taught to value the comforts and decencies of life, will not heedlessly involve himself and all that is dear to him in poverty, and its long train of miseries.

CAROLINE

I am very happy to hear that you think instruction may produce this desirable end, since the zeal for the education of the poor that has been displayed of late years gives every prospect of success; and in a few years more, it may perhaps be impossible to meet with a child who cannot read and write.

MRS B.

The highest advantages, both religious, moral, and political, may be expected to result from this general ardour for the instruction of the poor. No great or decided improvement can be effected in the manners of the people but by the education of the rising generation. It is difficult, if not impossible, to change the habits of men whose characters are formed, and settled; the prejudices of ignorance that have grown up with us, will not yield to new impressions; whilst youth and innocence may be moulded into any form you chuse to give them. . . .

CAROLINE

But, alas! how many years will elapse before these happy results can take place. I am impatient that benefits should be immediately and universally diffused; their progress is in general so slow and partial, that there is but a small chance of our living to see their effects.

MRS B.

There is some gratification in looking forward to an improved state of society, even if we should not live to witness it.

CAROLINE

Since it is so little in our power to accelerate its progress, we must endeavour to be contended: but I confess that I cannot help regretting the want of sovereign power to forward measures so conducive to the happiness of mankind.

MARY LAMB
(1764–1847)

Mary Lamb was born and brought up in the Inner Temple in London; her father John Lamb was the personal servant of the barrister and MP Samuel Salt, and her mother Elizabeth Field also came from a family of domestic servants. Samuel Salt secured places at the renowned school of Christ's Hospital for Mary's two brothers, and all the children had access to his library. Mary Lamb was to be especially close to her brother Charles, her junior by eleven years: she is the 'Cousin Bridget' of his *Essays of Elia*. The family's situation declined suddenly on the death of Salt in 1792, when, no longer able to live in the Temple, and with both parents frail physically and mentally, they became partially dependent upon Mary's earnings while Charles went through his unpaid apprenticeship as a trading-house clerk.

In 1796 the Lamb family was living in cramped rooms, Mary Lamb contributing to their earnings by working as a mantua-maker, to which she had been apprenticed in her teens. It was a hard and confined employment. On 22 September she suffered a fit of insanity in which she stabbed her mother to death and wounded her father. She would have been confined for life in a lunatic asylum but for the intervention of her brother Charles, who arranged for private care in a Quaker asylum in Hoxton and undertook to look after her for the rest of her life. As Jane Aaron points out, incarceration would have been mandatory four years later.[1] The causes of her imbalance are unclear, but there are signs in family correspondence that Mary thought that her mother treated her coldly, and resented the attention paid to the younger children (she was 31 at the time of the attack, and had always lived at home). Constantly liable to relapses, she spent periods of time in mental institutions, especially later in her life and after the death of her brother in 1834. She and Charles were continually in financial difficulty, partly (as he berated himself) as a result of his expenditure on alcohol. In 1823 they adopted the 15-year-old Emma Isola, daughter of a language-master at Cambridge, and she inherited their property after Mary Lamb's death. Mary Lamb's abilities and sympathetic temperament were held in high regard by William and Dorothy Wordsworth, Coleridge, Southey, Crabb Robinson, De Quincey, and Hazlitt, all of them friends of her brother.

Charles Lamb encouraged her literary habits, and when they were

---

[1] In Anne K. Mellor (ed.), *Romanticism and Feminism* (Bloomington, Ind.: Indiana University Press, 1988), 177.

commissioned by Mary Jane Godwin, Godwin's second wife, to write poetry and prose for the Godwins' Library for Children, the Lambs entered into the most successful brother-and-sister writing partnership of the early nineteenth century. Charles Lamb held strong views about the ruination of children's literature by Anna Laetitia Barbauld and Sarah Trimmer, so their entrance into this field was a challenge and an opportunity to put some of their ideas into practice. Mary Lamb's contributions to their joint volumes, however, were, by her own wish, unascribed. Of the twenty *Tales from Shakespeare* (1807), fourteen were by Mary: in a telling gender-division of labour, she took the comedies and romances, Charles took the tragedies. She wrote two-thirds of *Poetry for Children* (1809), and, of the ten tales making up *Mrs Leicester's School: or The History of Several Young Ladies Related by Themselves* (also 1809), Mary wrote seven. The premiss of this last volume of tales, which is clearly indebted to the structure of Sarah Fielding's *The Governess, or Little Female Academy* (1749), is that a teacher attempts to settle in a group of new pupils by proposing that they all tell their life-stories; the teacher is the amanuensis of these 'biographical conversations'. The girls are presented as historians, and their teacher hopes to be their 'faithful historiographer, as well as true friend'.[2] In a very different literary mode, Mary Lamb's own experience of seamstress-work formed the basis of the essay 'On Needlework', which appeared in the newly established *The British Lady's Magazine and Monthly Miscellany* in April 1815 under the pseudonym 'Sempronia'.

Three pieces of Mary Lamb's writing are included here. One of them, the story of Margaret Green from *Mrs Leicester's School*, is listed as Mary's in Lucas's standard edition of the Lambs' works, but it has sometimes been claimed for her brother. According to Henry Crabb Robinson, Charles Lamb was told that one Calvinist mother would not allow her children to read *Mrs Leicester's School* until she had torn out 'The Young Mahometan' and 'The Witch Aunt'. Delighted, Charles Lamb claimed them both.[3] It has been claimed that the tale must be Charles Lamb's because of its 'quirkiness' (Mary Lamb being noted for her 'naturalness'),[4] but these are distinctly gendered critical terms. In any event, the Calvinist mother was quite right to be disturbed by the story of Margaret Green. In spite of its assimilating, reassuringly Christian ending, this is a dangerous tale. Lamb's brilliantly economical evocation of childish loneliness and intellectual and emotional isolation poses many more questions than it

---

[2] *The Works of Charles and Mary Lamb*, ed. Thomas Hutchinson (London: Oxford University Press, Humphrey Milford, 1924), 340.

[3] *Henry Crabb Robinson on Books and Their Writers*, ed. Edith J. Morley (London: Dent, 1938), 833.

[4] Jonathan Wordsworth (ed.), *Mrs Leicester's School* (Poole: Woodstock, 1995), n.p.

resolves—questions about the imaginative desires of children, their need to identify and to belong, gender roles (it is very nearly an all-female narrative) and the part which organized religion plays in shaping and satisfying the individual. Margaret Green is as convincingly realized a child, in her short tale, as the young Jane Eyre; and her 'cure' is to be part of a joyous, instinctive, communicative, family life. The proclaimed moral of the tale is the danger of religious error; but whatever the 'serious' instruction of the physician's wife, and its satisfactory certainties for the young Margaret, the real message of the tale is that children want to belong, and that they will attach themselves to whatever creed meets their emotional and imaginative needs. Margaret Green's mother and her employer measure out their lives by sewing threads; and Margaret turns out to have a distinctly practical notion of what might be involved in walking across a bridge of silken threads. (The situation of the mother and daughter, the wonderful library, the pre-eminence of needlework, and the absence of men, all read as an imaginative translation of elements of the Lambs' childhood in the Inner Temple.) Superficially this is a piece of Christian propaganda for children, but in fact Mary Lamb makes the neediness of her narrator a way of exploring, under the surface, the constrictions on female emotional and intellectual life, the disappointing sterility encountered in the shut-up male library, the need for the little girl to identify herself with the infant Ishmael (cast out, with his mother, to starve, in the Old Testament story, but loved and protected by her, and prominent as a revered ancestor in Islamic tradition) in an attempt to overcome her own loveless state.

'Margaret Green: The Young Mahometan' is set here alongside the tale which precedes it in *Mrs Leicester's School*, 'Elinor Forester: The Father's Wedding Day'. Walter Savage Landor wrote to Henry Crabb Robinson in 1831 in raptures about *Mrs Leicester's School*, which Robinson had recommended to him: 'Never have I read anything in prose so many times over, within so short a space of time, as "The Father's Wedding-day." . . . Show me the man or woman, modern or ancient, who could have written this one sentence: "When I was dressed in my new frock, I wished poor mamma was alive, to see how fine I was on papa's wedding-day; and I ran to my favourite station at her bedroom door." How natural, in a little girl, is this incongruity—this impossibility! Richardson would have given his "Clarissa," and Rousseau his "Heloïse," to have imagined it.'[5] The emotional situation of Elinor Forester is strikingly similar to that of Margaret Green. Both little girls crave maternal affection; both find a refuge in

[5] *Diary, Reminiscences, and Correspondence of Henry Crabb Robinson, Barrister-at-Law, F.S.A.*, selected and ed. Thomas Sadler, 3rd edn., 2 vols. (1872; New York: AMS Press, 1967), ii. 110.

which to live out their inner thoughts; both are rescued by a sensitive but practical replacement-mother. In both stories, there is a genuine respect and affection for the sensitive rescuer, but a lingering awareness that, for all the needy child's complicity, a secret alternative world has been lost. In fact Elinor's tale ends more bleakly than Margaret's, because the little girl, her subversions neutralized, has been sent away from home to make room for her stepmother's new baby.

Finally, Lamb's essay 'On Needlework' examines the plight of another solitary and undervalued woman who may be rescued by more fortunate and more domestically secure women, if they choose. It may be read in conjunction with the passages from Priscilla Wakefield's *Reflections on the Present Condition of the Female Sex* which address the need for women in secure circumstances to support the labour of other women by employing them. Adam Smith's account of the division of labour makes Lamb, like Wakefield, aware of the advantages of specialization. One contemporary observer captured Mary Lamb's mood during work on this essay, which was, for her, unusual in speaking openly in a public forum of her personal experience of employment, and in advocating women's direct economic action. On 11 December 1814 Crabb Robinson called on her for a chat at 10 in the evening: 'She was not unwell, but she had undergone great fatigue from writing an article about needlework for the new *Ladies' British Magazine*. She spoke of writing as a most painful occupation, which only necessity could make her attempt. She has been learning Latin merely to assist her in acquiring a correct style. Yet, while she speaks of inability to write, what grace and talent has she not manifested in "Mrs Leicester's School," &c.'.[6] The composition of 'On Needlework' seemed to cause her unusual stress, and she suffered a severe relapse into insanity in mid-December, taking over two months to recover. Much later, Crabb Robinson went to see her in the weeks following Charles's death in 1834, and writes movingly and perceptively about her state of mind, and the way in which 'her mind seemed turned to subjects connected with insanity, as well as with her brother's death'.[7] She clearly associated Charles with her hold on sanity. He writes of her again in 1839, ill and 'inert' in mind: 'no one would discover what she once was'.[8] He was one of the nine mourners at her funeral in 1847; though 'mourners', he thought, was 'a most unsuitable word, for we all felt that her departure was a relief to herself and her friends'.[9]

~

[6] Ibid. i. 242.   [7] Ibid. ii. 155.   [8] Ibid. ii. 221.   [9] Ibid. ii. 279.

Elinor Forester: The Father's Wedding Day (1809)

When I was very young, I had the misfortune to lose my mother. My father very soon married again. In the morning of the day in which that event took place, my father set me on his knee, and, as he often used to do after the death of my mother, he called me his dear little orphaned Elinor, and then he asked me if I loved miss Saville. I replied 'Yes'. Then he said this dear lady was going to be so kind as to be married to him, and that she was to live with us, and be my mamma. My father told me this with such pleasure in his looks, that I thought it must be a very fine thing indeed to have a new mamma; and on his saying it was time for me to be dressed against his return from church, I ran in great spirits to tell the good news in the nursery. I found my maid and the house-maid looking out of the window to see my father get into his carriage, which was new painted; the servants had new liveries, and fine white ribbands in their hats; and then I perceived my father had left off his mourning. The maids were dressed in new coloured gowns and white ribbands. On the table I saw a new muslin frock, trimmed with fine lace, ready for me to put on. I skipped about the room quite in an ecstasy.

When the carriage drove from the door, the housekeeper came in to bring the maids new white gloves. I repeated to her the words I had just heard, that that dear lady, miss Saville, was going to be married to papa, and that she was to live with us, and be my mamma.

The housekeeper shook her head, and said, 'Poor thing! how soon children forget every thing!'

I could not imagine what she meant by my forgetting every thing, for I instantly recollected poor mamma used to say I had an excellent memory.

The women began to draw on their white gloves, and the seams rending in several places, Anne said, 'This is just the way our gloves served us at my mistress's funeral.' The other checked her, and said 'Hush!' I was then thinking of some instances in which my mamma had praised my memory, and this reference to her funeral fixed her idea in my mind.

From the time of her death no one had ever spoken to me of my mamma, and I had apparently forgotten her; yet I had a habit which perhaps had not been observed, of taking my little stool, which had been my mamma's footstool, and a doll, which my mamma had drest for me, while she was sitting in her elbow-chair, her head supported with pillows. With these in my hands, I used to go to the door of the room in which I had seen her in her last illness; and after trying to open it, and peeping through the keyhole, from whence I could just see a glimpse of the crimson curtains, I used to sit down on the stool before the door, and play with my doll, and sometimes sing to it mamma's pretty song, of 'Balow my babe';* imitating as well as I could, the weak voice in which she used to sing it to me. My mamma had a very sweet voice. I remember now the gentle tone in which she used to say my prattle did not disturb her.

When I was drest in my new frock, I wished poor mamma was alive to see how fine I was on papa's wedding-day, and I ran to my favourite station at her bed-room door. There I sat thinking of my mamma, and trying to remember exactly how she used to look; because I foolishly imagined that miss Saville was to be changed into something like my own mother, whose pale and delicate appearance in her last illness was all that I retained of her remembrance.

When my father returned home with his bride, he walked up stairs to look for me, and my new mamma followed him. They found me at my mother's door, earnestly looking through the keyhole; I was thinking so intently on my mother, that when my father said, 'Here is your new mamma, my Elinor,' I turned round, and began to cry, for no other reason than because she had a very high colour, and I remembered my mamma was very pale; she had bright black eyes, my mother's were mild blue eyes; and that instead of the wrapping gown and close cap in which I remembered my mamma, she was drest in all her bridal decorations.

I said, 'Miss Saville shall not be my mamma,' and I cried till I was sent away in disgrace.

Every time I saw her for several days, the same notion came into my head, that she was not a bit more like mamma than when she was miss Saville. My father was very angry when he saw how shy I continued to look at her; but she always said, 'Never mind. Elinor and I shall soon be better friends.'

One day, when I was very naughty indeed, for I would not speak one word to either of them, my papa took his hat, and walked out quite in a passion. When he was gone, I looked up at my new mamma, expecting to see her very angry too; but she was smiling and looking very good-naturedly upon me; and she said, 'Now we are alone together, my pretty little daughter, let us forget papa is angry with us; and tell me why you were peeping through that door the day your papa brought me home, and you cried so at the sight of me.' 'Because mamma used to be there,' I replied. When she heard me say this, she fell a-crying very sadly indeed; and I was so very sorry to hear her cry so, that I forgot I did not love her, and I went up to her, and said, 'Don't cry, I won't be naughty any more, I won't peep through the door any more.'

Then she said I had a little kind heart, and I should not have any occasion, for she would take me into the room herself; and she rung the bell, and ordered the key of that room to be brought to her; and the housekeeper brought it, and tried to persuade her not to go. But she said, 'I must have my own way in this;' and she carried me in her arms into my mother's room.

O I was so pleased to be taken into mamma's room! I pointed out to her all the things that I remembered to have belonged to mamma, and she encouraged me to tell her all the little incidents which had dwelt on my memory concerning her. She told me, that she went to school with mamma when she was a little girl, and that I should come into this room with her every day when papa was gone out, and she would tell me stories of mamma when she was a little girl no bigger than me.

When my father came home, we were walking in a garden at the back of our house, and I was shewing her mamma's geraniums, and telling her what pretty flowers they had been when mamma was alive.

My father was astonished; and he said 'Is this the sullen Elinor? what has worked this miracle?' 'Ask no questions', she replied, 'or you will disturb our new-born friendship. Elinor has promised to love me, and she says too that she will call me mamma.' 'Yes, I will, mamma, mamma, mamma,' I replied, and hung about her with the greatest fondness.

After this she used to pass great part of the mornings with me in my mother's room, which was now made the repository of all my playthings, and also my school-room. Here my new mamma taught me to read. I was a sad little dunce, and scarcely knew my letters; my own mamma had often said, when she got better she would hear me read every day, but as she never got better it was not her fault. I now began to learn very fast, for when I said my lesson well, I was always rewarded with some pretty story of my mother's childhood; and these stories generally contained some little hints that were instructive to me, and which I greatly stood in want of; for, between improper indulgence and neglect, I had many faulty ways.

In this kind manner my mother-in-law has instructed and improved me, and I love her because she was my mother's friend when they were young. She has been my only instructress, for I never went to school till I came here. She would have continued to teach me, but she has not time, for she has a little baby of her own now, and that is the reason I came to school.

Margaret Green: The Young Mahometan (1809)

My father has been dead near three years. Soon after his death, my mother being left in reduced circumstances, she was induced to accept the offer of Mrs Beresford, an elderly lady of large fortune, to live in her house as her companion, and the superintendent of her family. This lady was my godmother, and as I was my mother's only child, she very kindly permitted her to have me with her.

Mrs Beresford lived in a large old family mansion; she kept no company, and never moved except from the breakfast-parlour to the eating-room, and from thence to the drawing-room to tea.

Every morning when she first saw me, she used to nod her head very kindly, and say, 'How do you do, little Margaret?' But I do not recollect she ever spoke to me during the remainder of the day; except indeed after I had read the psalms and the chapters, which was my daily task; then she used constantly to observe, that I improved in my reading, and frequently added, 'I never heard a child read so distinctly.'

She had been remarkably fond of needlework, and her conversation with my mother was generally the history of some pieces of work she had formerly done; the dates when they were begun, and when finished; what had retarded their progress, and what had hastened their completion. If occasionally any other events were spoken of, she had no other chronology to reckon by, than in the recollection of what carpet, what sofa-cover, what set of chairs, were in the frame at that time.

I believe my mother is not particularly fond of needlework; for in my father's life-time I never saw her amuse herself in this way; yet, to oblige her kind patroness, she undertook to finish a large carpet, which the old lady had just begun when her eye-sight failed her. All day long my mother used to sit at the frame, talking of the shades of the worsted,* and the beauty of the colours;—Mrs Beresford seated in a chair near her, and, though her eyes were so dim she could hardly distinguish one colour from another, watching through her spectacles the progress of the work.

When my daily portion of reading was over, I had a task of needlework, which generally lasted half an hour. I was not allowed to pass more time in reading or work, because my eyes were very weak, for which reason I was always set to read in the large-print Family Bible. I was very fond of reading; and when I could unobserved steal a few minutes as they were intent on their work, I used to delight to read in the historical part of the Bible; but this, because of my eyes, was a forbidden pleasure; and the Bible never being removed out of the room, it was only for a short time together that I dared softly to lift up the leaves and peep into it.

As I was permitted to walk in the garden or wander about the house whenever I pleased, I used to leave the parlour for hours together, and make out my own solitary amusement as well as I could. My first visit was always to a very large hall, which, from being paved with marble, was called the marble hall. In this hall, while Mrs Beresford's husband was living, the tenants used to be feasted at Christmas.

The heads of the twelve Cæsars were hung round the hall. Every day I mounted on the chairs to look at them, and to read the inscriptions underneath, till I became perfectly familiar with their names and features.

Hogarth's prints were below the Cæsars:* I was very fond of looking at them, and endeavouring to make out their meaning.

An old broken battledore, and some shuttlecocks with most of the feathers missing, were on a marble slab in one corner of the hall, which constantly reminded me that there had once been younger inhabitants here than the old lady and her gray-headed servants. In another corner stood a marble figure of a satyr: every day I laid my hand on his shoulder to feel how cold he was.

This hall opened into a room full of family portraits. They were all in the dresses of former times: some were old men and women, and some were children. I used to long to have a fairy's power to call the children down from their frames to play with me. One little girl in particular, who hung by the side of a glass door which opened into the garden, I often invited to walk there with me, but she still kept her station—one arm round a little lamb's neck, and in her hand a large bunch of roses.

From this room I usually proceeded to the garden.

When I was weary of the garden I wandered over the rest of the house. The best suite of rooms I never saw by any other light than what glimmered through the tops of the window-shutters, which however served to shew the carved chimney-pieces, and the curious old ornaments about the rooms; but the worked furniture and carpets, of which I heard such constant praises, I could have but an imperfect sight of, peeping under the covers which were kept over them, by the dim light; for I constantly lifted up a corner of the envious cloth, that hid these highly-praised rarities from my view.

The bed-rooms were also regularly explored by me, as well to admire the antique furniture, as for the sake of contemplating the tapestry hangings, which were full of Bible history. The subject of the one which chiefly attracted my attention, was Hagar and her son Ishmael.* Every day I admired the beauty of the youth, and pitied the forlorn state of him and his mother in the wilderness. At the end of the gallery into which these tapestry rooms opened, was one door, which having often in vain attempted to open, I concluded to be locked; and finding myself shut out, I was very desirous of seeing what it contained; and though still foiled in the attempt, I every day endeavoured to turn the lock, which whether by constantly trying I loosened, being probably a very old one, or that the door was not locked but fastened tight by time, I know not,—to my great joy, as I was one day trying the lock as usual, it gave way, and I found myself in this so long desired room.

It proved to be a very large library. This was indeed a precious discovery. I looked round on the books with the greatest delight. I thought I would read them every one. I now forsook all my favourite haunts, and passed all my time here. I took down first one book, then another.

If you never spent whole mornings alone in a large library, you cannot conceive the pleasure of taking down books in the constant hope of finding an entertaining book among them; yet, after many days, meeting with nothing but disappointment, it becomes less pleasant. All the books within my reach were folios of the gravest cast. I could understand very little that I read in them, and the old dark print and the length of the lines made my eyes ache.

When I had almost resolved to give up the search as fruitless, I perceived a volume lying in an obscure corner of the room. I opened it. It was a charming print; the letters were almost as large as the type of the Family Bible. In the first page I looked into I saw the name of my favourite Ishmael, whose face I knew so well from the tapestry, and whose history I had often read in the Bible.

I sate myself down to read this book with the greatest eagerness. The title of it was 'Mahometism Explained'.* It was a very improper book, for it contained a false history of Abraham and his descendants.*

I shall be quite ashamed to tell you the strange effect it had on me. I know it was very wrong to read any book without permission to do so. If my time were to come over again, I would go and tell my mamma that there was a library in the house, and ask her to permit me to read a little while every day in some book that she might think proper to select for me. But unfortunately I did not then recollect that I ought to do this: the reason of my strange forgetfulness might be that my mother, following the example of her patroness, had almost wholly discontinued talking to me. I scarcely ever heard a word addressed to me from morning to night. If it were not for the old servants saying 'Good morning to you, miss Margaret,' as they passed me in the long passages, I should have been the greatest part of the day in as perfect a solitude as Robinson Crusoe. It must have been because I was never spoken to at all, that I forgot what was right and what was wrong, for I do not believe that I ever remembered I was doing wrong all the time I was reading in the library. A great many of the leaves in 'Mahometism Explained' were torn out, but enough remained to make me imagine that Ishmael was the true son of Abraham: I read here that the true descendants of Abraham were known by a light which streamed from the middle of their foreheads.

It said, that Ishmael's father and mother first saw this light streaming from his forehead, as he was lying asleep in the cradle.* I was very sorry so many of the leaves were torn out, for it was as entertaining as a fairy tale. I used to read the history of Ishmael, and then go and look at him in the tapestry, and then read his history again. When I had almost learned the history of Ishmael by heart, I read the rest of the book, and then I came to the history of Mahomet, who was there said to be the last descendant of Abraham.

If Ishmael had engaged so much of my thoughts, how much more so must Mahomet?* His history was full of nothing but wonders from the beginning to the end. The book said, that those who believed all the wonderful stories which were related of Mahomet were called Mahometans, and true believers:—I concluded that I must be a Mahometan, for I believed every word I read.

At length I met with something which I also believed, though I trembled as I read it:—this was, that after we are dead, we are to pass over a narrow bridge, which crosses a bottomless gulf. The bridge was described to be no wider than a silken thread; and it said, that all who were not Mahometans would slip on one side of this bridge, and drop into the tremendous gulf that had no bottom.* I considered myself as a Mahometan, yet I was perfectly giddy whenever I thought of passing over this bridge.

One day, seeing the old lady totter across the room, a sudden terror seized me, for I thought, how would she ever be able to get over the bridge. Then too it was, that I first recollected that my mother would also be in imminent danger; for I imagined she had never heard the name of Mahomet, because I foolishly conjectured this book had been locked up for ages in the library, and was utterly unknown to the rest of the world.

All my desire was now to tell them the discovery I had made; for I thought, when they knew of the existence of 'Mahometism Explained', they would read it, and become Mahometans, to ensure themselves a safe passage over the silken bridge. But it wanted more courage than I possessed, to break the matter to my intended converts; I must acknowledge that I had been reading without leave; and the habit of never speaking, or being spoken to, considerably increased the difficulty.

My anxiety on this subject threw me into a fever. I was so ill, that my mother thought it necessary to sleep in the same room with me.

In the middle of the night I could not resist the strong desire I felt to tell her what preyed so much on my mind.

I awoke her out of a sound sleep, and begged she would be so kind as to be a Mahometan. She was very much alarmed, for she thought I was delirious, which I believe I was; for I tried to explain the reason of my request, but it was in such an incoherent manner that she could not at all comprehend what I was talking about.

The next day a physician was sent for, and he discovered, by several questions that he put to me, that I had read myself into a fever. He gave me medicines, and ordered me to be kept very quiet, and said, he hoped in a few days I should be very well; but as it was a new case to him, he never having attended a little Mahometan before, if any lowness continued after he had removed the fever, he would, with my mother's permission, take me home with him to study this extraordinary case at his leisure; and added, that he could then hold a consultation with his wife, who was often very useful to him in prescribing remedies for the maladies of his younger patients.

In a few days he fetched me away. His wife was in the carriage with him. Having heard what he said about her prescriptions, I expected, between the doctor and his lady, to undergo a severe course of medicine, especially as I heard him very formally ask her advice what was good for a Mahometan fever, the moment after he had handed me into the carriage. She studied a little while, and then she said, A ride to Harlow fair would not be amiss.* He said he was entirely of her opinion, because it suited him to go there to buy a horse.

During the ride they entered into conversation with me, and in answer to their questions, I was relating to them the solitary manner in which I had passed my time; how I found out the library, and what I had read in the fatal book which had so heated my imagination,— when we arrived at the fair; and Ishmael, Mahomet, and the narrow bridge, vanished out of my head in an instant.

O what a cheerful sight it was to me, to see so many happy faces assembled together, walking up and down between the rows of booths that were full of showy things; ribbands, laces, toys, cakes, and sweetmeats! While the doctor was gone to buy his horse, his kind lady let me stand as long as I pleased at the booths, and gave me many things which she saw I particularly admired. My needle-case, my pin-cushion, indeed my work-basket, and all its contents, are presents which she purchased for me at this fair. After we returned home, she played with me all the evening at a geographical game, which she also bought for me at this cheerful fair.

The next day she invited some young ladies of my own age, to spend the day with me. She had a swing put up in the garden for us, and a room cleared of the furniture that we might play at blindman's-buff. One of the liveliest of the girls, who had taken on herself the direction of our sports, she kept to be my companion all the time I staid with her, and every day contrived some new amusement for us.

Yet this good lady did not suffer all my time to pass in mirth and gaiety. Before I went home, she explained to me very seriously the error into which I had fallen. I found that so far from 'Mahometism Explained' being a book concealed only in this library, it was well known to every person of the least information.

The Turks, she told me, were Mahometans, and that, if the leaves of my favourite book had not been torn out, I should have read that the author of it did not mean to give the fabulous stories here related as true, but only wrote it as giving a history of what the Turks, who are a very ignorant people, believe concerning the impostor Mahomet, who feigned himself to be a descendant of Ishmael. By the good offices of the physician and his lady, I was carried home at the end of a month, perfectly cured of the error into which I had fallen, and very much ashamed of having believed so many absurdities.

On Needlework (1815)

In early life I passed eleven years in the exercise of my needle for a livelihood. Will you allow me to address your readers, among whom might perhaps be found some of the kind patronesses of my former humble labours, on a subject widely connected with female life—the state of needlework in this country.

To lighten the heavy burden which many ladies impose upon themselves is one object I have in view; but, I confess, my strongest motive is to excite attention towards the industrious sisterhood to which I once belonged.

From books I have been informed of the fact, upon which *The*

British Lady's Magazine chiefly founds its pretensions, namely, that women have of late been rapidly advancing in intellectual improvement.* Much may have been gained for that class of females for whom I wish to plead. Needlework and intellectual improvement are naturally in a state of warfare. But I am afraid the root of the evil has not as yet been struck at. Workwomen of every description were never in so much distress for want of employment.

Among the present circle of my acquaintance I am proud to rank many that may truly be called respectable; nor do the female part of them, in their mental attainments, at all disprove the prevailing opinion of that intellectual progression which you have taken as the basis of your work; yet I affirm that I know not a single family where there is not some essential drawback to its comfort which may be traced to needlework done at home, as the phrase is for all needlework performed in a family by some of its own members, and for which no remuneration in money is received or expected.

In money alone, did I say? I would appeal to all the fair votaries of voluntary housewifery whether, in the matter of conscience, any one of them ever thought she had done as much needlework as she ought to have done. Even fancy work, the fairest of the tribe!—how delightful the arrangement of her materials! the fixing upon her happiest pattern, how pleasing an anxiety! how cheerful the commencement of the labour she enjoins! But that lady must be a true lover of the art, and so industrious a pursuer of a predetermined purpose, that it were pity her energy should not have been directed to some wiser end, who can affirm she neither feels weariness during the execution of a fancy piece, nor takes more time than she had calculated for the performance.

Is it too bold an attempt to persuade your readers that it would prove an incalculable addition to general happiness, and the domestic comfort of both sexes, if needlework were never practised but for a remuneration in money? As nearly, however, as this desirable thing can be effected, so much more nearly will women be upon an equality with men as far as respects the mere enjoyment of life. As far as that goes, I believe it is every woman's opinion that the condition of men is far superior to her own.

'They can do what they like,' we say. Do not these words generally mean, they have time to seek out whatever amusements suit their tastes? We dare not tell them we have no time to do this; for, if they should ask in what manner we dispose of our time, we should blush to enter upon a detail of the minutiae which compose the sum of a woman's daily employment. Nay, many a lady who allows not herself one quarter of an hour's positive leisure during her waking hours, considers her own husband as the most industrious of men, if he steadily pursue his occupation till the hour of dinner, and will be perpetually lamenting her own idleness.

Real business and *real leisure* make up the portions of men's time— two sources of happiness which we certainly partake of in a very inferior degree. To the execution of employment, in which the faculties of the body or mind are called into busy action, there must be a consoling importance attached, which feminine duties (that generic term for all our business) cannot aspire to.

In the most meritorious discharges of those duties, the highest praise we can aim at is to be accounted the help-mates of *man*; who, in return for all he does for us, expects, and justly expects, us to do all in our power to soften and sweeten life.

In how many ways is a good woman employed, in thought or action, through the day, in order that her *good man* may be enabled to feel his leisure hours *real substantial holiday*, and perfect respite from the cares of business! Not the least part to be done to accomplish this end is to fit herself to become a conversational companion; that is to say, she has to study and understand the subjects on which he loves to talk. This part of our duty, if strictly performed, will be found by far our hardest part. The disadvantages we labour under from an education differing from a manly one make the hours in which we *sit and do nothing* in men's company too often any thing but a relaxation; although, as to pleasure and instruction, time so passed may be esteemed more or less delightful.

To make a man's home so desirable a place as to preclude his having a wish to pass his leisure hours at any fireside in preference to his own, I should humbly take to be the sum and substance of woman's domestic ambition. I would appeal to our *British ladies*, who are generally allowed to be the most zealous and successful of all women in the pursuit of this object,—I would appeal to them who have been most successful in the performance of this laudable service, in behalf of father, son, husband, or brother, whether an anxious desire to perform this duty well is not attended with enough of *mental* exertion, at least, to incline them to the opinion that women may be more properly ranked among the contributors to, than the partakers of, the undisturbed relaxation of man.

If a family be so well ordered that the master is never called in to its direction, and yet he perceives comfort and economy well attended to, the mistress of that family (especially if children form a part of it) has, I apprehend, as large a share of womanly employment as ought to satisfy her own sense of duty; even though the needle-book and thread-case were quite laid aside, and she cheerfully contributed her part to the slender gains of the corset-maker, the milliner, the dress-maker, the plain-worker, the embroidress, and all the numerous classifications of females supporting themselves by *needlework*, that great staple commodity which is alone appropriated to the self-supporting part of our sex.

Much has been said and written on the subject of men engrossing to themselves every occupation and calling. After many years of observation and reflection, I am obliged to acquiesce in the notion that it cannot well be ordered otherwise.

If at the birth of girls it were possible to foresee in what cases it would be their fortune to pass a single life, we should soon find trades wrested from their present occupiers, and transferred to the exclusive possession of our sex. The whole mechanical business of copying writings in the law department, for instance, might very soon be transferred with advantage to the poorer sort of women, who with very little teaching would soon beat their rivals of the other sex in facility and neatness. The parents of female children, who were known to be destined from their birth to maintain themselves through the whole course of their lives with like certainty as their sons are, would feel it a duty incumbent on themselves to strengthen the minds, and even the bodily constitutions, of their girls, so circumstanced, by an education which, without affronting the preconceived habits of society, might enable them to follow some occupation now considered above the capacity or too robust for the constitution of our sex. Plenty of resources would then lie open for single women to obtain an independent livelihood, when every parent would be upon the alert to encroach upon some employment, now engrossed by men, for such of their daughters as would then be in exactly the same predicament as their sons now are. Who, for instance, would lay by money to set up his sons in trade; give premiums, and in part maintain them through a long apprenticeship; or, which men of moderate incomes frequently do, strain every nerve in order to bring them up to a learned profession; if it were in a very high degree probable that, by the time they were twenty years of age, they would be taken from this trade or profession, and maintained during the remainder of their lives by the *person whom they should marry*. Yet this is precisely the situation in which every parent, whose income does not very much exceed the moderate, is placed with respect to his daughters. Even where boys have gone through a laborious education, superinducing habits of steady attention, accompanied with the entire conviction that the business which they learn is to be the source of their future distinction, may it not be affirmed that the persevering industry required to accomplish this desirable end causes many a hard struggle in the minds of young men, even of the most hopeful disposition? What then must be the disadvantages under which a very young woman is placed who is required to learn a trade, from which she can never expect to reap any profit, but at the expense of losing that place in society, to the possession of which she may reasonably look forward, inasmuch as it is by far the most *common lot*, namely, the condition of a *happy* English wife?

As I desire to offer nothing to the consideration of your readers but what, at least as far as my own observation goes, I consider as truths confirmed by experience, I will only say that, were I to follow the bent of my own speculative opinion, I should be inclined to persuade every female over whom I hoped to have any influence to contribute all the assistance in her power to those of her own sex who may need it, in the employments they at present occupy, rather than to force them into situations now filled wholly by men. With the mere exception of the profits which they have a right to derive from their needle, I would take nothing from the industry of man which he already possesses.

'A penny saved is a penny earned,' is a maxim not true, unless the penny be saved in the same time in which it might have been earned. I, who have known what it is to work for *money earned*, have since had much experience in working for *money saved*; and I consider, from the closest calculation I can make, that a *penny saved* in that way bears about a true proportion to a *farthing earned*. I am no advocate for women, who do not depend on themselves for a subsistence, proposing to themselves to *earn money*. My reasons for thinking it not advisable are too numerous to state—reasons deduced from authentic facts, and strict observations on domestic life in its various shades of comfort. But, if the females of a family, *nominally* supported by the other sex, find it necessary to add something to the common stock, why not endeavour to do something by which they may produce money *in its true shape*?

It would be an excellent plan, attended with very little trouble, to calculate every evening how much money has been saved by needlework *done in the family*, and compare the result with the daily portion of the yearly income. Nor would it be amiss to make a memorandum of the time passed in this way, adding also a guess as to what share it has taken up in the thoughts and conversation. This would be an easy mode of forming a true notion, and getting at the exact worth of this species of *home* industry, and perhaps might place it in a different light from any in which it has hitherto been the fashion to consider it.

Needlework, taken up as an amusement, may not be altogether unamusing. We are all pretty good judges of what entertains ourselves, but it is not so easy to pronounce upon what may contribute to the entertainment of others. At all events, let us not confuse the motives of economy with those of simple pastime. If saving be no object, and long habit have rendered needlework so delightful an avocation that we cannot think of relinquishing it, there are the good old contrivances in which our grand-dames were used to beguile and lose their time—knitting, knotting, netting, carpet working, and the like ingenious pursuits,—those so-often-praised but tedious works, which are so long in the operation, that purchasing the labour has seldom been thought good economy, yet, by a certain fascination, they have been found to chain down the great to a self-imposed slavery, from which they considerately, or haughtily, excuse the needy. These may be esteemed lawful and lady-like amusements. But, if those works, more usually denominated useful, yield greater satisfaction, it might be a laudable scruple of conscience, and no bad test to herself of her own motive, if a lady, who had no absolute need, were to give the money so saved to poor needle-women belonging to those branches of employment from which she has borrowed these shares of pleasurable labour.

JANE AUSTEN
(1775–1817)

Born in the Rectory at Steventon, Hampshire, the seventh of the eight children of the Revd George Austen and Cassandra Leigh, Austen accompanied her elder sister Cassandra to boarding-schools in Oxford, Southampton, and Reading, and from the age of 11 was educated at home by her father. From one school, run by a Mrs Crawley, Jane and Cassandra had to be brought home after falling dangerously ill with a putrid fever. The family moved to Bath in 1801, and on the death of Austen's father in 1805 moved again to Southampton and finally to the village of Chawton, Hampshire, to a house owned by Austen's brother Edward Knight (born Austen, but adopted as a child by wealthy relatives whose estate he inherited). She never married, but she was involved in several more or less serious romantic entanglements, and in December 1802 accepted a proposal of marriage from the affluent and respectable Harris Bigg-Wither, only to refuse him, because she did not feel sufficiently attached, the next day. Austen's creative life began early, but it flourished in the security of Chawton Cottage, where she lived with her mother, her sister Cassandra, and their friend Martha Lloyd, from 1809 until her brief and unsuccessful removal to Winchester for medical attention in May 1817. She died in Winchester in July the same year, at the age of 41, probably from the as-yet-unrecognized Addison's disease.

Austen's juvenile writings reveal a precocious acuteness and wit: they include burlesques of the sentimental. She drafted first versions of novels in the 1790s (*Susan*, 1794; *Elinor and Marianne*, 1795; *First Impressions*, 1796–7), had *First Impressions* (the early form of *Pride and Prejudice*) rejected by the publisher Cadell in 1797, and sold *Susan* (the early form of *Northanger Abbey*) to the publishers Crosby & Co. for £10 in 1803. Purchase did not guarantee publication, however, and eventually Austen bought the novel back. *Sense and Sensibility* was published, at Austen's own expense, in 1811; the copyright of *Pride and Prejudice* was bought for £110 and the novel appeared in 1813; followed by *Mansfield Park* (1814), and *Emma* (1816). Her last completed novel, *Persuasion*, was published with her first, *Northanger Abbey*, the year after her death.

Austen is represented here in a way which strives to reconcile her special status in modern culture (and modern publishing) with the part she played in the culture of her own time. Two extracts from her novels will, it is hoped, interact with extracts from other writers included. The first extract, from *Mansfield Park*, presents the allure and danger of acting when indulged in a mixed domestic circle. Austen's heroine, Fanny Price, is the only one of her family party to refuse to take part in rehearsals for a private performance of a risqué play, *Lover's Vows* (adapted by Elizabeth Inchbald from the German original of Kotzebue), during the lengthy absence of the head of the family, her uncle and guardian Sir Thomas Bertram. Fanny is secretly in love with her cousin, Edmund; who is fascinated by the vivacious Mary Crawford; while Mary Crawford's witty brother, Henry, is pursuing a self-indulgent flirtation with Edmund's sister Maria, recently engaged to marry the lumpish but rich Mr Rushworth. The arrival of an empty-headed man of fashion, Mr Yates, has precipitated the whole group into enacting a play which is to expose the emotional tensions between them.

The second extract comes from one of the most emotionally charged episodes in Austen's fiction, the carefully structured scene from *Persuasion* in which the heroine, Anne Elliot, debates the strength of men's and women's love with a friend, Captain Harville, while their conversation is overheard by the man to whom she was once engaged, Captain Wentworth. Captain Harville is dispirited because the fiancé of his dead sister Fanny has all too quickly become engaged to another woman, Louisa Musgrove. Anne Elliot is drawn by her sympathy with his feelings to speak eloquently about the special love and faith of women; and in revealing how deeply she has reflected on this subject she in effect offers an impassioned self-defence to the listening man whom, years before, she had rejected because their marriage was not deemed prudent. Throughout the novel they have lived with her buried regret and his proud resentment. Commenting on the part of the exchange in which Captain Harville says that tales of women's inconstancy 'were all written by men', to which Anne readily agrees—'the pen has been in their hands'—Stuart Curran points out: 'By the final third of the eighteenth century, at least, a man must have been, like Captain Harville (and, for that measure, Captains Benwick and Wentworth), rather a long time at sea not to be aware that the culture of writing was becoming rapidly feminized.'[1]

∾

From *Mansfield Park* (1814)

Every thing was now in a regular train; theatre, actors, actresses, and dresses, were all getting forward: but though no other great impediments arose, Fanny found, before many days were past, that it was

[1] 'Women Readers, Women Writers', in Stuart Curran (ed.), *The Cambridge Companion to British Romanticism* (Cambridge: Cambridge University Press, 1993), 178.

not all uninterrupted enjoyment to the party themselves, and that she had not to witness the continuance of such unanimity and delight, as had been almost too much for her at first. Every body began to have their vexation. Edmund had many. Entirely against *his* judgment, a scene painter arrived from town, and was at work, much to the increase of the expenses, and what was worse, of the eclat of their proceedings; and his brother, instead of being really guided by him as to the privacy of the representation, was giving an invitation to every family who came in his way. Tom himself began to fret over the scene painter's slow progress, and to feel the miseries of waiting. He had learned his part—all his parts—for he took every trifling one that could be united with the Butler, and began to be impatient to be acting; and every day thus unemployed, was tending to increase his sense of the insignificance of all his parts together, and make him more ready to regret that some other play had not been chosen.

Fanny, being always a very courteous listener, and often the only listener at hand, came in for the complaints and distresses of most of them. *She* knew that Mr Yates was in general thought to rant dreadfully, that Mr Yates was disappointed in Henry Crawford, that Tom Bertram spoke so quick he would be unintelligible, that Mrs Grant spoilt every thing by laughing, that Edmund was behind-hand with his part, and that it was misery to have any thing to do with Mr Rushworth, who was wanting a prompter through every speech. She knew, also, that poor Mr Rushworth could seldom get any body to rehearse with him; *his* complaint came before her as well as the rest; and so decided to her eye was her cousin Maria's avoidance of him, and so needlessly often the rehearsal of the first scene between her and Mr Crawford, that she had soon all the terror of other complaints from *him*.—So far from being all satisfied and all enjoying, she found every body requiring something they had not, and giving occasion of discontent to the others.—Every body had a part either too long or too short;—nobody would attend as they ought, nobody would remember on which side they were to come in—nobody but the complainer would observe any directions.

Fanny believed herself to derive as much innocent enjoyment from the play as any of them;—Henry Crawford acted well, and it was a pleasure to *her* to creep into the theatre, and attend the rehearsal of the first act—in spite of the feelings it excited in some speeches for Maria.*—Maria she also thought acted well—too well;—and after the first rehearsal or two, Fanny began to be their only audience, and—sometimes as prompter, sometimes as spectator—was often very useful.—As far as she could judge, Mr Crawford was considerably the best actor of all; he had more confidence than Edmund, more judgment than Tom, more talent and taste than Mr Yates.—She did not like him as a man, but she must admit him to be the best actor, and on this point there were not many who differed from her. Mr Yates, indeed, exclaimed against his tameness and insipidity—and the day came at last, when Mr Rushworth turned to her with a black look, and said—'Do you think there is any thing so very fine in all this? For the life and soul of me, I cannot admire him;—and between ourselves, to see such an undersized, little, mean-looking man, set up for a fine actor, is very ridiculous in my opinion.'

From this moment there was a return of his former jealousy, which Maria, from increasing hopes of Crawford, was at little pains to remove; and the chances of Mr Rushworth's ever attaining to the knowledge of his two and forty speeches became much less. As to his ever making any thing *tolerable* of them, nobody had the smallest idea of that except his mother—*She*, indeed, regretted that his part was not more considerable, and deferred coming over to Mansfield till they were forward enough in their rehearsal to comprehend all his scenes, but the others aspired at nothing beyond his remembering the catchword, and the first line of his speech, and being able to follow the prompter through the rest. Fanny, in her pity and kind-heartedness, was at great pains to teach him how to learn, giving him all the helps and directions in her power, trying to make an artificial memory for him, and learning every word of his part herself, but without his being much the forwarder.

Many uncomfortable, anxious, apprehensive feelings she certainly had; but with all these, and other claims on her time and attention, she was as far from finding herself without employment or utility amongst them, as without a companion in uneasiness; quite as far from having no demand on her leisure as on her compassion. The gloom of her first anticipations was proved to have been unfounded. She was occasionally useful to all; she was perhaps as much at peace as any.

There was a great deal of needle-work to be done moreover, in which her help was wanted; and that Mrs Norris thought her quite as well off as the rest, was evident by the manner in which she claimed it: 'Come Fanny,' she cried, 'these are fine times for you, but you must not be always walking from one room to the other and doing the lookings on, at your ease, in this way,—I want you here.—I have been slaving myself till I can hardly stand, to contrive Mr Rushworth's cloak without sending for any more satin; and now I think you may give me your help in putting it together.—There are but three seams, you may do them in a trice.—It would be lucky for me if I had nothing but the executive part to do.— *You* are best off, I can tell you; but if nobody did more than *you*, we should not get on very fast.'

Fanny took the work very quietly without attempting any defence; but her kinder aunt Bertram observed on her behalf,

'One cannot wonder, sister, that Fanny *should* be delighted; it is all new to her, you know,—you and I used to be very fond of a play ourselves—and so am I still;—and as soon as I am a little more at leisure, *I* mean to look in at their rehearsals too. What is the play about, Fanny, you have never told me?'

'Oh! sister, pray do not ask her now; for Fanny is not one of those who can talk and work at the same time.—It is about Lovers' Vows.'

'I believe,' said Fanny to her aunt Bertram, 'there will be three acts rehearsed to-morrow evening, and that will give you an opportunity of seeing all the actors at once.'

'You had better stay till the curtain is hung,' interposed Mrs Norris—'the curtain will be hung in a day or two,—there is very little sense in a play without a curtain—and I am much mistaken if you do not find it draw up into very handsome festoons.'

Lady Bertram seemed quite resigned to waiting.—Fanny did not share her aunt's composure; she thought of the morrow a great deal,—for if the three acts were rehearsed, Edmund and Miss Crawford would then be acting together for the first time;—the third act would bring a scene between them which interested her most particularly, and which she was longing and dreading to see how they would perform.* The whole subject of it was love—a marriage of love was to be described by the gentleman, and very little short of a declaration of love be made by the lady.

She had read, and read the scene again with many painful, many wondering emotions, and looked forward to their representation of it as a circumstances almost too interesting. She did not *believe* they had yet rehearsed it, even in private.

The morrow came, the plan for the evening continued, and Fanny's consideration of it did not become less agitated. She worked very diligently under her aunt's directions, but her diligence and her silence concealed a very absent, anxious mind; and about noon she made her escape with her work to the East room, that she might have no concern in another, and, as she deemed it, most unnecessary rehearsal of the first act, which Henry Crawford was just proposing, desirous at once of having her time to herself, and of avoiding the sight of Mr Rushworth. A glimpse, as she passed through the hall, of the two ladies walking up from the parsonage, made no change in her wish of retreat, and she worked and meditated in the East room, undisturbed, for a quarter of an hour, when a gentle tap at the door was followed by the entrance of Miss Crawford.

'Am I right?—Yes; this is the East room. My dear Miss Price, I beg your pardon, but I have made my way to you on purpose to entreat your help.'

Fanny, quite surprised, endeavoured to show herself mistress of the room by her civilities, and looked at the bright bars of her empty grate with concern.

'Thank you—I am quite warm, very warm. Allow me to stay here a little while, and do have the goodness to hear me my third act. I have brought my book, and if you would but rehearse it with me, I should be *so* obliged! I came here today intending to rehearse it with Edmund—by ourselves—against the evening, but he is not in the way; and if he *were*, I do not think I could go through it with *him*, till I have hardened myself a little, for really there *is* a speech or two— You will be so good, won't you?'

Fanny was most civil in her assurances, though she could not give them in a very steady voice.

'Have you ever happened to look at the part I mean?' continued Miss Crawford, opening her book. 'Here it is. I did not think much of it at first—but, upon my word—.There, look at *that* speech, and *that*, and *that*. How am I ever to look him in the face and say such things? Could you do it? But then he is your cousin, which makes all the difference. You must rehearse it with me, that I may fancy *you* him, and get on by degrees. You *have* a look of *his* sometimes.'

'Have I?—I will do my best with the greatest readiness—but I must *read* the part, for I can *say* very little of it.'

'*None* of it, I suppose. You are to have the book of course. Now for it. We must have two chairs at hand for you to bring forward to the front of the stage. There—very good school-room chairs, not made for a theatre, I dare say; much more fitted for little girls to sit and kick their feet against when they are learning a lesson. What would your governess and your uncle say to see them used for such a purpose? Could Sir Thomas look in upon us just now, he would bless himself, for we are rehearsing all over the house. Yates is storming away in the dining room. I heard him as I came up stairs, and the theatre is engaged of course by those indefatigable rehearsers, Agatha and Frederick. If *they* are not perfect, I *shall* be surprised. By the bye, I looked in upon them five minutes ago, and it happened to be exactly at one of the times when they were trying *not* to embrace, and Mr Rushworth was with me. I thought he began to look a little queer, so I turned it off as well as I could, by whispering to him, "We shall have an excellent Agatha, there is something so *maternal* in her manner, so completely *maternal* in her voice and countenance." Was not that well done of me? He brightened up directly. Now for my soliloquy.'

She began, and Fanny joined in with all the modest feeling which the idea of representing Edmund was so strongly calculated to inspire; but with looks and voice so truly feminine, as to be no very good picture of a man. With such an Anhalt, however, Miss Crawford had courage enough, and they had got through half the scene, when a tap at the door brought a pause, and the entrance of Edmund the next moment, suspended it all.

Surprise, consciousness, and pleasure, appeared in each of the three on this unexpected meeting; and as Edmund was come on the very same business that had brought Miss Crawford, consciousness and pleasure were likely to be more than momentary in *them*. He too had his book, and was seeking Fanny, to ask her to rehearse with him, and help him prepare for the evening, without knowing Miss Crawford to be in the house; and great was the joy and animation of being thus thrown together—of comparing schemes—and sympathizing in praise of Fanny's kind offices.

She could not equal them in their warmth. *Her* spirits sank under the glow of theirs, and she felt herself becoming too nearly nothing to both, to have any comfort in having been sought by either. They must now rehearse together. Edmund proposed, urged, entreated it—till the lady, not very unwilling at first, could refuse no longer—and Fanny was wanted only to prompt and observe them. She was invested, indeed, with the office of judge and critic, and earnestly desired to exercise it and tell them all their faults; but from doing so every feeling within her shrank, she could not, would not, dared not attempt it; had she been otherwise qualified for criticism, her conscience must have restrained her from venturing at disapprobation. She believed herself to feel too much of it in the aggregate for honesty or safety in particulars. To prompt them must be enough for her; and it was sometimes *more* than enough; for she could not always pay attention to the book. In watching them she forgot herself; and agitated by the increasing spirit of Edmund's manner, had once closed the page and turned away exactly as he wanted help. It was imputed to very reasonable weariness, and she was thanked and pitied; but she deserved their pity, more than she hoped they would ever surmise. At last the scene was over, and Fanny forced herself to add her praise to the compliments each was giving the other; and when again alone and able to recall the whole, she was inclined to believe their performance would, indeed, have such nature and feeling in it, as must ensure their credit, and make it a very suffering exhibition to herself. Whatever might be its effect, however, she must stand the brunt of it again that very day.

The first regular rehearsal of the three first acts was certainly to take place in the evening; Mrs Grant and the Crawfords were engaged to return for that purpose as soon as they could after dinner; and every one concerned was looking forward with eagerness. There seemed a general diffusion of cheerfulness on the occasion; Tom was enjoying such an advance towards the end, Edmund was in spirits from the morning's rehearsal, and little vexations seemed every where smoothed away. All were alert and impatient; the ladies moved soon,* the gentlemen soon followed them, and with the exception of Lady Bertram, Mrs Norris, and Julia, every body was in the theatre at an early hour, and having lighted it up as well as its unfinished state admitted, were waiting only the arrival of Mrs Grant and the Crawfords to begin.

They did not wait long for the Crawfords, but there was no Mrs Grant. She could not come. Dr Grant, professing an indisposition, for which he had little credit with his fair sister-in-law, could not spare his wife.

'Dr Grant is ill,' said she, with mock solemnity. 'He has been ill ever since; he did not eat any of the pheasant today. He fancied it tough—sent away his plate—and has been suffering ever since.'

Here was disappointment! Mrs Grant's non-attendance was sad indeed. Her pleasant manners and cheerful conformity made her always valuable amongst them—but *now* she was absolutely necessary. They could not act, they could not rehearse with any satisfaction without her. The comfort of the whole evening was destroyed. What was to be done? Tom, as Cottager, was in despair. After a pause of perplexity, some eyes began to be turned towards Fanny, and a voice or two, to say, 'If Miss Price would be so good as to *read* the part.' She was immediately surrounded by supplications, every body asked it, even Edmund said, 'Do Fanny, if it is not *very* disagreeable to you.'

But Fanny still hung back. She could not endure the idea of it. Why was not Miss Crawford to be applied to as well? Or why had not she rather gone to her own room, as she had felt to be safest, instead of attending the rehearsal at all? She had known it would irritate and distress her—she had known it her duty to keep away. She was properly punished.

'You have only to *read* the part,' said Henry Crawford with renewed entreaty.

'And I do believe she can say every word of it,' added Maria, 'for she could put Mrs Grant right the other day in twenty places. Fanny, I am sure you know the part.'

Fanny could not say she did *not*—and as they all persevered—as Edmund repeated his wish, and with a look of even fond dependence on her good nature, she must yield. She would do her best. Every body was satisfied and she was left to the tremors of a most palpitating heart, while the others prepared to begin.

They *did* begin—and being too much engaged in their own noise, to be struck by unusual noise in the other part of the house, had proceeded some way, when the door of the room was thrown open, and Julia appearing at it, with a face all aghast, exclaimed, 'My father is come! He is in the hall at this moment.'

From *Persuasion* (1818)

Mrs Musgrove was giving Mrs Croft the history of her eldest daughter's engagement, and just in that inconvenient tone of voice which was perfectly audible while it pretended to be a whisper. Anne felt that she did not belong to the conversation, and yet, as Captain Harville seemed thoughtful and not disposed to talk, she could not avoid hearing many undesirable particulars, such as 'how Mr Musgrove and my brother Hayter had met again and again to talk it over; what my brother Hayter had said one day, and what Mr Musgrove had proposed the next, and what had occurred to my sister Hayter, and what the young people had wished, and what I said at first I never could consent to, but was afterwards persuaded to think might do very well,' and a great deal in the same style of open-hearted communication—Minutiæ which, even with every advantage of taste and delicacy which good Mrs Musgrove could not give, could be properly interesting only to the principals. Mrs Croft was attending with great good humour, and whenever she spoke at all, it was very sensibly. Anne hoped the gentlemen might each be too much self-occupied to hear.

'And so, ma'am, all these things considered,' said Mrs Musgrove in her powerful whisper, 'though we could have wished it different, yet altogether we did not think it fair to stand out any longer; for Charles Hayter was quite wild about it, and Henrietta was pretty near as bad; and so we thought they had better marry at once, and make the best of it, as many others have done before them. At any rate, said I, it will be better than a long engagement.'

'That is precisely what I was going to observe,' cried Mrs Croft. 'I would rather have young people settle on a small income at once, and have to struggle with a few difficulties together, than be involved in a long engagement. I always think that no mutual—'.

'Oh! dear Mrs Croft,' cried Mrs Musgrove, unable to let her finish her speech, 'there is nothing I so abominate for young people as a long engagement. It is what I always protested against for my children. It is all very well, I used to say, for young people to be engaged, if there is a certainty of their being able to marry in six months, or even in twelve, but a long engagement!'

'Yes, dear ma'am,' said Mrs Croft, 'or an uncertain engagement;

an engagement which may be long. To begin without knowing that at such a time there will be the means of marrying, I hold to be very unsafe and unwise, and what, I think, all parents should prevent as far as they can.'

Anne found an unexpected interest here. She felt its application to herself, felt it in a nervous thrill all over her, and at the same moment that her eyes instinctively glanced towards the distant table, Captain Wentworth's pen ceased to move, his head was raised, pausing, listening, and he turned round the next instant to give a look—one quick, conscious look at her.

The two ladies continued to talk, to re-urge the same admitted truths, and enforce them with such examples of the ill effect of a contrary practice, as had fallen within their observation, but Anne heard nothing distinctly; it was only a buzz of words in her ear, her mind was in confusion.

Captain Harville, who had in truth been hearing none of it, now left his seat, and moved to a window; and Anne seeming to watch him, though it was from thorough absence of mind, became gradually sensible that he was inviting her to join him where he stood. He looked at her with a smile, and a little motion of the head, which expressed, 'Come to me, I have something to say;' and the unaffected, easy kindness of manner which denoted the feelings of an older acquaintance than he really was, strongly enforced the invitation. She roused herself and went to him. The window at which he stood, was at the other end of the room from where the two ladies were sitting, and though nearer to Captain Wentworth's table, not very near. As she joined him, Captain Harville's countenance reassumed the serious, thoughtful expression which seemed its natural character.

'Look here,' said he, unfolding a parcel in his hand, and displaying a small miniature painting, 'do you know who that is?'

'Certainly, Captain Benwick.'*

'Yes, and you may guess who it is for. But (in a deep tone) it was not done for her. Miss Elliot, do you remember our walking together at Lyme, and grieving for him? I little thought then—but no matter. This was drawn at the Cape.* He met with a clever young German artist at the Cape, and in compliance with a promise to my poor sister, sat to him, and was bringing it home for her. And I have now the charge of getting it properly set for another! It was a commission to me! But who else was there to employ? I hope I can allow for him. I am not sorry, indeed, to make it over to another. He undertakes it— (looking towards Captain Wentworth) he is writing about it now.' And with a quivering lip he wound up the whole by adding, 'Poor Fanny! she would not have forgotten him so soon!'

'No,' replied Anne, in a low feeling voice. 'That, I can easily believe.'

'It was not in her nature. She doated on him.'

'It would not be the nature of any woman who truly loved.'

Captain Harville smiled, as much as to say, 'Do you claim that for your sex?' and she answered the question, smiling also, 'Yes. We certainly do not forget you, so soon as you forget us. It is, perhaps, our fate rather than our merit. We cannot help ourselves. We live at home, quiet, confined, and our feelings prey upon us. You are forced on exertion. You have always a profession, pursuits, business of some sort or other, to take you back into the world immediately, and continual occupation and change soon weaken impressions.'

'Granting your assertion that the world does all this so soon for men, (which, however, I do not think I shall grant) it does not apply to Benwick. He has not been forced upon any exertion. The peace turned him on shore at the very moment,* and he has been living with us, in our little family-circle, ever since.'

'True,' said Anne, 'very true; I did not recollect; but what shall we say now, Captain Harville? If the change be not from outward circumstances, it must be from within; it must be nature, man's nature, which has done the business for Captain Benwick.'

'No, no, it is not man's nature. I will not allow it to be more man's nature than woman's to be inconstant and forget those they do love, or have loved. I believe the reverse. I believe in a true analogy between our bodily frames and our mental; and that as our bodies are the strongest, so are our feelings; capable of bearing most rough usage, and riding out the heaviest weather.'

'Your feelings may be the strongest,' replied Anne, 'but the same spirit of analogy will authorise me to assert that ours are the most tender. Man is more robust than woman, but he is not longer-lived; which exactly explains my view of the nature of their attachments. Nay, it would be too hard upon you, if it were otherwise. You have difficulties, and privations, and dangers enough to struggle with. You are always labouring and toiling, exposed to every risk and hardship.

Your home, country, friends, all quitted. Neither time, nor health, nor life, to be called your own. It would be too hard indeed' (with a faltering voice) 'if woman's feelings were to be added to all this.'

'We shall never agree upon this question'—Captain Harville was beginning to say, when a slight noise called their attention to Captain Wentworth's hitherto perfectly quiet division of the room. It was nothing more than that his pen had fallen down, but Anne was startled at finding him nearer than she had supposed, and half inclined to suspect that the pen had only fallen, because he had been occupied by them, striving to catch sounds, which yet she did not think he could have caught.

'Have you finished your letter?' said Captain Harville.

'Not quite, a few lines more. I shall have done in five minutes.'

'There is no hurry on my side. I am only ready whenever you are.—I am in very good anchorage here,' (smiling at Anne) 'well supplied, and want for nothing.—No hurry for a signal at all.—Well, Miss Elliot,' (lowering his voice) 'as I was saying, we shall never agree I suppose upon this point. No man and woman would, probably. But let me observe that all histories are against you, all stories, prose and verse. If I had such a memory as Benwick, I could bring you fifty quotations in a moment on my side the argument, and I do not think I ever opened a book in my life which had not something to say upon woman's inconstancy. Songs and proverbs, all talk of woman's fickleness. But perhaps you will say, these were all written by men.'

'Perhaps I shall.—Yes, yes, if you please, no reference to examples in books. Men have had every advantage of us in telling their own story. Education has been theirs in so much higher a degree; the pen has been in their hands. I will not allow books to prove any thing.'

'But how shall we prove any thing?'

'We never shall. We never can expect to prove any thing upon such a point. It is a difference of opinion which does not admit of proof. We each begin probably with a little bias towards our own sex, and upon that bias build every circumstance in favour of it which has occurred within our own circle; many of which circumstances (perhaps those very cases which strike us the most) may be precisely such as cannot be brought forward without betraying a confidence, or in some respect saying what should not be said.'

'Ah!' cried Captain Harville, in a tone of strong feeling, 'if I could but make you comprehend what a man suffers when he takes a last look at his wife and children, and watches the boat that he has sent them off in, as long as it is in sight, and then turns away and says, "God knows whether we ever meet again!" And then, if I could convey to you the glow of his soul when he does see them again; when, coming back after a twelvemonth's absence perhaps, and obliged to put into another port, he calculates how soon it be possible to get them there, pretending to deceive himself, and saying, "They cannot be here till such a day," but all the while hoping for them twelve hours sooner, and seeing them arrive at last, as if Heaven had given them wings, by many hours sooner still! If I could explain to you all this, and all that a man can bear and do, and glories to do for the sake of these treasures of his existence! I speak, you know, only of such men as have hearts!' pressing his own with emotion.

'Oh!' cried Anne eagerly, 'I hope I do justice to all that is felt by you, and by those who resemble you. God forbid that I should undervalue the warm and faithful feelings of any of my fellow-creatures. I should deserve utter contempt if I dared to suppose that true attachment and constancy were known only by woman. No, I believe you capable of every thing great and good in your married lives. I believe you equal to every important exertion, and to every domestic forbearance, so long as—if I may be allowed the expression, so long as you have an object. I mean, while the woman you love lives, and lives for you. All the privilege I claim for my own sex (it is not a very enviable one, you need not covet it) is that of loving longest, when existence or when hope is gone.'

She could not immediately have uttered another sentence; her heart was too full, her breath too much oppressed.

'You are a good soul,' cried Captain Harville, putting his hand on her arm quite affectionately. 'There is no quarrelling with you.— And when I think of Benwick, my tongue is tied.'

Their attention was called towards the others.—Mrs Croft was taking leave.

'Here, Frederick, you and I part company, I believe,' said she. 'I am going home, and you have an engagement with your friend.— To-night we may have the pleasure of all meeting again, at your party,' (turning to Anne.) 'We had your sister's card yesterday, and I understood Frederick had a card too, though I did not see it—and you are disengaged, Frederick, are you not, as well as ourselves?'

Captain Wentworth was folding up a letter in great haste, and either could not or would not answer fully.

'Yes,' said he, 'very true; here we separate, but Harville and I shall soon be after you, that is, Harville, if you are ready, I am in half a minute. I know you will not be sorry to be off. I shall be at your service in half a minute.'

Mrs Croft left them, and Captain Wentworth, having sealed his letter with great rapidity, was indeed ready, and had even a hurried, agitated air, which shewed impatience to be gone. Anne knew not how to understand it. She had the kindest 'Good morning, God bless you,' from Captain Harville, but from him not a word, nor a look. He had passed out of the room without a look!

She had only time, however, to move closer to the table where he had been writing, when footsteps were heard returning; the door opened; it was himself. He begged their pardon, but he had forgotten his gloves, and instantly crossing the room to the writing table, and standing with his back towards Mrs Musgrove, he drew out a letter from under the scattered paper, placed it before Anne with eyes of glowing entreaty fixed on her for a moment, and hastily collecting his gloves, was again out of the room, almost before Mrs Musgrove was aware of his being in it—the work of an instant!

The revolution which one instant had made in Anne, was almost beyond expression. The letter, with a direction hardly legible, to 'Miss A. E.—' was evidently the one which he had been folding so hastily. While supposed to be writing only to Captain Benwick, he had been also addressing her! On the contents of that letter depended all which this world could do for her! Any thing was possible, any thing might be defied rather than suspense. Mrs Musgrove had little arrangements of her own at her own table; to their protection she must trust, and sinking into the chair which he had occupied, succeeding to the very spot where he had leaned and written, her eyes devoured the following words:

'I can listen no longer in silence. I must speak to you by such means as are within my reach. You pierce my soul. I am half agony, half hope. Tell me not that I am too late, that such precious feelings are gone for ever. I offer myself to you again with a heart even more your own, than when you almost broke it eight years and a half ago. Dare not say that man forgets sooner than woman, that his love has an earlier death. I have loved none but you. Unjust I may have been, weak and resentful I have been, but never inconstant. You alone have brought me to Bath. For you alone I think and plan.—Have you not seen this? Can you fail to have understood my wishes?—I had not waited even these ten days, could I have read your feelings, as I think you must have penetrated mine. I can hardly write. I am every instant hearing something which overpowers me. You sink your voice, but I can distinguish the tones of that voice, when they would be lost on others.—Too good, too excellent creature! You do us justice indeed. You do believe that there is true attachment and constancy among men. Believe it to be most fervent, most undeviating in

                                                                                    F.W.

'I must go, uncertain of my fate; but I shall return hither, or follow your party, as soon as possible. A word, a look will be enough to decide whether I enter your father's house this evening, or never.'

   Such a letter was not to be soon recovered from. Half an hour's solitude and reflection might have tranquillized her; but the ten minutes only, which now passed before she was interrupted, with all the restraints of her situation, could do nothing towards tranquillity. Every moment rather brought fresh agitation. It was an overpowering happiness.

MARY SHERWOOD
(1775–1851)

Born Mary Butt, the second child of the poet and divine George Butt and his wife Martha Sherwood, she was educated at home in Stanford, Worcestershire, in a highly disciplined way, until the age of 15, when she was sent to the school at Reading run by the French emigrés M. and Mme St Quintin; they later taught Mary Russell Mitford, Caroline Lamb, and Laetitia Elizabeth Landon. As a child she visited Anna Seward in Lichfield and became acquainted with her circle of literary ladies; a closer link in terms of her own writing was with Hannah More, whom she visited in 1799. Her education was thorough, including instruction in Latin, and she began to write stories and plays while still at school. She turned seriously to writing in 1793, and after her father's death in 1795 she moved with her mother and sister to Bridgnorth, where she learnt Greek and ran the parish Sunday School. In 1803 she married her cousin, Captain Henry Sherwood, an officer in the army. She left their first child in England in order to accompany her husband to India in 1805. Here Mary Sherwood had several more children, four of whom survived; and continued her charitable works, especially work for orphans, spurred on by strong evangelical convictions. She wrote many stories for use in the Sunday Schools and schools for native children converted to Christianity which she established. Returning to Britain in 1816 with her own four children and nine adopted European orphans, Sherwood continued to take in abandoned children sent from India, and in addition educated paying pupils. From her home in Worcestershire Mary Sherwood involved herself in prison reform and with the study of Hebrew, her ambition being to complete a dictionary of the prophetic books of the Bible. In 1848 the family moved to Twickenham, where Henry Sherwood died in 1849.

Sherwood's numerous stories and tracts made her a figure of lasting importance in nineteenth-century education. She first published *The Traditions* (1794), *Margarita*, and *Susan Gray* (1802), describing the last as 'the first of its kind—that is the first narrative allowing of anything like correct writing or refined sentiments, expressed without vulgarities, ever prepared for the poor, and having religion as its object'. The successful British publication of her Indian tale, *The Indian Pilgrim* (1815) was followed by the runaway success of *Little Henry and his Bearer*. This story appeared in about one hundred editions before 1884 and was widely translated. Just as successful were the three parts (1818, 1837, 1842) of *The History of the Fairchild Family; or, the Child's Manual: Being a Collection of Stories Calculated to Shew the Importance and Effects of a Religious Education*. E. I. Carlyle in the *Dictionary of National Biography* comments: 'Most children of the English middle-class born in the first quarter of the nineteenth century may be said to have been brought up on the "Fairchild Family".' Mary Sherwood published over ninety-five works, among the longer of which are *The Nun* and *The Lady of the Manor*; a selection was published in 1891 as *The Juvenile Library*.

The children of the Fairchild family—Emily, Lucy, and Henry— survive as remarkably lively and curious small consciousnesses in the face of a catalogue of moral instruction. Their parents, as in the following incident, are sincere and practical Christians. In 'The All-Seeing God', all the important action takes place in the child's guilty consciousness. Although the outcome seems to Emily to prove that the words of the sermon are indeed true, and that God sees all, the shock which causes her to spill red juice down her dress is caused by the cat and by her own nerves, and she catches fever through her own fearful attempts to conceal what Sherwood uncompromisingly sees as her wickedness. Sherwood creates a tale which is full of symbolic possibility, but which is never permitted to seem symbolic rather than actual. Even so, the stealing and compulsive consumption of the red fruit make one think of Christina Rossetti's 'Goblin Market', and the tale is replete with pre-adolescent anxiety. Sharing the secret with mother is the effective cure; although there is also a strong faith in the healing powers of outdoor nature and of loving companionship. As Sherwood's stories were retold in later selected editions and illustrated collections, the intense and explicit moralizing which is so striking in the 1818 original is erased, and many readers have approached Sherwood in a much lighter, easier, and grammatically sharpened form. The original text presented here is less appealing but much more faithful to Sherwood's troubling portrayal of a childish consciousness set amid a claustrophobic and spiritually punitive family life. The story as it is presented here ends in the original with an emotionally wrought 'Prayer' and a summarizing 'Hymn'.

～

From *The History of the Fairchild Family* (1818)

The All-Seeing God

I must now tell you of a sad temptation into which Emily fell about this time. It is a long story, but you shall have it all.

There was a room in Mrs Fairchild's house which was not often used: in this room was a closet full of shelves, where Mrs Fairchild used to keep her sugar, and tea, and sweetmeats, and pickles, and many other things. Now as Betty was very honest, and John too, Mrs Fairchild would often leave this closet unlocked for weeks together, and never missed any thing out of it. One day, at the time that damascenes were ripe, Mrs Fairchild and Betty boiled up a great many damascenes in sugar, to use in the winter;* and when they had put them in jars, and tied them down, they put them in the closet I before spoke of. Emily and Lucy saw their mamma do the damascenes, and helped Betty to cover them and carry them to the closet. As Emily was carrying one of the jars, she perceived that it was tied down so loosely that she could put in her finger and get at the fruit.

Accordingly she took out one of the damascenes, and ate it: it was so nice that she was tempted to take another; and was going even to take a third, when she heard Betty coming up: she covered the jar in haste, and came away. Some months after this, one evening, just about the time that it was getting dark, she was passing by the room where these sweetmeats were kept, and she observed that the door was open: she looked round to see if any body was near, but there was no one: her mamma and papa, and her brother and sister, were in the parlour and Betty was in the kitchen, and John was in the garden: no eye was looking at her, but the eye of God, who sees every thing we do, and knows even the secret thoughts of the heart; but Emily, at that moment, did not think of God. She passed through the open door, and went up to the closet: there she stood still again, and looked round, but saw no one. She then opened the closet door, and took two or three damascenes, which she ate in great haste. She then went to her own room, and washed her hands and mouth, and went down into the parlour, where her papa and mamma were just going to tea.

Although her mamma and papa never suspected what naughty thing Emily had been doing, and behaved just as usual to her, yet Emily felt frightened and uneasy before them; and every time they spoke to her, though it was only to ask her the commonest question, she stared and looked frightened, making out the words of King Solomon; 'The wicked flee when no man pursueth, but the righteous are bold as a lion.' (Prov. xxviii. 1.)

I am sorry to say, that the next day, when it was beginning to get dark, Emily went again to the closet, and took some more damascenes; and so she did for several days, though she knew she was doing wrong.

On the Sunday following, it happened to be so rainy that nobody could go to church; in consequence of which, Mr Fairchild called all the family into the parlour, and read the Morning Service, and a sermon. Some sermons are hard, are difficult for children to understand; but this was a very plain, easy sermon; even Henry could tell his mamma a great deal about it. The text was from Psalm cxxxix, 7th to 12th verses: 'Whither shall I go from thy Spirit? or whither shall I flee from thy presence? If I ascend up into heaven, thou art there: if I make my bed in hell, behold, thou art there: if I take the wings of the morning, and dwell in the uttermost parts of the sea, even there shall thy hand lead me, and thy right hand shall hold me:

if I say, Surely the darkness shall cover me, even the night shall be light about me; yea, the darkness hideth not from thee, but the night shineth as the day: the darkness and the light are both alike to thee.'

The meaning of these verses were explained in the sermon at full length. It was first shewn that God is a spirit: he has no body like us, no hands, or legs, or arms. Secondly, that there is no place where God is not: that if a person could go up into heaven, he would find God there; if he were to go down to hell, there also he would find God; that God is in every part of the earth, and of the sea, and of the sky; and that, being always present in every place, he knows every thing we do, and every thing we say, and even every thought of our heart, however secret we may think it. Then the sermon went on to shew how foolish and mad it is for people to do wicked things in secret and dark places, trusting that God will not know it. 'If I say, Surely the darkness shall cover me, even the night shall be light about me:' for no night is dark unto God: 'He will surely bring to light the hidden things of darkness, and will make manifest the counsels of the heart.' (I Cor. iv. 5.) Therefore 'woe unto them that seek deep to hide their counsel from the Lord, and their works are in the dark, and they say, 'Who seeth us? and who knoweth us?' (Isa. xxix. 15.), and the sermon showed that there is no place where God is not; that God is everywhere and knows everything we do, everything we say, and even every thought of our hearts.

All the time that Mr Fairchild was reading, Emily felt frightened and unhappy, thinking of the wickedness she was guilty of every day; and she even thought that she never would be guilty again of the same sin: but when the evening came, all her good resolutions left her, for she had not prayed to the Lord Jesus Christ to strengthen them; and she went again to the room, where the damascenes were kept. When she came to the door of the closet, she thought of the sermon which her papa had read in the morning, and stood still a few moments, to consider what she should do. 'There is nobody in this room,' she said; 'and nobody sees me, it is true; but God is in this room: he sees me, his eye is now upon me: I cannot hide what I am going to do from him: he knows every thing, and he has power to cast me into hell. I will not take any more damascenes; I will go back, I think. But yet, as I am come so far, and am just got to the closet, I will just take one damascene—it shall be the last; I shall never come again, without mamma's leave.' So she opened the closet door, and took one damascene, and then another, and then two more. Whilst she was taking the last, she heard the cat mew: she did not know that the cat had followed her into the room, and she was so frightened that she spilt some of the red juice upon her frock, but did not perceive it at the time; as it is said, 'The way of the wicked is darkness: they know not at what they stumble.' (Prov. iv. 19.) She then left the closet, and went, as usual, to wash her hands and mouth, and went down into the parlour.

When Emily got into the parlour, she immediately saw the red stain on her frock. She did not stay till it was observed, but ran out again instantly, and went up stairs, and washed her frock. As the stain had not dried in, it came out with very little trouble; but not till Emily had wet all the bosom of her frock, and sleeves; and that so much, that all her inner clothes were thoroughly wet, even to the skin: to hide this, she put her pinafore on, to go down to tea. When she came down—; 'Where have you been, Emily?' said her mamma; 'we have almost done tea.'

'I have been playing with the cat, up stairs, Mamma,' said Emily. But when she told this lie, she felt very unhappy, and her complexion changed once or twice from red to pale.

It was a cold evening, and Emily kept as much from the fire and candle as she could, lest any spots should be left in her frock, and her mamma should see them. She had no opportunity, therefore, of drying or warming herself, and she began to feel quite chilled and trembling: soon after a burning heat came in the palms of her hands, and a soreness about her throat: however, she did not dare to complain, but sat till bedtime, getting every minute more and more uncomfortable.

It was some time after she was in bed, and even after her mamma and papa came to bed, before she could sleep: at last she fell asleep; but her sleep was disturbed by dreadful dreams, such as she never had had before in her life. She fancied she had been doing something wrong, though her head was so confused that she did not know what, and that a dreadful Eye was looking upon her from above. Wherever she went, she thought this Eye followed her with angry looks, and she could not hide herself from it. It was her troubled conscience, together with an uneasy body, which gave her these dreadful dreams; and so horrible were they, that at length she awoke, screaming violently. Her mamma and papa heard her cry, and came running in to her, bringing a light; but she was in such a terror, that at first she did not know them, but kept looking up as if she saw something very horrible.

'Oh, my dear!' said Mrs Fairchild, 'this child is in a burning fever; only feel her hands.'

It was true, indeed; and when Mr Fairchild felt her, he was so much frightened that he resolved to watch by her all night, and in the morning, as soon as it was light, to send John for the doctor. And what do you think Emily felt all this time; knowing, as she did, how she had brought on this illness, and how she had deceived for many days this dear papa and mamma, who gave up their own rest to attend her; knowing also, as she did, how she had offended God by continuing so many days in sin; and particularly in committing that sin again, after having been warned of the greatness of it in the sermon which her papa had read in the morning?

Emily continued to get worse during the night; neither was the doctor able, when he came, to stop the fever, though he did all that he could. It would have grieved you to have seen poor Lucy and Henry. They could neither read nor play, they missed their dear sister so much. They kept crying to each other, 'Oh, Emily! dear Emily! there is no pleasure without our dear Emily!'

When the doctor came on the third morning, he found Emily so much worse, that, although he tried to hide it from Mr and Mrs Fairchild, he could not. He ordered her to be moved away from her brother and sister, for fear they should catch the fever. Accordingly she was taken into the very room where the sweetmeats were kept: the doctor chose that room, because it was very airy, and separate from the rest of the house.

For some hours Emily had not seemed to notice any thing that passed; neither did she seem to know that they were moving her: but when she came into the room, and saw the closet door (for the bed on which they laid her was just opposite the closet door), she looked this way, and that way, and tried to speak; but was so ill, and her head so confused, that she could not make any body understand what she wanted to say.

The next day, when the doctor came, Emily was so very ill that he thought it right that Lucy and Henry should be sent out of the house. Accordingly, John got the horse ready, and took them to Mrs Goodwill's. Poor Lucy and Henry! how they cried when they went out of the gate, thinking that perhaps they might never see their dear Emily any more! It was a terrible time for poor Mr and Mrs Fairchild: they had no comfort, but in praying and watching by poor Emily's bed. And all this grief Emily brought upon her friends by her own naughtiness! 'Woe unto them that seek deep to hide their counsel from the Lord, and their works are in the dark; and they say, Who seeth us? and who knoweth us?' (Isa. xxix. 15).

Emily had been exceedingly ill for nine days, and every one feared that if her fever continued a few days longer she must die, when, by the mercy of God, her fever suddenly left her, and she fell asleep, and continued sleeping for many hours. O how did her dear papa and mamma rejoice, when they found her sleeping so sweetly! They went into another room, and fell on their knees, and blessed and praised God. And Mr Fairchild pointed out these words to his wife: 'For the Lord will not cast off for ever; but though he cause grief, yet will he have compassion, according to the multitude of his mercies: for he doth not afflict willingly, nor grieve the children of men.' (Lament. iii. 31–33.)

When Emily awoke, she was very weak: but her fever was gone: she kissed her papa and mamma, and wanted to tell them of the naughty things she had done, which had been the cause of her fever: but they would not allow her to speak. How kindly did Mr and Mrs Fairchild watch over their dear little girl, and provide her with every thing that was thought good for her!

From that day she got better; and at the end of a week, from the time her fever left her, she was so well, that she was able to sit up, and tell her mamma all the history of her stealing the damascenes, and of the sad way in which she had got the fever. 'Oh, Mamma!' said Emily, 'what a wicked girl have I been! what trouble have I given to you, and to Papa, and to the Doctor, and to Betty! I thought that God would take no notice of my sin. I thought he did not see me when I was stealing in the dark; but I was much mistaken; his eye was upon me all the time, and he made me feel his anger. And yet how good, how very good it was of Him not to send me to hell for my wickedness! When I was ill, I might have died; and, oh! Mamma, Mamma! what would have become of me then!'

Mrs Fairchild cried very much when she heard her little girl talk in this way: she kissed her, and held her in her arms. 'My beloved child,' said Mrs Fairchild, 'God has been very good indeed to you:

he has brought you through a dreadful illness, and, what is better than this, he has brought you to a knowledge of your wickedness betimes. You might have gone on in your wickedness for many years, till you became a hardened sinner; and when you died, you would have gone to hell; but God, like a tender Father, has chastised you, my child.'—Then Mrs Fairchild shewed Emily these verses: 'And ye have forgotten the exhortation, which speaketh unto you as unto children: My son, despise not thou the chastening of the Lord, nor faint when thou art rebuked of him; for whom the Lord loveth he chasteneth, and scourgeth every son whom he receiveth. If ye endure chastening, God dealeth with you as with sons; for what son is he whom the father chasteneth not? But if ye be without chastisement, whereof all are partakers, then are ye bastards, and not sons. Furthermore, we have had fathers of our flesh, which corrected us; and we gave them reverence: shall we not much rather be in subjection unto the Father of spirits, and live? For they verily for a few days chastened us after their own pleasure; but he for our profit, that we might be partakers of his holiness. Now no chastening for the present seemeth to be joyous, but grievous: nevertheless, afterward it yieldeth the peaceable fruit of righteousness unto them which are exercised thereby.' (Heb. xii. 5–11.)

'Oh, Mamma!' said Emily, 'these are pretty verses; and when I am able, I will learn them, and I hope I shall never forget them.'

Mrs Fairchild then knelt down by Emily's bed, and prayed; after which, she sung a hymn. This prayer and hymn I shall put down in this place, that you may make use of it at any time when you may have been tempted to do any thing wrong, trusting that God could not see it.

MARY SHELLEY
(1797–1851)

Born in Somers Town, London, Mary Wollstonecraft Godwin, the only daughter of Mary Wollstonecraft and the philosopher William Godwin, lived with the consciousness of having been the cause of her mother's death. In 1801 her father married Mary Jane Clairmont, and Mary was brought up with Mary Wollstonecraft's illegitimate daugher Fanny Imlay, the second Mrs Godwin's children Charles and Clara Jane (later known as Claire) Clairmont, and the Godwins' son William. She was educated and encouraged in her literary interests by her father, and in 1808 her step-mother's publishing firm brought out her version of a comic song, *Mounseer Nongtongpaw; or the Discoveries of John Bull in a Trip to Paris*. Amid a busy and intellectually competitive family life she revered the memory of her mother, and her relationship with the poet Percy Bysshe Shelley, whom she eventually married, was emotionally and intellectually anchored in their admiration for Wollstonecraft's work. The two first met in 1812, when Percy Shelley became a friend of William Godwin, but they saw little of each other at this stage, and Mary spent much of the next two years visiting friends near Dundee. Only two months after her return to London in May 1814, however, she and Shelley (who was still married to Harriet Westbrook, with whom he had two infant children) eloped to the Continent, taking with them her half-sister Claire Clairmont. Her father was outraged, and refused to receive her when they returned to England after a few months spent travelling in France and the Rhineland.

Their first child, born prematurely in February 1815, when Mary Godwin was 17, died after a few days. After the birth of a second child, William, in 1816 the Shelleys, with Claire Clairmont, visited Geneva, where Claire's lover, Byron, was living. When Shelley's wife Harriet committed suicide in December 1816 (soon after the suicide of Mary Wollstonecraft's first daughter, Fanny Imlay), Mary married Shelley, and the following year gave birth to a daughter, Clara Everina. The years spent in Italy were unsettled (the Shelley household moved between Rome, Naples, Venice, Florence, Leghorn, Pisa, and Lerici), but intellectually and artistically stimulating: Mary Shelley wrote a second novel, *Mathilda*, which was rejected by her father, and two plays. The rift with Godwin caused continued pain, and Shelley's estranged father had reduced his allowance, making their finances at best unstable. Their daughter Clara died in 1817, followed by their son William the following year; only their fourth child, Percy Florence, born in 1819, survived infancy. The Shelleys' marriage was overshadowed by grief, mistrust, and jealousy: Claire Clairmont, and a succession of other emotionally engaging women, enervated and alienated Mary. It was traumatically ended in 1822 by Shelley's death in a sailing accident. Close to her twenty-fifth birthday, Mary Shelley faced an isolated and impecunious widowhood. She returned to London in 1823 and continued writing, partly to make money to support herself and her son. As a result she was able to send Percy Florence to Harrow and Cambridge, and saw him succeed to his grandfather's title and fortune in 1844. Six years later, at the age of 53, she died of a brain tumour.

Mary Shelley's account of her travels in 1814 was published, with contributions by Percy Shelley, in 1817 as *History of a Six Weeks Tour*. In the summer of 1816, on Lake Geneva, she began writing *Frankenstein; or the Modern Prometheus*, published anonymously in 1818. Dedicated to Godwin and with a preface written by her husband, it was reviewed as a work of the 'philosophical' school, its author assumed without question to be male. In addition to long works of fiction, including historical novels and the futuristic tale *The Last Man* (1826), she specialized in writing in the relatively new and lucrative popular form of the short tale, her work appearing frequently in periodicals and in the new fashionable embellished and illustrated annuals such as *The Keepsake* and *Heath's Book of Beauty*. She also contributed to Lardner's *Cabinet Cyclopaedia*. In 1839 she published an edition of Shelley's *Poetical Works* with year-by-year accounts of interests, reading, and composition: it kept his work alive. Soon afterwards she edited his *Essays, Letters from Abroad, Translations and Fragments* (1840), and published her own *Rambles in Germany and Italy* in 1844.

Two chapters from *Frankenstein*, in the 1818 edition, are included here, followed by the short story 'The Mortal Immortal', first published in *The Keepsake for 1834* (the text given here). At the start of the chapters from *Frankenstein*, the 17-year-old Victor Frankenstein has left his family in Geneva to study at the University of Ingoldstadt. He has long been interested in the natural sciences, but instead of being acquainted with the latest scientific advances he has been immersed in the work of Renaissance occultists and seekers after the elixir of life. Accordingly he is mocked by one of his professors, M. Krempe, but, treated more sympathetically by another, M. Waldman, he enters seriously upon his studies. At home he has left his recently bereaved and elderly father, two younger brothers, his close friend Henry Clerval, and his cousin Elizabeth Lavenza, whom he hopes to marry. The unhallowed investigation of the sources of life, and Victor Frankenstein's early interest in the writings of alchemists and occultists, are subjects continued in a different vein in the short story 'The Mortal Immortal'. Mary Shelley draws not only on her own earlier work and on the scientific debates which fascinated her and Shelley, but also on her father's novel *St Leon* (1799), in which the narrator wins physical immortality at the expense of his dearest domestic and social ties. The loneliness and emptiness of the sole survivor is a situation explored many times in Mary Shelley's work after her husband's death. The story of Bertha, attached to an ever-youthful husband, also allows Shelley to explore the progress of female physical ageing, and the psychological effects it has on women whose identity has depended on their beauty.

From *Frankenstein* (1818)

Chapter III

From this day natural philosophy, and particularly chemistry, in the most comprehensive sense of the term, became nearly my sole occupation.* I read with ardour those works, so full of genius and discrimination, which modern inquirers have written on these subjects. I attended the lectures, and cultivated the acquaintance, of the men of science of the university;* and I found even in M. Krempe a great deal of sound sense and real information, combined, it is true, with a repulsive physiognomy and manners, but not on that account the less valuable. In M. Waldman I found a true friend.* His gentleness was never tinged by dogmatism; and his instructions were given with an air of frankness and good nature, that banished every idea of pedantry. It was, perhaps, the amiable character of this man that inclined me more to that branch of natural philosophy which he professed, than an intrinsic love for the science itself. But this state of mind had place only in the first steps towards knowledge: the more fully I entered into the science, the more exclusively I pursued it for its own sake. That application, which at first had been a matter of duty and resolution, now became so ardent and eager, that the stars often disappeared in the light of morning whilst I was yet engaged in my laboratory.

As I applied so closely, it may be easily conceived that I improved rapidly. My ardour was indeed the astonishment of the students; and my proficiency, that of the masters. Professor Krempe often asked me, with a sly smile, how Cornelius Agrippa went on?* whilst M. Waldman expressed the most heartfelt exultation in my progress. Two years passed in this manner, during which I paid no visit to Geneva, but was engaged, heart and soul, in the pursuit of some discoveries, which I hoped to make. None but those who have experienced them can conceive of the enticements of science. In other studies you go as far as others have gone before you, and there is nothing more to know; but in a scientific pursuit there is continual food for discovery and wonder. A mind of moderate capacity, which closely pursues one study, must infallibly arrive at great proficiency in that study; and I, who continually sought the attainment of one object of pursuit, and was solely wrapt up in this, improved so rapidly, that, at the end of two years, I made some discoveries in the improvement of some chemical instruments, which procured me great esteem and admiration at the university. When I had arrived at this point, and had become as well acquainted with the theory and practice of natural philosophy as depended on the lessons of any of the professors at Ingolstadt, my residence there being no longer conducive to my improvements, I thought of returning to my friends and my native town, when an incident happened that protracted my stay.

One of the phænomena which had peculiarly attracted my attention was the structure of the human frame, and, indeed, any animal endued with life. Whence, I often asked myself, did the principle of life proceed? It was a bold question, and one which has ever been considered as a mystery; yet with how many things are we upon the brink of becoming acquainted, if cowardice or carelessness did not restrain our inquiries? I revolved these circumstances in my mind, and determined thenceforth to apply myself more particularly to those branches of natural philosophy which relate to physiology. Unless I had been animated by an almost supernatural enthusiasm, my application to this study would have been irksome, and almost intolerable. To examine the causes of life, we must first have recourse to death. I became acquainted with the science of anatomy: but this was not sufficient; I must also observe the natural decay and corruption of the human body. In my education my father had taken the greatest precautions that my mind should be impressed with no supernatural horrors. I do not ever remember to have trembled at a tale of superstition, or to have feared the apparition of a spirit. Darkness had no effect upon my fancy; and a church-yard was to me merely the receptacle of bodies deprived of life, which, from being the seat of beauty and strength, had become food for the worm. Now I was led to examine the cause and progress of this decay, and forced to spend days and nights in vaults and charnel houses. My attention was fixed upon every object the most insupportable to the delicacy of the human feelings. I saw how the fine form of man was degraded and wasted; I beheld the corruption of death succeed to the blooming cheek of life; I saw how the worm inherited the wonders of the eye and brain. I paused, examining and analysing all the minutiæ of causation, as exemplified in the change from life to death, and death to life, until from the midst of this darkness a sudden light broke in upon me—a light so brilliant and wondrous, yet so simple, that while I became dizzy with the immensity of the prospect which it illustrated, I was surprised that among so many men of genius, who had directed their inquiries towards the same science, that I alone should be reserved to discover so astonishing a secret.

Remember, I am not recording the vision of a madman. The sun does not more certainly shine in the heavens, than that which I now affirm is true. Some miracle might have produced it, yet the stages of the discovery were distinct and probable. After days and nights of incredible labour and fatigue, I succeeded in discovering the cause of generation and life; nay, more, I became myself capable of bestowing animation upon lifeless matter.

The astonishment which I had at first experienced on this discovery soon gave place to delight and rapture. After so much time spent in painful labour, to arrive at once at the summit of my desires, was the most gratifying consummation of my toils. But this discovery was so great and overwhelming, that all the steps by which I had been progressively led to it were obliterated, and I beheld only the result. What had been the study and desire of the wisest men since the creation of the world, was now within my grasp. Not that, like a magic scene, it all opened upon me at once: the information I had obtained was of a nature rather to direct my endeavours so soon as I should point them towards the object of my search, than to exhibit that object already accomplished. I was like the Arabian who had been buried with the dead, and found a passage to life aided only by one glimmering, and seemingly ineffectual, light.*

I see by your eagerness, and the wonder and hope which your eyes express, my friend,* that you expect to be informed of the secret with which I am acquainted; that cannot be: listen patiently until the end of my story, and you will easily perceive why I am reserved upon that subject. I will not lead you on, unguarded and ardent as I then was, to your destruction and infallible misery. Learn from me, if not by my precepts, at least by my example, how dangerous is the acquirement of knowledge, and how much happier that man is who believes his native town to be the world, than he who aspires to become greater than his nature will allow.

When I found so astonishing a power placed within my hands, I hesitated a long time concerning the manner in which I should employ it. Although I possessed the capacity of bestowing animation, yet to prepare a frame for the reception of it, with all its intricacies of fibres, muscles, and veins, still remained a work of inconceivable difficulty and labour. I doubted at first whether I should attempt the creation of a being like myself or one of simpler organization; but my imagination was too much exalted by my first success to permit me to doubt of my ability to give life to an animal as complex and wonderful as man. The materials at present within my command hardly appeared adequate to so arduous an undertaking; but I doubted not that I should ultimately succeed. I prepared myself for a multitude of reverses; my operations might be incessantly baffled, and at last my work be imperfect: yet, when I considered the improvement which every day takes place in science and mechanics, I was encouraged to hope my present attempts would at least lay the foundations of future success. Nor could I consider the magnitude and complexity of my plan as any argument of its impracticability. It was with these feelings that I began the creation of an human being. As the minuteness of the parts formed a great hindrance to my speed, I resolved, contrary to my first intention, to make the being of a gigantic stature; that is to say, about eight feet in height, and proportionably large. After having formed this determination, and having spent some months in successfully collecting and arranging my materials, I began.

No one can conceive the variety of feelings which bore me onwards, like a hurricane, in the first enthusiasm of success. Life and death appeared to me ideal bounds, which I should first break through, and pour a torrent of light into our dark world. A new species would bless me as its creator and source; many happy and excellent natures would owe their being to me. No father could claim the gratitude of his child so completely as I should deserve theirs. Pursuing these reflections, I thought, that if I could bestow animation upon lifeless matter, I might in process of time (although I now found it impossible) renew life where death had apparently devoted the body to corruption.

These thoughts supported my spirits, while I pursued my undertaking with unremitting ardour. My cheek had grown pale with study, and my person had become emaciated with confinement. Sometimes, on the very brink of certainty, I failed; yet still I clung to the hope which the next day or the next hour might realize. One secret which I alone possessed was the hope to which I had dedicated myself; and the moon gazed on my midnight labours, while, with unrelaxed and breathless eagerness, I pursued nature to her hiding places. Who shall conceive the horrors of my secret toil, as I dabbled among the unhallowed damps of the grave, or tortured the living animal to animate the lifeless clay? My limbs now tremble, and my eyes swim with the remembrance; but then a resistless, and almost frantic impulse, urged me forward; I seemed to have lost all soul or sensation but for this one pursuit. It was indeed but a passing trance, that only made me feel with renewed acuteness so soon as, the unnatural stimulus ceasing to operate, I had returned to my old habits. I collected bones from charnel houses; and disturbed, with profane fingers, the tremendous secrets of the human frame. In a solitary chamber, or rather cell, at the top of the house, and separated from all the other apartments by a gallery and staircase, I kept my workshop of filthy creation; my eyeballs were starting from their sockets in attending to the details of my employment. The dissecting room and the slaughter-house furnished many of my materials; and often did my human nature turn with loathing from my occupation, whilst, still urged on by an eagerness which perpetually increased, I brought my work near to a conclusion.

The summer months passed while I was thus engaged, heart and soul, in one pursuit. It was a most beautiful season; never did the fields bestow a more plentiful harvest, or the vines yield a more luxuriant vintage: but my eyes were insensible to the charms of nature. And the same feelings which made me neglect the scenes around me caused me also to forget those friends who were so many miles absent, and whom I had not seen for so long a time. I knew my silence disquieted them; and I well remembered the words of my father: 'I know that while you are pleased with yourself, you will think of us with affection, and we shall hear regularly from you. You must pardon me, if I regard any interruption in your correspondence as a proof that your other duties are equally neglected.'

I knew well therefore what would be my father's feelings; but I could not tear my thoughts from my employment, loathsome in itself, but which had taken an irresistible hold of my imagination. I wished, as it were, to procrastinate all that related to my feelings of affection until the great object, which swallowed up every habit of my nature, should be completed.

I then thought that my father would be unjust if he ascribed my neglect to vice, or faultiness on my part; but I am now convinced that he was justified in conceiving that I should not be altogether free from blame. A human being in perfection ought always to preserve a calm and peaceful mind, and never to allow passion or a transitory desire to disturb his tranquillity. I do not think that the pursuit of knowledge is an exception to this rule. If the study to which you apply yourself has a tendency to weaken your affections, and to destroy your taste for those simple pleasures in which no alloy can possibly mix, then that study is certainly unlawful, that is to say, not befitting the human mind. If this rule were always observed; if no man allowed any pursuit whatsoever to interfere with the tranquillity of his domestic affections, Greece had not been enslaved; Cæsar would have spared his country; America would have been discovered more gradually; and the empires of Mexico and Peru had not been destroyed.*

But I forget that I am moralizing in the most interesting part of my tale: and your looks remind me to proceed.

My father made no reproach in his letters; and only took notice of my silence by inquiring into my occupations more particularly than before. Winter, spring, and summer, passed away during my labours; but I did not watch the blossom or the expanding leaves—sights which before always yielded me supreme delight, so deeply was I engrossed in my occupation. The leaves of that year had withered before my work drew near to a close; and now every day shewed me more plainly how well I had succeeded. But my enthusiasm was checked by my anxiety, and I appeared rather like one doomed by slavery to toil in the mines, or any other unwholesome trade, than an artist occupied by his favourite employment. Every night I was oppressed by a slow fever, and I became nervous to a most painful degree; a disease that I regretted the more because I had hitherto enjoyed most excellent health, and had always boasted of the firmness of my nerves. But I believed that exercise and amusement would soon drive away such symptoms; and I promised myself both of these, when my creation should be complete.

Chapter IV

It was on a dreary night of November, that I beheld the accomplishment of my toils. With an anxiety that almost amounted to agony, I collected the instruments of life around me, that I might infuse a spark of being into the lifeless thing that lay at my feet.* It was already one in the morning; the rain pattered dismally against the panes, and my candle was nearly burnt out, when, by the glimmer of the half-extinguished light, I saw the dull yellow eye of the creature open; it breathed hard, and a convulsive motion agitated its limbs.

How can I describe my emotions at this catastrophe, or how delineate the wretch whom with such infinite pains and care I had endeavoured to form? His limbs were in proportion, and I had selected his features as beautiful. Beautiful!—Great God! His yellow skin scarcely covered the work of muscles and arteries beneath; his hair was of a lustrous black, and flowing; his teeth of a pearly whiteness; but these luxuriances only formed a more horrid contrast with his watery eyes, that seemed almost of the same colour as the dun white sockets in which they were set, his shrivelled complexion, and straight black lips.

The different accidents of life are not so changeable as the feelings of human nature. I had worked hard for nearly two years, for the sole purpose of infusing life into an inanimate body. For this I had deprived myself of rest and health. I had desired it with an ardour that far exceeded moderation; but now that I had finished, the beauty of the dream vanished, and breathless horror and disgust filled my heart. Unable to endure the aspect of the being I had created, I rushed out of the room, and continued a long time traversing my bed-chamber, unable to compose my mind to sleep. At length lassitude succeeded to the tumult I had before endured; and I threw myself on the bed in my clothes, endeavouring to seek a few moments of forgetfulness. But it was in vain: I slept indeed, but I was disturbed by the wildest dreams. I thought I saw Elizabeth, in the bloom of health, walking in the streets of Ingolstadt. Delighted and surprised, I embraced her; but as I imprinted the first kiss on her lips, they became livid with the hue of death; her features appeared to change, and I thought that I held the corpse of my dead mother in my arms; a shroud enveloped her form, and I saw the grave-worms crawling in the folds of the flannel. I started from my sleep with horror; a cold dew covered my forehead, my teeth chattered, and every limb became convulsed; when, by the dim and yellow light of the moon, as it forced its way though the window-shutters, I beheld the wretch—the miserable monster whom I had created. He held up the curtain of the bed; and his eyes, if eyes they may be called, were fixed on me. His jaws opened, and he muttered some inarticulate sounds, while a grin wrinkled his cheeks. He might have spoken, but I did not hear; one hand was stretched out, seemingly to detain me, but I escaped, and rushed down stairs. I took refuge in the courtyard belonging to the house which I inhabited; where I remained during the rest of the night, walking up and down in the greatest agitation, listening attentively, catching and fearing each sound as if it were to announce the approach of the demoniacal corpse to which I had so miserably given life.

Oh! no mortal could support the horror of that countenance. A mummy again endued with animation could not be so hideous as that wretch. I had gazed on him while unfinished; he was ugly then; but when those muscles and joints were rendered capable of motion, it became a thing such as even Dante could not have conceived.*

I passed the night wretchedly. Sometimes my pulse beat so quickly and hardly, that I felt the palpitation of every artery; at others, I nearly sank to the ground through languor and extreme weakness. Mingled with this horror, I felt the bitterness of disappointment: dreams that had been my food and pleasant rest for so long a space, were now become a hell to me; and the change was so rapid, the overthrow so complete!

Morning, dismal and wet, at length dawned, and discovered to my sleepless and aching eyes the church of Ingolstadt, its white steeple and clock, which indicated the sixth hour. The porter opened the gates of the court, which had that night been my asylum, and I issued into the streets, pacing them with quick steps, as if I sought to avoid the wretch whom I feared every turning of the street would present to my view. I did not dare return to the apartment which I inhabited, but felt impelled to hurry on, although wetted by the rain, which poured from a black and comfortless sky.

I continued walking in this manner for some time, endeavouring, by bodily exercise, to ease the load that weighed upon my mind. I traversed the streets, without any clear conception of where I was, or what I was doing. My heart palpitated in the sickness of fear; and I hurried on with irregular steps, not daring to look about me:

> Like one who, on a lonely road,
>   Doth walk in fear and dread,
> And, having once turn'd round, walks on,
>   And turns no more his head;
> Because he knows a frightful fiend
>   Doth close behind him tread.*

The Mortal Immortal: A Tale (1834)

July 16, 1833.—This is a memorable anniversary for me; on it I complete my three hundred and twenty-third year!

The Wandering Jew?—certainly not.* More than eighteen centuries have passed over his head. In comparison with him, I am a very young Immortal.

Am I, then, immortal? This is a question which I have asked myself, by day and night, for now three hundred and three years, and yet cannot answer it. I detected a gray hair amidst my brown locks this very day—that surely signifies decay. Yet it may have remained concealed there for three hundred years—for some persons have become entirely white-headed before twenty years of age.

I will tell my story, and my reader shall judge for me. I will tell my story, and so contrive to pass some few hours of a long eternity, become so wearisome to me. For ever! Can it be? to live for ever! I have heard of enchantments, in which the victims were plunged into a deep sleep, to wake, after a hundred years, as fresh as ever: I have heard of the Seven Sleepers—thus to be immortal would not be so burthensome:* but, oh! the weight of never-ending time—the tedious passage of the still-succeeding hours! How happy was the fabled Nourjahad!* —But to my task.

All the world has heard of Cornelius Agrippa.* His memory is as immortal as his arts have made me. All the world has also heard of his scholar, who, unawares, raised the foul fiend during his master's absence, and was destroyed by him. The report, true or false, of this accident, was attended with many inconveniences to the renowned philosopher. All his scholars at once deserted him—his servants disappeared. He had no one near him to put coals on his ever-burning fires while he slept, or to attend to the changeful colours of his medicines while he studied. Experiment after experiment failed, because one pair of hands was insufficient to complete them: the dark spirits laughed at him for not being able to retain a single mortal in his service.

I was then very young—very poor—and very much in love. I had been for about a year the pupil of Cornelius, though I was absent when this accident took place. On my return, my friends implored me not to return to the alchymist's abode. I trembled as I listened to the dire tale they told; I required no second warning; and when Cornelius came and offered me a purse of gold if I would remain under his roof, I felt as if Satan himself tempted me. My teeth chattered—my hair stood on end:—I ran off as fast as my trembling knees would permit.

My failing steps were directed whither for two years they had every evening been attracted,—a gently bubbling spring of pure living waters, beside which lingered a dark-haired girl, whose beaming eyes were fixed on the path I was accustomed each night to tread. I cannot remember the hour when I did not love Bertha; we had been neighbours and playmates from infancy—her parents, like mine, were of humble life, yet respectable—our attachment had been a source of pleasure to them. In an evil hour, a malignant fever carried off both her father and mother, and Bertha became an orphan. She would have found a home beneath my paternal roof, but, unfortunately, the old lady of the near castle, rich, childless, and solitary, declared her intention to adopt her. Henceforth Bertha was clad in silk—inhabited a marble palace—and was looked on as being highly favoured by fortune. But in her new situation among her new associates, Bertha remained true to the friend of her humbler days; she often visited the cottage of my father, and when forbidden to go thither, she would stray towards the neighbouring wood, and meet me beside its shady fountain.

She often declared that she owed no duty to her new protectress equal in sanctity to that which bound us. Yet still I was too poor to marry, and she grew weary of being tormented on my account. She had a haughty but an impatient spirit, and grew angry at the obstacles that prevented our union. We met now after an absence, and she had been sorely beset while I was away; she complained bitterly, and almost reproached me for being poor. I replied hastily,—

'I am honest, if I am poor!—were I not, I might soon become rich!'

This exclamation produced a thousand questions. I feared to shock her by owning the truth, but she drew it from me; and then, casting a look of disdain on me, she said—

'You pretend to love, and you fear to face the Devil for my sake!'

I protested that I had only dreaded to offend her;—while she dwelt on the magnitude of the reward that I should receive. Thus encouraged—shamed by her—led on by love and hope, laughing at my late fears, with quick steps and a light heart, I returned to accept the offers of the alchymist, and was instantly installed in my office.

A year passed away. I became possessed of no insignificant sum of money. Custom had banished my fears. In spite of the most painful vigilance, I had never detected the trace of a cloven foot; nor was the studious silence of our abode ever disturbed by demoniac howls. I still continued my stolen interviews with Bertha, and Hope dawned on me—Hope—but not perfect joy; for Bertha fancied that love and security were enemies, and her pleasure was to divide them in my bosom. Though true of heart, she was somewhat of a coquette in manner; and I was jealous as a Turk.* She slighted me in a thousand ways, yet would never acknowledge herself to be in the wrong. She would drive me mad with anger, and then force me to beg her pardon. Sometimes she fancied that I was not sufficiently submissive, and then she had some story of a rival, favoured by her protectress. She was surrounded by silk-clad youths—the rich and gay—What chance had the sad-robed scholar of Cornelius compared with these?

On one occasion, the philosopher made such large demands upon my time, that I was unable to meet her as I was wont. He was engaged in some mighty work, and I was forced to remain, day and night, feeding his furnaces and watching his chemical preparations. Bertha waited for me in vain at the fountain. Her haughty spirit fired at this neglect; and when at last I stole out during the few short minutes allotted to me for slumber, and hoped to be consoled by her, she received me with disdain, dismissed me in scorn, and vowed that any man should possess her hand rather than he who could not be in two places at once for her sake. She would be revenged!—And truly she was. In my dingy retreat I heard that she had been hunting, attended by Albert Hoffer. Albert Hoffer was favoured by her protectress, and the three passed in cavalcade before my smoky window. Methought that they mentioned my name—it was followed by a laugh of derision, as her dark eyes glanced contemptuously towards my abode.

Jealousy, with all its venom, and all its misery, entered my breast. Now I shed a torrent of tears, to think that I should never call her mine; and, anon, I imprecated a thousand curses on her inconstancy. Yet, still I must stir the fires of the alchymist, still attend on the changes of his unintelligible medicines.

Cornelius had watched for three days and nights, nor closed his eyes. The progress of his alembics was slower than he expected:* in spite of his anxiety, sleep weighed upon his eyelids. Again and again he threw off drowsiness with more than human energy; again and again it stole away his senses. He eyed his crucibles wistfully. 'Not ready yet,' he murmured; 'will another night pass before the work is accomplished? Winzy, you are vigilant—you are faithful—you have slept, my boy—you slept last night. Look at that glass vessel. The liquid it contains is of a soft rose-colour: the moment it begins to change its hue, awaken me—till then I may close my eyes. First, it will turn white, and then emit golden flashes; but wait not till then; when the rose-colour fades, rouse me.' I scarcely heard the last words, muttered, as they were, in sleep. Even then he did not quite yield to nature. 'Winzy, my boy,' he again said, 'do not touch the vessel—do not put it to your lips; it is a philter—a philter to cure love; you would not cease to love your Bertha—beware to drink!'

And he slept. His venerable head sunk on his breast, and I scarce heard his regular breathing. For a few minutes I watched the vessel—the rosy hue of the liquid remained unchanged. Then my thoughts wandered—they visited the fountain, and dwelt on a thousand charming scenes never to be renewed—never! Serpents and adders were in my heart as the word 'Never!' half formed itself on my lips. False girl!—false and cruel! Never more would she smile on me as that evening she smiled on Albert. Worthless, detested woman! I would not remain unrevenged—she should see Albert expire at her feet—she should die beneath my vengeance. She had smiled in disdain and triumph—she knew my wretchedness and her power. Yet what power had she?—the power of exciting my hate—my utter scorn—my—oh, all but indifference! Could I attain that—could I regard her with careless eyes, transferring my rejected love to one fairer and more true, that were indeed a victory!

A bright flash darted before my eyes. I had forgotten the medicine of the adept; I gazed on it with wonder: flashes of admirable beauty, more bright than those which the diamond emits when the sun's rays are on it, glanced from the surface of the liquid; an odour the most fragrant and grateful stole over my sense; the vessel seemed one globe of living radiance, lovely to the eye, and most inviting to the taste. The first thought, instinctively inspired by the grosser sense, was, I will—I must drink. I raised the vessel to my lips. 'It will cure me of love—of torture!' Already I had quaffed half of the most delicious liquor ever tasted by the palate of man, when the philosopher stirred. I started—I dropped the glass—the fluid flamed and glanced along the floor, while I felt Cornelius's gripe at my throat, as he shrieked aloud, 'Wretch! you have destroyed the labour of my life!'

The philosopher was totally unaware that I had drunk any portion of his drug. His idea was, and I gave a tacit assent to it, that I had raised the vessel from curiosity, and that, frighted at its brightness, and the flashes of intense light it gave forth, I had let it fall. I never undeceived him. The fire of the medicine was quenched—the fragrance died away—he grew calm, as a philosopher should under the heaviest trials, and dismissed me to rest.

I will not attempt to describe the sleep of glory and bliss which bathed my soul in paradise during the remaining hours of that memorable night. Words would be faint and shallow types of my enjoyment, or of the gladness that possessed my bosom when I woke. I trod air—my thoughts were heaven, and my inheritance upon it was to be one trance of delight. 'This it is to be cured of love,' I thought; 'I will see Bertha this day, and she will find her lover cold and regardless; too happy to be disdainful, yet how utterly indifferent to her!'

The hours danced away. The philosopher, secure that he had once succeeded, and believing that he might again, began to concoct the same medicine once more. He was shut up with his books and drugs, and I had a holiday. I dressed myself with care; I looked in an old but polished shield, which served me for a mirror; methought my good looks had wonderfully improved. I hurried beyond the precincts of the town, joy in my soul, the beauty of heaven and earth around me.

I turned my steps towards the castle—I could look on its lofty turrets with lightness of heart, for I was cured of love. My Bertha saw me afar off, as I came up the avenue. I know not what sudden impulse animated her bosom, but at the sight, she sprung with a light fawn-like bound down the marble steps, and was hastening towards me. But I had been perceived by another person. The old high-born hag, who called herself her protectress, and was her tyrant, had seen me, also; she hobbled, panting, up the terrace; a page, as ugly as herself, held up her train, and fanned her as she hurried along, and stopped my fair girl with a 'How, now, my bold mistress? whither so fast? Back to your cage—hawks are abroad!'

Bertha clasped her hands—her eyes were still bent on my approaching figure. I saw the contest. How I abhorred the old crone who checked the kind impulses of my Bertha's softening heart. Hitherto, respect for her rank had caused me to avoid the lady of the castle; now I disdained such trivial considerations. I was cured of love, and lifted above all human fears; I hastened forwards, and soon reached the terrace. How lovely Bertha looked! her eyes flashing fire, her cheeks glowing with impatience and anger, she was a thousand times more graceful and charming than ever—I no longer loved—Oh! no, I adored—worshipped—idolized her!

She had that morning been persecuted, with more than usual vehemence, to consent to an immediate marriage with my rival. She was reproached with the encouragement that she had shown him—she was threatened with being turned out of doors with disgrace and shame. Her proud spirit rose in arms at the threat; but when she remembered the scorn that she had heaped upon me, and how, perhaps, she had thus lost one whom she now regarded as her only friend, she wept with remorse and rage. At that moment I appeared. 'O, Winzy!' she exclaimed, 'take me to your mother's cot; swiftly let me leave the detested luxuries and wretchedness of this noble dwelling—take me to poverty and happiness.'

I clasped her in my arms with transport. The old lady was speechless with fury, and broke forth into invective only when we were far on our road to my natal cottage. My mother received the fair fugitive, escaped from a gilt cage to nature and liberty, with tenderness and joy; my father, who loved her, welcomed her heartily; it was a day of rejoicing, which did not need the addition of the celestial potion of the alchymist to steep me in delight.

Soon after this eventful day, I became the husband of Bertha. I ceased to be the scholar of Cornelius, but I continued his friend. I always felt grateful to him for having, unawares, procured me that delicious draught of a divine elixir, which, instead of curing me of love (sad cure! solitary and joyless remedy for evils which seem blessings to the memory), had inspired me with courage and resolution, thus winning for me an inestimable treasure in my Bertha.

I often called to mind that period of trance-like inebriation with wonder. The drink of Cornelius had not fulfilled the task for which he affirmed that it had been prepared, but its effects were more potent and blissful than words can express. They had faded by degrees, yet they lingered long—and painted life in hues of splendour. Bertha often wondered at my lightness of heart and unaccustomed gaiety; for, before, I had been rather serious, or even sad, in my disposition. She loved me the better for my cheerful temper, and our days were winged by joy.

Five years afterwards I was suddenly summoned to the bedside of the dying Cornelius. He had sent for me in haste, conjuring my instant presence. I found him stretched on his pallet, enfeebled even to death; all of life that yet remained animated his piercing eyes, and they were fixed on a glass vessel, full of a roseate liquid.

'Behold,' he said, in a broken and inward voice, 'the vanity of human wishes! a second time my hopes are about to be crowned, a second time they are destroyed. Look at that liquor—you remember five years ago I had prepared the same, with the same success;—then, as now, my thirsting lips expected to taste the immortal elixir—you dashed it from me! and at present it is too late.'

He spoke with difficulty, and fell back on his pillow. I could not help saying,—

'How, revered master, can a cure for love restore you to life?'

A faint smile gleamed across his face as I listened earnestly to his scarcely intelligible answer.

'A cure for love and for all things—the Elixir of Immortality. Ah! if now I might drink, I should live for ever!'

As he spoke, a golden flash gleamed from the fluid; a well-remembered fragrance stole over the air; he raised himself, all weak as he was—strength seemed miraculously to re-enter his frame—he stretched forth his hand—a loud explosion startled me—a ray of fire shot up from the elixir, and the glass vessel which contained it was shivered to atoms! I turned my eyes towards the philosopher; he had fallen back—his eyes were glassy—his features rigid—he was dead!

But I lived, and was to live for ever! So said the unfortunate alchymist, and for a few days I believed his words. I remembered the glorious drunkenness that had followed my stolen draught. I reflected on the change I had felt in my frame—in my soul. The bounding elasticity of the one—the buoyant lightness of the other. I surveyed myself in a mirror, and could perceive no change in my features during the space of the five years which had elapsed. I remembered the radiant hues and grateful scent of that delicious beverage—worthy the gift it was capable of bestowing—I was, then, IMMORTAL!

A few days after I laughed at my credulity. The old proverb, that 'a prophet is least regarded in his own country,'* was true with respect to me and my defunct master. I loved him as a man—I respected him as a sage—but I derided the notion that he could command the powers of darkness, and laughed at the superstitious fears with which he was regarded by the vulgar. He was a wise philosopher, but had no acquaintance with any spirits but those clad in flesh and blood. His science was simply human; and human science, I soon persuaded myself, could never conquer nature's laws so far as to imprison the soul for ever within its carnal habitation. Cornelius had brewed a soul-refreshing drink—more inebriating than wine— sweeter and more fragrant than any fruit: it possessed probably strong medicinal powers, imparting gladness to the heart and vigor to the limbs; but its effects would wear out; already were they diminished in my frame. I was a lucky fellow to have quaffed health and joyous spirits, and perhaps long life, at my master's hands; but my good fortune ended there: longevity was far different from immortality.

I continued to entertain this belief for many years. Sometimes a thought stole across me—Was the alchymist indeed deceived? But my habitual credence was, that I should meet the fate of all the children of Adam at my appointed time—a little late, but still at a natural age. Yet it was certain that I retained a wonderfully youthful look. I was laughed at for my vanity in consulting the mirror so often, but I consulted it in vain—my brow was untrenched—my cheeks—my eyes—my whole person continued as untarnished as in my twentieth year.

I was troubled. I looked at the faded beauty of Bertha—I seemed more like her son. By degrees our neighbours began to make similar observations, and I found at last that I went by the name of the Scholar bewitched. Bertha herself grew uneasy. She became jealous and peevish, and at length she began to question me. We had no children; we were all in all to each other; and though, as she grew older, her vivacious spirit became a little allied to ill-temper, and her beauty sadly diminished, I cherished her in my heart as the mistress I had idolized, the wife I had sought and won with such perfect love.

At last our situation became intolerable: Bertha was fifty—I twenty years of age. I had, in very shame, in some measure adopted the habits of a more advanced age; I no longer mingled in the dance among the young and gay, but my heart bounded along with them while I restrained my feet; and a sorry figure I cut among the Nestors of our village.* But before the time I mention, things were altered— we were universally shunned; we were—at least, I was—reported to have kept up an iniquitous acquaintance with some of my former master's supposed friends. Poor Bertha was pitied, but deserted. I was regarded with horror and detestation.

What was to be done? we sat by our winter fire—poverty had made itself felt, for none would buy the produce of my farm; and often I had been forced to journey twenty miles, to some place where I was not known, to dispose of our property. It is true we had saved something for an evil day—that day was come.

We sat by our lone fireside—the old-hearted youth and his anti-quated wife. Again Bertha insisted on knowing the truth; she recapitulated all she had ever heard said about me, and added her own observations. She conjured me to cast off the spell; she described how much more comely gray hairs were than my chestnut locks; she descanted on the reverence and respect due to age—how preferable to the slight regard paid to mere children: could I imagine that the despicable gifts of youth and good looks outweighed disgrace, hatred, and scorn? Nay, in the end I should be burnt as a dealer in the black art, while she, to whom I had not deigned to communicate any portion of my good fortune, might be stoned as my accomplice. At length she insinuated that I must share my secret with her, and bestow on her like benefits to those I myself enjoyed, or she would denounce me—and then she burst into tears.

Thus beset, methought it was the best way to tell the truth. I revealed it as tenderly as I could, and spoke only of a *very long life*, not of immorality—which representation, indeed, coincided best with my own ideas. When I ended, I rose and said.

'And now, my Bertha, will you denounce the lover of your youth?—You will not, I know. But it is too hard, my poor wife, that you should suffer from my ill-luck and the accursed arts of Cornelius. I will leave you—you have wealth enough, and friends will return in my absence. I will go; young as I seem, and strong as I am, I can work and gain my bread among strangers, unsuspected and unknown. I loved you in youth; God is my witness that I would not desert you in age, but that your safety and happiness require it.'

I took my cap and moved towards the door; in a moment Bertha's arms were round my neck, and her lips were pressed to mine. 'No, my husband, my Winzy,' she said, 'you shall not go alone—take me with you; we will remove from this place, and, as you say, among strangers we shall be unsuspected and safe. I am not so very old as quite to shame you, my Winzy; and I dare say the charm will soon wear off, and, with the blessing of God, you will become more elderly-looking, as is fitting; you shall not leave me.'

I returned the good soul's embrace heartily. 'I will not, my Bertha; but for your sake I had not thought of such a thing. I will be your true, faithful husband while you are spared to me, and do my duty by you to the last.'

The next day we prepared secretly for our emigration. We were obliged to make great pecuniary sacrifices—it could not be helped. We realised a sum sufficient, at least, to maintain us while Bertha lived; and, without saying adieu to any one, quitted our native country to take refuge in a remote part of western France.

It was a cruel thing to transport poor Bertha from her native village, and the friends of her youth, to a new country, new language, new customs. The strange secret of my destiny rendered this removal immaterial to me; but I compassionated her deeply, and was glad to perceive that she found compensation for her misfortunes in a variety of little ridiculous circumstances. Away from all tell-tale chroniclers, she sought to decrease the apparent disparity of our ages by a thousand feminine arts—rouge, youthful dress, and assumed juvenility of manner. I could not be angry—Did not I myself wear a mask? Why quarrel with hers, because it was less successful? I grieved deeply when I remembered that this was my Bertha, whom I had loved so fondly, and won with such transport—the dark-eyed, dark-haired girl, with smiles of enchanting archness and a step like a fawn—this mincing, simpering, jealous old woman. I should have revered her gray locks and withered cheeks; but thus!—It was my work, I knew; but I did not the less deplore this type of human weakness.

Her jealousy never slept. Her chief occupation was to discover that, in spite of outward appearances, I was myself growing old. I verily believe that the poor soul loved me truly in her heart, but never had woman so tormenting a mode of displaying fondness. She would discern wrinkles in my face and decrepitude in my walk, while I bounded along in youthful vigour, the youngest looking of twenty youths. I never dared address another woman: on one occasion, fancying that the belle of the village regarded me with favouring eyes, she bought me a gray wig. Her constant discourse among her acquaintances was, that though I looked so young, there was ruin at work within my frame; and she affirmed that the worst symptom about me was my apparent health. My youth was a disease, she said, and I ought at all times to prepare, if not for a sudden and awful death, at least to awake some morning white-headed, and bowed down with all the marks of advanced years. I let her talk—I often joined in her conjectures. Her warnings chimed in with my never-ceasing speculations concerning my state, and I took an earnest, though painful, interest in listening to all that her quick wit and excited imagination could say on the subject.

Why dwell on these minute circumstances? We lived on for many long years. Bertha became bed-rid and paralytic: I nursed her as a mother might a child. She grew peevish, and still harped upon one string—of how long I should survive her. It has ever been a source of consolation to me, that I performed my duty scrupulously towards her. She had been mine in youth, she was mine in age, and at last, when I heaped the sod over her corpse, I wept to feel that I had lost all that really bound me to humanity.

Since then how many have been my cares and woes, how few and empty my enjoyments! I pause here in my history—I will pursue it no further. A sailor without rudder or compass, tossed on a stormy sea—a traveller lost on a wide-spread heath, without landmark or star to guide him—such have I been: more lost, more hopeless than either. A nearing ship, a gleam from some far cot, may save them; but I have no beacon except the hope of death.

Death! mysterious, ill-visaged friend of weak humanity! Why alone of all mortals have you cast me from your sheltering fold? O, for the peace of the grave! the deep silence of the iron-bound tomb! that thought would cease to work in my brain, and my heart beat no more with emotions varied only by new forms of sadness!

Am I immortal? I return to my first question. In the first place, is it not more probable that the beverage of the alchymist was fraught rather with longevity than eternal life? Such is my hope. And then be it remembered, that I only drank *half* of the potion prepared by him. Was not the whole necessary to complete the charm? To have drained half the Elixir of Immortality is but to be half immortal— my Forever is thus truncated and null.

But again, who shall number the years of the half of eternity? I often try to imagine by what rule the infinite may be divided. Some-times I fancy age advancing upon me. One gray hair I have found. Fool! do I lament? Yes, the fear of age and death often creeps coldly into my heart; and the more I live, the more I dread death, even while I abhor life. Such an enigma is man—born to perish—when he wars, as I do, against the established laws of his nature.

But for this anomaly of feeling surely I might die: the medicine of the alchymist would not be proof against fire—sword—and the strangling waters. I have gazed upon the blue depths of many a placid lake, and the tumultuous rushing of many a mighty river, and have said, peace inhabits those waters; yet I have turned my steps away, to live yet another day. I have asked myself, whether suicide would be a crime in one to whom thus only the portals of the other world could be opened. I have done all, except presenting myself as a soldier or duellist, an object of destruction to my—no, *not* my fellow-mortals, and therefore I have shrunk away. They are not my fellows. The inextinguishable power of life in my frame, and their ephemeral existence, place us wide as the poles asunder. I could not raise a hand against the meanest or the most powerful among them.

Thus I have lived on for many a year—alone, and weary of myself—desirous of death, yet never dying—a mortal immortal. Neither ambition nor avarice can enter my mind, and the ardent love that gnaws at my heart, never to be returned—never to find an equal on which to expend itself—lives there only to torment me.

This very day I conceived a design by which I may end all— without self-slaughter, without making another man a Cain—an expedition, which mortal frame can never survive, even endued with the youth and strength that inhabits mine. Thus I shall put my immortality to the test, and rest for ever—or return, the wonder and benefactor of the human species.

Before I go, a miserable vanity has caused me to pen these pages. I would not die, and leave no name behind. Three centuries have passed since I quaffed the fatal beverage: another year shall not elapse before, encountering gigantic dangers—warring with the powers of frost in their home—beset by famine, toil, and tempest—I yield this body, too tenacious a cage for a soul which thirsts for freedom, to the destructive elements of air and water—or, if I survive, my name shall be recorded as one of the most famous among the sons of men; and, my task achieved, I shall adopt more resolute means, and, by scattering and annihilating the atoms that compose my frame, set at liberty the life imprisoned within, and so cruelly prevented from soaring from this dim earth to a sphere more congenial to its immortal essence.

MARY RUSSELL MITFORD
(1786–1855)

Born in Alresford, Hampshire, Mary Mitford was the only child of a spendthrift and gambler, Dr George Mitford, who came from a landed Northumberland family, had qualified as a doctor, and had married an heiress, Mary Russell. Her father having disposed of much of his wife's fortune, the 10-year-old Mary restored the family to (temporary) financial ease by winning £20,000 in the state lottery. From 1798 to 1802 she was sent to be educated by the French emigrée Mme St Quentin at her highly regarded new school in Hans Place, London (see also Sherwood and Landon). Meanwhile her parents had had a house built near Reading with their new money, and when the precocious Mary Mitford returned in 1802 she began an impressive course of reading and also began to write poetry. Later, during various visits to London, she made a range of literary and intellectual friends including the painters Sir William Elford and Benjamin Haydon, Thomas Moore, the editor of the *Morning Post*, James Perry, Lord Brougham, and Samuel Romilly. She was a great letter-writer and a lively conversationalist. By 1820 her father was in dire financial straits once again, and the family moved to a small cottage at Three Mile

Cross, Hampshire, where Mary Mitford lived for over thirty years. Made famous by her most successful work, *Our Village*, which Mitford dedicated to 'her beloved and venerable father', Three Mile Cross attracted many visitors, and Mitford became a celebrity here and during her visits to London. In London, in 1836, she met Elizabeth Barrett, and the two established a lively correspondence until Barrett's marriage to Robert Browning, of whom Mitford strongly disapproved (see Barrett, below). Barrett's sonnet 'To Mary Russell Mitford in her Garden' (1850) praises her as 'benignant' and natural, 'next to Nature's self in cheering the world's view'. Male connoisseurs of the literary woman seem to have found her less to their taste. William Bates's essay for *Maclise's Portrait Gallery*, for example, praises her as 'one of the most simple, graphic, and unaffected of our female writers',[1] but also devotes a paragraph to accounts of her 'roly-poly figure, most vexatiously dumpy' (this particular remark coming from her friend S. C. Hall).[2]

Despite Mitford's success, her father's improvidence prevented her accumulating what she earned, and she continued to write under financial pressure. The award of a government pension of £100 a year in 1837 helped, especially after the death of her father in 1842, when a subscription for her brought in £1,000. Her mother had died in 1829. In 1851 she moved to a cottage at Swallowfield, near Reading, where she died after a carriage accident, after being nearly incapacitated by rheumatism for several years.

Mitford published several collections of narrative and lyric poetry, including *Narrative Poems on the Female Character* (1813). After 1820, in an effort to make money to support herself and her parents, she tried her hand at tragedy, with some success: some of her plays were performed, *Julian* at Covent Garden in 1823 and *Rienzi* at Drury Lane in 1828. In 1854 she collected her plays as *The Dramatic Works of Mary Russell Mitford* (1854), for which she wrote an interesting Introduction. After the success of her most famous work, from which the stories included here come, she published other tales and sketches of rural and small town life, edited two series of American tales and the annual *Finden's Tableaux* (1838–41), and wrote for the *London Magazine* and the *Reading Mercury*. The most interesting of her later works is her three-volume *Recollections of a Literary Life: or, Books, Places and People* (1852).

The selection given here concentrates on *Our Village*, in its first form a

---

[1] *The Maclise Portrait-Gallery of 'Illustrious Literary Characters' with Memoirs Biographical, Critical, Bibliographical and Anecdotal Illustrative of the Literature of the Former Half of the Present Century by William Bates*, 2 vols. (London: Chatto and Windus, 1883), i. 66.

[2] Ibid. i. 65.

series of prose sketches of rural life which Mitford contributed to the *Lady's Magazine* in 1819, and which is credited with increasing the magazine's sales tenfold. Her stories told of village heroines and romances, natural history, odd and eccentric characters, rural incidents, cricket matches, and farm-labour, 'an attempt to delineate country scenery and country manners, as they exist in a small village in the south of England . . . written on the spot, and at the moment, and, in nearly every instance, with the closest and most resolute fidelity to the place and the people', as she declared in her Preface to the first collected edition (1824; the text followed here). Collections of them were published separately in 1824, 1826, 1828, 1830, and 1832, and there were numerous reprints and new selections throughout the century. Tributes from many of the leading literary figures of the day, including Felicia Hemans, Harriet Martineau, and Elizabeth Barrett, testified to their freshness, immediacy, and distinctive character. Elizabeth Barrett, feeling herself imprisoned by invalidism, thought *Our Village* liberating; it opened up to her, she wrote to Mitford in December 1840, flowers, grass, and summer. The stories were widely influential, one of the quiet literary revolutions of the nineteenth century. As she declared in the opening paragraph of the first tale, 'Our Village': 'Even in books I like a confined locality, and so do the critics when they talk of the unities. Nothing is so tiresome as to be whirled half over Europe at the chariot-wheels of a hero, to go to sleep at Vienna and awaken at Madrid; it produces a real fatigue, a weariness of spirit.' Instead she champions the novels of Austen and White's *Natural History of Selborne*, and in turn was a major influence on such works as Elizabeth Gaskell's *Cranford*.

In the two stories included here, the sequence 'Frost' and 'Thaw' and 'The First Primrose', the narrator of *Our Village* takes walks with her dog Mayflower and describes the people and things she encounters. A love of natural beauty is evident, and an interest in detail and idiosyncrasy which recalls Dorothy Wordsworth. The class-free socializings and investigations of Mayflower act as a way of drawing into the narrator's observations the antics of the working-class tearaway Jack Rapley and the hidden flowers of spring. All the narrator's sympathies are with this natural energy, but much of what she describes in society, such as the situation of little Lizzy, is circumscribed by decorum and convention. The men certainly seem to have a freer time of it, but in Mitford's world they are always regarded as secondary to the daily lives, loves, and foibles of women.

∼

'Frost' and 'Thaw' (1819)

FROST

January 23rd.—At noon to-day I and my white greyhound, May-flower, set out for a walk into a very beautiful world,—a sort of silent fairy-land,—a creation of that matchless magician the hoar-frost. There had been just snow enough to cover the earth and all its colours with one sheet of pure and uniform white, and just time enough since the snow had fallen to allow the hedges to be freed of their fleecy load, and clothed with a delicate coating of rime. The atmosphere was deliciously calm; soft, even mild, in spite of the thermometer; no perceptible air, but a stillness that might almost be felt; the sky, rather grey than blue, throwing out in bold relief the snow-covered roofs of our village* and the rimy trees that rise above them, and the sun shining dimly as through a veil, giving a pale fair light, like the moon, only brighter. There was a silence, too, that might become the moon, as we stood at our little gate looking up the quiet street; a sabbath-like pause of work and play, rare on a work-day; nothing was audible but the pleasant hum of frost, that low monotonous sound, which is perhaps the nearest approach that life and nature can make to absolute silence. The very waggons as they come down the hill along the beaten track of crisp, yellowish frost-dust glide along like shadows; even May's bounding footsteps fall like snow upon snow.

But we shall have noise enough presently: May has stopped at Lizzy's door;* and Lizzy, as she sat on the window-sill with her bright rosy face laughing through the casement, has seen her and disappeared. She is coming. No! The key is turning in the door, and sounds of evil omen issue through the keyhole—sturdy 'let me outs', and 'I will goes', mixed with shrill cries on May and on me from Lizzy, piercing through a low continuous harangue, of which the prominent parts are apologies, chilblains, sliding, broken bones, lollypops, rods, and gingerbread, from Lizzy's careful mother. 'Don't scratch the door, May! Don't roar so, my Lizzy! We'll call for you as we come back.'—'I'll go now! Let me out! I will go!' are the last words of Miss Lizzy. Mem. Not to spoil that child—if I can help it. But I do think her mother might have let the poor little soul walk with us to-day. Nothing worse for children than coddling. Nothing better for chilblains than exercise. Besides, I don't believe she has any—and as to breaking her bones in sliding, I don't suppose there's a slide on the common. These murmuring cogitations have brought us up the hill, and halfway across the light and airy common, with its bright expanse of snow and its clusters of cottages, whose turf fires send such wreaths of smoke sailing up the air, and diffuse such aromatic fragrance around. And now comes the delightful sound of childish voices, ringing with glee and merriment almost from beneath our feet. Ah, Lizzy, your mother was right! They are shouting from that deep irregular pool, all glass now, where, on two long, smooth, liny slides, half a dozen ragged urchins are slipping along in tottering triumph. Half a dozen steps bring us to the bank right above them. May can hardly resist the temptation of joining her friends, for most of the varlets are of her acquaintance, especially the rogue who leads the slide—he with the brimless hat, whose bronzed complexion and white flaxen hair, reversing the usual lights and shadows of the human countenance, give so strange and foreign a look to his flat and comic features. This hobgoblin, Jack Rapley by name, is May's great crony; and she stands on the brink of the steep, irregular descent, her black eyes fixed full upon him, as if she intended him the favour of jumping on his head. She does: she is down, and upon him; but Jack Rapley is not easily to be knocked off his feet. He saw her coming, and in the moment of her leap sprung dexterously off the slide on the rough ice, steadying himself by the shoulder of the next in the file, which unlucky follower, thus unexpectedly checked in his career, fell plump backwards, knocking down the rest of the line like a nest of card-houses. There they lie, roaring, kicking, sprawling, in every attitude of comic distress, whilst Jack Rapley and Mayflower, sole authors of this calamity, stand apart from the throng, fondling, and coquetting, and complimenting each other, and very visibly laughing, May in her black eyes, Jack in his wide, close-shut mouth, and his whole monkey-face, at their comrades' mischances. I think, Miss May, you may as well come up again, and leave Master Rapley to fight your battles. He'll get out of the scrape. He is a rustic wit—a sort of Robin Goodfellow*—the sauciest, idlest, cleverest, best-natured boy in the parish; always foremost in mischief, and always ready to do a good turn. The sages of our village predict sad things of Jack Rapley, so that I am sometimes a little ashamed to confess, before wise people, that I have a lurking predilection for him (in common with other naughty ones), and that I like to hear him talk to May almost as well as she does. 'Come, May!' and up she springs, as light as a bird. The road is gay now; carts and post-chaises, and girls in red cloaks, and, afar off, looking almost like a toy, the coach. It meets us fast and soon. How much happier the walkers look than the riders—especially the frost-bitten gentleman, and the shivering lady with the invisible face, sole passengers of that commodious machine! Hooded, veiled, and bonneted as she is, one sees from her attitude how miserable she would look uncovered.

Another pond, and another noise of children. More sliding? Oh! no. This is a sport of higher pretension. Our good neighbour, the lieutenant, skating, and his own pretty little boys, and two or three other four-year-old elves, standing on the brink in an ecstasy of joy and wonder! Oh what happy spectators! And what a happy performer! They admiring, he admired, with an ardour and sincerity never excited by all the quadrilles and the spread-eagles of the Seine and the Serpentine. . . .*

Now we have reached the trees,—the beautiful trees! never so beautiful as to-day. Imagine the effect of a straight and regular double avenue of oaks, nearly a mile long, arching overhead, and closing into perspective like the roof and columns of a cathedral, every tree and branch incrusted with the bright and delicate congelation of hoar-frost, white and pure as snow, delicate and defined as carved ivory. . . . At the end of this magnificent avenue, we are at the top of a steep eminence commanding a wide view over four counties—a landscape of snow. A deep lane leads abruptly down the hill; a mere narrow cart-track, sinking between high banks clothed with fern and furze and low broom, crowned with luxuriant hedge-rows, and famous for their summer smell of thyme. How lovely these banks are now—the tall weeds and the gorse fixed and stiffened in the hoar-frost, which fringes round the bright prickly holly, the pendent foliage of the bramble, and the deep orange leaves of the pollard oaks!* Oh, this is rime in its loveliest form! And there is still a berry here and there on the holly, 'blushing in its natural coral',* through the delicate tracery, still a stray hip or haw for the birds, who abound here always. The poor birds, how tame they are, how sadly tame! There is the beautiful and rare crested wren, 'that shadow of a bird',

as White of Selborne calls it,* perched in the middle of the hedge,
nestling as it were amongst the cold bare boughs, seeking, poor
pretty thing, for the warmth it will not find. And there, farther on,
just under the bank, by the slender runlet, which still trickles
between its transparent fantastic margin of thin ice, as if it were a
thing of life—there, with a swift, scudding motion, flits, in short low
flights, the gorgeous kingfisher, its magnificent plumage of scarlet
and blue flashing in the sun, like the glories of some tropical bird . . .

THAW

January 28th.—We have had rain, and snow, and frost, and rain
again; four days of absolute confinement. Now it is a thaw and a
flood; but our light gravelly soil, and country boots, and country
hardihood, will carry us through. What a dripping, comfortless day
it is! just like the last days of November: no sun, no sky, grey or blue;
one low, overhanging, dark, dismal cloud, like London smoke—
Mayflower is out coursing too, and Lizzy gone to school. Never
mind. Up the hill again! Walk we must. Oh what a watery world to
look back upon! Thames, Kennet, Loddon—all overflowed;* our
famous town, inland once, turned into a sort of Venice; C. park
converted into an island; and the long range of meadows from B. to
W. one huge unnatural lake, with trees growing out of it.* Oh what a
watery world!—I will look at it no longer. I will walk on. The road is
alive again. Noise is re-born. Waggons creak, horses splash, carts
rattle, and pattens paddle through the dirt with more than their
usual clink. The common has its old fine tints of green and brown,
and its old variety of inhabitants, horses, cows, sheep, pigs, and
donkeys. The ponds are unfrozen, except where some melancholy
piece of melting ice floats sullenly on the water; and cackling geese
and gabbling ducks have replaced the lieutenant and Jack Rapley.
The avenue is chill and dark, the hedges are dripping, the lanes are
knee-deep, and all nature is in a state of 'dissolution and thaw'.*

The First Primrose (1819)

March 6th.—Fine march weather: boisterous, blustering, much wind and squalls of rain; and yet the sky, where the clouds are swept away, deliciously blue, with snatches of sunshine, bright and clear, and healthful, and the roads, in spite of the slight glittering showers, crisply dry. Altogether, the day is tempting, very tempting. It will not do for the dear common, that windmill of a walk; but the close sheltered lanes at the bottom of the hill, which keep out just enough of the stormy air, and let in all the sun, will be delightful. Past our old house, and round by the winding lanes, and the workhouse, and across the lea, and so into the turnpike-road again—that is our route for to-day. Forth we set, Mayflower and I, rejoicing in the sunshine, and still more in the wind, which gives such an intense feeling of existence, and, co-operating with brisk motion, sets our blood and our spirits in a glow. . . .

Under this southern hedgerow nature is just beginning to live again: the periwinkles, with their starry blue flowers, and their shining myrtle-like leaves, garlanding the bushes; woodbines and elder-trees pushing out their small swelling buds; and grasses and mosses springing forth in every variety of brown and green. Here we are at the corner where four lanes meet, or rather where a passable road of stones and gravel crosses an impassable one of beautiful but treacherous turf, and where the small white farm-house, scarcely larger than a cottage, and the well-stocked rick-yard behind, tell of comfort and order, but leave all unguessed the great riches of the master. How he became so rich is almost a puzzle; for, though the farm be his own, it is not large; and though prudent and frugal on ordinary occasions, farmer Barnard is no miser. His horses, dogs, and pigs are the best kept in the parish—May herself, although her beauty be injured by her fatness, half envies the plight of his bitch Fly: his wife's gowns and shawls cost as much again as any shawls or gowns in the village; his dinner parties (to be sure they are not frequent) display twice the ordinary quantity of good things—two couples of ducks, two dishes of green peas, two turkey poults, two gammons of bacon, two plum-puddings; moreover, he keeps a single-horse chaise, and has built and endowed a Methodist chapel. Yet is he the richest man in these parts. Everything prospers with him. Money drifts about him like snow. He looks like a rich man. There is a sturdy squareness of face and figure; a good-humoured obstinacy; a civil importance. He never boasts of his wealth, or gives himself undue airs; but nobody can meet him at market or vestry without finding out immediately that he is the richest man there. They have no child to all this money; but there is an adopted nephew, a fine spirited lad, who may, perhaps, some day or other, play the part of a fountain to the reservoir.

Now turn up the wide road till we come to the open common, with its park-like trees, its beautiful stream, wandering and twisting along, and its rural bridge. Here we turn again, past that other white farm-house, half hidden by the magnificent elms which stand before it. Ah! riches dwell not there; but there is found the next best thing—an industrious and light-hearted poverty. Twenty years ago Rachel Hilton was the prettiest and merriest lass in the country. Her father, an old game-keeper, had retired to a village ale-house, where his good beer, his social humour, and his black-eyed daughter, brought much custom. She had lovers by the score; but Joseph White, the dashing and lively son of an opulent farmer, carried off the fair Rachel. They married and settled here, and here they live still, as merrily as ever, with fourteen children of all ages and sizes, from nineteen years to nineteen months, working harder than any people in the parish, and enjoying themselves more. I would match them for labour and laughter against any family in England. She is a blithe, jolly dame, whose beauty has amplified into comeliness: he is tall, and thin, and bony, with sinews like whipcord, a strong lively voice, a sharp weather-beaten face; and eyes and lips that smile and brighten when he speaks into a most contagious hilarity. They are very poor, and I often wish them richer; but I don't know—perhaps it might put them out.

Quite close to farmer White's is a little ruinous cottage, white-washed once, and now in a sad state of betweenity, where dangling stockings and shirts, swelled by the wind, drying in a neglected garden, give signal of a washerwoman. There dwells, at present in single blessedness, Betty Adams, the wife of our sometimes gardener. . . . Mrs Adams is a perfectly honest, industrious, painstaking person, who earns a good deal of money by washing and charing, and spends it in other luxuries than tidiness—in green tea, and gin, and snuff. Her husband lives in a great family, ten miles off. He is a capital gardener—or rather he would be so, if he were not too ambitious. He undertakes all things, and finishes none. But a smooth tongue, a knowing look, and a great capacity of labour, carry him through. Let him but like his ale and his master, and he will do work enough for four. Give him his own way, and his full quantum, and nothing comes amiss to him.

Ah, May is bounding forward! Her silly heart leaps at the sight of the old place—and so, in good truth, does mine. What a pretty place it was—or rather, how pretty I thought it! I suppose I should have thought any place so where I had spent eighteen happy years.* A large, heavy, white house, in the simplest style, surrounded by fine oaks and elms, and tall massy plantations shaded down into a beautiful lawn by wild overgrown shrubs, bowery acacias, ragged sweet-briers, promontories of dog-wood, and Portugal laurel, and bays, overhung by laburnum and bird-cherry; a long piece of water letting light into the picture, and looking just like a natural stream, the banks as rude and wild as the shrubbery, interspersed with broom, and furze, and bramble, and pollard oaks covered with ivy and honeysuckle; the whole enclosed by an old mossy park paling, and terminating in a series of rich meadows, richly planted. This is an exact description of the home which, three years ago, it nearly broke my heart to leave. What a tearing up by the root it was! I have pitied cabbage plants and celery, and all transplantable things, ever since; though, in common with them, and with other vegetables, the first agony of the transportation being over, I have taken such firm and tenacious hold of my new soil, that I would not for the world be pulled up again, even to be restored to the old beloved ground—not even if its beauty were undiminished, which is by no means the case; for in those three years it has thrice changed masters, and every successive possessor has brought the curse of improvement upon the place. . . . And yet I love to haunt round about it: so does May. Her particular attraction is a certain broken bank full of rabbit burrows, into which she insinuates her long pliant head and neck, and tears her pretty feet by vain scratchings: mine is a warm sunny hedgerow, in the same remote field, famous for early flowers. Never was a spot more variously flowery: primroses yellow, lilac white, violets of either hue, cowslips, oxlips, arums, orchises, wild hyacinths, ground ivy, pansies, strawberries, heart's-ease, formed a small part of the Flora of that wild hedgerow. How profusely they covered the sunny open slope under the weeping birch, 'the lady of the woods'*—and how often have I started to see the early innocent brown snake who loved the spot as well as I did, winding along the young blossoms, or rustling amongst the fallen leaves! There are primrose leaves already, and short green buds, but no flowers; not even in that furze cradle so full of roots, where they used to blow as in a basket. No, my May, no rabbits! no primroses! We may as well get over the gate into the woody winding lane, which will bring us home again.

Here we are making the best of our way between the old elms that arch so solemnly overhead, dark and sheltered even now. They say that a spirit haunts this deep pool—a white lady without a head. I cannot say that I have seen her, often as I have paced this lane at deep midnight, to hear the nightingales, and look at the glow-worms—but there, better and rarer than a thousand ghosts, dearer even than nightingales or glow-worms, there is a primrose, the first of the year; a tuft of primroses, springing in yonder sheltered nook, from the mossy roots of an old willow, and living again in the clear bright pool. Oh, how beautiful they are—three fully blown and two bursting buds! They are not to be reached. Who would wish to disturb them? There they live in their innocent and fragrant beauty, sheltered from the storms, and rejoicing in the sunshine, and looking as if they could feel their happiness. Who would disturb them? Oh, how glad I am I came this way home!

MARY HAYS
(1760–1843)

Born into a Dissenting family in Southwark, London, Mary Hays was brought up by her widowed mother. A romance with a local man, John Eccles, was opposed by both families because neither party was thought to have means or prospects; consent was eventually won, but Eccles died before they could marry. Many of Hays's letters to Eccles survive (in the Carl H. and Lily Pforzheimer Library, New York), and reveal a close intellectual as well as emotional bond. Hays turned to reading and study during several years of mourning, and in the late 1780s began to make friends in Dissenting intellectual circles, including the Unitarian Cambridge mathematician William Frend (1757–1841), to whom she became deeply attached. In her twenties she attended lectures on religion and politics at the Dissenting Academy in Hackney. Her first publication, a pamphlet, *Cursory Remarks on an Enquiry into the Expediency and Propriety of Public or Social Worship* (1792), by 'Eusebia', defended the public worship associated with Dissent against the attacks of Gilbert Wakefield; it brought her to the notice of radical Dissenters in the circle of the publisher Joseph Johnson, including Priestley, Godwin, Blake, and Paine. Hays wrote letters to Godwin (and to Frend) assessing and analysing her passion for Frend, and on parts of these she based her best-known work, the novel *Memoirs of Emma Courtney* (1796), which attracted criticism for its free-thinking heroine's frank avowal of passion for a man who has declared no attachment to her. She was greatly influenced by Mary Wollstonecraft's *Vindication*, and they became friends: it was Mary Hays who reintroduced Wollstonecraft and Godwin in 1796. Wollstonecraft also acted as literary adviser in the production of *Letters and Essays, Moral and Miscellaneous* (1793), which protests against the 'mental bondage' of women in a tyrannical male society. Hays attended Wollstonecraft on her birth/deathbed, and wrote an appreciative obituary for the *Monthly Magazine*, to which she was a regular contributor at this time. The reduced enthusiasm of her second obituary, written for *Annual Necrology, 1797–1798* (1800), is symptomatic of the pressures to which her endorsement of Wollstonecraft's views exposed her in an increasingly conservative society. Much of Hays's life was spent in London, and was supported by her writing; but she also worked as a schoolteacher in Oundle, and during a stay in Clifton in 1814 she befriended Hannah More, who published two of her works.

Hays's feminism, which is a feature of all her works, polemical and fictional, attracted ridicule as well as criticism. She was satirized as Lady Gertrude Sinclair in Charles Lloyd's novel *Edmund Oliver* (1798) and as Bridgetina Botherim in Elizabeth Hamilton's novel *Memoirs of Modern Philosophers* (1800), mocked for a squint which was easily used to suggest moral and intellectual wrong-headedness. A correspondence with Charles Lloyd the year after his satirical novel was published brought upon her a new embarrassment, for Lloyd claimed that she had declared love for him, Emma Courtney-style: the ensuing dispute involved Godwin, Southey, Coleridge, and Charles Lamb.

The six-volume *Female Biography: Or, Memoirs of Illustrious and Celebrated Women, of all Ages and Countries* (1803) showed Hays finding new, more acceptable, ways of focusing attention on women's history. In her Preface she addressed not just the female subject-matter but also the needs of the female reader:

Women, unsophisticated by the pedantry of the schools, read not for dry information, to load their memories with uninteresting facts, or to make an display of a vain errudition. A skeleton biography would afford to them but little gratification: they require pleasure to be mingled with instruction, lively images, the grace of sentiment, and the polish of language. Their understandings are principally access-ible through their affections: they delight in minute delineations of character; nor must the truths which impress them be either cold or unadorned. I have at heart the happiness of my sex, and their advancement in the grand scale of rational and social existence.[1]

Hays is represented here by substantial extracts from her narrative of the life of Caroline of Brunswick, wife of George, Prince of Wales, later George IV, published in her one-volume *Memoirs of Queens* (1821). Her importance as a biographer of women is difficult to capture in extracts: much of her work relies heavily and explicitly on earlier biographies, and she rarely expatiates at length on her own views of the lives she depicts. The effect of her writing is cumulative. So, Hays opens her account of Elizabeth I with a claim relevant to *Memoirs of Queens* as a whole, and to her account of Queen Caroline in particular: 'If the question respecting the equality of the sexes was to be determined by an appeal to the char-acters of sovereign princes, the comparison is, in proportion, manifestly in favour of woman, and that without having recourse to the trite and flip-pant observation, proved to have been ill founded, of male and female influence.' (70–1).

Hays wrote her radical and polemical account of Queen Caroline at the height of the debate about Caroline's rights and wrongs. Her arguments acquired an unexpected extra resonance when Caroline suddenly died in August 1821, a month after being turned away from Westminster Abbey during the coronation of George IV. Hays concludes her Preface by draw-ing attention to the difference in tone between the beginning of the account of Queen Caroline and the end; the explanation is 'that it was begun previous to the memorable trial; finished after it ended' (p. viii). In this most topical and most controversial of all the essays Hays explores the difficulties of Caroline's efforts to establish herself in the British court; her attachment to her daughter; the Prince of Wales's request, soon after the birth in 1796, for a formal separation; the rumours of Caroline's misconduct and supposed illegitimate child, and the various people encouraged to testify against her; the examination of reports by the friends of the Prince in 1806, and her acquittal; her enforced separation from her daughter and departure from Britain from 1814 to 1820; the marriage and early death of her daughter. Of the popular feeling in sup-port of Caroline, Hays comments: 'From the generosity inherent in the

[1] *Female Biography; or, Memoirs of Illustrious and Celebrated Women, of all Ages and Countries*, 6 vols. (London: for Richard Phillips by Thomas Davison, 1803), vol. i, p.iv.

British character, the situation of the princess of Wales, a contemned wife, a bereaved mother, a stranger deserted in a foreign land, outraged in every *womanly* and maternal feeling, had uniformly excited a strong popular sympathy: the affability of her manners increased this sympathy; and no tale of slander, however ingeniously invented, or industriously propagated, had been able to extinguish it, or prevent its manifestation' (121). The pages after the end of the extract selected here tell briefly of the evidence ('a torrent of odious obscenity, from the mouths of discarded servants, foreigners of the lowest classes, without credit or character', 131) brought against Caroline in support of the King's charges: 'To dwell upon the subject would be too disgusting', Hays maintains (131). The accusation is carried by a majority of nine but the parliamentary bill is abandoned, to the joy of the public, in what Hays describes as an ardent outpouring of 'national enthusiasm and popular sympathy' (133).

~

From *Memoirs of Queens* (1821)

Caroline, Wife of George IV

On the 8th of April, the marriage was celebrated between George, prince of Wales, and Caroline of Brunswick, to the apparent satisfaction of the family, the court, and the nation.*

But under these fair appearances evil lurked, that was not tardy in its manifestations. It had been understood by the prince that his debts, estimated at £700,000, were, on his marriage, to be paid by the nation; and when parliament voted the liberal sum of £60,000 annually, in quarterly payments, for the support of his establishment, and the gradual liquidation of the debts, he is said to have experienced disappointment. This, probably, with other circumstances, very early led to a coolness on his part towards his bride. On a subject so delicate, and on which but little with certainty can possibly be known, it would scarcely be prudent or proper to enlarge. The prince had appeared ever averse to marriage: rumours were in circulation respecting his having formed other attachments:* and for the caprices of the inclinations who can account? Marriages in his rank of life are not formed upon the sympathies and affections by which hearts and hands are united in humbler, more natural happier stations; yet, even when tenderness is wanting, respect and consideration for the feelings and claims of others are assuredly due and ought to be observed.

The circumstance that, when announced, afforded hope to the nation of a direct lineal succession to the crown, gave joy to all but those most interested in the accomplishment of that hope. The condescending and affable manners of the princess rendered her popular: by the king she was affectionately cherished as a daughter; by the other members of the family treated with complacency: but the heart which it was natural she should most wish to engage remained chill and alienated.

Her just expectations and dearest hopes were succeeded by disappointment and mortification. At a distance from her family and friends, in to her a foreign land, with strangers, among whom insidious enemies were suspected, she found herself, when the bridal compliments had scarcely passed, a neglected and contemned wife.* In the season most trying and affecting to the female mind, the prospect of becoming a mother, no tenderness sustained, no sympathy cheered her. A situation more truly desolate, not withstanding its external brilliancy, cannot well be imagined. The woman, in whatever rank, who is not supported by her husband's love and respect, can rarely hope for that of others; all are inclined to judge her with harshness; her misfortune is too frequently considered as her fault; if she complains she is thought to violate discretion; if she is silent, conjecture is busy against her. In a court, more especially, the favour of the reigning monarch, or of the apparent heir, spreads a lustre round its object: the apprehended disfavour, and courtiers have a quick and penetrating sight, casts over even merit the most distinguished a dark shadow. . . .

Magnanimously stifling her emotions, uncertain of the fate awaiting her, of her reception with the nation, of the strength and number of her enemies, with little other support than what conscious rectitude might afford her, the *queen of England*, as a stranger and a fugitive, landed from a packet on the British shores.

She confided in the justice of her cause and in the generous feelings of the nation, and her confidence was justified by the event. Her progress to the capital was as a triumph: the people crowded around her, persons of all ranks and professions, of both sexes and of every character and age.* One feeling seemed to pervade the mass, ardent sympathies, eager greetings, fervent blessings, were expressed and heard on every side. The sentiment, like a contagion, spread and diffused itself through the moral and political atmosphere of the kingdom.

Nearly exhausted with emotion and fatigue, the queen entered London, and, without a palace or residence of her own to receive her, accepted graciously and gratefully the asylum offered her by the respectable citizen who accompanied her in her voyage.*

Consternation seized her enemies and accusers, who appeared little to have foreseen or calculated upon the decided measures of the accused. The human mind is ingenious in self deception, it begins by imposing upon others, and ends in deceiving itself: of that which our passions and interests make us ardently wish to be true, we are not long in persuading ourselves; the process is easy and obvious to those who have looked into human character.

The queen, her magnanimity, her cause, now became the focus of public attention; defamation exerted her hundred tongues; slander poured her poison into every open ear; the ardent on both sides prejudiced the cause; reasoning is a slow process of which feeling gets the start; the candid paused, the wise doubted, and waited for evidence upon which to decide.

Burke, had he now lived, would have retracted his assertion, that the age of chivalry had passed away;* it revived, in all its impassioned fervour, amidst the soberest and gravest people in the civilized world. Every manly mind shrank from the idea of driving, by protracted and endless persecutions, a desolate unprotected female from her family, her rank, from society and from the world. *Woman* considered it as a common cause against the despotism and tyranny of man. Morals are of no sex, duties are reciprocal between being and being, or they are abrogated by nature and reason. Brute force may subjugate, but in knowledge only is real strength, and to truth and justice is the last and only legitimate appeal. With the feudal institutions fell the childish privileges and degrading homage paid to the sex; and to *equity* not gallantry do they now prefer their claim. Oppression and proscription, it is true, still linger, but old things appear to be passing away; and, in another century, probably, should the progress of knowledge bear any proportion to its accelerated march during the latter half of the past, all things will become new. We live in eventful times, and at a critical era of the world. Happy those who understand the signs of the times; who seek not to oppose to a flood feeble mounds and inadequate barriers; but who suffer its waters gently to flow and expand through prepared appropriate reservoirs and channels, carrying fertility as they glide.

The adversaries of the queen were in a perplexing dilemma, in a situation which their sagacity had not enabled them to foresee, or which they considered so improbable as scarcely to have provided against. To intimidate the intrepid princess was their first endeavour: she had left them, they declared, no alternative but to summon her to the bar of the nation, to answer there for her high misdemeanours and crimes. Volumes of evidence, it was stated, were already prepared, repeated and attested beyond all possibility of doubt. Their *green bag* was a Pandora's box, full of all mischief and evil, without even *hope* at the bottom.* Still, while they wielded the sword suspended from on high, they were too lenient to desire to strike; they wished to show all possible tenderness that the case would admit; and to relieve themselves, by a compromise, from the arduous duty that pressed upon them.

Their compromise was however refused with a dignity and firmness, that argued no consciousness of guilt, no dread of the threatened ordeal. It was proposed again from a less suspicious quarter; a respectable deputation from the Commons urged it with stronger arguments and higher offers; but not with better success. The queen had made up her mind to the event, and determined, by an appeal to the justice of the country, to put at once, if possible, a final period to the persecutions and anxieties of which she had been so long the victim.

And now another embarrassment arose. Upon the presumption of the truth of the facts alleged against the accused, of what description was her crime, under what law was it to be denounced, and what was its allotted punishment? It was not treason, because, in cases of this nature, it was declared by high law authority, that the woman could be implicated only through the man, and the man in question owed no allegiance to this country, of which he was not a subject.* It was no political offence, because time, circumstance, and place, rendered nugatory any apprehension of future evil being its result. It was no act of infidelity against a husband whose conduct left him without any right of appeal. No law existed to condemn a nominal wife placed in similar circumstances. If it was allowed to be a breach of morals, yet no legal penalty was annexed to such a breach.

Incontinence, whether in man or woman, is a moral offence and a violation of the most important branch of temperance, but it carries with it no civil disfranchisement, and its punishment is left to public opinion, to the usages and customs established in social intercourse,—and heavy enough upon *woman* does this chastisement fall. If higher virtues are to be expected from *queens*, on account of the eminence of their situation, and the greater importance of their example; the same reasoning, and the same rule, surely applies to *kings*. The case was novel, no precedent existed, unless we went back to the times of Henry VIII of wife-killing memory.* Catherine of Russia made no pretence to chastity, but she was not the less a great sovereign.* Our own Elizabeth, our *virgin* queen of glorious memory, has not, on this subject, left a fame like unsunned snow.*

What then was to be done? Why, a new law was to be made, an *ex post facto* law, after the alleged commission of the crime. And, previously, to render condemnation more sure, a private and *secret* tribunal was to try the cause upon evidence of accusation only; and thus, having pre-judged the business, and prejudiced the public mind by a declaration of that pre-judgement, these very men, with their minds thus biassed, were to take their place among the judges to whom the final award was to be referred. More, *much more*, might be said and urged on the same subject; but to enter into the detail of this extraordinary trial is not the purpose of the present memoir.

FELICIA HEMANS
(1793–1835)

The best-selling English-language poet of the nineteenth century, Felicia Dorothea Browne was one of the six children of a Liverpool merchant, George Browne, and his wife Felicity Wagner. When her father suffered business setbacks in 1800 the family moved first to Gwyrch, and in 1809 to Bronwhylfa, both in North Wales: her love for Wales is evident throughout her work. During her teenage years her father removed permanently to Quebec, his absence more than compensated for throughout her life by her mother, the daughter of the German and Tuscan consul in Liverpool and his Italian wife: she directed Hemans's education to reflect this background, making sure she was fluent in French, Italian, and

German even as a child. She also educated her in grammar, drawing, and music, and later added Spanish and Portuguese to her linguisitic skills. A local clergyman instructed her in Latin. Hemans's poems are full of reminders of this wide range of cultural reference.

As Felicia Browne, she published her first volume, *Poems*, in 1808, when she was 14. The collection, which was followed by another in the same year, was reviewed by Anna Laetitia Barbauld among others, and brought her to the attention of many well-connected subscribers and reviewers. One of the readers of her first collection was Percy Bysshe Shelley, who is said to have pursued her. When she was 15 she met Captain Alfred Hemans, an Irishman serving in the Royal Welsh Fusiliers, who had fought in the Peninsular Campaign with her brothers Thomas and George. They were married in 1812, just after Hemans had published a more accomplished volume of poetry, *The Domestic Affections*, and settled first in Daventry (where her husband was adjutant to the Northamptonshire Local Militia) and later back at her family's home in Wales; they had five sons before permanently separating in 1818, Captain Hemans following the example of his father-in-law by settling abroad, this time in Italy, and officially for the sake of his health. Incompatibility rather than villainy is suggested by the evidence, and Hemans is often thought to have been more deeply attached to her clearly talented and charismatic mother than to her military husband. After this, Hemans maintained a prolific output of poetry for many years, having to write in order to support and educate her children. Her health was weakened by whooping cough in 1829, scarlet fever in 1824, and the onset of tuberculosis, of which she died in 1835 at the age of 41. She moved to Liverpool after the death of her mother in 1827, met Wordsworth and Scott during a tour of the Lakes and Scotland in 1830, and moved to Dublin in 1831 to be near her brother George. Among her female writing friends were Joanna Baillie, Mary Russell Mitford, and Maria Jane Jewsbury.

Hemans's poetic output was prodigious, and is increasingly read and taught. Volumes are devoted to Italian art, modern Greece, historical events, the legends of other lands, national lyrics, and the affections of women: the most significant are *Welsh Melodies* (1822), *The Forest Sanctuary, and Other Poems* (1825), *Records of Woman* (1828; dedicated to Joanna Baillie), and *Songs of the Affections* (1830). As her reputation grew, she was able to earn money twice over for her work, publishing poems first in periodicals (especially *The New Monthly Magazine*) and then collecting them into volumes. A five-act tragedy, *The Vespers of Palermo*, was performed in London in 1823 and in Edinburgh in 1824, to unanimous disapproval; two other plays were not performed. Famously 'feminine', her poetry was thought graceful, rapturous, tender, and it was hugely popular, even more so in the United States than in Britain, sustaining its popularity for much of the nineteenth century. The facility with which she wrote marked her out as a true poet of feeling and natural inspiration: and, as her sales figures suggest, she exemplified for many what a poet ought to be. Wordsworth mourned her in 'Extempore Effusion upon the Death of James Hogg' (1835) as 'Sweet as the spring, as ocean deep'; Laetitia Elizabeth Landon's 'Stanzas on the Death of Mrs Hemans' are included in this collection. As 'Egeria' in Jewsbury's 'History of a Nonchalant' she strikes the narrator as 'totally different from any other woman I had ever seen . . . She did not dazzle; she subdued me'.[1]

Landon's essay 'On the Characteristics of Mrs Hemans's Writings' declares these to be: an expression of yearning for affection; 'the rich picturesque'; the polished versification which she defines as harmony; and morality.[2] Some modern critics have found more troubling and more ambivalent qualities in her work, especially her recurrence to scenes of female self-sacrifice and death. Superficially she endorses the ideal of the selfless woman, loyal through all betrayals and losses, but in repetition lies anxiety and discontent. The selection given here begins with three songs from *Welsh Melodies*, of which her biographer Henry Fothergill Chorley remarked: 'it was an instinct with Mrs. Hemans to catch the picturesque points of national character, as well as of national music; in the latter she always delighted'.[3] 'The Rock of Cader Idris' refers to a Welsh tradition that anyone spending a night on this mountain will die, go mad, or find poetic inspiration: the implications for the female poet describing a male poet's direct experience of this ordeal are interesting partly because Hemans does nothing to insist upon them. She does not complain of exclusion or profess inferiority; she does not ironize the male poet's awakened abilities. Perhaps she sees creativity as gender-neutral when it is set in the legendary past; perhaps she employs two different conventions of 'feminine' power—magic and nature—to suggest that male creativity depends upon the feminine. However one reads it, the poem contribtutes to a debate among women writers about the representation of male creativity, such as Barbauld's and Robinson's poems about Coleridge and Mary Shelley's portraits of Victor Frankenstein and Cornelius Agrippa. 'The Traveller at the Source of the Nile' reflects on the reported feelings of the explorer James Bruce of Kinnaird (another intrepid male) on reaching the end of his long quest; while the much-anthologized 'Casabianca'

---

[1] Maria Jane Jewsbury, *The Three Histories: The History of an Enthusiast, The History of a Nonchalant, The History of a Realist* (London: Frederick Westley and A. H. Davis, 1830), 231.

[2] *New Monthly Magazine*, 44 (May–Aug. 1835).

[3] *Memorials of Mrs Hemans*, 2 vols. (London: Saunders and Otley, 1836), i. 81.

(first published in an American collection of her poems in 1826) is based
on another Nile story, this time a tale of individual heroism in the Battle of
the Nile (1798). From *Records of Woman*, in which Hemans devotes a
series of nineteen poems to the portrayal of women characters from various historical periods, comes 'Properzia Rossi', the tale of a woman sculptor from Bologna; and 'Indian Woman's Death-Song', inspired by another
travel-account. The concentration on female loss and suffering in this
collection perhaps reflects her state of mind in the aftermath of her
mother's death, but they are recurrent preoccupations in all her poetry,
expressive either of a fetishization of female powerlessness or of a carefully modulated protest against it, depending on the reader's point of
view. Her lyrical gifts are shown to particular effect in 'An Hour of
Romance', and, from *Songs of the Affections*, 'Parting Words'. 'The
Haunted House' is notable for its metrical control, and another kind of
haunting is explored in 'Written After Visiting a Tomb', written in 1831
after a visit to the grave of Mary Tighe. 'The Last Song of Sappho',
finally, continues the fascination with the doomed and love-blighted figure
of the female poet seen in the works of Mary Robinson.

～

From *Welsh Melodies* (1822)

*The Sea-Song of Gafran**

Watch ye well! The moon is shrouded
   On her bright throne;
Storms are gathering, stars are clouded,
   Waves make wild moan.
'Tis no night of hearth-fires glowing,
And gay songs and wine-cups flowing;
But of winds, in darkness blowing,
   O'er seas unknown!

In the dwellings of our fathers,
   Round the glad blaze,
Now the festive circle gathers
   With harps and lays;
Now the rush-strewn halls are ringing,
Steps are bounding, bards are singing,
—Ay! the hour to all is bringing
   Peace, joy, or praise.

Save to us, our night-watch keeping,
    Storm-winds to brave,
While the very sea-bird sleeping
    Rests in its cave!
Think of us when hearths are beaming,
Think of us when mead is streaming,
Ye, of whom our souls are dreaming
    On the dark wave!

The Lament of Llywarch Hen

Llywarch Hen, or Llywarch the Aged, a celebrated bard and chief of the times of Arthur, was prince of Argoed, supposed to be a part of the present Cumberland.* Having sustained the loss of his patrimony, and witnessed the fall of most of his sons, in the unequal contest maintained by the North Britons against the growing power of the Saxons, Llywarch was compelled to fly from his country, and seek refuge in Wales. He there found an asylum for some time in the residence of Cynddylan, Prince of Powys, whose fall he pathetically laments in one of his poems.* These are still extant; and his elegy on old age and the loss of his sons, is remarkable for its simplicity and beauty.—See *Cambrian Biography*, and OWEN's *Heroic Elegies and other poems of Llywarch Hen.*

The bright hours return, and the blue sky is ringing
With song, and the hills are all mantled with bloom;
But fairer than aught which the summer is bringing,
The beauty and youth gone to people the tomb!
Oh! why should I live to hear music resounding,
Which cannot awake ye, my lovely, my brave?
Why smile the waste flowers, my sad footsteps surrounding?
—My sons! they but clothe the green turf of your grave!

Alone on the rocks of the stranger I linger,
My spirit all wrapt in the past as a dream!
Mine ear hath no joy in the voice of the singer,
Mine eye sparkles not to the sunlight's glad beam;
Yet, yet I live on, though forsaken and weeping!
—O grave! why refuse to the aged thy bed,
When valour's high heart on thy bosom is sleeping,
When youth's glorious flower is gone down to the dead!

Fair were ye, my sons! and all kingly your bearing,

As on to the fields of your glory ye trode!
Each prince of my race the bright golden chain wearing,
Each eye glancing fire, shrouded now by the sod!
I weep when the blast of the trumpet in sounding,
Which rouses ye not, O my lovely! my brave!
When warriors and chiefs to their proud steeds are bounding,
I turn from heaven's light, for it smiles on your grave!

The Rock of Cader Idris

It is an old tradition of the Welsh bards, that on the summit of the mountain Cader Idris, is an excavation resembling a couch;* and that whoever should pass a night in that hollow, would be found in the morning either dead, in a frenzy, or endowed with the highest poetical inspiration.

I lay on that rock where the storms have their dwelling,
    The birthplace of phantoms, the home of the cloud;
Around it for ever deep music is swelling,
    The voice of the mountain-wind, solemn and loud.
'Twas a midnight of shadows all fitfully streaming,
    Of wild waves and breezes, that mingled their moan;
Of dim shrouded stars, as from gulfs faintly gleaming;
    And I met the dread gloom of its grandeur alone.

I lay there in silence—a spirit came o'er me;
    Man's tongue hath no language to speak what I saw;
Things glorious, unearthly, pass'd floating before me,
    And my heart almost fainted with rapture and awe.
I view'd the dread beings around us that hover,
    Though veil'd by the mists of mortality's breath;
And I call'd upon darkness the vision to cover,
    For a strife was within me of madness and death.

I saw them—the powers of the wind and the ocean,
    The rush of whose pinion bears onward the storms;
Like the sweep of the white-rolling wave was their motion—
    I *felt* their dim presence, but knew not their forms!
I saw them—the mighty of ages departed—
    The dead were around me that night on the hill:
From their eyes, as they pass'd, a cold radiance they darted,—
    There was light on my soul, but my heart's blood was chill.

I saw what man looks on, and dies—but my spirit
  Was strong, and triumphantly lived through that hour;
And, as from the grave, I awoke to inherit
  A flame all immortal, a voice, and a power!
Day burst on that rock with the purple cloud crested,
  And high Cader Idris rejoiced in the sun;—
But oh! what new glory all nature invested,
  When the sense which gives soul to her beauty was won!

*Casabianca** (1826, 1829)

The boy stood on the burning deck
  Whence all but he had fled;
The flame that lit the battle's wreck
  Shone round him o'er the dead.

Yet beautiful and bright he stood,
  As born to rule the storm—
A creature of heroic blood,
  A proud, though child-like form.

The flames roll'd on—he would not go
  Without his father's word;
That father, faint in death below,
  His voice no longer heard.

He call'd aloud:—'Say, father! say
  If yet my task is done!'
He knew not that the chieftain lay
  Unconscious of his son.

'Speak, father!' once again he cried,
  'If I may yet be gone!'
And but the booming shots replied,
  And fast the flames roll'd on.

Upon his brow he felt their breath,
  And in his waving hair,
And look'd from that lone post of death
  In still yet brave despair;

And shouted but once more aloud,
  'My father! must I stay?'

While o'er him fast, through sail and shroud,
   The wreathing fires made way.

They wrapt the ship in splendour wild,
   They caught the flag on high,
And stream'd above the gallant child
   Like banners in the sky.

There came a burst of thunder-sound—
   The boy—oh! where was he?
Ask of the winds that far around
   With fragments strew'd the sea!—

With mast, and helm, and pennon fair,
   That well had borne their part;
But the noblest thing which perish'd there
   Was that young faithful heart!

An Hour of Romance (1827)

> 'I come
> To this sweet place for quiet. Every tree
> And bush, and fragrant flower, and hilly path,
> And thymy mound that flings unto the winds
> Its morning incense, is my friend.'
>
>   Barry Cornwall*

There were thick leaves above me and around,
   And low sweet sighs like those of childhood's sleep,
Amidst their dimness, and a fitful sound
   As of soft showers on water; dark and deep
Lay the oak shadows o'er the turf, so still
They seem'd but pictured glooms; a hidden rill
Made music, such as haunts us in a dream,
Under the fern-tufts; and a tender gleam
Of soft green light, as by the glow-worm shed,
   Came pouring through the woven beech-boughs down,
And steep'd the magic page wherein I read
   Of royal chivalry and old renown,
A tale of Palestine.* Meanwhile the bee
   Swept past me with a tone of summer hours—
   A drowsy bugle, wafting thoughts of flowers,

Blue skies, and amber sunshine: brightly free,
On filmy wings, the purple dragon-fly
Shot glancing like a fairy javelin by;
And a sweet voice of sorrow told the dell
Where sat the lone wood-pigeon.
                                        But ere long,
All sense of these things faded, as the spell
    Breathing from that high gorgeous tale grew strong
On my chain'd soul. 'Twas not the leaves I heard:—
A Syrian wind the lion-banner stirr'd,*
Through its proud floating folds. 'Twas not the brook
    Singing in secret through its grassy glen;—
    A wild shrill trumpet of the Saracen
Peal'd from the desert's lonely heart, and shook
The burning air.* Like clouds when winds are high,
O'er glittering sands flew steeds of Araby,
And tents rose up, and sudden lance and spear
Flash'd where a fountain's diamond wave lay clear,
Shadow'd by graceful palm-trees. Then the shout
Of merry England's joy swell'd freely out,
Sent through an Eastern heaven, whose glorious hue
Made shields dark mirrors to its depths of blue,
And harps were there—I heard their sounding strings,
As the waste echo'd to the mirth of kings.
The bright mask faded. Unto life's worn track,
What call'd me from its flood of glory back?
A voice of happy childhood!—and they pass'd,
Banner, and harp, and Paynim's trumpet's blast.*
Yet might I scarce bewail the splendours gone,
My heart so leap'd to that sweet laughter's tone.

Properzia Rossi (1828)

Properzia Rossi, a celebrated female sculptor of Bologna, possessed also of
talents for poetry and music, died in consequence of an unrequited
attachment.* A painting, by Ducis, represents her showing her last work, a
basso-relievo of Ariadne, to a Roman knight, the object of her affection.
who regards it with indifference.*

'Tell me no more, no more
Of my soul's lofty gifts! Are they not vain
To quench its haunting thirst for happiness?
Have I not loved, and striven, and fail'd to bind
One true heart unto me, whereon my own
Might find a resting-place, a home for all
Its burden of affections? I depart,
Unknown, though Fame goes with me; I must leave
The earth unknown. Yet it may be that death
Shall give my name a power to win such tears
As would have made life precious'.*

I

One dream of passion and of beauty more!
And in its bright fulfillment let me pour
My soul away! Let earth retain a trace
Of that which lit my being, though its race
Might have been loftier far. Yet one more dream!
From my deep spirit one victorious gleam
Ere I depart! For thee alone, for thee!
May this last work, this farewell triumph be—
Thou, loved so vainly! I would leave enshrined
Something immortal of my heart and mind,
That yet may speak to thee when I am gone,
Shaking thine inmost bosom with a tone
Of lost affection,—something that may prove
What she hath been, whose melancholy love
On thee was lavish'd; silent pang and tear,
And fervent song that gush'd when none were near,
And dream by night, and weary thought by day,
Stealing the brightness from her life away—
While thou—Awake! not yet within me die!
Under the burden and the agony
Of this vain tenderness—my spirit, wake!
Even for thy sorrowful affection's sake,
Live! in thy work breathe out!—that he may yet,
Feeling sad mastery there, perchance regret
Thine unrequited gift.

II

               It comes! the power
Within me born flows back—my fruitless dower
That could not win me love. Yet once again
I greet it proudly, with its rushing train
Of glorious images: they throng—they press—
A sudden joy lights up my loneliness—
I shall not perish all!
                    The bright work grows
Beneath my hand, unfolding, as a rose,
Leaf after leaf, to beauty—line by line
I fix my thought, heart, soul, to burn, to shine
Through the pale marble's veins. It grows!—and now
I give my own life's history to thy brow,
Forsaken Ariadne!—thou shalt wear
My form, my lineaments; but oh! more fair,
Touch'd into lovelier being by the glow
   Which in me dwells, as by the summer light
All things are glorified. From thee my woe
   Shall yet look beautiful to meet his sight,
When I am pass'd away. Thou art the mould,
Wherein I pour the fervent thoughts, th'untold,
The self-consuming! Speak to him of me,
Thou, the deserted by the lonely sea,
With the soft sadness of thine earnest eye—
Speak to him, lorn one! deeply, mournfully,
Of all my love and grief! Oh! could I throw
Into thy frame a voice—a sweet, and low,
And thrilling voice of song! when he came nigh,
To send the passion of its melody
Through his pierced bosom—on its tones to bear
My life's deep feeling, as the southern air
Wafts the faint myrtle's breath—to rise, to swell,
To sink away in accents of farewell,
Winning but one, *one* gush of tears, whose flow
Surely my parted spirit yet might know,
If love be strong as death!

III

Now fair thou art,

Thou form, whose life is of my burning heart!
Yet all the vision that within me wrought,
   I cannot make thee. Oh! I might have given
Birth to creations of far nobler thought;
   I might have kindled, with the fire of heaven,
Things not of such as die! But I have been
Too much alone! A heart whereon to lean,
With all these deep affections that o'erflow
My aching soul, and find no shore below;
An eye to be my star; a voice to bring
Hope o'er my path like sounds that breathe of spring!
These are denied me—dreamt of still in vain.
Therefore my brief aspirings from the chain
Are ever but as some wild fitful song,
Rising triumphantly, to die ere long
In dirge-like echoes.

IV

Yet the world will see

Little of this, my parting work! in thee.
   Thou shalt have fame! Oh, mockery! give the reed
From storms a shelter—give the drooping vine
Something round which its tendrils may entwine—
   Give the parch'd flower a rain-drop, and the meed
Of love's kind words to woman! Worthless fame!
That in *his* bosom wins not for my name
Th' abiding place it ask'd! Yet how my heart,
In its own fairy world of song and art,
Once beat for praise! Are those high longings o'er!
That which I have been can I be no more?
Never! oh, never more! though still thy sky
Be blue as then, my glorious Italy!
And though the music, whose rich breathings fill
Thine air with soul, be wandering past me still;
And though the mantle of thy sunlight streams
Unchanged on forms, instinct with poet-dreams.

Never! oh, never more! where'er I move,
The shadow of this broken-hearted love
Is on me and around! Too well *they* know
   Whose life is all within, too soon and well,
When there the blight hath settled! But I go
   Under the silent wings of peace to dwell;
From the slow wasting, from the lonely pain,
The inward burning of those words—'*in vain*'
   Sear'd on the heart—I go. 'Twill soon be past!
Sunshine and song, and bright Italian heaven,
   And thou, oh! thou, on whom my spirit cast
Unvalued wealth—who know'st not what was given
In that devotedness—the sad, and deep,
And unrepaid—farewell! If I could weep
Once, only once, beloved one! on thy breast,
Pouring my heart forth ere I sink to rest!
But that were happiness!—and unto me
Earth's gift is *fame*. Yet I was form'd to be
So richly bless'd! With thee to watch the sky,
Speaking not, feeling but that thou wert nigh;
With thee to listen, while the tones of song
Swept even as part of our sweet air along—
To listen silently; with thee to gaze
On forms, the deified of olden days—
This had been joy enough; and hour by hour,
From its glad well-springs drinking life and power
How had my spirit soar'd, and made its fame
   A glory for thy brow! Dreams, dreams!—The fire
Burns faint within me. Yet I leave my name—
   As a deep thrill may linger on the lyre
When its full chords are hush'd—awhile to live,
And one day haply in thy heart revive
Sad thoughts of me. I leave it, with a sound,
A spell o'er memory, mournfully profound;
I leave it, on my country's air to dwell—
Say proudly yet—''*Twas hers who loved me well!*'

Indian Woman's Death-Song (1828)

An Indian woman, driven to despair by her husband's desertion of her for another wife, entered a canoe with her children, and rowed it down the Mississippi towards a cataract. Her voice was heard from the shore singing a mournful death-song, until overpowered by the sound of the waters in which she perished. The tale is related in Long's 'Expedition to the Source of St Peter's River.'*

> 'Non, je ne puis vivre avec un cœur brise. Il faut que je retrouve
> la joie, et que je m'unisse aux esprits libres de l'air.'
> > 'Bride of Messina.' Translated by Madame de Stael*

> 'Let not my child be a girl, for very sad is the life of a woman.'
> > 'The Prairie'.*

Down a broad river of the western wilds,
Piercing thick forest-glooms, a light canoe
Swept with the current: fearful was the speed
Of the frail bark, as by a tempest's wing
Borne leaf-like on to where the mist of spray
Rose with the cataract's thunder. Yet within,
Proudly, and dauntlessly, and all alone,
Save that a babe lay sleeping at her breast,
A woman stood! Upon her Indian brow
Sat a strange gladness, and her dark hair waved
As if triumphantly. She press'd her child,
In its bright slumber, to her beating heart,
And lifted her sweet voice, that rose awhile
Above the sound of waters, high and clear,
Wafting a wild proud strain—a song of death.

'Roll swiftly to the spirits' land, thou mighty stream and free!
Father of ancient waters roll!* and bear our lives with thee!
The weary bird that storms have toss'd would seek the sunshine's
    calm,
And the deer that hath the arrow's hurt flies to the woods of balm.

'Roll on!—my warrior's eye hath look'd upon another's face,
And mine hath faded from his soul, as fades a moonbeam's trace:
My shadow comes not o'er his path, my whisper to his dream—
He flings away the broken reed. Roll swifter yet, thou stream!

'The voice that spoke of other days is hush'd within *his* breast,

But *mine* its lonely music haunts, and will not let me rest;
It sings a low and mournful song of gladness that is gone—
I cannot live without that light. Father of waves! roll on!

'Will he not miss the bounding step that met him from the chase?
The heart of love that made his home an ever-sunny place?
The hand that spread the hunter's board, and deck'd his couch of
    yore?—
He will not! Roll, dark foaming stream, on to the better shore!

'Some blessed fount amidst the woods of that bright land must flow,
Whose waters from my soul may lave the memory of this woe;
Some gentle wind must whisper there, whose breath may waft away
The burden of the heavy night, the sadness of the day.

'And thou, my babe! though born, like me, for woman's weary lot,
Smile!—to that wasting of the heart, my own! I leave thee not;
Too bright a thing art *thou* to pine in aching love away—
Thy mother bears thee far, young fawn! from sorrow and decay.

'She bears thee to the glorious bowers where none are heard to weep,
And where th' unkind one hath no power again to trouble sleep;
And where the soul shall find its youth, as wakening from a dream:
One moment, and that realm is ours. On, on, dark-rolling stream!'

The Traveller at the Source of the Nile (1829)

In sunset's light, o'er Afric thrown,
    A wanderer proudly stood
Beside the well-spring, deep and lone,
    Of Egypt's awful flood—
The cradle of that mighty birth,
So long a hidden thing to earth!

He heard its life's first murmuring sound,
    A low mysterious tone—
A music sought, but never found
    By kings and warriors gone.
He listen'd—and his heart beat high:
That was the song of victory!

The rapture of a conqueror's mood
    Rush'd burning through his frame,—

The depths of that green solitude
    Its torrents could not tame;
Though stillness lay, with eve's last smile,
Round those far fountains of the Nile.

Night came with stars. Across his soul
    There swept a sudden change:
E'en at the pilgrim's glorious goal,
    A shadow dark and strange
Breathed from the thought, so swift to fall
O'er triumph's hour—*and is this all?**

No more than this! What seem'd it *now*
    First by that spring to stand?
A thousand streams of lovelier flow
    Bathed his own mountain-land!
Whence, far o'er waste and ocean track,
Their wild, sweet voices, call'd him back.

They call'd him back to many a glade,
    His childhood's haunt of play,
Where brightly through the beechen shade
    Their waters glanced away;
They call'd him, with their sounding waves,
Back to his father's hills and graves.

But, darkly mingling with the thought
    Of each familiar scene,
Rose up a fearful vision, fraught
    With all that lay between—
The Arab's lance, the desert's gloom,
The whirling sands, the red simoom!

Where was the glow of power and pride?
    The spirit born to roam?
His alter'd heart within him died
    With yearnings for his home!
All vainly struggling to repress
That gush of painful tenderness.

He wept! The stars of Afric's heaven
    Beheld his bursting tears,

E'en on that spot where fate had given
        The meed of toiling years—
O Happiness! how far we flee
Thine own sweet paths in search of thee!

Parting Words (1830)

'One struggle more, and I am free.'
                        Byron*

Leave me! oh, leave me! Unto all below
Thy presence binds me with too deep a spell;
Thou makest those mortal regions, whence I go,
Too mighty in their loveliness. Farewell,
            That I may part in peace!

Leave me!—thy footstep, with its lightest sound,
The very shadow of thy waving hair,
Wakes in my soul a feeling too profound,
Too strong for aught that loves and dies, to bear—
            Oh! bid the conflict cease!

I hear thy whisper—and the warm tears gush
Into mine eyes, the quick pulse thrills my heart;
Thou bid'st the peace, the reverential hush,
The still submission, from my thoughts depart:
            Dear one! this must not be.

The past looks on me from thy mournful eye,
The beauty of our free and vernal days;
Our communings with sea, and hill, and sky—
Oh! take that bright world from my spirit's gaze!
            Thou art all earth to me!

Shut out the sunshine from my dying room,
The jasmine's breath, the murmur of the bee;
Let not the joy of bird-notes pierce the gloom!
They speak of love, of summer, and of thee,
            Too much—and death is here!

Doth our own spring make happy music now,
From the old beech-roots flashing into day?

Are the pure lilies imaged in its flow?
Alas! vain thoughts! that fondly thus can stray
    From the dread hour so near!

If I could but draw courage from the light
Of thy clear eye, that ever shone to bless!
—Not now! 'twill not be now!—my aching sight,
Drinks from that fount a flood of tenderness,
    Bearing all strength away!

Leave me!—thou com'st between my heart and Heaven;
I would be still, in voiceless prayer to die!—
Why must our souls thus love, and then be riven?
Return! thy parting wakes mine agony!
    Oh, yet awhile delay!

The Haunted House (1831)

    'I seem like one who treads alone
      Some banquet hall deserted,
    Whose lights are fled, whose garlands dead,
      And all but me departed.'*

                      Moore

See'st thou yon gray, gleaming hall,
Where the deep elm-shadows fall?*
Voices that have left the earth
    Long ago,
Still are murmuring round its hearth,
    Soft and low:
Ever there;—yet one alone
Hath the gift to hear their tone.
Guests come thither, and depart,
Free of step, and light of heart;
Children, with sweet vision bless'd,
In the haunted chambers rest;
One alone unslumbering lies
When the night hath seal'd all eyes,
One quick heart and watchful ear,
Listening for those whispers clear.

See'st thou where the woodbine-flowers
O'er yon low porch hang in showers?

Startling faces of the dead,
     Pale, yet sweet,
One lone woman's entering tread
     There still meet!
Some with young, smooth foreheads fair.
Faintly shining through bright hair;
Some with reverend locks of snow—
All, all buried long ago!
All, from under deep sea-waves,
Or the flowers of foreign graves,
Or the old and banner'd aisle,
Where their high tombs gleam the while;
Rising, wandering, floating by,
Suddenly and silently,
Through their earthly home and place,
But amidst another race.

Wherefore, unto one alone,
Are those sounds and visions known?
Wherefore hath that spell of power
     Dark and dread,
On *her* soul, a baleful dower,
     Thus been shed?
Oh! in those deep-seeing eyes,
No strange gift of mystery lies!
She is lone where once she moved
Fair, and happy, and beloved!
Sunny smiles were glancing round her,
Tendrils of kind hearts had bound her.
Now those silver chords are broken,
Those bright looks have left no token—
Not one trace on all the earth,
Save her memory of their mirth.
She is lone and lingering now,
Dreams have gather'd o'er her brow,
Midst gay songs and children's play,
She is dwelling far away,
Seeing what none else may see—
Haunted still her place must be!

Written After Visiting a Tomb
Near Woodstock, in the County of Kilkenny* (1831)

> 'Yes! hide beneath the mouldering heap,
> The undelighted, slighted thing;
> There in the cold earth, buried deep,
> In silence let it wait the Spring.'
> Mrs Tighe's 'Poem on the Lily.'*

I stood where the life of song lay low,
Where the dust had gather'd on Beauty's brow;
Where stillness hung on the heart of Love,
And a marble weeper kept watch above.

I stood in the silence of lonely thought,
Of deep affections that inly wrought,
Troubled, and dreamy, and dim with fear—
They knew themselves exiled spirits here!

Then didst *thou* pass me in radiance by,
Child of the sunbeam, bright butterfly!
Thou that dost bear, on thy fairy wings.
No burden of mortal sufferings.

Thou wert flitting past that solemn tomb,
Over a bright world of joy and bloom;
And strangely I felt, as I saw thee shine,
The all that sever'd *thy* life and *mine*.

Mine, with its inborn mysterious things,
Of love and grief its unfathom'd springs;
And quick thoughts wandering o'er earth and sky,
With voices to question eternity!

Thine, in its reckless and joyous way,
Like an embodied breeze at play!
Child of the sunlight!—thou wing'd and free!
One moment, *one* moment, I envied thee!

Thou art not lonely, though born to roam,
Thou hast no longings that pine for home;
Thou seek'st not the haunts of the bee and bird,
To fly from the sickness of hope deferr'd:

In thy brief being no strife of mind,
No boundless passion, is deeply shrined;
While I, as I gazed on thy swift flight by,
One hour of my soul seem'd infinity!

And she, that voiceless below me slept,
Flow'd not her song from a heart that wept?
—O Love and Song! though of heaven your powers,
Dark is your fate in this world of ours.

Yet, ere I turn'd from that silent place,
Or ceased from watching thy sunny race,
'Thou, even thou, on those glancing wings,
Didst waft me visions of brighter things!

Thou that dost image the freed soul's birth,
And its flight away o'er the mists of earth,
Oh! fitly thy path is through flowers that rise
Round the dark chamber where Genius lies!

The Last Song of Sappho (1832)

Suggested by a beautiful sketch, the design of the younger Westmacott. It
represents Sappho sitting on a rock above the sea, with her lyre cast at her
feet. There is a desolate grace about the whole figure, which seems
penetrated with the feeling of utter abandonment.*

Sound on, thou dark, unslumbering sea!
    My dirge is in thy moan;
My spirit finds response in thee
To its own ceaseless cry—'Alone, alone!'

Yet send me back one other word,
    Ye tones that never cease!
Oh! let your secret caves be stirr'd,
And say, dark waters! will ye give me *peace*?

Away! my weary soul hath sought
    In vain one echoing sigh,
One answer to consuming thought
In human hearts—and will the *wave* reply?

Sound on, thou dark unslumbering sea!
    Sound in thy scorn and pride!

I ask not, alien world! from thee
What my own kindred earth hath still denied.

And yet I loved that earth so well,
  With all its lovely things!
Was it for this the death-wind fell
On my rich lyre, and quench'd its living strings?

Let them lie silent at my feet!
  Since, broken even as they,
The heart whose music made them sweet
Hath pour'd on desert sands its wealth away.

Yet glory's light hath touch'd my name,
  The laurel-wreath is mine—
With a lone heart, a weary frame—
O restless deep! I come to make them thine!

Give to that crown, that burning crown,
  Place in thy darkest hold!
Bury my anguish, my renown,
With hidden wrecks, lost gems, and wasted gold.

Thou sea-bird on the billow's crest!
  Thou hast thy love, thy home;
They wait thee in the quiet nest,
And I, th' unsought, unwatch'd-for—I too come!

I, with this winged nature fraught,
  These visions wildly free,
This boundless love, this fiery thought—
Alone I come—oh! give me peace, dark sea!

HARRIETTE WILSON
(1786–1845)

Born and brought up in London, one of the fifteen children of a Swiss-born Mayfair shopkeeper, John Dubochet, and his wife Amelia Cook, who was the illegitimate daughter of a gentleman, Harriette Dubochet entered into a series of affairs with men of fashion and wealth, becoming the most celebrated courtesan of her times. During her upbringing she helped her mother and sisters in stocking-mending, by which the family made its living, and like her two elder sisters she left home when still young to seek a more traditional and more lucrative career. Her heyday was the first decade of the nineteenth century. Although good-looking she was not a great beauty, but she was witty and entertaining: Walter Scott, who met her in London in her late teens, remembered her as having 'the manners of a wild schoolboy'.[1] Her list of conquests included Lord Craven, the Hon. Frederick Lamb, the Duke of Argyle, the Marquis of Worcester, the Duke of Beaufort, the Duke of Wellington, Prince Esterhazy, Viscount Ponsonby, and the Duke of Leinster. In 1823 she married William Henry Rochfort, an Irish officer.

Harriette Wilson acquired lasting notoriety only when one man took advantage of what he assumed to be the powerlessness of her social situation. When the Duke of Beaufort reneged on the financial understanding they had reached, Wilson decided to capitalize on her connections, and wrote her *Memoirs of Harriette Wilson, Written by Herself* to extort money from those exposed. ('Two hundred pounds by return of post, to be left out'—'Publish and be damned', retorted the Duke of Wellington, securing the Wilson affair a place in the history of the language.) Extortion of this kind required publicity; and when publication went ahead, a sensation turned out to have been created, purchasers lining the streets outside the offices of John Joseph Stockdale, publisher, in Haymarket, London. The throng had to be controlled by a specially built barrier. Some estimates say that Wilson's earnings reached £10,000. The work was translated into French, and illustrations were commissioned. It also boasted, in respectable style, an 'editor' called Thomas Little, probably a composite, or Stockdale himself; the identity is less interesting than the appeal to recognized literary tradition, works such as Daniel Defoe's 'edited' memoirs of *Moll Flanders* (1722) springing to mind. Whether or not the 'editor' chastened Wilson's style, 'he' did nothing to impose a moralizing framework on the errant narrator's adventures. When more instalments of the memoirs were threatened, a group of gentlemen paid up. From about 1820 she lived mainly in Paris, and was snubbed on her return to London in 1830. Her last years were spent in obscurity. The *Memoirs*, meanwhile, frequently pirated, remained in the public eye, helped to define the Regency period for later writers, and were often used as anti-aristocratic propaganda by radical groups. Wilson went on to publish two *romans-à-clef*, *Paris Lions and London Tigers* (1825) and *Clara Gazul* (1830).

One of the most interesting narrative features of Wilson's *Memoirs* is the interwoven experiences of her sisters Fanny, Amy, and Sophia: they appeared of sufficient importance to require Thomas Seccombe in his

[1] *The Journal of Sir Walter Scott*, ed. W. E. K. Anderson (Oxford: OUP, 1972), 31.

notice of Harriette Wilson in the *Dictionary of National Biography* to enlighten readers as to their subsequent fortunes. In a small way this is a triumph of what would now be seen as fictional documentary. It is significant that the narrative of Wilson's liaisons with men should be combined in this way with the story of her relationships with her sisters, and in formal terms it challenges such male-authored works of 'whore biography' as John Cleland's *Fanny Hill; or, Memoirs of a Woman of Pleasure* (1748–9) by overturning the convention by which parallel female erotic experiences are used to maintain the stimulus of the narrative. Harriette Wilson fences with men, but seems to be hurt only by women.

In 1925 Virginia Woolf devoted a perceptive and evocative essay to Harriette Wilson, commenting on the special effort Wilson had to make as a narrator to 'make good her claim to a share in the emotions of human kind',[2] and concluding that 'gifts she had, gifts of dash and go and enthusiasm, which still stir among the dead leaves of her memoirs, and impart even to their rambling verbosity and archness and vulgarity some thrill of that old impetuosity, some flash of those fine dark eyes'.[3] It is not Wilson's love affairs which provide the work's interest, according to Woolf: 'It is when off duty, released from the necessity of painting the usual picture in the usual way, that she becomes capable of drawing one of those pictures which only seem to await some final stroke to become a page in *Vanity Fair* or a sketch by Hogarth.'[4]

Harriette Wilson offers her readers a fictional 'self' of some reflection and advance planning, but characterized more by verve and daring. The purpose of her *Memoirs* imposes on it some tedium of structure, but in its own way it is a heroic narrative of a woman keeping one step ahead of privileged men. It is also an expressively superficial evocation of Regency manners; and it looks back on the same Prince of Wales (at the time of publication, George IV) who took Mary Robinson as his mistress and whose marital conduct was excoriated by Mary Hays. Most importantly of all in terms of this collection, however, the *Memoirs of Harriette Wilson* suggest that the most successful and subversive thing a woman could do was simply to write.

∼

[2] Collected in *The Moment, Collected Essays*, 4 vols. (London: Hogarth Press, 1966–7), iii. 228.
[3] Ibid. iii. 229.
[4] Ibid.

From *Memoirs of Harriette Wilson,*
Written by Herself (1825)

I shall not say why and how I became, at the age of fifteen, the mistress of the Earl of Craven.* Whether it was love, or the severity of my father, the depravity of my own heart, or the winning arts of the noble Lord, which induced me to leave my paternal roof and place myself under his protection, does not now much signify: or if it does, I am not in the humour to gratify curiosity in this matter.

I resided on the Marine Parade, at Brighton;* and I remember that Lord Craven used to draw cocoa trees, and his fellows, as he called them, on the best vellum paper, for my amusement. Here stood the enemy, he would say; and here, my love, are my fellows: there the cocoa trees, etc. It was, in fact, a dead bore. All these cocoa trees and fellows, at past eleven o'clock at night, could have no peculiar interest for a child like myself, so lately in the habit of retiring early to rest. One night, I recollect, I fell asleep; and, as I often dream, I said, yawning, and half awake, 'Oh, Lord! oh, Lord! Craven has got me into the West Indies again.' In short, I soon found that I had made a bad speculation by going from my father to Lord Craven. I was even more afraid of the latter than I had been of the former; not that there was any particular harm in the man, beyond his cocoa trees; but we never suited nor understood each other.

I was not depraved enough to determine immediately on a new choice, and yet I often thought about it. How, indeed, could I do otherwise, when the Honourable Frederick Lamb was my constant visitor, and talked to me of nothing else?* However, in justice to myself, I must declare that the idea of the possibility of deceiving Lord Craven, while I was under his roof, never once entered into my head. Frederick was then very handsome; and certainly tried, with all his soul and with all his strength, to convince me that constancy to Lord Craven was the greatest nonsense in the world. I firmly believe that Frederick Lamb sincerely loved me, and deeply regretted that he had no fortune to invite me to share with him.

Lord Melbourne, his father, was a good man. Not one of your stiff-laced moralizing fathers, who preach chastity and forbearance to their children. Quite the contrary; he congratulated his son on the lucky circumstance of his friend Craven having such a girl with him.

'No such thing,' answered Frederick Lamb; 'I am unsuccessful there. Harriette will have nothing to do with me.'—'Nonsense!' rejoined Melbourne, in great surprise; 'I never heard anything half so ridiculous in all my life. The girl must be mad! She looks mad: I thought so the other day, when I met her galloping about, with her feathers blowing and her thick dark hair about her ears.'

'I'll speak to Harriette for you,' added His Lordship, after a long pause; and then continued repeating to himself, in an undertone, 'Not have my son, indeed! six feet high! a fine, straight, handsome, noble young fellow! I wonder what she would have!'

In truth, I scarcely knew myself; but something I determined on: so miserably tired was I of Craven, and his cocoa trees, and his sailing boats, and his ugly cotton nightcap. Surely, I would say, all men do not wear those shocking cotton nightcaps; else all women's illusions had been destroyed on the first night of their marriage!

I wonder, thought I, what sort of a nightcap the Prince of Wales wears? Then I went on to wonder whether the Prince of Wales would think me so beautiful as Frederick Lamb did? Next I reflected that Frederick Lamb was younger than the Prince; but then, again, a Prince of Wales!!!

I was undecided: my heart began to soften. I thought of my dear mother, and wished I had never left her. It was too late, however, now. My father would not suffer me to return; and as to passing my life, or any more of it, with Craven, cotton nightcap and all, it was death! He never once made me laugh, nor said nor did anything to please me.

Thus musing, I listlessly turned over my writing-book, half in the humour to address the Prince of Wales. A sheet of paper, covered with Lord Craven's cocoa trees, decided me; and I wrote the following letter, which I addressed to the Prince.

BRIGHTON

I am told that I am very beautiful, so, perhaps, you would like to see me; and I wish that, since so many are disposed to love me, one, for in the humility of my heart I should be quite satisfied with one, would be at the pains to make me love him. In the mean time, this is all very dull work, Sir, and worse even than being at home with my father: so, if you pity me, and believe you could make me in love with you, write to me, and direct to the post-office here.

By return of post, I received an answer nearly to this effect: I believe, from Colonel Thomas.*

Miss Wilson's letter has been received by the noble individual to whom it was addressed. If Miss Wilson will come to town, she may have an interview, by directing her letter as before.

I answered this note directly, addressing my letter to the Prince of Wales.

SIR,

To travel fifty-two miles, this bad weather, merely to see a man, with only the given number of legs, arms, fingers, etc., would, you must admit, be madness, in a girl like myself, surrounded by humble admirers, who are ever ready to travel any distance for the honour of kissing the tip of her little finger; but if you can prove to me that you are one bit better than any man who may be ready to attend my bidding, I'll e'en start for London directly. So, if you can do anything better, in the way of pleasing a lady, than ordinary men, write directly: if not, adieu, Monsieur le Prince.

I won't say Yours,
By day or night, or any kind of light;
*Because you are too impudent.**

It was necessary to put this letter into the post-office myself, as Lord Craven's black footman would have been somewhat surprised at its address. Crossing the Steyne,* I met Lord Melbourne, who joined me immediately.

'Where is Craven?' said His Lordship, shaking hands with me.

'Attending to his military duties at Lewes, my Lord.'

'And where's my son Fred?' asked His Lordship.

'I am not your son's keeper, my Lord,' said I.

'No! By the by,' inquired His Lordship, 'how is this; I wanted to call upon you about it. I never heard of such a thing, in the whole course of my life! What the Devil can you possibly have to say against my son Fred?'

'Good heavens! my Lord, you frighten me! I never recollect to have said a single word against your son, as long as I have lived. Why should I?'

'Why, indeed!' said Lord Melbourne. 'And since there is nothing to be said against him, what excuse can you make for using him so ill?'

'I don't understand you one bit, my Lord.' (The very idea of a father put me in a tremble.)

'Why,' said Lord Melbourne, 'did you not turn the poor boy out of your house, as soon as it was dark; although Craven was in town,* and there was not the shadow of an excuse for such treatment?'

At this moment, and before I could recover from my surprise at the tenderness of some parents, Frederick Lamb, who was almost my shadow, joined us.

'Fred, my boy,' said Lord Melbourne, 'I'll leave you two together; and I fancy you'll find Miss Wilson more reasonable.' He touched his hat to me, as he entered the little gate of the Pavilion, where we had remained stationary from the moment His Lordship had accosted me.

Frederick Lamb laughed long, loud, and heartily at his father's interference. So did I, the moment he was safely out of sight; and then I told him of my answer to the Prince's letter, at which he laughed still more. He was charmed with me for refusing His Royal Highness. 'Not,' said Frederick, 'that he is not as handsome and graceful a man as any in England; but I hate the weakness of a woman who knows not how to refuse a prince, merely because he is a prince.'

Frederick Lamb now began to plead his own cause. 'I must soon join my regiment in Yorkshire,' said he (he was, at that time, aide-de-camp to General Mackenzie);* 'God knows when we may meet again! I am sure you will not long continue with Lord Craven. I foresee what will happen, and yet, when it does, I think I shall go mad!'

For my part, I felt flattered and obliged by the affection Frederick Lamb evinced towards me; but I was still not in love with him.

At length the time arrived when poor Frederick Lamb could delay his departure from Brighton no longer. On the eve of it, he begged to be allowed to introduce his brother William to me.*

'What for?' said I.

'That he may let me know how you behave,' answered Frederick Lamb.

'And if I fall in love with him?' I inquired.

'I am sure you won't,' replied Fred. 'Not because my brother William is not likeable; on the contrary, William is much handsomer than I am; but he will not love you as I have done, and do still; and you are too good to forget me entirely.'

Our parting scene was rather tender. For the last ten days, Lord Craven being absent, we had scarcely been separated an hour during the whole day. I had begun to feel the force of habit; and Frederick Lamb really respected me, for the perseverance with which I had resisted his urgent wishes, when he would have had me deceive Lord Craven. He had ceased to torment me with such wild fits of passion as had, at first, frightened me; and by these means he had obtained much more of my confidence.

Two days after his departure for Hull, in Yorkshire, Lord Craven returned to Brighton, where he was immediately informed, by some spiteful enemy of mine, that I had been, during the whole of his absence, openly intriguing with Frederick Lamb. In consequence of this information, one evening, when I expected his return, his servant brought me the following letter, dated Lewes:

A friend of mine has informed me of what has been going on at Brighton. This information, added to what I have seen with my own eyes, of your intimacy with Frederick Lamb, obliges me to declare that we must separate. Let me add, Harriette, that you might have done anything with me, with only a little more conduct. As it is, allow me to wish you happy; and further, pray inform me, if, in any way, à la distance, I can promote your welfare.

CRAVEN

This letter completed my dislike of Lord Craven. I answered it immediately, as follows:

MY LORD,

Had I ever wished to deceive you, I have the wit to have done it successfully; but you are old enough to be a better judge of human nature than to have suspected me of guile or deception. In the plenitude of your condescension, you are pleased to add, that I 'might have done anything with you, with only a little more conduct', now I say, and from my heart, the Lord defend me from ever doing any thing with you again! Adieu.

HARRIETTE

My present situation was rather melancholy and embarrassing, and yet I felt my heart the lighter for my release from the cocoa trees, with its being my own act and deed. It is my fate! thought I; for I never wronged this man. I hate his fine carriage, and his money, and everything belonging to, or connected with him. I shall hate cocoa as long as I live; and, I am sure, I will never enter a boat again, if I can help it. This is what one gets by acting with principle.

The next morning, while I was considering what was to become of me, I received a very affectionate letter from Frederick Lamb, dated Hull. He dared not, he said, be selfish enough to ask me to share his poverty, and yet he had a kind of presentiment, that he should not lose me.

My case was desperate; for I had taken a vow not to remain another night under Lord Craven's roof. John, therefore, the black, whom Craven had, I suppose, imported, with his cocoa trees from the West Indies, was desired to secure me a place in the mail for Hull.

It is impossible to do justice to the joy and rapture which brightened Frederick's countenance, when he flew to receive me, and conducted me to his house, where I was shortly visited by his worthy general, Mackenzie, who assured me of his earnest desire to make my stay in Hull as comfortable as possible.

We continued here for about three months, and then came to London. Fred Lamb's passion increased daily; but I discovered, on our arrival in London, that he was a voluptuary, somewhat worldly and selfish. My comforts were not considered. I lived in extreme poverty, while he contrived to enjoy all the luxuries of life; and suffered me to pass my dreary evenings alone, while he frequented balls, masquerades, etc. Secure of my constancy, he was satisfied—so was not I! I felt that I deserved better from him.

I asked Frederick, one day, if the Marquis of Lorne was as handsome as he had been represented to me. 'The finest fellow on earth,' said Frederick Lamb, 'all the women adore him'; and then he went on to relate various anecdotes of His Lordship, which strongly excited my curiosity.*

Soon after this, he quitted town for a few weeks, and I was left alone in London, without money, or, at any rate, with very little; and Frederick Lamb, who had intruded himself on me at Brighton, and thus become the cause of my separation from Lord Craven, made himself happy; because he believed me faithful, and cared not for my distresses.

This idea disgusted me; and, in a fit of anger, I wrote to the Marquis of Lorne, merely to say that, if he would walk up to Duke's Row, Somerstown,* he would meet a most lovely girl.

This was his answer:

If you are but half as lovely as you think yourself, you must be well worth knowing; but how is that to be managed? not in the street! But come to No. 39 Portland Street, and ask for me.

L.

My reply was this:

No! our first meeting must be on the high road, in order that I may have room to run away, in case I don't like you.

HARRIETTE

The Marquis rejoined:

Well, then, fair lady, tomorrow, at four, near the turnpike, look for me on horseback; and then, you know, I can gallop away.

L.

We met. The Duke (he has since succeeded to the title) did not gallop away; and, for my part, I had never seen a countenance I had thought half so beautifully expressive. I was afraid to look at it, lest a closer examination might destroy all the new and delightful sensation his first glance had inspired in my breast. His manner was most gracefully soft and polished. We walked together for about two hours.

'I never saw such a sunny, happy countenance as yours in my whole life,' said Argyle to me.

'Oh, but I am happier than usual today,' answered I, very naturally.

Before we parted, the Duke knew as much of me and my adventures as I knew myself. He was very anxious to be allowed to call on me.

'And how will your particular friend, Frederick Lamb, like that?' inquired I.

The Duke laughed.

'Well, then,' said His Grace, 'do me the honour, some day, to come and dine or sup with me at Argyle House.'

'I shall not be able to run away, if I go there,' I answered, laughingly, in allusion to my last note.

'Shall you want to run away from me?' said Argyle; and there was something unusually beautiful and eloquent in his countenance, which brought a deep blush into my cheek.

'When we know each other better?' added Argyle, beseechingly.

'*En attendant*, will you walk again with me tomorrow?' I assented, and we parted.

I returned to my home in unusual spirits; they were a little damped, however, by the reflection that I had been doing wrong. I cannot, I reasoned with myself, I cannot, I fear, become what the world calls a steady, prudent, virtuous woman. That time is past, even if I was ever fit for it. Still I must distinguish myself from those in the like unfortunate situations, by strict probity and love of truth. I will never become vile. I will always adhere to good faith, as long as anything like kindness or honourable principle is shown towards me; and, when I am ill-used, I will leave my lover rather than deceive him. Frederick Lamb relies in perfect confidence on my honour. True, that confidence is the effect of vanity. He believes that a woman who could resist him, as I did at Brighton, is the safest woman on earth! He leaves me alone, and without sufficient money for common necessaries. No matter, I must tell him tonight, as soon as he arrives from the country, that I have written to, and walked with Lorne. My dear mother would never forgive me, if I became artful.

So mused, and thus reasoned I, till I was interrupted by Frederick Lamb's loud knock at my door. He will be in a fine passion, said I to myself, in excessive trepidation; and I was in such a hurry to have it over, that I related all immediately. To my equal joy and astonishment, Frederick Lamb was not a bit angry. From his manner, I could not help guessing that his friend Lorne had often been found a very powerful rival.

I could see through the delight he experienced, at the idea of possessing a woman whom, his vanity persuaded him, Argyle would sigh for in vain; and attacking me on my weak point, he kissed me, and said, 'I have the most perfect esteem for my dearest little wife, whom I can, I know, as safely trust with Argyle as Craven trusted her with me.'

'Are you quite sure?' I asked, merely to ease my conscience. 'Were it not wiser to advise me not to walk about with him?'

'No, no,' said Frederick Lamb; 'it is such good fun! bring him up every day to Somerstown and the Jew's Harp House,* there to swallow cyder and sentiment. Make him walk up here as many times as you can, dear little Harry, for the honour of your sex, and to punish him for declaring, as he always does, that no woman who will not love him at once is worth his pursuit.'

'I am sorry he is such a coxcomb,' said I.

'What is that to you, you little fool?'

'True,' I replied. And, at that moment, I made a sort of determination not to let the beautiful and voluptuous expression of Argyle's dark blue eyes take possession of my fancy.

'You are a neater figure than the Marquis of Lorne,' said I to Frederick, wishing to think so.

'Lorne is growing fat,' answered Frederick Lamb; 'but he is the most active creature possible, and appears lighter than any man of his weight I ever saw; and then he is, without any exception, the highest-bred man in England.'

'And you desire and permit me to walk about the country with him?'

'Yes; do trot him up here. I want to have a laugh against Lorne.'

'And you are not jealous?'

'Not at all,' said Frederick Lamb, 'for I am secure of your affections.'

I must not deceive this man, thought I, and the idea began to make me a little melancholy. My only chance, or rather my only excuse, will be his leaving me without the means of existence. This appeared likely; for I was too shy and too proud to ask for money; and Frederick Lamb encouraged me in this amiable forbearance!

The next morning, with my heart beating very unusually high, I attended my appointment with Argyle. I hoped, nay, almost expected, to find him there before me. I paraded near the turnpike five minutes, then grew angry; in five more, I became wretched; in five more, downright indignant; and, in five more, wretched again— and so I returned home.

This, thought I, shall be a lesson to me hereafter, never to meet a man: it is unnatural; and yet I had felt it perfectly natural to return to the person whose society had made me so happy! No matter, reasoned I, we females must not suffer love or pleasure to glow in our eyes until we are quite sure of a return. We must be dignified! Alas! I can only be and seem what I am. No doubt my sunny face of joy and happiness, which he talked to me about, was understood, and it has disgusted him. He thought me bold, and yet I am sure I never blushed so much in any man's society before.

I now began to consider myself with feelings of the most painful humility. Suddenly I flew to my writing-desk: he shall not have the cut all on his side neither, thought I, with the pride of a child. I will soon convince him I am not accustomed to be slighted; and then I wrote to His Grace, as follows:

It was very wrong and very bold of me, to have sought your acquaintance, in the way I did, my Lord; and I entreat you to forgive and forget my childish folly, as completely as I have forgotten the occasion of it.

So far, so good, thought I, pausing; but then suppose he should, from this dry note, really believe me so cold and stupid as not to have felt his pleasing qualities? Suppose now it were possible that he liked me after all? Then, hastily, and half ashamed of myself, I added these few lines:

I have not quite deserved this contempt from you, and, in that consolatory reflection, I take my leave—not in anger, my Lord, but only with the steady determination so to profit by the humiliating lesson you have given me, as never to expose myself to the like contempt again.

> *Your most obedient servant,*
> HARRIETTE WILSON

Having put my letter into the post, I passed a restless night; and, the next morning, heard the knock of the twopenny postman, in extreme agitation. He brought me, as I suspected, an answer from Argyle, which is subjoined.

You are not half vain enough, dear Harriette. You ought to have been quite certain that any man who had once met you, could fail in a second appointment, but from unavoidable accident—and, if you were only half as pleased with Thursday morning as I was, you will meet me tomorrow, in the same place, at four. Pray, pray, come.

> LORNE

I kissed the letter, and put it into my bosom, grateful for the weight it had taken off my heart. Not that I was so far gone in love, as my readers may imagine, but I had suffered severely from wounded pride, and, in fact, I was very much *tête montée.**

The sensations which Argyle had inspired me with, were the warmest, nay, the first of the same nature I had ever experienced. Nevertheless, I could not forgive him quite so easily as this, neither. I recollected what Frederick Lamb had said about his vanity. No doubt, thought I, he thinks it was nothing to have paraded me up and down that stupid turnpike road, in the vain hope of seeing him. It shall now be his turn: and I gloried in the idea of revenge.

The hour of Argyle's appointment drew nigh, arrived, and passed away, without my leaving my house. To Frederick Lamb I related everything—presented him with Argyle's letter, and acquainted him with my determination not to meet His Grace.

'How good!' said Frederick Lamb, quite delighted. 'We dine together today, at Lady Holland's; and I mean to ask him, before everybody at table, what he thinks of the air about the turnpike in Somerstown.'

The next day I was surprised by a letter, not, as I anticipated, from Argyle, but from the late Tom Sheridan, only son of Richard Brinsley Sheridan.* I had, by mere accident, become acquainted with that very interesting young man, when quite a child, from the circumstances of his having paid great attention to one of my elder sisters.

He requested me to allow him to speak a few words to me, wherever I pleased. Frederick Lamb having gone to Brocket Hall, in Hertfordshire,* I desired him to call on me.

'I am come from my friend Lorne,' said Tom Sheridan. 'I would not have intruded on you, but that poor fellow, he is really annoyed: and he has commissioned me to acquaint you with the accident which obliged him to break his appointment, because I can best vouch for the truth of it, having, upon my honour, heard the Prince of Wales invite Lord Lorne to Carlton House,* with my own ears, at the very moment when he was about to meet you in Somerstown. Lorne,' continued Tom Sheridan, 'desires me to say, that he is not coxcomb enough to imagine you cared for him; but, in justice, he wants to stand exactly where he did in your opinion, before he broke his appointment: he was so perfectly innocent on that subject. "I would write to her," said he, again and again; "but that, in all probability, my letters would be shown to Frederick Lamb, and be laughed at by them both. I would call on her, in spite of the devil, but that I know not where she lives."'

'I asked Argyle,' Tom Sheridan proceeded, 'how he had addressed his last letters to you? To the post-office, in Somerstown, was his answer, and thence they were forwarded to Harriette. He had tried to bribe the old woman there, to obtain my address, but she abused him, and turned him out of her shop. It is very hard,' continued Tom, repeating the words of his noble friend, 'to lose the goodwill of one of the nicest, cleverest girls I ever met with in my life, who was, I am certain, civilly, if not kindly disposed towards me, by such a mere accident. Therefore,' continued Tom Sheridan, smiling, 'you'll make it up with Lorne, won't you?'

'There is nothing to forgive,' said I, 'if no slight was meant. In short, you are making too much of me, and spoiling me, by all this explanation; for, indeed, I had, at first, been less indignant; but that I fancied His Grace neglected me, because—' and I hesitated, while I could feel myself blush deeply.

'Because what?' asked Tom Sheridan.

'Nothing,' I replied, looking at my shoes.

'What a pretty girl you are,' observed Sheridan, 'particularly when you blush.'

'Fiddlestick!' said I, laughing; 'you know you always preferred my sister Fanny.'

'Well,' replied Tom, 'there I plead guilty. Fanny is the sweetest creature on earth; but you are all a race of finished coquettes, who delight in making fools of people. Now can anything come up to your vanity in writing to Lorne, that you are the most beautiful creature on earth?'

'Never mind,' said I, 'you set all that to rights. I was never vain in your society, in my life.'

'I would give the world for a kiss at this moment,' said Tom; 'because you look so humble, and so amiable; but'—recollecting himself—'this is not exactly the embassy I came upon. Have you a mind to give Lorne an agreeable surprise?'

'I don't know.'

'Upon my honour I believe he is downright in love with you.'

'Well?'

'Come into a hackney-coach with me, and we will drive down to the Tennis Court, in the Haymarket.'*

'Is the Duke there?'

'Yes.'

'But—at all events, I will not trust myself in a hackney-coach with you.'

'There was a time,' said poor Tom Sheridan, with much drollery of expression, 'there was a time when the very motion of a carriage would—but now!'—and he shook his handsome head with comic gravity—'but now! you may drive with me, from here to St Paul's, in the most perfect safety. I will tell you a secret,' added he, and he fixed his fine dark eyes on my face while he spoke, in a tone, half merry, half desponding, 'I am dying; but nobody knows it yet!'

I was very much affected by his manner of saying this.

'My dear Mr Sheridan,' said I, with earnest warmth, 'you have accused me of being vain of the little beauty God has given me. Now I would give it all, or, upon my word, I think I would, to obtain the certainty that you would, from this hour, refrain from such excesses as are destroying you.'

'Did you see me play the methodist parson, in a tub, at Mrs Beaumont's masquerade, last Thursday?' said Tom, with affected levity.

'You may laugh as you please,' said I, 'at a little fool like me pretending to preach to you; yet I am sensible enough to admire you, and quite feeling enough to regret your time so misspent, your brilliant talents so misapplied.'

'Bravo! Bravo!' Tom reiterated, 'what a funny little girl you are! Pray, Miss, how is your time spent?'

'Not in drinking brandy,' I replied.

'And how might your talent be applied, Ma'am?'

'Have not I just given you a specimen, in the shape of a handsome quotation?'

'My good little girl—it is in the blood, and I can't help it—and, if I could, it is too late now. I'm dying, I tell you. I know not if my poor father's physician was as eloquent as you are; but he did his best to turn him from drinking. Among other things, he declared to him one day, that the brandy, Arquebusade, and eau-de-Cologne he swallowed, would burn off the coat of his stomach.* Then, said my father, my stomach must digest in its waistcoat; for I cannot help it.'

'Indeed, I am very sorry for you,' I replied; and I hoped he believed me; for he pressed my hand hastily, and I think I saw a tear glisten in his bright, dark eye.

'Shall I tell Lorne,' said poor Tom, with an effort to recover his usual gaiety, 'that you will write to him, or will you come to the Tennis Court?'

'Neither,' answered I; 'but you may tell His Lordship that, of course, I am not angry, since I am led to believe he had no intention to humble nor make a fool of me.'

'Nothing more?' inquired Tom.

'Nothing,' I replied, 'for His Lordship.'

'And what for me?' said Tom.

'You! what do you want?'

'A kiss!' he said.

'Not I, indeed!'

'Be it so, then; and yet you and I may never meet again on this earth, and just now I thought you felt some interest about me'; and he was going away.

'So I do, dear Tom Sheridan!' said I, detaining him; for I saw death had fixed his stamp on poor Sheridan's handsome face. 'You know I have a very warm and feeling heart, and taste enough to admire and like you; but why is this to be our last meeting?'

'I must go to the Mediterranean,' poor Sheridan continued, putting his hand to his chest, and coughing.

To die! thought I, as I looked on his sunk, but still very expressive dark eyes.

'Then God bless you!' said I, first kissing his hand, and then, though somewhat timidly, leaning my face towards him. He parted my hair, and kissed my forehead, my eyes, and my lips.

'If I do come back,' said he, forcing a languid smile, 'mind let me find you married, and rich enough to lend me an occasional hundred pounds or two.' He then kissed my hand gracefully, and was out of sight in an instant.

I never saw him again.

The next morning my maid brought me a little note from Argyle, to say that he had been waiting about my door an hour, having learned my address from poor Sheridan; and that, seeing the servant in the street, he could not help making an attempt to induce me to go out and walk with him. I looked out of the window, saw Argyle, ran for my hat and cloak, and joined him in an instant.

'Am I forgiven?' said Argyle, with gentle eagerness.

'Oh yes,' returned I, 'long ago; but that will do you no good, for I really am treating Frederick Lamb very ill, and therefore must not walk with you again.'

'Why not?' Argyle inquired. '*Apropos*,' he added, 'you told Frederick that I walked about the turnpike looking for you, and that, no doubt, to make him laugh at me?'

'No, not for that; but I never could deceive any man. I have told him the whole story of our becoming acquainted, and he allows me to walk with you. It is I who think it wrong, not Frederick.'

'That is to say, you think me a bore,' said Argyle, reddening with pique and disappointment.

'And suppose I loved you?' I asked, 'still I am engaged to Frederick Lamb, who trusts me, and—'

'If,' interrupted Argyle, 'it were possible you did love me, Frederick Lamb would be forgotten: but, though you did not love me, you must promise to try and do so, some day or other. You don't know how much I have fixed my heart on it.'

These sentimental walks continued more than a month. One evening we walked rather later than usual. It grew dark. In a moment of ungovernable passion, Argyle's ardour frightened me. Not that I was insensible to it: so much the contrary, that I felt certain another meeting must decide my fate. Still, I was offended at what, I conceived, showed such a want of respect. The Duke became humble. There is a charm in the humility of a lover who has offended. The charm is so great that we like to prolong it. In spite of all he could say, I left him in anger. The next morning I received the following note:

If you see me waiting about your door, tomorrow evening, do you not fancy I am looking for you; but for your pretty housemaid.

I did see him from a sly corner of my window; but I resisted all my desires, and remained concealed. I dare not see him again, thought I, for I cannot be so very profligate, knowing and feeling, as I do, how impossible it will be to refuse him anything, if we meet again. I cannot treat Fred Lamb in that manner! besides, I should be afraid to tell him of it: he would, perhaps, kill me.

But then, poor dear Lorne! to return his kisses, as I did last night, and afterwards be so very severe on him, for a passion which it seemed so out of his power to control!

Nevertheless we must part, now or never; so I'll write and take my leave of him kindly. This was my letter:

At the first, I was afraid I should love you, and, but for Fred Lamb having requested me to get you up to Somerstown, after I had declined meeting you, I had been happy: now the idea makes me miserable. Still it must be so. I am naturally affectionate. Habit attaches me to Fred Lamb.

I cannot deceive him or acquaint him with what will cause him to cut me, in anger and for ever. We may not then meet again, Lorne, as hitherto: for now we could not be merely friends: lovers we must be, hereafter, or nothing. I have never loved any man in my life before, and yet, dear Lorne, you see we must part. I venture to send you the inclosed thick lock of my hair; because you have been good enough to admire it. I do not care how I have disfigured my head, since you are not to see it again.

God bless you, Lorne. Do not quite forget last night directly, and believe me, as in truth I am,

Most devotedly yours,

HARRIETTE

This was his answer, written, I suppose, in some pique.

True, you have given me many sweet kisses, and a lock of your beautiful hair. All this does not convince me you are one bit in love with me. I am the last man on earth to desire you to do violence to your feelings, by leaving a man as dear to you as Frederick Lamb is; so farewell, Harriette. I shall not intrude to offend you again.

LORNE

Poor Lorne is unhappy; and, what is worse, thought I, he will soon hate me. The idea made me wretched. However, I will do myself the justice to say, that I have seldom, in the whole course of my life, been tempted by my passions or my fancies, to what my heart and conscience told me was wrong. I am afraid my conscience has been a very easy one; but, certainly, I have followed its dictates. There was a want of heart and delicacy, I always thought, in leaving any man, without full and very sufficient reasons for it. At the same time, my dear mother's marriage had proved to me so forcibly, the miseries of two people of contrary opinions and character, torturing each other to the end of their natural lives, that, before I was ten years old, I decided, in my own mind, to live free as air from any restraint but that of my conscience.

MARIA JANE JEWSBURY
(1800–1833)

The eldest of the seven children of Thomas Jewsbury, a mill owner, Maria Jane Jewsbury was born in Measham, Derbyshire, and educated at a school in Shenstone until she was 14. A setback in her father's business took the family to Manchester when she was about 18, and soon afterwards, in 1819, her mother died in childbirth, leaving her to take domestic responsibility for her sister Geraldine (later a well known novelist and reviewer, close friend of Jane Welsh Carlyle and friend of the Rossettis, the Kingsleys, Ruskin, and Huxley) and her other siblings. The change was a blow to her intellectual ambitions. Although she is the less well-known of the Jewsbury sisters, it was her achievements which opened up the literary world to her family. In August 1832 she married the Revd William Kew Fletcher, a chaplain of the East India Company, and she returned with him to Bombay, 'full of hope and belief', according to her friend Laetitia Elizabeth Landon.[1] She described the voyage from Gravesend in 'Extracts from a Lady's Log-Book'. Fourteen months later she died of cholera in Poona.

Jewsbury writes with a rare energy, and often with strikingly accomplished (as well as irresistible) humour. Alaric Watts, editor of the *Manchester Courier*, encouraged her writing, and his influence resulted in the publication of the varied and lively prose and verse pieces of *Phantasmagoria, or Sketches of Life and Literature* in 1825. It was dedicated to William Wordsworth, and led to a friendship with him and his family which was to shape her writing life, and partly to subdue her energy. She was ill for about two years and eventually convalesced emotionally and intellectually during a four-month stay with Felicia Hemans in Wales in 1827. Wordsworth dedicated his poem 'Liberty' to her (1829; annotated 1835), and, like other literary friends including Laetitia Elizabeth Landon, thought highly not only of her writings but also of her lively conversation and quick mind. She was a special friend of Wordsworth's daughter Dora. Landon quotes from some of Jewsbury's 'brilliant' letters at the end of her essay 'On the Character of Mrs Hemans's Writings' (1835), after commenting: 'I never met with any woman who possessed her powers of conversation. If her language had a fault, it was its extreme perfection. It was like reading an eloquent book—full of thought and poetry. . . . Greatly impressed as I was with her powers, it surprised me to note how much she

---

desponded over them.'[2] Elizabeth Barrett described her in a letter of June 1845 to Mary Mitford as 'a woman of more comprehensiveness of mind & of higher logical faculty than are commonly found among women', but (perhaps inevitably) thought her life, cut short, was one of 'aspiration' rather than achievement.[3]

Books of religious reflection (*Letters to the Young*, 1828) and poetry (*Lays of Leisure Hours*, 1829; dedicated to Felicia Hemans) were followed by the extended prose tales *The Three Histories: The History of an Enthusiast, the History of a Nonchalant, the History of a Realist* (1830), the most sustained exercise of her talents: the book went into three editions, and features a version of Felicia Hemans in the character of Egeria in 'The Nonchalant'. Jewsbury also wrote occasional pieces for *The Athenaeum* and for the literary annuals. In the postscript of a letter to Dora Wordsworth of 20 January 1829 she remarks of *Lays of Leisure Hours* 'pray remember that I only write verse to improve my prose';[4] and it is indeed for her prose that she deserves more recognition than she commonly receives.

Two pieces from *Phantasmagoria* are included here, along with a poem, 'To My Own Heart', from *Lays of Leisure Hours*. 'Writing a Love Tale' is a virtuoso piece of comic prose which purports to mock the author's limited powers. Its set-piece pastiches of current writing styles amply deserve to be better known; while the first part of the story brilliantly captures the delaying fetishisms of writing. Jewsbury demonstrates a knowledge of fiction far beyond the common range of the woman reader, and one would liken her wit to that of Jane Austen were that not to misrepresent Jewsbury's self-deprecating warmth. In complete contrast, 'Woman's Love' displays Jewsbury's sentimental feminism; but underneath the effusive style serious claims are being put forward for the revaluation of domestic affection. Jewsbury's way of dealing with the dispute between men and women for superiorty of intellect is characteristically conciliatory, and her closing restatement of the true glory of womanhood is a statement of faith rather than a secured conclusion. The mellifluousness of the style conceals tensions which were to be central to Victorian debates on the nature of women. Finally, 'To My Own Heart' explores these tensions in relation to Jewsbury's reflections on her own creativity, and is particularly interesting when read in conjunction with

[2] Ibid. 184.

[3] *The Letters of Elizabeth Barrett Browning to Mary Russell Mitford: 1836–1854*, ed. Meredith B. Raymond and Mary Ross Sullivan, 3 vols. (Winfield, Kan.: Wedgestone Press, 1983), iii. 118.

[4] *Maria Jane Jewsbury: Occasional Papers*, selected with a Memoir by Eric Gillett (London: Oxford University Press, Humphrey Milford, 1932), p. li.

Elizabeth Barrett's early poems of tempest, inner strife, and uneasy, self-conscious subjugation.

～

Writing a Love Tale (1825)

> The vein, which makes flesh a deity;
> A green goose, a goddess; pure, pure idolatry;—
> God amend us, God amend! we are much out o' the way.
>
> SHAKESPEARE*

When a youth of little more than sixteen, I had obtained much distinction in my own set, which consisted of four persons besides myself, by the extraordinary facility with which I wrote rhymes on all subjects, and produced essays on 'Pride', 'Indolence', 'Humanity', and the like. These from time to time 'graced the columns' of the —— *Weekly Advertiser*,* and were much admired by all who read them. Many a young lady cut them out of the newspaper, in order to preserve them amongst her frills and ribbons; and one or two honoured me so far as to paste them in a small brown paper book, made for the purpose. Let no fair reader start at the vulgarity of the plan:—in those days, Albums, like veils, were a distinction. At length, I longed to shine in more elaborate composition,—to be read by readers of finer taste,—to obtain admiration of a more public nature than I had yet acquired by my three page essays, which commenced with a definition, and closed with a comparison; or by my lines to 'Delia', a 'Dead Lamb', or the 'Moon'.* I was seized with an unaccountable ambition to write a LOVE TALE—a *real* Love Tale, that should make, when finished, a very elegant sentimental-looking volume, and beguile fair ladies of sighs and sixpences, to the infinite satisfaction of my heart and pocket. No sooner imagined, than in imagination effected. A month's pocket-money went for the purchase of pens and paper, the *best* paper, and the *best* pens (Love in those days was always in my mind associated with gilt edge), my desk was re-lined, and the outside polished;—a capacious black leather folio was purchased to receive the MSS—red tape to tie each chapter separately,—and two new penknives, one for erasing, and the other for mending pens.

To find a study was the next concern. I remember debating long between the rival claims of a lumber closet with a sky-light, and an old summer-house, the door of which was off the hinges, and the windows minus of glass, excepting four panes, which were badly cracked. Nevertheless, the summer-house carried the day. It was in the garden;—it was covered with ivy;—it looked ruinous, alias poetical and picturesque. Then ensued the delights of contriving, of revolving ways and means;—of getting up to put them in practice;— the delight, the unspeakable delight, of propping the door,—and patching the windows, and whitewashing the walls, and stopping the rat holes! Then followed the furnishing; a matter requiring greater consideration than such as depended entirely upon my own skill and perseverance. At last, this too was achieved. By dint of exploring— begging—borrowing, and occasionally stealing, the summer-house was furnished,—rather an equivocal term I admit, since the chair was rheumatic in the joints, and the table fastened to the wall on account of a slight deficiency of leg. These were trifles. Buffon, I remembered, spent the better part of fifty years in a study which contained only a single chair, a table, his desk, and a print of Newton, hanging opposite to him.* Now the accommodations of *my* study were, at least, equal to those of his, and its ornaments far superior, for I had portraits of dogs and horses, besides caricatures innumerable, pasted upon the walls, not to mention all my own poetry and essays. I never recollect being so thoroughly happy as during the week which these preparations occupied. It is true I laugh at the freak *now*, but I cannot do so without coveting the simple, devoted energy which made the occupation its own reward.

At length all was ready, and one fine morning in May I took possession in form and for the first time. Everything succeeded *à merveille*.* The table did not give way—and the chair stood steadily;—the sun shone brightly, and the four cracked panes admitted a very pleasant light—quite sufficient—too much light, I was convinced, injured the eyesight. I sat down to my desk;—spread before me the whitest, glossiest, superbest (see Milton in extenuation of the superlatives) quire of gilt edge;*—dipped the stateliest-looking pen in the ink, and then, and for the first time, asked myself—what I had got to say? A question which I found it very much easier to ask, than to answer satisfactorily. I laid down the pen, and began to consider. 'What did I want to write?' A Love

Tale—certainly—a Love Tale, after the most approved fashion, with a proper complement of heroes, heroines, misfortunes, and marriages. A Love Tale, interspersed as usual, with interesting dialogue, and picturesque description. I resumed the pen. Alas, I was farther than ever from knowing how to use it. Difficulties suggested themselves which I had not before contemplated;—difficulties too, neither so palpable nor of such easy remedy as the broken door and cracked window. I thought over all the tales, novels, and romances which I had read (they were not a few), but the more I thought, and the more I remembered, the more difficult seemed the task I had vowed to accomplish. There must be a well-woven plot;—one, if not two;—there must be a variety of characters introduced, and they must act and talk in character;—there must be interest, and pathos, and style, and fine language, and fifty other essentials which had never entered into my previous calculations. Had I mistaken my talents? was the next reflection that occurred. A glance at the essays which adorned my walls reassured me; and again I took up the pen; but again and again I laid it down, unable to produce anything worthy (as I then thought) of myself and my subject. The fever for writing a Love Tale soon passed its crisis, but not before I had made an effort in every known, and unknown, style of composition. A few days since, I found the identical quire of gilt edge, bearing in its blotted pages lamentable proof of my early and disappointed ambition. The reader may be amused by a few specimens, though I doubt not he has already perused similar effusions in print, for that 'there is nothing new under the sun' is especially true of novels.* The opening specimen is exceedingly grand, for, like most young writers in their first piece, I *began* with the sublime, in order to *end* with the ridiculous. Here follows the proof.

SORROWS OF THE SOUL, OR, MAGDALENA THE MYSTERIOUS

Loud blew the wind,—fast poured the rain from a midnight sky,— fiercely bellowed the thunder;—not a star peeped forth from its cloudy tabernacle, upon the dark dwellings of the earth, when Magdalena, in all the radiant charms of grace, beauty, virtue, and simplicity, stood before the gate of the Castle of Colberando, a stranger, an outcast, a pilgrim, and an orphan. All was dark, except here and there the twinkling of a solitary light, illumining a window of the Castle; all was still, except the roaring of the thunder, and the chirping of the poor birds half drowned in their nests by the rain, which fell in torrents. Alas! sighed Magdalena, once, ah once! I had a home, a father, a mother, a brother, a sister, and a lover (here her voice faltered), a lover dearer and nobler than all! But now!—now I am desolate!—alone!—forgotten!—forsaken!—(and the fair Magdalena leaned against a tree and sobbed bitterly) by all—and for ever! Say not so, my beloved! my angel! my Magdalena! (said a voice from the other side of the tree)—say not, think not so harshly of your own, your adoring Palladio Giovanni!—No—no—

> My flower perennial
> My bud of beauty, my imperial rose,
> My passion flower! oh, I will wear thee on
> My heart, and thou shalt never never fade!—
> I'll love thee mightily, my queen, and in
> The sultry hours, I'll sing thee to thy rest,
> With music sweeter than the wild bird's song;
> And I will swear thine eyes are like the stars,—
> (They are! they are! but softer!) and thy shape
> Fine as the vaunted nymphs who poets feigned
> Dwelt long ago in woods of Arcady.*

To say nothing of the natural and novel circumstance of making the hero and heroine soliloquize, quote poetry, and make love in a thunder-storm, I suppose the having so speedily tacked the catastrophe to the commencement left me unable to find a middle for the tale, and induced me to forgo the precious fragment. The next is much superior, and bears, I think, a slight resemblance to a style of composition which, as it has been very popular of late years, must, of necessity, be in good taste.

DUMB DEBORAH

There is a fair spot lying between two lofty mountains, which, sheltered from the ruthless blast of winter, and the fierce and scorching heat of summer, goes and has gone, from time immemorial, by the name of THE EVERGREEN GLEN. There, first appears the pale, pensive, primrose, the maiden-eyed violet, and that poet's darling, the daisy. There too, in that green and graceful valley, nestling in the long grass, or gambolling about like their fellow innocents, the young lambs, are seen in the short sweet sunny days of spring, the bright-eyed and fair-haired children of the neighbouring cottagers. There, in that sequestered spot, hallowed and sheltered from the approach of the enfeebling follies and corroding cares of the world,— springing up in sunshine and serenity of spirit,—a creature of calm, quiet, inward happiness,—a pure child of nature,—grew like a fair flourishing flower,—DUMB DEBORAH! She was lovely in spite of her infirmity;—by some she was loved the better for it,—for, O! there is in the human heart a deep and holy feeling which leads it to send forth its sympathies in the fullest measure to those whose natural birthright of the five senses has been by aught diminished! The quiet, uncomplaining tranquillity of the dumb female establishes a peculiar claim to the affections of man. It is natural that *he* should love her for her very silentness. So Deborah loved, and though—

She never *told* her love,*

was beloved again, firmly, fondly, and fervently. O, words are needless to communicate the feelings of the heart! There is the language of the eye, far more touching, and far less equivocal, than that of the lips,—the language of

The silent stars that wink and listen*

and of the sweet, sweet flowers of the earth. But Deborah, the beautiful, yet bereaved Deborah, had another language,—that of the fingers.

I am exceedingly surprised that I had not courage to finish the above, as I am convinced that judiciously finished, i.e. well spangled with epithets and alliterations, it might have made a very pretty, popular, and pathetic tale. The next specimen is of a totally different nature: I believe I meant it to be that style of writing which we now distinguish by the epithet powerful.

THE CURSE OF SOLITUDE

I stood alone! alone in the Great Desert of Africa! alone in that interminable sea of sand, which no wind can cool,—no water moisten,— which spreads, and spreads, beyond the reach of eyesight, beyond the sphere of thought;—black, barren, blasted, and fiery, like *the vision of an undone eternity*.* I stood alone! Not a tree,—not a flower,—not a herb,—not a single blade of grass, refreshed my sight. Not a breath broke the awful, the invulnerable silence! Not a trace of life,—not a vestige of humanity, no, not even a shadow of savage existence, was visible. I looked around;—but the sun pouring down his red, ruthless, rays, alone returned my glance. *It was as though a demon glared upon me!* I shouted; there was no echo to my voice. The silence smote upon my soul, terrible as a young earthquake. Again, and again, I shouted. Again, and again it returned, each time more terrible than before. Oh the weight of that Solitude! It was as though the earth and the ocean lay upon my soul!—as though the heavens, with all the stars, had fallen upon them to increase the load! Oh the curse of that Solitude! that aimless,—objectless, solitude! I could have hailed with rapture the slimy track of the serpent,—or the lair of the lion, though strewed with the bleaching bones of my species;—aye, I could have loved the presence of my mortal foe, though he had met me thirsting for my blood. At length I slept;—and, suddenly, a dream came over my tortured spirit. I dreamed that I was still alone—still in the desert—when, on its farthest verge, a spotless form appeared. As she stood, flowers of every clime sprung up on the before blasted sand. She came nearer, and *every step she approached, I felt a diminution of torture*. She bent over me, and I longed to awake.—She wreathed my hot dry hair with roses, dropping with the morning dew;—her hand touched my scorched and blackened brow;—it was as though the stream of a summer brook had flowed over it.

'Enough, enough, my little lad'—such subjects require the grasp of a mightier hand than thine. Let us see what comes next—and (rejoice, reader, if you will)—last also. The antipodes of the Curse of Solitude—a plain unaffected tale of everyday life, everyday people, everyday conversation. A tale of dialogue, in which the hero and heroine talk rationally, and in short sentences, as people who intend to be listened to, should do in real life.

WILFRID WINSTANLIE

'My dear Rosa, you cannot surely be serious.'
'Unquestionably I am.'
'You will not see me again of a month?'
'Exactly so.'
'Exactly?—Torture and Tartars!'
'Exactly as I have said, Wilfrid.'

'Rosa, have you any heart?'

'Yes.'

'Where, pray?'

'Here.'

'Are you quite sure?'

'Quite.'

'Rosa, dearest Rosa! will nothing make you repent?'

'Of what?'

'Of your cruelty.'

'Propriety, Wilfrid.'

'Cruelty, Rosa.'

'Prudence, for both of us.'

'Misery for me.'

'Wilfrid, will you listen to reason?'

'Rosa, will you listen to love?'

'No.'

'Do.'

'For a moment I beseech you, be calm.'

'Torture and Tartars!—Calm!—Calm!'

'Wilfrid.'

'Rosa.'

Leaving these lovers to cross-examine each other, according to their leisure and pleasure, I shall no farther expose my early efforts in love writing. At the same time, as many persons may be surprised to find in these volumes such a very small proportion of love, prose and poetry,* I may as well confess the honest truth, which is—that the failures now faithfully narrated so completely dispirited me, that since the days of the summer-house I have abstained from anything of the kind. I know this confession will lower me in the opinion of the fair sex, but honesty is the best policy. The object of my youthful ambition remains unattained—I *cannot* write a Love Tale; and I sit down for life with the mortifying reflection that a peculiar talent is necessary, which has not been bestowed upon me.

Woman's Love (1825)

> The very first
> Of human life, must spring from woman's breast,
> Your first small words be taught you from her lips,
> Your first tears quenched by her, and your last sighs
> Too often breathed out in a woman's hearing.
> When men have shrunk from the ignoble care
> Of watching the last hours of him who led them.
>
>   BYRON*

It would be easy to enumerate the authors who have described Woman as otherwise than 'in love.' It would be too easy to enumerate the books in which Woman is *prominently* brought forwards in any of the great relative characters of life;—as the daughter, the wife, the mother, the sister, the matron, or the friend; and yet wherever she is so introduced by a master hand, the absorbing interest of the book centres in her. Fifty other females may have, or want lovers, and we care nothing for them or their troubles. It is *her* actions, *her* faith, *her* love, and *her* sufferings, which sink into our hearts, ay, and abide there, long after we have closed the book. Elizabeth, in the pride and pomp of royalty, even Elizabeth, yielding to womanly affection, fades from our minds before the influence of her humble rival, the imprudent, but the delicate, the devoted Amy, who loved her husband's honour far better than her own aggrandisement.* No one cares about Rose Bradwardine, when Flora MacIvor stands before us—in sublime self-devotedness to the cause of her royal friends;* and who ever restrained his tears when the high-souled Rebecca presented the casket of jewels to Rowena, sent her farewell to Wilfrid, and went forth a wanderer with her father?*

Jeannie Deans, the heroine of sisterly affection, is more to us than Effie Deans, the victim of unhappy passion;*—and Immalie, in her island of flowers, a fairy thing of love and happiness, excites nothing of that agony of interest, which the same Immalie excites in the dungeon of the Inquisition, with her dead child lying in her bosom.* Who has not (whilst *reading* the plays at least) felt more for the lovely and loving Desdemona, than the lovely and loving Juliet? for Imogene, the neglected wife, than Ophelia,* the neglected mistress? And to leave off *putting cases*, who does not sympathise more strongly in those true tales, which history has preserved for us of Woman's Love, manifested in the relative duties and relative characters of life, than in any or all the creations of the sublimest genius, the purest fancy? She, who 'had no ornament but her children'*—she who, even in the presence of Cyrus, 'saw *him* only who had said he would give a thousand lives for her ransom'*—she who died to give her husband courage, and pronounced that death 'not painful.'* These and a thousand other instances which shine, and will shine on the page of history 'as the stars for ever and ever,' come home to the human heart with a far deeper and divine influence, than all the love of mere lovers. The reasons are plain. Pure and fervent as their love may be, it is still selfish; possessing no higher motive than personal will and pleasure. It has not yet become sacred as a duty, and settled as a habit; nor has it yet passed through long years of need, sickness, sorrow, and adversity, and come out impressed with the broad seal of constancy. Lovers' Love may exhibit the 'freshness and glory of a dream;'* but it is from the nature of things unproved, and therefore from books as in real life, we have far deeper satisfaction in contemplating that love which has passed its trial hour, undimmed, and undiminished.

There is another reason: if we cannot all invent, we can all observe; and he must be singularly unfortunate in his society, who does not know living instances of women whose love bears an analogy, at least, to that of which we have been speaking. His sphere is indeed confined, to say no worse of it, if he knows no woman who could, were it her duty, die *with* a husband and *for* a child—no wife who has found the devoted specious lover change into the unworthy, brutal husband, and has yet endured her lot with unrepining patience, and met the world with smiles of seeming cheerfulness, and

> learned the art
> To bleed in secret, yet conceal the smart.*

And, higher and harder task; denied herself the privilege of friendship, and never told her *grief*.*—No intellectual and accomplished mother, who has surrendered early affluence, and accustomed comforts, the pleasures of society, the indulgence of refined taste, and become a menial as well as mother to her children, and entered into all the harassing details of minute daily economy, not with mere dogged submission, but with active cheerful interest! Does he not know some daughter, who has secluded herself from youthful companions and youthful pleasures, that she may employ her health and spirits, her days and nights, in soothing a parent to whom 'the grasshopper is become a burden,'* and existence a pain, but who can, nevertheless, depart quietly to his long home, because his last steps thither are supported by a beloved and affectionate child? Does he not know some sister, whose mild influence has controlled the follies, and whose tenderness, though at the risk of personal blame, has shielded the faults of a brother? Or has he never seen an instance of female friendship? His lip may curl at the idea, but there *is* such a thing as female friendship;—not often, I grant, between young ladies, but between the young and the old,—the matron who has safely trodden the ways of life, and the young blooming girl, who is just entering upon them. It is a beautiful, ay, and it is a frequent sight, to behold the calm gravity of age, tempering the enthusiasm of youth; and the bright influence of youth shedding, as it were, a sunset radiance over the sombre sky of age. But to come rather closer to the feelings of our sceptic;—to touch upon his personal experience. If he ever lay upon a bed of sickness, what eyes became dim with weeping, what cheeks pale with watching, over him?—What hand administered the medicine and smoothed the pillow?—Whose form glided round his bed with the quiet care of a mortal, and yet ministering spirit?—Whose tear soothed his dejection?—Whose smile calmed his temper?—Whose patience bore with his many infirmities?—Unless he live in a desert island, he will reply— Woman's! Woman's!

But to know to the full extent of such knowledge, how noble, how sacred a thing is Woman's Love, it must be contemplated when strengthened by the bonds of duty, when called forth by the ties of nature. Some may think it needless to lay such strong and repeated stress upon this condition; but for my own part I do not believe that in the hearts of *true* women, and such alone are worthy of mention, Love, the passion of Love, has before marriage by any means the power generally supposed. I verily think that many a most exemplary wife, has been as the mistress—

Uncertain, coy, and hard to please.*

No *true* woman will either do or suffer for the fondest and most faithful lover, a thousandth part of what she will do and suffer for a husband who is only moderately kind. No.—Love must with woman become a duty, a habit, a part of existence, a condition of life, before we can know how completely it unites and exemplifies the natures of the Lion and the Dove, the courage which no danger can dismay, with the constancy no suffering can diminish.

It has been much the fashion, of late, to write and talk about women's minds, and to make comparative estimates of the power of female and masculine intellect: Some, with pleasant malice, have made the scale preponderate on the gentleman's side; others, with pleasant gallantry, have made it preponderate on that of the lady. Women of genius, never argue for the recognised *equality* of female intellect; and men of genius, never argue for its recognised *inferiority*; but, as in political questions, those dispute loudest who have least at stake. 'Master and mistress minds,' move in their separate spheres, like the rulers of distinct and distant kingdoms, seldom wishing, and scarcely ever tempted, to disturb each other's sovereignty. It is amongst those who reside in the nooks and corners of Parnassus,* that disputes and litigations arise. We can fancy such small occupiers of intellectual territory, as Hayley, and Miss Seward, extremely agitated about the mutual recognition of rights, and claims, and divisions.* We can only fancy Shakspeare and Madame de Stael,* regarding them with contempt and indifference. But by all means let the dispute go forwards, and if women are stimulated to give proof by their exertions, that there *is* such a thing as female genius,—and men are stimulated to give proof by *their* surpassing productions, that there is no genius in the world but what is masculine, the public will be the gainer any way. We shall have more clever people to write,—more clever books to be read. Without hazarding an opinion on the subject, for the very sufficient reason of not understanding its merits, I return to my own, my favourite theme, that with which I begun, and with which I would close,—Woman's Love.'

Let man take his claimed superiority, and take it as his hereditary, his inalienable right. Let him have for his dower, sovereignty in science, in philosophy, in learning, in arts, and in arms; let him wear, unenvied, the ermine, the lawn, and the helmet;* and wield, unrivalled, the sword, the pen, and the pencil. Let him be supreme in the cabinet, the camp, and the study; and to woman will still remain a 'goodly heritage,'* of which neither force nor rivalry can deprive her. The heart is *her* domain; and there she is queen. To acquire over the unruly wills and tempers of men, an influence which no man, however great, however gifted, can acquire;—to manifest a faith which never fails; a patience that never wears out, a devotedness which can sacrifice, and a courage which can suffer;—to perform the same, unvarying, round of duties, without weariness,—and endure the same unvarying round of vexations, without murmuring;—to requite neglect with kindness, and injustice with fidelity;—to be true, when all are false,—and firm, when all is hopeless;—to watch over the few dear objects of regard, with an eye that never sleeps, and a care that cannot change;—to think, to act, to suffer, to sacrifice, to live, to die, for them, their happiness and safety,—These are Woman's true triumphs;—this, this, this, is WOMAN'S LOVE.

To my Own Heart (1829)

I am a little world made cunningly.*

Come, let me sound thy depths, unquiet sea
Of thought and passion; let thy wild waves be
Calm for a moment. Thou mysterious mind—
No human eye may see, no fetters bind;
Within me, ever near me as a friend
That whilst I know I fail to comprehend;
Fountain, whence sweet and bitter waters flow,
The source of happiness, the cause of woe,—
Of all that spreads o'er life enchantment's spell,
Or bids it be anticipated hell;—
Come let me talk with thee, allotted part
Of immortality—my own deep heart!
Yes, deep and hidden now, but soon unsealed,
Must thou thy deepest thoughts and secrets yield:
Like the old sea, put off the shrouding gloom
That makes thee now a prison-house and tomb;
Spectres and sins that undisturbed have lain,
Must hear the judgment-voice and live again.
Then woe or bliss for thee:—thy ocean-mate,
Material only in its birth and fate,
Its rage rebuked, its captive hosts set free,
And homage paid, shall shrink away, and be

With all the mutinous billows o'er it hurled,
Less than a dew-drop on a rose impearled!
But thou—but thou—or darker, or more fair
The sentence and the doom that waits thee there.
No rock will hide thee in its friendly breast,
No death dismiss thee to eternal rest;
The solid earth thrilled by the trumpet's call,
Like a sere leaf shall tremble ere it fall,—
From heaven to hell one Eye extend and shine,
That can forgotten deeds and thoughts divine—
How wilt thou brook that day, that glance, frail heart of mine?

Spirit within me, speak; and through the veil
That hides thee from my vision, tell thy tale;
That so the present and the past may be
Guardians and prophets to futurity.
Spirit by which I live, thou art not dumb,
I hear thy voice; I called and thou art come;
I hear thy still and whispering voice of thought
Thus speak, with memories and musings fraught:—

'Mortal, Immortal, would desires like these
Had claimed thy prime, employed thine hours of ease!
But then, within thee burned the enthusiast's fire,
Wild love of freedom, longings for the lyre;—
And ardent vision of romantic youth,
Too fair for time, and oh! too frail for truth!
Aspirings nursed by solitude and pride,
Worlds to the dreamer, dreams to all beside;
Bright vague imaginings of bliss to be,
None ever saw, yet none despaired to see,
And aimless energies that bade the mind
Launch like a ship and leave the world behind.
But duty disregarded, reason spurned,
Knowledge despised, and wisdom all unlearned,
Punished the rebel who refused to bow,
And stamped Self-Torturer on the enthusiast's brow.

'No earthly happiness exists for such,
They shrink like insects from the gentlest touch;
A breath can raise them, but a breath can kill,

And such wert thou—how sad the memory still!
Without a single real grief to own,
Yet ever mourning fancied joys o'erthrown;—
Viewing mankind with delicate disdain.
Unshared their pleasures, unrelieved their pain;
Self, thy sole object, interest, aim, end, view,
The circle's centre, oft the circle too.
''Tis past! 'tis past!—and never more may rise
The wasted hours I now have learned to prize;
Youth, like a summer sun, hath sunk to rest,
But left no glory lingering in its west.
Maturer life hath real sorrows brought,
And made me blush for those that such once thought;
Fancy is bankrupt of her golden schemes,
Tried in the world they proved but glittering dreams;
Remembrance views with unavailing tears,
The accusing phantoms of departed years,
While Hope too often lays her anchor by,
Or only lifts to heaven a troubled eye;
Too oft forebodings agonize the soul,
As lamentation filled the prophet's roll.

'Why do I speak of this? though sad, though true,
I know a calmer mood, a brighter view:
The restless ocean hath its hours of rest,
And sleep may visit those by pain opprest;
More shade than sunlight o'er his heart may sweep,
Who yet is cheerful, nay, may seldom weep;
And he may learn, though late, and by degrees,
To love his neighbour and desire to please;
Rejoice o'er those who never go astray,
And those who do, assist to find their way:
Life he may look on with a sobered eye,
And how to live, think less than how to die;
Love all that's fair on earth, or near or far,
Yet deem the fairest but a shooting star,
And strive to point his spirit's inward sight,
To orbs for ever fixed, for ever bright;
Mourn countless sins, yet trust to be forgiven,
And feel a hesitating hope of heaven!'

LAETITIA ELIZABETH LANDON
(1802–1838)

The poet who became known by her initials, L.E.L., was born in Chelsea, London, the eldest child of initially affluent parents: her father John Landon, well connected and well travelled, was a partner in the army agency of Adair & Co. in Pall Mall, and her Welsh mother, Katherine Jane Bishop, was the daughter of a close friend of Sarah Siddons. When she was 5 Landon attended the school of Frances Rowden in Hans Place for a few months; then, when she was 7, the family moved to East Barnet, where her cousin Elizabeth taught or perhaps accompanied her in grammar, literature, history, and geography, and she had a master for French and music. Financial difficulties brought on by the end of the war against Napoleonic France prompted moves first to Fulham in 1814 then to Old Brompton in 1815, and the voraciously literary and curious Landon had to forgo further instruction.

A neighbour in Old Brompton was William Jerdan, editor since 1817 of the growingly influential *Literary Gazette*, and in 1820 her first published poem, 'Rome', appeared in that magazine. Many more followed after favourable notice in the *Gazette* of her first volume, *The Fate of Adelaide, a Swiss Romantic Tale, and Other Poems* (1821; dedicated to Sarah Siddons) and her poems, published weekly in the *Literary Gazette*, quickly became both popular and fashionable. She also wrote reviews, and by her earnings sought to contribute to her family's support. Collections of poetry followed: *The Improvisatrice; and Other Poems* (1824: the title poem is a personal history by an 'impassioned' young Italian woman, and this proved to be financially and critically her breakthrough volume), *The Troubadour; Catalogue of Pictures, and Historical Sketches* (1825), *The Golden Violet, with its Tales of Romance and Chivalry* (1827), *The Venetian Bracelet, The Lost Pleiad, a History of the Lyre, and Other Poems* (1829), *The Vow of the Peacock, and Other Poems* (1835), and *The Zenana, and Other Poems* (posthumous; edited, with a memoir, by Emma Roberts, 1839). In 1831 she took on the editorship of the illustrated annual *Fisher's Drawing Room Scrap-Book*, to which she also contributed many poems. In 1832 she began contributing poems and short stories to the *New Monthly Magazine*, and edited another annual, *Heath's Book of Beauty for 1833*. She wrote prose tales for children (*Traits and Trials of Early Life*, 1836), novels (*Romance and Reality*, 1831; *Francesca Carrera*, 1834; *Ethel Churchill*, 1837), and a play (*The Triumph of Lucca or Castruccio Castrucani*, 1837). Landon was an iconic but overworked figure in the newly burgeoning world of 'polite' occasional and illustrative literature concentrated in the lavish annuals, gift-books, and sentimental ephemera which were the great publishing successes of the late 1820s and 1830s: these publications made her enough money to support her mother and to buy her brother a church living, but they also candied much of her poetry. Her critical reputation was high at the time of her death: reviewers thought her novels revealed abilities which had been obscured in her poetry, and that her later poems showed more depth of feeling and thought.

Landon included among her writing friends Mary Russell Mitford, Maria Jane Jewsbury, Jane Porter, Agnes Strickland, and Anna Maria Hall. Her father died in 1824 and Landon went to live with her grandmother in Sloane Street, London. On her grandmother's death in 1826 she rented an attic apartment in the school and boarding house in Hans Place, Knightsbridge, where she had been a schoolgirl; among the other female lodgers were Emma Roberts and her sister. 'The society here was of the most pleasant description, and afforded relaxation from literary employment of a quiet, tasteful, and intelligent kind', observes the writer of the memoir prefixed to her novel *Romance and Reality* when it appeared in Bentley's Standard Novels in 1848 (vol. iii in the series; pp. xvi–xvii). Even so, Landon's reputation was tainted by rumours which illustrate the difficulties often facing young, attractive, single women writers in her time: 'envy, malice, and all uncharitableness,—these are the fruits of a successful literary career for a woman', she is reported to have said.[1] Her familiarity with William Jerdan and the Irish artist Daniel Maclise was misinterpreted; and rumours about her relationship with the journalist William Maginn, fuelled by the jealousy of his wife, led in 1835 to her breaking off her engagment to the literary reviewer and (much later) biographer of Dickens, John Forster. Two years after this she met Captain George Maclean, Governor of Cape Coast Castle, the principal British settlement on the Gold Coast of West Africa (in what is now Ghana); they were not well suited and not in love, and the marriage, which took place on 7 June 1838, was delayed by rumours that he already had a wife in Africa, and by his misgivings about her stained reputation. Having agreed to spend at least three years on the continent which she had described in her (anonymous) 1832 essay 'On the Ancient and Modern Influence of Poetry' as 'the least civilized quarter of the globe', as seeming 'formed from the dregs of the other parts', and entirely deficient in 'that soil of mind wherewith the intellect works',[2] and planning to continue her literary

[1] S. C. Hall, *A Book of Memories of Great Men and Women of the Age* (London: Virtue, 1871), 264.

[2] Jerome McGann and Daniel Riess (eds.) *Letitia Elizabeth Landon: Selected Writings* (Peterborough, Ont.: Broadview, 1997), 161.

career, Landon sailed with her husband to Cape Coast, arrived on 16 August, and on 15 October was found dead in circumstances which made her even more of a sensation and which caused extreme unease among her friends and admirers. She held in her hand a bottle of prussic (hydrocyanic) acid, but there are reports of bruising on her face and hands, and the coroner's verdict of death by accidental overdose was brought—on the day of her death—without a post-mortem. Her husband claimed that she had accidentally taken an overdose of a medicine (and this remains a likely supposition), but theories of suicide and murder at the hands of his discarded black mistress were rife. An unpublished thesis by Anne Ethel Wyly in 1942 argues that the true cause of death was an epileptic seizure.[3]

Isobel Armstrong offers a useful way in to Landon's work in commenting on her way of risking, almost courting, triteness: 'Her simplicity is rigorous because, though she refuses to write anything that cannot be said simply, the implications of her diction are far from simple; her syntax is condensed, ellipical.'[4] Selected here are 'Lines of Life' from the collection *The Venetian Bracelet* (1829), 'Felicia Hemans' from *Fisher's Drawing Room Scrap-Book for 1838* (1837), and 'Night at Sea', written on 15 August 1838 during the voyage to Africa and sent to Henry Colburn, editor of the *New Monthly Magazine*, in which it appeared in 1839. Landon's status as a poet is often disputed even by those who automatically cede her a place in anthologies because of her contemporary importance, although it has been strengthened by the publication of the 1997 selection of her work edited by Jerome McGann and Daniel Riess. The scope of the present collection allows readers to consider alongside her poetry a sample of her prose, and although there is no space here for her longer fiction these novels and extended prose pieces, especially *Romance and Reality*, deserve exhumation. During her brief time in Africa Landon was working on a series of essays on the female characters of Walter Scott, some of which had already been published in the *New Monthly Magazine*. This unfinished series was a new direction in Landon's writing, and reveals her gifts in critical prose, more familiar to most modern readers from her essay on Hemans. Scott had been a favourite since childhood, and she uses the essays to comment more generally on the situation of women. She declares in her account of Flora MacIvor, for example: 'Generally speaking, the female character is developed through the medium of affection—till she loves, she has rarely felt, consequently rarely thought much—for

[3] 'Letitia Elizabeth Landon: Her Career, Her "Mysterious" Death, and Her Poetry', Ph.D. Thesis (Durham, NC: Duke University).

[4] Paula R. Feldmen and Theresa M. Kelley (eds.), *Romantic Women Writers: Voices and Countervoices* (Hanover, NH: University Press of New England, 1995), 26.

thoughts are but the representatives of past feelings—it is the heart that awakens the mind in woman.'[5] The essay printed here is about Diana Vernon, dashing and tantalizing heroine of *Rob Roy* (1817) and a great favourite of the nineteenth-century male imagination.

⁓

Lines of Life (1825, 1829)

Orphan in my first years, I early learnt
To make my heart suffice itself, and seek
Support and sympathy in its own depths.

Well, read my cheek, and watch my eye,—
    Too strictly schooled are they,
One secret of my soul to show,
    One hidden thought betray.

I never knew the time my heart
    Looked freely from my brow;
I once was checked by timidness,
    'Tis taught by caution now.

I live among the cold, the false,
    And I must seem like them;
And such I am, for I am false
    As those I most condemn.

I teach my lip its sweetest smile,
    My tongue its softest tone;
I borrow others' likeness, till
    Almost I lose my own.

I pass through flattery's gilded sieve,
    Whatever I would say;
In social life, all, like the blind,
    Must learn to feel their way.

I check my thoughts like curbed steeds
    That struggle with the rein;
I bid my feelings sleep, like wrecks
    In the unfathomed main.

---

[5] [Samuel] Laman Blanchard, *The Life and Literary Remains of L.E.L.*, 2 vols. (London: Henry Colburn, 1841), ii. 84.

I hear them speak of love, the deep,
    The true, and mock the name;
Mock at all high and early truth,
    And I too do the same.

I hear them tell some touching tale,
    I swallow down the tear;
I hear them name some generous deed,
    And I have learnt to sneer.

I hear the spiritual, the kind,
    The pure, but named in mirth;
Till all of good, ay, even hope,
    Seems exiled from our earth.

And one fear, withering ridicule,
    Is all that I can dread;
A sword hung by a single hair
    For ever o'er the head.*

We bow to a most servile faith,
    In a most servile fear;
While none among us dares to say
    What none will choose to hear.

And if we dream of loftier thoughts,
    In weakness they are gone;
And indolence and vanity
    Rivet our fetters on.

Surely I was not born for this!
    I feel a loftier mood
Of generous impulse, high resolve,
    Steal o'er my solitude!

I gaze upon the thousand stars
    That fill the midnight sky;
And wish, so passionately wish,
    A light like theirs on high.

I have such eagerness of hope
    To benefit my kind;
And feel as if immortal power
    Were given to my mind.

I think on that eternal fame,
    The sun of earthly gloom,
Which makes the gloriousness of death,
    The future of the tomb—

That earthly future, the faint sign
    Of a more heavenly one;
—A step, a word, a voice, a look.—
    Alas! my dream is done!

And earth, and earth's debasing stain,
    Again is on my soul;
And I am but a nameless part
    Of a most worthless whole.

Why write I this? because my heart
    Towards the future springs,
That future where it loves to soar
    On more than eagle wings.

The present, it is but a speck
    In that eternal time,
In which my lost hopes find a home,
    My spirit knows its clime.

Oh! not myself,—for what am I?—
    The worthless and the weak,
Whose every thought of self should raise
    A blush to burn my cheek.

But song has touched my lips with fire,
    And made my heart a shrine
For what, although alloyed, debased,
    Is in itself divine.

I am myself but a vile link
    Amid life's weary chain;
But I have spoken hallowed words,
    Oh do not say in vain!

My first, my last, my only wish,
    Say will my charmed chords
Wake to the morning light of fame,
    And breathe again my words?

Will the young maiden, when her tears
    Alone in moonlight shine—
Tears for the absent and the loved—
    Murmur some song of mine?

Will the pale youth by his dim lamp,
    Himself a dying flame,
From many an antique scroll beside,
    Choose that which bears my name?

Let music make less terrible
    The silence of the dead;
I care not, so my spirit last
    Long after life has fled.

Felicia Hemans (1837)

No more, no more—oh, never more returning,
    Will thy beloved presence gladden earth;
No more wilt thou with sad, yet anxious yearning
    Cling to those hopes which have no mortal birth.
Though art gone from us, and with thee departed.
    How many lovely things have vanished too;
Deep thoughts that at thy will to being started,
    And feelings, teach us our own were true.
Thou hast been round us, like a viewless spirit,
    Known only by the music on the air;
The leaf or flowers which thou hast named inherit
    A beauty known but from thy breathing there:
For thou didst on them fling thy strong emotion,
    The likeness from itself the fond heart gave;
As planets from afar look down on ocean,
    And give their own sweet image to the wave.

And thou didst bring from foreign lands their treasures,
    As floats thy various melody along;
We know the softness of Italian measures,
    And the grave cadence of Castilian song.*
A general bond of union is the poet,
    By its immortal verse is language known,
And for the sake of song do others know it—

One glorious poet makes the world his own.
And thou—how far thy gentle sway extended!
    The heart's sweet empire over land and sea;
Many a stranger and far flower was blended
    In the soft wreath that glory bound for thee.
The echoes of the Susquehanna's waters
    Paused in the pine-woods words of thine to hear;*
And to the wide Atlantic's younger daughters
    Thy name was lovely, and thy song was dear.

Was not this purchased all too dearly?—never
    Can fame atone for all that fame hath cost.
We see the goal, but know not the endeavour,
    Nor what fond hopes have on the way been lost.
What do we know of the unquiet pillow,
    By the worn cheek and tearful eyelid pressed,
When thoughts chased thoughts, like the tumultuous billow,
    Whose very light and foam reveals unrest?
We say, the song is sorrowful, but know not
    What may have left that sorrow on the song;
However mournful words may be, they show not
    The whole extent of wretchedness and wrong
They cannot paint the long sad hours, passed only
    In vain regrets o'er what we feel we are.
Alas! the kingdom of the lute is lonely—
    Cold is the worship coming from afar.

Yet what is mind in woman, but revealing
    In sweet clear light the hidden world below,
By quicker fancies and a keener feeling
    Than those around, the cold and careless, know?
What is to feed such feeling, but to culture
    A soil whence pain will never more depart?
The fable of Prometheus and the vulture
    Reveals the poet's and the woman's heart.*
Unkindly are they judged—unkindly treated—
    By careless tongues and by ungenerous words;
While cruel sneer, and hard reproach, repeated,
    Jar the fine music of the spirit's chords.
Wert thou not weary—thou whose soothing numbers

Gave other lips the joy thine own had not?
Didst thou not welcome thankfully the slumbers
    Which closed around thy mourning human lot?

What on this earth could answer thy requiring,
    For earnest faith—for love, the deep and true,
The beautiful, which was thy soul's desiring,
    But only from thyself its being drew.
How is the warm and loving heart requited
    In this harsh world, where it awhile must dwell.
Its best affections wronged, betrayed, and slighted—
    Such is the doom of those who love too well.
Better the weary dove should close its pinion,
    Fold up its golden wings and be at peace:
Enter, O ladye, that serene dominion
    Where earthly cares and earthly sorrows cease.
Fame's troubled hour has cleared, and now replying,
    A thousand hearts their music ask of thine.
Sleep with a light, the lovely and undying
    Around thy grave—a grave which is a shrine.

Night at Sea (1838)

The lovely purple of the noon's bestowing
    Has vanished from the waters, where it flung
A royal colour, such as gems are throwing
    Tyrian or regal garniture among.*
'Tis night, and overhead the sky is gleaming,
    Through the slight vapour trembles each dim star;
I turn away—my heart is sadly dreaming
    Of scenes they do not light, of scenes afar.
            My friends, my absent friends!
                Do you think of me, as I think of you?

By each dark wave around the vessel sweeping,
    Farther am I from old dear friends removed,
Till the lone vigil that I now am keeping,
    I did not know how much you were beloved.
How many acts of kindness little heeded,
    Kind looks, kind words, rise half reproachful now!

Hurried and anxious, my vexed life has speeded,
　And memory wears a soft accusing brow.
　　　My friends, my absent friends!
　　　　Do you think of me, as I think of you?

The very stars are strangers, as I catch them
　Athwart the shadowy sails that swell above;
I cannot hope that other eyes will watch them
　At the same moment with a mutual love.
They shine not there, as here they now are shining,
　The very hours are changed.—Ah, do ye sleep?
O'er each home pillow, midnight is declining,
　May some kind dream at least my image keep!
　　　My friends, my absent friends!
　　　　Do you think of me, as I think of you?

Yesterday has a charm, to-day could never
　Fling o'er the mind, which knows not till it parts
How it turns back with tenderest endeavour
　To fix the past within the heart of hearts.
Absence is full of memory, it teaches
　The value of all old familiar things;
The strengthener of affection, while it reaches
　O'er the dark parting, with an angel's wings.
　　　My friends, my absent friends!
　　　　Do you think of me, as I think of you?

The world with one vast element omitted—
　Man's own especial element, the earth,
Yet, o'er the waters is his rule transmitted
　By that great knowledge whence has power its birth.
How oft on some strange loveliness while gazing
　Have I wished for you,—beautiful as new,
The purple waves like some wild army raising
　Their snowy banners as the ship cuts through.
　　　My friends, my absent friends!
　　　　Do you think of me, as I think of you?

Bearing upon its wing the hues of morning,
　Up springs the flying fish, like life's false joy,
Which of the sunshine asks that frail adorning
　Whose very light is fated to destroy.

Ah, so doth genius on its rainbow pinion,
   Spring from the depths of an unkindly world;
So spring sweet fancies from the heart's dominion,—
   Too soon in death the scorched up wing is furled.
         My friends, my absent friends!
            Whate'er I see is linked with thoughts of you.

No life is in the air, but in the waters
   Are creatures, huge and terrible and strong,
The sword-fish and the shark pursue their slaughters,
   War universal reigns these depths along.
Like some new island on the ocean springing,
   Floats on the surface some gigantic whale,
From its vast head a silver fountain flinging
   Bright as the fountain in a fairy tale.
         My friends, my absent friends!
            I read such fairy legends while with you.

Light is amid the gloomy canvass spreading,
   The moon is whitening the dusky sails,
From the thick bank of clouds she masters, shedding
   The softest influence that o'er night prevails.
Pale is she like a young queen pale with splendour,
   Hunted with passionate thoughts too fond, too deep,
The very glory that she wears is tender,
   The eyes that watch her beauty fain would weep.
         My friends, my absent friends!
            Do you think of me, as I think of you?

Sunshine is ever cheerful, when the morning
   Wakens the world with cloud-dispelling eyes;
The spirits mount to glad endeavour, scorning
   What toil upon a path so sunny lies.
Sunshine and hope are comrades, and their weather
   Calls into life the energies of earth;
But memory and moonlight go together,
   Reflected in the light that either brings.
         My friends, my absent friends!
            Do you think of me then? I think of you.

The busy deck is hushed, no sounds are waking
   But the watch pacing silently and slow;

The waves against the sides incessant breaking,
  And rope and canvass swaying to and fro.
The topmast sail seems some dim pinnacle
  Cresting a shadowy tower amid the air;
While red and fitful gleams come from the binnacle,*
  The only light on board to guide us—where?
      My friends, my absent friends!
         Far from my native land, and far from you.

On one side of the ship, the moonbeam's shimmer
  In luminous vibration sweeps the sea,
But where the shadow falls, a strange pale glimmer
  Seems glow-worm like amid the waves to be.
All that the spirit keeps of thought and feeling,
  Takes visionary hues from such an hour;
But while some fantasy is o'er me stealing,
  I start, remembrance has a keener power.
      My friends, my absent friends,
        From the fair dream I start to think of you!

A dusk line in the moonlight I discover,
  What all day long vainly I sought to catch;
Or is it but the varying clouds that hover
  Thick in the air, to mock the eyes that watch?
No! well the sailor knows each speck appearing.
  Upon the tossing waves, the far-off strand
To that dusk line our eager ship is steering.
  Her voyage done—to-morrow we shall land.

Rob Roy: Diana Vernon (1838)

Many and opposite are the lots in life, and unequal are the portions
which they measure out to the children of earth. We cannot agree
with those who contend that the difference after all is but in outward
seeming. Such an assertion is often the result of thoughtlessness—
sometimes the result of selfishness. It is one of the good points of
human nature, that it revolts against human suffering. Few there are
who can witness pain, whether of mind or of body, without pity, and
the desire to alleviate; but such is our infirmity of purpose, that a

little suffices to turn us aside from assistance. Indolence, difficulties, and contrary interests come in the way of sympathy, and then we desire to excuse our apathy to ourselves. It is a comfortable doctrine to suppose that the evil is made up by some mysterious allotment of good; it is an excuse for non-interference, and we let conscience sleep over our own enjoyments, taking it for granted others have them also—though how we know not. It was much this spirit that made the young French queen exclaim, when she heard that the people were perishing for want of bread, 'why do they not eat buns!'*

But there is a vast difference in the paths of humanity; some have their lines cast in pleasant places, while others are doomed to troubled waters. Of one person, that question might well be asked, which Johnstone, the old Scotch secretary, put to Sir Robert Walpole, 'What have you done, sir, to make God Almighty so much your friend?' while another would seem 'the very scoff and mockery of fortune.'* It must, however, be admitted, that the hard circumstances form the strong character, as the cold climes of the north nurture a race of men, whose activity and energies leave those of the south far behind. Hence it is that the characters of women are more uniform than men; they are rarely placed in circumstances to call forth the latent powers of the mind. Diana Vernon's character would never have grown out of a regular education of geography, history, and the use of the globes, to say nothing of extras, such as Poonah work, or oriental tinting.* Miss Vernon is the most original of Scott's heroines, especially so, when we consider the period to which she herself belongs, or that at which such a spirited sketch was drawn.* The manners of Scott's own earlier days were formal and restrained. An amusing story is told in his life of Lord Napier, which will admirably illustrate the importance attached to minutiæ. His lordship suddenly quitted a friend's house, where he was to have paid a visit, without any cause satisfactory to a host being assigned. But much ingenuity might have been exerted without the right cause being discovered; it was, that his valet had not packed up the set of neckcloths marked the same as the shirts.*

Within the last few years what alterations have taken place in 'the glass of fashion, and the mould of forms.'* The Duchess of Gordon brought in a style—bold, dashing, and reckless, like herself.* The Duchess of Devonshire took the opposite—soft, languid, and flattering:* the exclusives established a stoical school—cold, haughty, and *impayable*.* The reform era has brought a more popular manner. There has been so much canvassing going on, that conciliation has become a habit, and the hustings has remodelled the drawing-room.

But Diana Vernon is a creature formed by no conventional rules; she has been educated by her own heart amid hardships and difficulties; and if nature has but given the original good impulse, and the strength of mind to work it out, hardships and difficulties will only serve to form a character of the loftiest order. Again, there is that tender relationship between the widowed father and the only girl, in which Scott so much delights.* But, if the cradle be lonely which lacks a mother at its side, still more lonely is the hour when girlhood is on the eve of womanhood.

> 'On the horizon like a dewy star,
> That trembles into lustre.'*

No man ever enters into the feelings of a woman, let his kindness be what it may; they are too subtle and too delicate for a hand whose grasp is on 'life's rougher things.'* They require that sorrow should find a voice; now the most soothing sympathy is that which guesses the suffering without a question. But Diana Vernon has been brought up by a father, who, whatever might be his affection, has had no time for minute and tender cares. Engaged in dark intrigues, surrounded by dangers, he has been forced to leave his child in situations as dangerous as his own, nay, a thousand times worse—what is an outward to an inward danger? The young and beautiful girl is left to herself—in a wild solitude, like Osbaldistone-hall—with a tutor like Rashleigh.*

Take the life of girls in general; how are they cared for from their youth upwards. The nurse, the school, the home circle, environ their early years; they know nothing of real difficulties, or of real cares; and there is an old saying, that a woman's education begins after she is married.* Truly, it does, if education be meant to apply to the actual purposes of life. How different is the lot of a girl condemned from childhood upwards to struggle in this wide and weary world! Bitter, indeed, is the fruit of the tree of knowledge to her; at the expense of how many kind and beautiful feelings must that knowledge be obtained; how often will the confidence be betrayed, and the affection misplaced; how often will the aching heart turn on itself for comfort, and in vain; for, under its first eager disappointment, youth wonders why its kindliness and its generous emotions have been given, if falsehood and ingratitude be their requital. How often will the right and the expedient contend together, while the faults of others seem to justify our own, and the low, but distinct voice within us, be half lost, while listening to the sophistry of temptation justifying itself by example; yet how many nobly support the trial, while they have learned of difficulties to use the mental strength which overcomes them, and have been taught by errors to rely more decidedly on the instinctive sense of right which at once shrinks from their admission.

What to Diana Vernon was the craft and crime of one like Rashleigh, which her own native purity would at once detect and shun—as the dove feels and flies from the hawk before the shadow of his dark wings be seen on the air? What the desolate loneliness of the old hall, and the doubts and fears around her difficult path—what but so many steps towards forming a character high-minded, steadfast, generous and true; a lovely and lonely flower over which the rough winds have past, leaving behind only the strength taught by resistance, and keeping fresh the fairness—blessing even the rock with its sweet and healthy presence.

ANNA JAMESON
(1794–1860)

The eldest of the five daughters of the miniature-painter and Irish patriot D. Brownell Murphy and his English wife, Anna Jameson was born in Dublin but was brought up in England after her parents left Ireland in 1798, living for four years in Whitehaven, Cumbria, then in Newcastle upon Tyne, before moving in 1803 to London, settling first in Hanwell and a few years later in the area around Pall Mall. She and her sisters were educated at home by a governess from whom she took some pride in concealing her meditative and imaginative inner life: in London, she pursued her own studies in modern languages and became fascinated by Eastern lore and antiquities. At 16 she became governess to the family of the Marquis of Winchester for four years, and in 1821 fell in love with a talented young Cumbrian barrister and protégé of William Wordsworth, Robert Jameson. Their engagement floundered, but was resumed after she had travelled on the Continent for a year, taken a new position as governess to the Littleton family for four years, and written her first work, *A Lady's Diary*, a travel account suffused with romantic sorrow and ending with the death of the young author. It was later reissued (and is generally known) as *The Diary of an Ennuyée* in 1826 and was very successful.

The Jamesons married in 1825 and settled in Chenies Street, London, but were not happy. In 1829 Robert Jameson accepted a judicial post in Dominica, and his wife returned to her father's house and turned seriously to her literary career, although the separation from her husband was still regarded by both as a temporary matter of practicality. She travelled in Europe with her father and his patron Sir Gerard Noel. In 1833 her husband returned from Dominica and they spent a few months together before he took a more advantageous post in Canada. Anna Jameson visited Germany in 1833, publishing her experiences as *Visits and Sketches* the following year. After uncertainty on her part and affectionate assurances on his she joined her husband in Canada for about eighteen months in 1836–8, but it was a miserable period, alleviated by the formation of new friendships and journeys to explore the initially unappealing land. Her experiences formed the basis of *Winter Studies and Summer Rambles* (1838). Before her departure her husband legally bound himself to pay her an annuity of £300. Described by Anna Jameson's niece and biographer Gerardine Macpherson, in a scrupulousiy tactful analysis of incompatibility, as 'one of those strangely constituted persons to whom absence is always necessary to reawaken affection, and who prize what they are not in possession of',[1] Robert Jameson eventually became Attorney-General of Canada, while his wife returned to the absorbing domestic circle formed by her sisters, mother, and ailing father, to pursue an active social and literary life in Britain, Italy, and Germany. Gerardine Macpherson describes her aunt's life as one 'of steady work, unostentatious and unceasing', and her biography as 'the story of one who kept a stout heart through all the troubles that befell her; who kept her unhappiness to herself, and sought unceasingly to give happiness to all who belonged to her; who never used her pen to strike or to wound, nor took advantage of its power to avenge herself on any who wronged her; and who was, all her life long, the chief support and consolation of her family'.[2]

Among the friends to whom she returned from Canada were Joanna Baillie, Lady Byron (an eventual bitter estrangement from whom, she said, broke her heart), Elizabeth Barrett, Ottilie von Goethe, Harriet Martineau; more generally, her circle of literary acquaintances included some of the greatest names of her time in Britain and Germany. She visited

---

[1] *Memoirs of the Life of Anna Jameson* (London: Longmans, Green, and Co., 1878), 98.

[2] Ibid., p. xi.

Germany in 1833 and 1845, spent two years there (1834–5); and in 1847 travelled to Italy with her niece Gerardine (then Bate: Macpherson by the time she wrote her memoir) in order to collect materials for her work on the history of sacred art: they travelled from Paris to Pisa with the newly married Brownings. On the death of her father in 1842 the family moved from Notting Hill to a smaller house in Ealing. Having persuaded her to give up her entitlement to the promised annuity, her husband made no financial provision for her on his death in 1854; friends raised an annuity of £100, and she had a government pension also for £100 per year. Jameson's interests were social as well as literary and artistic, and in later years she became involved in the organization of sick-care. In her two lectures 'Sisters of Charity' (1855) and 'The Communion of Labour' (1856) she promoted reappraisal based on her observation of work done in other European cities. Working hard, she caught a chill walking home from the British Museum in 1860, and died of bronchitis a week later. Gerardine Macpherson concludes her biography with the distressed response of Elizabeth Barrett Browning, herself ill in Rome, to the sudden loss of 'that noble human creature . . . that dearest friend!'.[3]

Jameson is one of the pioneers of women's criticism of the visual arts, but her most important works in this mode—especially *Sacred and Legendary Art* (four parts, 1848–60)—fall outside the period covered in this anthology. Best known among her earlier works is *Characteristics of Women, Moral, Poetical, and Historical* (1832), a series of essays on Shakespeare's heroines which she dedicated to the actress Fanny Kemble, niece of Sarah Siddons; the year after this, she collaborated with her artist father in the production of *The Beauties of the Court of King Charles the Second*. A telling insight into her working methods and the typical scope of her work is provided in *A Commonplace Book of Thoughts, Memories, and Fancies, Original and Selected* (1854), in which she writes: 'I have been accustomed to make a memorandum of any thought which might come across me—(if pen and paper were at hand), and to mark (and *remark*) any passage in a book which excited either a sympathetic or an antagonistic feeling. This collection of notes accumulated insensibly from day to day. The volumes on Shakespeare's Women, on Sacred and Legendary Art, and various other productions, sprung from seed thus lightly and casually sown, which, I hardly know how, grew up and expanded into a regular, readable form, with a beginning, a middle, and an end' (p. v). The sample of her work included here comes from *The Diary of an Ennuyée*, and amid the posturings of heartbreak gives, in a different voice entirely, strikingly

---

[3] *Memoirs of the Life of Anna Jameson*, 314.

spirited discussions of the paintings she saw and of the representations of women in Renaissance art.

~

From *The Diary of an Ennuyée* (1826)

Florence

I have not written a word since we arrived at Sienna. What would it avail me to keep a mere journal of suffering? O that I could change as others do, could forget that such things have been which can never be again! that there were not this tenacity in my heart and soul which clings to the shadow though the substance be gone!

This is not a mere effusion of low spirits, I was never more cheerful; I have just left a gay party, where Mr Rogers (whom by special good fortune we meet at every resting place, and who dined with us to-day) has been entertaining us delightfully.* I disdain low spirits as a mere disease which comes over us, generally from some physical or external cause; to prescribe for them is as easy as to disguise them is difficult: but the hopeless, cureless sadness of a heart which droops with regret, and throbs with resentment, is easily, very easily disguised, but not so easily banished. I hear every body round me congratulating themselves, and *me* more particularly, that we have at last reached Florence, that we are so far advanced on our road homewards, that soon we shall be at Paris, and Paris is to do wonders—Paris and Dr R** are to *set me up* again, as the phrase is.* But I shall never be set up again, I shall never live to reach Paris: none can tell how I sicken at the very name of that detested place; none seem aware how fast, how very fast the principle of life is burning away within me: but why should I speak? and what earthly help can now avail me? I can suffer in silence, I can conceal the weakness which increases upon me, by retiring, as if from choice and not necessity, from all exertion not absolutely inevitable; and the change is so gradual, none will perceive it till the great change of all comes, and then I shall be at rest.

Florence looked most beautiful as we approached it from the south, girt with her theatre of verdant hills, and glittering in the sunshine. All the country from Sienna to Florence is richly cultivated;

diversified with neat hamlets, farms and villas. I was more struck with the appearance of the Tuscan peasantry on my return from the Papal dominions than when we passed through the country before: no where in Tuscany have we seen that look of abject negligent poverty, those crowds of squalid beggars which shocked us in the Ecclesiastical States.* In the towns where we stopped to change horses, we were presently surrounded by a crowd of people: the women came out spinning, or sewing and plaiting the Leghorn hats;* the children threw flowers into our barouche, the men grinned and gaped, but there was no vociferous begging, no disgusting display of physical evils, filth, and wretchedness. The motive was merely that idle curiosity for which the Florentines in all ages have been remarked. I remember an amusing instance which occurred when I was here in December last. I was standing one evening in the Piazza del Gran Duca, looking at the group of the Rape of the Sabines:* in a few minutes a dozen people gathered round me, gaping at the statue, and staring at that and at me alternately, either to enjoy my admiration, or find out the cause of it: the people came out of the neighbouring shops, and the crowd continued to increase, till at length, though infinitely amused, I was glad to make my escape.

I suffered from cold when first we arrived at Florence, owing to the change of climate, or rather to mere weakness and fatigue: to-day I begin to doubt the possibility of outliving an Italian summer. The blazing atmosphere which depresses the eyelids, the enervating heat, and the rich perfume of the flowers all around us, are almost too much.

April 20.—During our stay at Florence, it has been one of my favourite occupations to go to the Gallery or the Pitti Palace,* and placing my portable seat opposite to some favourite pictures, minutely study and compare the styles of the different masters. By the style of any particular painter, I presume we mean to express the combination of two separate essentials—first, his peculiar conception of his subject; secondly, his peculiar method of executing that conception, with regard to colouring, drawing, and what artists call handling. The former department of style lies in the mind, and will vary according to the feelings, the temper, the personal habits, and previous education of the painter: the latter is merely mechanical, and is technically termed the *manner* of a painter; it may be cold or warm, hard, dry, free, strong, tender: as we say the cold manner of

Sasso Ferrato, the warm manner of Giorgione, the hard manner of Holbein, the dry manner of Perugino, the free manner of Rubens, the strong manner of Carravaggio,* and so forth; I heard an amateur once observe, that one of Morland's Pig-sties was painted with great *feeling:** all this refers merely to mechanical execution.

I am no connoisseur; and I should have lamented as a misfortune, the want of some fixed principles of taste and criticism to guide my judgment; some nomenclature by which to express certain effects, peculiarities, and excellencies which I felt, rather than understood; if my own ignorance had not afforded considerable amusement to myself, and perhaps to others. I have derived some gratification from observing the gradual improvement of my own taste: and from comparing the decisions of my own unassisted judgment and natural feelings, with the fiat of profound critics and connoisseurs: the result has been sometimes mortifying, sometimes pleasing. Had I visited Italy in the character of a ready-made connoisseur, I should have lost many pleasures; for as the eye becomes more practised, the taste becomes more discriminative and fastidious; and the more extensive our acquaintance with the works of art, the more limited is our sphere of admiration; as if the circle of enjoyment contracted round us, in proportion as our sense of beauty became more intense and exquisite. A thousand things which once had power to charm, can charm no longer; but, *en revanche*,* those which *do* please, please a thousand times more: thus what we lose on one side, we gain on the other. Perhaps, on the whole, a technical knowledge of the arts is apt to divert the mind from the general effect, to fix it on petty details of execution. Here comes a connoisseur, who has found his way, good man! from Somerset House, to the Tribune at Florence:* see him with one hand passed across his brow, to shade the light, while the other extended forwards, describes certain indescribable circumvolutions in the air, and now he retires, now advances, now recedes again, till he has hit the exact distance from which every point of beauty is displayed to the best possible advantage, and there he stands— gazing, as never gazed the moon upon the waters, or love-sick maiden upon the moon! We take him perhaps for another Pygmalion?* We imagine that it is those parted and half-breathing lips, those eyes that *seem* to float in light; the pictured majesty of suffering virtue, or the tears of repenting loveliness; the divinity of beauty, or '*the beauty of holiness*,'* which have thus transfixed him? No such

thing: it is the *fleshiness* of the tints, the *vaghezza* of the colouring,*
the brilliance of the carnations, the fold of a robe, or the foreshorten-
ing of a little finger. O! whip me such connoisseurs! the critic's
stop-watch was nothing to this.*

Mere mechanical excellence, and all the tricks of art have their
praise as long as they are subordinate and conduce to the general
effect. In painting as in her sister arts it is necessary

> Che l'arte che tutte fa nulla si scuopre.*

Of course I do not speak here of the Dutch school, whose highest
aim, and highest praise, is exquisite mechanical precision in the
representation of common nature and still life: but of those pictures
which are the productions of mind, which address themselves to the
understanding, the fancy, the feelings, and convey either a moral or a
poetical pleasure.

In taking a retrospective view of all the best collections in Italy and
of the Italian school in particular, I have been struck by the endless
multiplication of the same subjects, crucifixions, martyrdoms, and
other scripture horrors;—virgins, saints, and holy families. The
prevalence of the former class of subjects is easily explained, and has
been ingeniously defended; but it is not so easily reconciled to the
imagination. The mind and the eye are shocked and fatigued by
the succession of revolting and sanguinary images which pollute the
walls of every palace, church, gallery, and academy, from Milan to
Naples. The splendour of the execution only adds to their hideous-
ness; we at once seek for nature, and tremble to find it. It is hateful to
see the loveliest of the arts degraded to such butcher-work. I have
often gone to visit a famed collection with a secret dread of being led
through a sort of intellectual shambles, and returned with the feeling
of one who had supped full of horrors.* I do not know how *men* think,
and feel, though I believe many a man, who with every other feeling
absorbed in overpowering interest, could look unshrinking upon a
real scene of cruelty and blood, would shrink away disgusted and
sickened from the cold, obtrusive, *painted* representation of the same
object; for the truth of this I appeal to men. I can only see with
woman's eyes, and think and feel as I believe every woman *must*,
whatever may be her love for the arts. I remember that in one of the
palaces at Milan—(I think it was in the collection of the Duca
Litti)—we were led up to a picture defended from the air by a plate

of glass, and which being considered as the gem of the collection, was reserved for the last as a kind of bonne bouche.* I gave but one glance, and turned away loathing, shuddering, sickening. The cicerone looked amazed at my bad taste, he assured me it was *un vero Correggio*, (which by the way I can never believe,) and that the duke had refused for it I know not how many thousand scudi.* It would be difficult to say what was most execrable in this picture, the appalling nature of the subject, the depravity of mind evinced in its conception, or the horrible truth and skill with which it was delineated. I ought to add that it hung up in the family dining-room and in full view of the dinner-table.

There is a picture among the chefs-d'œuvres in the Vatican, which, if I were pope (or Pope Joan)* for a single day, should be burnt by the common hangman, 'with the smoke of its ashes to poison the air,'* as it now poisons the sight by its unutterable horrors. There is another in the Palazzo Pitti, at which I shiver still, and unfortunately there is no avoiding it, as they have hung it close to Guido's lovely Cleopatra.* In the gallery there is a Judith and Holofernes which irresistibly strikes the attention—if any thing would add to the horror inspired by the sanguinary subject, and the atrocious fidelity and talent with which it is expressed, it is that the artist was a *woman*.* I must confess that Judith is not one of my favourite heroines; but I can more easily conceive how a woman inspired by vengeance and patriotism could execute such a deed, than that she could coolly sit down, and day after day, hour after hour, touch after touch, dwell upon and almost realize to the eye such an abomination as this.

We can study anatomy, if (like a certain princess) we have a taste that way,* in the surgeons' dissecting-rooms; we do not look upon pictures to have our minds agonized and contaminated by the sight of human turpitude and barbarity, streaming blood, quivering flesh, wounds, tortures, death, and horrors in every shape, even though it should be all very *natural*. Painting has been called the handmaid of nature;* is it not the duty of a handmaid to array her mistress to the best possible advantage? At least to keep her infirmities and deformities from view and not to expose her too undressed?

But I am not so weak, so cowardly, so fastidious, as to shrink from every representation of human suffering, provided that our sympathy be not strained beyond a certain point. To *please* is the genuine aim of painting, as of all the fine arts; when pleasure is conveyed through deeply excited interest, by affecting the passions, the senses, and the imagination, painting assumes a higher character, and almost vies with tragedy: in fact, it *is* tragedy to the eye, and is amenable to the same laws. The St Sebastians of Guido and Razzi; the St Jerome of Domenichino; the sternly beautiful Judith of Allori; the Pietà of Raffaelle; the San Pietro Martire of Titian;* are all so many tragic *scenes*, wherein whatever is revolting in circumstances or character is judiciously kept from view, where human suffering is dignified by the moral lesson it is made to convey, and its effect on the beholder at once softened and heightened by the redeeming grace which genius and poetry have shed like a glory round it.

Allowing all this I am yet obliged to confess that I am wearied with this class of pictures, and that I wish there were fewer of them.

But there is one subject which never tires, at least never tires *me*, however varied, repeated, multiplied. A subject so lovely in itself that the most eminent painter cannot easily embellish it, or the meanest degrade it; a subject which comes home to our own bosoms and dearest feelings; and in which we may 'lose ourselves in all delightfulness'* and indulge unreproved pleasure. I mean the *Virgin and Child*, or in other words, the abstract personification of what is loveliest, purest, and dearest, under heaven—maternal tenderness, virgin meekness, and childish innocence, and the *beauty of holiness* over all.

It occurred to me to-day, that if a gallery could be formed of this subject alone, selecting one specimen from among the works of every painter, it would form not only a comparative index to their different styles, but we should find, on recurring to what is known of the lives and characters of the great masters, that each has stamped some peculiarity of his own disposition on his Virgins; and that, after a little consideration and practice, a very fair guess might be formed of the character of each artist, by observing the style in which he has treated this beautiful and favourite subject.

HANNAH KILHAM
(1774–1832)

Born and brought up in Sheffield, Hannah Spurr was the seventh child of Peter Spurr, a tradesman, and his wife Hannah Brittlebank, who died in 1786, leaving the 12-year-old Hannah in charge of the domestic comforts of her father and elder brothers. Her father died two years later, and Hannah was sent at the age of 14 to a boarding-school in Chesterfield, where she proved herself to be a rapid learner. She became very interested in religious matters, and, to the strong disapproval of her Church of England family, began regularly to attend the early morning services of John Wesley. In this she was partly developing an interest shown by her mother, who had been sympathetic to Wesley's ideas, but she became more deeply involved, formally becoming a Wesleyan Methodist in 1794. Four years later, at the age of 24, in April 1798 she became the second wife of Alexander Kilham, a preacher and the founder of the Methodist New Connection, a group which sought to secede from the Anglican Church. Her husband died eight months later, in December the same year, and in April 1799 she gave birth to their daughter, Mary, who died the following winter. She set up a day-school in Nottingham, and during holidays in Epworth, Alexander Kilham's childhood home, she met and was influenced by the thinking of the Quakers. In 1802 she joined the Society of Friends. It was through William Allen, a Quaker and president of the African Institution, that she became interested in the problems facing the British colony of Sierra Leone in the aftermath of the abolition of the maritime slave trade and the attempts of Allen and others to educate Africans. Having moved back to Sheffield, she became an active and influential philanthropist, establishing a Society for the Bettering of the Condition of the Poor.

Hannah Kilham began her strikingly unusual publishing career with several educational works, including *Scripture Selections* (1817), *Lessons on Language* (1818), and *First Lessons in Spelling* (1818). She became best known, however, for her pioneering work in the languages of Africa. Having Christian instruction as her ultimate aim, she began to investigate the utility of producing grammars of as-yet unwritten African languages, to be used in missionary schools. During the winter of 1819–20 she employed two West African sailors to instruct her in Mande and Wolof and to help her 'reduce' the languages for the purposes of instruction. In 1820 she published *Ta-Re Wa-Lof, Ta-re boo Juk-a. First Lessons in Jaloff* [Wolof]; in 1823 *African Lessons in Three Parts*; in 1827 *African Lessons, Mandingo and English, and African School Tracts*. Her pamphlets promoted the vernacular as the first medium of instruction, since Kilham felt strongly that Africans should be taught by means of their own language. Her books aimed to break down different African languages into teaching elements with English translations, an idea which seems obvious today but which presumed a worth in the 'barbaric' African languages which was simply not taken for granted by her contemporaries. Her immediate precursors in this work were men: Henry Brunton of the Edinburgh Missionary Society had analysed the Soso language in the 1790s; the botanist Thomas Winterbottom had published work on the Temne, Bullom, and Soso languages; and just before Kilham's work the naturalist and ethnographer Thomas Bowdich had published a vocabulary of Wolof and Fula. Kilham is unusual not only because of her gender but also because of the intended readership and beneficiaries of her linguistic work. Earlier guides had been intended for the colonialists, not for the Africans. Although one must always be aware of what was intended by the declaredly benevolent mission of 'educating' the African peoples, Kilham's task was innovative and distinctive in that she set out to provide a tool which would enable Africans to help themselves, rather than a tool to smooth the negotiations of European domination. It is very important to have some sense of this distinction when approaching the writings included here, parts of which seem at first sight indistinguishable from the common run of European representations of the peoples of Africa.

In order to achieve her goals Kilham had to be persistent and courageous. After nearly ten years of lobbying, in 1824 she set sail with three missionaries of the Society of Friends and two African sailors for Sierra Leone, one of the few new British colonies established in the last years of the eighteenth century. The government of the colony was undergoing change, and the abolition of the slave trade was bringing thousands of recaptured slaves to the capital, Freetown, where the Anglican Church Missionary Society had established a school to teach freed slave children. Sierra Leone was known for its high mortality rates among colonialists and missionaries. As Moira Ferguson has explained: 'Only five or six white European women lived in the colony at any given time in the early nineteenth century . . . By 1826 sixty-five of the seventy-nine Church Missionary Society missionaries, wives, and instructors who had come to work in Sierra Leone were dead.'[1] Kilham's visit was not very satisfactory: she and her party were given a base in the settlement of Bathurst (now Banjul in the Gambia), and when she returned in June 1824 the group's activities did not seem successful, and two of the party did not survive

---

[1] 'Hannah Kilham: Gender, the Gambia, and the Politics of Language', in Alan Richardson and Sonia Hofkosh (eds.), *Romanticism, Race, and Imperial Culture, 1780–1834* (Bloomington, Ind.: Indiana University Press, 1996), 123.

their return visit. On her return to Britain she reported to the Committee for African Instruction, published as *Reports on a Recent Visit* (1824). She then spent several months in Ireland working with the British and Irish Ladies' Society in famine relief. After this, she sailed again for an even more internally unstable Sierra Leone in November 1827, and in the two working months before her return in February 1828 visited a greater range of villages and towns, composed lists and categories of the major languages, and set up a school in Portuguese Town. Complicating her work at this time was the fact that she was gradually moving away from the beliefs and teachings of the Quakers. After returning and reporting again to the Committee for the Promotion of African Instruction—and publishing *Report on a Recent Visit to Africa* (1827) and *Specimens of African Languages, Spoken in the Colony of Sierra Leone* (1828)—she made her third and final visit to Sierra Leone in 1830. Her *The Claims of West Africa to Christian Instruction through the Native Languages* appeared this same year. This time she founded a large school at the mountain village of Charlotte, where she was the only European: her pupils were children rescued from slave ships and entrusted to her care by permission of the Governor. From Charlotte she travelled in Liberia, and visited schools in Monrovia. During her return voyage to Sierra Leone, however, the ship was struck by lightning, and Kilham, deeply traumatized by the experience, died three days later, at sea. *Extracts from the Letters of Hannah Kilham, now at Sierra Leone*, reprinted from the *Friends' Magazine*, appeared as a pamphlet in 1831; and in 1837 Kilham's memoirs and diaries, which she had kept since 1816, were published, edited by her stepdaughter Sarah Biller.

The wider implications of Kilham's linguistic plans bore directly on the autonomy of the people of Sierra Leone: their consequences have been seen as proto-nationalistic. The extracts selected here come from the 24-page pamphlet *Report on a Recent Visit to the Colony of Sierra Leone* (1828), addressed to the Committee for African Instruction as well as to 'other Friends concerned in promoting its objects'. Kilham observes carefully and with compassion, and writes eloquently about the need to set in place improvements which can be maintained and directed by Africans themselves. She is alert to the need for regulation (as in her anxiety about the well-being of the slave children freed only to be in effect re-enslaved by their new protectors) but she is also interested in sustainable social amelioration which does not depend on a permanent domination by Europeans.

≈

From *Report on a Recent Visit to the Colony of Sierra Leone* (1828)

To the Committee for African Instruction, and other Friends concerned in promoting its objects.

ALTHOUGH gratefully sensible of the obligations under which I am placed towards Friends, who have kindly favoured my desire to visit the Coast of Africa, I yet feel so deeply impressed with the conviction that the *cause itself* only, is worthy of notice in this Report, that most gladly would I lose sight of my own individual engagement in it, only to acknowledge that infinite Mercy, by which an unworthy servant has been protected and sustained: preserved and restored from sickness by land, and delivered from the dangers of an awful storm at sea, when the waves seemed ready to overwhelm, and ourselves as at the very gate of death. And thankfully would I acknowledge also, the deep sense with which my mind has been impressed, of the little moment of all transitory sufferings or enjoyments, in comparison of the concerns which we shall feel to be of everlasting interest, in that swiftly approaching hour when we shall each have to stand as alone before our Judge.

We were favoured, after a rapid passage to Sierra Leone, with a safe and pleasant landing, on First day morning the 9th of 12th month, 1827.

In anchoring at this Port, the fine open view of Free Town,* in which are many handsome buildings, the fresh and beautiful foliage of trees in its vicinity, and the mountains covered with verdure, rising in majestic grandeur in the bounds of our view, presented a scene so interesting, that, together with the attraction felt towards the dear children on the coast, it was not easy to imagine there could be any *unconquerable* difficulty as to European residence in the country; still it could not be concealed from the most sanguine, that, even in *approaching* these shores, the influence of the heat was felt to be greatly relaxing, and experience must confirm the conviction of the precariousness of European life on this coast, and of the great claim which the instruction of Native Teachers presents, for the prompt and efficient help of the friends of Africa.

It was a great comfort to us soon to meet some our dear friends on shore. Several of the Missionaries had been seriously ill during the rains (which had ceased only three weeks) but they were now recovered, excepting one who was still sick at Wellington.* With some of the Missionaries I had been previously acquainted in England, and with others had had the advantage of friendly open communication on the way, on subjects of importance, and of mutual interest. My kind friends J. and A. Weeks, invited me immediately to take up my abode with them: (A.W. I had previously known in Africa and in England). Although their hospitality and friendship in this distant land were truly consoling, and I felt it as a claim for thankfulness to Him, who is present to help and protect as well when far off from near relatives and home, as in any other circumstances, yet I could not at once conclude upon any thing more than to remain with them for the present, and wait to see whether Free Town or the village districts, would be most favourable for pursuing the objects in view.

On the day after our landing I visited the Free Town Eastern School, which, since the removal of a number of the Free Town children to this school, in the early part of last year, had been conducted by J. and A. Weeks, with two Native Assistants. The school contained about 200 Children, Boys on one side and Girls on the other, without farther division than a few slight posts, at a distance from each other. The room had been built for the purpose, ample and commodious, and very pleasantly situated near the sea. The scholars are chiefly the children of the American settlers,* together with a few others sent from Native districts in the vicinity of Sierra Leone, and boarded in Free Town at the expense of their parents, for the advantage of having them sent to the day schools.

The attention and intelligence of the Boys in this school delighted me; and never did I see a company of children in any school whose countenances struck me as more expressive of a lively disposition to imbibe instruction, and quick capacity for receiving it. They answered with readiness from the Scriptures, questions on many interesting and important subjects, and evidently enjoyed the opportunity given them of receiving farther instruction. The Girls joined in attending to the questions thus proposed by J. W. to the whole school, but, though the countenances of many of them were intelligent and interesting, they did not appear to have attained to the same scriptural knowledge with the Boys. They had, during the late rains, been under many disadvantages; the almost constant sickness of A. W. preventing her being able to attend the school during a great part of the season.

There was another School for Boys and Girls in Free Town (now called the Western School) in which the number of Scholars was rather larger than in this. The Boys taught by a Native Teacher and his Assistant, and the Girls by M. Taylor, the widow of a Missionary, and S. Fox, the wife of the Master of the Boys school, as her Assistant. Some changes have since taken place in the arrangement of the Schools, on account of the return of J. and A. Weeks to England, for the recovery of their health. No Europeans being at liberty to take charge of the school on their departure, the Boys of both schools were placed under the care of the Native Teacher, George Fox, who had his education in England, and the Girls under M. Taylor, with the Native Assistants in each school.

For several days during the school vacation, which commenced on the 15th, J. W. assembled a large company of little children, together with a number of the other scholars, to try the effect of some parts of the infant School system, and with a success so interesting, that we could not but greatly desire such a school for the junior children could be formed in that place.

The engagements I had in view in Sierra Leone were, first, the obtaining an outline of the principal languages spoken by the Liberated Africans and others in the Colony, so as, by taking down in writing, in an easy and distinct orthography, the numerals and some of the leading words, to identify, so far as might be practicable, the dialects of the different tribes, to form an idea of the number of distinct languages spoken in Sierra Leone; and to consider what prospect there might be of proceeding to reduce those of most importance to a written form. Also to prepare such an outline for elementary instruction in each language, as might introduce the pupils in the Liberated African Schools, to a better knowledge of English than they at present possess.

From observations made in Sierra Leone, and from subsequent reflection, it has appeared quite likely that this purpose may be effected, if the children can learn at first only fifty or sixty leading words, besides the numerals, each in their own language, and the correspondent words in English. This would indeed seem but as a small beginning, but so many leading words *attained* and *understood*, would soon introduce to an extension of their knowledge. At present the Liberated African children are learning English under the same disadvantages, which English children would have in learning French, were French books only given to them, without any English translation. The children in the villages have but little opportunity of hearing *conversation* in English, excepting in the barbarous broken form of it, which prevails in that district, and which consists of but a very limited number of words (some suppose not more than fifty): the written language of their English books of course appears quite as a foreign tongue in comparison with this; therefore, although many learn in time to *read* and to *spell*, those who are thus circumstanced cannot be expected to *understand* what they read. The children of the Free Town schools have superior advantages in this respect—their parents being chiefly from the American Continent or Islands, they are brought up by them in *speaking* as well as reading the English language.

The School vacation in Free Town having commenced so soon after my arrival in Sierra Leone, my friends J. and A. Weeks, kindly accompanied me to several villages of Liberated Africans in pursuance of the objects in view. The first place which we visited was Wellington, of which Thomas Macfoy, a native of the West Indies, is Superintendent. From his Register of the names and native countries of the people under his care, I found an unexpected facility in obtaining a knowledge of how many tribes were resident in the village, and the number of persons belonging to each. From these various tribes T. Macfoy sent out for the most intelligent individuals as interpreters, yet in some instances it seemed necessary for himself or J. Weeks to act as an *intermediate interpreter*, for such of them as could not understand any other than the broken English. Besides Wellington, we visited in this engagement Allen's Town, Leopold, Regent, and Gloucester; and J. W. went alone to Charlotte, to ascertain whether any other tribes were to be met with there.* Sketches were taken down of the numbers, and of some leading words in twenty-five languages, and J. W. suggested, that by an arrangement which would present at one view a few words in each language, one elementary book might serve for a whole school, although the children might be of many different tribes. The idea was adopted, and a manuscript was afterwards, during my passage home, arranged in that order. Two of the dialects taken down in the villages, had been omitted, as being too similar to some others, to be regarded as distinct; and three having been added in Free Town, the whole prepared for the proposed elementary book, including the Jalof, Mandingo, Timmani, and Sussu, previously printed,* were thirty in number, and, with the addition of the English, they are now presented to the notice of the Committee, under the title of 'Specimens of African Languages,' & c. . . .

From the report of the Liberated African School of Leopold, printed last year, I was painfully struck with the proportion of deaths among the children, and with the number at that time sick. Observing that other schools had not made any point of reporting on the state of the children's health, I could not but feel it a matter of importance that such reports should be regularly required on behalf of all the liberated African children, both with respect to health, and to their state of instruction; and should it appear that there is more of sickness among these children, than even their debilitated state on arrival will account for, farther enquiry should undoubtedly be made as to the cause, or causes.

That some of these poor little children do appear on arrival only like moving skeletons, is indeed true. Nothing but the very representation of death, could equal the worn and wretchedly emaciated appearance, that some of these presented when I lately saw them, having but within a few weeks been received from the Slave Ship. There are sometimes melancholy instances of a feverish, ravenous appetite, inducing these miserable little victims of oppression, as soon as they land and are brought within sight of poultry and other kinds of food, to fall upon stealing it, half roasting it if possible, and eagerly devouring it, yet still feeling always in want, and always out of health.

The breaking up of the schools of liberated African children some time ago, and their distribution as apprentices to such as would take them, is the more to be lamented, as there are not at present any means of collecting these children or ascertaining that they are well treated; some arrangement to bring them occasionally into view, is greatly wanted; some of the people who take them, after having paid ten shillings for an indenture, imagine that they have by this means purchased the children, and made them their own property. . . .

My mind has for years been impressed with a conviction, that our great duty toward Africa, is to strengthen the hands of the people, *to promote each other's good*; and, if we may be so permitted, to be instrumental in leading some to the acknowledgment of Christianity from experimental feeling, who may become humble instruments in the Divine hand of spreading the Truth and the love of it, and especially among the rising generation in Africa. It is the Africans themselves that must be the travellers, and Instructors, and Improvers of Africa:—let Europeans aid them with Christian kindness, as senior brethren would the younger and feebler members of their Father's family—but let it be kept in mind to what perpetual interruption every purpose must be subject, that is made dependant upon European life on the African shores.

Let a full and fair opportunity be given, if by Divine favour and assistance it may be so permitted, for preparing Agents of intelligence and Christian feeling from among the Natives themselves. Let them be trained in habits which will lead them to the exercise of their own understanding, and let them be taught to make good use of their own resources, and not disposed to look to others to do for them, what is within their own power by proper exertion and attention, to do for themselves,—and, above all, may they be taught to feel and thankfully acknowledge, that their beneficent Creator, the Father of all the families of the earth, wills the happiness and redemption of all—that all mankind are indeed in a fallen state and prone to evil—but that the effects of our first Parents' fall are not more universal, than the blessing of an universal opening to Redemption by Christ Jesus;—that, a measure of His divine light and renewing power is imparted to 'every man that cometh into the world,'* and would lead all if yielded to, to salvation, from sin and misery, and would conduct to final happiness:—but where men will 'love darkness rather than light, because their deeds are evil,' and 'will not come unto the light, lest their deeds be reproved,'* then, although the light may still in degree continue to shine, its power and efficiency will not be felt; it will shine only as on the darkness that 'comprehendeth it not'*—and the offers of mercy and redemption afforded, will, if thus slighted and neglected, rise up against them to their condemnation.

I left Sierra Leone, in company with my friends J. and A. Weeks, on the 20th of 2d month, and it seems due from me here to acknowledge, that soon after coming on board, I was favoured with a sense of the overshadowing of Divine care and goodness, so indubitable and consoling, that my mind was covered with thankfulness, and with a feeling of peace inexpressible.

ELIZABETH BARRETT
(1806–1861)

Born in Coxhoe, County Durham, the eldest of the eleven children of a wealthy plantation-owner, Edward Barrett Moulton-Barrett, and his wife Mary Graham Clarke, Elizabeth Barrett won widespread recognition in her own time as one of the most important poets of the nineteenth century. Her family moved to a large house on her father's estate at Hope End in Hertfordshire when she was 3: here, in her teens, she injured her spine in an accident and was treated as an invalid for many years. Educated at home by a private tutor, she could read Homer in the original when she was 8. After the death of their mother in 1828 the Barrett children were increasingly restricted by their protective father. The abolition of the slave trade in 1834 lessened Edward Moulton-Barrett's profits, and the family moved to Wimpole Street, London. In 1840 Elizabeth Barrett was traumatized by the death of her favourite brother, Bro, and her habits of confinement and intensive reading were confirmed. The isolation in which she wrote has been seen as the epitome of the increasing retirement of women writers towards the end of the period represented here. Barrett did, however, form close friendships, later with Anna Jameson and at this period of seclusion with Mary Russell Mitford and John Kenyon. She met Mitford in May 1836, and, as their letters show, a close and deeply affectionate friendship sprang up between them, despite or because of a twenty-year age difference: between 1836 and 1846 they wrote to each other two or three times a week. In May 1845 she met the poet Robert Browning who had been a correspondent and admirer of her verse, and after a few days he declared his love for her. After months of planning during a secret engagement she married him in 1846 and travelled immediately to Italy, settling in Florence, where their son Pen was born in 1849. Mary Mitford, who disliked Browning, broke off their friendship.

Barrett's later works—especially *Sonnets from the Portuguese* (1850), *Casa Guidi Windows* (1851), and *Aurora Leigh* (1857)—are widely known, and fall outside the scope of this anthology. She appears here because the poetry which she published before her breakthrough collection (the two-volume *Poems*, 1844) deserves more attention than it commonly receives. Her first poem, *The Battle of Marathon*, was privately printed in 1820, when she was 14; six years later appeared the weighty *An Essay on Mind*. In 1833 she published *Prometheus Bound, and Miscellaneous Poems*, followed by *The Seraphim and Other Poems* (1838). These early works reveal both her lyricism and her preoccupation with her place as a woman poet in the context of a literary tradition which she sees as predominantly male. They tell of dreams, visions, interrupted access of various kinds, anticipated or actual exclusion and 'waywardness'.

All but the last of the poems selected here were written when Barrett was in her twenties. As the first poem, 'Mine is a wayward lay', makes clear, Barrett's speaker wants to flaunt her originality and her right to song, while distrusting its acceptability. Her song is dependent on the approving reception of the loved one she addresses; it is also imagined as an echo of something more genuine, the feelings of her heart, and, in the second stanza, is seen as less eloquent than the conventional physical registers of faith and love. Barrett's emphasis on 'unfashioned' simplicity provides a telling contrast to the more ambitious poems which follow, parts of which read like studied attempts to outdo her Romantic male predecessors such as Coleridge, Percy Shelley, and Keats. That these are dreams and visions, and fragments, makes them, by convention, provisional and exploratory. It also allows the poet to incorporate or to imitate the voices of those to whom she listens.

When critics discuss Barrett's early work, they usually turn to one ambitious poem, 'The Tempest', based on memories of a storm Barrett witnessed in 1826, in which two women died. As Angela Leighton points out in her discussion of 'The Tempest', Barrett replaces the female victims with a single male figure, imaginatively associated with her father, and exploits a traditional link between storm and the creative power to express her guilty excitement at claiming for herself the authority of the poet and the father.[1] The other poems included in the selection below make it possible to examine these ideas more fully, and to see 'The Tempest' as part of an ongoing questioning of the relationships between the physical and the imaginative or spiritual worlds, and between Barrett and poetic tradition. They also loosen the grip which Barrett's father has exercised upon traditional views of her creative imagination. 'The Dream' anticipates some of the ideas of 'The Tempest', but the elements are significantly rearranged, and the meditation seems more broadly cultural than autobiographical. It is, as it happens, a more successful poem, designedly disjointed in a way which calls into question its apparently secure Christian ending. The corpse which draws critics to 'The Tempest', meanwhile, is also a feature of 'The Dream' and 'The Vision of Fame', and in the latter poem is a female skeleton, the remains of a dream vision which seems at first to be about art or poetry. There may be a punitive male system in the superstructure of this meditation, but the visionary and her temptation are alike female. Continuing Barrett's fascination with the macabre, 'A Vision of Life and Death' tells of a 'mystic

[1] Angela Leighton, *Elizabeth Barrett Browning* (Brighton: Harvester, 1986), 46–51.

strife' between the two female figures of life and death, but also of a struggle between the poet and her soul, whose cryptic account of her wanderings surely frustrates the questioning self who begins the poem in enforced deafness and silence.

Finally, 'L.E.L.'s Last Question' carries forward Barrett's interest in poetic fame, in minstrelsy, in awakening from dreams, and in the resolution of awkward questioning into Christian assurance (although here the assurance is rather a guilty one, and the questioning does not cease: it is taken up by a neglected Christ). The poem, written in 1839, slightly oversteps the chronological barrier of this collection, but it is an important addition to the group of works which reflect on the fates of other women writers. 'Female elegy' may not be a definable literary category, but it is striking how open this poem is to the words of another. Writing to Mary Russell Mitford in July 1841, Barrett provides one of the best contexts in which to read her elegy:

Poor wretched L E L—I grieve for her. But I hold stedfastly—perversely perhaps you think—(yet dont!) that her faults were not *of* her poetry but *against* it. . . .

But poor poor L E L—I feel all you say of the material unworked. She might indeed have achieved a greatness which her fondest admirers can scarcely consider achieved now. And do you know (ah—*I* know that you wont agree with me!) I have sometimes thought to myself that if I had those two powers to choose from—Mrs Hemans's and Miss Landon's—I mean the *raw* bare powers—I would choose Miss Landon's. I surmise that it was more elastic, more various, of a stronger web. I fancy it would have worked out better—had it *been* worked out—with the right moral and intellectual influences in application. As it is, Mrs Hemans has left the finer poems.[2]

In the poem which sprang from these complex feelings about a woman poet's flawed creativity Barrett astutely and poignantly questions Landon's substitution of emotional and 'romantic' support for the praise and gratitude owed by the country she is leaving. The decision to freeze the image of Landon lonely on the sea, between a native land and an exotic but murderous exile, is inspired; and the ending, which on first reading subsumes Landon's plea to Christ's, also, more subtly, makes her words his.

∼

[2] *Elizabeth Barrett to Miss Mitford: the Unpublished Letters of Elizabeth Barrett Browning to Mary Russell Mitford*, ed. Betty Miller (London: Murray, 1954), 78.

To—— (1826)

Mine is a wayward lay;
And, if its echoing rimes I try to string
  Proveth a truant thing,
Whenso some names I love, send it away!

For then, eyes swimming o'er,
And claspèd hands, and smiles in fondness meant,
  Are much more eloquent:—
So it had fain begone, and speak no more!

Yet shall it come again,
Ah, friend beloved! if so thy wishes be,
  And, with wild melody,
I will, upon thine ear, cadence my strain—

Cadence my simple line,
Unfashioned by the cunning hand of Art,
  But coming from my heart,
To tell the message of its love to thine!

As ocean shells, when taken
From Ocean's bed, will faithfully repeat
  Her ancient music sweet—
Ev'n so these words, true to my heart, shall waken!

Oh! while our bark is seen,
Our little bark of kindly, social love,
  Down life's clear stream to move
Toward the summer shores, where all is green—

So long thy name shall bring
Echoes of joy unto the grateful gales,
  And thousand tender tales,
To freshen the fond hearts that round thee cling!

Hast thou not looked upon
The flowerets of the field in lowly dress?
  Blame not my simpleness—
Think only of my love!—my song is gone.

The Dream: A Fragment (1826)

I had a dream!—my spirit was unbound
From the dark iron of its dungeon, clay,
And rode the steeds of Time;—my thoughts had sound,
And spoke without a word,—I went away
Among the buried ages, and did lay
The pulses of my heart beneath the touch
Of the rude minstrel Time, that he should play
Thereon a melody which might seem such
As musing spirits love—mournful, but not too much!

I had a dream—and there mine eyes did see
The shadows of past deeds like present things—
The sepulchres of Greece and Hespery,*
Aegyptus, and old lands, gave up their kings,
Their prophets, saints, and minstrels, whose lute-strings
Keep a long echo—yea, the dead, white bones
Did stand up by the house whereto Death clings,
And dressed themselves in life, speaking of thrones,
And fame, and power, and beauty, in familiar tones!

I went back further still, for I beheld
What time the earth was one fair Paradise—
And over such bright meads the waters welled,
I wot the rainbow was content to rise
Upon the earth, when absent from the skies!
And there were tall trees that I never knew,
Whereon sate nameless birds in merry guise,
Folding their radiant wings, as the flowers do,
When summer nights send sleep down with the dew.

Anon there came a change—a terrible motion,
That made all living things grow pale and shake!
The dark Heavens bowed themselves unto the ocean,
Like a strong man in strife—Ocean did take
His flight across the mountains; and the lake
Was lashed into a sea where the winds ride—
Earth was no more, for in her merry-make
She had forgot her God—Sin claimed his bride,
And with his vampire breath sucked out her life's fair tide!

Life went back to her nostrils, and she raised
Her spirit from the waters once again—
The lovely sights, on which I erst had gazed,
Were *not*—though she was beautiful as when
The Grecian called her 'Beauty'—* sinful men
Walked i' the track of the waters, and felt bold—
Yea, they looked up to Heaven in calm disdain,
As if no eye had seen its vault unfold
Darkness, and fear, and death!—as if a tale were told!

And ages fled away within my dream;
And still Sin made the heart his dwelling-place,
Eclipsing Heaven from men; but it would seem
That two or three dared commune face to face,
And speak of the soul's life, of hope, and grace.
Anon there rose such sounds as angels breathe—
For a God came to die, bringing down peace—
'Pan *was not*'; and the darkness that did wreathe
The earth, passed from the soul—Life came by Death!

The Vision of Fame (1826)

Did ye ever sit on summer noon,
　　Half musing and half asleep,
When ye smile in such a dreamy way,
　　Ye know not if ye weep—

When the little flowers are thick beneath,
　　And the welkin blue above;*
When there is not a sound but the cattle's low,
　　And the voice of the woodland dove!

A while ago, and I dreamed thus—
　　I mused on ancient story,—
For the heart like a minstrel of old doth seem,
　　It delighteth to sing of glory.

What time I saw before me stand
　　A bright and lofty One;
A golden lute was in her hand,
　　And her brow drooped thereon.

But the brow that drooped was raisèd soon,

Showing its royal sheen—
It was, I guessed, no human brow,
 Though pleasant to human een.

And this brow of peerless majesty
 With its whiteness did enshroud
Two eyes that, darkly mystical,
 Gan look up at a cloud.

Like to the hair of Berenice,*
 Fetched from its house of light,
Was the hair which wreathed her shadowless form—
 And Fame the ladye hight!

But as she wended on to me,
 My heart's deep fear was chidden;
For she called up the sprite of Melody,
 Which in her lute lay hidden.

When ye speak to well-belovèd ones,
 Your voice is tender and low:
The wires methought did love her touch—
 For they did answer so.

And her lips in such a quiet way
 Gave the chant soft and long,—
You might have thought she only breathed,
 And that her breath was song:—

'When Death shrouds thy memory,
 Love is no shrine—
The dear eyes that weep for thee
 Soon sleep like thine!
The wail murmured over thee
 Fainteth away;
And the heart which kept love for thee
 Turns into clay!

'But wouldst thou remembered be,
 Make me thy vow;
This verse that flows gushingly
 Telleth thee how—
Linking thy hand in mine,
 Listen to me,

So not a thought of thine
   Dieth with thee—

'Rifle thy pulsing heart
   Of the gift, love made;
Bid thine eye's light depart;
   Let thy cheek fade!
Give me the slumber deep,
   Which night-long seems;
Give me the joys that creep
   Into thy dreams!

'Give me thy youthful years,
   Merriest that fly—
So the word, spoke in *tears*,
   Liveth for ay!
So thy sepulchral stone,
   Nations may raise—
What time thy soul hath known
   The *worth of praise!*'

She did not sing this chant to me,
   Though I was sitting by;
But I listened to it with chainèd breath,
   That had no power to sigh.

And ever as the chant went on
   Its measure changed to wail;
And ever as the lips sang on
   Her face did grow more pale.

Paler and paler—till anon
   A fear came o'er my soul;
For the flesh curled up from her bones,
   Like to a blasted scroll!

Aye I silently it dropped away
   Before my wondering sight—
There was only a bleachèd skeleton
   Where erst was ladye bright!

But still the vacant sockets gleamed
   With supernatural fires—

> But still the bony hands did ring
> > Against the shuddering wires!

> Alas, alas! I wended home,
> > With a sorrow and a shame—
> Is Fame the rest of our poor hearts?
> Woe's me! for THIS IS FAME!

The Tempest: A Fragment (1833)

Mors erat ante oculos. LUCAN lib. ix*

The forest made my home—the voiceful streams
My minstrel throng: the everlasting hills,—
Which marry with the firmament, and cry
Unto the brazen thunder, 'Come away,
Come from thy secret place, and try our strength,'—
Enwrapped me with their solemn arms. Here, light
Grew pale as darkness, scarèd by the shade
O' the forest Titans.* Here, in piny state,
Reigned Night, the Aethiopian queen, and crowned
The charmèd brow of Solitude, her spouse.

A sign was on creation. You beheld
All things encoloured in a sulph'rous hue,
As day were sick with fear. The haggard clouds
O'erhung the utter lifelessness of air;
The top boughs of the forest, all aghast,
Stared in the face of Heaven; the deep-mouthed wind,
That hath a voice to bay the armèd sea,
Fled with a low cry like a beaten hound;
And only that askance the shadows flew
Some open-beakèd birds in wilderment,
Naught stirred abroad. All dumb did Nature seem,
In expectation of the coming storm.

It came in power. You soon might hear afar
The footsteps of the martial thunder sound
Over the mountain battlements; the sky
Being deep-stained with hues fantastical,
Red like to blood, and yellow like to fire,
And black like plumes at funerals; overhead

You might behold the lightning faintly gleam
Amid the clouds which thrill and gape aside,
And straight again shut up their solemn jaws,
As if to interpose between Heaven's wrath
And Earth's despair. Interposition brief!
Darkness is gathering out her mighty pall
Above us, and the pent-up rain is loosed,
Down trampling in its fierce delirium.

Was not my spirit gladdened, as with wine,
To hear the iron rain, and view the mark
Of battle on the banner of the clouds?
Did I not hearken for the battle-cry,
And rush along the bowing woods to meet
The riding Tempest—skyey cataracts
Hissing around him with rebellion vain?
Yea! and I lifted up my glorying voice
In an 'All hail'; when, wildly resonant,
As brazen chariots rushing from the war,
As passioned waters gushing from the rock,
As thousand crashèd woods, the thunder cried:
And at his cry the forest tops were shook
As by the woodman's axe; and far and near
Staggered the mountains with a muttered dread.

All hail unto the lightning! hurriedly
His lurid arms are glaring through the air,
Making the face of Heaven to show like hell!
Let him go breathe his sulphur stench about,
And, pale with death's own mission, lord the storm!
Again the gleam—the glare: I turned to hail
Death's mission: at my feet there lay the dead!
The dead—the dead lay there! I could not view
(For Night espoused the storm, and made all dark)
Its features, but the lightning in its course
Shivered above a white and corpse-like heap,
Stretched in the path, as if to show his prey,
And have a triumph ere he passed. Then I
Crouched down upon the ground, and groped about
Until I touched that thing of flesh, rain-drenched,

And chill, and soft. Nathless, I did refrain
My soul from natural horror! I did lift
The heavy head, half-bedded in the clay,
Unto my knee; and passed my fingers o'er
The wet face, touching every lineament,
Until I found the brow; and chafed its chill,
To know if life yet lingered in its pulse.
And while I was so busied, there did leap
From out the entrails of the firmament,
The lightning, who his white unblenching breath
Blew in the dead man's face, discovering it
As by a staring day. I knew that face—
His, who did hate me—his, whom I did hate!

I shrunk not—spake not—sprang not from the ground!
But felt my lips shake without cry or breath,
And mine heart wrestle in my breast to still
The tossing of its pulses; and a cold,
Instead of living blood, o'ercreep my brow.
Albeit such darkness brooded all around,
I had dread knowledge that the open eyes
Of that dead man were glaring up to mine,
With their unwinking, unexpressive stare;
And mine I could not shut nor turn away
The man was my familiar. I had borne
Those eyes to scowl on me their living hate,
Better than I could bear their deadliness:
I had endured the curses of those lips
Far better than their silence. Oh, constrained
And awful silence!—awful peace of death!
There is an answer to all questioning,
That one word—*death*. Our bitterness can throw
No look upon the face of death, and live.
The burning thoughts that erst my soul illumed
Were quenched at once; as tapers in a pit
Wherein the vapour-witches weirdly reign
In charge of darkness. Farewell all the past!
It was out-blotted from my memory's eyes
When clay's cold silence pleaded for its sin.

Farewell the elemental war! farewell
The clashing of the shielded clouds—the cry
Of scathèd echoes! I no longer knew
Silence from sound, but wandered far away
Into the deep Eleusis of mine heart,*
To learn its secret things. When armèd foes
Meet on one deck with impulse violent,
The vessel quakes thro'all her oaken ribs,
And shivers in the sea; so with mine heart:
For there had battled in her solitudes,
Contrary spirits; sympathy with power,
And stooping unto power;—the energy
And passiveness,—the thunder and the death!

Within me was a nameless thought: it closed
The Janus of my soul on echoing hinge,*
And said 'Peace!' with a voice like War's. I bowed,
And trembled at its voice: it gave a key,
Empowered to open out all mysteries
Of soul and flesh; of man, who doth begin,
But endeth not; of life, and *after life*.

Day came at last: her light showed grey and sad,
As hatched by tempest, and could scarce prevail
Over the shaggy forest to imprint
Its outline on the sky—expressionless,
Almost sans shadow as sans radiance:
An idiocy of light. I wakened from
My deep unslumb'ring dream, but uttered naught.
My living I uncoupled from the dead,
And looked out, 'mid the swart and sluggish air,
For place to make a grave. A mighty tree
Above me, his gigantic arms outstretched,
Poising the clouds. A thousand muttered spells
Of every ancient wind and thund'rous storm
Had been off-shaken from his scatheless bark.
He had heard distant years sweet concord yield,
And go to silence; having firmly kept
Majestical companionship with Time.
Anon his strength waxed proud: his tusky roots

Forced for themselves a path on every side,
Riving the earth; and, in their savage scorn,
Casting it from them like a thing unclean,
Which might impede his naked clambering
Unto the heavens. Now blasted, peeled, he stood,
By the gone night, whose lightning had come in
And rent him, even as it rent the man
Beneath his shade: and there the strong and weak
Communion joined in deathly agony.
There, underneath, I lent my feverish strength,
To scoop a lodgement for the traveller's corse.
I gave it to the silence and the pit,
And strewed the heavy earth on all: and then—
I—I, whose hands had formed that silent house,—
I could not look thereon, but turned and wept!

O Death—O crownèd Death—pale-steeded Death!
Whose name doth make our respiration brief,
Muffling the spirit's drum! Thou, whom men know
Alone by charnel-houses, and the dark
Sweeping of funeral feathers, and the scath
Of happy days,—love deemed inviolate!
Thou of the shrouded face, which to have seen
Is to be very awful, like thyself!—
Thou, whom all flesh shall see!—thou, who dost call,
And there is none to answer!—thou, whose call
Changeth all beauty into what we fear,
Changeth all glory into what we tread,
Genius to silence, wrath to nothingness,
And love—not love!—thou hast no change for love!
Thou, who art Life's betrothed, and bear'st her forth
To scare her with sad sights,—who hast thy joy
Where'er the peopled towns are dumb with plague,—
Where'er the battle and the vulture meet,—
Where'er the deep sea writhes like Laocoon*
Beneath the serpent winds, and vessels split
On secret rocks, and men go gurgling down,
Down, down, to lose their shriekings in the depth!
O universal thou! who comest ay

Among the minstrels, and their tongue is tied;
Among the sophists, and their brain is still;
Among the mourners, and their wail is done;
Among the dancers, and their tinkling feet
No more make echoes on the tombing earth;
Among the wassail rout, and all the lamps
Are quenched, and withered the wine-pouring hands!
Mine heart is armèd not in panoply
Of the old Roman iron, nor assumes
The Stoic valour.* 'Tis a human heart,
And so confesses, with a human fear;—
That only for the hope the cross inspires,
That only for the MAN who died and lives,
'Twould crouch beneath thy sceptre's royalty,
With faintess of the pulse, and backward cling
To life. But knowing what I soothly know,
High-seeming Death, I dare thee! and have hope,
In God's good time, of showing to thy face
An unsuccumbing spirit, which sublime
May cast away the low anxieties
That wait upon the flesh—the reptile moods;
And enter that eternity to come,
Where live the dead, and only Death shall die.*

L.E.L.'s Last Question

Do you think of me as I think of you? From her poem
written during the voyage to the Cape (1839)

'Do you think of me as I think of you,
My friends, my friends?' She said it from the sea,
The English minstrel in her minstrelsy—
While under brighter skies than erst she knew,
Her heart grew dark, and gropèd as the blind,
To touch, across the waves, friends left behind—
'Do you think of me as I think of you?'

It seemed not much to ask—*as I of you*—
We all do ask the same—no eyelids cover
Within the meekest eyes that question over—
And little in this world the loving do,

But sit (among the rocks?) and listen for
The echo of their own love evermore—
Do you think of me as I think of you?

Love-learnèd, she had sung of only love—
And as a child asleep (with weary head
Dropped on the fairy-book he lately read),
Whatever household noises round him move,
Hears in his dream some elfin turbulence—
Even so, suggestive to her inward sense,
All sounds of life assumed one tune of love.

And when the glory of her dream withdrew,
When knightly gestes and courtly pageantries
Were broken in her visionary eyes
By tears, the solemn seas attested true—
Forgetting that sweet lute beside her hand,
She asked not 'Do you praise me, O my land,'
But, 'Think ye of me, friends, as I of you?'

True heart to love, that pourèd many a year
Love's oracles for England, smooth and well,—
Would God, thou hadst an inward oracle
In that lone moment, to confirm thee dear!
For when thy questioned friends in agony
Made passionate response, 'We think of thee,'
Thy place was in the dust—too deep to hear!

Could she not wait to catch the answering breath?—
Was she content with that drear ocean's sound,
Dashing his mocking infinite around
The craver of a little love?—beneath
Those stars, content—where last her song had gone?
They, mute and cold in radiant life, as soon
Their singer was to be, in darksome death!

Bring your vain answers—cry. 'We think of thee!'
How think ye of her?—in the long ago
Delights!—or crowned by new bays?—not so—
None smile, and none are crowned where lyeth she—
With all her visions unfulfilled, save one,
Her childhood's, of the palm-trees in the sun—
And lo!—their shadow on her sepulchre!

Do you think of me as I think of you?—
O friends, O kindred, O dear brotherhood
Of the whole world—what are we that we should
For covenants of long affection sue?—
Why press so near each other, when the touch
Is barred by graves? Not much, and yet too much,
This, 'Think upon me as I think of you.'

But, while on mortal lips I shape anew
A sigh to mortal issues, verily
Above the unshaken stars that see us die,
A vocal pathos rolls—and He who drew
All life from dust, and *for* all, tasted death,
By death, and life, and love appealing, saith,
Do you think of me as I think of you?

HARRIET MARTINEAU
(1802–1876)

Born into a prominent Unitarian family in Norwich, Martineau was the
sixth of the eight children of Thomas Martineau, a cloth manufacturer,
and his wife Elizabeth Rankin, the eldest daughter of a sugar refiner from
Newcastle upon Tyne. She received a reasonably good education, taught
by her two elder brothers and sister before going to school from the age of
11. According to her *Autobiography*, she was a religious and sickly child
with a strong need for approbation and affection. The deafness which was
to afflict her for the rest of her life became noticeable when she was 12,
and by the time she was 16 it was a serious impairment. The collapse of
her father's business in 1829 left her to support herself first by needlework; academically gifted, she turned to writing, and between 1829 and
1833 reviewed extensively for the *Monthly Repository*. At the age of 20 she
published three articles in the *Monthly Repository*: entitled 'Female
Writers on Practical Divinity' and signed 'Disciplus', they include discussions of the religious thinking of Hannah More and of Martineau's fellow
Unitarian Anna Laetitia Barbauld. In 1826 her only romantic involvement
came to an end when her betrothed, John Worthington, became insane
and died. Believing herself ill-suited to married life, she later declared
herself 'probably the happiest single woman in England' (*Autobiography*,
133). She travelled in the United States from 1834 to 1836, visiting New

Orleans, Cincinnati, Chicago, and Lake Michigan; and in Egypt and the
Holy Land in 1846–7. In between these travels, she spent from 1839 to
1844 as an invalid in Tynemouth, cared for by her sister and brother-in-
law. In 1844 she settled in Ambleside, Cumbria, where she built a house,
The Knoll, and became a friend of the Wordsworths. In 1855, given only a
short time to live, she wrote her autobiography, but lived for another
twenty years, cared for by two nieces, and writing about the Lakes, Comte,
India, farming, and a range of other topics. She insisted on making her
living by writing, three times turning down the offer of a civil list pension
(that useful prop for Burney, Hamilton, and several other women writers
of this period). Her autobiography was eventually published, posthumously, in 1877.

The twenty-four stories of different lengths which made up *Illustrations of Political Economy* (1832–4), in which she was influenced and
encouraged by Jane Marcet, made Martineau's name. She had prepared
thoroughly, reading Jeremy Bentham, Adam Smith, and Malthus, but she
found it difficult to persuade a publisher to support the idea of political
economy written for a general market and intended most of all to help the
poor. From the appearance of the first story, however, the work was a huge
success, and Martineau calculated that it earned her £10,000 in all. Earning an income was no longer to be a problem. Eager readers included the
young Princess Victoria; while the French king Louis-Philippe and the
Emperor of Russia both ordered translations of Martineau's work to be
made part of the school curriculum. She won praise from prominent
economists, including Richard Cobden, Peel, and John Stuart Mill. *Society in America* (1837) and *A Retrospect of Western Travel* (1838) extended
her reputation for social criticism: unlike many commentators, she judged
the United States by its own standards as set out in the Declaration of
Independence, thereby freeing herself from any suspicion of Eurocentric
carping, and securing the works' considerable impact. Her novels include
Deerbrook (1839) and *The Hour and the Man* (1841), and among her many
works of descriptive and argumentative prose are *Eastern Life, Past and
Present* (1848), a history of contemporary England, and a translation of
Auguste Comte's *Positive Philosophy* (1851). In *Letters on the Laws of
Man's Nature and Development* (1851) she declared herself free of Christianity, and a narrative of her move away from the Unitarianism of her
upbringing is central to the *Autobiography*.

Included here are a tale from *Illustrations of Political Economy* and
extracts from two chapters of *Society in America*. In the Preface to the first
volume of *Illustrations of Political Economy* Martineau criticizes system-
atizing approaches to economics, arguing: 'We cannot see why the truth
and its application should not go together,—why an explanation of the

principles which regulate society should not be made more clear and interesting at the same time by pictures of what those principles are actually doing in communities' (i, p. xii). By combining instruction and fiction, she wrote explicitly for all social classes, arguing that all, even the educated, are ignorant of the principles of political economy: 'If it concerns all that the advantages of a social state should be preserved and improved, it concerns them likewise that Political Economy should be understood *by all.*' (i, p. xvi). Here Martineau is in dialogue with the extract from her mentor Jane Marcet's *Conversations on Political Economy* included in the material selected from Marcet in this anthology: Marcet's shrewd little girls had seen clearly that economic knowledge might be socially liberating for the working classes, and their teacher, Mrs B., had gone to some trouble to impose limits on it. Each of Martineau's twenty-four tales is made up of several numbers, and addresses a specific economic question. Trade Unionism is addressed in the twelve numbers of 'A Manchester Strike', for example, while the tale excerpted here, 'A Mushroom City', is the second of the seven numbers of 'Cinnamon and Pearls', published in 1833 and addressing the economic relationship between Britain and the colonies. Martineau summarized the principles illustrated in 'A Mushroom City' thus: 'The duty of government being to render secure the property of its subjects, and their industry being their most undeniable property, all interference of government with the direction and the rewards of industry is a violation of its duty towards its subjects. Such interference takes place when some are countenanced by legislation in engrossing labours and rewards which would otherwise be open to all;—as in the case of privileged trading corporations' (vii. 134). The tale of Rayo is part of an attack on the injustice and bad economic sense of detaching a workforce from the products of its labours, and from all hope of honest proportionate reward. Rayo is eventually caught trying to steal a pearl which he sees as his only chance of securing a comfortable future for his family.

Martineau's *Society in America* is an impressively wide-ranging survey, and although critical of many institutions and practices of the United States is written from a markedly liberal perspective. Its indictment of the situation of black citizens and of women is a striking contribution and carries forward the association of womanhood and slavery to be found in the writings of Wollstonecraft and More. As was widely reported, Martineau had combined these concerns when she addressed the Boston Female Anti-Slavery Society in 1835; she also notably feminizes the spirit of Abolitionism (p. 522 below). In the first of the two extracts below, Martineau trains her fire on the situation of black people not in the slave-owning states but in the supposedly less contentious New England. In her investigation of the situation of women, Martineau adopts a similarly abrupt and lucid style, eschewing the traditional voice of the 'feminine' observer in order to claim political equality in her style alone. She has already stated, in the chapter entitled simply 'Woman', that 'The Americans have, in the treatment of women, fallen below, not only their own democratic principles, but the practice of some parts of the Old World.' Arguing that 'the intellect of woman is confined', that 'marriage is the only option left open to woman', and that 'the morals of women are crushed', Martineau develops at a safe geographical and political distance a critique which holds for her own country too. As she declares in her *Autobiography:* 'My business in life has been to think and learn, and to speak out with absolute freedom what I have thought and learned' (p. 133).

∾

From *Illustrations of Political Economy* (1832–1834)

A Mushroom City (1833)

After the usual expenditure of anxiety, prudence, jealousy, wrath and cunning, the letting of the Pearl banks had been accomplished.* A great speculator had offered government a certain sum for the whole fishery of the season, and had then let the different banks to various merchants, to whom the gracious permission was given to make what they could of the natives of the land as well as of the sea;—not only to appropriate the natural wealth of the region, but to bring its inhabitants as near to the brink of starvation as they pleased in their methods of employing their toil. Pearls seem to be thought beautiful all over the world where they have been seen. Empresses in the north, ladies of all degree in the east and west, and savages between the tropics, all love to wear pearls; and where is there a woman, in an Esquimaux hut or a Welsh farmhouse, who would not wear pearls if she could obtain them? And why should not all have pearls who wish for them, if there is a boundless store, and labourers enough willing and ready to provide them? Alas! there are not only few wearers of pearls because the interests of the many are not consulted, but the labourers who obtain them are by the same cause kept bare of almost the necessaries of life, going forth hungry and half naked to their toil, and returning to seek rest amidst the squalidness of poverty, while hundreds and thousands of their families and neighbours stand on the shore envying them as they depart, and preparing to be jealous of them on their return; both parties being, all the while, the natural owners of the native wealth of their region. And why is all this injustice and tyranny? That a few, a very few, may engross a resource which should enrich the many. Yet, not many things are more evident than that to impoverish the many is the most certain method of ultimately impoverishing the few; and the reverse. If the government would give away its pearl banks to those who now fish those banks for the scantiest wages which will support life, government would soon gain more in a year from the pearls of Ceylon than it has hitherto gained by any five fisheries. If buyers might bid for pearls from every quarter of the world to those who might sell any where, and after their own manner, Cingalese huts of mud and rushes would grow into dwellings of timber and stone; instead of bare walls, there would be furniture from a thousand British warehouses; instead of marshes, there would be rice-fields; instead of rickety coasting boats, there would be fleets of merchantmen riding in the glorious harbours of the island; instead of abject prayers from man to man as the one is about to suffer the dearth which the other inflicts, there would be the good will and thanksgiving which spring from abundance; instead of complaints on the one hand of expensive dependence, and murmurs about oppression on the other, there would be mutual congratulation for mutual aid. Ceylon would over pay, if required, in taxes, if not in advantageous commerce, any sacrifice of the monopolies by which she has been more thoroughly and ingeniously beggared than any dependency on which British monopoly has exercised its skill; and Britain might disburthen her conscience of the crime of perpetuating barbarism in that fairest of all regions, for whose civilization she has made herself responsible.* There are many methods of introducing civilization; and some very important ones have been tried upon this beautiful island, and with as much success as could be expected: but the most efficacious,—the prime method,—is only beginning to be tried,—the allowing the people to gain the property which nature has appointed as their share of her distribution. Let the Cingalese gather their own pearls, exchange their own timber, sell their own dyes wherever and in whatsoever manner they like, and they will soon understand comfort, and care for luxuries, like all who have comforts and luxuries within their reach; and with these desires and attainments will come the perceptions of duty,—the new sense of obligation which it is the object of all plans of civilization to introduce.

Great pains had been taken to civilize Rayo. He had been schooled and watched over—he could read, and he respected the religion of his priest; he was willing to toil, and had a taste for comfort. But, beyond the hope of acquiring a hut and a mat or two, there was little stimulus to toil, and as little to conduct himself with a view towards any future circumstances. Strangers not only carried away the wealth of the land, but they prevented that wealth from growing, and therefore the labour of the inhabitants from obtaining a wider field. As pearls were fished ten years before, so they would be fished ten years hence, for any probability that he saw to the contrary. A thousand divers carried away a pittance then, insufficient to bring over to them the desirable things which were waiting on the shores of the neighbouring continent for a demand; and a like pittance might such another thousand carry away in time to come; in like manner might they sigh for foreign commodities, and in like manner might foreign commodities be still waiting, wrought or unwrought, for a demand. Therefore was Rayo still in a state of barbarism, though he understood and praised the trial by jury, and could read the prayers of his church. He was in a state of barbarism, for these accomplishments had no influence on his conduct and his happiness. He was selfish in his love; fraudulent with an easy conscience in his transactions of business; and capable of a revenge towards his superiors as remorseless as his deportment was gentle and polished. No circumstance had ever produced so happy an effect upon him as his advancement to be a pearl-diver, an advancement in dignity, if not in gain. It was the last promotion he was ever likely to obtain; but, besides that it softened his heart by occasioning his immediate marriage, it gave him the new object of distinguishing himself, and opened the possibility of his profiting by some stray pearl, or by some chance opportunity of speculating on a lot of oysters. He walked to join his company on the beach with a demeanour unlike that by which Rayo was commonly known; and his young wife looked after him with a new feeling of pride.

He was sure to be as safe as on shore, for the Charmer was to go in the same boat, and no shark binder of the whole assemblage was more confident of having effectually bound the sharks than Marana's father.* All were confident; and the crowds on the beach looked as joyous for the night as if the work was going on for their sakes. A city of bowers seemed to have sprung up like Jonah's gourd,* or like the tabernacles which, in old times of Jewish festivals, made Jerusalem a leafy paradise for a short season of every year. Talipot tents,* and bamboo huts dressed with greens and flowers were clustered around the sordid dwellings on the sands. Throngs of merchants and craftsmen, black, tawny, and white, with their variety of costumes, mingled in this great fair. The polisher of jewels was there with his glittering treasure. The pearl-driller looked to his needles and pearl dust, while awaiting on his low seat the materials on which he was to employ his skill. The bald, yellow-mantled priest of Budhoo passed on amidst obeisances in one place, as did the Catholic pastor in another. The white vested Mahomedan, the turbaned Hindoo, the swathed Malay merchants exhibited their stores, or looked passively on the gay scene. The quiet Dutchman from the south sent a keen glance through the market in quest of precious stones in the hands of an ignorant or indolent vender. The haughty Candian abated his fierceness, and stepped out of the path of the European;* while the stealthy Cingalese was in no one's path, but won his way like a snake in the tall grass of the jungle. The restless lessees of the banks, meanwhile, were flitting near the boats, now ranged in a long row, each with its platform, ropes and pullies; each with its shark-binder, its pilot, its commander, its crew of ten, and its company of ten divers. The boat-lights were being kindled, one by one, and scattering a thousand sparkles over the rippling tide. It was just on the stroke of ten, and the signal gun was all that was waited for. The buzz of voices fell into a deep silence as the expectation became more intense. Those who were wont to make the heavens their clock and the stars its hour-hand, looked up to mark the precise inclination of the Southern Cross;* while those who found an index in the flow of the tide, paced the sands from watermark to watermark. Yet more turned their faces southward towards the dark outline of hill and forest that rose on the horizon, and watched for the land breeze. It came,—at first in light puffs which scarcely bowed the rushes around the lagoons, or made a stir among the stalks in the rice-ground. Moment by moment it strengthened, till the sails of the boats began to bulge, and every torch and faggot of cocoa-nut leaves on the beach slanted its forks of flame towards the sea, as if to indicate to the voyagers their way. Then the signal-gun boomed, its wreath of smoke curled lazily upward and dispersed itself in the clear air, while a shout, in which every variety of voice was mingled, seemed to chase the little fleet into the distance. The shouting ceased amidst the anxiety of watching the clusters of receding lights, which presently looked as if they had parted company with those in the sky, and had become a degree less pure by their descent. Then rose the song of the dancing-girls, as they stood grouped, each with a jewelled arm withdrawn from beneath her mantle, and her jet-black hair bound with strings of pearl. Mixed with their chaunt, came the mutterings and gabblings of the charmers who remained on shore, contorting their bodies more vehemently than would have been safe on any footing less stable than terra-firma.

The most imposing part of the spectacle was now to the people at sea. As their vessels were impelled by an unintermitting wind through the calmest of seas, they were insensible to motion, and the scene on shore, with its stir and its sound, seemed to recede like the image of a phantasmagoria, till the flickering lights blended into one yellow haze in which every distinct object was lost. It became at length like a dim star, contrasting strangely in brightness and in hue with the constellation which appeared to rise as rapidly as majestically over the southern hills, like an auxiliary wheeling his silent force to restore the invaded empire of night. Night now had here undisputed sway; for the torches which flared at the prows of the boats were tokens of homage, and not attempts at rivalship of her splendours.

Sailing is nearly as calculable a matter on these expeditions as a journey of fifty miles in an English mail-coach. There is no need to think about the duration of the darkness, in a region where the days and nights never vary more than fifteen minutes from their equal length; and as for a fair wind, if it is certain that there will be one to carry you straight out at ten to-night, it is equally certain that there will be an opposite one to bring you straight in before noon to-morrow. Nature here saves you the trouble of putting engine and paddle-box into your boat, in order to be able to calculate your going forth and your return. By the time the amber haze in the east was parting to disclose the glories of a tropical sunrise, the fleet was stationed in a circle over the banks. Every stray shark had received its commands to close its jaws, and hie back to Adam's Bridge;* and on each side of every platform stood five men, every one with his foot slung on the pyramidal stone, whose weight must carry him nine fathoms down into the regions of monstrous forms and terrifying motions.

Rayo was one who was thus in readiness. He stood next to the Charmer,—Marana's father,—over whom a change seemed to have come since he left the land. It might be from the fasting necessary to his office; it might be from the intensity of his devotion; but it might also be from fear, that his hands shook as he fumbled among his sacred furniture, and his voice quavered as he chaunted his spells. Rayo perceived his disorder, and a qualm came over the heart of the young diver,—a qualm such as assails the servile agent of a rich man's prosperity much sooner than one in whom independence brings bravery. Rayo looked keenly at the Charmer; but the Charmer avoided meeting his eye, and it was not permitted to interrupt his incantation.

It was, perhaps, not the better for Rayo that the opposite five went first,—it gave more time for the unstringing of his nerves. The splash of the thousand men who descended within the circle took away his breath as effectually as the closing waters were about to deprive him of it. It was a singular sight to see the half of this vast marshalled company thus suddenly engulphed, and to think of them, in one moment after, as forming a human population at the bottom of the sea. To be a subject of the experiment was to the full as strange as to witness it, as Rayo found, when the minute of his companions' submersion was at length over, and a thousand faces (very nearly scarlet, notwithstanding their tawny skins) rushed up through the green wave. Spouting, dripping, and panting, they convulsively jerked their burden of oysters out upon the platform, and then tried to deliver their news from the regions below; but for this news their comrades must not wait. Down went Rayo, to find out the difference between three fathoms and nine. How far the lively idea of a shark's row of teeth might have quickened his perceptions, he did not himself inquire; but he was conscious of a more dazzling flash before his eyes, a sharper boring of the drum of his ear, and a general pressure so much stronger than ever before, that it would have been easy for him to believe, if he had been a Hindoo, like his neighbours, that he supported the tortoise that supported the elephant that supported the globe.* He could see nothing at first in the dizzy green that was suffocating and boiling him; but that did not signify, as he had no time to look about him. He thought he was descending clean into a shark's jaws, so sharp was that against which his left great toe struck, when his descent from the ninth heaven to the ninetieth abyss was at length accomplished. (How could any one call it nine fathoms?). On meeting this shark's tooth, or whatever it was, yelling was found to be out of the question. It was luckily forgotten in the panic, that the rope was to be pulled in case of accident;—luckily, as there was no alternative between Rayo's losing all credit as a diver, and the fishing being at an end for that day, from his spreading the alarm of a shark. He did not pull the rope; he only pulled up his left leg vigorously enough to assure himself that it was still in its proper place; by which time he discovered that he had only mistaken a large, gaping oyster for a hungry shark. Rayo's great toe being not exactly the viand that this oyster had a longing for, it ceased to gape, and Rayo manfully trampled it under foot, before wrenching it from the abode of which its seven years' lease had this day expired. These oysters required a terrible wrenching, considering that there was no taking breath between. Now he had got the knack. A pretty good handful, that!— St Anthony!* where did that slap in the face come from—so cold and stunning? Rayo's idea of a buffet from the devil was, that it would be hot; so he took heart, and supposed it was a fish, as indeed it was. He must go now,—O! O! he must go. He should die now before he could get up through that immeasurable abyss. But where was the rope? St Anthony! where was the rope? He was lost! No! it was the rope slapped his face this time. Still he was lost! A shadowy, striding mountain was coming upon him,—too enormous to be any fish but a whale. Suppose Rayo should be the first to see a whale in these seas! St Anthony! It was one of his companions. If they were not gone up yet, could not he stay an instant longer, and so avoid being made allowance for as the youngest diver of the party? No, not an instant. He rather thought he must be dead already, for it was hours since he breathed. He was alive enough, however, to coil himself in the rope. Then he went to sleep for a hundred years; then,—what is this? dawn? A green dawn?—brighter,— lighter,—vistas of green light everywhere, with wriggling forms shooting from end to end of them. Pah! here is a mouthful of ooze. Rayo should not have opened his mouth. Here is the air at last! Rayo does not care; the water does as well by this time. If he is not dead now water will never kill him, for he has been a lifetime under it.

'Well, Rayo,' says the captain, 'you have done pretty well for the first time. You have been under water a full minute, and one man is up before you. Here comes another.'

'A full minute!'

Even so. Who has not gone through more than this in a dream of less than a minute? and yet more if he has been in sudden peril of instant death, when the entire life is lived over again, with the single difference of all its events being contemporaneous? Since it is impossible to get into this position voluntarily, let him who would know the full worth of a minute of waking existence, plunge nine fathoms deep,—not in the sandy ooze of a storm-vext ocean, where he might as well be asleep for anything that he will see,— but in some translucent region which Nature has chosen for her treasury.

Rayo had re-discovered one of the natural uses of air; but he was in despair at the prospect before him. Forty or fifty such plunges as that to-day! and as many more to-morrow, and almost every day for six weeks! Forty or fifty life-times a-day for six weeks! This is not the sort of eternity he had ever thought of desiring, and if purgatory is worse, Father Anthony has not yet spoken half ill enough of it. Rayo had better turn priest: he could speak eloquently now on any subject connected with duration.

From *Society in America* (1837)

Citizenship of People of Colour

Before I entered New England, while I was ascending the Mississippi, I was told by a Boston gentleman that the people of colour in the New England States were perfectly well-treated; that the children were educated in schools provided for them; and that their fathers freely exercised the franchise. This gentleman certainly believed he was telling me the truth. That he, a busy citizen of Boston, should know no better, is now as striking an exemplification of the state of the case to me as a correct representation of the facts would have been. There are two causes for his mistake. He was not aware that the schools for the coloured children in New England are, unless they escape by their insignificance, shut up, or pulled down, or the school-house wheeled away upon rollers over the frontier of a pious State, which will not endure that its coloured citizens should be educated.* He was not aware of a gentleman of colour, and his family, being locked out of their own hired pew in a church, because their white brethren will not worship by their side. But I will not proceed with an enumeration of injuries, too familiar to Americans to excite any feeling but that of weariness; and too disgusting to all others to be endured. The other cause of this gentleman's mistake was, that he did not, from long custom, feel some things to be injuries, which he would call anything but good treatment, if he had to bear them himself. Would he think it good treatment to be forbidden to eat with fellow-citizens; to be assigned to a particular gallery in his church; to be excluded from college, from municipal office, from professions, from scientific and literary associations? If he felt himself excluded from every department of society, but its humiliations and its drudgery, would he declare himself to be 'perfectly well-treated in Boston?' Not a word more of statement is needed.

A Connecticut judge lately declared on the bench that he believed people of colour were not considered citizens in the laws.* He was proved to be wrong. He was actually ignorant of the wording of the acts by which people of colour are termed citizens. Of course, no judge could have forgotten this who had seen them treated as citizens: nor could one of the most eminent statesmen and lawyers in the country have told me that it is still a doubt, in the minds of some high authorities, whether people of colour are citizens. He is as mistaken as the judge. There has been no such doubt since the Connecticut judge was corrected and enlightened. The error of the statesman arose from the same cause; he had never seen the coloured people treated as citizens. 'In fact,' said he, 'these people hold an anomalous situation. They are protected as citizens when the public service requires their security; but not otherwise treated as such.' Any comment would weaken this intrepid statement.

The common argument, about the inferiority of the coloured race, bears no relation whatever to this question. They are citizens. They stand, as such, in the law, and in the acknowledgment of every one who knows the law. They are citizens, yet their houses and schools are pulled down, and they can obtain no remedy at law. They are thrust out of offices, and excluded from the most honourable employments, and stripped of all the best benefits of society by fellow-citizens who, once a year, solemnly lay their hands on their hearts, and declare that all men are born free and equal, and that rulers derive their just powers from the consent of the governed.

This system of injury is not wearing out. Lafayette, on his last visit to the United States, expressed his astonishment at the increase of the prejudice against colour.* He remembered, he said, how the black soldiers used to mess with the whites in the revolutionary war. The leaders of that war are gone where principles are all,— where prejudices are nothing. If their ghosts could arise, in majestic array, before the American nation, on their great anniversary, and hold up before them the mirror of their constitution, in the light of its first principles, where would the people hide themselves from the blasting radiance? They would call upon their holy soil to swallow them up, as unworthy to tread upon it. But not all. It should ever be remembered that America is the country of the best friends the coloured race has ever had. The more truth there is in the assertions of the oppressors of the blacks, the more heroism there is in their friends. The greater the excuse for the pharisees of the community,* the more divine is the equity of the redeemers of the coloured race. If it be granted that the coloured race are naturally inferior, naturally depraved, disgusting, cursed,—it must be granted that it is a heavenly charity which descends among them to give such solace as it can to their incomprehensible existence. As long as the excuses of the one party go to enhance the merit of the other, the society is not to be despaired of, even with this poisonous anomaly at its heart.

Happily, however, the coloured race is not cursed by God, as it is by some factions of his children. The less clear-sighted of them are pardonable for so believing. Circumstances, for which no living man is answerable, have generated an erroneous conviction in the feeble mind of man, which sees not beyond the actual and immediate. No remedy could ever have been applied, unless stronger minds than ordinary had been brought into the case. But it so happens, wherever there is an anomaly, giant minds rise up to overthrow it: minds gigantic, not in understanding, but in faith. Wherever they arise, they are the salt of their earth, and its corruption is retrieved. So it is now in America. While the mass of common men and women are despising, and disliking, and fearing, and keeping down the coloured race, blinking the fact that they are citizens, the few of Nature's aristocracy are putting forth a strong hand to lift up this degraded race out of oppression, and their country from the reproach of it. If they were but one or two, trembling and toiling in solitary energy, the world afar would be confident of their success. But they number hundreds and thousands; and if ever they feel a passing doubt of their progress, it is only because they are pressed upon by the meaner multitude. Over the sea, no one doubts of their victory. It is as certain as that the risen sun will reach the meridian. Already are there overflowing colleges, where no distinction of colour is allowed;* —overflowing, *because* no distinction of colour is allowed. Already have people of colour crossed the thresholds of many whites, as guests, not as drudges or beggars. Already are they admitted to worship, and to exercise charity, among the whites.

The world has heard and seen enough of the reproach incurred by America, on account of her coloured population. It is now time to look for the fairer side. The crescent streak is brightening towards the full, to wane no more. Already is the world beyond the sea beginning to think of America, less as the country of the double-faced pretender to the name of Liberty, than as the home of the single-hearted, clear-eyed Presence which, under the name of Abolitionism, is majestically passing through the land which is soon to be her throne.

Political Non-Existence of Women

One of the fundamental principles announced in the Declaration of Independence is, that governments derive their just powers from the consent of the governed. How can the political condition of women be reconciled with this?

Governments in the United States have power to tax women who hold property; to divorce them from their husbands; to fine, imprison, and execute them for certain offences. Whence do these governments derive their powers? They are not 'just,' as they are not derived from the consent of the women thus governed.

Governments in the United States have power to enslave certain women; and also to punish other women for inhuman treatment of such slaves. Neither of these powers are 'just;' not being derived from the consent of the governed.

Governments decree to women in some States half their husbands' property; in others one-third. In some, a woman, on her marriage, is made to yield all her property to her husband; in others, to retain a portion, or the whole, in her own hands. Whence do governments derive the unjust power of thus disposing of property without the consent of the governed?

The democratic principle condemns all this as wrong; and requires the equal political representation of all rational beings. Children, idiots, and criminals, during the season of sequestration, are the only fair exceptions.

The case is so plain that I might close it here; but it is interesting to inquire how so obvious a decision has been so evaded as to leave to women no political rights whatever. The question has been asked, from time to time, in more countries than one, how obedience to the laws can be required of women, when no woman has, either actually or virtually, given any assent to any law. No plausible answer has, as far as I can discover, been offered; for the good reason, that no plausible answer can be devised. The most principled democratic writers on government have on this subject sunk into fallacies, as disgraceful as any advocate of despotism has adduced. In fact, they have thus sunk from being, for the moment, advocates of despotism. Jefferson in America, and James Mill at home, subside, for the occasion, to the level of the author of the Emperor of Russia's Catechism for the young Poles.*

Jefferson says, 'Were our State a pure democracy, in which all the inhabitants should meet together to transact all their business, there would yet be excluded from their deliberations,

'1. Infants, until arrived at years of discretion;

'2. Women, who, to prevent depravation of morals, and ambiguity of issue, could not mix promiscuously in the public meetings of men;

'3. Slaves, from whom the unfortunate state of things with us takes away the rights of will and of property.'*

If the slave disqualification, here assigned, were shifted up under the head of Women, their case would be nearer the truth than as it now stands. Woman's lack of will and of property, is more like the true cause of her exclusion from the representation, than that which is actually set down against her. As if there could be no means of conducting public affairs but by promiscuous meetings! As if there would be more danger in promiscuous meetings for political business than in such meetings for worship, for oratory, for music, for dramatic entertainments,—for any of the thousand transactions of civilized life! The plea is not worth another word.

Mill says, with regard to representation, in his Essay on

Government, 'One thing is pretty clear; that all those individuals, whose interests are involved in those of other individuals, may be struck off without inconvenience. . . . In this light, women may be regarded, the interest of almost all of whom is involved, either in that of their fathers or in that of their husbands.'*

The true democratic principle is, that no person's interests can be, or can be ascertained to be, identical with those of any other person. This allows the exclusion of none but incapables.

The word 'almost,' in Mr Mill's second sentence, rescues women from the exclusion he proposes. As long as there are women who have neither husbands nor fathers, his proposition remains an absurdity.

The interests of women who have fathers and husbands can never be identical with theirs, while there is a necessity for laws to protect women against their husbands and fathers. This statement is not worth another word.

Some who desire that there should be an equality of property between men and women, oppose representation, on the ground that political duties would be incompatible with the other duties which women have to discharge. The reply to this is, that women are the best judges here. God has given time and power for the discharge of all duties; and, if he had not, it would be for women to decide which they would take, and which they would leave. But their guardians follow the ancient fashion of deciding what is best for their wards. The Emperor of Russia discovers when a coat of arms and title do not agree with a subject prince. The King of France early perceives that the air of Paris does not agree with a free-thinking foreigner. The English Tories feel the hardship that it would be to impose the franchise on every artizan, busy as he is in getting his bread.* The Georgian planter perceives the hardship that freedom would be to his slaves. And the best friends of half the human race peremptorily decide for them as to their rights, their duties, their feelings, their powers. In all these cases, the persons thus cared for feel that the abstract decision rests with themselves; that, though they may be compelled to submit, they need not acquiesce.

It is pleaded that half of the human race does acquiesce in the decision of the other half, as to their rights and duties. And some instances, not only of submission, but of acquiescence, there are. Forty years ago, the women of New Jersey went to the poll, and voted, at state elections.* The general term, 'inhabitants,' stood unqualified;—as it will again, when the true democratic principle comes to be fully understood. A motion was made to correct the inadvertence; and it was done, as a matter of course; without any appeal, as far as I could learn, from the persons about to be injured. Such acquiescence proves nothing but the degradation of the injured party. It inspires the same emotions of pity as the supplication of the freed slave who kneels to his master to restore him to slavery, that he may have his animal wants supplied, without being troubled with human rights and duties. Acquiescence like this is an argument which cuts the wrong way for those who use it.

But this acquiescence is only partial; and, to give any semblance of strength to the plea, the acquiescence must be complete. I, for one, do not acquiesce. I declare that whatever obedience I yield to the laws of the society in which I live is a matter between, not the community and myself, but my judgment and my will. Any punishment inflicted on me for the breach of the laws, I should regard as so much gratuitous injury; for to those laws I have never, actually or virtually, assented. I know that there are women in England who agree with me in this—I know that there are women in America who agree with me in this. The plea of acquiescence is invalidated by us.

It is pleaded that, by enjoying the protection of some laws, women give their assent to all. This needs but a brief answer. Any protection thus conferred is, under woman's circumstances, a boon bestowed at the pleasure of those in whose power she is. A boon of any sort is no compensation for the privation of something else; nor can the enjoyment of it bind to the performance of anything to which it bears no relation. Because I, by favour, may procure the imprisonment of the thief who robs my house, am I, unrepresented, therefore bound not to smuggle French ribbons? The obligation not to smuggle has a widely different derivation.

I cannot enter upon the commonest order of pleas of all;—those which relate to the virtual influence of woman; her swaying the judgment and will of man through the heart; and so forth. One might as well try to dissect the morning mist. I knew a gentleman in America who told me how much rather he had be a woman than the man he is;—a professional man, a father, a citizen. He would give up all this for a woman's influence. I thought he was mated too soon. He should have married a lady, also of my acquaintance, who would not at all object to being a slave, if ever the blacks should have the upper hand; 'it is so right that the one race should be subservient to the other!' Or rather,—I thought it a pity that the one could not be a woman, and the other a slave; so that an injured individual of each class might be exalted into their places, to fulfil and enjoy the duties and privileges which they despise, and, in despising, disgrace.

The truth is, that while there is much said about 'the sphere of woman,' two widely different notions are entertained of what is meant by the phrase. The narrow, and, to the ruling party, the more convenient notion is that sphere appointed by men, and bounded by their ideas of propriety;— a notion from which any and every woman may fairly dissent. The broad and true conception is of the sphere appointed by God, and bounded by the powers which he has bestowed. This commands the assent of man and woman; and only the question of powers remains to be proved.

That woman has power to represent her own interests, no one can deny till she has been tried. The modes need not be discussed here: they must vary with circumstances. The fearful and absurd images which are perpetually called up to perplex the question,—images of women on woolsacks in England, and under canopies in America,* have nothing to do with the matter. The principle being once established, the methods will follow, easily, naturally, and under a remarkable transmutation of the ludicrous into the sublime. The kings of Europe would have laughed mightily, two centuries ago, at the idea of a commoner, without robes, crown, or sceptre, stepping into the throne of a strong nation. Yet who dared to laugh when Washington's super-royal voice greeted the New World from the presidential chair, and the old world stood still to catch the echo?

The principle of the equal rights of both halves of the human race is all we have to do with here. It is the true democratic principle which can never be seriously controverted, and only for a short time evaded. Governments can derive their just powers only from the consent of the governed.

EMMA ROBERTS
(*c.*1794–1840)

Emma Roberts's father, Captain William Roberts, died before she was born, in Methley, near Leeds: she was brought up in Bath by her mother, who had literary interests, and moved to London to pursue her own writing career. She met Laetitia Elizabeth Landon while studying in the British Museum, and they briefly lodged in the same house. Like Landon, she wrote for the annuals. After the death of her mother in 1828 she accompanied her sister, who had married a captain in the 61st Bengal Infantry, to India, and for three years lived in various army stations in Upper India. A collection of verse, *Oriental Scenes, Dramatic Sketches and Tales, with Other Poems*, was published in Calcutta in 1830 (and in London in 1832). In 1831 her sister died and Roberts moved to Calcutta, where she edited the *Oriental Observer* before returning to England in 1832. Continuing her journalistic work, she wrote a series of articles about India for the *Asiatic Journal*, and in 1835 collected them to be published in three volumes as *Scenes and Characteristics of Hindostan, with Sketches of Anglo-Indian Society*. After editing Landon's *The Zenana* (1839), for which she wrote a memoir of her friend, and Maria Eliza Rundell's *New System of Domestic Cookery* she set off again in September 1839 to travel to India by the overland route, arriving in Bombay in November and settling in the suburb of Parell, where she edited the weekly newspaper *The Bombay United Service Gazette* and became involved in work to improve employment for Indian women. She became ill during a visit to Sattara in April 1840, was taken to Poona to convalesce at the house of a friend, but died in September and was buried near Maria Jane Jewsbury, who also died in Poona. She had nearly completed the writing for her new book, *Notes of an Overland Journey through France and Egypt to Bombay*, which was published posthumously in 1841.

Roberts also appears in this collection as the editor (1840) of Rundell's *New System of Domestic Cookery*, for which she wrote a lively new introduction and many new recipes: see the next section, 'Household Words'. The extracts in the present section are from *Scenes and Characteristics of Hindostan*, and come from chapter 2, 'Bengal Bridals and Bridal Candidates'. In her account of Bengal bridals Roberts wittily debunks received opinion about the availability of rich old men and the value of British brides, shrewdly traces the typical progress of a betrothal in British India, before moving closer to her own direct experience to evaluate marriages of convenience and the sorry situation of the sister of the bride. Finally, she classifies 'the spinsterhood of India' and draws attention to the uneasy position, socially and economically, of women of mixed race, arguing that British India has become gradually less willing to accept these people.

The near-total critical neglect of Roberts's brilliant prose is difficult to explain. Perhaps humorous writing by women is most easily appreciated when it seems either coolly detached or reassuringly self-deprecating. Roberts, however, is sparkling and authoritative, evocative and pragmatic, all at the same time. There is more than a touch of Austen in her observations and in her style of irony: her comments on the situation of women, likewise, have a comparable mix of tartness and compassion. She is always alert to practicalities: her work is full of accounts of the mismatch between dressmaking patterns and available fabrics or between 'French white and pearl white' on a threadbare wedding gown, the complex arrangements and ill humour involved in bringing together neighbours in remote stations, the profits made by traders who buy cheaply in the Indian markets, and tradesmen's chests full of 'stationery, pen-knives, soap, lavender-water, tooth-brushes, hair-brushes, small looking-glasses, and minor articles of hardware . . . trumpery of various kinds, the sweepings of London shops, condemned to return to their boxes until, in some miserable time of scarcity, they are purchased for want of better things' (30). It is easy to see why she wanted to edit, and augment, Rundell's *New System of Domestic Cookery* in 1840, and why she argues for the centrality of domestic management to all women's affairs.

Her views on Indians will elicit differing responses from readers. She is resolutely non-interventionist, seeking neither to 'improve' nor to soften what she sees, and this robs her style of certain pieties to which readers have long been accustomed. (We are used to deploring them, but their absence can be unsettling.) She uses the exotic sparingly but knowingly, employing it to register an absolute cultural difference which precludes any attempt at a synthesizing Eurocentric analysis. She also observes Indians' 'misunderstandings' or debased applications of European ways and commodities in a way which suggests their cultural inferiority while unmistakably mocking the self-importance of fashionable London ways, as when she lingers on the broken-down carriage at the centre of her comic account of a Hindu marriage procession, all noise and turmeric, an account which then gives way to a night-scene steeped in the descriptive conventions of the oriental exotic. The irony also cuts both ways when she comments on the shortage of sewing thread for English ladies' pastime-needlework: 'The natives twist all the thread they use as they need it from the raw material, division of labour being very ill-understood in Hindostan,—in consequence perhaps of the dearth of political economists' (261). The difficulty in pinning down her views is partly traceable to the design of her work. This study of Hindostan is aptly titled 'scenes and characteristics': Roberts swerves from large-scale cultural analysis, preferring to move informally from one localized observation to the next. She eschews analytical system in a way which invites reflection on the preferred historiographical and sociological styles of women of her time. Like many writers in this anthology, she associates female writing with close observation of manners and social foibles. But what is actually presented in her work is a pioneering account of domestic life in British India and an attention to the lives of European and Indian women which suggests many parallels between experiences conventionally addressed separately. It is also an instinctively anti-institutional and anti-centralizing account, notably putting its faith in the critical judgements of people reading books independently of received opinion and hype. Like Martineau, Roberts is an atypical travel-writer in that she is unwilling to use instances of native or foreign idiosyncrasy to validate the home team. Hindostan frustrates, baffles, and amuses her; but underlying her determined encounter with this mixed and—to her—contradictory culture is an always-nearly-visible battle with the culture of home.

~

From *Scenes and Characteristics of Hindostan* (1835)

Bengal Bridals and Bridal Candidates

Few opinions can be more erroneous than those which prevail in Europe upon the subject of Indian marriages. According to the popular idea, a young lady visiting the Honourable Company's territories,* is destined to be sacrificed to some old, dingy, rich, bilious nawaub, or, as he is styled on this side of the Atlantic, 'nabob,'* a class of persons unfortunately exceedingly rare. Ancient subjects devoted to the interests of the conclave in Leadenhall-street,* belonging to both services, are doubtless to be found in India, some dingy, and some bilious, but very few rich; and, generally speaking, these elderly gentlemen have either taken to themselves wives in their younger days, or have become such confirmed bachelors, that neither flashing eyes, smiling lips, lilies, roses, dimples, &c. comprehending the whole catalogue of female fascinations, can make the slightest impression upon their flinty hearts. Happy may the fair expectant account herself, who has the opportunity of choosing or refusing a *rara avis* of this nature,*—some yellow civilian out of debt, or some battered brigadier, who saw service in the days of sacks and sieges, and who comes wooing in the olden style, preceded by trains of servants bearing presents of shawls and diamonds! Such prizes are scarce. The damsel, educated in the fallacious hope of seeing a rich antiquated suitor at her feet, laden with 'barbaric pearl and gold,'* soon discovers to her horror that, if she should decide upon marrying at all, she will be absolutely compelled to make a love-match, and select the husband of her choice out of the half-dozen subalterns who may offer; fortunate may she esteem herself if there be one amongst them who can boast a staff-appointment, the adjutancy or quarter-mastership of his corps.* Formerly, when the importations of European females were much smaller than at present, men grew grey in the service before they had an opportunity of meeting with a wife, there consequently was a supply of rich old gentlemen ready at every station to lay their wealth at the feet of the new arrival; and as we are told that 'mammon wins its way where seraphs might despair,'* it may be supposed that younger and poorer suitors had no chance against these wealthy wooers. The golden age has passed away in India; the silver fruitage of the rupee-tree has been plucked, and love, poverty-stricken, has nothing left to offer but his roses.

In the dearth of actual possessions, expectancies become of consequence; and now that old civilians are less attainable, young writers rank amongst the eligibles.* A supply of these desirables, by no means adequate to the demand, is brought out to Calcutta every year, and upon the arrival of a young man who has been lucky enough to secure a civil appointment, he is immediately accommodated with a handsome suite of apartments in Tank-square, styled, *par distinction*, 'the Buildings,'* and entered at the college, where he is condemned to the study of the Hindoostanee and Persian languages, until he can pass an examination which shall qualify him to become an assistant to a judge, collector, or other official belonging to the civil department. A few hours of the day are spent under the surveillance of a moonshee,* or some more learned pundit, and the remainder are devoted to amusements. This is the dangerous period for young men bent upon making fortunes in India, and upon returning home. They are usually younger sons, disregarded in England on account of the slenderness of their finances, or too juvenile to have attracted matrimonial speculations. Launched into the society of Calcutta, they enact the parts of the young dukes and heirs-apparent of a

London circle; where there are daughters or sisters to dispose of. The '*great parti*'* is caressed, fêted, dressed at, danced at, and flirted with, until perfectly bewildered; either falling desperately in love, or fancying himself so, he makes an offer, which is eagerly accepted by some young lady, too happy to escape the much-dreaded horrors of a half-batta station.* The writers, of course, speedily acquire a due sense of their importance, and conduct themselves accordingly. Vainly do the gay uniforms strive to compete with their more sombre rivals; no dashing cavalry officer, feathered, and sashed, and epauletted, has a chance against the men privileged to wear a plain coat and a round hat; and in the evening drives in Calcutta, sparkling eyes will be turned away from the military equestrian, gracefully reining up his Arab steed to the carriage-window, to rest upon some awkward rider, who sits his horse like a sack, and, more attentive to his own comfort than to the elegance of his appearance, may, if it should be the rainy season, have thrust his white jean trowsers into jockey boots, and introduced a black velvet waistcoat under his white calico jacket. Figures even more extraordinary are not rare; for, though the ladies follow European fashions as closely as circumstances will admit, few gentlemen, not compelled by general orders to attend strictly to the regulations of the service, are willing to sacrifice to the Graces. An Anglo-Indian dandy is generally a very grotesque personage; for where tailors have little sway, and individual taste is left to its own devices, the attire will be found to present strange incongruities.

When a matrimonial proposal has been accepted, the engagement of the parties is made known to the community at large by their appearance together in public. The gentleman drives the lady out in his buggy. This is conclusive; and should either prove fickle, and refuse to fulfil the contract, a breach of promise might be established in the Supreme Court, based upon the single fact, that the pair were actually seen in the same carriage, without a third person. The nuptials of a newly-arrived civilian, entrapped at his outset, are usually appointed to take place at some indefinite period, namely, when the bridegroom shall have got out of college. It is difficult to say whether the strength of his affection should be measured by a speedy exit, or a protracted residence, for love may be supposed to interfere with study, and though excited to diligence by his matrimonial prospects, a mind distracted between rose-coloured billet-doux, and long rolls of vellum covered with puzzling characters in Arabic and Persian, will not easily master the difficulties of Oriental lore.

The allowances of a writer in the Buildings are not exceedingly splendid; writers do not, according to the notion adopted in England, step immediately into a salary of three or four thousand a year, though, very probably with the brilliant prospect before them which dazzled their eyes upon their embarkation, not yet sobered down to dull reality, they commence living at that rate. The bridegroom elect, consequently, is compelled to borrow one or two thousand rupees to equip himself with household goods necessary for the married state, and thus lays the foundation for an increasing debt, bearing an interest of twelve per cent at the least. The bride, who would not find it quite so easy to borrow money, and whose relatives do not consider it necessary to be very magnificent upon these occasions, either contrives to make her outfit (the grand expense incurred in her behalf) serve the purpose, or should that have faded and grown old-fashioned, purchases some scanty addition to her wardrobe. Thus the bridal paraphernalia, the bales of gold and silver muslins, the feathers, jewels, carved ivory, splendid brocades, exquisite embroidery, and all the rich products of the East, on which our imaginations luxuriate when we read of an Indian marriage, sinks down into a few yards of white sarsnet.* There is always an immense concourse of wedding-guests present at the ceremony, but as invitations to accompany a bridal-party to the church are of very frequent occurrence, they do not make any extraordinary display of new dresses and decorations. Sometimes, the company separate at the church-door; at others, there is some sort of entertainment given by the relatives of the bride; but the whole business, compared with the pomp and circumstance attending weddings of persons of a certain rank in England, is flat, dull, and destitute of show. . . .

The greatest drawback upon the chances of happiness in an Indian marriage, exists in the sort of compulsion sometimes used to effect the consent of a lady. Many young women in India may be considered almost homeless; their parents or friends have no means of providing for them except by a matrimonial establishment; they feel that they are burthens upon families who can ill afford to support them, and they do no not consider themselves at liberty to refuse an offer, although the person proposing may not be particularly agreeable to them. Mrs Malaprop tells us, that it is safest to begin with a little aversion,* and the truth of her aphorism has been frequently exemplified in India; gratitude and esteem are admirable substitutes for love—they last much longer, and the affection, based upon such solid supports, is purer in its nature, and far more durable, than that which owes its existence to mere fancy. It is rarely that a wife leaves the protection of her husband, and in the instances that have occurred, it is generally observed that the lady has made a love-match.

But though marriages of convenience, in nine cases out of ten, turn out very happily, we are by no means prepared to dispute the propriety of freedom of choice on the part of the bride, and deem those daughters, sisters, and nieces most fortunate, who live in the bosoms of relatives not anxious to dispose of them to the first suitor who may apply. It is only under these happy circumstances that India can be considered a paradise to a single woman, where she can be truly free and unfettered, and where her existence may glide away in the enjoyment of a beloved home, until she shall be tempted to quit it by some object dearer far, than parents, friends, and all the world beside.

There cannot be a more wretched situation than that of a young woman who has been induced to follow the fortunes of a married sister, under the delusive expectation that she will exchange the privations attached to limited means in England for the far-famed luxuries of the East. The husband is usually desirous to lessen the regret of his wife at quitting her home, by persuading an affectionate relative to accompany her, and does not calculate before-hand the expense and inconvenience which he has entailed upon himself by the additional burthen.

Soon after their arrival in India, the family, in all probability, have to travel to an up-country station,—and here the poor girl's troubles begin: she is thrust into an outer cabin in a budgerow,* or into an inner room in a tent; she makes perhaps a third in a buggy, and finds herself always in the way; she discovers that she is a source of continual expense; that an additional person in a family imposes the necessity of keeping several additional servants, and where there is not a close carriage she must remain a prisoner. She cannot walk out beyond the garden or the verandah, and all the out-of-door recreations, in which she may have been accustomed to indulge in at home, are denied her.

Tending flowers, that truly feminine employment, is an utter impossibility; the garden may be full of plants (which she has only seen in their exotic state) in all the abundance and beauty of native luxuriance, but except before the sun has risen, or after it has set, they are not to be approached; and even then, the frame is too completely enervated by the climate to admit of those little pleasing labours, which render the green-house and the parterre so interesting. She may be condemned to a long melancholy sojourn at some out-station, offering little society, and none to her taste.

If she should be musical, so much the worse; the hot winds have split her piano and her guitar, or the former is in a wretched condition, and there is nobody to tune it; the white ants have demolished her music-books, and new ones are not to be had. Drawing offers a better resource, but it is often suspended from want of materials; and needle-work is not suited to the climate. Her brother and sister are domestic, and do not sympathize in her *ennui*; they either see little company, or invite guests merely with a view to be quit of an incumbrance.

If the few young men who may be at the station should not entertain matrimonial views, they will be shy of their attention to a single woman, lest expectations should be formed which they are not inclined to fulfil. It is dangerous to hand a disengaged lady too often to table, for though no conversation may take place between the parties, the gentleman's silence is attributed to want of courage to speak, and the offer, if not forthcoming, is inferred. A determined flirt may certainly succeed in drawing a train of admirers around her; but such exhibitions are not common, and where ladies are exceedingly scarce, they are sometimes subject to very extraordinary instances of neglect. These are sufficiently frequent to be designated by a peculiar phrase; the wife or sister who may be obliged to accept a relative's arm, or walk alone, is said to be 'wrecked,' and perhaps an undue degree of apprehension is entertained upon the subject; a mark of rudeness of this nature reflecting more discredit upon the persons who can be guilty of it, than upon those subjected to the affront. Few young woman, who have accompanied their married sisters to India, possess the means of returning home; however strong their dislike may be to the country, their lot is cast in it, and they must remain in a state of miserable dependence, with the danger of being left unprovided for before them, until they shall be rescued from this distressing situation by an offer of marriage. . . .

The spinsterhood of India is composed of three different classes; the first consists of the daughters of civil and military servants, merchants, and others settled in India, who have been sent to England for education, and who generally return between the ages of sixteen and twenty; these may be said to belong to the country, and to possess homes, although upon the expectation of the arrival of a second or third daughter, they are often disposed of after a very summary fashion. In the second are to be found the sisters and near relatives of those brides who have married Indian officers, &c. during the period of a visit to the mother-country, and who, either through affection for their relatives, or in consequence of having no provision in England, have been induced to accompany them to the Eastern world. The third is formed of the orphan daughters, legitimate and illegitimate, of Indian residents, who have been educated at the presidencies.* This latter class is exceedingly numerous, and as they are frequently destitute of family connexions, those who are not so fortunate as to possess relatives in a certain rank in life, see very little of society, and have comparatively little chance of being well-established. The progress of refinement has materially altered the condition of these young ladies, but has acted in a manner the very reverse of improvement, as far as their individual interests are concerned.

A considerable number, having no support excepting that which is derived from the Orphan Fund, reside at a large house at Kidderpore, about a mile and a-half from Calcutta, belonging to that institution; others who may be endowed with the interest of a few thousand rupees, become parlour-boarders at schools of various degrees of respectability, where they await the chance of attracting some young officer, the military being objects of consideration when civilians are unattainable.

Formerly it was the practice to give balls at the establishment at Kidderpore, to which vast numbers of beaux were invited; but this undisguised method of seeking husbands is now at variance with the received notions of propriety, and the Female Orphan School has assumed, in consequence of the discontinuance of these parties, somewhat of the character of a nunnery. In fact, the young ladies immured within the walls have no chance of meeting with suitors, unless they should possess friends in Calcutta to give them occasional invitations, or the fame of their beauty should spread itself abroad. Every year, by increasing the number of arrivals educated in England, lessens their chance of meeting with eligible matches.

The prejudices against 'dark beauties' (the phrase usually employed to designate those who are the inheritors of the native complexion) are daily gaining ground, and in the present state of female intellectuality, their uncultivated minds form a decided objection. The English language has degenerated in the possession of the 'country-born;' their pronunciation is short and disagreeable, and they usually place the accent on the wrong syllable: though not so completely barbarized as in America, the mother, or rather father-tongue, has lost all its strength and beauty, and acquired a peculiar idiom.

There are not many heiresses to be found in India, and those who are gifted with property of any kind, almost invariably belong to the dark population, the daughters or grand-daughters of the Company's servants of more prosperous times, the representatives of merchants of Portuguese extraction, or the ladies of Armenian families. These latter named are frequently extremely handsome, and nearly as fair as Europeans; but though adopting English fashions in dress, they do not speak the language, and sing in Hindoostanee to their performances on the piano. They mix very little in the British society of Calcutta, and usually intermarry with persons belonging to their own nation, living in a retired manner within the bosoms of their families, without being entirely secluded like the females of the country in which their ancestors have been so long domiciled.

The daughters and wives of the Portuguese, a numerous and wealthy class, are quite as tawny, and not so handsome, as the natives; they usually dress in a rich and tawdry manner, after the European fashion, which is particularly unbecoming to them: they form a peculiar circle of their own, and though the spinster portion of this community, it is said, prefer British officers to husbands of Portuguese extraction, unions between them are extremely rare.

HOUSEHOLD WORDS

My heart's in the kitchen, my heart is not here,
My heart's in the kitchen, though following the *dear*,
Thinking on the roast meat, and musing on the fry,
My heart's in the kitchen whatever I spy.

(Maria Jane Jewsbury, in pastiche of Burns's
'My heart's in the Highlands')

Periodicals and reviews in this period typically present the book-buying woman as a fanciful, potentially suggestible creature, in search of amusement and the reification of romantic passion. Even in her *Reflections on the Condition of Women*, Priscilla Wakefield (see above) comments that 'nothing can be more distant from the plain, sober, useful qualities of a housewife, than the excellencies of the heroine of a novel' and that those enchanted by novels underestimate 'the modest virtues of industry, frugality, and simplicity of behaviour' (148). A rise in the romance of housecraft is discernible in the mid-nineteenth century, however, and heroines with a sharp eye for the details of domestic management were increasingly apparent in the generation following Wakefield's own. In recognition of this alternative model of the female consumer of books, the final selection of materials in this anthology ranges over the domestic instruction offered to women by women.

Although it seems obvious that those in charge of domestic matters should be accepted as authorities upon them, most manuals for female instruction in the arts of cookery, household management, marital harmony, infant health, and family husbandry were written, promoted, and distributed by men, such as A. F. M. Willich, author of the redoubtable *Domestic Encyclopaedia* (1802). In some works new pressure is brought to bear on the subject of domestic accomplishment, bringing it within the scope of new scientific and social developments. The celebrity French chef Louis Eustache Ude declares in his cookbook: 'If Poetry be, as has been said, the offspring of Love, why should we not call Cookery the sister of Chemistry? for surely we may do so with equal reason and justice'. Drawing on art rather than on science for his elevation of the discipline, Jean-Anthelme Brillat-Savarin argues in *La Physiologie du gout* (1825): 'cookery is the most ancient of arts, and, of all the arts, has contributed most to civil society'.[1] The place of cookery in the larger life and identity

---

[1] Trans. as *The Philosopher in the Kitchen* (Harmondsworth: Penguin, 1970, 1988).

of society—or, more narrowly, the nation—had long been accepted, by women as well as by men. Hannah Glasse's *The Art of Cookery, Made Plain and Easy* (1747) is explicitly anti-French; whereas the superiority of French cooking, and recipes from Spain, Italy, Switzerland, and Portugal, are prominent in Martha Bradley's *The British Housewife: or, the Cook, Housekeeper's and Gardener's Companion*, published in weekly parts in 1756.

Furthermore, the practice of domesticity was changing. As Bridget Hill argues, 'there was a great deal of new housework created by standards of genteel living introduced in the course of the eighteenth century'.[2] Eighteenth-century women of all social levels except the highest were active in maintaining and managing their homes, and these were practical guides; as, in a different market niche, was *The Complete Servant* (1825) by avowed practitioners Samuel and Sarah Adams. The form reached even higher popularity and influence in the Victorian period, with Eliza Acton's *Modern Cookery for Private Families* (1845), Alexis Soyer's *Gastronomic Regenerator* (1846) and *Modern Housewife* (1850), and Isabella Beeton's *Household Management* (1861); with Beeton, most strikingly of all, the model consumer of these books was definably middle class.

The period 1778–1838 has a modest share of commercially successful women advisers on domestic economy, of varying socio-political hues. They address an increasing class of women, not new, but distinctive enough to be definable: women educated (or feeling themselves to have been educated) for show rather than for use; encouraged to improve themselves by marriages which they were ill-equipped, emotionally and practically, to sustain; and faced not with a natural transfer of knowledge from mother to daughter but with social expectations which had changed, or which had changed them, so that they had managed not to acquire skills once thought essential. Whether this market of women was real, or created, is difficult to ascertain, so one must be cautious in reading levels of actual domestic competence or otherwise into these works. The works sampled below address female readers in a way which may seem initially restrictive, but which actually opens up many of the key concerns driving women's writing and thinking as they have been represented in this anthology. The emphasis on household skills may seem intrinsically conservative, and it was undoubtedly used to steer young women away from reading and thinking, as in 'The Polished Grisette', a poem by one Captain Thomas Morris, published in *The Spirit of the Public Journals for 1798*:

> Mothers, however trade improve your store,
> Make your girls housewives, and they need no more;

[2] *Women, Work, and Sexual Politics in Eighteenth-Century England* (Oxford: Blackwell, 1989), 116.

> Their best accomplishments are household arts;
> Novels and tricks at school make vicious hearts.
>
> (189–90)

As the selection provided here will suggest, however, the promotion of household arts formed a significant part of, and in many cases extended, the discussion of women's wider roles within society. As in modern publishing, works of this kind, marketed if not always designed as stand-alone guides to domestic success, rarely enter into explicit dialogue with each other; but there is dialogue, all the same, not only at the level of dispute about individual recipes or systems of accounting, but also at the level of what might be called domestic ideology. Introductory comments on each extract attempt to clarify what is at stake. More generally, it is worth noticing the ways in which advisers adopt the forms of address and intimacy developed in novels and familiar correspondence; how women's importance in the maintenance of the realm is configured, or deflected; how class and gender roles are regulated; and how the arts of domestic management are shaped by the language of social change, political contest, and intellectual self-development. The roles and capabilities of women are always in sharp focus. These works do not always further the debate about the rights and wrongs of women, though some of them explicitly do; but they offer some of the clearest available evidence that the debate created various kinds of felt need—anxiety, curiosity, resignation, resolve.

The extracts provided here are from one of Hannah More's *Cheap Repository Tracts*, 'The Cottage Cook'; from Maria Eliza Rundell's hugely successful and frequently reprinted *New System of Domestic Cookery*; from the characteristically spiky preface written by Emma Roberts for the 1840 edition of Rundell's work; from Christian Isobel Johnstone's brilliant extension of the character of Meg Dods from Scott's novel *St Ronan's Well*; from the best-seller of another stalwart of female manners, Mrs William Parkes; from the anonymous *Domestic Economy and Cookery for Rich and Poor* of 1827, the running commentary of which is the most combative of domestic writings 'by a Lady' of the period; and from the careful and more conservative *Home Book*, also anonymous, of 1829. As an indication of the perceived modern status of these works it is worth noting that only Hannah More and Emma Roberts among the authors represented here are to be found in reference books on women writers (and they are included for works which have nothing to do with domestic economy).

Hannah More's one-penny tract, *The Cottage Cook; or, Mrs. Jones's Cheap Dishes; Shewing the Way to do much good with little Money*, is exceptional among the works included here in being written for the instruction both of the affluent and of the poor. It teaches the Mrs Joneses of the community how to overcome indolence and do good by offering guidance and practical instruction. It also enjoins prudence and good management upon the poor, and extends Mrs Jones's advice by appending useful recipes and hints. More's greatest strength in this tract is to see how one problem or shortcoming impinges upon or even causes another; her evocation of the community of Weston, likewise, strives to promote a recognition of mutual responsibility. Her classes of people are not expected to mingle, but they are expected to be mindful of each other. The construction of the public oven is a triumph of community vision; while the restoration of female education in practical household skills is a reminder of More's belief that education should be regulated by social class and expectation. If this seems a limiting educational goal, nevertheless More allows women to determine it for themselves. Mrs Jones sets out to acquire practical skills which she then passes on to the women of the parish; she praises the recipes given in another *Cheap Repository Tract*, attributed to a 'Mrs White'; and she strikes a blow for English cookery by producing cheap soup which is declared to be just as savoury as any dish indebted to the refinements of Sir John's French cook. The vicar initiates and validates Mrs Jones's good works; in effect, however, More's tract claims his authority for itself.

The next extract comes from one of the most important domestic manuals of the period, *A New System of Domestic Cookery: Founded upon Principles of Economy; and Adapted to the Use of Private Families*, 'by a Lady' (1808). The 'lady' was Maria Eliza Rundell (1745–1828), who, after a long legal battle with the publisher, John Murray, eventually earned £1,000 for a work which sold between 5,000 and 10,000 copies each year for many years. Intended, according to the Advertisement, for the guidance of Rundell's own daughter, it is a practical guide to cookery, and includes a wide range of recipes. Rundell's introduction to it, however, is more generally interesting as a record of the perceived state of domestic knowledge among young women, and as a reflection on the same concerns about inappropriate ambition and female self-delusion which preoccupy many novelists and social commentators of the same period.

A mark of the importance of Rundell's work is the number of new augmented editions which appeared over the years. Among these, a special interest attaches to the sixty-sixth edition, in which many new recipes and a vibrant new preface are added by Emma Roberts. Roberts shares Rundell's unease about women's ignorance of culinary and domestic skills; the situation, as she represents it, is getting worse. Roberts's wit and range of reference, however, provide a reflection on the women of her day which deserves excavation; in choosing to write in this way in this context she implicitly demonstrates the interconnectedness of women's intellectual and practical accomplishments.

The next extract comes from the most original cookery book of the period, sometimes referred to in histories of the form as actually the work of the woman named on the title page, 'Mrs Margaret Dods, of the Cleikum Inn, St Ronan's'. The real author, for whom it was printed in Edinburgh in 1826, was Christian Isobel Johnstone (1781–1857), a prolific radical novelist, journalist, and editor, and its full title is *The Cook and Housewife's Manual; Containing the Most Approved Modern Receipts for Making Soups, Gravies, Sauces, Ragouts, and Made-Dishes; and for Pies, Puddings, Pastry, Pickles, and Preserves: also for Baking, Brewing, Making Home-Made Wines, Cordials, &c. The Whole Illustrated by Numerous Notes, and Practical Observations, on all the Various Branches of Domestic Economy*. It went into eleven editions. Born in Fife, Christian Isobel Johnston was divorced from her first husband in obscure circumstances, and married a schoolmaster, John Johnstone, in 1812. After she had published two novels, *The Saxon and the Gael* (1814) and *Clan-Albin: A National Tale* (1815), she helped her husband edit the new *Inverness Courier*. They moved to Edinburgh in 1824, where she published other novels, edited with her husband the *Edinburgh Weekly Chronicle, The Schoolmaster*, and *Johnstone's Magazine*, and from 1834 was a major contributor to the radical *Tait's Magazine*, set up in rivalry to the Tory *Blackwood's*. Her other works include collections of stories and journalism such as *The Edinburgh Tales* (1845), didactic tales for children such as *The Diversions of Hollycot; or, The Mother's Art of Thinking* (1828), and an edition of the works of the radical poet Robert Nicoll (1842).

The fiercely independent and plain-speaking inn-keeper Meg Dods, who has avoided marital dominion and whose kitchen is her 'pride and glory', is the central comic character in Scott's tragedy of modern manners and spa-town folly, *St Ronan's Well* (1823). She has seen her Cleikum Inn and its home cooking supplanted by the frippery of the assorted fashionables at the new spa-town built a mile and a half away, but her worth is recognized by those who value more substantial and traditional fare. In basing *The Cook and Housewife's Manual* on the authority of Meg Dods, Christian Johnstone allies it with the old ways, culinary and social. In Scott's novel, cookery is already a hot topic. Johnstone seizes on the suggestion that eating habits are a key indicator of the state of society as a whole: she builds on Scott's politicization of the subject.

Johnstone's introduction describes the effects of the catastrophe of *St Ronan's Well* on the spirits of one of Meg Dods's devotees, the meddlesome, irritable elderly 'nabob' Peregrine Touchwood, who is described at the end of the novel as 'still alive, forming plans which have no object, and accumulating a fortune, for which he has apparently no heir'. In Johnstone's fiction, to Touchwood's refuge at the Cleikum Inn comes a form of salvation in the shape of 'the celebrated churchman and gourmand, Dr Redgill', with whom Touchwood sets up a dining club, joined by another character from the novel, the fashionable and mildly dissipated young soldier Captain Jekyl. The Cleikum Club begins its gourmandizing with an address on the history of cooking from Peregrine Touchwood, from which the extract here is taken. Johnstone repeatedly undermines her male speaker by having Meg Dods, who does the work on which he theorizes, interject exclamations and practical asides. The passage is also interesting for parodying the 'stages of society' model of the Scottish Enlightenment, one of the male narratives of history which several female historians represented in this anthology have questioned.

If one can imagine the Meg Dods system of cookery being bought for wives by hopeful husbands, the next extract comes from a work addressed with great skill to the wives themselves. Mrs William Parkes's *Domestic Duties; or, Instructions to Young Married Ladies, on the Management of their Households, and the Regulation of their Conduct in the Various Relations and Duties of Married Life* (1825) sounds distinctly militaristic, but its discipline was clearly welcome, for it went into eleven editions by 1862. She was a recognized authority, and her contributions on cookery, servants, and health helped sell Thomas Webster's commodious 1264-page *Encyclopaedia of Domestic Economy* in 1844, after her death. *Domestic Duties* is a wide-ranging work written in the form of a dialogue between the newly married Mrs L. and a mentor, Mrs B., experienced but unstuffy. In one of their early conversations about keeping up friendships after marriage Mrs L. exclaims 'Well! there is more liberality in these sentiments than I was led to expect' (11), and so there usually is. Parkes is especially strong on advice concerning the regulation of a married lady's time and on the conduct of different kinds of entertainment. In the section chosen here she advises on that high-point of a young wife's social responsibilities, the ball.

The anonymous author of *Domestic Economy and Cookery for Rich and Poor* offers one of the most intellectually alert of all accounts of domestic management and mismanagement in this period. The subtitle of the work gives some indication of its scope: *Containing an Account of the Best English, Scotch, French, Oriental, and Other Foreign Dishes; Preparations of Broths and Milks for Consumption; Receipts for Sea-Faring Men, Travellers, and Children's Food. Together with Estimates and Comparisons of Dinners and Dishes. The Whole Composed with the Utmost Atttention to Health, Economy, and Elegance*. The extract below comes from the introductory chapter of this compendious and discursive volume, and is notably freethinking, directly addressing the evils of inadequate and inappropriate female education, the hypocrisy of polite society, and the prejudice of the British against all things foreign. Hannah More's side-swipe at French cooks, made at the height of post-revolutionary fears, is replaced here by praise for French economy and by a willingness to see the good in the customs of other countries and other religious traditions. In a later section of the work, 'Oriental Cookery', the author gives instruction in the adaptation of methods and recipes from Hindu, Muslim, nomadic Arab, and Levantine cookery: although there was a great deal of interest in the styles of cookery developed for European tastes in British India, recipes for kedgeree, curry dishes, and chutney being brought back to Britain by employees of the East India Company, this range is out of the ordinary, and is interesting for its ethnic even-handedness. Her historical and ethnographic range is difficult to represent in extracts, but some sense of it may be captured here. Her work, like that of Roberts, is proof that the management of the small economy of the household can encompass social and political enquiry. Women's domestic calling is not questioned; their domestic passivity is.

The final extracts come from *The Home Book: or, Young Housekeeper's Assistant: Forming a Complete System of Domestic Economy, and Household Accounts. With Estimates of Expenditure, &., &c. in every department of housekeeping, founded on forty-five years personal experience*, again 'by a Lady'. Addressed to the author's daughter, the work aims to supply new wives with ready-made regimes for the smooth running of their households, and with tips for preserving marital harmony. Instruction is given in the duties to be expected of each servant, arrangements with tradesmen, dinner parties, childcare, the management of the dairy, and how to find a house. The personal address is appealing and reassuring; the advice somewhat conservative in its assumptions about suitable female behaviour and topics of concern. Two parts of *The Home Book* are sampled here. The first is from the opening discussion of the proper management of servants and kitchen economy. Servants are a constant preoccupation in household literature of the day: like Fanny Price's mother in *Mansfield Park*, women seem always to be lamenting their laziness or malpractice, and they are a constant threat to female domestic rule. On this matter *The Home Book* offers firm precepts: respect is to be earned, and authority is to be established from the start. The second extract comprises the whole of the chapter devoted to matrimonial duty. Like many novelists and critics of novels it warns against idealistic expectations of romantic love, but its recommendations of 'conciliating conduct' are more direct than many women writers seem willing to endorse. Given in its entirety, and with its pointedly turned ending, the chapter is an exemplum of what it is not possible to say. Matrimonial duty in two pages may suggest brilliant concision or extreme repression; but what is most interesting in this volume is the acceptance that it can be addressed, or needs to be addressed, at all. As in Hannah More's tale of Mrs Jones, household skill is taken to include personal relationships, and this, in the superficially conscribing form of the household manual, allows us to see the traces of debates on female ability and the proper roles of women. *The Home Book* is a forerunner of advice-books setting out to integrate all aspects of women's experience; and underlying its declared compliance in the mores of contemporary society is an assumption that all aspects of this experience are important.

~

HANNAH MORE, from *The Cottage Cook; or, Mrs Jones's Cheap Dishes* (1797)

Mrs Jones was a great merchant's lady. She was liberal to the poor, but as she was too much taken up with the world, she did not spare so much of her time and thoughts about doing good as she ought, so that her money was often ill bestowed. In the late troubles,* Mr Jones, who had lived in a grand manner, failed, and he took his misfortunes so much to heart that he fell sick and died. Mrs Jones retired on a very narrow income to the small village of Weston, where she seldom went out except to church. Though a pious woman she was too apt to indulge her sorrow; and though she did not neglect to read and pray, yet she gave up a great part of her time to melancholy thoughts, and grew quite inactive. She well knew how sinful it would be for her to seek a cure for her grief in worldly pleasures, which is a way many people take under afflictions, but she was not aware how wrong it was to weep away that time which might have been better spent in drying the tears of others.

It was happy for her that Mr Simpson, the vicar of Weston, was a pious man. One Sunday he happened to preach on the good Samaritan. It was a charity sermon, and there was a collection at the door. He called on Mrs Jones after church, and found her in tears. She told him she had been much moved by his discourse, and she wept because she felt very keenly for the poor in these dear times, yet she could not assist them. 'Indeed Sir,' added she, 'I never so much regretted the loss of my fortune, as this afternoon, when you bade us *go and do likewise.*'* 'You do not,' replied Mr Simpson 'enter into the spirit of our Saviour's parable, if you think you cannot *go and do likewise* without being rich. In the case of the Samaritan you may observe, that charity was afforded more by kindness, and care, and medicine, than by money. You, Madam, were as much concerned in my sermon as Sir John with his great estate; and, to speak plainly, I have been sometimes surprized that you should not put your[self] in the way of being more useful.'

'Sir,' said Mrs Jones 'I am grown shy of the poor since I have nothing to give them.' 'Nothing, Madam,' replied the Clergyman, 'do you call your time, your talents, your kind offices, nothing? I will venture to say that you might do more good than the richest man in the parish could do by merely giving his money. Instead of sitting here brooding over your misfortunes, which are past remedy, bestir yourself to find out ways of doing much good with little money; or even without any money at all. You have lately studied oeconomy for yourself. Instruct your poor neighbours in it. They want it almost as much as they want money. You have influence with the few rich persons in the parish. Exert that influence. Betty, my housekeeper, shall assist you in any thing in which she can be useful. Try this for one year and if you then tell me that you should have better shewn your love to God and man, and been a happier woman had you continued gloomy and inactive, I shall be much surprized.'

The Sermon and this discourse made so deep an impression on Mrs Jones, that she formed a new plan of life, and set about it at once, as every body does who is in earnest. Her chief aim was the happiness of her poor neighbours in the next world; but she was also very desirous to promote their present comfort. The plans she pursued with a view to the latter object shall be explained in this little book. . . .

Patty Smart and Jenny Rose were thought to be the two best managers in the parish. They both told Mrs Jones that the poor will get the coarse pieces of meat cheaper, if the gentlefolks did not buy them for soups and gravy. Mrs Jones thought there was reason in this. So away she went to Sir John, the Squire, the Surgeon, the Attorney, and the Steward, the only persons in the parish who could afford to buy costly things. She told them that if they would all be so good as to buy only prime pieces, which they could very well afford, the coarse and cheap joints would come more within the reach of the poor. Most of the gentry readily consented. Sir John cared not for what his meat cost him, but told Mrs Jones in his gay way, that he would eat any thing, or give any thing, so that she would not teaze him with long stories about the poor. The Squire said, he should prefer vegetable soups, because they were cheaper, and the Doctor, because they were wholesomer. The Steward chose to imitate the Squire; and the Attorney found it would be quite ungenteel to stand out. So gravy soups became very unfashionable in the parish of Weston; and I am sure if rich people did but think a little on this subject, they would be as unfashionable in many other places.

When wheat grew cheaper Mrs Jones was earnest with the poor women to bake large brown loaves at home, instead of buying small white ones at the shop. Mrs Betty had told her, that baking at home would be one step towards restoring the good old management. Only [Pa]tty Smart and Jenny Rose baked at home in the whole parish, and who lived so well as they did? Yet the general objection seemed reasonable. They could not bake without yeast, which often could not be had, as no one brewed but the great folks and the public houses. Mrs Jones found, however, that Patty and Jenny contrived to brew as well as to bake. She sent for these women, knowing that from them she should get truth and reason. 'How comes it,' she said to them, 'that you two are the only poor women in the parish who can afford to brew a small cask of beer? Your husbands have not better wages than other men.' 'True Madam,' said Patty, 'but they never set foot in a public house. I will tell you the truth. When I first married, our John went to the Chequers every night, and I had my tea and fresh butter twice a-day at home. This slop, which consumed a deal of sugar, began to *rake* my stomach sadly, as I had neither meat nor milk; at last (I am ashamed to own it) I began to take a drop of gin to quiet the pain, and in time I looked for my gin as regularly as for my tea. At last the gin, the ale-house, and the tea began to make us both sick and poor. I had like to have died with my first child. Parson Simpson then talked so finely to us that we resolved, by the grace of God, to turn over a new leaf, and I promised John if he would give up the Chequers, I would break the gin bottle, and never drink tea in the afternoon, except on Sundays when he was at home with me. We have kept our word, and both our eating and drinking, our health and our conscience are the better for it. Though meat is sadly dear we can buy two pounds of fresh meat for less than one pound of fresh butter, and it gives five times the nourishment. And dear as malt is, I contrive to keep a drop of drink in the house for John, and John will make me drink half a pint with him every evening, and a pint a day when I am a nurse.'

As one good deed as well as one bad thing brings on another, this conversation set Mrs Jones on enquiring why so many ale-houses were allowed. She did not chuse to talk to Sir John on this subject, who would only have said 'let them enjoy themselves, poor fellows; if they get drunk now and then, they work hard.' But those who have this false good-nature forget, that while the man is *enjoying himself,* as it is called, his wife and children are ragged and starving. True christian good-nature never indulges one at the cost of many, but is kind to all. The Squire, who was a friend to order, took up the matter. He consulted Mr Simpson. 'The Lion,' said he 'is necessary. It stands by the road side; travellers must have a resting place. As to the Chequers and the Bell they do no good but much harm.' Mr Simpson had before made many attempts to get the Chequers put down; but unluckily it was Sir John's own house, and kept by his late butler. Not that Sir John valued the rent, but he had a false kindness which made him support the cause of an old servant, though he knew he kept a disorderly house. The Squire, however, now took away the licence from the [Bell]. And a fray happening soon after at the Chequers (which was near the church) in time of divine service, Sir John was obliged to suffer the house to be put down as a nuisance. You would not believe how many poor families were able to brew a little cask when the temptations of those ale houses were taken out of their way. Mrs Jones in her evening walks had the pleasure to see many an honest man drinking his wholesome cup of beer by his own fire side, his rosy children playing about his knees, his clean chearful wife singing her youngest baby to sleep, rocking the cradle with her foot, while with her hands she was making a dumpling for her kind husband's supper. Some few, I am sorry to say, though I don't chuse to name names, still preferred getting drunk once a week at the Lion, and drinking water at other times.

The good women now being supplied with yeast from each other's brewings, would have baked, but two difficulties still remained. Many of them had no ovens, for since the new bad management had crept in, many cottages have been built without this convenience. Fuel also was scarce at Weston. Mrs Jones advised the building of a large parish oven. To the oven, at a certain hour, three times a week, the elder children carried the loaves which their mothers had made at home, and paid a halfpenny, or a penny, according to their size, for the baking.

Mrs Jones found that no poor woman in Weston could buy a little milk, as the farmers' wives did not care to rob their dairies. This was a great distress, especially when the children were sick. So Mrs Jones advised Mrs Sparks at the Cross to keep a couple of cows, and sell out the milk by halfpennyworths. She did so, and found, that though this plan gave her some additional trouble, she got full as much by it as if she had made cheese and butter. She also sold rice at a cheap rate, so that with the help of the milk and the publick oven, a fine rice pudding was to be had for a trifle.

The girls' school in the parish was fallen into neglect, for though many would be subscribers, yet no one would look after it. I wish this was the case at Weston only. It was not in Mr Simpson's way to see if girls were taught to work. This is ladies' business. Mrs Jones consulted her counsellor Mrs Betty, and they went every Friday to the school, where they invited mothers as well as daughters to come, and learn to cut out to the best advantage. Mrs Jones had not been bred to these things, but by means of Mrs Cooper's excellent cutting out book,* she soon became mistress of the whole art. She not only had the girls taught to make and mend but to wash and iron too. She also allowed the mother, or eldest daughter of every family, to come once a week, and learn how to dress *one cheap dish*. One Friday, which was cooking day, who should pass by but the Squire, with his gun and his dogs. He looked into the school for the first time. 'Well, madam,' said he, 'what good are you doing here? What are your girls learning and earning? Where are your manufactures? Where is your spinning and your carding?' 'Sir,' said she, 'this is a small parish, and you know ours is not a manufacturing country; so that when these girls are women, they will not be much employed in spinning. However, we teach them a little of it, and more of knitting, that they may be able to get up a small piece of household linen once a year, and provide the family with stockings, by employing the odds and ends of their time in these ways. But there is a manufacture which I am carrying on, and I know of none within my own reach which is so valuable.' 'What can that be?' said the Squire. 'To MAKE GOOD WIVES FOR WORKING MEN' said she. 'Is not mine an excellent staple commodity? I am teaching these girls the art of industry and good management. It is little encouragement to an honest man to work hard all the week, if his wages are wasted by a slattern at home.' 'What have you got on the fire, madam?' said the Squire, 'for your pot really smells as savoury, as if Sir John's French Cook had filled it.' 'Sir,' replied Mrs Jones, 'I have lately got acquainted with Mrs White, who has given us an account of her cheap dishes, and wise cookery, in one of the Cheap Repository little books. Mrs Betty and I have made all her dishes, and very good they are, and we have got several others of our own. Every Friday we come here and dress one. These good women see how it is done, and learn to dress it at their own houses. I take home part for my own dinner, and what is left I give to each in turn. I hope I have opened their eyes on a sad mistake they had got into, *that we think any thing is good enough for the poor.*'

'Pray Mrs Betty,' said the Squire, 'oblige me with a bason of your soup.' The Squire found it so good after his walk, that he was almost sorry he had promised to buy no more legs of beef, and declared that not one sheep's head should ever go to his kennel again. He begged his cook might have the receipt, and Mrs Jones wrote it out for her. She has also been so obliging as to favour me with a copy of all her receipts. And as I hate all monopoly; and see no reason why such cheap, nourishing, and savoury dishes should be confined to the parish of Weston, I print them, that all other parishes may have the same advantage. Not only the poor, but all persons with small incomes may be glad of them. 'Well, madam,' said Mr Simpson, who came in soon after, 'which is best, to sit down and cry over our misfortunes, or to bestir ourselves to do our duty to the world?' 'Sir,' replied Mrs Jones, 'I thank you for the useful lesson you have given me. You have taught me that our time and talents are to be employed with zeal in God's service, if we wish for his favour here or hereafter, and that one great employment of them, which he requires, is the promotion of the present, and much more, the future happiness of all around us. You have taught me that much good may be done with little money, and that the heart, the head, and the hands are of some use, as well as the purse.'

May all who read this account of Mrs Jones, *go and do likewise*! . . .

FRIENDLY HINTS

The difference between eating bread new and stale, is one loaf in five.

If you turn your meat into broth it will go much farther than if you roast or bake it.

If you have a garden, make the most of it. A bit of leek or an onion makes all dishes savoury at small expence.

If the money spent on fresh butter were spent on meat, poor families would be much better fed than they are.

If the money spent on tea were spent on home-brewed beer, the wife would be better fed, the husband better pleased, and both would be healthier.

Keep a little Scotch barley, rice, dry pease, and oatmeal in the house. They are all cheap and don't spoil. Keep also pepper and ginger.

Pay your debts, serve God, love your neighbour.

MARIA ELIZA RUNDELL, from *A New System of Domestic Cookery* (1808)

Miscellaneous Observations for the Use of the Mistress of the Family

In every rank, those deserve the greatest praise who best acquit themselves of the duties which their station requires. Indeed, this line of conduct is not a matter of choice but of necessity, if we would maintain the dignity of our character as rational beings.

In the variety of female acquirements, though domestic occupations stand not so high in esteem as they formerly did, yet, when neglected, they produce much human misery. There was a time when ladies knew nothing *beyond* their own family concerns; but in the present day there are many who know nothing *about* them. Each of these extremes should be avoided; but is there no way to unite in the female character cultivation of talents, and habits of usefulness? Happily there are still great numbers in every situation, whose example proves that this is possible. Instances may be found of ladies in the higher walks of life, who condescend to examine the accounts of their house-steward, and, by overlooking and wisely directing the expenditure of that part of their husband's income which falls under their own inspection, avoid the inconveniences of embarrassed circumstances. How much more necessary, then, is domestic knowledge in those whose limited fortunes press on their attention considerations of the strictest economy! There ought to be a material difference in the degree of care which a person of a large and independent estate bestows on money-concerns, and that of a person in confined circumstances; yet both may very commendably employ some portion of their time and thoughts on this subject. The custom of the times tends in some measure to abolish the distinctions of rank: and the education given to young people is nearly the same in all; but though the leisure of the higher may be well devoted to different accomplishments, the pursuits of those in a middle line, if less ornamental, would better secure their own happiness and that of others connected with them. We sometimes bring up children in a manner calculated rather to fit them for the station we wish, than that which it is likely they will actually possess; and it is in all cases worth the while of parents to consider whether the expectation or hope of raising their offspring above their own situation be well founded.

EMMA ROBERTS, from her Preface to Rundell, *A New System of Domestic Cookery* (1840)

While man has been characterized as a cooking animal,* the capabilities of woman to undertake even the minor branches of the culinary art have been doubted and denied. All gastronomes of a refined grade unite in denouncing she-cooks; and M. Ude, when he wishes to express his contempt for any commonplace dish, says, 'A woman can do it.'* An observation of Dr Johnson's shows upon how very low a scale that learned person rated the culinary talents of the sex. 'Women,' he remarks, 'can spin very well, but they cannot write a book of cookery.'* Women have written more extraordinary things since his time; and Mrs Rundell's excellent work—a work which far surpassed all its predecessors, and continues to be the best treatise extant concerning the art—shows that the Doctor did not do justice to feminine ingenuity.

The present collection of receipts will be found to possess strong claims to recommendation, having been carefully collected from family MSS, and vouched for by the parties by whom they have been contributed. Nor is the compiler wholly destitute of practical knowledge of the art, since, during her residence in India, she enjoyed constant opportunities of improving her acquaintance with culinary science, and of ascertaining her own skill in a species of useful knowledge scarcely sufficiently studied by the young ladies of the present day. Although the style of living adopted by British residents in India is generally luxurious, native cookery differs so widely from the European style, that it is necessary to teach the servants the method of preparing the elegant novelties continually introduced at home; and the experience previously obtained in England having been found exceedingly useful upon many occasions, the results are given with some degree of confidence.

The number and value of the receipts contained in the present volume, never before published, will offer a sufficient excuse for what at the first blush might appear to be a work of supererogation. Without wishing to disparage any one of the numerous modern productions which have preceded this attempt at instruction, it may be said that there is still room for a new effort; and being desirous to afford to others the advantage of her own experience, and to show that a life devoted to literature is not incompatible with the study and practice of domestic economy, the author trusts that no further explanation or apology will be necessary for a work undertaken with a view to general utility.

If our ancestors made the structure of pyramids of pastry, and the manufacture of oceans of syllabub, too exclusively the aim of female education, the present generation have fallen as unwisely into the contrary extreme. Young ladies of our time pride themselves upon knowing nothing whatever concerning an art which most assuredly ought to be deemed essential in the mistress of a family. Generally speaking, there is a universal distaste amongst the educated classes of the female community of England to the details of housekeeping. We hear upon all sides complaints of the trouble of ordering a dinner; and the consequence is, that dinners are seldom well arranged, or the most made of the materials provided. There are comparatively few persons among the merely respectable classes of society who can afford to keep professed cooks—their wages being too high, and their methods too extravagant. It follows, therefore, that a plain cook, plain enough in most cases, is alone attainable, who can put a dinner on the table in a very slovenly manner, and knows nothing beyond the commonest operations. It would, however, be considered *infra dig.** in the young ladies of the family to afford the slightest assistance, or to employ themselves in instructing some clever and industrious domestic, willing to qualify herself for a cook's place. The misfortune of losing a tolerable cook is in such cases irreparable: the customary arrangements are disturbed; and the mistress of the house, dependent upon her domestic, must be content to put up with an inferior and distasteful mode of living. It is a very common, but a very erroneous supposition, that attention to culinary affairs is unladylike, and beneath the dignity of a gentlewoman. There can be no question that elegance, comfort, social enjoyment, and, it may be added, health, materially attend upon attention to the table. . . .

Physicians have asserted that it is less difficult to get a hogshead of claret out of a man's constitution than a round of beef; but, generally speaking, M. Ude is in the right when he declares the faculty to be most unjustly the opponents of cooks. He is right also in stating that the cultivation of the art is retarded by the hostility of the fair sex.* In the higher ranks an idea is entertained that any consideration connected with eating is injurious to the delicacy of the feminine character; this notion being strengthened, as it descends, by an indisposition to undertake the toils which attention to the table must necessarily involve. Eating is an unpoetical thing: Lord Byron disliked to see women eat;* and ladies, sheltering themselves under such high authority, neglect the cares of the table, and make their male relatives suffer from their over-refinement, if such it may be called, which limits the bill of fare to a joint of beef or mutton.

Nothing can be more erroneous than the supposition, too commonly entertained amongst young ladies, that living on air, or vegetables, or a non-descript ambrosial kind of food, which they sometimes affect, will add to their personal attractions. A generous diet is in most instances absolutely essential to the complexion; while indigestion, brought on by a regimen ill adapted to the constitution of the party pursuing it, is frequently destructive to symmetry of form. Rout cakes,* when taken as the only diet, have proved as detrimental, with this difference, bringing on lingering illness instead of sudden death, as the most solid kind of animal food; and ladies and gentlemen, afraid of becoming stout, have seriously injured their health by taking a cup of gruel or a piece of dry bread, immediately before dinner, in order to damp the appetite. The happy medium between injurious abstinence and injurious excess is unfortunately too seldom preserved; but there cannot be a doubt that light and nourishing food may be eaten, if the quantity be too large, with greater impunity than when its solidity renders it less easily digestible.

CHRISTIAN ISOBEL JOHNSTONE, from *The Cook and Housewife's Manual* (1826)

Peregrine Touchwood's Address

Gentlemen,—Man is a cooking animal;* and in whatever situation he is found, it may be assumed as an axiom, that his progress in civilization has kept exact pace with the degree of refinement he has attained in the science of gastronomy. From the hairy man of the woods, gentlemen, digging his roots with his claws, to the refined banquet of the Greek, or the sumptuous entertainment of the Roman; from the ferocious hunter, gnawing the half-broiled bloody collop,* torn from the still reeking carcass, to the modern *gourmet*, apportioning his ingredients, and blending his essences, the chain is complete! *First*, We have the brutalized digger of roots; then the sly entrapper of the finny tribes; and next the fierce foul feeder, devouring his ensnared prey, fat, blood, and muscle! ('What a style o' language!' whispered Mrs Dods; 'but I maun look after the scouring o' the kettles.') The next age of cookery, gentlemen, may be called the pastoral, as the last was that of the hunter.* Here we have simple, mild broths, seasoned, perhaps, with herbs of the field; decoctions of pulse; barley-cake, and the kid seethed in milk. I pass over the ages of Rome and Greece, and confine myself to the Gothic and Celtic tribes, among whom gradually emerged what I call the chivalrous or feudal age of cookery,—the wild boar roasted whole, the stately crane, the lordly swan, the full-plumaged peacock, borne into the feudal hall by troops of vassals, to the flourish of trumpets, warlike instruments, marrow-bones and cleavers. ('Bravo!' cried Jekyl.) Cookery as a domestic art, contributing to the comfort and luxury of private life, had made considerable progress in England before the Reformation; which event threw it back some centuries. We find the writers of those ages making large account of an art, from which common sense, in all countries, borrows its most striking illustrations and analogies. ('Only hear till him!' whispered Meg.) The ambitious man seeks to rule the roast.*—The meddling person likes to have a finger in the pie;—Meat and mass hinder no business;—The rash man gets into a stew, and cooks himself a pretty mess;—A half-loaf is better than no bread;—There goes reason to the roasting of an egg;*—Fools make feasts, and wise men eat them;—The churl invites a guest, and sticks him with the spit;*—The belly is every man's master;—He who will not fight for his meat, what will he fight for?—A hungry man is an angry man;—It's ill talking between a full man and a fasting; and, finally, It is the main business of every man's life to make the pot boil; or, as the Scots more emphatically have it, 'to make the pat play brown,'* which a lean pot never will do.

'And that's as true,' said Meg. 'A fat pat boiling, popples and glances on the tap, like as mony brown lammer-beads.'*

'Hush!—The science, as we noticed, gentlemen, had made considerable advance in England, when the Reformation not only arrested its progress, but threatened forever to extinguish the culinary fire. Gastronomy, violently expelled from monasteries and colleges, found no sanctuary either in the riotous household of the jolly cavalier, or in the gloomy abode of the lank, pinched-visaged round-head; the latter, as the poet has it, eager to

> "——Fall out with mince-meat, and disparage
> His best and dearest friend, plum-porridge;"*

the former broaching his hogshead of October,* and roasting a whole ox, in the exercise of a hospitality far more liberal than elegant.

'But, gentlemen, the genial spark was still secretly cherished in our seats of learning. Oxford watched over the culinary flame with zeal proportioned to the importance of the trust.* From this altar were rekindled the culinary fires of episcopal palaces, which had smouldered for a time. Gastronomy once more raised her parsley-wreathed front in Britain; and daily gained an increase of devoted, if not yet enlightened worshippers.'

'Ay, that will suffice for a general view of the subject,' cried Dr Redgill; 'let us now get to the practical part of the science,—arrange the dinners,— the proof of the pudding is the eating.'

Touchwood had a high disdain for what he called 'the bigotry of the stewpan' in Dr Redgill, who, like a true churchman, had a strong leaning 'to dishes as they are.'* Jekyl was to the full as flighty and speculative as the Doctor was dogmatic. The young man had French theory,—the *beau ideal* of gastrology floating in his brains. His experience in the most fashionable clubs, and taverns, and bachelor-establishments about the metropolis, had been great; but it was fortunately modified by a course of peninsular practice;* and, upon the whole, he was found a most efficient member of the club in all that regarded modern improvements, though rather intolerant of Scottish national dishes.

The culinary lectures of Touchwood, whose eloquence for six long weeks fulminated over the Cleikum kitchen, extended to such unreasonable compass, that a brief syllabus of the course is all we can give, without unduly swelling this Manual, and losing sight of the purpose for which it was intended; namely, a Practical System of Rational Cookery and Domestic Economy.

MRS WILLIAM PARKES, from *Domestic Duties* (1825)

Evening Parties

Mrs B. As the company is generally numerous at balls, it is neither necessary, nor is it expected, to be so select as at smaller parties. On these occasions the rooms may be well filled, although too great a crowd should be avoided. The majority ought, of course, to be juvenile, and the number of gentlemen should be equal to, or even exceed, that of the ladies.

I need scarcely remind you of the great advantage of being beforehand, in all the necessary preparations for parties of every kind. Early in the day, the sofas, chairs, and tables should be removed, as well as every other piece of furniture which is likely either to be in the way or to be injured: forms should be placed around the walls of the room, as occupying less space than chairs, and accommodating more persons with seats. A ball room should be brilliantly lighted, and this is done in the best style by a chandelier suspended from the centre of the ceiling, which besides adds much to the elegant appearance of the room. Lustres placed on the mantlepiece, and branches on tripods in the corners of the room, are also extremely ornamental.

Mrs L. I hope you also recommend chalking the floor, which is not only very ornamental but useful, as I know by experience, in preventing those awkward and disagreeable accidents which a slippery floor inevitably occasions amongst the lively votaries of Terpsichore.*

Mrs B. A chalked floor is useful too in disguising, for the time, an old or ill coloured floor, which would otherwise form a miserable contrast to the elegant chandeliers, and the well dressed belles and beaux. When the season will allow it, we must not forget to fill the fire-place with flowers and plants, which, indeed, form an appropriate and pleasing ornament on the landing-places, and in other parts of the house through which the guests may have to pass.

In consulting the beauty of the fair visitants, those flowers should be selected which reflect colours in harmony with the human complexion; as, for example, the Rose, the early white Azalea, the white and pink Hyacinth, and other flowers of similar tints. There should not be an over proportion of green; for, as this colour reflects the blue and yellow rays, it is by no means favourable to the female complexion; and still worse are yellow and orange coloured groups, whether of natural or artificial flowers. In some degree, however, the flowers should be chosen to harmonize also with the colour of the paper, or the walls of the ball-room.

The music should always be good, as much of the pleasure of dancing depends upon it. Violins, with harp and flute accompaniments, form the most agreeable band for dancing.

The lady of the house, who is expected to appear in rather conspicuous full dress, should be in readiness to receive her guests in good time; allowing herself a few minutes' leisure to survey her rooms, to ascertain that every thing is in proper order, and nothing defective in any of her arrangements. The arrival of her guests will be between the hours of nine and twelve.

A retiring room should be in readiness for ladies who may wish to disburthen themselves of shawls and cloaks; and here a female should be in attendance to receive them, and to perform any little office of neatness which a lady's dress may accidentally require. Tea and coffee may also be presented in this room, if any be deemed necessary; but of late the custom of introducing these refreshments at balls has been nearly abolished.

Three male servants, at least, are necessary, and as many more as the sphere of life of the individual who gives the ball sanctions. One servant should attend at the door of the house; and receiving the names of the company as they arrive, he should transmit them to another, who should conduct the party into the anti-room, while he in turn communicates their arrival to a third at the drawing-room door, who should announce them to the lady of the house. Her station should be as near the entrance of the room as possible, that her friends may not have to search for her to whom, of course, they first wish to pay their respects, and from whom they expect their welcome. As soon as a sufficient number of dancers are arrived, the young people should be introduced to partners, that they may not, by any unreasonable delay of their expected amusement, lose their self-complacency, and cast the reflection of dulness on the party. When the lady of the house is a dancer, she generally commences the dance; but when this is not the case, her husband should lead out the greatest stranger, or person of highest rank present: and while one dance is proceeding, la Maitresse du bal, if a French term be allowable, should be preparing another set of dancers to take the place of those upon the floor, as soon as they have finished. Nothing displays more want of management and method, than a dead pause after a dance; while the lady, all confusion at so disagreeable a circumstance, is begging those to take their places who have perhaps never been introduced to partners. There should be no monopoly of this delightful recreation, but all the dancers in the party should enjoy it in regular succession.

Refreshments, such as ices, lemonade, negus, and small rout cakes, should be handed round between every two or three dances, unless a room be appropriated for such refreshments. Supper should be announced at half-past twelve or at one o'clock, never later: and each gentleman should then be requested to take charge of a lady to the supper-room. Both with regard to the pleasure of her company, and her own comfort, La Maitresse would do well to discountenance the habit, which is sometimes sanctioned, of the gentlemen remaining long in the supper room after the ladies have retired.

Mrs L. Indeed, I entirely agree with you in this opinion, for when the gentlemen remain in the supper-room, it frequently causes a formal party of silent and listless fair ones, who seem to consider this temporary suspension of their amusement as an evil of sufficient magnitude to rob their countenances of the smiles of cheerfulness and good-humour, which they had worn during the preceding part of the evening. As our gentle islanders lose half their charms when they lose their good-humour, it is charitable to them to prevent, if possible, this half-hour of discomfiture. Of what, my dear madam, should a supper for such a party consist? Is it an expensive addition to the entertainment?

Mrs B. The variety of little delicacies of which suppers generally consist, makes them rather expensive. The table is usually crowded with dishes, which, however, contain nothing of a more solid nature than chickens, tongue, collared eels, prawns, lobsters, trifles, jellies, blanchmange, whips, fruit, ornamental confectionery, &c. French wines are frequently presented at suppers. As it would be scarcely possible to seat a very large party at once at a supper table, it is advisable to keep one part of the company dancing in the ball room, whilst another is at supper: and, even in this case, the gentlemen need not be seated, nor sup until the ladies have retired. Very little apparent exertion is necessary in the lady of the house, yet should she contrive to speak to most of her guests some time during the evening, and to the greatest strangers she should pay more marked attention.

From *Domestic Economy and Cookery for Rich and Poor* (1827)

No nation has written more on the subject of economy than our own, and no nation has practised it less. Indeed, the mass of the population can receive little or no benefit from the clearest general precepts. When they are told economy is a good and useful thing, that it will secure a comfortable subsistence to their children in their infancy, and themselves in their old age, they hear and believe; but this will never teach them that 3lbs of one sort of meat may be had for the same price as one of another,[1] or that they may make wholesome

---

[1] Were I not afraid of frightening my readers, I should have added, and that they may make one of these pounds go farther than three cooked in the ordinary way. This, however, the receipts will show. I once saw a French family, consisting of six grown persons, a child, and a jack-daw, who, by the by, was the heaviest of the eight on the meat, dine on one pound of lean veal, made into a rich ragout, with mushrooms, morels, &c. (see receipt) and goose fat, the properties of which I have amply enlarged upon. This may astonish my country folks, as I assure them it did me; and in the expectation that the moral of it may impress itself on others as it did on myself, I place it thus forward as being the first thing that opened my eyes to the advantages of French

beer for themselves, at one eighth of the price that they pay, as their forefathers did, and their neighbours do, for poisonous porter. Such precepts must proceed from those that have devoted a considerable portion of their time to domestic concerns; and in no work can they with more propriety be given than in a cookery-book, from the hands it is likely to fall into, from its embracing the objects of expenditure more than any other, and because the waste of the necessaries of life is, of all others, the most injurious.

The arrangement of those receipts has been no trifling labour. I indulge, however, in the hope that, by pointing out the means of preventing waste, I may be enabled, in some degree, to diminish the cares of the rich, and encrease the happiness of the poor. The dishes of our own and other countries which are given, have been all dressed in my own kitchen; and the foreign ones which are not yet used in England I have had proved. I have assigned a reason for every thing, *as far as the limits would permit*, that the cook may understand what she does, and why she does it. In gardening, agriculture, &c. analysis and generalisation have been introduced, to the great ease of the learner, and advantage of the community. In cookery, generalisation has certainly been recommended, but very little practised, because that art, though indebted to some professional men, as Dr Hill, (Mrs Glasse,) Dr Hunter, and Dr Kitchener, for the three best cookery-books we have at present,* engages still less than any other the attention of those whose education renders them best calculated to simplify and improve. Not that cookery is in itself any ways inferior to many others in which they pride themselves in excelling, but they neglect it from the very reason that should have induced them to lend their assistance to it, namely, its universal practice; and in this consideration I perhaps may be excused when I say, that I treat more of universals than the few who have restricted that term to themselves. As I shall have frequently to use the word economy, let it be understood that it is not saving I mean. Saving is the privation of a comfort or luxury; economy, the procuring it at the least expence.

Though deeply impressed with the importance of economy, and though convinced of the facility with which it may be practised, and of the happiness which may be the result, still it is with a feeling far

cookery. I may further add, that this entire family was enjoying perfect health, and had never heard of many of those disorders, which, under the different appellation of nervous, bilious, &c. are so prevalent in this country.

short of confidence that I propose the following system, when I look around me on the habitual extravagance of every rank, the depravity of servants, the inability of women to manage their own affairs, and the rooted prejudice against improvement,—a prejudice that has prevented our people from benefiting by the better customs of their neighbours, which the profusion of money, and local and accidental circumstances, have prevented them from discovering, or (more hopeless still) have brought into disuse. The middling classes, so far from wishing to save, seem to consider profusion a mark of affluence. The higher orders, who are above this vanity, are, in most cases, equally ignorant of the state of their establishments: while the poor are proportionably more extravagant than either. In fact, I know not where anything like economy is to be found amongst us, except in the reduced families of the higher, and sometimes of the middling ranks. It is worse than ridiculous to hear the English boasting of their charitable and benevolent institutions, and valuing themselves on a comparison with the virtuous and unobtrusive frugality of the French, and indeed of every other nation, when there is twice as much wasted by their menials as would, if fitly administered, maintain in honest independence the wretches whose name is a sanction for drunkenness in a tavern, or dissipation at a masquerade. 'A French family would live well on what is daily wasted in an English kitchen.'*

This national blemish has originated amongst the rich, in the enormous disproportion between the wealth of this and of other countries; amongst the poor, in the demand for workmen, and the consequent high price of labour which attends a flourishing state. The habits of extravagance thus acquired, in subsequent reduction, by fall of wages, sickness, or any other cause, are no less heavy and calamitous than they were criminal before. The manhood of such persons is a succession of intemperance and want; their age is spent in a workhouse. But we must contrast them with the working classes of other countries, to be awakened to the wretchedness of a condition to which, unfortunately, its very prevalence renders us callous. To these causes, and, in a great measure, to the fall of the Roman Catholic religion, I am inclined to attribute the manifest decline of the culinary art. The frequency of fasts and jours-maigres* forced the people to exert their ingenuity in dressing vegetables, fish, eggs, &c.; and Friar's chicken, Pope's posset, Bishop, and Monk, are reliques that have not been swept away with their cells and monasteries; whilst New-College pudding, Oxford John, Dean's particulars, &c., still grace their ancient halls.* In an old family register. I find, besides many other dainties requisite for a bishop's table, that capon was a standing dish, and formed a considerable portion of his *kain*.[1] I do not believe, that now-a-days, a single capon would be procured for money, from Tweed to John-o'-Groats. To the patriotic zeal of the monks,[2] are we much more indebted for fine breeds of animals, than to the Agricultural Society of the present day. They discovered a spring of action, as yet wholly overlooked, by the less scientific members of that society; for they received no poultry, as kain, under an enormous weight; and I saw, a few years ago, at Paisley Abbey, a pretty tolerable sized ring for measuring eggs, beneath which, the friars used to place a basin; the eggs that fell through were, of course, not counted, being broken, and only fit for puddings.

With respect to servants, their depravity is too notorious to require exposure or minute detail. Its evil effects are so universally, and so severely felt, that the bare mention of a chance for ameliorating it, would, it might be supposed, be seized with avidity. This, however, is far from being the case, because the real root of the evil is in the factitious state of society, and want of proper education.

But, at all events, the more we can be useful to ourselves, and the more we can do without servants, the happier we shall be. It would be quite Quixotic to call society by its right name, or to think even of the pains and assumed happiness it costs; but let those who have the

[1] A portion of rent or tithe paid in kind.
[2] The monks on the continent, at this moment, are reputed the best of cooks. I may say that I never saw a better dressed or better served dinner than one that was begged, cooked, and served by a mendicant friar. He came to Rome once a-week, went his rounds, and brought his gleanings to an *Abbate* who patronized him. The door was then shut, the outer cloak thrown off, and half a dozen bags, plump as their carrier, displayed themselves to the enraptured eyes of the benevolent host. Fearing that the load under which the frater's shoulders themselves were made to bend, would completely overwhelm the credulity of my readers, I abstain from the bill of lading. Suffice it to say, that for a dinner of ten dishes, no one ingredient was wanting, not even oil. The receipt for one of them—baked curds—I regret I have lost. I shall refer to the receipts for a *Quarter of kid dressed à l'Isaac*, which was truly savory. I had an opportunity of witnessing several sights of the kind, being introduced by the friendly Abbate as the Sorella——.

greatest trial and exertion to maintain themselves in it, and who are, consequently, most dependent on servants, mark some point at which they judge the pleasure of society to be more than counterbalanced by its pains. Let such persons, then, summon up courage, and retire from it at once, and save, for the support of their children, the substance they lavished on strangers, that ridiculed them while they fed on their misapplied bounty. Let them not suppose, that, in the parade of society, there is any thing captivating beyond idea. It is afflicting to think, that the mind, which we are accustomed to call free and uncontrolled, should not only be less free than the body, but that the means of enslaving it should be greater: 'when goods increase, they are increased that eat them; and what good is there to the owners thereof, save the beholding them with their eyes.'* I should recommend that no servant be taken, without a character of three years at least; that no master or mistress give a good character to bad servants, for the sake of getting rid of them; and that no servant be taken from the recommendation of trades-people.[1] Were these simple maxims attended to, the result, I have no doubt, would answer the most sanguine expectations. Servants would then seldom quit their places; they would have an interest in pleasing their masters; and masters have always an interest in overlooking a few faults, that they may not be put to the inconvenience of changing. In short, servants would consider their places as their homes. The system of giving false characters,[2] seems now quite a matter of course. Indeed, a brother, a husband, or a father of a family, would risk much in refusing one to an impertinent fellow. The only means of remedying this, is requiring testimonials of a period of residence in one family

---

[1] Though it is not my plan to enter particularly into the subject of servants, yet there is an abuse too serious to be omitted, as it is not generally known, though I do not see how it is to be remedied. A gentleman runs about to a dozen coachmakers to save a couple of pounds on his carriage, and (say) it costs him 200*l.* The coachman before he drives it from the tradesman's door, receives, perhaps, 200 shillings, though the tradesman has to wait for his money, and long enough too sometimes. He has likewise to supply the coachman with tickets for drink when he chooses to pay him a visit, with dinners, civilities, and whatever else may be going on, and to pay him three times the value of the old harness, should that be unfortunately a perquisite. The cause of this is, that the coachmaker has warranted the coach to run for a certain period, and of course he must season the coachman as well as the coach.

[2] A case of false character has lately been tried, and 700*l.* damages were adjudged against a person who gave a character for honesty to a servant whom it was proved he knew to be dishonest. A few such examples would have a very salutary effect.

of a considerable length; surely people could not falsify in this respect. If a man, who knows himself wholly deficient, in point of honesty, find his master give him the character of an honest servant, what inducement can he have to forego a practice that adds to his stock, and detracts not from his good name?

But it requires something more than precept and the terror of true characters to constitute a well-principled and a well-regulated family—the good conduct and good principles in the master and mistress, of which servants are the best judges. What can oral precepts do, when constant practical ones are in opposition to them? or with what reverence can servants look up to those whose duplicity and petty frauds they daily witness? How can they receive benefit from their instructions, when they merely recommend honesty and truth? This remark I would address more particularly to the mistress, as her conduct is an example to her husband, as well as to others, from the persuasive and engaging delicacy that belongs to the female character;—the only return, and a poor one it is, that woman receives in lieu of every thing society denies. And besides, it is her virtues alone that can be displayed in the most necessary and endearing offices of domestic life, in the management of the household, in the toils and anxieties of bringing up a family, and in the tender and indefatigable watchfulness of a sick bed. Evil example is generally considered much more contagious than good; but, placing the standard a good way below perfection, as is requisite to make the cases admit of comparison, I think it is just the reverse. I could mention instances of prudent women whose example has influenced their neighbourhood for miles around; and, while no female tongue could allow them the slightest praise, mothers became more attentive to their families, and mistresses to their households.

Another fundamental error is the ignorance in which the wife is kept of the real state of her husband's affairs, of whose ruin she may thus be the innocent and unconscious cause. Men often seem more anxious to conceal from their wives, than from others, the embarrassment they should wish them alone to know. They have buoyed them up with expectations, the failure of which mortifies their own pride. With the rent-roll let the debts and mortgages be produced, and at all events, let the young wife, before she runs into the heedless expense, find some means to ascertain whether there be incumbrances, and to what extent. If example be required, I will produce that of a lady of more than patrician birth, and of a mind as elevated as her rank. Suspecting, from several circumstances, the embarrassed state of her husband's affairs, she went into the steward's office, and, locking the door after her, declared that she would not quit the place till he made her acquainted with her real situation. Her suspicions being more than confirmed, she prevailed on her husband to go and pay some visit, and then immediately dismissed the carriages, horses, servants, hounds, and all the et cetera of expense, and when her husband returned, received him with open arms to a state of peace and comfort to which his former condition rendered him a stranger, and which pomp and festivity had served at best to interrupt. The creditors, by wisely trusting their honour and discretion, saved their own money, and prevented the ruin of the family. It was, however, a long and painful task of fourteen years. With less labour the fortune might have been triply earned; but it had more value as the work of integrity. Had the lady been a merchant's daughter, in all probability the family would have been ruined; for what judgment or feeling can be expected from boarding-school discipline? Many mistresses, who subscribe to the Bible Society, have servants at home without a Bible. Let them take home a common Bible, and books, of which there are many suited to their capacity, both engaging and instructing. These books should be changed at proper intervals (say once a week) and some of them examined as to their contents to secure their perusal. Thus mistresses would gain a knowledge of the dispositions of their servants, and obtain intellectual authority over them, the reaction of which, by requiring in her the same moral superiority and a regard for the principles which she nurtures, would extend its beneficial influence to the society in which she moves, to her children, and even to her children's children. Let us not regard remote causes as insignificant. The highest flights of genius, and the profoundest arguments of philosophy, are but assemblages of minute and individually inconsequent relations. By this discipline, servants also will have their minds occupied and improved, and consequently their happiness increased. Is not idleness the source of all evil? What then can be expected from a number of idle people sitting down together from three to five hours every evening, deprived by dependence and distrust of every sense of honour, with no spur to improvement, and every incentive for vice? As their service is indispensable to our comfort, their comfort, morals, and happiness, are indispensable to our tranquillity. Their life, however, is far from being happy, and, though our happiness is intimately connected with theirs, we seem not to have a care on the subject. We are exalted by their degradation, but let it not appear that we are happy by their misery. There is a great deal of time, precious to their families, wasted by well meaning and virtuous women in running after charitable institutions, whilst their children are suffering from neglect, or abandoned to neglectful servants, and whilst there is perhaps twenty times the value of their alms wasted in their kitchens, not from any particular mismanagement, but from the want of attention to economy and knowledge of it so universal in this country. I do not mean to say that charities are always prejudicial: there are many on the contrary highly meritorious; such as schools of all descriptions, when food and clothes are not given; relief in all cases of accident, unforeseen calamity, fires, &c. But the constant and systematic practice of alms-giving, the Foundling and Lying-in Hospitals, and the like, are checks to industry, and premiums for vice, and are as remote from the spirit, as from the letter of the Scripture, on the authority of which they are generally maintained. There are [those], who are carried away by what they call tender sympathies, and who give some from their abundance, some from their necessity, and some forgetting that justice is before liberality; and there are [those], I am sorry to say, whose sole aim is a fair report, who would think it very harsh that the poor should be taught to have an honest contempt for the bread of charity, and that they should save even from their needful to support their aged parents, or to keep in store for their own necessities. But what could such people think of any one who would say, that, 'If any man provide not for his own, and especially for his own kindred, he hath denied the faith: he is worse than an infidel?'

Women, guided by judgment and reason (as well as by the best intentions), will begin with studying and practising economy in their own families, and they will then instruct the poor or peasantry around them to increase their means by diminishing their waste and their wants, and to pride themselves on independence. But, till women's minds are more improved, and their views more extended, they naturally will endeavour to render themselves as necessary to the poor as the poor are to them.

From *The Home Book; or, Young Housekeeper's Assistant* (1829)

On Servants

When you have settled this business [agreement with each servant about terms and duties], then order your dinner, and fix the hour. A week's experience will enable you to judge what is consumed in the family daily, and what quantity of each article to order; and as servants are occasionally apt to forget or misunderstand verbal instructions, I have, of late years, adopted a plan which has proved of very considerable utility. I keep a number of pieces of paper, about three inches square, strung together by the corners, hanging in my dressing-room; on one of which I write my orders for dinner, in the manner specified in No. II in the Appendix; and there can then be no plea for forgetfulness or misapprehension. You must next visit your Larder, prepared with a pencil and slip of paper, on which to write your orders for the Cook. See what cold meat is in the house; if there be enough for the servants' dinner, or if you would have any of it hashed for the parlour; examine what cold vegetables, pies, or puddings remain. While you are doing this, you will be able to see, at a glance, if the Larder be kept clean and in order. The Meat, &c. should always be put away after dinner, in common white, or in Welsh dishes, which are better, because stronger, that the table-service may be washed immediately after use, and safely put away. I should also recommend you to have a sufficient quantity of common yellow dishes and plates for kitchen use, and to give strict order that the table-service be kept for the parlour table only. Look into the bread-pan, to see if the loaves are fairly cut, and not used while new; and also that the pieces of bread are not more numerous than might be expected to have been left from the day before; if the servants refuse to eat those bits, let them be made into a pudding for the kitchen, with one or two eggs, before they become too hard for use. To avoid this evil, however, I should recommend that the loaf be brought into the dining-room, that the servant may cut just what may be wanted. Some Footmen, without considering the number of persons to be at table, will pile up the basket with large pieces of bread, the half of which, perhaps, not being eaten, goes amongst what is called the 'broken victuals,' which the Cook may either with, or without, your permission, give to some poor person. That the poor should have the crumbs from your table, is very right; but it should always be by your express orders; for the term *broken victuals* is sometimes understood in so very comprehensive a sense, as to include cold meat, potatoes, greens, butter, bread, soap, and candles, which are conveyed out of the house once or twice in a week, to sell at shops where such articles are regularly purchased.

LETTER VIII

MY BELOVED CHILD,

In my introductory Letter, I briefly touched upon those important duties which will devolve upon you by marriage; but I should not be doing my duty, if I did not enlarge on the subject, as it is of the utmost consequence to your future happiness, that you should fully understand all those points, which are most likely to secure, or to destroy it. I am sorry to say that many young women enter the marriage state, without considering either the nature or extent of those duties, which they are thus called upon to fulfil; it seems to them, that if they are chaste and correct in their conduct, moderate in their expenses, and regular in the arrangement of their household, they perform all the duties of a good Wife. But though these are deeply essential to that character, yet they are very insufficient to secure happiness in the married life. When I say *happiness*, I do not allude to that state of exquisite and unfading bliss which some romantic girls expect will be their lot, when united to the object of their affections; but I mean that reasonable degree of felicity which may exist, though intermingled with many sorrows, and which, in a great measure, depends on the conduct of the Wife. It is not to be supposed that a well educated young woman will suddenly fall into those great and fatal errors, which too frequently destroy the peace of whole families; but it is certain that trifles, or what many people consider as such, will as effectually destroy all comfort in the marriage state. It is, therefore, the more requisite that when a female takes upon herself the character of a Wife, she should know, and continually consider, that her happiness chiefly depends on those quiet, unpretending, fire-side duties, which are rather to be felt than described. Let me then recommend to you to make a resolution, at the very commencement of your married life, never to attempt, nor even wish, to gain what is called the management of your Husband; on the contrary, endeavour to regulate your own conduct according to his opinion: never needlessly oppose him in any object he may have in view, but rather cheerfully give up your own will, than enter into an argument with him. If he should be of a hasty temper, it is the more necessary to be always upon your guard to avoid giving a sharp reply to any remark he may make; for it must be considered, that men constantly engaged in worldly concerns, meet with many vexations which women can have no idea of. It is, therefore, not to be wondered at, if they should sometimes return home with a cloud on their brow; or occasionally utter a sharp word, perhaps, without being conscious of it. If that should be the case at any time with your Husband, and he is received by you with affection and a smiling countenance, the cloud will soon pass off, and he will feel the delight of knowing, that at home he is sure to meet a balm for all vexations; that at his own dear fire-side he will find a thousand little attentions, which too many women do not consider as part of a Wife's duty. These must prove of far more advantage than appears at the first view, as they will shew to a Husband, that even in his absence he occupies the affectionate thoughts of his Wife; and that she is ever studious to supply him with whatever may, by any possibility, contribute either to his comfort or convenience.

In the article of dress, you should be guided not less by his circumstances, than by his taste and mode of thinking; for what pleasure could you possibly experience in being attired in the most fashionable and extravagant style, in comparison with the satisfaction of proving to your Husband, that your chief duty was to please him, whose approbation was dearer to you than the admiration of all the world. Many women fall into the dangerous error of dressing well when they go into public, and neglecting almost propriety when at home, and expecting to be seen only by their Husbands. This conduct is such a very bad compliment, that he would almost be justified in supposing, that her attention to dress before marriage, was designed as a bait to gain a partner, and not thought necessary afterwards to keep his love. Perfect candour and unbounded confidence should be established between a married couple, more particularly on the side of the female; let me, therefore, advise you to have no concealments from your Husband; never be made a party in the secret of any friend of which he may not be a partaker. If any domestic bickerings should arise, or unhappiness of a more serious nature, study to conceal it from the world as long as possible, and do not impart the circumstance to any one, even of your most intimate friends. Call to mind the terms of the marriage contract, so solemnly pronounced at the altar, when you took your Husband for better, or for worse, and you will feel it your duty, as well as your interest, to conceal his faults and infirmities, and not to lessen him in the estimation of his friends. Such imprudent confidence, when adopted by a thoughtless young woman, tends only to increase the evil complained of, and sometimes causes the entire destruction of that marital happiness, which might have been preserved by silence, and prudent conciliating conduct on her part. During the days of courtship, it is natural to suppose that both parties will endeavour to appear as amiable as possible; and studiously to avoid betraying those points in their dispositions which they feel conscious might lessen their attractions. But it is to be expected that, after marriage, circumstances will arise to call forth the latent errors of temper, which were not previously visible; and when the discovery is made, it will be wisdom in each party to make allowances for the frailty of human nature. If such occurs to yourself, consider that the happiness of your life depends on preserving the love of your Husband, and keep a guard in your mind against the beginnings of discontent; for it was truly said by the wisest man that ever lived, that 'The beginning of strife is as the letting out of water.'*

Be careful to avoid every thing that may disoblige, or wear the face of unkindness or neglect; be always ready to receive your Husband's friends with complacency; and, however inconvenient it may be to have an unexpected guest brought home to dinner, let not your countenance inform him how unwelcome he is. If your entertainment be not so good as you would wish, utter no such freezing expression as, 'If I had been aware of your visit, I would have provided better;' but, with a hearty good will, set before him what you have, and let it be seasoned with good humour. If he be a man of sense and feeling, he will assuredly think his dinner, however simple, with such accompaniments, far preferable to an entertainment of two courses, with a frowning countenance at the head of the table. It is, I think, unnecessary to give more particulars concerning your matrimonial duties, and I conclude by recommending you to take *Discretion* as your guide in every part of your conduct; it is a comprehensive word, and not one of those virtues which come into practice only occasionally, or in particular circumstances; for it is requisite *at all times, in all places, and upon all occasions.*

EXPLANATORY NOTES

6 *Drury-Lane theatre*: after the proliferation of theatres in the Elizabethan and Jacobean periods, Charles II introduced a system of theatre licensing in 1660, so that in 1777 only the theatres of Drury Lane (opened in 1663) and Covent Garden in London held royal patents. Every new play performed had to be licensed by the Lord Chamberlain's office. Drury Lane had been managed for many years by David Garrick (see next note) until his retirement in 1776. For the history of the theatre, its several destructions and reinventions, and its significance in the careers of many of the dramatists and actors mentioned in the text and notes of this anthology, see W. Macqueen-Pope, *The Theatre Royal* (London: W. H. Allen, 1945).

Mr Garrick performs Ranger: the leading actor of his time and a family friend of the Burneys, David Garrick (1717–79) had frequently performed the part of the frolicsome opportunist and rake Ranger, in Benjamin Hoadly's bedroom farce *The Suspicious Husband* (1747). In May and June 1776, it was one of the performances marking his retirement from the stage.

Clarinda: usually seen as a mistake on Burney's part, which it may well be, since Ranger dances not with Clarinda, the young friend of the Stricklands' ward Jacintha, at the end of *The Suspicious Husband*, but with Mrs Strickland, in whose bedroom he has just been discovered. It is also possible, however, that Evelina's breathless sentences convey the excited rush of her ideas, and that she envies Clarinda as a lively young woman-about-town rather than as Ranger's dance-partner.

7 *Portland chapel . . . houses built of brick*: properly St Paul's, Great Portland Street; Pall Mall, SW1, named after a croquet-like Italian game and laid out in 1661, was a fashionable walk at this time, lined with expensive shops and fine houses. Kensington Gardens was also a fashionable parade, having been extended and altered in 1730–3. The Palace in the next sentence is Buckingham House, which stood on the site of the present Buckingham Palace, principal residence of the British monarch. Buckingham House was built by John Sheffield, 1st Duke of Buckingham, in 1702–5, and bought by George III in 1762. It was also known as the Queen's House because it became Queen Charlotte's in 1775 until her death in 1818, upon which the Prince Regent began the alteration works which eventually produced Buckingham Palace.

the mercers: dealers in textiles, especially expensive fabrics such as velvets and silk.

8 *suit of linen . . . evening*: a linen gown complete with underskirt of the same fabric.

my hair dressed: in the late 1770s this was a lengthy process, the fashion being for ladies to support two- or three-feet high structures of wire and padding around which their hair would be arranged. The hair was greased then powdered, and would stay in place for days or sometimes weeks.

10 *minuets were over . . . wait for our things*: a minuet was the slow stately dance in triple measure, fashionable throughout the eighteenth century, and customarily the opening dance of a gathering: it would be followed by more energetic dances, and the order, which Evelina recounts later, was a matter of strict form.

16 *tomorrow, and tomorrow, and tomorrow*: from Macbeth's reaction to the reported death of his wife, *Macbeth*, v. v. 19.

19 *her handkerchief off her neck*: a square of linen or silk, often embroidered, worn around the neckline of a lady's gown.

25 *my friend . . . the South Sea Company*: Macaulay is addressing the Revd Dr Wilson, with whom she and her daughter had taken up residence in Bath. The South Sea Company, originally the idea of Robert Harley, 1st Earl of Oxford (1661–1724; chief minister to Queen Anne, 1711–14), was set up in 1711: supposedly poised to take advantage of huge trading possibilities and riches in South America, it was always a monetary rather than a trading corporation. Supported for several years by government policy and intervention, it attracted thousands of investors, becoming increasingly fraudulent until its collapse in 1820–1. For a few shrewd observers at the time, including Robert Walpole and Daniel Defoe, it represented public gambling on a catastrophic scale, but for most contemporaries it was a story of perfidy among the few (directors) rather than, as Macaulay argues here, greed and self-delusion among the many. For details of this infamous episode in the history of finance—still the defining disaster of British speculation—see John Carswell, *The South Sea Bubble* (1960; Stroud: Alan Sutton, 1993).

The pernicious policy . . . happier times: Macaulay refers to the practice of raising funds for the finance of wars, begun, she argues, by William III (king 1688–1702). The expensive war against France from 1689 to 1697, for which between four and five million pounds were needed each year, drove key aspects of William's constitutional and financial policy. The best account of the operation and implications of this new system remains that of Sir David Lindsay Keir in *The Constitutional History of Modern Britain, 1485–1951*, 5th edn., revised (London: Adam and Charles Black, 1953), 274–5: '[Money for the war] was largely raised by a land tax of four shillings in the pound, the incidence of which further embittered the relations of the Tory landed class who paid the tax, and the Whig moneyed class which lent to the government and drew the interest on their investment from the proceeds of taxes paid by the landowners. By an astonishing financial effort, three-fourths of the cost of the war was met by current taxation. For this lavish financial support there was a serious constitutional price to be paid. It involved the foundation of a permanent system of estimate, appropriation, and audit . . . The effect was to consolidate parliamentary control over its finances.' Keir goes on to support the main thrust of Macaulay's argument: 'It might perhaps be supposed that the complete assumption of control by Parliament over the raising of money by tax or loan—and its expenditure as well—were expedients applying only to extraordinary revenue. In theory, this is true. Yet even the "ordinary" revenue of the Crown entered on a new phase of its history after 1688' (275).

25 *the eleventh year of Queen Anne*: 1713, the year before Anne was succeeded by the first of the Hanoverian monarchs, George I, in whose reign the South Sea Bubble was blown and burst.

26 *all the duties upon wines . . . Peru in Mexico, in South America*: the South Sea Company was granted the revenues raised by the duties on all these imported goods, and granted a monopoly to set up a trade with the 'South Sea', meaning the eastern coast of South America. When Macaulay refers to the 'coast of Peru in Mexico', she is using 'Mexico' very vaguely to indicate South America as a whole: so vaguely that an editor might be tempted to suppose 'in' a misprint for 'and', were it not for the fact that the South Sea affair was never associated with Mexico.

navy bills, debentures, and other public securities: all ways of dealing in government bonds. Navy bills were bills issued by the Admiralty in place of ready-money payments, or drawn by a naval officer on the Admiralty; debentures were vouchers certifying that the designated person was owed money, especially by the royal household, the Exchequer, or other government office.

Sir John Blount . . . a scrivener: apprenticed to a scrivener—that is, a professional scribe or clerk—as a young man, John Blunt (1665–1733) took up the same profession, also acting as a financier and gradually buying up extensive real estate in London. He was a director of the South Sea Company from 1711 to 1721 and a leading exponent of the South Sea scheme in 1719–20. Made a baronet in 1720, he was arrested in January 1721 and subjected to financial penalties, upon which he left London for Bath, later (in 1732) being prosecuted for misuse of arms in the Court of Chivalry. According to John Carswell, his gross assets in 1721 stood among the highest of those involved in the South Sea scheme, at £184,043 (*South Sea Bubble*, 246). His nephew, Charles Blunt, committed suicide during the collapse of the Company, in September 1720.

Mississippi scheme . . . in that kingdom: the Scottish financier and theorist of finance John Law (1671–1729) settled in France in 1712, under the regency of Philip of Orleans, set up the Banque Générale in 1716, gained this bank a controlling interest in the Mississippi Company, renamed the Compagnie de l'Orient, in 1717, and created a speculative surge which collapsed in 1720, to the ruin of thousands. Before its collapse, the Mississippi scheme was an object of great envy and rivalry in Britain and increased the allure of the South Sea scheme.

the peace of Utrecht . . . any commercial advantage: the Treaty of Utrecht brought to an end the War of the Spanish Succession (1702–13) between England and France, by which England's American trade had been threatened. The treaty secured a separation of the French and Spanish thrones, the independence of the Netherlands, and the cessation of French support for the Jacobite cause. It helped make Britain a world power, bringing gains in the Caribbean and North America and granting the right to trade with the Spanish colonies for thirty years, opening up commercial exploitation of South America. Macaulay's point is that this advantageous treaty made the South Sea scheme unnecessary. Her distinction between Law's scheme and the South Sea scheme is perfectly valid, and was later commented on by others who wished to distinguish the entirely fictitious trade of the South Sea Company from the genuine, though disastrously oversubscribed, trade to Louisiana proposed by Law. For an account of some Romantic Period uses of the image and reputation of John Law, see Fiona Robertson, 'Of Speculation and Return: Scott's Jacobites, John Law, and the Company of the West', *Scottish Literary Journal*, 24 (1997), 1–24.

tricks of the alley . . . credulous individuals: Change Alley, Cornhill, London EC3, is named after the Royal Exchange where, from 1697, brokers wishing to buy and sell shares on behalf of clients had to register. In 1707 the original limit on the number of brokers, 100, was removed. The present-day Stock Exchange, in Capel Court, EC2, was not established until 1801, although when Macaulay was writing its immediate predecessor had recently been set up, in Threadneedle Street in 1773.

27 *Gibraltar and Port Mahon . . . places in Peru*: it was rumoured that the soldier and statesman James, 1st Earl Stanhope (1673–1721), leader of the Whig opposition in 1711 and later chief minister to George I, had arranged a deal with Spain by which Britain would give up Gibraltar and Port Mahon in exchange for four ports in Chile and Peru, protecting and enlarging the 'South Sea' trade. Stanhope was to become one of the genuine casualties of the affair, dying from a cerebral haemorrhage after a heated parliamentary exchange about the South Sea Company.

obliged to stop payment and abscond: that is, the bankers and goldsmiths were unable to honour requests to sell shares, and made themselves scarce. The Sword Blade Company was the most prominent of the financial institutions involved. Macaulay's phrasing is followed closely in Charles Mackay's account of the collapse in *Memoirs of Extraordinary Popular Delusions and the Madness of Crowds* (London: George Routledge and Sons, 1841), 66.

Lady-day and Michaelmas of the ensuing year: two of the dates on which debts traditionally fell due.

28 *the King . . . to hasten his return*: the king, George I, also the Elector of Hanover, could speak no English on his accession to the throne in 1714 and remained closely tied to Hanover. He returned on 11 November

1720, amid fears of violent riots and attacks on the directors of the Company.

28 *East-India company . . . bank of England*: one of the first joint-stock companies, the East India Company was set up in 1600 by a group of London merchants, acquired exclusive rights over the trade to Asia, and in the second half of the eighteenth century took over responsibility for the military protection and, gradually, the administration of India. The Company was in trouble throughout the 1770s when Macaulay was writing, a new administrative and colonial rationale being imposed by the East India Act of 1784. The Bank of England was established in 1694 to raise funds for the war against France: in 1706 it began to act as the direct agent of the government in the circulation of Exchequer Bills; eventually, in 1751, it took over the management of the National Debt.

Knight, Surman, and Turner: Robert Knight (1675–1744) was Cashier of the South Sea Company from 1711 to 1721, and had been an associate of John Blunt (see note to page 26) from 1709 or earlier as an employee of the Sword Blade Bank; a central figure in the South Sea fraud of 1720–1, in January 1721 he packed up all his documents and set sail, in disguise, for Calais; imprisoned in Antwerp, he became the centre of a diplomatic row before taking refuge in France a few months later and resuming his business career, not returning to Britain until he was granted a royal pardon in 1742. Robert Surman (d. 1759), from 1715 a clerk in the Sword Blade Bank, was Deputy Cashier of the South Sea Company from 1718 until his dismissal, with penalties, in 1721, when his gross assets stood at £158,262 (Carswell, *South Sea Bubble*, 254); he later returned as a partner in new banking ventures. The speculator John Turner was a director of the South Sea Company from 1718 to 1721, earning the less spectacular but high sum of £19,579 by 1721 (Carswell, *South Sea Bubble*, 254).

the persons . . . taken into custody: the banker and stockbroker George Caswall (d. 1742)—like John Blunt, a Baptist—was a director of the Company from 1711 to 1718, had been a Lombard Street banker since 1700, and was closely involved with the politician and First Minister Harley, whose career he helped support; knighted in 1718, he had ceased to be a director of the Company at the time of its collapse, but was a senior partner in its bank, the Sword Blade Bank, and was involved in shady stock transactions; an MP 1717–21, he was expelled from the Commons and imprisoned in March 1721, but returned as an MP 1722–42. John Lambert (1666–1723), of Huguenot descent, was an international stockbroker and commodity dealer closely associated with John Law (see note to p. 26), and a director of the South Sea Company from 1711 to 1721; he was especially notable for holding Company stock as a nominee for many foreign residents through his worldwide financial contacts, and, like John Blunt, Robert Surman, and Theodore Janssen, was worth a huge sum (£189,451: Carswell, *South Sea Bubble*, 252) in 1721.

Sir Theodore Janssen . . . apprehended: the four directors of the Company

named here were all MPs, and were called to account for their actions to
the House of Commons. They were tried and expelled by a secret committee of thirteen, empowered to requisition papers, records, and individual testimony. Like Lambert, of Huguenot descent, the financier and
author Theodore Janssen (1654–1748) took English citizenship in 1685
and was knighted in 1696; a director of the Bank of England in 1694–9,
1700–1, 1707–11, and 1718–19, he was a director of the South Sea Company from 1711 to 1718 and again from 1719 to 1721, and an MP 1715–
21, when he was expelled from the House of Commons; with extensive
trade connections and landowning interests, his gross assets stood higher
than those of any of the other directors Macaulay mentions here,
at £243,109 in 1721 (Carswell, *South Sea Bubble*, 251). Macaulay's
grandfather Jacob Sawbridge (d. 1748), a banker and stockbroker
associated with the Sword Blade Company from 1704, a director of
the South Sea Company from 1711 to 1721, and an MP 1715–21, had
amassed £121,689 by 1721 (Carswell, *South Sea Bubble*, 253). He lost all
but £5,000 after his trial in 1721. The barrister and financier Robert
Chaplin (d. 1728), who inherited and acquired extensive property
and was made a baronet in 1715, was a director of the Company from
1718 to 1721, an MP from 1715, and in 1721 was expelled from the
Commons, and imprisoned, for acquiring fictitious South Sea stock.
Francis Eyles (d. 1735), was a cloth merchant, an MP from 1715 until
his expulsion in 1721, and a director of the South Sea Company from
1715 to 1721.

29 *Mr Aislabie . . . the tower*: probably the greatest outcry of the South Sea
affair was caused by the involvement of the Chancellor of the Exchequer,
John Aislabie (1670–1742), 'very justly regarded as perhaps the greatest
criminal of all' (Mackay, *Extraordinary Popular Delusions*, 79). He had
been the principal parliamentary advocate of the Company, and, it
emerged, large quantities of stock had been transferred into his name. In
1721 he resigned as Chancellor, was tried, and was found guilty. On his
imprisonment in the Tower of London there were bonfires and popular
rejoicing; but when the affair died down he was left with £120,000 and
retired to improve and landscape his estate at Studley Royal, North
Yorkshire.

the Prince of Wales . . . the Duke of Chandos . . . the Duke of Bridgwater:
later George II (1683–1760), the Prince of Wales succeeded his father in
1727; James Brydges (1673–1744), 8th Lord Chandos, created Duke of
Chandos in 1719 and an MP from 1698 to 1714; Scroope Egerton, 4th
Earl and 1st Duke of Bridgwater (1681–1745). The same three examples
of speculation fever in high life are given by Mackay, *Extraordinary Popular Delusions*, 52.

30 *the aera of the Revolution*: that is, the Glorious Revolution of 1688–9, in
which the Roman Catholic James VII and II, brother of Charles II, was
deposed in favour of his Protestant daughter, Mary, and her husband
William of Orange.

31 *pensioners from sitting in parliament*: with a derogatory implication in this
    context, a pensioner means one who is in receipt of a pension or regular
    payment; hence a hireling or retainer set up with a parliamentary seat and
    expected to vote in the interests of the person paying him.

    duration of parliaments . . . a venal majority: as a general rule, the longer
    the term of office of a parliament, the greater the security and opportun-
    ities for corruption of the parliament: the greater, also, it was thought,
    the influence of the Crown. The Septennial Act of 1716 had extended the
    life of an elected parliament from three to seven years.

    Dr Sherlock . . . Sarum . . . London: Thomas Sherlock (1678–1761) had a
    prominent clerical and political career in the reigns of Anne, George I,
    and George II. A supporter of Walpole and the rights of the Crown, he
    became Bishop of Bangor in 1727, of Salisbury (Sarum) in 1734, and
    London in 1748.

32 *the whig banners*: although the eighteenth-century Whigs were pre-
    dominantly Anglican, they were sympathetic to the claims of the Dis-
    senters. The great eighteenth-century Whig families—the Rocking-
    hams, Temples, Newcastles—ruled England in the reigns of George I
    and II.

    the minister . . . parliament: a reference to the defeat of the great Whig
    statesman Sir Robert Walpole, 1st Earl of Orford (1676–1745), First
    Lord of the Treasury and Chancellor of the Exchequer 1715–17 and
    1721–42, after the longest ministry in English history, the result of the
    Excise Crisis of 1733.

    Davenant: Charles Davenant (1656–1714), who had a notable career in
    politics and government administration, was an MP, a commissioner of
    excise, and inspector-general of exports and imports. His most important
    contributions to economic thought were made in the late 1690s, in the
    context of the end of the War of the Grand Alliance (against France): *An
    Essay on Ways and Means of Supplying the War* (1695), *Essay on the East-
    India Trade* (1696), and *Discourses on the Public Revenues and on the Trade
    of England* (1698). A five-volume edition of his works was published in
    1771, a mark of recognition of his advanced economic principles, espe-
    cially his questioning of mercantilism, in the period immediately before
    the work of Adam Smith. Macaulay's apparently historical reference
    responds to a revival of interest in Davenant's work.

33 *the customs . . . excise*: custom is the duty levied on imports from foreign
    countries, excise the duty on goods produced in Britain, levied either
    during manufacture or before sale to British consumers. Under discus-
    sion here is the Excise Crisis of 1733.

    his Majesty's civil list: the civil list is the money voted by parliament to the
    monarch, which, after crises in the reign of William and Mary, leading to
    the Civil List Act of 1698, was primarily devoted to the costs of the royal
    household. Civil list monies had increased during every reign since that
    of William and Mary.

the vitals of the commonwealth: like many phrases in this discussion, this recalls the language, and carries forward the concerns, of Shakespeare's *Richard II*, especially the gardener's speeches in III. iv.

34 *the country party*: differentiated by their attitudes towards the executive, the Court party supported the king's ministers while the Country party opposed them: this opposition usually involved attacks on alleged corruption and the economic power of the state. For many historians, the court/country split is more significant in eighteenth-century politics than the division between Whigs and Tories, since country Whigs and country Tories often joined together on key issues.

35 *Pope . . . a softer man*: Alexander Pope's *Epistles to Several Persons*, 'Epistle II: To a Lady' (1735), ll. 271–2: 'Heav'n, when it strives to polish all it can | Its last best work, but forms a softer Man'.

36 *Rousseau . . . compositions*: the innovative and controversial French writer Jean-Jacques Rousseau (1712–78), best known for his novels *Julie, ou la nouvelle Héloïse* (1761) and *Émile* (1762), *The Social Contract* (1762), and the *Confessions* (1770, published 1781).

the schools: in ancient Greece and Rome, the place in which philosophers taught their hearers; hence a body of scholars, a faculty.

38 *Addison . . . graces of person*: Addison's *Guardian* essay 155, 'The Utility of Learning to the Female Sex'.

their summum bonum: the chief good, especially as the end or ultimate determining principle in an ethical system.

the man of ton . . . despises in women: 'ton' means everything—dress, manners, opinions—that is stylish and in vogue.

Chesterfield: Philip Dormer Stanhope, 4th Earl of Chesterfield (1694–1773), MP, ambassador, Lord Lieutenant of Ireland, and Secretary of State (1746–8), became celebrated after his death for the long series of private letters shaping the education and morals of his illegitimate son Philip Stanhope (born 1732). They were widely read, eleven editions appearing in Britain and Ireland by 1800. Chesterfield's authority and information were widely admired, but many of his views sparked controversy.

'Women . . . in serious matters': Chesterfield presents this information to his son as something 'that will be very useful for you to know, but which you must, with the utmost care, conceal; and never seem to know': *Lord Chesterfield's Letters*, ed. and introd. David Roberts (Oxford: Oxford University Press, 1992), 91.

41 *Epic poetry . . . the old Romance*: as contrasted in Samuel Johnson's *Dictionary* (1755), epic is 'narrative; comprising narrations, not acted, but rehearsed', while romance is 'a military fable of the middle ages; a tale of wild adventures in war and love'.

46 *The Novel . . . is written*: according to Johnson, a novel is something 'new, not ancient; a small tale, generally of love'.

47 *especially collegians*: members of the colleges of the two ancient English universities, Oxford and Cambridge.

52 *the Pleiades . . . the Bear . . . the Pole star*: the Pleiades is a cluster of about 500 stars in the constellation of Taurus; the Great Bear, Ursa Major, is the third-largest of the constellations, lying in the northern hemisphere of the sky; Polaris, the Pole Star, lies within one degree of the north celestial pole, in the constellation Ursa Minor.

Orion . . . Sirius, the dog-star: Orion, the hunter, is a prominent constellation on the celestial equator; also known as Alpha Canis Majoris or the Dog Star, Sirius, in the constellation Canis Major, is the brightest star visible to the naked eye after the Sun.

54 *an Ice-House*: a structure, often partly or wholly underground, in which ice was stored in winter for use throughout the year. See Monica Ellis, *Ice and Icehouses through the Ages* (Southampton: Southampton Industrial Archaeology Group, 1982), and Sylvia P. Beamon and Susan Roajof, *The Ice-Houses of Britain* (London: Routledge, 1990).

55 *fettered Sampson . . . Gaza's wealthy sons*: after his betrayal by Delilah, the Israelite hero Samson was blinded and fettered to the columns of the temple of the Philistines in Gaza; his strength restored by God, he destroyed the temple and all in it: Judges 16. The story is presented by Milton's tragic drama *Samson Agonistes* (1647–53?) which may be Barbauld's main source here.

or he who sat . . . sinewy grasp: Samson again. As McCarthy and Kraft point out (*Poems of Anna Letitia Barbauld*, 293–4), this is an allusion to 'Deianira to Hercules', related by Ovid in *Heroides*, ll. 113, 115 ('Ah, how often, while with dour finger you twisted the thread, have your too strong hands crushed the spindle!').

C[oleridge]: the poet, philosopher, and critic Samuel Taylor Coleridge (1772–1834). Barbauld and Coleridge met in Bristol in August 1797, and the manuscript of this poem is dated September 1797. It was first published in the *Monthly Magazine* in April 1799.

56 *Circe . . . still subservient*: in Greek mythology, Circe is a sorceress of the island of Æaea: she turned the companions of Ulysses into swine.

57 *Miss C.*: Sarah Grace Carr (d. 1837), eldest of the five daughters of Barbauld's friend Frances Carr, and a favourite, to judge from a letter of 1801 in which she is imagined 'skimming along the shore like a swallow, or walking, with naked feet like a slender heron in the water, or nestling among the cliffs' (*The Works of Anna Laetitia Barbauld*, ed. Lucy Akin, ii. 120). In adulthood a close friend of Maria Edgeworth, in 1821 she married Dr Stephen Lushington; through their connection a selection of Barbauld's and Edgeworth's letters to her is included in Walter Sidney Scott (ed.), *Letters of Maria Edgeworth and Anna Letitia Barbauld, Selected from the Lushington Papers* (London: Golden Cockerel Press, 1953).

58 *Dorking . . . south*: all places in Surrey: Dorking, 25 miles from London;

Norbury Park, near Mickleham, a few miles from Dorking, is famous for its trees; Box Hill, nearby, is a picturesque expanse of down and woodland; Reigate, 21 miles from London; Leith tower is the tower on the top of Leith Hill, 4½ miles south-west of Dorking, the highest hill in South-East England, on clear days offering views to central London and the English Channel.

blockaded by our fleets: when Barbauld wrote this, the British fleet was attempting to prevent French trade in an effort to cut short the war begun in 1793.

Notre Dame, and the Tuileries . . . the source of the Loire: Notre Dame is the Gothic cathedral church of Paris; the Tuileries, a royal palace in Paris built in the sixteenth century and destroyed by fire in the nineteenth, was invaded by revolutionary crowds in June 1792, saw the massacre of the royal Swiss Guards two months later, and was abandoned by the royal family as they attempted to flee to safety; the Loire, the longest river in France, rises in the mountains of the Massif Central.

the Delta and the seven-mouthed Nile: the arable farming of Egypt was effectively confined to the Nile valley and its delta; the Nile, a river-system nearer its source, becomes so again near the Mediterranean coast of Egypt.

59 *Cicero, the Roman orator*: Marcus Tullius Cicero (106–43 BC), Roman orator, statesman, and man of letters.

his orations against Catiline: among the most famous of Cicero's speeches, the four *In Catilinam*, delivered to the Roman senate in 63 BC, were explorations and attacks on the political ambitions of Lucius Sergius Catilina and his supporters. Catiline was killed in battle against the state a few months later.

his expedition into Gaul: the campaigns of the Roman general and statesman Gaius Julius Caesar (100–44 BC) in 58–50 BC, part of the extension of Roman power in western Europe.

the youth of Macedon . . . Bucephalus . . . Darius . . . his behaviour: Alexander III, the Great, king of Macedon (356–323 BC), his horse Bucephalus, and Darius I, the Great, king of Persia (c. 550–486 BC), who invaded Greece but was defeated at Marathon in 490 BC.

the sea-fight of Actium: the battle which brought the end of the Roman Republic and introduced the Empire was fought at sea off the promontory of Actium in the south of Epirus, off the west coast of Greece, on 2 September 31 BC. Octavian's victory over Antony and Cleopatra was precipitated by the flight of Cleopatra's ships and by Antony's decision to follow them.

like the descendants of Banquo in Macbeth: the eight kings who process before Macbeth, followed by Banquo, in *Macbeth*, IV. i.

60 *Homer . . . 'Guess!'*: the circumstances of the life (and even the existence) of Homer, the Greek epic poet of the eighth century BC, are shrouded in

mystery; at least four city-states—Smyrna, Colophon, Ephesus, and Chios—have been claimed as his birthplace.

60 *Louis the Fourteenth . . . man in the iron mask*: during the reign of 'le roi soleil' Louis XIV (1638–1715, king from 1643), a mysterious state prisoner was held in various gaols for over forty years, dying in 1703. He wore a mask not of iron but of black velvet, and his name has never been revealed: according to Voltaire, he was an illegitimate brother of the king.

Catharine of Russia . . . Semiramis . . . Aristotle . . . Lord Bacon: Catherine II, the Great (1729–96), empress of Russia from 1762 after the dethronement and later murder of her husband, Peter III, greatly expanded the territories and European power of the Russian Empire and was notorious for her love affairs; Semiramis, the semi-legendary queen of Assyria in the ninth century BC, also reigned after her husband, Ninus, with whom she is said to have founded Babylon. The second of Barbauld's comparisons is between the Greek philosopher and scientist Aristotle (384–322 BC), pupil of Plato and tutor to Alexander the Great, and the English statesman and philosopher Francis Bacon, 1st Baron Verulam, Viscount St Albans (1561–1626), best known for his *Essays* (1597).

a whispering-gallery: a gallery or dome, ususually circular or elliptical, in which a whisper or other faint sound made at one point can be heard at another, where the direct sound would be inaudible. The best-known example is in the dome of St Paul's Cathedral in London.

'Rura mihi et rigui placeant in vallibus amnes': by the Roman poet Virgil (Publius Vergilius Maro, 70–19 BC), author of the *Aeneid*, the *Georgics*, and the *Eclogues*. In his *Life of Virgil*, the fourth-century Latin grammarian Aelius Donatus describes him as shy and retired, avoiding the public life of Rome, and as resembling a countryman in appearance.

62 *the storm of war*: the war of the allies Britain, Russia, Prussia, Austria, and Spain against France had begun for Britain in 1793, and by 1811 most of the others had surrendered to the armies of Napoleon (Russia in 1807, Spain in 1808, Austria in 1809). The Peace of Amiens had brought nearly fourteen months of peace in 1802–3, but war had dominated the past eighteen years.

63 *the Despot's sway . . . obey*: the Despot defeating the feminized Freedom here is Napoleon Bonaparte (1769–1821), who had become First Consul of France in 1799, Consul for Life in 1802, and Emperor of France in 1804.

64 *So sing thy flatterers*: those who thought Britain impregnable in her naval superiority, allowing the island nation to avoid invasion and the threat of civil war. Barbauld's slighting reference to the country 'sporting' in wars would be especially stinging to patriotic sensibilities.

The tempest blackening in the distant West: at the end of lines replete with allusions to economic and financial disasters caused by the war, which seriously impeded international trade, ruined individuals and businesses, and threatened a collapse of the currency, Barbauld alludes to the danger that war would break out between Britain and the United States, as it did in June 1812.

the dim cold Crescent . . . Muse unpaid: the once-great Ottoman Empire was in dangerous decline during these years, although the risk to the balance of power in Europe throughout the nineteenth century was more political than cultural. Barbauld's emphasis here is on the scientific and artistic stagnation which she sees as a threat to Britain also. See Donald Quataert, *The Ottoman Empire, 1700–1922* (Cambridge: Cambridge University Press, 2000), chs. 3 and 4.

the streaming radiance pours: that is, that although the United States has taken up the torch of Britain's cultural and political achievements, the inspiration and the ideas should still be traced back to Britain.

65 *Thy Lockes, thy Paleys*: the philosopher John Locke (1632–1704), author of *An Essay Concerning Human Understanding* (1690), one of the most important and influential of all English philosophical works, and *Two Treatises of Government* (1689), which discusses the rights of individuals and the function of political authority; and the Yorkshire-born cleric and Anglican apologist William Paley (1743–1805), a Fellow of Christ's College, Cambridge, an advocate of church reform, the abolition of the slave trade, and resistance to the radicalism of Thomas Paine: his major works are *Evidences of Christianity* (1794) and *Natural Theology* (1802).

Of Hagley's woods the enamoured virgin dream: the Palladian manor of Hagley Hall, 2 miles from Stourbridge, Worcestershire, was built in 1756–60 for George Lyttleton, 1st Lord Lyttleton (1709–73). The grounds, laid out by Lyttleton, were praised by James Thomson in *Spring* (1728), ll. 901–59.

Thomson's glass . . . Nature to discern: one of the most popular and most frequently reprinted of eighteenth-century poems, *The Seasons* (1730), by the Scottish poet James Thomson (1700–48), comprised *Winter* (1726), *Summer* (1727), *Spring* (1728), and *Autumn* (1730).

loved Joanna . . . pomp shall rise: Joanna Baillie (1762–1851), referred to as writing 'storied groups' because of her declared aim to write a comedy and a tragedy on the theme of each of the passions (such as hatred, love, and fear).

Basil . . . Ethwald . . . the mystic glass: the heroes of Baillie's tragedies *Count Basil* (1798) and *Ethwald* (1802), especially the scene in *Ethwald*, IV. iii, in which Ethwald is shown a mystic image of himself as king.

66 *Gothic night . . . where Science reigns*: a reference to the overthrow of the Roman Empire by the Goths, destroying its culture and social order (hence 'night'): the empires of Europe, and particularly Britain, face a comparable extinction.

Europe sit in dust, as Asia now: the perceived decline in the ancient cultures of Asia was manifested in the loss of its great buildings. The greatest influence on Barbauld's poem, and on many other Romantic Period representations of empire and history, is *Les Ruines; ou Meditations sur les Revolutions des Empires* (1791) by Constantin François, comte de Volney, commonly known as Volney's *Ruins of Empires*.

66 *the blue mountains*: in central Pennsylvania.

Isis . . . Runnymede . . . Cam's slow waters . . . realms of mind: the Isis is the Thames at Oxford, Runnymede where King John was forced to sign the Magna Carta, designed to protect the rights of feudal landowners against infringement by the Crown, in 1215, the Cam the river which runs through Cambridge, with Oxford England's 'realms of mind' since the Middle Ages, and the only English universities before the establishment of University College London in 1828 and the University of Durham in 1832.

Newton's awful brow: the English scientist and mathematician Sir Isaac Newton (1642–1727), professor of mathematics and a Fellow of Trinity College, Cambridge, is buried in Westminster Abbey. He is best known for his law of gravitation (see *Philosophiae Naturalis Principia Mathematica*, 1687) and for his study of the nature of light (*Opticks*, 1703).

Clarkson . . . Jones: the passionate abolitionist campaigner and philanthropist Thomas Clarkson (1760–1846), friend of the Wordsworths, and in 1808 the author of *The History of the Rise, Progress and Accomplishment of the Abolition of the African Slave-Trade*; the pioneering linguist and orientalist Sir William Jones (1746–94), who founded the Asiatic Society of Bengal in 1784 and conducted influential research into Hindu and Muslim law, publishing a range of works including *The Mahomedan Law of Succession* (1782), *Al Sirajiyyah; or the Mohamedan Law of Inheritance* (1792), and *Institutes of Hindu Law, or the Ordinances of Menu* (1796).

Cowper's strains: the poet William Cowper (1731–1800), known for his devotional and autobiographical poetry, and a great influence on the 'conversational' style of Wordsworth and Coleridge: especially significant here, McCarthy and Kraft suggest (314), are his *Olney Hymns* (1779).

Roscoe . . . Ceres . . . wreath before: Barbauld added a note here: 'The Historian of the age of Leo has brought into cultivation the extensive tract of Chatmoss.' Author of the badly received *The History of the Life and Pontificate of Leo the Tenth* (1805) and a friend of Barbauld, the Dissenting Liverpool historian William Roscoe (1753–1831) was also known as an agricultural pioneer, having cultivated the poor moorland soil of his land at Chat Moss, in Lancashire, to produce crops. Ceres is the Roman goddess of crops and agriculture.

Skiddaw . . . Lodore: the mountain of Skiddaw in the English Lake District is described more fully in the note to p. 305. Lodore is a high waterfall in the Lake District.

Dun Edin . . . pale moonlight: Edinburgh, visited by Barbauld in 1794, its 'brow' being Arthur's Seat; Scott, *The Lay of the Last Minstrel* (1805), Canto II, ll. 1–2.

67 *Johnson's form . . . Howard's sainted feet*: in the nave of St Paul's Cathedral, London, stand marble statues of the poet, lexicographer, essayist, and moralist Samuel Johnson (1709–84: buried in Westminster Abbey) and the prison reformer John Howard (1726–90), the inspiration for Elizabeth Inchbald's play *Such Things Are*. John Bacon's monument to John Howard was the first monument to be erected in St Paul's, in 1795. The same sculptor created the monument to Samuel Johnson.

Chatham . . . Fox . . . Garrick spoke: William Pitt, 1st Earl of Chatham (1708–78) formerly Prime Minister and the father of Pitt the Younger; the reformist Whig leader Charles James Fox (1749–1806), who led the opposition to Pitt the Younger and championed the rights of the American colonies, Ireland, and India; for the actor David Garrick (1717–79), see note to p. 6.

Nelson . . . fulfilled his own: Barbauld annotated this reference: 'Every reader will recollect the sublime telegraphic dispatch, "England expects every man to do his duty".' Horatio Nelson (1758–1805), revered admiral of the naval campaign against Napoleon, especially at Cape St Vincent (1797) and Copenhagen (1801), was killed by a French sniper during the battle of Trafalgar, won by his fleet, after issuing this order. He was given a state funeral at St Paul's Cathedral and quickly became an icon of British heroism.

68 *Moore . . . fame absolved*: Barbauld added the note: ' "I hope England will be satisfied," were the last words of General Moore.' General Sir John Moore (1761–1809) died at the battle of Corunna after evacuating the survivors among his troops: his army had just failed to prevent Napoleon's capture of Madrid, to the disgust of the patriotic press in Britain. To describe him as 'gallant', and almost in the same breath as Nelson, was practically to guarantee outrage at this time.

Davy's lips . . . disclosed: the leading English chemist Sir Humphry Davy (1778–1829), experimenter and friend of leading radicals and prominent aristocratic sponsors, greatly extended the popularity of the science through his lectures and publications, which included *Researches, Chemical and Philosophical: Chiefly Concerning Nitrous Oxide and its Respiration* (1799); the 'mute crowds' hanging on his words are the lay audiences drawn by his famous public lectures at the new (1801) Royal Institution in London. They included many women, among them Jane Marcet.

Franklin . . . Priestley . . . proudly claim: the American statesman and scientist Benjamin Franklin, FRS (1706–90) known for his researches into electricity and actively involved in the Declaration of Independence in 1776; the Unitarian minister, scientist, linguist, and political thinker Joseph Priestley, FRS (1733–1804), who supported the principles of the French Revolution and argued for the separation of church and state. As well as his important work in isolating several gases, most famously oxygen, he discovered photosynthesis, and corresponded with Franklin on the subject of electricity. Priestley and his wife Mary Wilkinson were long-standing friends of the Barbaulds from their years at Warrington Academy, but he was not unequivocally 'claimed' by his country, having had his house in Birmingham sacked by crowds in 1791 and emigrating to the United States in 1794.

68 *Reynolds . . . Raphael*: Sir Joshua Reynolds (1723–92) was president of the Royal Academy and the leading portrait painter of his time; Raphael (1483–1520) was the most influential artist of the High Renaissance, and revolutionized portrait-painting. For Reynolds, Raphael was the key exponent of what he called the 'great style' in painting, and he features frequently in the series of lectures which Reynolds delivered at the Royal Academy from 1769 to 1790 (collected as *Discourses on Art*).

Eyptian granites and the Etruscan vase: typical treasures of the British Museum, founded upon the collections of Sir Hans Sloane in 1753 and opened to the public in 1759, but, until 1808, only for three hours a day and after approval of a written application. Especially relevant is Sir William Hamilton's collection of antique vases, acquired in 1772, and the Egyptian treasures requisitioned from the French after their defeat at Alexandria in 1801, which included the Rosetta Stone.

Alexander's ashes lay: when Barbauld wrote, a granite sarcophagus brought to the British Museum in 1802 was believed to be that of Alexander the Great.

There walks a Spirit o'er the peopled earth: probably an imagined 'spirit of civilization' (in a neutral sense: 'progress' is not always implied), although the overtones of the spirit of liberty have misled readers from the poem's first publication. The gendering of the poem's other spirits is helpful here. In ll. 8 and 9 'Freedom' is feminine, and this—male—spirit, though fertile and enriching, is also 'moody and viewless', random, 'capricious', and an enabler of tyrants.

Babel's towers . . . obelisks invade the skies: in Genesis 11: 1–9, the tower of the temple of Marduk, near the ancient city of Babylon, was built with the ambition that it should reach heaven, an ambition punished by God. A popular artistic motif, and one of particular relevance to poetry because God's punishment caused people to be unable to understand each other's language, it was a common type of over-presumption.

Tyrian purple . . . Egypt's virgins weave the linen vest: the city and seaport of Tyre in the Al Janub province of Lebanon, south of Beirut, was a major commercial centre of the Phoenicians and noted for its production of silk garments, glassware, and—the main point of Barbauld's reference here—purple dye.

69 *Ophir . . . the Nile*: Ophir was famous for the quality of its gold, and features several times in the Bible—for example in 1 Kings 9:28, 10:11—although its actual location is disputed. Here Barbauld favours the main contender, Eastern Africa.

Tadmor . . . Marius . . . Carthage weeps: Tadmor is the biblical name for the ancient Syrian city of Palmyra, incorporated into the Roman Empire in AD 17 but a major power in the third century; the Roman general and politician Gaius Marius (157–86 BC) weeps over the fall of the ancient city of Carthage in Tunisia, by tradition founded by the Phoenicians and destroyed by the Romans in the Punic Wars (146 BC), as related by Plutarch, *Lives*, ix. 577.

vale of Tempe, or Ausonian plains: vale of Tempe in Thessaly, 'Ausonian' is Virgilian for 'Italian'.

Batavia's dykes . . . Arno's purple vale: Holland was known as the Batavian Republic during Napoleon's occupation; the valley of the Arno, in Tuscany, is known for its wine-production, hence the 'purple' from grapes.

Enna's plains or Baia's viny coast: in classical myth, Enna is a valley in Sicily; Baia is a resort town in the Bay of Naples.

Venice . . . Campania's plain: in this vision of the Spirit's desertion of southern Europe for northern Europe, the grandeur of Venice declines, her 'marriage' with the Adriatic, which had been the basis of her sea-power and commerce, fails, and she falls into decay; while the plain of Campania is brooded over by Death.

Hercynian groves . . . impulse moves: the Black Forest, Germany.

70 *Odin's daughters breathe distilled perfumes*: Norse god of war, poetry, knowledge, and wisdom; the growth of northern Europe's economy brings luxury goods, Persian carpets, textiles, and perfumes, to the peoples of Scandanavia. A reference to the prosperous Gustavan period in eighteenth-century Sweden.

'build the lofty verse': Milton, *Lycidas*, l. 11, 'build the lofty rhyme'.

the 'Æolian shell . . . altered voice her own: the muse of poetry is no longer characterized by the 'liquid' and 'soft' notes of Italy, but by the more guttural tones of the Germanic nations, and speaks more of war than of love. 'Æolian' means governed by the god of winds, Æolus.

Tully's eloquence and Maro's song: the orator Cicero Marcus Tullius (see note to p. 59) and the poet Publius Vergilius Maro (see note to p. 60), commonly known as Cicero and Virgil.

Bonduca . . . shriek of war: the first-century British warrior queen Boudicca, queen of the Iceni, led an uprising against the Roman occupation, and is said to have poisoned herself when it was quashed.

the northern Bear: the North Star, part of the constellation Ursa Minor.

71 *Andes' heights . . . Chimborazo's summits treads sublime*: the major mountain system which stretches the length of the Pacific coast of South America, and the inactive volcano Chimborazo, the highest peak of the Andes in Ecuador.

La Plata . . . Potosi . . . ore: the city of La Plata in Argentina, south of Buenos Aires, and the city of Potosi in south-central Bolivia. These are all sites of European colonial despoilation of the natural and human resources of South America, commonly used in eighteenth-century poetry to symbolize the evils brought by European conquest.

71 *Thy world, Columbus, shall be free*: Barbauld means especially the lands of Spanish and Portuguese South America, some of which were beginning to sue for independence. Venezuala declared independence in the year of Barbauld's poem. The cause of the South American colonies was a favourite one for writers such as Robert Southey, and there was general approval when independence was won for many states in the 1820s. Britain and Spain had long been imperial rivals in the Americas.

76 *the evening moth, of mealy wing*: 'mealy' means soft, pale, and powdery, like meal.

Dr Darwin: the physician, poet, and scientific theorist Erasmus Darwin (1731–1802), grandfather of Charles Darwin, and promulgator of scientific ideas in poetry, often, as in *Loves of the Plants* (1789) and *Zoonomia* (1794–6), to heated controversy. He also wrote on female education (*Plan for the Conduct of Female Education in Boarding Schools*, 1797) and agricultural theory (*Phytologia*, 1800). The reference here is to his *Economy of Vegetation* (1791), i. 196.

Walcot's beautiful 'Ode to the Glow-worm': the reference is to l. 9, 'Hanging thy lamp upon the moisten'd blade', of 'Ode to the Glow-Worm' by 'Peter Pindar', the pseudonymn of John Wolcot (1738–1819), in *The Works of Peter Pindar* (1816).

Written . . . Coast of Sussex: this sonnet is not one of the original collection, but was included as an effusion of the hero, Sommers Walsingham, in Smith's *Montalbert: A Novel* (1795). Smith gives the compositional history in a note, commenting that it was 'written on the coast of Sussex during very tempestuous weather in December 1791'.

77 *'Nature's soft nurse'*: that is, sleep, as in the King's soliloquy in 2 *Henry IV*, III. i. 6.

Enshrines thy image in thy Mother's heart: this is one of several sonnets addressed to her second daughter Anna Augusta de Foville, who died a few months after a difficult childbirth in April 1795, aged 20. She had married the French émigré Alexandre Marc-Constant de Foville in August 1793. Augusta was always Smith's favourite daughter, and is said to have resembled her (though not in physical strength), being 'the only one [of Smith's children] who did not resemble Benjamin [her estranged husband] in features or colouring' (Loraine Fletcher, *Charlotte Smith: A Critical Biography* (Basingstoke: Macmillan, 1998), 8).

Mr White . . . before Midsummer: *The Natural History of Selborne* (1789) by Gilbert White (1720–93), on singing birds and the missel thrush (a variant spelling of 'mistle thrush', which is a large thrush, with a spotted breast, which feeds on mistletoe berries): see *The Natural History of Selborne*, ed. W. S. Scott (London, 1962), 89.

78 *starwort fair*: a plant with starlike flowers, usually referring to greater stichwort, *Stellaria holostea*, which has small white flowers.

79 *mast*: deriving from an Old English word, this means the fruit of the beech, oak, chestnut, and other forest trees.

   the lighter ashes . . . jetty keys: a key is the samara, or winged seed, of trees including the sycamore and, as here, the ash; jetty means black.

   willow wren and halcyon saw: a halcyon, originally from the Greek, is a kingfisher.

   shieldrake . . . teal . . . water rail . . . widgeon hide: these are all varieties of freshwater duck.

80 *Sachem's diadem*: the headdress, signifying sovereignty, of an Iroquois Indian.

81 *the stare . . . yaffil . . . aspin gray*: starling; northern dialect for the green woodpecker; and the aspen, the poplar tree *Populus*.

85 *The writer . . . the subject on which the work is founded*: Inchbald was 34 when she wrote the five-act *Such Things Are*, played at Covent Garden in 1787 and published the following year.

86 *Howard . . . sufferings of the prisoner*: Inchbald goes on to give a sketch of Howard's life, concluding: 'He fell a sacrifice to his humanity; for visiting a sick patient at Cherson, who had a malignant fever, he caught the infection, and died January the 20th, 1790.'

   Sumatra: a large island of Indonesia, off the Malay peninsula; the plot of Inchbald's play involves a tyrannical sultan who turns out to be a Christian impostor who has seized power after being disappointed in love (and who is redeemed by the rediscovery of his beloved). The play emphasizes the effects of his rule on the prisons, visited by Mr Haswell (the character modelled on the prison reformer John Howard).

87 *the year of the great eclipse*: possibly 1715, famous for the careful observation it attracted in England, some results of which were published by Halley in his *Philosophical Transactions*.

94 *the death of the late earl*: Dorriforth's relative, the young Lord Elmwood, who was engaged to marry Miss Fenton, has died soon after coming into his estate. As a result, Dorriforth gives up the priesthood in order to inherit the title and preserve the Catholic line.

96 *the serpent's skin*: meaning that she is a tempter, more like the devil in disguise than an angel; there may also be a play on the sheep skin adopted by the meek, Hebrews 11: 37.

97 *Lord Frederick Lawnly by her side*: Lord Frederick is the young, hand-some, man of fashion whom Miss Milner has appeared most to favour among her suitors. His presence is assumed to be a sting to Dorriforth: see next note.

99 *'it was very lucky you were not there'*: Dorriforth has already fought a duel with Lord Frederick in protection of his ward, withholding his fire as a

matter of conscience. It is taken to be an affront that Miss Milner should maintain any friendly informal contact with Lord Frederick.

101 *being a heretic*: Miss Milner is the daughter of a Catholic father and a Protestant mother, and, as was traditional among English Catholic families at this time, has been brought up in her mother's faith, and has attended a Protestant boarding-school before becoming the ward of her father's friend Mr Dorriforth.

105 *the advantage of a good education*: the moral declared at the end of *A Simple Story* reads: 'And Mr Milner, Matilda's grandfather, had better have given his fortune to a distant branch of his family . . . so he had bestowed upon his daughter A PROPER EDUCATION.'

106 *Thus Milton . . . the true Mahometan strain . . . the wing of contemplation*: referring to the widespread Christian misconception that Islam denied women souls, and quoting from *Paradise Lost*, iv. 297–8.

Lord Bacon . . . ignoble creature!: from the *Essays* (1606), xiv, 'Of Atheism', 89, by Francis Bacon (see note to p. 60). Wollstonecraft's references in this section are traced by Janet Todd and Marilyn Butler (eds.), *The Works of Mary Wollstonecraft*, vol. v (London: William Pickering, 1989).

107 *'To whom thus Eve . . . and her praise'*: *Paradise Lost*, iv. 634–8 (Wollstonecraft's emphasis).

'Hast thou not . . . rational delight—': *Paradise Lost*, viii. 381–92 (Wollstonecraft's emphasis).

108 *Rousseau's opinion respecting men*: for Rousseau, see note to p. 36. See his *Émile*, I. i. 76 and III. iv. 16–154.

109 *Dr Gregory*: *A Father's Legacy to his Daughters* (1774) by the Scottish professor of medicine John Gregory (1724–73).

110 *Standing armies . . . robust men*: a permanent professionalized army, a relatively new phenomenon, in contrast to armies recruited to fight in particular wars.

112 *The poet . . . 'If weak women . . . more in fault than they'*: from the comic narrative poem 'Hans Carvel' (1701) by Matthew Prior (1664–1721), ll. 11–12.

113 *China . . . made a God*: Chinese emperors were considered to be divine.

114 *You . . . in England and in America*: Wollstonecraft addresses her lover Gilbert Imlay, an American timber-merchant and land-speculator whom she had met in Paris in 1792. For the offence caused by Wollstonecraft's depiction of the women of Gothenburg, see *A Short Residence in Sweden, Norway and Denmark, and Memoirs of the Author of 'The Rights of Woman'*, ed. Richard Holmes (London: Penguin, 1987), 36–43.

115 *lead frail women astray*: a paraphrase of Prior's lines (see note to p. 112).

116 *very picturesque*: referring to a theory of landscape highly influential and widespread in the eighteenth century, and broadly characterized by principles of contrast, variety, and pleasing irregularity; addressed by William Gilpin in *Three Essays* (1792) and by Uvedale Price in *Essay on*

the Picturesque (1794, 1797–8). Here Wollstonecraft uses it to refer to the simple graces of peasant deportment.

the human face divine . . . varying lineaments: see *Paradise Lost*, iii. 44.

119 *the Federation at the Champ de Mars, and the National Assembly of France, with indifference?*: the Fête de la Fédération, an elaborate festival held on the Champ de Mars on 14 July 1790 to mark the first anniversary of the fall of the Bastille; it was subsequently held annually, a ritualistic proclamation of national unity. The National Assembly was the title adopted on 17 June 1789 by the Third Estate of the French parliament.

'Who shall decide . . . like you and me?': the opening two lines of Pope, *Epistles to Several Persons*, Epistle III, 'To Bathurst'.

120 *old gloomy Gothic fabric . . . laid in ruins*: architectural Gothic, pervasive from the mid-twelfth century in France until the sixteenth century, characterized by pointed arches, rib vaults, and flying buttresses: here associated with the medieval, Roman Catholic, and monastic. Williams's imagined contrast with the temple of Freedom is prophetic: many French churches were renamed temples in 1793, the cathedral of Notre-Dame in Paris becoming 'Temple de la Raison'.

a society of philosophers in our country . . . the nation: a reference to the acclamation of the French Revolution by the Revolution Society, led by the political pamphleteer and leading Dissenter Richard Price (1723–91), whose sermon on the anniversary of the Glorious Revolution was published as *A Discourse on the Love of Our Country* in 1789 and formed the initial focus of attack in Edmund Burke's *Reflections on the Revolution in France* (1790).

'While ev'n the peasant . . . himself as man': from Oliver Goldsmith, *The Traveller, or a Prospect of Society* (1764), ll. 333–4.

121 *cotillon is adapted to a national tune*: a dance of French origin for four or eight persons.

Jack the Giant-killer, with swords of sharpness: the hero of the old nursery-tale, one of whose magical possessions was a sword which could cut through everything (unlike the swords of the children in the streets).

the image of a friend . . . happiness: Williams refers to the hero of the story she is about to tell, Monsieur du Fossé, imprisoned because of his family's wrath at his love-match with a woman they deemed unsuitable, after the issue of one of the infamous French *lettres de cachet*.

the equinoctial gales: occuring when the centre of the sun crosses the celestial equator on about 21 March and 23 September each year.

122 *some points from the wind*: nautical terminology, meaning that the National Assembly was increasingly off course. Rumours of crimes and assassinations are not obviously justified by this stage in the Assembly's history: in late September 1790, the period of Williams's voyage, a Fayettist ministry had been formed after the resignation of the Minister of Finance, Necker, on 4 September.

124 *'and passions are the elements of life'*—: Pope, *Essay on Man*, I (1733), 170.

a young gentleman . . . the Bishop de Sens . . . 'among the faithless': the nephew of Étienne-Charles de Loménie de Brienne (1727–94), friend of the *philosophes*, appointed archbishop of Sens in January 1788, he introduced the notorious May Edicts, opposed by the nobility, and resigned in August 1788; arrested in November 1793, he died soon afterwards. The second part of the sentence adapts lines describing Abdiel in Milton's *Paradise Lost*, v. 896–7.

Madame Roland, the wife of the late minister: Jeanne Marie Roland de la Platière (1754–93), executed on 8 November, directed the political career of her husband, twice Minister of the Interior, and was a great influence upon the policies of the moderate Girondin group of bourgeois revolutionaries. The daughter of a Parisian engraver, she married in 1780, and her salon became the meeting-place of revolutionaries and intellectuals. She was arrested and imprisoned on the outbreak of the Jacobin-inspired insurrection on 31 May 1793 which led to the expulsion of leading Girondins from the Convention on 2 June. Her opponents spread rumours about her sexual profligacy, and correspondence which came to light in the mid-nineteenth century suggests a romantic involvement with the Girondin François Nicolas Léonard Buzot, beginning in the autumn of 1792. Buzot committed suicide in 1794. See Ida A Taylor, *A Life of Madame Roland* (London, 1911), Una Pope-Hennessy, *Madame Roland: A Study in Revolution* (London, 1917), Charles A. Le Guin, *Roland de la Platière: A Public Servant in the Eighteenth Century*, Transactions of the American Philosophical Society, NS 56, part 6 (Philadelphia: American Philosophical Society, 1966).

125 *the prison of St Pelagie*: Madame Roland was first imprisoned in the Abbaye, Paris, a recognized political prison, but was moved to the prison of Sainte-Pélagie, 'among prostitutes and assassins', according to her biographer Madeleine Clemenceau-Jacquemaire, *The Life of Madame Roland*, trans. Laurence Vail (London: Longmans, Green and Co., 1930), 284. During the five months of her imprisonment Madame Roland wrote her memoirs, *Appel à l'impartiale posteritie*, published in translation in Britain by Joseph Johnson in 1795.

reading Plutarch: the Greek historian, biographer, and moral philosopher (*c.*46–120), best known for his series of biographies, *Parallel Lives*, in which the stories of Greek statesmen and soliders are paired with the stories of comparable Romans. Plutarch concentrated on the personalities of each figure rather than on the political context: Madame Roland is therefore seen seeking out the human circumstances behind great public events.

the murder of the Gironde . . . the Conciergerie . . . to perish: the group of deputies to the National Convention known as the Girondins were increasingly critical of the emergency powers and centralizing policies introduced by the Montagnards, and many of them were purged from the

Convention after the *journée* (a day of action of great political significance) of 2 June 1793, which was followed by the imprisonment and execution of many. Roland de la Platière and Madame Roland were central to the Girondin group.

the night on which I was myself arrested: along with her mother and sister, Williams was arrested and sent to the Luxembourg prison in Paris in October 1793, later being transferred to a British convent and in November placed under house arrest.

126 *her figure would have softened . . . her judges*: possibly hinting at an unexplored aspect of the Roland story. Madame Roland's fellow prisoner Honoré Riouffe commented on her appearance that day: 'On the day of her condemnation she was clad in white, her black dishevelled hair falling to her girdle. She would have softened the most ferocious hearts' (trans. Laurence Vail in Clemenceau-Jacquemaire, *Life*, 318). Williams's description, however, seems to hint at pregnancy, for which appeals to a woman's 'figure' were recognized code. No biographical information on Roland at the time of her imprisonment and execution suggests that she might have been pregnant, but neither have I found any biographical account which draws on Williams's testimony.

127 *put an end to his existence*: Jean-Marie Roland de la Platière (1734–93) had been Minster of the Interior 1792–3, escaped proscription in June 1793 by fleeing from Paris just before his wife's arrest, and committed suicide on 15 November after hearing the news of her execution.

this child . . . those who gave her birth: after her mother's final letter to her, written on 8 October, Marie-Thérèse-Eudora Roland (1781–1858), later Madame Champagneux, was taken into the protection of one of her mother's oldest friends, the botanist Louis Bosc d'Antic. In his grief Bosc fell unrequitedly in love with her, and took up an appointment as consul to the United States, soon after which, at 15, Eudora married. She publicly disavowed the depiction of her parents in Lamartine's *Girondins* (see Le Guin, *Roland de la Platière*, 123), and after the death of her own daughter in 1832 lived in virtual seclusion.

130 *vera incessu patuit Dea*: she showed herself a true goddess by her gait (Virgil, *Aeneid*, i. 405).

Armida accoutred in Clarinda's armour: in Tasso's *Gerusalem Liberata* (1581), Armida is a beautiful sorceress with whom Rinaldo falls in love; on his escape she follows him, sets fire to her palace, and is killed in combat. The reference here relies on her difference from Clarinda, an Amazon or warrior-woman in the same epic.

132 *polemics . . . can give in to*: the practice of controversial discussion, especially in theology.

133 *the gauntlope of a public school*: 'gauntlope' is a variant form of 'gauntelote', a gauntlet; a public school means a school to which rich fee-paying parents would send their sons.

133 *his weapons for the 'wordy war'*: a common phrase, translated by Pope
from Homer in *Odyssey*, Book 1, found in Horace, and found in a range
of contemporary poets from Burns to Crabbe.

the ipse dixit of his instructors: a dogmatic statement or assertion (literally,
'he himself said it').

134 *Portia ... Cornelia ... our justification*: the resouceful and intelligent
heroine of Shakespeare's *The Merchant of Venice*, Portia, disguises herself as the advocate Balthazar in order to confound in court Shylock's
demand for a pound of Antonio's flesh; Cornelia, daughter of the Roman
general Scipio Africanus Major, was noted for her virtue and abilities,
and is reported to have replied to a Roman matron's request to see her
jewels by bringing before her her two sons.

to fight pro aris et focis: to fight for hearth and home (literally, for altars in
private houses, symbolizing the sanctity of home, and firesides or
hearths).

entering the lists with them: a term used in accounts of medieval jousting,
referring to the palisades enclosing a tilting-ground.

135 *The Comforter*: an obsolete term for a small spaniel. There are references
in Holinshed's *Chronicles* to 'The spaniell gentle, or comforter' (i. 387),
but by the 'modern naturalist' Hawkins may mean Ralph Beilby, whose
General History of Quadrupeds was illustrated by Thomas Bewick (Newcastle upon Tyne, 1790), and which refers (p. 364), to 'The comforter . . .
generally kept by the ladies as an attendant of the toilette or the drawing-
room.'

the dear Chloe, or the charming Bijou: both given as fashionable, if affected,
names for lapdogs in Susan Ferrier's novel *Marriage* (1818), for example.

139 *Deal . . . open for the sea*: near Dover, the coastal town of Deal in Kent was
reputed to have been the site of Julius Caesar's landing in Britain in 55
BC.

140 *cabinet pictures . . . only from a distance*: pictures suitable for a small room
or private apartment; sometimes 'cabinet' denoted a room devoted to the
display of works of art, not on a grand public scale but tastefully set.

Hardwick . . . the unfortunate Mary: the Elizabethan mansion of Hardwick Hall, built in the 1590s for Elizabeth, Countess of Shrewsbury, lies a
few miles north-west of Mansfield in Nottinghamshire. Contrary to Radcliffe's vivid account, it was never one of the prisons of Mary Stuart. In
Memoirs of the Family of Cavendish in 1708 Bishop Kennet had asserted
that Mary's chamber and rooms of state were preserved as she had used
them at Hardwick, and this became an article of faith for eighteenth-
century Marians. George Talbot, Earl of Shrewsbury, and his second
wife Elizabeth were Mary's keepers from early 1569, seven months after
her escape to England, to 1584, three years before her execution at Foth-
eringhay. Over the years of their custodianship she was moved forty-six
times between several of their estates in the midlands, especially Tutbury

Castle, Wingfield Manor, Chatsworth, and Sheffield. When Hardwick Hall opened to visitors, it became one of the sites most often visited for its associations with Mary Stuart. The poet Thomas Gray wrote in December 1762 that it contained 'the very canopies, chair of state, footstool, lit-de-repos, oratory, carpets, & hangings, just as she left them . . . all preserv'd with religious care' (Jayne Elizabeth Lewis, *Mary Queen of Scots: Romance and Nation* (London and New York: Routledge, 1998), 111). Horace Walpole was convinced that the bedroom was Mary's when he visited Hardwick in 1760. What seems to have happened is that Mary's actual apartments at Chatsworth were left unchanged until the remodelling of that house in the late seventeenth century; as the new Hardwick Hall was constructed, items were moved across, and the second-floor rooms of Hardwick grew into a themed but cumulative reconstruction. For details of her actual places of captivity during this period, see Elizabeth Eisenberg, *The Captive Queen in Derbyshire* (Derby: J. H. Hall, 1984).

Elizabeth, Countess of Shrewsbury . . . the present edifice: the formidable and often-married 'Bess of Hardwick'—Elizabeth Hardwick Talbot, Countess of Shrewsbury (1520–1608)—was left a very rich widow after the death of her estranged husband in 1590, and set about building a new mansion at Hardwick. See David N. Durant, *Bess of Hardwick: Portrait of an Elizabethan Dynast* (1977; rev. edn. London and Chester Springs: Peter Owen, 1999).

Harewood . . . that veil Elfrida: Ælfthryth (*c*.945–1000), second wife of King Eadgar and mother of Æthelred the Unready, her story was known through the mainly fabulous account of life given by the historian William of Malmesbury. The story was popular on the stage during Radcliffe's youth, with performances of William Mason's dramatic poem *Elfrida*, the female lead played to great acclaim by Elizabeth Hartley (mentioned by Robinson: see note to p. 173). Radcliffe is clearly thinking of romanticized versions of the story, such as Mason's, rather than any verifiable historical basis for Elfrida's fate. The ruins of Harewood Castle lie in the Capability Brown-designed grounds of Harewood House (1759–72), Wharfedale, Yorkshire.

141 *The scene of Mary's arrival . . . my Lord Keeper . . . surrounding attendants*: for Mary's keeper, see notes to p. 140. When the Shrewsburys' marriage broke down in 1584, after years of strife, the Earl was rumoured to have had an affair with Mary Stuart.

worked by herself: Hardwick Hall has a scarce-rivalled collection of sixteenth- and seventeenth-century embroideries, all made for, and usually by, the same household. Only two panels are positively identified as Mary's, but these were probably only added to the collection late in the nineteenth century, and would not have been among the ones Radcliffe saw. Embroidery was a major part of the captive queen's life, as she is reported to have testified in a letter written by Nicholas White to Sir

William Cecil in 1569: 'She said that all the day she wrought with the needle, and that the diversity of the colours made the work seem less tedious, and continued so long at it till very pain did make her to give it over; and with that laid her hand upon her left side and complained of an old grief newly increased there' (J. D. Leader, *Mary Queen of Scots in Captivity* (Sheffield, 1880), 42). Of the contents of Mary's supposed chambers at Hardwick, Mark Girouard comments: 'The famous embroidered hangings of heroines of antiquity . . . now framed in the Hall and on the Chapel landing, were shown to eighteenth-century visitors as the work of Mary; this they certainly were not, but they were equally certainly made for Chatsworth in and around 1575. Other embroideries at Hardwick carrying dates in the 1570s, and probably many of the undated ones, must originally have been at Chatsworth. So must many of the portraits, including the full-length one of Mary herself and much of the furniture; the inventory of Chatsworth made in 1601 shows that it was relatively unfurnished, and it must have been partially stripped to furnish Hardwick. More Elizabethan fittings came later, such as the overmantel in the Withdrawing Chamber, and, possibly, Mary's own coat of arms, the Marriage of Tobias chimneypiece in the Blue Room, and the intarsia panels on the Chapel staircase. So if Mary were to visit Hardwick today she would find much that would be familiar to her' (*Hardwick Hall* (London: National Trust, 1989), 41).

141 *1584 . . . 1587*: Elizabeth I (1533–1603) ordered or endorsed many executions, including that of her closest male relative Thomas Howard, Duke of Norfolk, beheaded for his part in plots involving Mary in June 1572. Radcliffe's teacher Sophia Lee had based her novel *The Recess* (1783–5) on the supposition that Mary had married Norfolk and with him had twin daughters, the heroines of the tale.

142 *many portraits . . . beautiful chin*: the Long Gallery in Hardwick Hall contains a large collection of royal and family portraits; on the same floor, at the back of the Hall, is the room known as 'Queen Mary's Bedchamber'. The portraits referred to in this paragraph depict the scholar and statesman Sir Thomas More (1478–1535), friend of Henry VIII but executed for his opposition to the Act of Supremacy (the portrait is a copy of a lost Holbein depicting More and his family); Lady Jane Grey (1537–54), named as his successor by Edward VI, Queen of England for nine days in July 1553 and executed by Edward's half-sister Mary 1; and Edward's other half-sister Elizabeth I (see previous note), the portrait mentioned here being possibly by Nicholas Hilliard and his apprentice Rowland Lockey. The dignified full-length painting of Mary referred to here is still at Hardwick Hall, and has been attributed to Rowland Lockey: it is one of several painted not at the end of her life but posthumously, and known as the 'Sheffield' portraits because they were thought to derive from her years there.

Middleton: the former silk and cotton town about 6 miles from Manchester; and, like Manchester, in 1816 one of the birthplaces of Trade Unionism.

church . . . the Duke of Devonshire: the church at Middleton has a striking tower, a sixteenth-century rood screen, and a stained-glass window commemorating the battle of Flodden Field (1513).

143 *Manchester . . . science, letters and taste*: the growth of Manchester into the leading financial, business, and cultural centre of the north-west of England began in the mid-eighteenth century and was due to its pre-eminence in cotton manufacturing. The first Manchester cotton-mill was built in 1781, and Arkwright's mill, which was to be the first to use steam power, in 1783; the extensive system of waterways which was crucial to its success had already begun, with the first section of the Duke of Bridgewater's canal open in 1761. Architecturally, not much remains of eighteenth-century Manchester, most of the great civic buildings dating from the Victorian period, but the urban blight which was to make the city a symbol of the social problems brought by industrialization was only beginning to look possible at the time of Radcliffe's description. Cultur-ally, the city was thriving, leading to the establishment of the Portico Library as a social and literary institution in 1806 and the City Art Gallery, built for the Royal Manchester Institution in 1825–9; though it was not represented in parliament until 1832.

a neighbouring place . . . the Slave Trade: from 1648 Liverpool was a major port serving transatlantic trade, throughout the eighteenth century trad-ing in sugar, tobacco, cotton, and rum, but more notoriously in slaves. Overtaking Bristol, by the middle of the century it conducted more trade in slaves than any other port in Europe and in 1800 accounted for about three-quarters of the whole British slave trade.

144 *a scene of dreadful contention*: referring to a banquet attended by Emily in *The Mysteries of Udolpho*, vol. ii, ch. 10, in which her aunt's husband Montoni, suspecting his guests of an attempt to poison him, confines them in the castle and then accuses his wife of hatching the plot, for which he imprisons her in the east turret. The phrase is also echoed in 'the scenes of terrible contention' between Montoni and his wife in vol. ii, ch. 9.

145 *a former conversation of Annette . . . unpleasant emotions*: on their first night at Udolpho, Annette, a specialist in tales of haunted chambers, tells Emily what Montoni's servants believe about the ghost of the mysterious Signora Laurentini, adding: 'They say, too, there is an old chapel adjoin-ing the west side of the castle, where, any time at midnight, you may hear such groans!—it makes one shudder to think of them!—and strange sights have been seen there—' (vol. ii, ch. 5).

149 *a recollection . . . apartment of the castle*: a reminder of the most icono-graphic of the mysteries of Udolpho, an object of display, first assumed to be a portrait, hidden behind a black veil: early in her stay at the castle, Emily has looked behind the veil, and fainted in horror.

150 *Montoni and Cavigni*: the moody and handsome Montoni, owner of the Castle of Udolpho, is an Italian relation of Emily's maternal aunt and has married her paternal aunt Madame Cheron; aged about 40, he has a younger friend, Cavigni, more sociable and insinuating in manner but also dangerous.

155 *I am hungry . . . seize all the meat*: the bad harvests of 1794–5 led to acute food shortages, especially shortages of the staple cereals and bread, on which the diet of the poor largely depended; because of the war with France overseas supplies had been disrupted, and the government acted too slowly to avoid widespread shortages and famine. Price inflation and a harsh winter further exacerbated the problem, and rioting, against which More's poem warns, was commonplace.

156 *says the wise man*: 'Better is a dinner of herbs where love is, than a stalled ox and hatred therewith' (Proverbs 15 : 17)

157 *For a mittimus hangs o'er each rioter's head*: a legal term, 'mittimus' is a warrant issued under the hand and seal of a Justice of the Peace or other officer of the law, directing the keeper of a prison to take into custody and hold the person specified in the warrant. By the Riot Act of 1715, an assembly of twelve or more persons had to disperse within an hour if ordered to do so by a magistrate; if they resisted, and were dispersed by force, the authorities or troops involved were indemnified against the consequences. Preventative legislation was increased in 1795 with the Seditious Meetings and Assemblies Act; and the Habeas Corpus Act, which restricted the detention of individuals without charge, was suspended from 1794 to 1801.

if I rise, I'm a Turk: a Muslim, used here as in the phrase 'to turn Turk', meaning to become renegade.

many members of both Houses . . . the trade itself: calls for an end to the highly lucrative and economically ingrained trade in African slaves began in Britain in the 1780s, with the formation of a committee in London made up mainly of Quakers, and spread until abolitionism was a national cause, promoted by key figures such as Thomas Clarkson and William Wilberforce (1759–1833). It attracted notably large numbers of women, for whom this was an acceptably humanitarian political cause, in tune with the vogue for sentimentalism. Parliamentary debate, led by Wilberforce, continued throughout the 1790s, although the trade was not abolished until 1806–7. Slavery itself was not abolished in the British Empire until the legislation of 1834 and 1838.

158 *the two notorious grounds of inhumanity and impolicy*: common touchstones of the moral and economic debate about the slave trade.

first of the first, as our good old divines say: not a precise biblical allusion, but redolent of Old Testament genealogies.

159 *their nightly labours*: their attendance at balls, routs, receptions, and the theatre.

so little clothing . . . the humane beholder: in contrast to the elaborate costuming in vogue when Burney's Evelina goes to London, the clothing of the fashionable woman attending a ball or evening party in the early 1800s was flimsy and revealing. The first chapter of Walter Scott's *Waverley* (1814), refers to 'the primitive nakedness of a modern fashionable at a route'.

at other tables . . . to be at liberty: a reference to the addictions of card-playing and gambling, often seen as the most prevalent and socially destructive vices of the eighteenth century. Fashionable women's involvement in private gambling parties (as opposed to those held in gentlemen's clubs) was indisputable—the Duchess of Devonshire (see note to p. 173) being the most prominent high-society female gambler—and, as was the case with many other anti-domestic influences, the moral danger posed to women was a keynote of the campaigns against it. Gambling had also become thoroughly politicized through Edmund Burke's metaphors of gambling for French revolutionary finance, in *Reflections*. To this may be added the hint of danger to a young woman's morality, as in Pope's *Rape of the Lock*.

160 *the law-maker is the law-breaker*: the traditional saying 'Law makers should not be law breakers' is recorded in the *Oxford Dictionary of English Proverbs*, revd. F. P. Wilson (Oxford: Clarendon, 1970).

they come out: meaning to come into public society, to become fully adult in the eyes of society.

161 *has increased, is increasing, and ought to be diminished*: echoing the terms of the lawyer and MP John Dunning (1731–83), whose Commons motion deploring the increasing influence of the Crown was carried on 6 April 1780.

162 *the black factor to allow the African slaves a ton to a man*: the calculations for human cargo in the slave trade rightly aroused compassion, a width of 13 inches being allowed for a woman and 15 inches for a man: the destined slaves were chained except for brief daily exercise, and illness and death were commonplace.

166 *Genius, in a garret, starving!*: the icon of this tradition was Robinson's fellow Bristolian, the poet Thomas Chatterton (1752–70), who had achieved success in his home city but died in poverty in London, of arsenic poisoning.

167 *Commerce drooping, Credit failing!*: for the economic crises of the year 1795, see note to p. 155.

Placemen, mocking subjects loyal: a deprecatory term for one who holds an appointment in the service of sovereign or state because of private interest rather than ability or suitability for the post.

Separations; Weddings Royal!: 1795 was the year in which George Augustus Frederick, Prince of Wales, from 1811 Prince Regent and from 1820 George IV (1762–1830), married Caroline of Brunswick, disastrously for both: see notes to Mary Hays's biographical account of Caroline, pp. 402–6. Robinson's conjunction hints at rumours about the Prince's relationship with Mrs Fitzherbert (see note to p. 402), from whom he had separated in June 1794. In a bad couple of years for royal relationships, there had also been the recent scandal of the marriage of the Prince's younger brother Augustus Frederick to Lady Augusta Murray in 1793; deemed unsuitable, it was annulled at the insistence of George III in 1794, after the birth of a son.

168 *Sappho Discovers her Passion*: the love of the Greek poet of Lesbos, Sappho (fl. *c*.610–*c*.580 BC), for the young boatman Phaon is described by Ovid in the *Heroides*, but may be entirely mythical.

my chilled breast . . . rise?: as Judith Pascoe points out, this is a recollection of Pope, *Sappho to Phaon*, l. 126 ('Grief chilled my breast, and stopped my freezing blood').

170 *To the Aeolian Harp*: a stringed instrument over which the breeze plays, creating random musical sounds, named after Aeolus, the Greek god of winds. The poem dates from the same year as Coleridge's 'The Aeolian Harp', the best known of Romantic usages of the aeolian harp as an image of (possibly passive, though god-given) creativity.

the lorn Philomel . . . parting rays!: 'his' because only male nightingales sing; in Greek legend the gods turn Philomela into a nightingale after she has been raped by her brother-in-law Tereus, King of Thrace, who cuts out her tongue to prevent her telling of his crime.

the sunny people move: insects in the sun.

wound the breast of love: a reference to the thorn in Philomel's breast.

o'er frozen Scythia reigns: the ancient Greek name for the region around the Black Sea coast of Russia and the Caucasus mountains.

a daemon in a form divine!: in ancient Greek mythology a daemon was a spirt, a genius; the term was taking on the connotations of evil which dominate its modern usage. 'The human form divine' is from Milton, *Paradise Lost*, iii. 44.

171 *my dying parents saw it shine*: Robinson adds a note here: '"Sex mihi natales ierant, cum lecta parentis | Ante diem lacrymas ossa bibere meas. | Arsit inops frater, victus meretricis amore; | Mistaque cum turpi damna podore tulit." Ovid.' From *Heroides*, xv. 61–2: 'Scarce was I in my sixth year, when the ashes of a deceased parent drank my tears. My brother next, despising wealth and honour, burnt with an ignoble flame, and obstinately plunged himself into shameful distresses': Sappho's brother Charaxos was seduced by a courtesan, Rhodope, and squandered all his money on her.

maternal griefs were mine!: Sappho had one daughter, Cleïs, although it is not clear from her poems what 'maternal griefs' Robinson might mean here. In *Sappho of Lesbos: A Psychological Reconstruction of her Life* (London: Rich and Cowan, 1938), Margaret Goldsmith creates a character for Cleïs, making her the dupe of Rhodope (see previous note), a rival for the affections of Sappho's beloved young female scholar, Atthis, and intellectually a disappointment to her learned mother (207–9, 253).

172 *the Leucadian Rock Before She Perishes*: Robinson's note reads: 'Leucata was a promontory of Epirus, on the top of which stood a temple dedicated to Apollo. From this promontory despairing lovers threw themselves into the sea, with an idea that, if they survived, they should be cured of their hopeless passions. The Abbé Barthelemi says, that, "many escaped, but others having perished, the custom fell into disrepute; and at length was wholly abolished."—*Vide Travels of Anacharsis the Younger*.' Leucadia is one of the Ionian islands off the west coast of Greece.

the cool concave owns her tempered rays!: 'concave' refers to the sky, while 'tempered' means diminished.

the waves Lethean roll: in classical myth, Lethe is the river of forgetfulness over which the dead must cross on their way to Hades, the underworld.

173 *Miss Farren and the late Mr Henderson*: Elizabeth Farren (1759–1829) started acting as a child, and made her adult debut at the Haymarket in 1777. She specialized in the portrayal of fine ladies, and, after leaving the stage in 1797, married the recently widowed Earl of Derby. When Robinson wrote these memoirs, therefore, she was a particularly respectable actor to mention, and someone whose beauty and more fortunate later career gives point to the tale of the Prince of Wales's pursuit of Robinson. There is a portrait of Elizabeth Farren as Hermione, the part Robinson describes here, by Johann Zoffany, *c.*1780, National Gallery of Victoria, Melbourne. John Henderson (1747–85) was a protégé of Garrick, first appeared on the stage in 1772, and in 1777 achieved great success as Shylock at the Haymarket. During the relatively brief period at which he was near the top of his profession, he became particularly associated with the role of Falstaff.

Palmira ... the Zaphna of Mr J. Bannister: characters in the tragedy *Mahomet the Imposter*, adapted by J. Miller and J. Hoadly from the French of Voltaire. John Bannister (1760–1836) first appeared on the stage in 1778. Overshadowed by John Henderson (see previous note) in tragedy, he specialized in comic roles, and became one of the managers of Drury Lane.

Duchess of Devonshire ... friendship: Georgiana Cavendish, Duchess of Devonshire (1757–1806), was the eldest daughter of John, 1st Earl Spencer, and made the most glittering aristocratic match of her generation in 1774. The leading figure in London society, she was known for her intellectual ability, wrote poetry herself, and dabbled in politics, especially as a supporter of Fox in 1784. A conspicuously impressive friend for Robinson to mention, she too was to have the experience of being pursued by the Prince of Wales, but not Robinson's experience of disgrace.

The Winter's Tale ... their Majesties: George III (1738–1820), who succeeded his grandfather in 1760, and his queen since 1761, Charlotte Sophia, princess of Mecklenburg-Strelitz.

Perdita ... Hermione ... Mrs Hartley: Perdita is the daughter of

Hermione and Leontes in *The Winter's Tale*. Elizabeth Hartley (1751–1824), née White (and possibly not actually married), played at Covent Garden from 1772, and became a favourite model of Sir Joshua Reynolds.

173 *the green-room . . . Mr Smith*: the green-room is a room in a theatre provided for the accommodation of the actors when they are not required on stage. The elegant William Smith (1730–1819), nicknamed 'Gentleman Smith', first appeared at Covent Garden in 1753, to which he returned in 1788 after many years performing at Drury Lane. In this production he played Leontes, the jealous husband of Hermione.

Lord Viscount Malden, now Earl of Essex: George Capel Coningsby, Viscount Malden (1757–1839), from 1799 5th Earl of Essex. His second wife was the singer Catherine Stephens: again, Robinson seems especially interested in impeccably aristocratic figures who take a serious matrimonial or artistic interest in female performers. She would also have been taking special care over her description of the man widely believed to have replaced the Prince of Wales as her lover. Robinson is still described in biographies of the Prince of Wales in terms which make her care understandable: see, for example, Saul David, *Prince of Pleasure: The Prince of Wales and the Making of the Regency* (1998; London: Abacus, 1999), 22 and 23, where she is described as 'already a skilled courtesan' at the time of the Prince's pursuit, and as 'eccentric'.

Colonel . . . Lake . . . Mr Legge . . . Lord Lewisham: Gerard Lake (1744–1808), first equerry and one of the most respected members of the Prince's household, was at this stage a lieutenant-colonel, and beginning a brilliant miltiary career; he later became commander-in-chief of the forces in India, and the 1st Viscount Lake of Delhi and Leswarree. The statesman George Legge, later 3rd Earl of Dartsmouth (1755–1810) took the courtesy title of Lord Lewisham to serve as MP for Stafford; from 1782 he was lord of the bedchamber to the Prince of Wales.

174 *my chair*: a Sedan chair, a closed vehicle seating one person, borne on two poles by two bearers. Sedan chairs were often hired on the spot after gatherings like these, so Robinson is again subtly underlining her social status.

signed FLORIZEL: the successful lover of the exiled and unknown Perdita in *The Winter's Tale*. The nickname is still commonly used in accounts of the amorous adventures of the Prince of Wales.

175 *the late Mr Meyer*: Jeremiah Meyer (1735–89), was a highly regarded miniature-painter and enamel-portraitist, appointed as one of the court artists of George III in 1764. Born in Germany, he took British nationality in 1762. He painted a miniature of the Prince for Robinson, which she later displayed to Marie Antoinette during her visit to Paris.

Je ne change qu'en mourant: I will be unchanging until death (literally, moribund).

176 *his Royal Highness still resided in Buckingham House*: see note on Buckingham House, p. 7 above. The Prince of Wales did not set up his own establishment at Carlton House, on the south side of Pall Mall near St James's Palace, until 1781.

the Irish Widow: the character of Widow Brady, written for the leading actor Anne Barry, in the two-act farce *The Irish Widow* (1772) by David Garrick. Something of a showpiece for Barry, it required verve and versatility, and included 'breeches' scenes for which Robinson was well known.

177 *a female who lodged in Maiden Lane*: Maiden Lane, WC2, lying between Covent Garden and the Strand, was at this time a cul-de-sac. It would have been associated with tradespeople of modest social standing, with one of whom Mr Robinson's mistress lodges, and a convenient location for someone who worked at or for the theatre; but it was not necessarily a low address. We know it had a barber's shop at number 21, for the artist J. M. W. Turner, a barber's son, was born in the rooms above it in 1775, and would have been growing up there at the time Robinson describes.

180 *that republic Addison display'd*: Joseph Addison (1672–1719), with reference here to views he expressed in *The Free-Holder, or Political Essays* (1715–16).

181 *a larum to my heart*: a call to arms, a battle-cry, and by extension any sound which warns of danger.

the corpuscular philosophy: the theory promulgated by the Irish physicist and chemist Robert Boyle (1627–91), which sought to account for all natural phenomena by the position and motion of corpuscles, or invisible particles.

182 *the bard | On Cambria's height I struck the lyre*: Wales, or 'Cambria', was increasingly known for its bardic tradition in the eighteenth century, an upsurge of interest in Welsh poetry and language inspiring Thomas Gray's Pindaric ode *The Bard* (1757), which fixed the romantic image. When Yearsley was writing the creation of a national history and culture was being promoted by the forger Iolo Morganwg, and was to continue for the first third of the nineteenth century.

186 *O Mā ā ndā ā a . . . thirsted after knowledge*: the name of the Rajah's confidant echoes the name of one of the mountains in northern India, Mount Mandara (Mandara Parvata). Frequently mentioned in ancient books, prayers, liturgies, and civil and religious ceremonies, this mountain is associated with Hindu narratives of the origins of the seven ancestors of the Brahmins.

187 *the Persian writers . . . conquerors of the world*: a brief note by Hamilton refers readers at this point to 'Richardson's Introduction to the Persian Dictionary'; that is, *A Dictionary, Persian, Arabic and English. To which is prefixed A Dissertation on the Languages, Literature and Manners of the Eastern Nations*, 2 vols. (Oxford: Clarendon Press, 1777) by John

Richardson (1741–1811?): it was based on the *Thesaurus* of F. à Mesgniea Meninski.

187 *performed Poojah to the Goddess of Liberty*: that is, puja, or sacrifice, one of the Hindu rites most frequently performed in all ceremonies, public and private.

the favoured race of Brahma . . . the Mussulmans: one of the highest deities of Hindu belief, Brahma, rides on a swan, and his emblem is the water-lily; he has taken as his wife his daughter, Sarasvati, and in punishment has no temple, worship, or sacrifice. He is the author and creator of all things, the dispenser of gifts and favours, and the disposer of destiny.

188 *See Halhed's Gentoo Laws*: Vivādārnavesetu's *A Code of Gentoo Laws, or Ordinations of the Pundits*, trans. and ed. Nathaniel Brassey Halhed (1776, new edition 1781). A leading orientalist scholar, Halhed also published a translation of the mystical *Upanishads* in 1787 and a grammar of Bengali in 1778. See Rosanne Rocher, *Orientalism, Poetry, and the Millenium: The Checkered Life of N. B. Halhed, 1751–1830* (Delhi: Motilal Banarsidass, 1983). Halhed was a follower of the prophet Richard Brothers, and while MP for Lymington in Hampshire moved that the House of Commons hear a reading of Brothers's prophecies, a reportedly impassioned proposal that failed to find a seconder. In 1802 Joanna Southcott was sending him copies of her books, and he was invited to be present at one of the trials of her writings. He met Southcott in 1804 and became one of her converts.

the shores of Hindostan!: literally the land of the Hindus, loosely the whole of the Indian subcontinent but more specifically India north of the Deccan plateau.

the profligate court of Delhi: traditionally the capital of Muslim India during the Tughluq Dynasty (1321–1421), and from the Rajah's point of view the greatest threat to Hindu tradition. 'In manners the Delhi Court became the Versailles of India', comments Percival Spear in 'The Mughals and the British', in A. L. Basham (ed.), *A Cultural History of India* (Oxford: Clarendon Press, 1975), 354.

189 *that tribunal, from whose decision there lies no appeal*: the English House of Lords, which was doubled in size during the premiership of Pitt the Younger. This created a far more powerful unelected group, many members of which owed their rank to personal favour, and were far from independent in the way they carried out their constitutional or legal roles.

All laws . . . in the name of the whole: a highly ironic account of the British parliamentary system in 1796. An antiquated electoral system, dating back to the Restoration of 1660, was becoming increasingly anomalous in the context of the rapid expansion of industrial towns and cities. Manchester, for example, returned no MP. In the counties, freeholders of land worth forty shillings a year (that is, most landowners and non-tenant farmers) could vote: counties returned the same number of MPs whatever their population, so that Rutland, with 600 inhabitants, was on a par with Yorkshire, with 16,000. In the boroughs, there was no such uniformity in the franchise, and in effect the MPs for many boroughs were under the control of the major landowner. The franchise was widest in the 'scot and lot' and 'potwalloper' boroughs; in the more common 'freeman' boroughs the range of freemen varied considerably; boroughs in which the franchise depended upon the holding of land by burgage tenure were open to corruption by the sale of this tenure; while in other boroughs only a specified corporation of individuals was eligible to vote. Some boroughs were under the control of the Treasury or the Admiralty. Most notorious of all were the 'rotten' boroughs such as Old Sarum, which had no inhabitants at all. Even in general elections, seats would only rarely be contested. As pressure to reform the system grew, leading eventually to the first Reform Act of 1832, elections were contested more and more.

the third estate: the British House of Commons.

190 *the Governor General*: originally there were three co-equal presidencies in British India (Calcutta, Madras, Bombay), but by the Regulating Act of 1773 a central Governor-General and Council were created in Calcutta, with control over the other two presidencies. After the impeachment of Warren Hastings, the East India Act of 1784 moved the Governor-Generalship to Bengal and revised the structure of administration; this system stayed in place until the Indian Mutiny of 1858.

a notch: according to *OED2*, this instance in Hamilton's novel is the only recorded use of the obsolete variant of 'Nautch', an Indian exhibition of dancing, performed by professional dancing girls.

either were, or, had been Dancers: professional dancing girls, not noblewomen. In Hindu tradition, groups of eight, twelve, or more dancing girls or *devadasis* were attached to every temple, first reserved for the use of the Brahmins but subsequently recognized as prostitutes. The Rajah's confusion is clarified by a comment by the Abbé J. A. Dubois in his *Hindu Manners, Customs, and Ceremonies*, trans. Henry K. Beauchamp, 3rd edn. (Oxford: Clarendon Press, 1906), 586: 'The courtesans are the only women in India who enjoy the privilege of learning to read, to dance, and to sing. A well-bred and respectable woman would for this reason blush to acquire any one of these accomplishments.'

191 *the Omrahs . . . royal Musmud . . . than have submitted!*: an omrah is a high-ranking Mughal official; Sultan Mahmud (1436–69) was the first Khalji ruler of Malwa.

a group of Bibbys: this variant form is not recorded in *OED2*, a reminder of Hamilton's marginal status. It is a variant of 'Bibi' or 'Beebee', the chief's wife or the mistress of a household in India.

192 *green horses of Surraya . . . the sacred stream*: the sun-god Surya; the rivers of the Ganges, the Jumna, the Sarsvati, the Indus, and others, are held sacred; to drink or bathe is to be sanctified.

194 *Nature is an oeconomist*: an oeconomist is one who manages a household, including managing the household expenses; 'political economy', which has come to take over the primary meaning of the term 'economy', was used to refer to the art or practical science of managing the resources of the nation, especially the production and distribution of wealth. In its turn, the original meaning of 'economy' came to be seen as a subcategory of political economy, as in the term 'home economics'.

195 *the pith or medullary substance*: the pith is the central column of cellular tissue in the stems and branches of plants; the medulla, usually in biology the marrow of bones, refers in botanical contexts to the pith.

sun-flower . . . perspire nineteen times . . . hours: the annual herb *Helianthus annuus* is a native of the western Americas, though the word 'sunflower' existed before the plant to which it now refers was first seen by Europeans: in herbal medicine the sunflower is used to induce perspiration.

proceeds from the corollas only: in botany, the corolla is the whorl of leaves forming the inner envelope of the flower: generally, the petals or the most conspicuous part of the flower.

197 *Doctor Adam Smith . . . good of the whole*: professor of logic and of moral philosophy, the social theorist and economic thinker Adam Smith (1723–90) was best known for his *Theory of Moral Sentiments* (1759) and *The Wealth of Nations* (1776).

207 *'Father . . . pass from me'*: the words of Christ recorded in Matthew 26: 39, Mark 14: 23, and Luke 22: 42.

209 *My secret troubles cannot be revealed*: from the start of the play, De Monfort has been represented as haughty, capricious, and distrustful: reunited here with his sister, he has also been forced to meet the Marquis Rezenvelt, of whom he has harboured an irrational hatred since childhood, exacerbated by the consciousness that he owes his life to Rezenvelt's forbearance in combat. In Act III, scene ii, Rezenvelt sums up the situation: 'In short, I still have been th'opposing rock, | O'er which the stream of his o'erflowing pride | Hath foam'd and bellow'd'.

213 *with gibing brow*: 'gibing' is a variant spelling of 'jibing', meaning jeering or taunting.

218 *'Fair as the forms that, wove in Fancy's loom, | Float in light visions round the poet's head'*: William Mason, 'Elegy IV. On the Death of a Lady' (1760), ll. 11–12.

219 *'Nought's had . . . in doubtful joy'*: *Macbeth*, III. ii. 4–7.

220 *'How now . . . What's done, is done'*: the continuation of the last speech quoted, *Macbeth*, III. ii. 8–12.

'Canst thou not minister to a mind diseased?' &c.: from Macbeth's discussion of his wife's malady, with implicit reference to his own troubled thoughts, *Macbeth*, V. iii. 40.

221 *'Here's the smell . . . This little hand'*: *Macbeth*, V. i. 55–7.

'*Will all . . . Clean from this hand?*': after the murder of Duncan, *Macbeth*, II. ii. 61–2.

222 '*The grief . . . bids it break*': from Malcolm's speech, *Macbeth*, IV. iii. 209–10, in which he breaks the news to Macduff of the slaughter of his wife and children.

'*For mine own good . . . as go o'er*': *Macbeth*, III. iv. 135–7.

Unlike the first frail pair . . . mutual accusation: Milton's *Paradise Lost*, ix. 1187–9: 'Thus they in mutual accusation spent | The fruitless hours, but neither self-condemning, | And of their vain contest appeared no end.'

226 *the flam full in her face to light her*: 'flam' is an abbreviated form of 'flambeau', a flaming torch.

little better than a blackamoor: in some of its earlier occurrences having no derogatory force at all, this general term for a black-skinned person, especially a black African, became, as is obvious here, highly dismissive.

227 *a nabob in the kitchen*: by transfer from the title of a Muslim official acting as the deputy governor of a province, a 'nabob' denoted a person of high rank or wealth, especially someone who had returned from India with a large fortune acquired there: such is the fiction Thady promotes among the lower servants. For an actual nabob in the kitchen, Peregrine Touchwood, see the extract from Christian Isobel Johnstone in the 'Household Words' section.

the barrack-room your honour's talking on: Edgeworth's own note explains: 'Formerly it was customary, in gentlemen's houses in Ireland, to fit up one large bedchamber with a number of beds for the reception of occasional visitors. These rooms were called Barrack rooms.'

an innocent: deriving from the term for an artless or child-like person, someone simple or half-witted.

229 *Lady Cathcart's conjugal imprisonment*: Edgeworth, the 'male' editor, takes the opportunity to expand on the legal helplessness of married women. As George Watson points out in his edition of *Castle Rackrent* (Oxford: Oxford University Press, 1964, 1980), 122: 'The story is told in detail in an obituary of Elizabeth Malyn, Lady Cathcart (1692?–1789) in the *Gentleman's Magazine*, 59 (1789), 766–7. She was the widow of the 8th Baron Cathcart (d. 1740), her third husband, when she married Colonel Hugh Macguire, an Irish soldier-adventurer and fortune-hunter, in 1745. When she refused to give him her property and jewels he abducted her from their home in Hertfordshire to a castle in Co. Fermanagh, where he kept her confined till his death in 1764, when she returned to England, dying childless in 1789.'

230 *likely to call a man out for it afterwards*: that is, challenge him to a duel.

'*my pretty Jessica!*': *Merchant of Venice*, V. i. 21.

231 *within ames-ace . . . his enemies*: 'i.e. ambs-ace, a double ace, the lowest

possible throw at dice, or next to nothing' (George Watson, note to his edition of *Castle Rackrent*, 122).

232 *waked the same night*: meaning that, as was traditional, relatives and friends had kept watch through the night over his corpse until burial, an observance often accompanied by drinking and feasting.

the Curragh, where his cattle were well known: the Curragh is a plain in Co. Kildare in the Republic of Ireland noted for the breeding of racehorses: the Irish Derby is run annually on its racecourse. Originally meaning simply 'possessions', especially livestock, the term 'cattle' has only gradually taken on specifically bovine connotations, and here means 'horses'.

stud sold at the cant . . . county: a cant is an Irish term for the disposal of property at a public auction.

233 *no vails . . . at parting*: a gratuity, a tip, customarily given to servants on the departure of a guest, and in the seventeenth and eighteenth centuries often the only tangible element of a servant's pay. This is a serious snub, especially from Thady's point of view.

234 *Gil Blas . . . archbishop of Grenada . . . if you were*: picaresque narrative by Alain René Lesage (1688–1747), translated by Tobias Smollett in 1749.

235 *"Sad was the hour, and luckless was the day"*: Collins, *Persian Eclogues*, 'Eclogue the Second: Hassan; or, The Camel-Driver' (1742), l. 13, and repeated throughout.

lost at Newmarket . . . the word: since the reign of Charles II the centre of horseracing in England.

a Clarence Hervey of a man—: the romantic hero of *Belinda*, Clarence Hervey is a devotee of Rousseau.

236 *the torpedo, the coldest of cold creatures*: a flat fish with an almost circular body and tapering tail, which is distinguished by the ability to emit electric discharges, stunning its prey.

in petto as my ultimate remedy: in her own breast.

237 *the noble lord upon the woolsack*: the Lord Chancellor of England sits on a wool-stuffed cushion, called the woolsack, when presiding over the House of Lords.

238 *absolutely gold stick in waiting*: the bearer of a gilt rod carried on state occasions by the colonel of the Life Guards.

239 *"necessity had no law"*: in varying forms, a proverbial expression current since the sixteenth century.

heir at law: the heir apparent, who succeeds by right of blood (such as an eldest son), as opposed to an heir presumptive who is only the heir if closer issue does not appear (such as the nephew of an unmarried man), and therefore is always in danger of being displaced.

Harriet Freke: an account of her follows after a few paragraphs. She is a composite figure, not a portrait of any one feminist free-thinker.

240 *a vile Cassandra . . . be born alive*: the daughter of Priam of Troy and his

wife Hecuba, Cassandra was granted the gift of accurate prophecy by Apollo, but with the accompanying curse that what she prophesied would not be believed.

the old dowager . . . chief mourner: the term can be used loosely to mean simply a widow, but here it is used in its strict sense to indicate a widow who has some title or property (a dower) that has come to her from her husband, and which she holds in her own right, independently of any help offered by his heirs.

a plus forte raison: all the more so.

her airs and tracasseries for three or four years: a French term meaning worries, vexations.

241 *Corinthian brass . . . harum scarum manners into fashion*: 'brass' carries connotations of effrontery, as in 'as sounding brass', 1 Corinthians 13: 1; harum scarum comes from 'hare 'em, scare 'em', and means wild rash manners.

242 *"touch the brink of all we hate"*: Pope, *Epistles to Several Persons*, Epistle II, 'To a Lady: Of the Characters of Women', l. 52.

the cosmogony-man in the Vicar of Wakefield: cosmogony is the study of the subject of the generation or creation of the universe, a cosmogonist someone with a theory, system, or account of that generation; *The Vicar of Wakefield* is a novel, published in 1766, by Oliver Goldsmith (1730–74).

sterling gold . . . counters: imitation coin of brass or an inferior metal used to represent gold.

out-Heroded Herod upon the occasion: Herod, King of Judea at the time of the Nativity, ordered the Massacre of the Innocents when told by the three Magi that a greater king was about to be born: Matthew 2: 16.

stars . . . than ourselves: another reference to Prior's 'Hans Carvel': see note to p. 112.

the continent . . . a black fillet . . . than ever: a fillet is a headband.

243 *a faro bank*: a house where faro is played, faro being a gambling card-game in which players bet on the order in which cards will appear when taken from the top of the pack.

the House of Commons . . . Sheridan's speech: the dramatist and politition Richard Brinsley Sheridan (1751–1816) was from 1780 MP for Stafford and an eloquent parliamentarian. His most famous speech, referred to here, was the so-called 'Begums speech' of February 1787, in which he addressed the House of Commons for six hours, arguing for the impeachment of Warren Hastings, Governor-General of Bengal, for misappropriation of funds and immoral colonial management.

244 *Sloane-street . . . quite out of town*: built in 1760, Sloane Street, SW1, links Knightsbridge and Sloane Square. Apart from a small stretch of the South Bank, Georgian London did not extend much further south than this.

244 *sir Bertrand, or of some German horrifications*: Barbauld's tale 'Sir Bertrand' was included in the *Miscellaneous Pieces in Prose* which she published with her brother John Aikin in 1773.

tout de bon . . . and all that: all good things.

245 *"doated upon folly"*: not an exact quotation, but a self-conscious adoption of biblical phraseology, as in, for example, Ezekiel 23: 20, Jeremiah 10: 11.

246 *Knightsbridge*: the street stretching from Hyde Park Corner to Kensington Road in London.

a cock crowed . . . sister's house: meaning that dawn has come, and the time for evil spirits has passed.

not guilty of a bull, was I?: a bull is a verbal blunder, arising from an inadvertent contradiction of ideas, for which the Irish are said to be proverbial. With her father, Maria Edgeworth published *An Essay on Irish Bulls* in 1802.

247 *to be elected for a borough*: for the frequently corrupt and unreformed system of elections to boroughs, see the note to p. 189. Such an election would be a matter of patronage, not public service, and bore no obligation to represent the people. The eighteenth-century view was that parliament represented property, not people.

248 *chasse-café*: a draft of liquor taken to remove the taste of coffee or tobacco.

the princess Scheherazade . . . her story: narrator of *The Arabian Nights' Entertainment*, Scheherazade was the wife of the Sultan Shahriyar, the legendary king of Samarkand: she broke the king's practice of having his brides executed after the consumation of the marriage by telling stories every night. The allusion is to an exemplary female storyteller but also to a woman fighting for her life.

252 *the French are destroying themselves*: a reference to the growing factionalism of revolutionary France in 1792, and more generally to the view that France was in the throes of self-destruction.

for England was never in a more flouishing state than it is at present: in February 1792 William Pitt declared in his Budget speech: 'There never was a time in the history of our country, when from the situation in Europe we might more reasonably expect fifteen years of peace.' (G. R. Balleine, *Past Finding Out: The Tragic Story of Joanna Southcott and her Successors* (London: SPCK, 1956), 13.) The general expectation was that this period of peace would allow Britain to focus on internal affairs, such as calls for social and parliamentary reform and the consolidation of economic prosperity.

Plymtree . . . Exeter: Southcott's sister Susanna lived in Plymtree, 12 miles from Exeter: Southcott was at this time employed as a daily maid by the Taylor family, who had an upholstery business in Exeter.

253 *to sift you as wheat*: recalling Amos 9: 9: 'I will command, I will sift the house of Israel among all nations, like as corn is sifted in a sieve.'

the May following: that is, May 1796.

what will happen in Italy or England, I shall believe you: in the summer of 1796 it would have seemed inconceivable that Britain should sue unsuccessfully for peace with France and that the French army would conquer Italy. Lord Malmesbury's peace mission to Paris was unsuccessful and the French acquired a new general, Napoleon Bonaparte. The prophecy which most seems to have convinced or puzzled observers was Southcott's prediction of the unexpected death of the Bishop of Exeter in December 1796: and see Jeremiah 28: 15–17.

254 *Let . . . stand*: the omitted name is that of the Reverend Joseph Pomeroy (1750–1837), the eloquent and handsome Anglican vicar of St Kew, near Bodmin in Cornwall, who was closely involved with the early years of Southcott's mission and very important to her as a possible believer and legitimator. Their close discussions waned after the death of his wife in 1799, when, her biographers suggest, she may have considered him a worthy match.

255 *the words of David, 'Since godly men . . . One just and faithful friend'*: no precise reference found: Southcott appears to be amalgamating the pleas and assertions of many of David's Psalms, notably nos. 55, 56, 71, and 94.

the 12th chapter of Revelations . . . longing to be delivered: the woman described in Revelation 12: 1 (clothed in the sun) and 12: 2 ('And she being with child cried, travailing in birth, and pained to be delivered').

And seen without a glass: that is, without obstacle, more clearly than in 1 Corinthians 13: 12 ('For now we see through a glass darkly').

256 *the Scriptures . . . to complete his happiness*: see God's words in Genesis 2: 18 ('I will make him an help meet for him'), and the creation of Eve, Genesis 2: 22.

when the seven thousand years are ended: seven is the mystical number signifying completion and perfection, and although only a thousand years are specified in Revelation 20, there are many sevens (churches, candlesticks, angels, vials, plagues), a seventh seal, and seven thousand men (Revelation 11).

257 *written by the Prophets, 'in the latter days . . . prudent men shall be hid'*: see Isaiah 29: 14: 'for the wisdom of their wise men shall perish, and the understanding of their prudent men shall be hid.'

258 *the division must have taken place in hell already*: meaning that not until the Day of Judgement are the souls of the damned finally judged.

I cannot build . . . such sandy foundation: alluding to the house built on sand, Matthew 7: 26.

259 *the fulfilment of the Gentiles, and the calling in of the Jews*: from Christ's words in the Temple, Luke 21, especially verses 22 ('For these be the days of vengeance, that all things which are written may be fulfilled') and 24 ('and Jerusalem shall be trodden down of the Gentiles, until the times of the Gentiles be fulfilled').

259 *any that were sealed*: prompted by the many references to the 'sealing' of writings and people in the Book of Revelation (see 1: 2–4, 7: 3–9, 9: 4), Southcott issued seals to her believers. She had found a seal bearing the initials 'I.C.', which she came to believe represented 'Jesus Christ', and had used this to seal her early prophecies: subsequently it was used to stamp the issued seals. With the name of the sealed person, the date, and the signature of Southcott, these folded documents bore the words 'The Sealed of the Lord, the Elect and Precious, Man's Redemption to inherit the Tree of Life, to be made Heirs of God and Joint Heirs with Jesus Christ'. A photograph of one issued in December 1803 to John Bird may be seen in Balleine, *Past Finding Out*, facing p. 41.

The Lord . . . with Satan about Job: as told in Job 1: 8–12.

tempted forty days by the Devil: the story of Christ in the Wilderness, told in Mark 1: 13 and Luke 4: 2.

260 *began with the Devil and the woman*: the serpent's persuasion of Eve in Genesis 3, and enmity decreed between them for ever after, Genesis 3: 15 (see note to p. 264).

261 *For the great A line a child could read*: the top line of the card used in eyesight-tests always reads 'A'.

as Isaiah speaks . . . which was the last: see Isaiah 66, and the note to p. 257 above. 'That the last may be first, and the first last' is repeated several times in the ensuing debate: see Matthew 12: 45, 19: 30, 20: 16, Luke 11: 26, 13: 30.

mouth of the lion . . . Paw of the Bear . . . heart, ear, and life: see the lion and the bear in Amos 5: 19 ('As if a man did flee from a lion, and a bear met him').

262 *the woman mentioned in the Revelations . . . arguments*: the wife of the Lamb, Revelation 19: 8, and the woman in Revelation 12.

bring in a bill against Him and shame Him to His Face: to bring in the warrant initiating prosecution.

Foley or Bruce . . . allowed me: the Reverend Thomas Philip Foley (1758–1835), a Fellow of Jesus College, Cambridge, came from a wealthy family, and became an Anglican minister in Suffolk. He was a believer in the prophet Richard Brothers, many of whose followers converted to Southcottianism, and has been described as 'the strategist of the [Southcottian] movement at its inception': J. D. M. Derrett, *Prophecy in the Cotswolds 1803–1947: Joanna Southcott and Spiritual Reform* (Shipston-on-Stour, Warwickshire: for the Blockley Antiquarian Society by P. I. Drinkwater, 1994), p. xi. The Reverend Stanhope Bruce, also previously a follower of Richard Brothers, was the Anglican minister of Inglesham.

264 *Jezebel . . . Naboth . . . his vineyard*: Jezebel, wife of Ahab, killed the prophets, and Naboth: 1 Kings 18: 4, 19: 2, 21, 2 Kings 9: 21, 30.

He shall bruize thy head: Genesis 3: 15: 'And I will put enmity between thee and the woman, and between thy seed and her seed; it shall bruise thy head, and thou shalt bruise his heel.' See also Revelation 12: 9 and 20: 2, and Galatians 4: 4.

see the Gallows and the Fires . . . O Satan: a reference to the punishments for those suspected of witchcraft and devil-worship.

265 *Pomeroy . . . Manley . . . Mossop . . . Bruce*: for Pomeroy and Bruce, see notes to pp. 254 and 262. Manley is unidentified. The Reverend John Mossop, an Anglican vicar whom Southcott met when she was staying with connections of Stanhope Bruce in Market Deeping, near Peterborough, became one of her converts.

279 *Mr Belzoni . . . a toad of enormous size*: see Giovanni Battista Belzoni (1778–1823), *Narrative of the Operations and Recent Discoveries within the Pyramids, Temples, Tombs and Excavations in Egypt and Nubia, and of a Journey to the Coast of the Red Sea, in Search of the Ancient Berenice; and another to the Oasis of Jupiter Ammon* (London: John Murray, 1820).

the assertions of some naturalists . . . in a state of solitary confinement: Oliver Goldsmith refers to the toad's 'patient, solitary life' in *A History of the Earth, and Animated Nature*, 8 vols. (London: J. Nourse, 1774–7), vii. 94, and reports tales of centuries-old toads from other observers, vii. 101–2.

280 *a present to the British Museum . . . the 500th edition . . . pretend not to say*: like the claim that the manuscripts have been 'faithfully rendered from the original hieroglyphic character', this is a spoof of the fashion for fake ancient documents such as James Macpherson's Ossian poems, Thomas Chatterton's Rowley poems, and William Beckford's *Vathek*.

287 *the Furies agitate*: the Furies is the Roman name for the three Erinyes, merciless goddesses of vengeance, of Greek mythology: Tisiphone, the Avenger of Blood; Alecto, the Implacable; and Megaera, the Jealous.

289 *in the northern sky . . . lightning plays*: the aurora borealis, or northern lights, bands or streamers of light in the sky around the North Pole.

295 *immortal roses . . . lucid myrtles in the breezes play*: the Roman goddess of beauty and love, Venus, was associated with the rose and the myrtle: the myrtle is 'lucid' because when it is viewed in strong light, its leaves are seen to have innumerable small punctures.

the sandy Garamantian wild: the deserts of modern-day northern Libya.

When Macedonia's lord . . . fatigue beguiled: the reference is to the story whereby Alexander the Great, King of Macedonia, made a journey of pilgrimage to the temple of the Egyptian god Ammon (the Greek form of the name Amun or Amon).

296 *Sent by the hand of Love . . . her wondering eyes*: the turtle-dove, associated with courting couples. To set food before her echoes the actions of Christ (as in George Herbert's 'Love: III').

298 *There, as I whilom sung*: fomerly; a term in fashion after stanza 2 of Byron's *Childe Harold's Pilgrimage*, Canto 1, which begins 'Whilome in Albion's isle there dwelt a youth'.

There all thy charms, Narcissus, still abound!: in Greek mythology, the beautiful youth Narcissus spurned the love of the nymph Echo and was punished by being made to fall in love with his own reflection; he died gazing at it, and at death was changed into a flower.

Thy flowers, Adonis, bright vermilion show: in Greek mythology, Aphrodite fell in love with the beautiful Adonis, and when he was killed by a wild boar while hunting he was restored to life for part of the year in the shape of the flower anemone.

Beloved by Phoebus his Acanthus shines: the nymph Acantha, loved by Apollo Phoebus, was made immortal as a flower.

Reseda . . . his golden rays: Tighe notes here that the plant referred to is *reseda luteola*. Reseda is the English garden plant Mignonette.

302 *We had before seen the lake only as one wide plain of water*: Loch Lomond, which the Wordsworths and Coleridge approached via Glasgow and Dumbarton. As the road follows the western edge of the Loch, and approaches Luss, the view across the Loch becomes more broken up by a series of small islands than is the case further south.

Rydale-water: Rydal Water, one of the smallest of the English Lakes, is next to the lake of Grasmere, where the Wordsworths were living in 1803, and overlooked by Dorothy's home during the last forty years of her life, Rydal Mount.

the holms of Windermere: holm or holme is the term used in Cumberland for an island, here those in Windermere, the largest lake in England, and, at 10½ miles long, the longest of the English Lakes.

what a place for William!: her brother William Wordsworth, who liked to row out to the little island in the middle of the lake of Grasmere.

303 *Luss . . . that country begins*: it was traditional at this time to view Luss as the border between Highland and Lowland Scotland, a difference which is geological (marked, as Carol Kyros Walker points out, by the Highland Boundary Fault, roughly from Dumbarton, 10 miles south of Luss, to Stonehaven on the east coast) but more profoundly, especially for observers in 1803, cultural and linguistic, English giving way to Gaelic as the first language of the inhabitants.

the Highland dress and philabeg: 'philabeg' is an erroneous but at this time common form of 'filibeg', a kilt, from the Gaelic *feileadh-beag*.

another gentleman's house . . . prettily in a bay: Camstraddan House and bay.

a nice-looking white house, by the road-side: this is still an inn today, the Colquhoun Arms Hotel.

clean for a Scotch inn: like Dr Johnson during his Scottish tour with

Boswell in 1773, Dorothy Wordsworth discovered the truth of the popular wisdom that there was little comfort or cleanliness to be expected in Scottish inns.

304 *'built its own bower' . . . the riggins . . . village*: 'riggins' means 'rigging', the ridge or roof of a building.

Inch-ta-vannach . . . towers above the rest: as island in Loch Lomond.

305 *Ben Lomond . . . as Skiddaw does from Derwent-water*: the highest peak in this area at 974 metres, Ben Lomond lies on the upper north-east side of Loch Lomond. Derwentwater is in the north-west of the English Lake District, near the town of Keswick: at 931 metres, the mountain of Skiddaw lies to the north of it and is the highest peak in the area. Dorothy Wordsworth is perhaps reminded of this scene because of the combination of the many small islands on Derwentwater and the presence to the north of this large peak and the Skiddaw Fells. This is also the home of the 'floating island', a tangled mass of weeds buoyed up by marsh gas, which periodically surfaces near Lodore.

306 *the dropsy . . . whisky-drinking*: a morbid condition, the accumulation of fluid in the serous cavities or connective tissue of the body.

307 *Sir James Colquhoun*: a local landowner, who had a house on the peninsula looking towards Ben Lomond.

308 *Dumbarton rock with its double head*: the large isolated rock of Dumbarton, in the Clyde, has two summits, the higher of which is known as Wallace's Seat. The Wordsworths had climbed to the top and judged the view to be 'sufficient recompense'.

the Tor of Glastonbury from the Dorsetshire hills: a strong suggestion that Dorothy Wordsworth is associating this Scottish tour with an earlier period of intense creativity between her brother and Coleridge. The reference is to Glastonbury Tor, east of the ancient town of Glastonbury in Somerset, as seen afar from the Quantock Hills, Dorset, 20 miles to the west. The Quantocks, near Nether Stowey, are where Dorothy, William, and Coleridge lived and walked during their work on *Lyrical Ballads* in 1796–7.

309 *Ruth . . . A home in every glade*: the reference to her brother William's poem 'Ruth' (1800) continues the transatlantic links in this passage. Ruth is wooed by a man who has served as a soldier in America and leaves her family to follow him, but he deserts her.

310 *one single horse and outlandish Hibernian vehicle*: an Irish jaunting car hired by Coleridge; it was an open two-wheeled cart pulled by a single horse, caused them considerable discomfort, and was conspicuous for its meanness among the more fashionable carriages usually hired by visitors to Scotland.

311 *Floating Island*: see note to p. 305 above.

315 *NATURAL PHILOSOPHY*: the enquiry into the properties and powers of nature, loosely corresponding to what we now call 'science', although the

term was becoming increasingly unstable in this period as the modern branches of science became more sharply defined and more specialized.

316 *the philosopher's stone, or the secret of making gold?*: sought by alchemists, a substance capable of turning base metal into gold; recently a favourite topic in the 1790s, as in William Godwin's novel *St Leon* (1799).

so complete a revolution . . . to which art is entirely subservient: the so-called 'chemical revolution', beginning in the 1770s, consisted of a number of distinct discoveries—the French chemist Antoine Laurent Lavoisier's identification of oxygen, the British John Dalton's theory of 'atomic weights', the identification of gases by Joseph Priestley and Joseph Black—and, more generally, of a new interest in systematic classification and nomenclature, by which the science in effect equipped itself with a vocabulary and an experimental methodology equal to the growing interest in it. The precise rhetoric of classification and description helped to distinguish it from 'art'. In a passage of which Mrs B. would have approved, Jan Golinski comments: 'Chemistry indeed appeared capable of working miracles. It was widely believed to have proved the most spectacularly successful science of recent times. The new discoveries had placed unprecedented powers in the hands of the chemist and promised revelations of the inmost secrets of matter. It was mainly to chemistry, therefore, that hopes for further scientific progress turned in the first two decades of the nineteenth century' (*Science as Public Culture: Chemistry and Enlightenment in Britain, 1760–1820* (Cambridge: Cambridge University Press, 1992), 236).

317 *the steam engine . . . chemistry*: the first successful steam engine was developed by the British engineer Thomas Newcomen in 1712 and improved by other engineers; the first steam locomotive, developed by the Cornish engineer Richard Trevithick, was built in 1804 for an ironworks.

318 *Within these thirty years especially . . . elementary bodies*: Lavoisier's system of chemical classification replaced earlier theories of the 'elements'.

320 *the evils arising from an excess of population . . . on my mind*: the arguments put forward by Thomas Robert Malthus in his *Essay on the Principles of Population* (1798) had a great impact on social and economic thought. Malthus argued that unchecked population growth would inevitably overtake any growth in the supply of food; instead of progress and improvement, therefore, mankind could only expect social conflict and want. Aspects of Malthus's thinking, which presented social inequality as natural and necessary, appealed to conservative models of society; for Caroline, always more radical and more compassionate than Mrs B., they evoke images of suffering among the poor. As David M. Knight observes of Caroline and Emily during their chemistry lessons: 'The girls are exceedingly sharp, and would be very welcome in any tutorial group' (*Science in the Romantic Era* (Aldershot: Ashgate Variorum, 1998), 261).

a great number of commons inclosed and cultivated: the enclosure of traditionally common land was a major part of the agrarian change which transformed Britain by 1815. Open fields were surrounded by hedge-rows, banks, and walls, and landownership was concentrated in the hands of the few, with the loss of small plots of land cultivated by rural workers, and the loss of grazing rights. Debate raged between those who thought that the increased efficiency of agriculture represented progress, and those who argued that it had increased rural poverty and social hardship.

321 *my favourite Goldsmith . . . bare worn common is deny'd'*: a reference to the effects of the enclosure of common land in Oliver Goldsmith, 'The Deserted Village' (1770), ll. 303–8.

   Finchley Common . . . the inhabitants of that parish: the eastern part of present-day Finchley, in north London, once consisted mainly of Finchley Common, which was crossed by the Great North Road and was a notorious haunt of highwaymen. It was enclosed in 1816.

329 *'Balow my babe'*: 'balow' is a lulling word, used in lullabies; the most probable referent here is part of the song known as 'Lady Bothwell's Lament' from Allan Ramsey's *Tea-Table Miscellany* (1733), ii. 13: 'Balow my boy, ly still and sleep'.

332 *the shades of the worsted*: worsted is a fine and soft woollen yarn which at this time was often used, as here, for needlework and embroidery.

   Hogarth's prints were below the Cæsars: prints from the works of the English painter and engraver William Hogarth (1697–1764) were very popular; narrative and anecdotal, they satirized social abuses, as in the celebrated sequences 'A Harlot's Progress' (*c.*1731), 'A Rake's Progress' (*c.*1735), and 'Marriage à la Mode' (*c.*1742–4).

333 *Hagar and her son Ishmael*: Genesis 16: 10, 11, 21: 14. Hagar, an Egyptian maidservant of Abraham's wife Sarah, was given to Abraham and bore him a son, Ishmael. Later Sarah sent Hagar and Ishmael into the desert, but through God's protection they were kept alive.

334 *'Mahometism Explained'*: *Mahometism Fully Explained*, translated by a Mr Morgan (London: W. Mears, 1723–5), from the Arabic of Muhammad Rabadan (fl. 1603).

   a false history of Abraham and his descendants: a descendant of Noah in Old Testament history, Abraham's son Ishmael is identified in the Koran as the father of the Arab nations, and Abraham as 'the Chosen', one of the six great prophets of Allah and the leader of mankind (Koran II: 124). Through the Koran, Allah explains that the revelations made by the prophets to Jews and Christians were accurate, but were corrupted as texts and misconstrued by these religions; and that Abraham's pure monotheism had been lost by the times of Muhammad.

335 *this light streaming from his forehead . . . asleep in the cradle*: a story not told of Ishmael in the Koran, but reminiscent of the story of Moses.

   Mahomet: the chief spokesman and interpreter of Islam, Muhammad (570–632), was born in Mecca, and at the age of 40 realized his prophetic mission and went into seclusion in a cave on Mount Hira, where he was visited by the archangel Gabriel, the first of a series of revelations and teachings recorded in the Koran from 610. Persecuted in Mecca, in 622 he migrated to Medina (in the flight known as the Hijara), where he built the first mosque, established traditions of prayer, and in 630 conquered Mecca, uniting the tribes of Arabia.

335 *no wider than a silken thread . . . gulf that had no bottom*: as told in the Koran and in later writings of Islam, the wrongdoings and good deeds of all Muslims are weighed on the day of reckoning: warnings of the last judgement describe the soul crossing a vast bridge as sharp as a sword, as thin as a hair, and as long as a caravan's journey. The punishment for evil is to fall into the burning pit beneath.

336 *A ride to Harlow fair would not be amiss*: the old village of Harlow, near Bishop's Stortford in Hertfordshire.

338 *The British Lady's Magazine . . . advancing in intellectual improvement*: the first series of this monthly periodical, running from 1 January 1815 to 31 December 1819, is one of the most interesting publications aimed at women readers in this period. It developed, and continued in its second series, into a more traditionally and frivolously feminine work, with a greater emphasis on fashions and entertainment, but when Mary Lamb addressed its readership she was writing for a work which displayed on its first page an altered piece of Milton, 'Greatness of mind, and nobleness their seat | In *her* build loveliest'. The 'Introductory Address' of the editor, John Souter, declared in the first issue of the magazine that 'the Principal inducement to the dedication of a new Journal to the sex exclusively, originates in a firm conviction, that the female is partaking, to an unprecedented extent, in that taste for intellectual acquirement, so perceptible in every department of civilized life', giving women a part in 'the progressive march of science, literature, policy, morals, manners, religion, and, in short, [in] whatever may reasonably be expected to please or inform' (see further Alvin Sullivan (ed.), *British Literary Magazines: The Romantic Age, 1789–1836* (Westport, Conn., and London: Greenwood Press, 1983), 62–6). It contained articles on a wide range of topics, and was open-minded in its range of views, explicitly aiming to equip women with the information to form their own ideas.

345 *the feelings it excited in some speeches for Maria*: Maria Bertram has recently become engaged to marry Mr Rushworth, and ought to be scrupulous in her behaviour to other men. She is playing the part of the fallen woman Agatha in dramatic dialogue with her illegitimate son Frederick, played by Henry Crawford.

347 *the third act . . . how they would perform*: in Inchbald's adaptation Amelia (played by Mary Crawford), daughter of the Baron Wildenheim, resists marriage to her father's choice, the foolish Count Cassel, because she is in love with her tutor, Anhalt (played by Edmund Bertram). In Act III she openly declares her love to Anhalt, and although Inchbald had

greatly toned down her expressions from Kotzebue's original, her declaration breaks all acceptable codes of behaviour for an unmarried woman
such as Mary Crawford.

350 *the ladies moved soon*: it was usual for gentlemen to sit over port while the
ladies retired.

353 *Captain Benwick*: as references later in the exchange reveal, Captain
Benwick is an indulgent lover of poetry or rather of poetical sentiment.
He had been engaged to Captain Harville's sister Fanny, and on her death
the summer before the present action had taken up residence with the
Harvilles in Lyme Regis. First attracted to Anne, he has now fallen in
love with Louisa Musgrove, Anne's rival for Captain Wentworth's affections, during her convalesence after a serious fall.

at the Cape: the Cape of Good Hope, a crucial sea-route to Asia, was
disputed during the wars with France. The British army had held Cape
Colony from 1795 to 1802.

354 *The peace turned him on shore at the very moment*: the peace of Amiens in
1802.

360 *damescenes in sugar, to use in the winter*: properly damascene plum, now
usually called a damson: a small plum, but sometimes distinguished from
damson by extra size and sweetness.

369 *natural philosophy . . . my sole occupation*: as in Marcet's usage (see note to
p. 315), natural philosophy means the physical sciences.

the university: the Bavarian university of Ingoldstadt, closed in 1800, and
notorious as the home of the Order of the Illuminists, one of the experimental mystical sects held responsible by the Abbé de Barruel and others
for the intellectual inception of revolutionary ideas in France.

In M. Waldman I found a true friend: the mild and benevolent M. Waldman, professor of natural philosophy, becomes Frankenstein's mentor: he
lectures with particular eloquence on modern chemistry.

how Cornelius Agrippa went on?: the original for stories about 'the sorcerer's apprentice', Cornelius Agrippa (1486–1535) was a German cabal-
ist, author of *De Occulta Philosophia Libri Tres* (1529).

371 *I was like the Arabian . . . seemingly ineffectual, light*: referring to the live
burials described in the fourth voyage of Sinbad the Sailor in the *Arabian
Nights*.

my friend: Frankenstein is addressing Robert Walton, leader of an expedition to the North Pole, who has rescued and befriended him.

374 *If this rule were always observed . . . been destroyed*: after gradual Roman
infiltration of the ancient Greek civilizations, complete by the first
century BC, the Romans created Greece (Achaea) as a province in 27
BC; in southern America, the ancient cultures of Mexico and Peru were
destroyed by the Spanish conquests led by Cortés and Pizarro
respectively.

375 *the instruments of life . . . lay at my feet*: as Marilyn Butler points out in her edition of the 1818 *Frankenstein* (Oxford: Oxford University Press, 1993), prominent among scientific experiments into the nature of life were those of Luigi Galvani (1737–98): 'Galvani's experiments explored the role of "animal electricity" in the nerves and muscles of small creatures such as frogs. To animate a much larger animal (such as the eight-foot Creature) Frankenstein may have calculated he needed a gigantic Voltaic battery. It is at this point in the story, at the culmination of the experiment, with the sentence "It was on a dreary night . . . ", that the original tale began' (255).

376 *such as even Dante could not have conceived*: referring to the descriptions of hell and purgatory in the *Divine Comedy* of Dante Alighieri (1265–1321).

377 *Like one . . . close behind him tread*: Mary Shelley's note gives the source, Coleridge's 'Rime of the Ancient Mariner' (1798), ll. 446–51.

The Wandering Jew?—certainly not*: referred to frequently in medieval literature, the Wandering Jew was said to have insulted Christ as he bore the cross, and was condemned to wander the world until the Day of Judgement; according to some variants of the tradition, he fell into a trance at the end of every hundred years and awoke as a young man.

the Seven Sleepers . . . so burthensome*: seven Christian youths of Ephesus who fled persecution to a cave in Mount Celion, and awoke 200 years later.

the fabled Nourjahad!*: Frances Sheridan's play *Illusion, or the Trances of Nourjahad* (1813) was initially attributed to Byron, and is attacked in his poem 'The Devil's Drive' of the same year.

Cornelius Agrippa*: for this link between the two Shelley tales extracted here, see note to p. 369 above.

379 *jealous as a Turk*: by tradition, Turks were held to be barbarous and cruel, ruled by sudden passions.

380 *The progress of his alembics . . . expected*: an alembic, of which the mage here has several on the go, is an apparatus formerly used in distilling, consisting of a gourd-shaped vessel or cucurbit which is surmounted by a head or cap (the alembic proper) the beak of which conveys the vapour to a receiver in which it is condensed.

384 *'a prophet is least regarded in his own country'*: Luke 4: 24, 'no prophet is accepted in his own country'.

385 *among the Nestors of our village*: in Homeric legend, the eldest of the Greek kings to take part in the Trojan War, and characterized as garrulous but wise, counselling moderation.

392 *our village*: based on Three Mile Cross, in the parish of Shinfield, on the A33 3½ miles south of Reading, Berkshire. Mitford's cottage, now named The Mitford, is on the east side of the main road.

at Lizzy's door: Lizzy is the carpenter's daughter, described in the opening tale of the series, 'Our Village', as 'the plaything and queen of the village, a child three years old according to the register, but six in size and strength and intellect, in power and in self-will'; in her appearance, energy, and affection, she is presented as an image of Englishness.

393 *a sort of Robin Goodfellow*: in English folklore, another name for the mischievous spirit Puck.

394 *the quadrilles and the spread-eagles of the Seine and the Serpentine . . .*: the fancy footwork of skaters on the frozen river Seine in Paris and the Serpentine in London; a quadrille would be an especially ambitious manœuvre, since it is a square-dance for four couples; a spread-eagle is a figure in elaborate skating.

the pollard oaks: oaks which have been polled, that is, cut back in order to thicken the growth of the young branches.

'blushing in its natural coral': perhaps a recollection of the blushing coral in the description of Venus in Christopher Marlowe's *Hero and Leander* (1598), l. 32.

395 *'that shadow of a bird', as White of Selborne calls it*: 'the feeble little golden-crowned wren, that shadow of a bird', is commented on as very rare in *The Natural History of Selborne*, 75.

Thames, Kennet, Loddon—all overflowed: the Thames here is a red herring; the Kennet and Loddon are the two main rivers in the countryside around Three Mile Cross.

C. park . . . meadows from B. to W. . . . out of it: the scope of Mitford's reference is imprecise, but C. park is likely to be either Stanbury Park, near Three Mile Cross, or the larger Stratfield Saye Park, further south, both on the Loddon; while, again depending on the area flooded, the towns could be Basingstoke to Wokingham or Burghfield to Winnersh.

'dissolution and thaw': 'a man of continual dissolution and thaw', as Falstaff describes himself in *The Merry Wives of Windsor*, III. v. 101.

398 *the old place . . . eighteen happy years*: a reference to the larger house nearer Reading which the Mitfords were forced to give up in 1820.

399 *the weeping birch, 'the lady of the woods'*: so called by Samuel Taylor Coleridge in 'The Picture or the Lover's Resolution', ll. 136–7.

402 *Caroline of Brunswick . . . the nation*: Princess Caroline Amelia Elizabeth of Brunswick-Wolfenbüttel (1768–1821) was born into the reigning family of a small vassal state of Prussia in northern Germany: she married the Prince of Wales, her cousin, on 8 April 1795, all contracts having been signed before the two met. The Prince had been persuaded into the marriage by the promise of money to ease his huge debts; his first reaction on seeing his bride was to ask his attendant to pour him a glass of brandy. For a fuller account of the events Hays relates, see Flora Fraser, *The Unruly Queen: The Life of Queen Caroline* (London: Macmillan, 1996).

402 *his having formed other attachments*: in canon law, the Prince had long been rather more than attached, being already secretly married to the twice-widowed Roman Catholic Maria Fitzherbert, to whom an Anglican clergyman had joined him in December 1785. In English parliamentary law, which technically overruled canon law, this match was illegal: marriage to a Catholic had been forbidden by the provisions of the Bill of Rights in 1689, and by the 1772 Royal Marriages Act the heir to the throne was required to obtain the sovereign's consent to any marriage. Maria Fitzherbert had by this time retired to the country upon the Prince's affair with Frances, Lady Jersey, who became his mistress—and a very controlling one—in 1784, but after his marriage to Caroline he continued to refer privately to her as his wife and sought to return to her. Lady Jersey's constant presence at Carlton House was an open scandal at the time.

403 *a neglected and contemned wife*: in effect the Prince and Princess of Wales lived separate lives at Carlton House from 1796, and were rarely thereafter at the same residence at the same time: in May that year *The Times* printed a 'rumour of a separation in high life'. George III refused the Prince's request for a separation as early as June 1796, and again in 1798. Despite the lack of a formal settlement, from 1798 to 1804 Caroline took up a separate residence at Montague House, near Greenwich Park.

Her progress to the capital . . . character and age: having sailed from Calais to Dover on 5 June 1820, Caroline was greeted by cheering crowds on her landing, and by crowds, public dignitaries, and bell-ringing at every stop on her route to the capital through Canterbury, Rochester, Stroud, Gravesend, and Dartford. To ministerial alarm, officers of a cavalry regiment accompanied her party to Sittingbourne; at Gravesend her carriage was pulled through the town by groups of citizens; and from Dartford a huge procession followed her into London, where she was greeted by radical MPs including William Cobbett. Her cause was a rallying-point for anti-establishment protest of all varieties, and her return to Britain after all the desperate attempts to keep her away provoked carnival and unrest throughout the country.

404 *the respectable citizen who accompanied her in her voyage*: this was the former mayor of London and radical MP Alderman Matthew Wood, who sailed with Caroline from Calais to Dover, accompanied her to London, and gave her lodgings in his house at 77 South Audley Street, Mayfair (now, perhaps, a misleadingly impeccable address, but it was disturbing to many that the queen should be forced to accept the hospitality of a commoner). A contemporary drawing in the Mansell Collection depicts Alderman Wood supporting Caroline as her party landed on the beach at Dover: it is one of the prints in Joanna Richardson, *The Disastrous Marriage: A Study of George IV and Caroline of Brunswick* (London: Jonathan Cape, 1960), facing 192.

Burke . . . chivalry had passed away: commenting on the treatment of Queen Marie Antoinette at the hands of the Paris crowds who had cheered her on her marriage years earlier, Edmund Burke had exclaimed in his *Reflections on the Revolution in France* (1790): 'But the age of chivalry is gone' (ed. Conor Cruise O'Brien (London: Penguin, 1968), 170). Hays thus explicitly links the indignities suffered by Caroline with the fate of the executed French queen.

405 *Their green bag . . . Pandora's box . . . at the bottom*: a bag made of green material, formerly used by barristers and lawyers to carry documents and papers. During the queen's trial, the green bags containing papers from the scandals of 1806 and 1813, one each for the House of Lords and the House of Commons, became a national obsession: they 'caught the imagination of the public and of the influential cartoonists of the day as a synonym for Government dirty business' (Fraser, *Unruly Queen*, 369). Fraser's biography includes a print of one of these cartoons, George Cruikshank's 'Ah! Sure such a pair was never seen so justly form'd by nature' (British Museum), p. 18.

the man in question . . . not a subject: Caroline's Italian lover, whom she had first employed as a courier in 1814, was the strikingly handsome Bartolomeo Pergami, Barone Pergame della Franchina (1784–1842), sixteen years her junior. As her defence lawyers stated in her trial, by a statute of Edward III 'the act of a person having no allegiance to the British Crown could not be high treason' (Fraser, *Unruly Queen*, 378–9).

406 *Henry VIII of wife-killing memory*: two of the six wives of Henry VIII (1491–1547), Anne Boleyn (*c.*1504–36; married 1533) and her young cousin Catherine Howard (d. 1542; married 1540) were executed after being found guilty of infidelity. Henry's first wife, Catherine of Aragon, died in 1536 after their divorce, while his third, Jane Seymour, died a few months after their marriage, giving birth to his only son, Edward (later VI).

Catherine of Russia . . . a great sovereign: see note to p. 60.

Our own Elizabeth . . . unsunned snow: an indirect allusion to Proverbs 26: 1, 'as snow in summer', and referring to Elizabeth I's fabled virginity.

409 *Gafran*: a Welsh chieftain of the fifth century who went with his family to discover the 'Gwerddonan Llion' or islands of the souls of the Druids.

410 *Llywarch Hen . . . prince of Argoed . . . the present Cumberland*: 'Llywarch the Old', one of the four great Welsh poets of the late sixth century, is also the subject of a group of poems and 'the typical old man of Powysian legend, as Nestor of the Homeric epics', comments H. I. Bell, *The Development of Welsh Poetry* (Oxford: Clarendon Press, 1936), 28: metrically distinctive and often elegiac in tone, his work has continued to appeal to a non-Welsh readership, perhaps because 'generations which have grown up under the influence of the Romantic movement find the mood of wistful or passionate regret here expressed more readily comprehensible than the stark epic compactness of the *Gododdin* and Taliesin's historical odes or the remoter and more mysterious atmosphere of the latter's mythological poetry' (28).

410 *Cynddylan, Prince of Powys . . . one of his poems*: the subject of a cycle of poems in the 'Llywarch Hen' group (see previous note) is the death of the prince Cynddylan and the destruction of Pengwern (Shrewsbury) and Eglwyseu Bassa (Baschurch); the narrator is Cynddylan's sister, Heledd.

411 *Cader Idris . . . resembling a couch*: 'the chair of Idris', a mountain ridge in north-west Wales, the highest point of which is Pen-y-Gader.

412 *Casabianca*: the 10-year-old Giacomo Casabianca, son of Louis de Casabianca, Admiral of the French flagship *Orient*, was killed by exploding gunpowder during the battle of the Nile in 1798.

413 *'I come | To this sweet place . . . Barry Cornwall*: 'A Haunted Stream' (1822) by Barry Cornwall (1787–1874), ll. 111–12.

A tale of Palestine: Scott's novel *The Talisman*, one of his *Tales of the Crusaders* (1825).

414 *A Syrian wind the lion-banner stirr'd*: the banner of the English crusaders in the Holy Land, and more particularly of Richard the Lionheart. During the absence of the hero of *The Talisman*, the Scottish knight Sir Kenneth (Prince David of Scotland in disguise), the standard of the English troops is torn down.

A wild shrill trumpet of the Saracen . . . burning air: properly Sala-Ed-Din Yusuf Ibn Ayub (1137–93), Sultan of Egypt and captor of Jerusalem, Saladin is the charismatic central figure of *The Talisman*.

Paynim's trumpet's blast: a paynim is an archaic and poetic term for a pagan or heathen, especially a Saracen.

Properzia Rossi . . . an unrequited attachment: for an account of Properzia Rossi, see Giorgio Vasari, *Lives of the Most Eminent Painters, Sculptors, and Architects* (1568), 10 vols. (London: Warner, 1912), v. 123–8.

painting, by Ducis . . . a basso-relievo of Ariadne . . . with indifference: the painter is the French painter Jean-Louis Ducis (1775–1847). Ariadne, the daughter of King Minos of Crete, helped Theseus escape from the maze of the Minotaur, but was abandoned by him on the island of Naxos. Dionysos later took pity on her, and she married him.

415 *'Tell me no more . . . would have made life precious'*: untraced in earlier works, and probably written by Hemans.

419 *Long's 'Expedition to the Source of St Peter's River'*: Major Stephen H. Long led trans-Mississippi expeditions in 1819 and 1823, the results of which were reported in S. H. Long and Edwin James, *Account of an Expedition from Pittsburgh to the Rocky Mountains* (Philadelphia, 1823) and S. H. Long and W. H. Keating, *Narrative of an Expedition to the Lake of the Woods* (Philadelphia, 1824).

'Non, je ne puis vivre . . . Madame de Stael: 'No, I cannot live with a broken heart. I must rediscover joy and join the free spirits of the air.' The French novelist, poet, and writer on politics, philosophy, and

literature Germaine de Staël (1766–1817) was the daughter of Louis XVI's finance minister Jacques Necker, and an important *salonière* who drew together key European thinkers first in pre-revolutionary Paris and later at her estate near Geneva. She was a great influence on women writers in Britain, especially Felicia Hemans and Laetitia Elizabeth Landon. The work referred to here is her translation of Friedrich Schiller's drama *Die Braut von Messina* (1803).

'Let not my child be a girl . . . The Prairie': in James Fenimore Cooper's novel, *The Prairie* (1827), ch. 26, Tachechana, abandoned wife of the Teton chief Mahtoree, gives up her baby son with the words 'Let him not be a girl, for very sad is the life of a woman.'

Father of ancient waters roll!: the 'Great Water' and 'Father of Waters' are Amerindian names for the Mississippi river, the major river of North America.

421 *and is this all?*: in his *Travels to Discover the Source of the Nile* (1790), the explorer James Bruce of Kinnaird gives a striking account of his feelings on the night of 4 November 1770, when the goal for which he had sacrificed so much was within sight: 'I was, at that very moment, in possession of what had, for many years, been the principal object of my ambition and wishes: indifference, which, from the usual infirmity of human nature, follows, at least for a time, complete enjoyment, had taken place of it. The marsh, and the fountains, upon comparison with the rise of many of our rivers, became now a trifling object in my sight [he compares the sources of the Tweed, Clyde, Annan, Rhine, Rhone, and Soane, with that of the Nile] . . . I began, in my sorrow, to treat the inquiry about the source of the Nile, as a violent effort of a distempered fancy' (selected and ed. C. F. Beckingham (Edinburgh: Edinburgh University Press, 1964), 163).

422 *'One struggle more, and I am free' Byron*: the first line of Byron's lyric poem 'To Thyrza' (1811–12), and sometimes given as its title.

423 *'I seem like one who treads alone . . . departed.' Moore*: 'The Light of Other Days' or 'Oft, in the Stilly Night', by Thomas Moore, ll. 19–20.

yon gray, gleaming hall . . . fall: Wavertree Hall, in the village of Wavertree now incorporated to the city of Liverpool. Hemans lived in Wavertree for nearly three years in 1828–31, at 17 High Street: her house, or townish 'cottage', was indentified, and photographed, by the Liverpool librarian and antiquarian George T. Shaw in his pamphlet *The Liverpool Homes of Mrs Hemans* (Liverpool: F. & E. Gibbons, 1897), written as part of a plea for the recognition of houses in Liverpool which should have London 'blue plaque' status.

425 *Woodstock, in the County of Kilkenny*: near Clonamery in County Kilkenny lies the estate of Woodstock, the house of which, seat of the Tighe family, was destroyed in 1922. Flaxman's effigy of Mary Tighe is in the mausoleum of the village church in Inistioge ('Teoc's or Tighe's island'), with other memorials to her.

425 *'Yes! hide beneath . . . Poem on the Lily'*: dated May 1809, 'The Lily' is one of the poems included in Mary Tighe's collection *Psyche* (1811).

426 *Suggested by a beautiful sketch . . . utter abandonment*: a sketch of Sappho by the English sculptor Sir Richard Westmacott (1775–1856), son of the sculptor of the same name: best known for the tomb of Charles James Fox in Westminster Abbey and the statue of Achilles in Hyde Park, he specialized in the neoclassical manner and had a very successful practice in London.

430 *the Earl of Craven*: William, 7th Baron and 1st Earl Craven (1770–1825), who succeeded to the baronetcy in 1770 and was created Earl in 1801; in 1807 he married the celebrated actress Louisa Brunton. As his drawings of cocoa trees and his 'fellows' (either slaves or soldiers) suggest, he had property in the West Indies. The topics of conversation which bore Wilson may reflect the tastes of the family, for the Earl's younger brother was the traveller and writer Keppel Richard Craven (1779–1851).

the Marine Parade, at Brighton: after the houses fronting the Steine (see note to p. 432), the most fashionable address in Regency Brighton, on the central seafront. In the year of the Prince of Wales's first visit to the small town of Brighthelmston, 1783, the population was 3,500; by 1801, the era that Harriette Wilson describes here, it had doubled to 7,339; by 1821, a few years before the publication of her memoirs, it was 24,429.

the Honourable Frederick Lamb . . . nothing else?: the handsome and popular Frederick James Lamb (1782–1853) was the third son of Peniston, 1st Viscount Melbourne. Educated at Eton, the University of Glasgow, and the University of Cambridge, he graduated in 1803 and took up a highly successful career in the diplomatic service, becoming a minister and ambassador. In 1839 he was created a peer, Baron Beauvale, married a 20-year-old heiress at the age of 60 in 1841, and in 1848 succeeded his brother (see note to p. 433) to become the 3rd Viscount Melbourne. Wilson's reference to his father in the next paragraph is to the 1st Viscount Melbourne (1748–1819).

432 *Colonel Thomas*: from the context, one of the household of the Prince of Wales. It was usual for military officers to be attached to the household for a few years, as was Colonel Lake (see note to p. 173).

you are too impudent: it is improbable that Harriette Wilson's connection with the Prince stopped here, and there is evidence that he was one of those who discreetly paid up in advance of publication. 'Mrs Arbuthnot in April, 1826, records that the Prime Minister, Canning, gave "a sum of money out of the *secret service* to stop Miss Harriette Wilson's pen"' (Philip Lindsay, *The Loves of Florizel* (London: Hutchinson, 1951), 98 n.). Saul David also notes that the Prince was reportedly petrified when Wilson threatened to publish a second volume of revelations in 1828 (*The Prince of Pleasure and the Making of the Regency* (London: Little, Brown, 1998), 286).

the Steyne: now known as the 'Old Steine', in the centre of Brighton, this was a stretch of ground, once open but by this time enclosed by wooden palings and later by iron railings, a fashionable promenading-ground made up of a series of walkways and gardens and dominated by the Prince's lavish fantasy-oriental Royal Pavilion (John Nash, 1815–22). Until its enclosure it was used by fishermen as a place to dry their nets, and it can be seen as a large open space in E. Cobby's map in *The Brighthelmston Directory for 1800*, included in Sue Farrant, *Georgian Brighton, 1740 to 1820* (Brighton: Centre for Continuing Education, University of Sussex, 1980), 37.

433 *although Craven was in town*: that is, in London, at this time an eight-hour journey from Brighton, and absent from his house on Marine Parade.

aide-de-camp to General Mackenzie: an officer acting as the confidential assistant to the general (not identified).

introduce his brother William to me: his elder and (later) more famous brother William Lamb (1779–1848), 2nd Viscount Melbourne and husband of the writer and mistress of Byron, Lady Caroline Lamb. In 1825 he was an MP but not yet prominent in national politics; he went on to become Home Secretary in Grey's ministry in 1830, and Prime Minister from 1834 to 1841.

435 *the Marquis of Lorne . . . excited my curiosity*: Marquess of Lorne is one of the ancient creations (1470) attached to the family of Campbell of Argyll, one of the grandest of Scottish ducal families. The man who so appealed to Wilson was George William Campbell (1766–1839), from 1806 6th Duke of Argyll. He married in 1810. The good looks were partly inherited from his mother, Elizabeth Gunning, one of the greatest beauties of the court of George III.

Duke's Row, Somerstown: a comedown for a man of Argyll's status. The area of Somers Town, London, lying between the present-day St Pancras Station and Crowndale Road, bordered to the west by Hampstead Road, and separated from Bloomsbury by Euston Road, was at this time mainly inhabited by the working classes but also by a large influx of French emigrés in the 1790s and Spanish liberal refugees from 1823. William Godwin and his daughter Mary Shelley lived here. The land to the east was a slightly shady area used for blood sports and fighting. So much of this district was altered (indeed, chosen for social 'cleansing') in the nineteenth century to make room for Euston, St Pancras, and King's Cross stations (and, more recently, the new British Library) that precise locations here are more than usually nebulous. There is still a Duke's Road, a small road to the south of Euston Road near Euston station, which may—Euston Road having been present in Wilson's time, from 1757—have been part of, or a route to, Duke's Row.

437 *the Jew's Harp House*: demolished in 1812, the Jew's Harp, Marylebone Park, was an eighteenth-century tavern, tea-garden, and pleasure ground, near the present-day Broad Walk in Regent's Park.

439 *very much tête montée*: literally 'excited head': over-excited, agitated.

440 *Tom Sheridan, only son of Richard Brinsley Sheridan*: the son of the Irish dramatist and theatre manager Richard Brinsley Sheridan (1751–1816), best known for *The Rivals* and *The School for Scandal* among many other plays; he was also an MP and politician (see note to p. 243). His son Tom Sheridan was consumptive, and an inveterate gambler, frequently in debt.

Brocket Hall, in Hertfordshire: the seat of the Melbourne family (not an ancient aristocratic family: Frederick's and William's great-grandfather was an attorney), where both boys spent their childhood.

Carlton House: a short-lived magnificence with beautiful and extensive wooded gardens and lavish interior, the Prince of Wales's residence on the south side of Pall Mall was reconstructed on the site of an early eighteenth-century house at huge expense over nearly thirty years from 1783, by Henry Holland, and was the scene for splendid receptions and balls. It was demolished after the Regent became king in 1820 and decided that it was insufficiently regal: Buckingham Palace was begun instead. On the site of Carlton House now lie the two terraces of Carlton House Terrace (John Nash, 1827–32).

441 *the Tennis Court, in the Haymarket*: the Haymarket, SW1, home of the Theatre Royal, Haymarket, and a host of inns and shops, was still bustling with wagons of hay and straw at this time, the market only being moved to Cumberland Park in 1830. The tennis court was presumably one of its centres of entertainment, or perhaps a tavern, though the area was well known as the haunt of prostitutes.

442 *the brandy, Arquebusade, and eau-de-Cologne . . . his stomach*: conventional and unconventional liquors, harquebusade-water being a lotion used to treat gunshot or other wounds, and eau-de-Cologne a perfume made of aromatic oils and spirit.

448 *The vein, which makes flesh a deity . . . SHAKSPEARE*: a reference to Berowne's speech in *Love's Labour's Lost*, IV. iii. 70, 'This is the liver-vein, which makes flesh a deity'.

the——Weekly Advertiser: the missing place is presumably Manchester.

my lines to 'Delia', a 'Dead Lamb', or the 'Moon': parodying the stylized sentimental poems to female friendship, objects of tender pathos, and rhapsodic reflection associated with female writers.

449 *Buffon . . . a print of Newton, hanging opposite to him*: the highly influential French naturalist Georges Louis Leclerc, comte de Buffon (1707–88), best known for the 44-volume *Histoire naturelle* (1749–1804). For Newton, see note to p. 66.

à merveille: marvellously, wonderfully.

superbest (see Milton in extenuation of the superlatives) quire of gilt edge: an allusion to the 'grand style' of Milton's *Paradise Lost*, although in fact Milton uses more comparative than superlative forms; a quire is 24 sheets of writing paper.

450 *'there is nothing new under the sun' . . . novels*: Ecclesiastes 1: 9; 'novels' were by etymological tradition expected to offer something 'new'.

451 *My flower perennial . . . in woods of Arcady*: Barry Cornwall, 'The Falcon: A Dramatic Sketch', ii. 120–30, from *A Sicilian Story* (1820).

452 *She never told her love*: from Viola's speech about the unrequited and unexpressed love of her fictitious sister, *Twelfth Night*, II. iv. 110.

The silent stars that wink and listen: Thomas Moore, 'The Light of the Haram', l. 461.

like the vision of an undone eternity: Jewsbury mimics the style of Charles Robert Maturin's novel *Melmoth the Wanderer* (1820), ch. 3, which is a series of fragments from the manuscript of the Englishman Stanton. The phrase is taken up by Carlos Wilcox in *The Age of Benevolence*, i. 1197.

454 *in these volumes . . . love, prose and poetry*: the two volumes of *Phantasma-goria* (1825) in which this piece first appeared.

455 *The very first . . . who led them. BYRON*: from Byron's *Sardanapalus: A Tragedy* (1821), I. ii. 509–15.

Elizabeth . . . Amy . . . own aggrandisement: the story of Amy Robsart, wife of Elizabeth I's favourite Robert Dudley, Earl of Leicester, from 1550 to 1560; when she died in mysterious circumstances, she was widely rumoured to have been murdered on her husband's orders so that he might marry the queen; the story is told in Scott's novel *Kenilworth* (1821).

Rose Bradwardine . . . Flora MacIvor . . . her royal friends: the two heroines of Walter Scott's first novel *Waverley* (1814), respectively the daughter of the old Jacobite Baron Bradwardine and the fascinating, passionately Jacobite sister of one of the Highland chiefs prominent in the rising of 1745–6. Edward Waverley falls in love with Flora MacIvor but marries the loyal and more domesticated Rose.

Rebecca . . . Rowena . . . with her father: the two heroines, the Jewish Rebecca and the high-born Saxon Rowena, of Scott's novel *Ivanhoe* (1819), both love the Saxon knight Wilfrid of Ivanhoe. Ivanhoe has always been in love with Rowena, and marries her, but the emotional tension of the last pages of the novel comes from a charged meeting between the two women. Many readers had different views on the hero's choice of wife, and Thackeray published a corrective version, *Rebecca and Rowena*, in 1850. Jewsbury is expressing a commonly held critical view.

Jeannie Deans . . . the victim of unhappy passion: in Scott's novel *The Heart of Midlothian* (1818) a younger sister, Effie Deans, has an illegitim-ate child and is convicted, wrongly, of the murder of that child. Her sister, Jeannie, walks from Edinburgh to London to seek a pardon from the queen.

Immalie, in her island of flowers . . . dead child lying in her bosom: while Jewsbury's references so far are to accepted touchstones of literary culture in the 1820s, this reference to the central female figure of Charles Robert Maturin's *Melmoth the Wanderer* (1820) is a rare occurence, especially from a woman reader. The child of nature Immalie is seen with her dead baby in the prisons of the Inquisition in ch. 37. Jewsbury has already written a pastiche of the novel in 'The Curse of Solitude', above.

455 *Desdemona . . . Juliet . . . Imogene . . . Ophelia*: in reserving a higher sympathy for wives, Jewsbury refers to the heroines of *Othello, Romeo and Juliet, Cymbeline*, and *Hamlet*.

456 *She, who 'had no ornament but her children'*: in Greek mythology, Niobe, Queen of Thebes, was punished for her boastfulness by the loss of her beloved children, killed by Apollo and Artemis. She was turned into a stone figure which wept tears.

she who . . . 'saw him . . . give a thousand lives for her ransom': stories about the Persian prince Cyrus the Younger (d. 401 BC) are given in Xenophon.

she who . . . 'not painful': as related by Pliny the Younger, Arria, wife of Cæcinna Pætus, fatally stabs herself to inspire her dying husband with courage, assuring him 'Pætus, it is not painful'. Jewsbury might have found the tale under the title 'Female Fortitude' in Anna Laetitia Barbauld (ed.), *The Female Speaker* (London: J. Johnson, 1811), 160–3.

the 'freshness and glory of a dream': a misquotation from 'Ode [Intimations of Immortality]', l. 5 ('The glory and the freshness of a dream') published in 1807 by Jewsbury's friend William Wordsworth.

learned the art . . . conceal the smart: Alaric Watts, 'A Sketch from Real Life' (1828), ll. 23–4.

never told her grief: another reference to the situation of Viola in *Twelfth Night*: see note to p. 452.

457 *'the grasshopper is become a burden'*: Ecclesiastes 12: 5, warning of the times of old age to come, 'when they shall be afraid of that which is nigh, and fears shall be in the way, and the almond tree shall flourish, and the grasshopper [an agent of destruction in the Bible] shall be a burden, and desire shall fail: because man goeth to his long home, and the mourners go about the streets'.

Uncertain, coy, and hard to please: referring to woman in her hours of ease, Scott's *Marmion* (1808), canto 6, stanza xxx.

458 *'Master and mistress minds' . . . Parnassus*: Mount Parnassus in central Greece was held sacred by the ancients, and regarded as a symbol of poetry because of its association with Apollo and the Muses.

such small occupiers . . . Hayley, and Miss Seward . . . divisions: the poet and biographer William Hayley (1745–1820) was popular but not very highly regarded critically: his *The Triumphs of Temper* (1781) went into 24 editions by 1817. The poet Anna Seward (1742–1809), often called the 'Swan of Lichfield', also had considerable poetic success in her day, and was best known for her *Monody on the Death of Major Andre* (1781).

Madame de Stael: see note to p. 419.

the ermine, the lawn, and the helmet: ermine is used to trim the ceremonial robes of peers of the realm; lawn is a kind of fine linen, used for the sleeves of a bishop's gown; the helmet is the mark of a military man.

will still remain a 'goodly heritage,': Psalms 16: 6, Jeremiah 3: 19.

459 *I am a little world made cunningly*: the opening of the fifth of John Donne's *Holy Sonnets*.

466 *A sword hung . . . o'er the head*: Damocles, a flatterer at the court of the fourth-century tyrant Dionysus I, was seated at the banqueting table with a sword suspended by a single hair over his head.

468 *the grave cadence of Castilian song*: the language of Castile is the standard spoken and literary Spanish; translations and imitations of Spanish literature were fashionable at this time, popularized by Robert Southey and John Gibson Lockhart.

469 *Susquehanna's waters . . . words of thine to hear*: the Susquehanna is a major river of southern Pennsylvania; Hemans's poetry enjoyed a widespread and lasting popularity in the United States.

The fable of Prometheus and the vulture . . . woman's heart: in Greek mythology, the Titan Prometheus first made man from clay and stole fire from the gods to give to him; in punishment, Zeus had him chained to a rock where, each day, an eagle (or vulture in some versions) ate his liver, which grew again each night. He was eventually rescued by Hercules.

470 *Tyrian or regal garniture among*: for Tyre and its association with purple dye (the colour of the garments of emperors and kings), see note to p. 68.

473 *the binnacle*: a box on the deck of a ship near the helm in which the compass is placed.

474 *'why do they not eat buns!'*: now usually translated as 'cake', this was a remark attributed to Queen Marie Antoinette and thought to reveal her ignorance of the social conditions of the people of Paris, who were rioting because of a shortage of bread.

Johnstone . . . Sir Robert Walpole . . . 'the very scoff and mockery of fortune': for Walpole, see note to p. 32.

Poonah work, or oriental tinting: Poona, in the Bombay Presidency (now in Maharashatra State), gave its name to poona painting, an imitation of oriental work in which pictures of flowers and birds were produced on rice paper or other thin paper by the application of thick body-colour with little or no shading or background. It was fashionable in England in the early nineteenth century.

the period to which she herself belongs . . . sketch was drawn: *Rob Roy* is set in the period of the Jacobite uprising of 1715, and was published in 1817.

Lord Napier . . . the shirts: a story told by John Gibson Lockhart in *Memoirs of the Life of Sir Walter Scott, Bart.*, 7 vols. (Edinburgh: Cadell, 1837), ii. 2n., of Francis, Lord Napier, Lord–Lieutenant of Selkirkshire.

474 *'the glass of fashion, and the mould of forms'*: Ophelia's speech, *Hamlet*, III. i. 155.

The Duchess of Gordon . . . reckless, like herself: the unconventional, boisterous, witty but notoriously coarse Scottish aristocrat Jane Maxwell (?1749–1812), married the 4th Duke of Gordon in 1767; ambitious and highly influential in the social circles of London and Edinburgh, she was estranged from her husband for several years before her death.

The Duchess of Devonshire . . . flattering: see note to p. 173.

475 *the exclusives . . . impayable*: an exclusive, first recorded in this sense in 1825, was society slang for 'an exclusive person'; *impayable* means 'priceless'.

that tender relationship . . . Scott so much delights: the best examples are Rose Bradwardine and her father in *Waverley*, Julia Mannering and her father in *Guy Mannering*, Sir Arthur Wardour and his daughter Isabella in *The Antiquary*, Rebecca and Isaac in *Ivanhoe*, Margaret Ramsay and her father in *The Fortunes of Nigel*, Bridgenorth and Alice in *Peveril of the Peak*, and Simon Glover and Catharine in *The Fair Maid of Perth*.

'On the horizon . . . trembles into lustre': precise reference untraced, but this may be an imprecise recollection or adaptation of lines from Mary Robinson's poem 'The Progress of Liberty' (published in 1806), ll. 371–2: 'like a dewy star, | Gleams 'midst surrounding darkness'.

'life's rougher things': instead of the traditional 'finer things'.

Osbaldistone-hall . . . Rashleigh: the family home of the Osbaldistones in Northumberland; and the scheming, clever, manipulative brother who seeks to seduce Diana Vernon, taking advantage of his tutelage of her.

an old saying . . . begins after she is married: a familiar saying, but not recorded in any collections of proverbs.

479 *Mr Rogers . . . entertaining us delightfully*: the poet, banker, and connoisseur of the visual arts Samuel Rogers (1763–1855) was a fixture of polite society and known for his sociable breakfast parties. Best known for his poem *The Pleasures of Memory* (1792), he was a key figure in the establishment of the National Gallery, and his artistic interests would complement Jameson's own.

*Paris and Dr R**. . . as the phrase is*: to be 'set up' was usually associated with financial recoveries at this time but here means to retrieve one's health and spirits.

480 *the Ecclesiastical States*: at this time the pre-unification Italy was a collection of states, most under Austrian rule. The Ecclesiastical or Papal States centred on Rome.

plaiting the Leghorn hats: originally imported from Leghorn in Tuscany, these were hats or bonnets plaited from straw made from a particular kind of wheat, cut when green then bleached.

the Piazza del Gran Duca . . . the Rape of the Sabines: Giambologna's marble statue, *The Rape of the Sabine Women* (1583), depicting the abduction of the women of the Sabine territory by the invading Roman troops of Romulus, is in the Loggia della Signoria off the Piazza della Signoria, Florence. The Palazzo Vecchio, from 1550 to 1560 the residence of the grandduke Cosimo I de Medici, is also in this piazza, as is Giambologna's equestrian statue of Cosimo I.

the Gallery or the Pitti Palace: Italy's foremost gallery, the Uffizi (the 'offices' of the Florentine state, designed by Giorgio Vasari as the secretariat of Cosimo I), has as its core collections the private collections of the Medici and Lorraine granddukes. Over the Ponte Vecchio, the Palazzo Pitti was built in 1457 by the banker Luca Pitti and acquired by Cosimo I in the 1540s: the Medicis, and later the House of Lorraine, lived there until 1868: the art collections of the Pitti were also open to visitors. The Brownings' house in Florence is nearby.

481 *Sasso Ferrato . . . Giorgione . . . Holbein . . . Perguino . . . Rubens . . . Carravaggio*: Giovanni Battista Salvi (1609–85), known as Sassoferrato, an Italian painter and draughtsman; Giorgio da Castelfranco, known as Giorgione (?1478–1510): the painter and designer Hans Holbein (1497/8–1543), best known in Britain for his work, especially portraits, at the court of Henry VIII; the Umbrian painter Pietro Vanucci Perugino (active *c.*1472, d. 1523), known for his rigid, static classical style of composition ('dry', for Jameson); the Flemish artist and leading artist of his day Sir Peter Paul Rubens (1577–1640), known for his draughtsmanship and luminous use of colour; and the controversial, innovative stylist Michelangelo Merisi da Carravaggio (1573–1610).

one of Morland's Pig-sties was painted with great feeling: the painter George Morland (1763–1804) was best known for his genre paintings of low or vulgar, often rustic, life. Scorned by Sir Joshua Reynolds but taken up by a circle of aristocratic connoisseurs led by the Prince of Wales in the 1790s, genre painting was in fact undergoing a major revaluation in this period.

en revanche: in return, by way of compensation.

from Somerset House, to the Tribune at Florence: government offices since the demolition of the former palace in 1775, the north wing of Somerset House in the Strand was the home of the Royal Academy of Arts from 1771 to 1836. Designed by Buonalenti in about 1589 as a showcase for some of the Medicis' greatest treasures, the Tribune in the Uffizi has at its centre a masterpiece of Greek sculpture, the Medici Venus of the third century BC, and its walls are hung with sixteenth-century portraits, including fine paintings of women such as Bronzino's *Eleonora di Toledo* and *Lucrezia Panciatichi*.

another Pygmalion?: in Greek mythology, a king of Cyprus who fell in love with the statue of a beautiful woman, brought to life by Aphrodite; in some accounts he was also the sculptor of the statue, though Jameson's connoisseur would not be so creative.

481 *'the beauty of holiness'*: 1 Chronicles 16: 29, 2 Chronicles 20: 21, Psalms 29: 2, 96: 9.

482 *the vaghezza of the colouring*: vagueness.

the critic's stop-watch was nothing to this: see Richard Brinsley Sheridan's *The Critic* (1781), I. i, where 'the watch, you know, is the critic'.

In painting as in her sister arts . . . Che l'arte che tutte fa nulla si scuopre: roughly, all art and skill whatever is as nothing when unpicked.

intellectual shambles . . . supped full of horrors: the shambles is the area of towns in which animals are slaughtered; the quotation from *Macbeth*, v. v. 13.

483 *a kind of bonne bouche*: a morsel taken after a meal in order to leave a pleasant taste in the mouth.

un vero Correggio . . . thousand scudi: a genuine work of the great Emilian painter Antonio Allegri Correggio (1494–1534), known for his dynamic and subtle works in oil and fresco and especially for his beautiful female nudes; a scudo is an old Italian silver coin.

Pope Joan: the mythical female Pope, said to have been born in Germany of English parents and elected to the papacy in 855 as John VIII: the story was disproved by the Calvininst scholar David Blondel in 1647 but continued to cause debate until the work of Dollinger in 1863.

'with the smoke of its ashes to poison the air': a misquotation of Thomas Campbell's poem 'Lochiel's Warning' (1802), l. 77 ('With the smoke of its ashes to poison the gale').

There is another . . . Guido's lovely Cleopatra: the Italian painter Guido Reni (1575–1642) was underappreciated in Jameson's time: several of his works are in the Palatine (or Pitti) Gallery in Florence.

a Judith and Holofernes . . . the artist was a woman: the widow of Manasseh, Judith entered the camp of the Assyrian general Holofernes and dined with him alone, taking advantage of his intended seduction to kill and decapitate him, escaping with his head, which she displayed on the ramparts of the besieged city of Bethulia. She, her maidservant, and Holofernes were a popular subject of Renaissance art. The painting referred to here is the *Judith and Holofernes* of Artemisia Gentileschi (*c.*1597–after 1651), daughter of Orazio Gentileschi: she worked in Florence, *c.*1621–4.

if (like a certain princess) we have a taste that way: not identified.

Painting has been called the handmaid of nature: as in the penultimate stanza of Thomas Campbell's 'Stanzas to Painting' (1803): 'Then blest be Nature's guardian Muse, | Whose hand her perished grace redeems!'

484 *The St Sebastians of Guido and Razzi; the St Jerome of Domenichino; the sternly beautiful Judith of Allori; the Pietà of Raffaelle; the San Pietro Martire of Titian*: an especially popular subject in Renaissance and baroque art, the third-century martyr St Sebastian was executed with

arrows because of his Christian beliefs, restored to life, then clubbed to death on the orders of the emperor Diocletian; the references here are to Guido Reni (see note to previous page) and the Italian monk, writer, and scholar Girolamo Silvano Razzi (*c*.1527–1611). St Jerome (*c*.342–420) was one of the four fathers of the Western Church, and translated the Bible into the Latin Vulgate; a popular figure in Christian art and legend, he was commonly depicted in his study, an ascetic elderly man, or as a repentant hermit in the desert, in either location accompanied by a tamed lion: the representation here is by Domenico Zampieri, known as Domenichino (1581–1641), artist of the Bolognese school, most valued in the eighteenth and nineteenth centuries for his atmospheric landscapes. For Judith, see note to the previous page; the *Judith* Jameson means, by Cristoforo Allori (1577–1621), son of the more famous late Mannerist Alessandro Allori, is in the Sala dell'Educazione di Giove in the Palatine (Pitti) Gallery, Florence. The *pietà* (from the Italian for pity or compassion) represented Mary mourning her dead son, a composition popular in early German and Renaissance Italian art and especially associated with Michelangelo; here the work is by Raffaello Sanzio, known as Raphael (1483–1520), one of the major painters of the High Renaissance. The Venetian painter Tiziano Vecellio , known as Titian (?1477–1576) and the dominant force in northern Italian art of his time, painted the altarpiece of the *Death of St Peter Martyr* (1525–30) in SS Giovanni e Paolo, Venice, destroyed by fire in 1867; the murdered Dominican St Peter Martyr (1206–52) is traditionally represented carrying a palm and cross, and as having a hatchet or knife in his head.

'lose ourselves in all delightfulness': not traced.

488 *Free Town*: the capital of Sierra Leone, on the African West Coast bordering Guinea to the north and Liberia to the south-east; Sierra Leone was founded as a colony for liberated slaves in 1787, subsequently becoming a British colony in 1808, a British protectorate in 1896, and independent in 1961.

489 *Wellington*: as with later places mentioned in Kilham's account, this town is no longer identifiable under this name. Kilham mentions several places which were obviously given colonial names to honour key British figures of the time: here, Arthur Wellesley, Duke of Wellington and victor of the battle of Waterloo.

the children of the American settlers: homeless freed slaves were settled on the site of Freetown by the British in 1787. In neighbouring Liberia, a group of liberated American slaves landed in 1822 to found a colony negotiated with the indigenous peoples by the American Colonization Society.

491 *Allen's Town, Leopold, Regent, and Gloucester . . . Charlotte . . . there*: see note to p. 489. As with Wellington, these are obsolete colonial names, in honour of Prince Leopold, the Prince Regent, the Duke of Gloucester, and Princess Charlotte, only daughter of the Prince Regent.

492 *the Jalof, Mandingo, Timmani, and Sussu, previously printed*: all languages now grouped under the Niger-Congo *phylum* (or major language family): Jolof (also referred to in Kilham's account as Wolof), Malinke or Maninka (of the Mande or Mende people of present-day Sierra Leone), and Susu.

493 *'every man that cometh into the world'*: an amalgam of biblical phrases rather than a saying from the Bible; given the origins of Kilham's next two quotations, the language loosely recalls St John, especially 11: 27.

'will not come unto the light, lest their deeds be reproved': John 3: 20.

shine only as on the darkness that 'comprehendeth it not': John 1: 5.

498 *Hespery*: a poetic name for the lands of the West, used by the Greeks to refer to Italy and by the Romans to refer to Spain.

499 *The Grecian called her 'Beauty'*:—in Greek stories of creation, notably Hesiod's *Theogony*, the earth is the goddess Gaia: see Homer, *Odyssey*, XI. 576.

the welkin blue above: the welkin is a term used mainly in a poetic context to mean the apparent arch or vault of heaven overhead.

500 *Like to the hair of Berenice*: the third-century Egyptian queen, wife of Ptolemy III, dedicated her hair as a votive offering for the safe return of her husband from his conquest of Asia. The hair was stolen, and, according to legend, placed in the heavens: the constellation Coma Berenices is named after her.

502 *Mors erat ante oculos.* LUCAN, lib. ix: 'death was before his eyes', from Lucan, *Pharsalia*, ix. 763.

the forest Titans: in Greek mythology, the six sons and six daughters of Uranus and Gaia, overthrown by the Olympians.

505 *the deep Eleusis of mine heart*: the Attic town of Eleusis was the site of a temple to the corn goddess Demeter.

The Janus of my soul on echoing hinge: in Roman mythology, Janus is the god of gates, doorways, and bridges, and is represented as having two heads, facing in opposite directions.

506 *writhes like Laocoon*: the son of Priam of Troy and priest of Apollo, Laocoon and his two sons were squeezed to death by serpents while he was making a sacrifice to the sea god Poseidon; the event is depicted in an early sculpture now in the Vatican.

507 *in panoply of the old Roman iron ... Stoic valour*: in a full suit of iron armour; the Stoics were a school of Greek philosophers founded by Zeno (fl. *c.*300 B.C.), known for austerity and endurance, and more generally used to describe physical and emotional self-deniers.

only Death shall die: an allusion to the tenth of Donne's 'Holy Sonnets', 'Death be not proud', the last line of which is 'And death shall be no more; death, thou shalt die.'

512 *the letting of the Pearl banks had been accomplished*: the main sources of information on the economy of Ceylon consulted by Martineau were Anthony Bertolacci, *A View of the Agricultural, Commercial, and Financial Interests of Ceylon: with an Appendix, containing some of the Principal Laws and Usages of the Candians; Port and Custom-house Regulations, &c.* (London: Black, Parbury, and Allen, 1817) and Robert Percival, *An Account of the Island of Ceylon, containing its History, Geography, Natural History, with the Manners and Customs of its Various Inhabitants; to which is added, the Journal of an Embassy to the Court of Candy* (London: C. and R. Baldwin, 1803).

513 *that fairest of all regions . . . made herself responsible*: since 1972 the Republic of Sri Lanka, the island-state of Ceylon off the south-east coast of India became a British colony in 1796.

514 *the Charmer . . . father*: Rayo's father-in-law is a snakecharmer.

515 *like Jonah's gourd*: in Jonah 4: 6, God creates a great gourd which offers the prophet Jonah shelter from the sun, then causes it to wither, teaching Jonah the importance of mercy to the repentant citizens of Ninevah.

Talipot tents: the huge leaves of the south Indian tea-palm, *Corypha umbraculifera*, used here to form a tent.

The haughty Candian . . . path of the European: a native of Kandy, formerly the centre of an independent Singhalese mountain kingdom in the heart of Sri Lanka.

the Southern Cross: Crux, the smallest constellation in the sky, used as a pointer to the south celestial pole.

516 *Adam's Bridge*: or Rama's Bridge, a chain of sandbanks over 30 miles long, north-west of Sri Lanka.

517 *a Hindoo . . . the elephant that supported the globe*: the elephant is a key supportive figure in Indian art and custom, and in Hindu tradition bears the earth on its head.

518 *St Anthony!*: the father of Christian monasticism, St Anthony the Abbot (*c.*251–356), perhaps recalled by Martineau in this tale because he resisted temptation, including a nugget of gold.

520 *a pious State, which will not endure that its coloured citizens should be educated*: the district school system in Massachusetts, established in 1789, was made compulsory in 1827; in 1855 the state banned segregation in all schools.

A Connecticut judge . . . citizens in the laws: slavery was not abolished in Connecticut until 1848, 68 years after Massachusetts and 21 after New York. The 'eminent statesman' is probably Henry Clay (1777–1852), with whom Martineau had stayed in Kentucky.

521 *Lafayette . . . increase of the prejudice against colour*: the French soldier and statesman Marie Joseph du Motier, marquis de Lafayette

(1757–1834) fought in support of the American Revolution, became a lifelong friend of George Washington, and visited the USA for the last time, July 1824–Sept. 1825.

521 *the pharisees of the community*: one of the ancient Jewish sects, distinguished by strict observance of tradition and written law.

522 *overflowing colleges . . . allowed*: an exaggeration: Oberlin, the USA's first co-educational college (est. 1833) first admitted black students in 1835, while in 1867 Howard University was established to provide higher education for black Americans.

523 *Jefferson . . . James Mill . . . the Emperor of Russia's Catechism for the young Poles*: Thomas Jefferson (1743–1826), principal drafter of the Declaration of Independence and third President of the United States; the 'Essay on Government' contributed to the *Encyclopaedia Britannica* by the Scottish philosopher, historian, and economist James Mill (1773–1836), best known for his *History of British India* (1817–19); Peter I, the Great, of Russia (1672–1725).

Infants . . . the rights of will and of property: the edition used by Martineau was *Memoirs, Correspondence, and Private Papers of Thomas Jefferson, Late President of the United States*, ed. Thomas Jefferson Randolph, 4 vols. (London: Colburn and Bentley, 1829), quoted here from iv. 295.

524 *Mill says . . . that of their husbands*: *An Essay on Government*, introd. Ernest Barker (Cambridge: Cambridge University Press, 1937), 45.

The English Tories . . . getting his bread: a reference to the opposition of the Tory party to parliamentary reform.

Forty years ago . . . state elections: in 1800 women voted in local elections for the first time in Elizabethtown, New Jersey. Not until 1869 was the first law to enfranchise women enacted, in the then territory of Wyoming, while the right to vote in national elections was not secured until the Nineteenth Amendment in 1920.

526 *images of women on woolsacks in England, and under canopies in America*: that is, women presiding as the chief legal officers of their country. The first woman justice of the US Supreme Court was Sandra Day O'Connor in 1981.

529 *the Honourable Company's territories*: for the administration and territories of the East India Company, see note to p. 28.

'nabob': see note to p. 227.

the conclave in Leadenhall-street: on the corner of Lime Street and Leadenhall Street, EC3, until 1862, stood East India House, headquarters of the East India Company and workplace of Mary Lamb's brother Charles, John Stuart Mill, and Thomas Love Peacock.

a rara avis of this nature: a rare bird, hence a phenomenon or prodigy.

530 *laden with 'barbaric pearl and gold'*: Milton, *Paradise Lost*, ii. 4.

subalterns . . . a staff-appointment, the adjutancy or quarter-mastership of his corps: a subaltern is a junior officer below the rank of captain; a staff appointment is to a group of officers assisting a general or other commanding officer, but not in command themselves; an adjutancy is the post of an officer assisting the commanding officer, undertaking such tasks as communicating orders and conducting correspondence; the quartermaster of a corps is the regimental officer responsible for assigning quarters, laying out the camp, and looking after rations, clothing, and equipment.

that 'mammon wins its way where seraphs might despair': Byron, *Childe Harold's Pilgrimage*, canto 1 (1812), stanza 9.

young writers rank amongst the eligibles: a writer was a clerk, sent out from Britain, in the service of the East India Company.

apartments in Tank-square . . . 'the Buildings': the government offices in Calcutta.

a moonshee: the Urdu and Arabic term *munshi* referred to a native secretary or language-teacher in India.

531 *The 'great parti'*: a person regarded as eligible in the marriage market.

horrors of a half-batta station: not a particular kind of military station but a station on the dreaded half-pay. 'Batta' was an extra allowance paid to Indian regiments on campaign, which grew to be a constant addition to the pay of officers serving in India; half-batta was half-pay.

532 *white sarsnet*: or sarsenet, a very fine and soft silk now used mainly as lining material.

533 *Mrs Malaprop . . . a little aversion*: a comment by Mrs Malaprop, famed for her misapplication of long words, in Sheridan's comedy *The Rivals* (1775), II. ii.

a budgerow: or budgero, an Anglo-Indian term derived from the Hindi or Bengali *bajura*, a heavy barge commonly used by Europeans travelling on the Ganges.

535 *educated at the presidencies*: in the territory of the East India Company there were three divisions or districts, each governed by a president.

544 *her money was often ill bestowed. In the late troubles*: the economic problems and bad harvests of the middle years of the 1790s, which led to widespread rural hardship.

go and do likewise: Luke 10: 37.

548 *Mrs Cooper's excellent cutting out book*: not identified.

551 *man has been characterized as a cooking animal*: by James Boswell, in *The Journal of a Tour to the Hebrides, with Samuel Johnson* (London: Charles Dilly, 1785), 25.

M. Ude . . . 'A woman can do it': this is probably a reported remark, for in print there is no such encouragement to female endeavour in *The French Cook*, by Louis Eustache Ude, 'ci-devant cook to Louis XVI and the Earl of Sefton, and steward to his late Royal Highness the Duke of York', who uniformly treats cooks as professionals, and therefore as men. None of his many recipes allows for delegation in the kitchen. Indeed, Ude takes a rather combative line on women, and some of his asides reveal much about women's dietary habits: luncheon, for example, is said to be largely a lady's meal, taken in order to avoid the appearance of over-eating at dinner.

551 *'Women . . . cannot write a book of cookery'*: James Boswell's *Life of Johnson* (1794) records a conversation of 15 April 1778, prompted by Dilly's observation that the cookery book of Mrs Glasse was in fact written by Dr Hill. Johnson declares that he will write a cookery book of his own, to which Anna Seward replies 'That would be Hercules with the distaff indeed'. Johnson's response is 'No, Madam. Women can spin very well; but they cannot make a good book of Cookery'. *Boswell's Life of Johnson*, ed. R. W. Chapman (London: Oxford University Press, 1953, 1965), 943.

553 *infra dig.*: beneath one's dignity.

most unjustly the opponents of cooks . . . hostility of the fair sex: for Ude's work, see note to p. 551. 'The Ladies of England are unfavourably disposed towards our art', Ude notes, largely because 'they are not introduced to their parents' table till their palates have been completely benumbed by the strict diet observed in the Nursery and Boarding-Schools' (8th edn. (London: William H. Ainsworth, 1827), p. xxxv).

Lord Byron disliked to see women eat: in a letter of 25 September 1812 Byron writes to Lady Melbourne that 'a woman should never be seen eating or drinking, unless it be *lobster sallad & Champagne*, the only truly feminine & becoming viands' ('*Famous in my time*', vol. ii of *Byron's Letters and Journals*, ed. Leslie A. Marchand (London: John Murray, 1973), 208).

Rout cakes: rich cakes made for the fashionable large assemblages or evening parties known as routs, in vogue during the eighteenth and nineteenth centuries.

554 *Man is a cooking animal*: see note to p. 551.

the half-broiled bloody collop: a collop need not refer to a piece of raw meat, though that is the implication here; it is a thick-cut slice or chunk.

the pastoral . . . the hunter: a pastiche of the stages of human society as described in Scottish Enlightenment works such as Adam Ferguson's *Essay on the History of Civil Society* (1767).

555 *The ambitious man seeks to rule the roast*: first recorded in the fifteenth century (*Oxford Dictionary of English Proverbs*) and meaning to have full sway, to be master; the proverb has shifted in current usage, now usually given as 'to rule the roost'.

There goes reason to the roasting of an egg: the proverbs in this list are: 'to have a finger in the pie' (sixteenth century); 'meat and mass never hindered any man' (seventeenth century); 'half a loaf is better than no bread' (sixteenth century); and 'There is reason in roasting of eggs' (seventeenth century).

The churl . . . sticks him with the spit: 'Set a fool to make feasts, and a wise man to eat them' (seventeenth century); the churl and spit appears to be an amalgam of various proverbs, but has no independent corroboration.

'to make the pat play brown': the proverbs in this list are a mixed group. No independent corroboration is found for 'belly is every man's master' or 'he who will not fight for his meat'. 'A hungry man, an angry man' (sixteenth century) and 'It is ill speaking between a full man and a fasting' (seventeenth century) are included in the *Oxford Dictionary of Proverbs*, 3rd edn. The last phrase seems to respond to the proverbial warning 'When the pot's full, it will boil over' (eighteenth century).

as mony brown lammer-beads: lamber-beads, an obsolete northern dialect variant of amber-beads: the term would perhaps be familiar to Johnstone's readers from occasional uses in the novels of Walter Scott (see *The Heart of Midlothian* (1818), ch. 13, and *The Bride of Lammermoor* (1819), ch. 12).

"—— Fall out with mince-meat . . . plum-porridge": a misquotation from Samuel Butler's *Hudibras* (1662), i. 226–7: 'Quarrel with minced-pies, and disparage | Their best and dearest friend—plum-porridge.'

his hogshead of October: a hogshead was a large cask, the standard measure varying by liquid and region but being about 52½ imperial gallons; the liquid here is ale brewed in October.

Oxford watched . . . importance of the trust: during the English Civil Wars, the city and university of Oxford were known for their staunch royalism. Louis Eustache Ude makes a similar point about the decline of French cookery during the Revolution, and its promising resurgence after the Restoration, *French Cook*, p. xlviii.

556 *a strong leaning 'to dishes as they are'*: the fiction, especially the political fiction, of the 1790s, often used this opposition, as in William Godwin's *Things as They Are; or, Caleb Williams* (1794) and Robert Bage's *Hermsprong; or, Things as They Are Not* (1796); see also Inchbald's comedy *Wives As They Were, and Maids As They Are* (1797).

a course of peninsular practice: Jekyll has served in the Peninsular Campaign against Napoleon under the Duke of Wellington.

557 *the lively votaries of Terpsichore*: one of the nine muses of ancient Greece, Terpsichore is the muse of dancing and the dramatic chorus.

560 *Dr Hill, (Mrs Glass,) Dr Hunter, and Dr Kitchener . . . we have at present*: Hannah Glasse (1707/8–70) came from a Northumbrian family, and took up paid employment on the early death of her husband, including dressmaking work for the royal household: she is best known for her writings on domestic economy, especially the highly successful *The Art of Cookery*

(1747), which went into thirty-four editions by 1842, *The Servant's Directory* (1760), and *The Compleat Confectioner* (1770). Alexander Hunter (1729–1809), a doctor, published anonymously, as 'Ignotus', *Culina Famulatrix Medicinæ: or, Receipts in Cookery* (1804), which appeared in various expanded and augmented forms. William Kitchiner (?1775–1827) also trained as a doctor and became a writer and celebrated epicure, especially notable for his interest in the connections between good food and good health, and famed for his luncheon and dinner parties: his key work in this field is *Apicius Redivivus, or the Cook's Oracle* (1817).

561 *'A French family . . . wasted in an English kitchen'*: it was a commonplace in eighteenth-century England to contrast plump John Bull with images of French poverty and emaciation. See the Englishman quoted by Helen Maria Williams (p. 122 above). Here the commonplace is turned to the advantage of the French.

fasts and jours-maigres: a period of abstinence as part of religious observance, and a religious 'jour' or day of abstinence, especially from meat.

562 *New-College pudding, Oxford John, Dean's particulars . . . ancient halls*: exotic still, New-College Pudding is a prepared pineapple, filled with lemon sorbet and drenched in Kirsch; Oxford John consists of slices of mutton or lamb with a seasoned coating, pan-fried; no recipe for Dean's particulars, however, is given in Ursula Aylmer and Carolyn McCrum (eds.), *Oxford Food: An Anthology* (Oxford: Bodleian Library and Ashmolean Museum, 1995), though its name suggests that, like 'Warden's Savoury' (61), it may have been applied to a dish the name of which the chef had forgotten, or perhaps to a happy improvisation.

563 *'when goods increase . . . beholding them with their eyes'*: Ecclesiastes 5: 11.

570 *'The beginning of strife is as the letting out of water'*: Proverbs 17: 14.

The Oxford World's Classics Website

www.worldsclassics.co.uk

- Information about new titles
- Explore the full range of Oxford World's Classics
- Links to other literary sites and the main OUP webpage
- Imaginative competitions, with bookish prizes
- Peruse *Compass*, the Oxford World's Classics magazine
- Articles by editors
- Extracts from Introductions
- A forum for discussion and feedback on the series
- Special information for teachers and lecturers

www.worldsclassics.co.uk

American Literature

British and Irish Literature

Children's Literature

Classics and Ancient Literature

Colonial Literature

Eastern Literature

European Literature

History

Medieval Literature

Oxford English Drama

Poetry

Philosophy

Politics

Religion

The Oxford Shakespeare

A complete list of Oxford Paperbacks, including Oxford World's Classics, OPUS, Past Masters, Oxford Authors, Oxford Shakespeare, Oxford Drama, and Oxford Paperback Reference, is available in the UK from the Academic Division Publicity Department, Oxford University Press, Great Clarendon Street, Oxford OX2 6DP.

In the USA, complete lists are available from the Paperbacks Marketing Manager, Oxford University Press, 198 Madison Avenue, New York, NY 10016.

Oxford Paperbacks are available from all good bookshops. In case of difficulty, customers in the UK can order direct from Oxford University Press Bookshop, Freepost, 116 High Street, Oxford OX1 4BR, enclosing full payment. Please add 10 per cent of published price for postage and packing.